CROSS OF FIRE
&
WHIRLPOOL

Colin Forbes writes a novel every year. For the past twenty-seven years he has earned his living solely as a full-time writer.

Forbes visits all the locations which will appear in a new novel. He says, 'It is essential for me to see for myself where the book will take place. Only in this way can I conjure up the unique atmosphere of the chosen locales.'

He has explored most of Western Europe, the east and west coasts of America, and has made excursions to Africa and Asia. Each new book appears on all major bestsellers lists. He is translated into thirty languages.

Surveys have shown his readership is divided equally between women and men.

COLIN FORBES

CROSS OF FIRE

&

WHIRLPOOL

PAN BOOKS

Cross of Fire first published 1992 by Pan Books.
First published in paperback by Pan Books 1993.
Whirlpool first published 1991 by Pan Books.
First published in paperback by Pan Books 1992.

This omnibus first published 2005 by Pan Books
an imprint of Pan Macmillan Ltd
Pan Macmillan, 20 New Wharf Road, London N1 9RR
Basingstoke and Oxford
Associated companies throughout the world
www.panmacmillan.com

ISBN 0 330 44369 0

A CIP catalogue record for this book is available from
the British Library.

Printed and bound in Great Britain by
Mackays of Chatham plc, Chatham, Kent

CROSS OF FIRE

For Jane

Contents

Prologue

November. Paula Grey was fleeing for her life . . .

Under a stormy sky, in Suffolk, England, she ran across the spongy marsh towards a dense copse of evergreen trees. Above the whine of the wind coming off the sea she heard again the baying of the hounds, the shouts of the men pursuing them.

She glanced over her shoulder. Her friend, Karin Rosewater, was some distance behind her, having trouble negotiating the treacherous ground. Paula thought of going back, urging her to hurry – but the sinister men chasing them were closing in.

'Head for the trees, Karin,' she shouted.

But her voice was carried away on the rising wind. She ran on, ran all-out, gasping for breath, with fear. Then she was inside the shelter of the black firs. Clad in denims and a windcheater, she ran deeper inside the small wood. The barking of the savage dogs was closer. There was no escape.

There *had* to be. Hidden inside the firs she looked up at a giant spreading its branches like hands reaching out to grasp her. Her denims were tucked inside leather boots with indented rubber soles. She grabbed at a low branch, hauled herself up the huge trunk, forcing herself to move fast. Her boots were wet from splashing through a creek a short distance back. She continued her climb like an agile monkey, thanking God she was slim and fit.

Near the top of the fir, which rose above the surrounding

trees, she perched herself, legs straddled over a branch, back leant against the trunk as she waited to get her breath. Looking down, she saw she was concealed from the ground except for one small gap. She stared out across the marsh towards the river Alde as dusk descended. To her horror, she saw Karin running in the open, heading for a small boat moored in a creek snaking in from the yacht basin. Close behind her followed the hunters. Paula heard a sound below, glanced down, stiffened with fright.

A large Alsatian, released by its handler, was sniffing round the base of the fir. She waited for its head to lift, to stare up at her refuge. Two of the pursuers appeared. Tall men wearing Balaclava helmets with slits for vision, camouflage jackets tucked into military-style boots. Both men held rifles.

Paula reached quietly into her shoulder bag, took out her .32 Browning automatic. Then she heard the sound of more men treading through the undergrowth. She was out-numbered. The Alsatian was moving in circles as though baffled. It ran away out of sight. Paula remembered the creek she had splashed through by chance. The beast had lost her scent. The two hunters moved away. She let out a sigh of relief.

Still seated, she stretched up to her full height, gazing in the direction of Aldeburgh, the strange town by the sea. Its huddle of rooftops had disappeared in the dark. She had a brief glimpse of a belt of sea with whitecaps and then that, too, disappeared in the moonless night.

Where is Karin? she asked herself.

As though in reply to her anxious question she heard a penetrating scream piercing the silence of the marshes. It came from the direction where Karin had run for the boat. The agonized scream was choked off. The return of silence sounded dreadful. God! Had they reached Karin? What had they done to her?

Shivering with cold, she buttoned the windcheater up to her neck, checked the time by the illuminated hands of her watch. 5.30 p.m. Experience warned her she must wait inside her refuge. The hunters knew there had been two women. And she still caught the distant sound of a dog barking.

Her legs were beginning to ache – reaction from the desperate run across the marshes, from the strain of keeping still, straddled over the branch. The wind stirred the smaller branches, brushed her face with prickly twigs. She waited until 6.30 p.m. before hauling out the mobile phone from her pocket. There had been no sign or sound of the hunters for three-quarters of an hour. She was frozen stiff as she dialled the number of SIS headquarters at Park Crescent.

Robert Newman, world-famous foreign correspondent, drove his Mercedes 280E at speed through the night along the A1094, hardly slowed as he turned into Aldeburgh High Street, which was eerily deserted. By chance he had called in at Park Crescent when the phone message for help had come through from Paula.

Beside him sat Marler, slim, compact, small, and the most deadly marksman in Western Europe. His Armalite rifle rested on his lap. In the rear sat Harry Butler, in his thirties, clean-shaven, well built, and a man of few words. Beside him sat his younger partner, Pete Nield, slimmer, a snappy dresser with a neat black moustache.

In a shoulder holster Newman, of medium height and in his early forties, his favourite Smith, & Wesson Special. Butler was armed with a 7.65mm Walther, and Nield also had a Walther.

Newman was the only member of the team not permanently employed by the Secret Service, but was fully vetted
and had helped with a number of dangerous missions. He
was also fond of Paula, another member of the SIS.

'You'll wake the dead,' Marler drawled in his upper crust
voice.

'At eight in the evening the place is dead,' Newman
snapped.

'You seem to know your way,' Marler observed.

'I should. I've spent time here recuperating. Most of it
walking. I reckon I can take us straight to that copse of trees
Paula described over the phone . . .'

'If she's still there. It's a God-awful night. Wind howling
like a banshee. Wonder what it's all about.'

'We'll know when we find her,' Newman said grimly
and hoped Marler would shut up.

Newman was driving with his headlights undimmed. In
the beams Marler saw the High Street as a collection of
shops and houses, old and with the roofs going up and
down. A weird atmosphere.

'Dotty sort of place,' he commented.

'Quaint is the word,' Newman growled. 'We're nearly at
the end of the line for driving. We hoof it from the end of
the town, which is here . . .'

The road surface beyond where the town stopped
abruptly had deteriorated. In the headlight beams it was a
wide track of gravel. As they alighted they heard above the
wind the boom of surf waves hitting the unseen beach. It
was a wild night. Newman checked his watch. 8 p.m. It had
been about 6.30 p.m. when Paula had phoned.

'Where does that track lead to?' Marler enquired. 'And
what is that huge bank with cranes atop it?'

'Reinforcing the sea defences. If it breaks through it will
flood the marshes we have to cross.' He switched off the

4

headlights, locked the car, stood for a moment to get back his night vision. 'The track leads to the Slaughden Yacht Club. Slaughden village slid into the sea years ago. Like Dunwich further up the coast. I can see the copse of firs. Let's pray to God Paula is still there. Alive . . .'

He led the way off the road down on to the marsh. The other three men automatically spread out to make a difficult target. In her brief message Paula had warned of men with guns. Using a powerful flashlight, Newman picked his way across the ooze, stepping from grassy stump to grassy stump. One wrong step and he'd sink into the slime of mud.

The night air was bitterly cold but Newman had called at his flat to put on ankle-length boots. Like the others he wore a padded windcheater. Torch in left hand, revolver in the other, he was the first to reach and enter the fir copse. He began to call out softly. 'Paula . . . It's Bob . . . Paula . . .'

His boots pressed down the mush of dead bracken. He swivelled his torch upwards at the foot of a giant fir. The beam shone on his face. He stiffened as a fragment of the fir fell to the ground.

'Bob! I'm up here! I'm coming down. God! It's freezing . . .'

He was carrying an overcoat he'd grabbed during the brief visit to his South Ken. flat *en route* to Suffolk. He wrapped it round her as she jumped to the ground. She threw her arms around him and he hugged her tight.

'It's all right now, Paula.'

'There were men with rifles . . .'

'And we have men with guns. Myself, Marler, Butler, and Nield.'

'We must look for Karin at once.'

'It's dark. Pitch black . . .'

5

'We *must* look,' she insisted, freeing herself from his grip. 'I saw the direction where she went. I know the area. Give me the torch. *Please*, Bob . . .'

They emerged from the copse and Newman's three companions were waiting for him. Shining the flashlight downwards Paula moved stiffly but at surprising speed across the marsh towards the yacht basin where a number of craft were moored to buoys, their hulls covered with sheeting for winter.

Aching in every limb, Paula gradually loosened up as she pressed on over the grassy tufts, avoiding pools of oily water. The others followed, using their own flashlights. Within five minutes Paula had scrambled up the embankment hemming in the anchorage. Switching off the flashlight, she stood on the narrow footpath following the ridge of the embankment. Her eyes swiftly became accustomed to the dark, and her sense of direction had been good. She was close to the craft she had seen Karin running towards before that hellish scream.

Switching on the flash again, she hurried along the footpath. Every step was an effort after her long vigil up in the fir but her determination carried her forward with Newman close behind. The elevated footpath was even more exposed to the wind blowing in from the sea. Out in the anchorage the masts of the moored craft swayed back and forth. She stopped, directed the beam down towards the small craft moored in a creek some distance from the main river.

'What is it?' Newman asked, raising his voice.

'Look. That craft is empty. That was the one she was running towards.'

'You heard a scream,' he reminded her quietly. 'I don't want to assume the worst, but it will be easier to search the area in daylight.'

'I'm going down there,' she replied stubbornly.

Before he could grab her arm she had scrambled down the wet grassy bank to the edge of the creek. He looked back quickly. Marler was crouched further back on the footpath, Armalite held at the ready, scanning the whole marshland. Butler and Nield were similarly crouched, spaced well out. Their rear was safe. He scrambled down after her.

'I can't understand it,' Paula said, half to herself.

She was gazing at the empty hull, moving the beam back and forth. Newman stood beside her, began playing the beam of his own flash over a wider area. The beam passed over another nearby creek, then swivelled slowly back.

'Go and join Harry and Pete,' he advised in a sombre tone. 'Tell Marler to come and join me now.'

'Whatever it is I must see it. I'm a big girl now. So, what is it?'

Newman switched off his flash. Tucking it inside the pocket of windcheater, he cupped his hands to call out to Marler.

'Leave Harry and Pete where they are. Come down here quickly . . .

'What is it, for God's sake?'

Paula tugged at his sleeve in frustration. He ignored her until Marler had joined them. As always, Marler was calm and controlled.

'Something up? If so, what? If I may be so bold as to enquire.'

'Come with me. Stay back, Paula . . .'

Switching on his flash, he trod carefully at the edge of the marsh towards the next isolated creek. Marler kept close to his heels and Paula followed him. Newman stopped, looked back at Paula, shook his head in resignation, aimed his flash.

At the edge of the creek of stagnant water covered with green slime were the relics of a rowing boat. Most of its structure had rotted away and it was half buried in mud. The basic structure stood out like the ribs of a prehistoric beast. Reeds had recently been torn up and thrown over the ruin. Newman steadied his torch. Paula gasped, then got a grip on herself. At the prow nearest to them a pair of training shoes projected, toes pointed at the sky. Newman knew the trainers had to be occupied by a pair of feet.

Marler moved forward after handing his Armalite to Newman. He used his bare hands to remove the mess of reeds carefully from the stern. By the light of Newman's steady beam they saw dark hair exposed, a white blotchy face staring upwards, the tongue protruding horribly from the half-open mouth. Marler continued removing more reeds, exposing the torso clad in a dark blue windcheater. Then the boat lost balance, toppled the corpse out sideways.

A macabre movement, the body rolled as though alive, ended up on its back, lying on damp reeds. Paula sucked in her breath. By the light of Newman's flash Marler bent over the pathetic figure clad in denims below the windcheater.

'It's Karin,' Paula whispered. 'She's dead, isn't she?'

'Fear so,' Marler answered quietly. 'Dead as a doornail,' he added under his breath.

'How did she . . .' Paula began.

'Strangled,' Marler replied.

The flashlight focused on the girl's bruised, swollen throat. The protruding tongue flopped over the lower lip. Newman put his arm round Paula, forced her back up to the footpath on the embankment.

'We'd better get back to the car. I need my mobile phone to call the police.'

'You've forgotten – I've got one.'

Paula pulled her own instrument from underneath her

windcheater. She handed it to Newman as she stood very still, staring down where Marler, realizing he could do no more, had stood up, was brushing stray reeds off his raincoat.

'Then I can call from here,' Newman said, taking hold of the phone.

'You won't know the number.'

'On the way I stopped briefly at a call box, checked the number of Ipswich police headquarters. Your message to Park Crescent mentioned a scream which was choked off. I suspected we might face something like this.'

He pressed buttons after extending the aerial. He had to wait a minute before the desk sergeant answered. 'I want to report a murder. Location . . .'

Part One

Nightmare for Paula

Chapter One

'I sense a crisis situation in Germany,' Tweed said, to take his mind off his anxiety about Paula. He paced the floor of his first-floor office at the Park Crescent HQ.

The Deputy Director of the SIS was of medium height, well built, ageless. He wore horn-rims and could pass people in the street without being noticed – a trait which had so often helped him in his job.

The only other occupant was his faithful assistant, Monica. A middle-aged woman with her grey hair tied in a bun, she sat behind her desk as her chief continued. He checked his watch. 10 p.m.

'Thank God Paula is safe. That call from Newman was brief. If she's injured he'd keep it from me until they get back here. I wonder what happened up in Suffolk.'

'You'll hear when she gets back and tells you. What made you use the word crisis about Germany?'

'The urgent call from Chief Inspector Kuhlmann of the German Kriminalpolizei. His request for me to meet him in the utmost secrecy in three days' time in Luxembourg City. Why there? I could have flown to his HQ in Wiesbaden.'

'Again, you'll only know when you meet him.'

'What could have gone wrong in Suffolk?' Tweed repeated. 'Paula only dashed off up there because she knows I am investigating the disturbing rumours from France. Karin Rosewater told her she was on the track of a connec-

13

tion with the rising chaos in the French Republic. What connection could there be between Suffolk and France?'

'Maybe all three situations are linked,' Monica suggested. 'Suffolk, France, and this trip to see Kuhlmann.'

'That I find in the realms of fantasy.'

It was a remark he was to regret later. The phone rang, Monica took the call, looked pleased, said come up now.

'Paula, Newman, and Marler have arrived . . .'

'Bob must have driven his Merc to the limit . . .'

As the trio came into the room Tweed noticed Paula's grim expression. Nodding to him she said nothing as she sagged at her desk. Marler perched on the edge of her desk, giving her moral support. Newman threw his windcheater over the back of a chair, sat down, began to talk while Monica hurried out to make coffee. Tweed leaned back in his swivel chair, listened without interruption, glancing occasionally at Paula.

'. . . so, after we found the body I called Ipswich police,' Newman continued. 'We left Butler and Nield to show the police the location when they arrived. We took Paula to the local hotel, the Brudenell, booked a room so she could have a hot bath, then drove straight back here. That's it.'

'Not quite all, I suspect.' Tweed looked at Paula. 'I must first say how very sorry I am about the fate of your friend, Karin Rosewater.'

'It was cold-blooded murder. I'm all right now. The hot bath revived me. Like you, I'm an owl, so we can get on with it now. You'll have questions.'

'Why did Karin come over to see you?'

'She knew I was employed by what she thought was a highly organized security service. She didn't know I was SIS, of course. She said she had been asked by what she called the authorities to investigate the deteriorating situation in France. She asked me to go with her to Dunwich in

Suffolk. A tiny scrap of a village down the coast below Southwold.'

'I know Dunwich. Why there?'

'Then you probably know most of Dunwich is buried under the sea – erosion over the years. At her suggestion we hired wetsuits and drove up there. Some organization is exploring underwater, trying to locate and map this sunken village. I thought she was crazy, asked her why. She said she couldn't say but would I help? She said there was a connection with what is happening in France.'

'Did she elaborate on that odd remark?'

'No. I was going to pump her later during dinner but as it turned out...' She paused, swallowed. 'Karin phoned ahead before we left London to someone she knew in Southwold. When we arrived at Aldeburgh a seaman was waiting for us with a rubber dinghy with a powerful outboard engine. Karin took us up the coast over a calm sea until we were opposite Dunwich, then cut the engine and we went over there in our wetsuits.'

'How far offshore?' asked Newman.

Paula drank half the large mug of coffee Monica had served. 'About half a mile, maybe less.'

'Go on,' urged Tweed. 'Anyone else about when you arrived?'

'Absolutely no one. There was a long rope curled up in the dinghy with an iron hook at one end, the other attached to the dinghy. Karin threw it overboard, then said we could find our way back up to the dinghy fast if we had to. And by God, later we had to.'

'What happened underwater?' Tweed prodded.

'To start with it was fascinating. Horribly cold but there are surprisingly well-preserved relics of the sunken village. Even an old church tower, which was upright, which I thought strange. We swam among the relics and the rocks

15

and then I thought I saw a great white whale. I nearly jumped out of my wetsuit but it remained quite motionless, as though it was anchored. That was when the floating cavalry appeared – men in wetsuits, one with a knife between his teeth.'

'You mean they were hostile?' Marler drawled.

'I mean they were trying to kill us, for God's sake. We managed to evade them by swimming fast among the relics. Karin led me to where the iron hook rested – she'd attached it to a window in the church. We shinned up the rope, climbed back into the dinghy and had the shock of our lives.'

'Have more coffee,' Tweed advised.

He was watching closely for signs of reaction. She'd had a punishing experience and he was ready to send her home. But she seemed determined to tell her story.

Even under stress, she was attractive. In her early thirties, she had raven-black hair, good bone structure, was slim with an excellent figure and of medium height. She put down her mug.

'The sea was no longer deserted. Not far from our dinghy a large vessel was floating. Weird. I've never seen anything like it. Beautiful lines but something sinister about it. Not like an ordinary ship.'

'Hovercraft?' Newman suggested.

'Absolutely not. High out of the water. Something odd about the hull.'

'Hydrofoil?' Marler queried.

'No!' She waved an impatient hand. 'I know what both look like. The hull seemed to be split in two.'

'Why not tell us what happened next?' Tweed coaxed.

'Three of the men in wetsuits came up to the surface close to the dinghy. Karin slashed the anchor rope, I started up the outboard, and we beat the hell south for Aldeburgh.'

'Why go all that way?' Tweed asked.

'Because I'd left the car in a public car park just outside Aldeburgh near the marshes. I thought we could just make it before night came. Luckily we had a good start on the hunters. When we reached the beach at Aldeburgh we had another shock.'

'More coffee.' Monica had refilled her mug. Paula had another drink of the hot, soothing liquid. Eyes half closed, Tweed waited and watched her as she continued.

'That peculiar ship had caught up with us. Again it was lying about half a mile out as we hit the beach. We saw them lowering dinghies with outboard motors as dusk came. No one was about. We stripped off our wetsuits, dropped them on the beach and pulled on our everyday clothes we'd left there. The dinghies were closing in when we started running for the car park. I glanced back and saw them scrambling ashore – this time men wearing Balaclavas and carrying rifles. No time to get the car open and started. I ran faster than Karin, heading across the marshes for the copse of firs . . .'

Sipping more coffee, her voice lowered as she described the last horrific scenes – Karin making the mistake of fleeing for a boat, the dreadful scream . . .

'Shouldn't we stop now till the morning?'

Tweed made the suggestion as Paula paused for a couple of minutes, staring into space.

'No. Ask me questions. Please. I don't went to be alone yet. It helps me to talk.'

'As you wish. Tell me something about Karin Rosewater. Why the mix of nationalities in her name?'

'She's married to an Englishman, Victor. He's a captain with the British Army in Germany. Military Intelligence.

He's liaison officer at a Nato air base near Freiburg in southern Germany. Has an apartment in Freiburg.'

'And Karin was German?'

'Her mother was French, her father German. She's from Colmar in Alsace.'

'Everything close to the Swiss border,' Tweed mused.

'What's the significance of that?' Paula asked.

'Probably nothing. Just a geographical comment. Were you close friends?'

'Yes and no. I met her during that holiday I took in Germany. We got on well. Seemed to be on the same waveband. We agreed to keep in touch.'

'Exactly how and where did you meet?'

Tweed was becoming intrigued. He felt something important was eluding him.

'At a party at the air base. Lots of people there. Oh, I've just remembered. Otto Kuhlmann was there. We had a long chat. He explained he was there on duty, but didn't say why.'

'What about her husband, Victor? You met him?'

'Yes.' Paula pulled a face. 'I didn't like him too much. I'm not sure why.' She stifled a yawn. 'Just not my type, I suppose.'

'And while you were with Karin over here did she tell you what "authorities" – that was the word you used – had asked her to investigate the deteriorating situation in France?'

'No. She didn't refer to it again. And afterwards we were preoccupied with what happened.'

'When you first met her did you get any inkling whether she had some sort of job?'

'No, I didn't. I thought she was a housewife. I feel I'm being interrogated. Not that I mind. But that's how it feels.' She managed a wan smile.

18

'You *are* being interrogated. You may know more than you think you do. Now, it's late. I really think you ought to go home. Marler, would you escort her?'

'My pleasure. You've really put her through the mill.'

'That's all right,' Paula assured him as she stood up and slipped on her windcheater which had been drying on the radiator where Monica had placed it. 'There's something funny going on, isn't there? I don't just mean the brutal murder of Karin – that is bad enough. But why was she interested in the underwater exploration of a sunken village?'

'You need sleep. Don't worry about it. You've done wonderfully well in a desperate situation.'

It was unusual for Tweed to pay her such a compliment. She smiled gratefully, said goodnight, and left the room with Marler.

'There is something funny about this whole business,' Newman said grimly, repeating Paula's thought.

He was alone with Monica and Tweed, who had resumed pacing slowly round the large room. He was frowning and Monica kept quiet, knowing he was thinking hard.

'You're right, Bob,' Tweed said eventually. 'One key question I'd like to know the answer to – were those killers trying to liquidate only Karin, or Paula as well? The answer to that would tell me not only what happened. But *why*.'

'From what she told me in the car they were after both of them,' Newman responded.

'And the other mystery is what is the link between Suffolk and France? Karin told Paula she was hired by authorities to report on the French situation. Also, who owns that strange ship – and what kind of a vessel could it be?'

'Lots of questions,' Monica commented, 'and absolutely no answers.'

Tweed paused, looked down at Newman. 'You left Butler and Nield to cope with the police. What story will they tell them?'

'I covered that carefully, not knowing what we'd got ourselves into. I had to warn them to tell the truth – up to a point. That Paula and Karin were interested in underwater exploration, that they travelled to Dunwich in the outboard, went under the sea, were chased by men with knives, fled back to Aldeburgh where they'd left their car, hadn't time to use the car so they fled over the marshes.'

'So far, so good. It covers all the evidence the police will unearth. The two wetsuits left on the beach, the abandoned outboard. Even the car parked near the marshes.'

'I had to think fast and that's the way I thought. But I left out this business of Karin investigating the situation building up in France, that she was working for someone unknown. You'd better warn Paula in the morning – she's bound to be interviewed by the police soon.'

'I'll call her tonight by the time she's just reached her flat in Putney. Just in case they discover her address and tackle her there.'

Tweed resumed his slow pacing, hands clasped behind his back. Monica realized he was staring into space.

'What's on your mind?' she enquired after a moment.

'Those men in Balaclava helmets – with guns and savage dogs. That suggests a high degree of organization. I just wonder who is behind all this, who is their employer. Bob, while I'm in Luxembourg City, would you please drive back to Aldeburgh, make a few discreet enquiries. Don't forget Dunwich. The trouble started there. Why?'

'I might take Paula with me. She needs some action to get her mind off her awful experience.'

'I may need to leave her here.' Tweed paused. 'There is something you don't know. I've sent the new man, Francis Carey, into France to nose around.'

'After only six months with the SIS?' Newman sounded doubtful. 'Has he enough experience in case he walks into a dangerous situation? What qualifications has he for such a mission?'

'His father was English but his mother French. He spent part of his childhood in Bordeaux. He can pass easily for a Frenchman. He's cautious by nature, but persistent. He's attractive to women – Paula would confirm that. So he'll probably pick up a girlfriend. A couple is less conspicuous than a single man.'

'Theoretically, it sounds a perfect choice.' Newman shook his head. 'But I've met him, talked to him. In an emergency I think he could panic.'

'I wish you hadn't said that . . .'

'Which means you don't disagree.'

'Well, he's there now with a transmitter. He's sent several coded reports from the Bordeaux region. There are serious and growing riots – over the issue of deporting foreign immigrants. Someone is stirring up hatred of the Algerians, for a start. There is a lot of talk in the bars that men high up are plotting a coup. I might just know when I get back from Luxembourg City. In the meantime we'd better get some rest. Tomorrow may hold some unpleasant news. I just have that feeling . . .'

Chapter Two

The following evening it was bitterly cold in the old city of Bordeaux, a port situated inland on the wide Garonne river. In the Bar Miami Francis Carey looked at his watch. 10.30 p.m. Soon he'd be able to go off duty and hurry back to his cheap apartment.

He had got himself a job as barman at the Miami, which was always crowded, after making casual enquiries about the place in his fluent French. It was one of several bars he'd checked out before taking the job. He had heard this bar was popular with low-ranking officers of the French Army who regularly patronized the Miami.

At that hour – and because of the weather – the long room parallel to the bar was packed. Every chair and stool was occupied, many stood with their drinks. The noise was deafening as Frenchmen talked and joked. Carey, a thin man in his late twenties, with dark hair and a long lean face, polished glasses rapidly for new customers as he mentally wrestled with two problems.

He had found himself a French girlfriend, Isabelle Thomas. She had a job in an advertising agency, long titian hair, a pallid complexion, a good figure she liked to display to advantage. She appeared to have fallen for him heavily, which had not been his hope when he picked her up as good cover. And any moment now she would walk in so he could take her out for a quick meal. He dreaded her arrival. And he wanted to postpone their date.

Returning to his modest apartment in a large old block on the rue Georges Bonnac after a shopping trip that morning, he'd detected traces of the place being searched. The compact transmitter he used to send coded signals to Park Crescent had been concealed inside a battered old suitcase hidden on the top of the huge museum piece of a wardrobe. Before leaving for the supermarket in the Mériadeck Centre Commercial, a vast newish concrete complex, he'd attached a hair to the suitcase. When he returned he'd had trouble opening the door. His first suspicion that something was wrong.

A closer check on the apartment inside confirmed his suspicions. The hair half-inserted inside the suitcase had vanished. At first he'd assumed Madame Argoud, the mean old biddy who ran the *pension*, had been nosy. But Argoud was short and fat. Carey was tall and still had had to stand on a chair to reach the suitcase pushed out of sight on top of the wardrobe.

Now he was wondering whether he should have packed up, left the *pension* that morning and moved to another part of the sprawling city. All his training with SIS had emphasized this point. *You never take one single unnecessary risk in hostile territory. You act to remove the risk instantly . . .*

Had he left it too late? Continuing to polish glasses at speed, he checked over the crowded room again. No one who seemed out of place. And had he been wise to trust Isabelle to send the message if anything happened to him? 'If I disappear and don't phone you,' as he had put it.

Two Army lieutenants came in, walked straight to the bar, ordered drinks. He served them as they talked, paid, and drank.

'Soon we'll be drinking in Paris, Anton. They say the women there are quite something.'

'Paris? You mean on leave? We haven't any due.'

23

'So they haven't told you? Well, I am in a specialist unit. Forget what I said.'

The officer turned to stare at Carey. The barman was using a cloth to wipe the counter.

'Haven't seen you here before,' the lieutenant said.

'It's a new job,' Carey answered easily. 'My girlfriend moved, so I moved to be closer to her.'

'And I'll bet you're very close to her at night!'

The officer grinned lewdly, finished his drink, the two men left. An odd remark that – about Paris – Carey thought. I'll quote it in my next signal. He froze as he saw Isabelle pushing her way through the crowd towards him, a wide smile on her full red lips. A fat man leaning on the bar belched and Carey forced himself not to show repugnance. A mixed stench of garlic and anisette turned his stomach. He'd gone off French smells after his years in England. Isabelle perched on a stool and he poured her a Pernod.

'Will you be free soon?' she asked eagerly. 'I know a small restaurant where we can get a super meal.'

'Pay for your drink. The boss is looking. I'll give it to you later.'

'No need. You can buy the dinner. Here it is.'

Further along the counter the chief barman, a short fat man with greasy hair, a long moustache and a stomach which bulged against his apron noted the transaction with satisfaction. No free drinks in his bar – not even for Henri's bedmate.

'Just a few more minutes and we can go,' Carey said, automatically polishing the counter.

He glanced at the door, wondering why a hush had descended on the room. Everyone was looking at two men who had just entered. Both wore belted grey trench coats with wide lapels, trilby hats pulled down over their foreheads, and dark glasses. Why in winter and at night would

24

they sport tinted glasses? Carey was suddenly afraid as they pushed their way steadily towards him.

'Get well away from me, Isabelle,' he ordered. 'No questions. Just move – and take your glass with you.'

Unlike some women she did exactly what he told her to without asking any questions. She had melted into the crowd by the time the two men reached the bar opposite Carey. The crowd, still silent, continued to watch their backs.

'DST.' The taller of the two heavily built men flashed a folder. 'You are Henri Bayle?'

DST. *Direction de la Surveillance du Territoire* – French counter-espionage. And they had the name he had assumed, the name on his papers skilfully forged in the Engine Room in the basement at Park Crescent. He nearly produced his papers to confirm his identity and then decided that would be a mistake at this stage. He continued polishing the counter as he replied.

'That's me. What can I do for you?'

'You are coming with us. For interrogation. Where is your jacket and coat?'

'I only have a jacket. It's out at the back. I'll go and fetch it.'

'Stay where you are,' the taller man snapped. He looked at the chief barman who had edged close. 'Go and bring this man's jacket. He's leaving with us . . .'

'You have a problem?' Carey enquired.

'No. You are the problem.'

Carey put on the jacket his boss had thrown on the bar counter, walked to the flap exit, lifted it and walked out with an escort on either side. He was careful not to look for Isabelle. As they came close to the door he rammed his elbow into the stomach of the man on his left, shoved his way through the crowd and out into the bitter air. A foot reached out, tripped him up. The foot was planted on his back as he lay on the flagstones, trying to get his breath back.

'Stupid, that,' the tall man remarked as he came out.

Carey looked up and saw two more men similarly dressed. They had been waiting for him outside. Hauled to his feet, he was thrown into the rear of a parked Citroën. As the car moved off one man sat on either side of him. Their two companions occupied the front seats. They arrived at the Gare St Jean and the Citroën turned down the deserted ramp leading to the quiet station entrance below street level.

Behind them as they drove away from the bar Isabelle followed on her moped, easily keeping the Citroën in view along the dark empty streets. She was puzzled when the Citroën disappeared down the ramp. Where were they taking Henri? Could they be moving him somewhere by train? If so, why? She parked her moped by the station wall, attached the safety chain, clasped her windcheater close to her neck against the bitter wind off the Atlantic.

As the Citroën descended down the ramp Henri gritted his teeth to conceal his fear. It was like entering a dimly lit cavern. No passengers were about at that hour. The tall man repeated for the third time the question he had asked as they drove to the Gare.

'Who were you communicating with when you used that transmitter we found in your apartment?'

'I'm a radio ham. I talk to other hams all over the world.'

'You're lying. That's the last time I'm going to ask.'

'How did you get into my apartment?' Henri demanded.

'Haven't you heard of skeleton keys? I'm sure you have. This is the end of the line. Get out.'

The Citroën had parked near the entrance to the ticket hall. Behind, the cavern was disturbing darkness. Carey followed the shorter man out on to the sidewalk. His arm was gripped in a vice. The tall man stayed inside the car, pointed an automatic at him.

'Get rid of him, Louis. He isn't going to talk.'

'You can go now,' Louis told Carey. 'You get out to the street that way. Shove off before we change our minds.'

Carey walked into the deep shadow and stopped as something moved, a shadow among the shadows. Hands grasped him round the neck. Carey tried to kick his attacker in the groin, slipped and fell. The shadowy figure knelt on top of him, hands still grasping his neck, thumbs pressed expertly on his windpipe. Carey tried to scream. Only a gurgle emerged as the remorseless pressure increased. Carey began to lose consciousness. He choked for dear life, his clenched fists hammering futilely against his assailant. Even when Carey had gone limp the strangler continued exerting pressure. When another minute had passed he rose to his feet, vanished into the darkness.

Louis pressed the button on his flashlight, walked forward, bent down over the prone form, checked its neck pulse. He strolled back to the car, climbed back into the rear.

'No neck pulse,' he reported to the tall man.

'Kalmar – whoever he may be – did another good job. For a big fat fee, I'm sure. What will we get? A pat on the back.' He addressed the driver. 'Back to the barracks.'

Isabelle pressed herself against the wall at the top of the ramp as the Citroën drove off. She had caught a glimpse of Henri getting out of the car by the glow of the courtesy light inside the car when the rear door was opened.

She crept slowly down the ramp, stopped to 1isten. The silence frightened her. She pulled out the flashlight her mother insisted she carried, switched it on, walked on to the bottom of the ramp. Swivelling the beam, she ventured into the shadows.

She almost tripped over the body, gave a little cry as she aimed the beam downwards. Henri was on his back, his tongue protruding obscenely from his slack open mouth. His throat was badly bruised.

She forced herself to kneel beside him, felt his wrist pulse. But she knew he was dead. Numb with terror and grief, she felt inside the breast pocket where he kept his papers, his wallet. Both had gone. She had no way of knowing that within minutes Kalmar would be throwing them from the bridge into the Garonne.

She kissed the cold head, her eyes closed to avoid seeing the distorted face. Standing up, she stumbled back up the ramp to where she had left her moped. She was unlocking her moped chain when a drunk holding a bottle staggered across the wide *place* from the Bar Nicole. Tears were streaming down Isabelle's face as she began to wheel her machine to the street. The drunk leered at her.

'Lost your boy friend, girlie? Maybe we could have fun together . . .'

'*Drop dead.*'

She started up her moped and rode off towards her home. The wind raked her damp face as tears continued to pour down her cheeks. She remembered what she had just said to the drunk. It was poor Henri who was dead and she had been in love with him.

At least she could do one last thing for him. Carry out his request if anything happened to him. On her way to work the following morning she would phone the London number he had given her in secrecy, would tell whoever answered what had happened to him.

Chapter Three

'Kuhlmann has changed the rendezvous at the last moment,' Tweed announced to Monica and Paula. 'That is quite out of character. He must be a very worried man. Geneva – not Luxembourg City – is the meeting place. Tomorrow morning at the Hotel des Bergues.'

'What time would you like to leave?' Monica asked, her hand poised over the phone.

'I'd like to leave this evening.' Tweed turned to Paula. 'Yesterday was a bit gruelling for you – I spent most of the day drilling you in what to say to Chief Inspector Buchanan.'

'And I'm grateful. I'm sure I'm word perfect. It was clever of you to tell Buchanan when he phoned I was out of town and you didn't know where . . .'

She broke off as the door opened, Newman and Marler came in, sat down and looked at Tweed. As Monica lowered her voice on the phone Tweed warned Newman quickly.

'Bob, I've got a bit of a shock for you. The man who is investigating Karin Rosewater's murder is our old friend, Chief Inspector Roy Buchanan.'

'He's no friend of mine. The last time we met he had me marked as number one suspect in a murder case. May I look forward to a repeat performance?' He frowned. 'Just a minute. Buchanan is Homicide, New Scotland Yard. There hasn't been time for the locals to request the Yard's aid. It was only the day before yesterday we found Karin's body.'

'I asked Buchanan that very question when he phoned to come and interview Paula yesterday. Apparently he'd just solved another murder case in Suffolk and was still there. Most of the senior officers at Ipswich HQ are down with flu. Hence the Chief Constable asked Buchanan if he'd stand in temporarily.'

'What lousy luck . . .'

'And he's on his way here now. Which is why I left a message on your answerphone to get here as early as you could this morning. Both you and Marler have a lot to grasp before Buchanan descends. Yesterday Paula and I went over how she would handle it – his questioning. Briefly, no mention of Karin being hired by some mysterious authority to check the state of France. Just a friend of Paula's who shared her interest in underwater exploration. I'm going to point Buchanan in the direction of Paula so he questions her first. You two can then follow her lead. Volunteer nothing – answer any questions he asks and shut up.'

'I say,' Marler protested, 'we're not exactly amateurs at this game.'

Tweed leaned forward over his desk. 'And neither is Buchanan, so don't you forget it . . .'

The phone rang, Monica took the call, listened, grimaced at Tweed, who nodded and relaxed in his chair.

'They're on the way up,' Monica said as she replaced the receiver. 'The Heavenly Twins – Chief Inspector Buchanan, with his ever-faithful sidekick, Sergeant Warden.'

'We must welcome them. Make coffee, if you would.'

Tweed rose behind his desk as Monica opened the door and two men entered. Buchanan was a tall slim man in his forties with a deceptively relaxed manner which had trapped more than a few suspects. Warden, an inch or two shorter, had a poker face and rarely showed any kind of reaction. He carried a notebook. Greeting them amiably,

Tweed ushered them into two chairs he had earlier placed so they half-faced Paula and himself.

'We are all ready for you,' Tweed began amiably, 'and Paula is ready to answer your questions.'

'Really?' Buchanan's tone was cynical as he glanced round the room. 'You mean you're going to co-operate without waving the Official Secrets Act in my face? Something General & Cumbria Assurance have been known to resort to.'

Tweed smiled at this reference to the cover name for the SIS, the name on the brass plate on the front door.

'Monica will be bringing coffee,' Tweed continued his welcoming act. 'It's a raw day.'

'It must have been a raw day, Miss Grey, when you went scuba diving at Dunwich. At least that was the story Mr Harry Butler told me at Ipswich police headquarters two days ago.'

'Miss Grey?' She gave him her best smile. 'I recall it was Paula last time we met.'

'This is a formal inquiry into a cold-blooded case of murder. How do you think she was killed?'

He's going for the jugular for openers, Tweed thought. Trying to throw her off balance with a brutal approach.

'She appeared to have been strangled,' Paula replied quietly.

'By an expert. One might almost say a professional.'

'What makes you say that?' Tweed interjected sharply.

'The autopsy report. It was carried out by Dr Kersey. You may have heard of him – one of the leading pathologists.' Buchanan jingled loose change in his pocket.

'What does he base that conclusion on?' Tweed persisted.

Buchanan faced him and his alert grey eyes showed a trace of amusement. He was well aware Tweed had intervened to take the pressure off Paula for a moment.

'The way the strangler had used his thumbs to press on the windpipe to bring about death as swiftly as possible. Kersey suspects some of the bruising was inflicted after death – an attempt to cover up the skill with which the strangulation was carried out. Now, if you don't mind, I'd like to continue asking Miss Grey certain questions. After all, she was at the scene of the crime. You weren't.'

'I wasn't actually at the scene of the crime as you said,' Paula contradicted him. 'I was shivering with cold and fright near the top of a fir tree.'

'But you saw the murder take place?'

'I did not. Would you like me to explain how Karin and I came to be there?'

'You're willing to make a statement?'

Buchanan glanced at Warden who sat with his notebook on his lap, then at Tweed; expecting opposition. Tweed, playing with a pen, merely nodded.

Paula told her story tersely and without a wasted word. While she talked Buchanan never took his eyes off her but she stared back. The Chief Inspector crossed his legs, perched the cup and saucer Monica had given him on his knee, sipped the beverage as Paula concluded.

'. . . I wish to God now I'd insisted Karin and I spent the day shopping in London.'

'I hadn't heard you were interested in underwater exploration,' Buchanan remarked.

'But you don't know all that about me. I've made my statement.'

'And these mysterious men in disguise who hunted you with rifles . . .' There was a hint of sarcasm in his tone and he paused, hoping Paula would rise to the bait. When she remained silent he pressed on. 'Who could they have been? Why would they want to kill the two of you? When you were racing back to Aldeburgh with the other outboard dinghies in pursuit why didn't you head for the shore earlier and run for it?'

Warden smiled to himself. A typical Buchanan tactic. Without warning he was putting on the pressure to break her down with a barrage of queries. Pressure had broken many witnesses before.

'I've made my statement,' Paula repeated. 'In that statement I answered all but one of those three questions but I'll humour you. You don't mind if I repeat myself, Chief Inspector?'

'Not at all,' Buchanan replied agreeably.

'I've no idea who the killers were. I've no idea why they came after us. The third question was not covered in my statement. If you knew that part of the world you'd know that south of Dunwich is one of the loneliest stretches of coast in the world. I felt we had to get to the parked car to escape.'

'And the three dinghies these men used to pursue you at sea had appeared after you had dived below the surface?'

'I refer you to my statement.'

'Karin's husband, Captain Victor Rosewater, is stationed at a Nato base in southern Germany. Someone will have to tell him what's happened.'

'I've already done that. It wasn't a pleasant duty.'

'You left that out of your statement,' Buchanan pointed out.

'It's been added to the statement now.'

'How did he react?'

This was the unexpected question she'd been dreading. Something which hadn't arisen when she'd had her long session with Tweed. She hesitated for a second, used her hand to straighten a pleat in her blue skirt.

'He expressed complete disbelief. I don't think he'd taken it in by the time the conversation ended.'

Buchanan smoothed his brown, neatly cut hair, stroking the back of his neck. Warden recognized the gesture: frustration. Buchanan suddenly looked over his shoulder at Newman.

'Have you anything to add to the latter part of Miss Grey's statement? After all, you were there at the crucial time. I have a further question when you've explained your own version of events.'

'I have nothing to add to Paula's very lucid description of what took place. And your other question?'

'The timing seems wrong. I was at Ipswich police HQ when your call came through. I was passing the duty sergeant's desk and he'd also gone down with flu. So I took your call . . .'

'Funny, I didn't recognize your voice,' Newman interjected, playing for time.

'Probably because I used my official voice. I recognized yours. The call was timed at exactly 8.20 p.m. From Miss Grey's account you must still have been on the marshes. So how did you know the right number to phone?'

'Driving out to find Paula we passed a call box. I stopped the car, went back, checked the number in the phone directory.'

'Why? At that stage?'

Buchanan's tone was whiplash. Newman smiled, lit a cigarette, blew smoke rings.

'I refer you to Paula's statement. You're a detective. You should have worked that out for yourself. When she called for help she mentioned hearing Karin scream. I feared the worst, thought we might need the police.'

'I see.' He turned suddenly to Paula. 'Were you carrying a weapon?'

'No,' she lied promptly.

'What about you, Newman – and the others?'

34

Buchanan had twisted round in his chair again. His gaze swept over Marler, rested on Newman.

'We were all armed. I don't have to explain why, do I?'

'What weapon were you equipped with?'

Buchanan was addressing Marler who had been sitting like a statue. He was smoking a king-size cigarette. Marler flicked ash from the cigarette into a glass bowl, looked at Buchanan with amusement.

'For the record,' he drawled, 'as if it mattered, I had my favourite weapon. An Armalite.'

The cup and saucer on Buchanan's knee jiggled. Warden, intrigued, leaned forward. It was the first time he had ever seen his chief rattled. Buchanan recovered quickly, nodded in response before he replied.

'A strange weapon to be hawking round the countryside.'

'You think so?' Marler's tone was still bantering. 'I would have thought it logical when we'd heard the men hunting Paula were carrying rifles. I'm quite a fairish shot, you know.'

Buchanan put down his cup and saucer on a table. Standing up, he addressed Paula, his tone neutral.

'We'll have your statement typed out and then maybe you would be good enough to drop in at the Yard to sign it.'

'Have it brought here,' Tweed said quietly. 'Something urgent cropped up yesterday. Paula will be occupied for some time to come.'

'As you wish.' Buchanan walked to the door Warden had opened. He turned round before leaving. 'I would like to thank everyone for their co-operation. And yours especially, Tweed . . .'

He said nothing more until he had climbed behind the wheel of his Volvo parked further along the Crescent. He was fixing his seat belt when Warden asked his question.

'What do you think, Chief?'

'Paula Grey was lying.'

'Really, I didn't get that impression.'

'She was lying by omission. Her statement bore all the hallmarks of having been carefully rehearsed. Probably with Tweed. There's a lot they haven't told us. You noticed Newman said very little? Just said he agreed with Paula's version. Not like him to keep so quiet.'

'That Marler is a saucy sod.'

'Oh, that was a clever tactic. A way of terminating the interview.'

'And you let him get away with it? Not like you.'

'I realized we'd get no more out of them at this stage. We'll leave them alone for a while, let them think we swallowed it, hook, line and sinker.'

'What about the mysterious men in Balaclavas carrying rifles? Sounded a load of codswallop to me.'

'There you could be wrong. It's so bizarre I do believe it happened. I think we may have stumbled on to something big. We'll go back to the Yard, you pick up your own car, then we drive back to Suffolk. Separately, we scour the area, ask questions – especially about underwater exploration. Even with the two of us we'll have our hands full. It's a very large area . . .'

'Well, that went well,' Newman commented after their visitors had left.

'You think so?' Tweed queried. 'Buchanan wasn't fooled. He'll be back. What we've gained is a breathing space so we can get to the bottom of what is happening – here and in France. Where were you yesterday, Bob?'

'Marler and I went to Aldeburgh. We avoided the marshes where the police have cordoned off the killing ground. And someone is financing a new expedition to explore that sunken village of Dunwich. Ever heard of Lord Dane Dawlish?'

Tweed ticked off items on his fingers. 'Self-made million-aire. Has armament factories in Scotland, at Thetford in Norfolk, in Belgium, and at Annecy in southern France. Made his original fortune out of the property boom in the eighties. A tough ruthless character. I suppose he had to be to get where he has. That's it.'

'I think I ought to try and get an interview with him,' Newman suggested.

'I might do better at that,' Paula intervened. 'I hear he has a soft spot for girlfriends.'

'How could you present yourself?'

'I know the editor of *Woman's Eye*. I could go as a reporter to write an article on his achievements.'

'Hold off, Bob,' Tweed advised. 'For the moment. I'll decide who goes when I get back from Geneva – and Paula is coming with me. One step at a time. I want to hear what is disturbing the Germans first.'

The phone rang, Monica answered it, saying it was General & Cumbria Assurance. She listened for a short time, then put her hand over the receiver and looked at Paula.

'Could you take this? It's a girl. Speaking in French.'

Paula took the receiver, perched herself on the edge of Monica's desk. She spoke in French.

'This is General & Cumbria. Who is this?'

'My name is Isabelle Thomas.' There was a choking sound. 'I'm sorry about that. I'm upset. Do please excuse me. Did you know Henri Bayle?'

Paula put her hand over the receiver. 'Henri Bayle?'

'Francis Carey, the undercover man I sent to the south of France,' Tweed confirmed.

'Sorry,' Paula continued, 'the line crackled. You did say

Henri Bayle? Yes, I work with him. I know all about him. I'm the General Manager . . .'

'Henri is dead . . .' Isabelle's voice broke again. 'It was awful. He's been murdered . . .'

'Isabelle, where are you speaking from?' Paula enquired quickly.

'From the main Post Office.'

'That's all right. Sorry to interrupt. Do go on,' Paula said in a businesslike tone. 'This is appalling news. I need to know as much as you can tell me.'

She listened while Isabelle, calmer under Paula's controlled reaction, related her story, starting from the arrival of the DST men at the Bar Miami. Paula was scribbling in shorthand on a pad Monica had pushed in front of her. The room had gone quiet. Everyone sensed the tension in the conversation as Paula encouraged the French girl to go on. Eventually she started checking Isabelle's story.

'You did say two DST men? Your *Direction de la Surveillance du Territoire*?'

'Yes, it was them. I was close enough to Henri in the crowded bar to catch what they said. I don't understand why they would . . .' Another choking sound. 'I was in love with Henri.'

'So you're very upset – as I would be.' A vital question: 'Have you informed the local police?'

'No. Should I?'

'Under no circumstances. Don't do that. Tell no one.'

'I haven't even told my mother. I'm so confused.'

'I can understand that. I may know what happened,' Paula lied. 'Whatever you do, tell no one,' she repeated. 'We will try and send someone to meet you. He will introduce himself as . . . Alain Dreyfus.' The first name which came into her head. 'Have patience, Isabelle. It could be a short

38

time before we can contact you. Now, would you give me your address and phone number?'

She wrote the details down carefully, asked Isabelle to repeat the address to make sure she had it down correctly.

'Isabelle, have you got a job? I see. Don't throw it up. Carry on your life as usual – as far as you can, considering the terrible bereavement you have suffered. And no police. Why was Henri working for an insurance company? He was checking on a suspicious death where a claim for insurance had been made.'

'I must get back to my job now,' Isabelle said in a lacklustre voice. 'I have at least done what Henri asked me to if something happened to him.'

'You did the right thing. We will investigate. But, don't forget, no police . . .'

She put down the phone and sighed heavily. She was wearing a white blouse with a pussy bow. She fiddled with the bow before she looked at Tweed.

'God! I hope I handled that reasonably well. You do realize what has happened?'

'With no time to think you reacted brilliantly. And am I right in assuming Francis Carey is dead?'

'Yes. Murdered through the agency of two DST men who took him from a bar to the Gare St Jean late in the evening yesterday. In Bordeaux . . .'

She gave a terse account of what Isabelle had told her. Tweed listened with an expressionless face. When she had finished he drummed the fingers of his right hand lightly on the desk top and looked at Newman.

'I fear you were right. Carey was too inexperienced to send him on that mission. My deadly mistake.'

'Rubbish!' Newman snapped. 'Not too long ago Harry Masterson, an area chief in Europe, experienced as hell, was also murdered. It's part of the risk run by anyone belonging to SIS. I'm sure you warned Carey before he agreed to go. So stop blaming yourself.'

Tweed was suddenly galvanized into action. 'Two DST men? It's unbelievable. Monica, try and get me René Lasalle on the scrambler now. We'll soon find out the truth . . .'

There was silence as Monica dialled the number. Paula sat at her desk, plucking at the pleats of her skirt, playing back in her mind the conversation with the distraught Isabelle. Monica nodded to Tweed, indicating the DST chief in Paris was on the line.

'René,' Tweed began in a decisive tone, 'Tweed here on scrambler . . . You are too? Good. I sent an agent to the south of France as we agreed. I've just heard he was murdered last night in Bordeaux – at the main station. After being hustled out of a bar by two men who said they were DST . . .'

'Good God! You did say DST? That's impossible. No DST men are operating in the Bordeaux area. I should know.'

'Then they were impersonators . . .'

'That I will not tolerate. As soon as this call is ended teams will be flown to Bordeaux to investigate. But I need more information, if you are willing to reveal that.'

'Certainly. The agent was masquerading – with papers – under the name Henri Bayle. He was working as a barman at some dive called the Bar Miami. From the timing I was given the murder must have taken place something in the region of 11 p.m. Apparently in some underground entrance which is reached by a ramp. Someone other than the two fake DST officers actually committed the murder.'

'And who told you this?'

'An informant whose name I would sooner not give. The informant sounds reliable. Carey was due to transmit a radio signal last night and nothing came. I assumed it was inconvenient.'

'And you heard this news when?'

'Five minutes ago.'

'My teams will be flying there immediately. Tweed, I would appreciate it very much if you could fly to Paris to see me. There are developments you should know – and they may be linked with this assassination. I send you my sympathy. But, most important, can we meet?'

'Yes. Very soon. I have to fly elsewhere in Europe first. May I call you as soon as I can come on to Paris?'

'Please do.' Lasalle's tone became grim. 'Events here are taking a desperate turn. A crisis is upon us. Hurry, my friend. *Au revoir . . .*'

Tweed stared into the distance after putting down the phone. He seemed to have forgotten the presence of everyone else in the room.

'Any instructions?' asked Monica.

'Yes. I've decided Paula is coming with me to Geneva and to Paris. Book another room at the Hotel des Bergues in Geneva, get her a ticket on my flight. Get us both open air tickets to Paris. Book two rooms at that small hotel in Paris, the Madeleine. It's fairly close to the rue des Saussaies – to Lasalle.'

'What is this Lasalle business?' Newman asked.

'The second man who has used the word crisis in the past few days. First Kuhlmann, now Lasalle. Something explosive is building up in Europe.'

'I've just remembered something Karin said,' Paula reported. 'It was while were hurriedly changing into our clothes after hitting the beach at Aldeburgh with those men coming after us. Drove it out of my mind.'

'What was it?' Newman asked.

'She said the French Army was the danger. The units stationed in the south. In our anxiety to escape it completely slipped my mind. I was never able to ask her what she meant.'

'My next objective,' Newman decided. 'While Tweed is haring over Europe.'

'What objective?' Tweed asked.

'To interview the commander of that army . . .'

Chapter Four

Gun barrels. Row upon row of lethal firepower projecting menacingly from the huge assembly of tanks Newman was escorted past by a French Army lieutenant.

He had driven from Bordeaux to the heavily guarded entrance of the Third Corps. After flying to Bordeaux he had been surprised by the speed with which the commander of this great battle array had agreed to an interview.

'You represent *Der Spiegel*, Mr Newman? Then I am sure the General will be pleased to see you,' the suave voice had responded. 'I am Major Lamy. You are in Bordeaux? Shall we say 2 p.m? Yes, today. That is agreed . . .'

GHQ, Third Corps, was located in hilly country east of Bordeaux. During his drive in a hired Citroën Newman had passed through fields laid out with grids of vineyards, a distant view of the turrets of a large chateau.

'This way, Mr Newman,' the lieutenant said in French, walking between four lines of tanks, gun barrels precisely aligned parallel to each other. Uniformed soldiers ran in the distance. Newman had an impression of a highly organized military machine run by a man who tolerated no waste of time. Escorted inside a single-storey building guarded by sentries, he was led along a wide corridor to a heavy wooden mahogany door, elaborately carved with Napoleonic-style eagles. More like the door he'd expect to have seen inside the chateau he had passed.

'The General is expecting you. Just walk in,' the lieutenant invited, taking hold of the handle.

'How does he know I've arrived?' Newman enquired.

'The officer in the guard room had obtained a newspaper photo of you from the library. When you got out of your car he radioed to the General's aide-de-camp.'

'Radioed? Haven't you heard of the telephone?'

'Phones can be tapped.'

'And why was I body-searched before I was permitted to enter?'

'More security. You were checked for weapons, for a concealed tape-recorder. Normal procedure against the danger of saboteurs. The General is waiting . . .'

The door was closed behind him as Newman walked alone into a long room with a polished woodblock floor. A very long room with a large Louis Quinze desk at the far end. Behind the desk sat a stocky figure wearing the uniform of a full general. Standing behind the tall-backed Louis Quinze chair was a thin erect man, also in uniform and with the rank of major.

But what caught Newman's attention was the framed silhouette hanging from the wall behind the chair. A large black silhouette, unmistakably of General Charles de Gaulle, head and shoulders, in profile and wearing his képi.

'Welcome to Third Corps, Mr Newman. Please do sit down. I hope you won't mind but we checked with *Der Spiegel* that you were reporting for them.'

'General Charles de Forge?' Newman enquired, remaining on his feet.

'Of course. This is Major Lamy, my Chief of Intelligence.'

De Forge had a strong hawk-like face, longish and with a firm jaw. His eyes were a piercing blue and he stared penetratingly at Newman as he rose, extended a hand. His grip was so firm Newman's fingers would have suffered had he not been prepared for it.

Lamy sported a dark smear of a moustache and his expression was sardonic as he nodded to Newman who now sat down.

'I can't interview you, General, with someone else present.'

De Forge, his manner aloof, stared at Newman. Leaning against the imperial high-backed chair, he exuded dynamic energy under the control of an iron will. There was something almost presidential about his manner.

'Major Lamy is one of my closest associates.'

'Nevertheless,' Newman insisted, 'I made it quite clear on the phone – and the call was with Lamy – that the interview was to be personal. That means alone.'

'Lamy, you'd better leave us. Reporters seem to think they out-rank generals.'

'I have heard rumours,' Newman began after the Intelligence officer had shut the door, 'that you have strong views on the present position in France. When I was at the gate I was body-searched. The lieutenant used a word I didn't quite grasp. Saboteurs.'

'The scum are everywhere. France is polluted with alien elements that should be removed. Algerians, Arabs – God knows what else.'

'That sounds lile the programme of the new party, *Pour France*, an extremist group akin to *Action Direct*.'

Newman's French was fluent. He thought he detected a hint of surprise in the penetrating eyes. De Forge waved a well-shaped hand.

'I am a servant of the Republic. Politics does not interest me. But I must correct you. *Pour France* is a party whose popularity is growing hourly. If their views coincide with mine, that is irrelevant.'

'You're not concerned in any way with politics, or so you say. Have you any views on the new Germany?'

It was like pressing a button. De Forge leaned forward, gesticulating with a clenched fist. But his voice remained calm as he launched his attack.

'We have to be on our guard. The present Chancellor is a man of peace, but who follows him? A new Bismarck who will attempt to use the tremendous power of unified Germany to take back Alsace-Lorraine from us again? I draw your attention to the *Siegfried* movement which is growing stronger daily. An underground organization which may surface at any time. France must be prepared for a fresh onslaught. I repeat, *Siegfried* is a great menace to us – to your own country. We must be strong. You want to see how strong we are?'

'I did see your tanks . . .'

'I refer to our methods of training an élite army – ready for any emergency. Come with me, Mr Newman . . .'

De Forge stood up, placed his képi over his high forehead. He glanced at the silhouette of General de Gaulle and smiled coldly.

'He was a great man. Maybe it is time for a second de Gaulle to arise. Come!'

De Forge led the way from his office out of the building to where a vehicle like a jeep was parked. Jumping with agility behind the wheel he beckoned for Newman to join him in the passenger seat. Curious, Newman climbed up. He had barely sat down when the vehicle began moving at high speed.

Uniformed men on motorcycles appeared as outriders with sirens screaming, ahead of the General and behind his vehicle. The racing cavalcade swept through the gates of the main entrance which had been opened, continued into the countryside.

Newman, holding on with his right hand to avoid being tipped out, glanced at the General. His hawkish profile was calm despite the fact that he obviously enjoyed moving at high speed. The cavalcade swung off the road up a track across a field towards a forest, slowed down.

'Just where are we going?' Newman demanded.

'To show you the punishment well. Men have to be tough to form an élite strike force. Discipline, order, and stability are our watchwords.'

'I seem to recall the leader of *Pour France* used the same slogan.'

Swivelling the wheel, de Forge stared at Newman and his expression was bleak. He stopped the vehicle in the middle of the evergreen forest in a clearing. There was something sinister about the atmosphere, the way the outriders formed a circle a distance away from an old stone well.

'This part of the interview is off the record,' de Forge ordered.

'I didn't agree to that condition earlier. You can't impose it now.'

De Forge paused as though about to change his mind, to drive back to GHQ. Newman, sensing the change of mood, jumped out of the vehicle, strode over to the well. De Forge followed him. He wore riding boots polished so they gleamed like glass. In his right hand he carried a whip which he slashed against the boots. Newman had to admit it was an impressive performance. Whatever else the General was, he was a natural leader.

Newman examined the ancient well. The main structure had crumbling walls but the windlass, operated by a handle, was brand new. Attached to one end of the windlass was a gauge measured in metres. Two ropes dangled tautly into the depths. Newman picked up a small stone, dropped it down the side. It seemed for ever before he heard a faint distant splash.

'Don't drop a large stone,' de Forge warned and smiled his cold smile. 'You might hit the prisoner.'

'Prisoner?'

'This is the punishment well. If a soldier fails to carry out an order – or doesn't perform up to scratch on the obstacle course – he spends some time down the punishment well. A defaulter is now suspended just above the stagnant water.'

'Why two ropes?'

'One is attached round his neck like a noose. It has a special adjustable slip knot which can be tightened or loosened from here. He is in no danger. Just a touch of terror.'

'And the second rope?' Newman asked in a tight voice.

'Attached to a harness round his chest. The main support between the defaulter and eternity. Later he will be hauled up by the harness rope.'

'And that gauge?' Newman persisted.

'That tells us how close to the water the prisoner has been lowered.'

Newman peered over the rim into the black hole. It was so dark he could see no sign of the poor devil hanging in space. He heard an engine sound. Out of the corner of his eye he saw Major Lamy arrive in another jeep-like vehicle, the sardonic officer crouched over the wheel like a bird of prey.

De Forge strode over to him. There was a brief conversation. Lamy picked up a microphone. An aerial extended upwards automatically. Lamy was speaking into the mike, then replaced it and drove away. De Forge strode back.

'You see now how we have built the most powerful army in Europe.'

'I think it's barbaric . . .'

Nothing further was said between the two men while de Forge drove Newman back to GHQ. The sinister outriders, wearing tinted goggles, accompanied them. Racing up to the entrance, de Forge stopped with a jerk which would have hurled Newman to the ground had he not been prepared for just such a manoeuvre. De Forge stared straight ahead as he spoke.

'You leave here.'

Newman jumped out, de Forge raced into GHQ through the gates which had been opened at his approach. Walking towards his parked Citroën, Newman had to pass between the circle of outriders who had remained. Behind tinted glasses unseen eyes stared at him. Careful not to touch a motorcycle, he slipped through a gap, took out his key and inserted it into the lock of the Citroën.

The key did not slip in easily as it had done earlier. Newman grunted, punctuating his thought. He opened the door, slipped behind the wheel, closed the door, started the engine. The accelerator seemed slower to respond. He drove off, waited until he had rounded two distant bends, well clear of GHQ, parked on the grass verge.

Getting out, he extracted his pencil flash, crawled under the chassis, examined it carefully. No sign of a bomb. It would have been a bomb activated by remote radio control – he had realized earlier there would be no danger of an explosion with the motoryclists so close. I'm getting paranoid, he thought. De Forge is just an egomaniac who likes to show off.

He drove on towards Bordeaux. Five minutes later, moving along the deserted road, he saw a black Berliet van, a large wide vehicle, appear in his rear-view mirror. The type of vehicle used by the CRS, the French paramilitary police brought in to quell mob violence. Surely de Forge hadn't managed to persuade them to become his allies? Then he recalled the phoney DST men who had taken Francis Carey from the Bar Miami. Had the vehicle been hijacked?

It was closing up on him rapidly, huge in his mirror. In the cab sat the driver and two men wearing Balaclavas which concealed their faces. One held what looked like a long truncheon. Standard CRS equipment for beating back a seething mob.

Newman had an excellent memory for routes. He had only to drive along a new complex route once to be able to remember every detail on the return trip. He rammed his foot down and again there wasn't the normal reaction he'd experienced when driving out to the GHQ, the same burst of speed.

Newman knew exactly what had happened. He recalled the change in de Forge's manner when he had refused to accept the 'off the record' condition imposed so belatedly. The arrival of the cynical Lamy, de Forge's conversation with him, Lamy's use of the radio to send back a message. They had used skeleton keys to open his car, had tampered with the accelerator. He glanced in the mirror again. The black Berliet van was moving like a shell from a gun, was almost in his boot.

He pressed his foot all the way down, coaxed more speed out of the damaged mechanism. Newman swung round a bend, sped on, recognizing exactly where he was. Could he reach the bridge in time? It would be a matter of seconds. No bookmaker would give odds on him for this race for survival.

The two Balaclava-masked passengers in the cab leaned forward. Newman could sense their savage eagerness to get at him. The gap between the two vehicles had temporarily widened with his recent pressure on the accelerator. Two more bends.

The Berliet was closing the gap again, filling his rear-view mirror like a mobile hulk. He swung round the first bend, his foot pressed down with all his strength. Ahead lay the last bend. It seemed to creep towards him as the Berliet almost touched his rear bumper. He swung the wheel, negotiated the last bend and the narrow hump-backed stone bridge was a hundred yards away. Newman tightened his grip on the wheel, forced himself to ignore the mirror.

On his outward journey he had slowed to cross the narrow bridge, just sliding both sides of the car between the stone walls without scraping the Citroën. Now he had to judge in centimetres, taking the bridge at a belting speed. He risked a brief final glance in the mirror. The Berliet was about to ram him. The wheels of the Citroën mounted the near side of the hump-back, raced over the crest. The solid stone walls flashed past him in a blur. He gripped the wheel more firmly as he felt the Citroën descending. He almost lost control but his nerve held. He was beyond the bridge.

In his rear-view mirror he saw the Berliet reach the bridge. Because he'd had plenty of time Newman had not taken the main road to Third Corps GHQ; he had driven along a more devious route to see the vineyards and maybe a chateau. The driver of the Berliet saw the bridge too late. The wide van roared up the near side, metal screaming as it grated against the stone. The van stopped abruptly, jammed between the walls. The left-hand wall broke under the pressure, fell into the gorge below and took with it a portion of the floor of the bridge. The Berliet swayed, hung tilted at an angle over the drop for a fraction of a second, then followed the wall, turning over in mid-air, smashing into the rockstrewn gorge with a noise like a bomb detonating.

Newman stopped the Citroën, jumped out, climbed a bank which gave him a view down into the gorge. The Berliet lay motionless. Nothing moved. No one emerged from the metal coffin.

Newman shrugged, got back behind the wheel and drove on to Bordeaux. When Tweed heard he was flying to the city he had given him the address of Isabelle Thomas, Francis Carey's girlfriend. It was time someone paid her a visit to see how she was bearing up – and perhaps gain more information.

Chapter Five

The first surprise Tweed and Paula had when they arrived in Geneva at the Hotel des Bergues was the sight of Chief Inspector Kuhlmann sitting reading a newspaper in a chair near reception. He had arrived much earlier than they'd expected.

The second surprise was his reaction. He glanced up and then ignored them, turning to a fresh page of his paper. Paula looked at Tweed.

'Don't say a word to him,' he warned. 'And don't look at him again . . .'

Tweed registered for his room. When Paula followed his example Tweed wondered why she stood well back as she filled in the form. The receptionist handed her a key.

'What room did you say?' she asked in a loud voice. 'I have left my reading glasses behind.'

'Room Number 135,' the receptionist repeated in an equally carrying voice.

Tweed hurried to her room as soon as he had swiftly unpacked. Her room was also a large double – the only rooms Monica had been able to reserve. Situated at a corner overlooking the rue du Mont-Blanc on one side and the river itself across the street where the main entrance was located, it was more like a suite.

'Very de luxe,' Paula glowed. 'And look at the lights across the river.'

Beyond the uncurtained windows neon of various colours illuminated the distant buildings in the dark, the signs reflected like coloured snakes in the water. Tweed nodded appreciation, his thoughts eleswhere.

'Otto Kuhlmann has already phoned me,' Paula went on. 'He asked when we would be leaving for dinner, said he'd be waiting in the lobby, then rang off abruptly.'

'He's acting mysteriously. Maybe he's going to join us so I think we need somwhere discreet.'

'I'd already caught on to that. I hope you don't mind, but after his call I booked a corner table for three at Les Armures. It's a fashionable restaurant in the Old Town, near the Cathedral. I hope you approve.'

'An excellent choice. Do you want to change?'

'I want food. I'm hungry. And I sense Otto is wanting to see us urgently. He used that word when he called me.'

'Put on your coat and let's move . . .'

Kuhlmann standing just outside the entrance, wearing a black overcoat and a black wide-brimmed hat pulled down over his broad forehead. Short in stature, he had very wide shoulders, a large head and reminded Paula once more of old films she'd seen of Edward G. Robinson. The same tough face, firm mouth, the suggestion of great physical and mental strength. Again he ignored them as he stood under the canopy, peering to left and right as though waiting for someone else.

Paula approached the Mercedes cab which drove forward. As the driver darted to open a rear door for her she spoke in a clear penetrating voice.

'Could you take us to Les Armures, please? It's a restaurant in the Old Town near the Cathedral.'

'I know it well, Madame . . .'

She settled back in the warmth of the car with Tweed beside her as the car left the kerb. It had been freezing cold even during the short time she had stood on the pavement. A raw east wind was blowing from off the lake – probably from Siberia, she thought.

'I hope he caught on,' she whispered.

'Oh, he'd catch on, if that is his idea . . .'

Crossing the wide Rhône bridge, the car followed a zigzag course to the restaurant. It had begun to drizzle. The cobbled streets had a greasy shine under the glow of the street lamps. The Old City was perched on a hill facing the main part of Geneva across the river. It rose steeply, climbing to the summit, the Cathedral. The car continued its swerving pace round hairpin bends between rows of old houses huddled together. Tweed glanced at Paula.

Her reaction to the dreadful experience in Suffolk had been remarkable. The way she had taken command of the situation back at the hotel, relaying to Kuhlmann her room number. And later when they left she had cleverly informed him of their destination.

He knew what she was attempting and admired her for it. She was proving to him that despite her ordeal she was capable of doing her job.

Paula stared out of the window as the Mercedes continued its endless ascent of the narrow cobbled streets. At night the Old City had a sinister atmosphere. No one about. Shadowed alleyways and the occasional flight of precipitous staircases.

The Mercedes slowed, stopped close to a narrow street running alongside a large raised platform supporting old cannons. The driver twisted round to speak.

'It is only a short walk under the Arsenal,' he said, indicating the platform.

'I know,' Tweed said and paid him.

The driver ran to open the rear door, Paula stepped out,

followed by Tweed who stood in the drizzle, pulling up his overcoat collar as the Mercedes drove off. He appeared to be listening to the heavy silence which had fallen.

'Trouble?' Paula enquired, sheltering on the platform.

'No. I wanted to make sure we hadn't been followed. 'Let's get inside and hope Kuhlmann joins us . . .'

Les Armures, 1 Puits-St-Pierre, showed a welcoming glow of light behind old windows. They entered through a revolving door, passed a bar with wood-topped stools. Paula revelled in the sudden warmth, took off her coat and handed it to a waiter who hurried forward. The room was packed with tables, most of them occupied. A babble of voices mingled with the clink of glasses.

'You have a table for three. The name is Grey,' Paula told the waiter who was relieving Tweed of his coat.

As the waiter escorted them Paula had a glimpse through an archway into another room, the *Salle des Artistes*. Elephant tusks decorated the wall of the inner room. Paula had requested a secluded table and they were shown to a corner table with crossed muskets on the wall. She sat in a chair, leaving the corner chair for their guest while Tweed occupied the flanking seat.

'This place is just as I remember it,' Paula remarked before studying the large menu. 'And still popular.'

'A good place to talk,' Tweed replied.

The warmth, the babble of voices created an atmosphere of people enjoying themselves. Mostly locals, Tweed judged. He was studying the menu when Paula saw Otto Kuhlmann enter. He paused by the bar, scanning the crowded room. She guessed he had checked the faces of everyone in the room before he handed over his coat and hat and joined them in the corner chair.

'I had company,' the German began in English, explaining his precautions. 'A motorcyclist tagged my cab.'

'How did you shake him?' Tweed asked.

'By directing my cab to stop at the tunnel of steps below the Cathedral. Then I ran up the steps and he was unable to follow on his machine. He's lost.'

'Something to drink,' Tweed suggested.

'Let's start with Kir Royale,' Paula said promptly and Kuhlmann nodded agreement as he produced his trademark, a large cigar.

'Down to business. I hope you don't mind the cigar – I have denied myself since leaving Wiesbaden, hoping to avoid identification. Somewhere I slipped up – but the people we are dealing with are ruthless and thorough.'

He paused while Tweed gave the drinks order. They were served almost at once. Paula drank half the mix of champagne and blackcurrant liqueur, put down her glass.

'I needed that. Now, Otto. And do smoke your cigar.'

'As I said on the phone, Tweed, a crisis is building in the new Germany. We have a dangerous enemy we can't locate. Extreme elements of the Paris press are painting a picture of an aggressive Germany which wishes to take revenge on France for historic defeats.'

'That's ridiculous, Otto,' Tweed protested. 'We know Germany has the most peaceful intentions of any nation in Europe.'

'True, but there is a brilliantly orchestrated campaign to portray us as dangerous.'

'Under the present Chancellor? That's absurd.'

'I know. The propaganda is insidious, worthy of the infamous Goebbels. It is suggested a new Bismarck may take over later. That he will want to take back from France Alsace-Lorraine – which Germany annexed in 1871.'

'Surely such an obvious lie can be countered.'

'There is more.' Kuhlmann drank the rest of his Kir Royale, paused while Paula ordered another round. 'I have to tell you there is a new underground movement being organized by someone outside Germany. Organized in cells made up of terrorists. Where they are coming in from we can't trace. It is called the *Siegfried* movement. And has extreme right-wing characteristics. We know arms and explosives are being smuggled in and stored for future use on a large scale. Again, we can't detect the source.'

'You must have some idea who is behind this conspiracy,' Tweed said quietly.

'As I said earlier, certain extremist elements of the Paris press are stoking the fires.' He puffed at his cigar as they ordered food, said he would have the same. 'All this is very confidential, you will have realized. Even more top secret is the fact that I've travelled here as the personal representative of the Chancellor.'

Paula stared at him over the rim of her second Kir Royale. With his thick dark hair, equally dark eyebrows, his wide mouth clamped tight on his cigar, Kuhlmann looked very grim.

'I see, Otto,' Tweed said quietly. 'Have you an idea of the view of the President of France?'

'He can't believe there is any such conspiracy. He is extremely annoyed at what certain French newspapers have said. He thinks it best not to comment – that would draw more attention to their aggressive statements. Also, he has his own problems.'

'Which ones are you referring to?' Tweed pressed.

'The growing popularity of this new party, *Pour France*. They advocate deporting all foreigners – Algerians, etc. That strikes a chord with many and he doesn't know how to react.'

'So I come back to my earlier question. Who exactly in France is behind this conspiracy, all these lies about Germany?'

'Emile Dubois, driving force behind *Pour France*, is one, I would guess. But there are disturbing rumours that some Cabinet Ministers in Paris support Dubois secretly. There is a fog over France and it is very difficult to penetrate it, to find out what is really happening. Which is why I have taken the enormous risk of sending in an agent secretly to investigate.'

The *émince de veau Zürichoise* with *rosti* had been served after Kuhlmann had revealed his role as representative of the German Chancellor. Now Paula sat very still, food poised on her fork. She was wondering whether Tweed would tell Otto about Francis Carey. 'Define the risk for me,' Tweed said.

'Supposing he was caught, his mission exposed. Can you imagine what the French press would make of it? *German Secret Agent Spies On France.* I could write the headlines myself.'

'You must be – determined – to take that risk.'

'Maybe desperate would be a better word.' Kuhlmann waved his cigar and grinned for the first time. 'His real name is Stahl. He has entered France from here – Switzerland – under an assumed name with forged papers. He may escape undetected. Stahl's mother was French, his father German. And he comes from Alsace which, as you know, is a real hotch-potch of French and German names.' He turned to Paula. 'Hotch-potch? Is that right?'

'Perfect, Otto.' Paula placed a reassuring hand on his thick wrist. She knew he prided himself on his English, on mastering colloquialisms. 'Just as all your English has been since we started talking.'

'Why are you telling me all this?' Tweed asked briskly. 'Why me?'

'Because I know you have established an excellent network of agents inside France. There you are ahead of us.

I'm hoping if Stahl fails you will succeed. Providing you agree to help.'

'I agree. Paula, show Otto that photograph you have of yourself and your friend.'

Paula blinked, opened her shoulder bag, took out an envelope from a zipped pocket. Inside the envelope was the only photo she had of Karin Rosewater – taken while she had spent time with Karin on holiday in Freiburg near the Black Forest. She passed over the envelope to Kuhlmann.

He extracted the photograph, held it in the palm of his large hand. The only reaction was his teeth clamping tighter on his cigar. He looked at Tweed, at Paula.

'You know the girl with you in this snap?'

'Do you, Otto?' Tweed asked quietly.

Kuhlmann stubbed out the cigar, began to eat the superbly cooked veal and the speciality Swiss potato which was so crisp and tasty. He drank some of the champagne Tweed had ordered earlier. Paula pursed her lips, glancing at Tweed. Kuhlmann put down his knife and fork, wiped his mouth with his napkin.

'Yes, I know her,' he said eventually. 'What puzzles me is how you know her. It seems an amazing coincidence.'

'I have bad news for you, Otto.'

'Tell me.' Kuhlmann put down the glass he had been about to drink from.

'She is dead . . .'

Kuhlmann listened with an impassive expression as Tweed related tersely what had happened in Suffolk. He also referred to the mysterious 'authority' Karin had mentioned to Paula.

'She was talking about me,' Kuhlmann said grimly. 'I remember now, Paula, you were at that party at the Nato base in southern Germany when Karin was there. That was why I was also there. To protect her cover she never came

near Wiesbaden. We'd meet for a few minutes at a party –
prearranged. Chat like acquaintances for just a short time.
She reported to me, I gave her fresh instructions.'

'You weren't going to mention her,' Tweed commented.
'Only Stahl.'

'Deliberately. I was fond of her – and she was a brave
lady. Want to hear how I recuited her?'

'I'd like very much to hear that,' Paula broke in.

'She was a brilliant linguist. Her husband, Victor Rosewater, is with British Military Intelligence. He has had
occasion to visit Wiesbaden in connection with his work. I
was invited to their home. One day when I arrived Karin
was on her own. She told me she'd worked for the BND at
Pullach near Munich . . .' Tweed glanced at Paula. The BND
was German counter-espionage. 'She pressed me to let her
help with my work,' Kuhlmann continued. 'Karin could be
very persuasive. And I was needing an operative to back up
Stahl. She seemed the perfect choice. I regret I hired her to
check on the situation in France – working with Stahl.'

'Did her husband know what she was doing?' Tweed
asked.

'Victor Rosewater? I warned her not to tell him. And
there the arrangement fitted so well. Rosewater spends a lot
of time away from home – tracking the IRA units operating
in Germany, I gathered.'

'Anyone else except yourself and Stahl know what she
was doing?' Tweed persisted.

'No one. Security seemed watertight.'

'Why didn't the Chancellor involve the BND in this?'

Kuhlmann waved a dismissive hand. 'They are up to
their necks checking dubious characters infiltrating from
Eastern Europe since unification. Also, for some reason the
Chancellor seems to trust me. God knows why.'

'Because you're so reliable, like a bulldog which never

gives up,' Paula said and gave him her warmest smile. 'Now do get on with your meal.'

'We'll do what we can to unravel this mystery,' Tweed assured. 'If you want to let me know how we can contact Stahl it would be helpful. It's up to you.'

Kuhlmann took out a notepad, tore off a sheet, rested it on the cardboard back so there would be no impression, wrote rapidly, gave the folded sheet to Tweed.

'Thank you for your offer of help. We need it. That gives you Stahl's present address, the name he's operating under, his phone number. The codeword which will identify you as safe is Gamelin. Now maybe we can relax – even if only for tonight. I return to Wiesbaden tomorrow. One more thing – Stahl reports *Siegfried* have hired the most ruthless assassin on the continent. Someone called Kalmar.'

'That's a new name.'

'To me, too. And Stahl said contact between *Siegfried* and Kalmar is maintained here in Geneva. Now, I'm going to finish this excellent meal . . .'

At Kuhlmann's suggestion they left separately as they had arrived. Tweed asked the waiter to phone for a taxi. Paula kissed Kuhlmann on the cheek, told him to take care of himself. Just before they left, Tweed leaned close to the German, whispered.

'Warn Stahl that however he communicates with you not to use a radio transmitter. Detector vans could locate him.'

'You have a reason for that advice?'

'I have . . .'

Kuhlmann left the restaurant ten minutes after Tweed and Paula were driven away in a taxi. Tweed had insisted on paying the bill. The German did not call for a cab. He walked in the drizzle through the silence and the dark of the Old Town. He chose to descend by a route opposite to the way the cab had brought him to the foot of the tunnel

below the Cathedral. Walking down the deserted Grand
Rue, his mind was full of the death of Karin Rosewater. But
as he pursued a devious route through side alleys he kept a
lookout for the motorcyclist who had followed him earlier.

He had seen no sign of the tracker when eventually he
crossed the Rhône footbridge to the Hotel des Bergues.
Tweed had really said very little, but the German felt now
resolving the crisis depended largely on the Englishman.

Chapter Six

Seen on a street plan Bordeaux is a city going nowhere. Driving round the city Newman had the same impression. Moving along a main street leading from the Gare St Jean towards his hotel, the Pullman, small narrow streets led off on both sides, radiating like the sails of a windmill.

The ancient city comprised old blocks, five or six storeys high, built of grey stone. The walls were stained with the grime of ages, hadn't been cleaned for years. Shutters hung at drunken angles. Nowhere was there any sign of paint being used for a decade. Some were uninhabited ruins, stark walls which looked like the relics of bombing, but he suspected they were simply relics of neglect.

It was like driving through a monstrous prison as he jammed on the brakes once again. Traffic everywhere, filling the streets, parked nose to tail on the sidewalks. Most bore signs of collisions – dented chassis, battered doors. The leaden sky added to the atmosphere of dreariness.

Newman had a room at the Pullman, one of the better hotels. But he had also taken a room at a small dump of a lodging house where he'd been able to register in a false name. All the old biddy who ran the place wanted was money in advance. He had bought a shabby suitcase from a sleazy second-hand shop, had filled it with a selection of clothes taken from his suitcase at the Pullman, carried to his car in one of the ubiquitous plastic bags.

It was a precaution – taking a room at the lodging house.

The murder of Francis Carey had made him take certain precautions. Now he was driving to a rendezvous with Isabelle Thomas, Carey's girlfriend. He had phoned her at the address provided by Tweed, they had agreed to meet at a bar named by Isabelle, the Bar Rococo, at six in the evening. She had told him how she would be dressed. He turned down the street she had named, saw a car leaving a 'slot' on the sidewalk, drove in fast. A woman with a fur round her neck behind the wheel of a Renault leaned out of her window.

'That was my slot, you bastard. Get out of the way.'

Newman gave her a broad smile. 'First come, first served,' he rejoined.

He locked his car and waited to make sure she wasn't going to follow up her insult with physical damage to his vehicle. She made an obscene gesture, drove away. Bordeaux drivers' manners . . .

The Bar Rococo was of a higher class than he'd expected. Large bulbous pots stuffed with green ferns obscured a clear view inside. The tables had clean red check cloths. The waiters' green aprons were also spotless. He wandered among the ferns and stopped. She fitted her description, but again he was surprised – she was so attractive and well dressed. Could this be her?

'Isabelle Thomas?' he enquired politely in French.

'Yes.' Her tone was guarded.

'Good, I'm Alain Dreyfus,' he went on, giving the code name Paula had arranged with her from London. 'May I sit down?'

'Certainly, Mr Robert Newman. And we can speak in English,' she continued in that language.

It was his third surprise. She smiled as she saw his expression when he was sitting opposite her.

'Actually, I recognize you from pictures I've seen in the

foreign press. You are Robert Newman, aren't you? And your profession?'

She was covering herself again, wondering if she had made a bad mistake. He smiled reassuringly. Inwardly he felt annoyed she had penetrated his real identity so quickly.

'I am Robert Newman, foreign correspondent. Is it safe to talk here?'

'That is why I chose this rendezvous. It early. We are almost the only people here. And, as you see, the heavy lace curtains conceal us from the street.'

She was more than attractive, she was beautiful, Newman was thinking. She had a mane of titian hair, a slim, tall neck, good bone structure, greenish eyes, and a clear complexion. Very little make-up: just a touch of red lipstick on her firm mouth. She struck him as a woman of character. In her late twenties. And what she said about the place was true – there was no one else anywhere near them.

'An aperitif?' he suggested as a waiter hovered.

'Why don't we go straight on to a bottle of wine? You choose. Doesn't matter what we decide to eat as far as I'm concerned.'

'We'll have a 1979 red Bordeaux,' he told the waiter in French. 'Leave the menu. We'll order later.'

'Pushing the boat out a bit, aren't we?' she teased him.

'I've had a long day.'

'Do you mind if I start talking about what happened?'

'I wish you would. But first, let me ask you something. Was Henri your first serious boyfriend?'

'No.' Her expression changed, became intense. 'I was engaged to be married to a soldier with the Third Army Corps. A tank commander. It ended tragically.'

'You want to tell me how?'

'Someone should know about General Charles de Forge.' Her tone dripped contempt. 'Joseph Roux was his name, would have become mine – Roux. I have never told this to anyone. As a foreign correspondent you might like to add to your experience. It's a pretty horrific story. I don't want to spoil your meal.'

'I've developed a pretty strong stomach. Go on.'

'Joseph was very independent-minded. De Forge has what he calls the punishment well . . .'

'I've heard some details about it.'

'You have? Your contacts must be pretty good. Joseph was among a group of troops addressed by the General one day. De Forge likes the sound of his own voice. He was damning the Jews, said they ought to be eliminated from French life. After he'd finished speaking he asked if there were any questions. You're not supposed to react to that. Joseph did.'

'What did he say?'

'That he thought he was in the Army. That politics was nothing to do with the military. And in any case he had two good friends who were Jews. He said that anti-Semitism was a curse, that it was anti-French. De Forge was livid. He gave the order at once.'

She paused, drank some wine, her hand trembled slightly. She tightened her grip on the glass, was careful to stand it back on the table without trembling.

'What order?' Newman asked quietly. 'If you want to go on with this.'

'Now I've started,' she said firmly. 'They took him to the punishment well immediately. Joseph was hung in the well by his thumbs.' She leaned forward, her gaze intense. 'Can you imagine hanging for six hours by your thumbs? And Joseph was a big man.'

'Quite horrible – and barbaric.'

'That's how de Forge maintains what he likes to call iron discipline. Some of his officers call him the Iron Man.'

'Go on about Joseph. What happened next?'

'After the six hours they hauled him up out of the well. He was kept in the military hospital at GHQ and then discharged from the Army with a big pension.'

'What sort of state was he in?' Newman asked gently.

'I wasn't allowed to visit him in hospital. When he came home both thumbs were horribly distended. My doctor examined him and said he would be a cripple for life. Nothing could be done for him. Joseph was a very active man and they'd reduced him to a wreck. That's what he said to me, "I'm a shipwreck for ever."'

'What did his parents say? Do?'

'Joseph was an orphan. We had been living together in an apartment. A very unpleasant officer, a Major Lamy, told him just before he left hospital that if he ever told anyone what had happened his pension would stop at once.'

'What was Joseph's reaction?

'At first he thought we could get married and live on the pension.'

'Which is why he kept quiet about the atrocity?'

'There was more to it than that . . .'

She paused as the waiter served the grilled red mullet and *pommes natures* they had both ordered. Newman disliked the way the fish's head leered at him. He cut it off, hid it under the tail.

'You were saying?' he coaxed her.

'Joseph was very self-conscious about his handicap. He thought it made him look like a freak. The idea of being interviewed by reporters – then photographed – horrified him.' She gulped, drank more wine. Something even grimmer was coming Newman sensed. She ate for a few minutes, then put down her knife and fork.

'He became very depressed. There was so much he was unable to do for himself. I knew something was going to happen when we stopped making love. He said he was no good to me any more. I argued that was nonsense. One evening after dark he said he was going to go out by himself, to have a drink in a bar, to learn to lead a normal life. I was glad.'

She drank more wine and stared at Newman as he refilled her glass. She was nerving herself to tell him something. He let her take her time.

'Joseph fooled me with his story about going to a bar. He had secretly bought two heavy iron weights from a hardware shop. He drove to a bridge over the Garonne, got out, attached the weights with rope to each ankle, lifted himself and the weights somehow over the side of the bridge, and went down into the Garonne. Divers brought up his body later that night. A woman had seen him go over and called the police. So, you see, General Charles de Forge is a murderer.'

'How long ago?' Newman asked, for something to say.

'Two years. It seems like two weeks. I lived for revenge until I met Henri. And now Henri is gone – murdered by the Government's DST. What is happening?'

Newman changed the direction of the conversation, asking her about herself. She had returned to living at home with her mother in a Bordeaux apartment. At the moment her mother was visiting relatives in Arcachon, a port and seaside town on the Atlantic coast west of Bordeaux.

She worked as an account executive for an agency. Yes, she was young to hold such a job, but they had found women directors of client firms preferred dealing with their own sex. Especially when they were advertising women's clothes and underwear.

'You must earn a good salary,' Newman suggested.

'Far more than most girls my age. Which is perhaps why I have few friends.'

'Is there somewhere private we could go to chat and be sure we're not overheard?'

Newman looked round. The restaurant was filling up. At tables close by every chair was taken. He wondered why it was called a bar and voiced the question aloud.

'They have a large bar downstairs which is very popular. As to somewhere quiet . . .' She considered, watching Newman while she drank the rest of her coffee. 'I told you my mother has gone to Arcachon – so there is no one at the apartment. We could go there . . .'

At Isabelle's suggestion – when he said he disliked parking in the street – he drove the Citroën round the end of the grey apartment block inside an alley leading to a courtyard. He parked the car out of sight of the street.

She was waiting for him, one of the huge tall double doors unlocked, closed it behind him and led the way across an interior yard. The apartment was on the first floor at the top of a flight of bleak stone steps. He realized it overlooked the street when she ushered him inside. Lace curtains masked the tall windows.

'Don't switch on any lights in here,' he warned.

'OK. But why?'

'The place will look empty from the street. We need somewhere not overlooking it.'

'The kitchen. Then we can have more coffee . . .'

He perched on a stool at an island unit after taking off his trench coat. Underneath he wore an English business suit, a blue bird's-eye. The kitchen was a different world from the living room which was furnished with heavy, old-fashioned furniture; it was equipped with the latest facilities, including a hood over the cooker. He opened his onslaught when she had placed a brown mug of steaming coffee in front of him, had settled herself on a stool facing her guest.

'How many people knew of your friendship with Henri?'

'No one really. I told you I have few friends.'

'What about your mother?'

'Not her.' She made a move. 'We don't see eye to eye on many things. I never let her know what happened. She would have criticized my choice of a barman.' She warmed her hands round her mug, shapely hands. 'I did think it funny that Henri was just a barman – he seemed so intelligent. When I said so he shrugged, said he was travelling round France to get experience of the world.'

'Are you actually saying that no one else in the whole world knew about you and Henri?'

'Yes. When we went out he asked me to choose places to eat I'd never been before. I didn't ask him why.'

'Someone must have betrayed Henri to the DST. From what you've said you're the only one who could have done that.'

Her face flushed. She stared at Newman as though unable to believe her ears. Newman stared back as she continued.

'How much did they pay you for your services?'

Her hand tightened on the handle of her mug. For a moment he thought he was going to get the contents in his face and prepared to duck.

'You swine!' she hissed in her well-modulated voice. 'I could kill you for what you've just said. Why? in the name of God, why do you say such terrible things?'

'Because you're the obvious betrayer. Making up to him, gaining his confidence – when all the time you were an agent of the DST . . .'

She slipped off her stool, ran round the island. On the

way she tipped the contents of her mug into the sink. She was slimly built, almost as tall as Newman, wore a mini-skirt which exposed her excellent legs. She came at him like a tigress.

He stood upright just in time as she aimed the mug to smash it against his head. He grabbed her arms, forced them to her sides, surprised at her strength, her agility. She aimed her knee at his groin, he took the thrust in the side of his leg, held her prisoner until she stopped struggling, breathing heavily.

'And you're a damned good actress, I'll give you that,' he goaded her.

She dipped her titian-maned head, prepared to butt him under the chin. He swivelled her through a hundred and eighty degrees, holding her arms against her sides, his head pushing against hers, pressing himself into her back. A faint whiff of perfume drifted to his nostrils. She relaxed, unable to fight any more. Her voice was controlled now, loaded with venom.

'Get out of here,' she ordered him. 'I never want to see you again. I thought you were a friend . . .'

'I am,' he said quietly, his mouth close to her ear, 'but I had to be sure of you. To test you to breaking point. I believe you now, Isabelle. Sorry I upset you, but I repeat, I had to be certain of you.'

She relaxed in his arms completely. Her tone held a hint of amusement.

'Maybe you'd better let me go. If anyone came in and found us like this they'd think we were lovers.'

'Not a bad idea – as far as I'm concerned. But I'm here for professional reasons. Behave? If I let you go?'

'If I must.'

She turned round and gave him a glowing smile, tears in her eyes. She collapsed with emotion, buried her head against his chest. He stroked her hair as she shook with relief, let her get it out of her system. She let go of him, ran to the sink, turned on the tap, splashed her face with huge quantities of cold water. Drying herself, she opened a drawer, took out a brush and attacked her mane with the aid of a mirror on the wall.

When she had finished smartening her appearance, Newman pushed his mug of coffee over the island.

'I've had enough. The rest is yours.'

She drank greedily, watching him over the rim as she had done in the Bar Rococo drinking wine. When she had emptied the mug she asked her question.

'Who, then, do you think could have betrayed Henri – if he was doing something against the French state?'

'Tell me why he chose to work in the Bar Miami,' Newman suggested, folding his arms, leaning against the island.

'He never said. But I met him there often, sometimes sitting at a table while I waited for him to come off duty. A lot of French officers in the Army use that bar. I had the impression they interested him.'

'He asked them questions?'

'Sometimes, yes. Innocuous questions as though he was being companionable. Were they on leave? Things like that.' She frowned. 'I've just remembered something. Shortly before the two DST men arrested him he was serving two French lieutenants. I was out of sight but close. You know how in a crowded bar for no reason there is sometimes a brief hush in the conversation?'

'I know exactly what you mean.'

'That happened on that night. I heard one lieutenant tell his fellow officer he was with a specialist unit, that soon he'd be in Paris – and not on leave. Henri was intrigued by that remark.'

73

'So am I. But how could you tell Henri was intrigued?'

She looked wistful, had perched herself on a counter top, her long legs swinging.

'Because by then I knew him well. His every little gesture. Henri was polishing a glass. He was very quick. When the lieutenant made that remark for a second Henri stopped polishing the glass, then polished it furiously.'

'I see.'

Newman saw more than that. He thought he'd learned how Carey had been detected. A trifle too much enthusiasm talking to officers, asking the odd question. Someone had reported his interest.

'Let's go sit on the couch in the living room,' Isabelle suggested, her eyes smoky.

Newman frowned as she switched off the kitchen light before opening the door, followed her. She seemed to be interested in him. Business and pleasure didn't mix – and he sensed that despite her outer poise she was in an emotional state. Little wonder after what he had put her through.

He kept close to her to avoid furniture until he became accustomed to the dark. Isabelle wandered over to one of the tall windows, glanced down through the curtains, stiffened. Newman saw how her silhouette froze.

'What is it?' he said and joined her quickly.

'Those two men standing in that shop doorway. They are the DST men who took Henri away.'

'How can you be sure?'

'The way the tall one moves. He turned to the shorter man to say something. It is them, Robert. I may call you Robert?'

Newman was staring down into the street. He knew the temperature outside was arctic, compounded by the wind-chill factor. So why should two men take up a position opposite the entrance to the apartment block? A couple of friends who had met by chance? Then they'd head for the nearest bar. Newman looked up and down the narrow street. Fifty yards away from where the men stood a solitary Renault was parked. The shorter of the waiting couple thrust gloved hands into the pockets of his wide-lapelled trenchcoat, huddled his shoulders, stared at the entrance opposite.

'I know it's them,' Isabelle insisted. 'I was close to them when they came up to Henri. That's how they were dressed then.'

'Does anyone at the Bar Miami know your address?'

'The chief barman. I left a silk scarf there once. I phoned him, he said they'd found it. He asked for my address – there was an expensive scarf ring attached to it. He made me repeat my address when I went to collect it.'

'And he'd know you were Henri's girlfriend?'

'He could hardly avoid realizing that.'

'You have to leave here. Tonight. Can you go out to Arcachon and stay with your mother? I'll drive you there. Do you want to pack? Urgently?'

'So many questions, Robert . . .'

'My friends call me Bob. Now, can you?'

'Yes. But not with my mother. I have a sister with an apartment there where I could stay – Lucille, my sister, is abroad and left me the keys. The advertising agency is having a slack time and owes me two weeks' holiday. I could phone them, say I'm leaving for San Trop. I can pack in ten minutes, maybe less.'

'Is there some way we can get to my car in the alley without using the main entrance? Those aren't real DST men – they're far more dangerous. DST don't go round murdering people.'

'Yes, Bob. There is a back way direct into the alley. I have a key.'

'Next point. Have you two sharp knives? I suppose you wouldn't have a French coat I could wear?'

'There is one which Henri left. He was about your size. In a wardrobe in the bedroom. And a hat, if you want one. We'll be lucky if that fits . . .'

Closing the door, when they were inside the bedroom, she switched on the light, went to a huge, old-fashioned wardrobe, took out a dark overcoat, a trilby hat – both shabby. Carey's method of passing for a Frenchman. Newman slipped on the coat, pulled up the collar. Rather tight under the arms but it would pass in the dark. He rammed the hat on his head, pulled the brim low over his forehead.

'It's not big enough,' Isabelle decided.

'Big enough at night. Now, the knives.'

She was a girl who never wasted time asking unnecessary questions, which impressed Newman. In the kitchen she opened a drawer, stood back, invited him to take his pick. The wooden box divided into compartments fitted snugly inside the drawer contained an amazing selection. He chose two short-bladed knives with strong handles, slid them blade first carefully inside the coat pockets.

'Show me how to get out of the rear entrance. While I'm away do your packing. Oh, I suppose you haven't an empty bottle of wine?'

'Only in the trash can. I could wash and clean it thoroughly.'

'I'll be drinking out of it. Fill it with water . . .'

She led him down to the rear entrance, unlocked the door and he found himself in the alley leading to the main street.

A raw wind slashed at his face. Newman cowered under his floppy hat, staggering slowly along the sidewalk, waving the bottle with his left hand. The wind grew in fury, sheets of newspaper flew in the air, Newman leaned against a wall, tilted the bottle, drank from the neck. He stumbled into the deserted street closer to the parked Renault.

Behind him the two men in trench coats peered out at his erratic progress. Newman rammed the hat tighter over his head as the wind almost blew it away. He spun round in a drunken circle. The trench coat men had retreated deep into the shelter of their doorway.

He lurched across to the car, sprawled on the cobbles alongside the rear wheel of the Renault. Letting go of the bottle, he grasped the first knife, plunged the blade deep into the tyre, the handle protruding close to the cobbles in the direction the car would move. Swiftly he gripped the second knife, repeated his performance, driving the second knife alongside the first. The wind was blowing away the bottle when he grabbed it by the neck, staggered to his feet. No sign of Trenchcoats.

He began his weaving walk back the way he had come, watching the doorway from under the brim of his hat. Still no sign of the enemy. He resisted the temptation to move faster, arrived at the entrance to the alley, tottered out of sight.

Now he ran to the rear entrance in the alley, took the key Isabelle had handed him from his trouser pocket, and within a minute was back inside her mother's apartment. She was standing by the window in the living room, turning round as he entered.

'God! You just made it. They both peered out as you made the alley . . .'

'You're supposed to be packing.'

'I'm ready. Can we make a run for it now?'

'Now . . .'

She wrapped a silk shawl round her head, concealing her

titian mane. A blue coat buttoned to her neck completed the transformation. As protection against the wind she had changed her mini for a knee-length blue skirt.

'My trenchcoat,' Newman reminded her.

'Packed in my case, plus Henri's shaving kit and the pyjamas he left behind – hidden where my mother would not find them. It will get you through the night in Arcachon . . .'

The alley was deserted as they hurried to the parked Citroën in the courtyard. They'd have the description of his car, Newman thought grimly – and its registration number. Plenty of time to record that while de Forge took him to see the punishment well. Undoubtedly passed to the phoney DST men. Best to assume the worst.

He drove out of the alley with Isabelle beside him. She was careful not to look towards the doorway sheltering the watchers as Newman swung the vehicle in the opposite direction. He glanced back, saw the two men running for the parked Renault.

The two men dived into the front of the car. Behind its wheel the taller man started up the engine, released the brake, pressed his foot down. The car sped forward maybe a dozen yards and then the rear wheel's tyre collapsed as the knives penetrated it. The driver cursed as the car slewed towards the sidewalk, the wheel rims grinding on the cobbles.

Newman saw what happened in his mirror, increased speed along the deserted street as the wind hammered at the windscreen. With Isabelle's guidance, he soon left the outer suburbs behind and was racing along the N650 – towards the Atlantic, towards Arcachon.

'Has your mother friends in Bordeaux who could let enquirers know her address?' Newman asked.

'No. She doesn't like her city neighbours, lets them know

nothing of her affairs. No one knows she has relatives in Arcachon. No one can say anything.'

It seemed she would be safe in Arcachon, Newman hoped. He was also wondering whether the police had acted on his anonymous call to the Prefecture in Bordeaux. His call had been made from the Post Office before driving on to the Bar Rococo.

He had told them about the CRS Berliet truck crashing into the gorge, had given them an idea of the location. Whose bodies would they find inside?

Chapter Seven

General Charles de Forge sat in his high-backed chair, his hands rested on the arms as he fired questions at Major Lamy, standing facing him across the large desk. It was early evening, the only illumination a desk lamp which threw Lamy's saturnine face into sharp relief.

'Most unfortunate about that Berliet truck. Has Newman got away?'

'Only for the moment, sir. We're watching the airport, the main rail stations – a small army of our men in plain clothes. All with his description.'

'And the Berliet?'

'Dealt with. The bodies removed to the usual place.'

'And that spy? Henri Bayle, wasn't that his name? I understand he had a mistress.'

'Her apartment is being watched. I hope to have news of her detention. After being questioned – if necessary under pressure – she will be disposed of.'

De Forge stood up, walked round his desk, hands clasped behind his back. He paced slowly up and down the long room.

'It is the details which have to be attended to. Never forget that, Lamy.'

'What I don't understand, General, is why you agreed to see Newman, then changed your mind about him.'

'Because I have a fingertip feeling about people. I hoped an article in *Der Spiegel*, angled my way, would add to the growing anxiety and confusion in Germany. Later, he seemed hostile. My decision, as always, was logical. Now, I will address my troops . . .'

The tank commanders assembled in the drill hall had been served a good meal. De Forge often quoted maxims of Napoleon. One of his favourites was 'an army marches on its stomach'. A loud cheer went up as de Forge appeared in full uniform on the raised platform at the end of the hall. Then the chant began.

'*Pour France . . . Pour France . . . Pour France . . .*'

De Forge silenced them by raising his right hand, palm open, shoulder high. The soldiers, who had jumped to their feet at his appearance, sat down and leaned forward. At the end of the front row a certain Lieutenant Berthier, lean and clean-shaven with fair hair cut very short, watched his commander intently.

'Soldiers of France,' de Forge began in his magnetic voice, 'the time is approaching for action. Paris – not Berlin – will become the capital of the New Europe. It will be your skill, your courage which will bring all this about. And you are not alone – your help in bringing in the harvest assures us of the support of the farmers. And beyond that we have our friends in high places – in Paris. You are the iron barrier against which the foreign scum will break their unwashed skulls . . .'

He had to pause as his audience broke into a thunder of cheering and applause. He continued speaking for another half hour, a natural orator of compelling power. His climax, which lifted off the roof, was typical.

'None of this is for me, as you well understand. It is for France . . .!'

He acknowledged the three minutes of wild applause with a solemn, aloof expression, hands clasped behind his back, then walked off the platform, disappearing through a side door where Major Lamy waited.

'They would die for you, my General,' Lamy commented.

'They may have to. Now, drive me to the villa of Mademoiselle Jean Burgoyne. I need some active relaxation.'

De Forge was married but rarely visited his wife, Josette. She lived in an expensive apartment in Bordeaux where she held 'salons' – parties for influential and artistic celebrities. He had married her because she had been the daughter of the Minister of Defence at that time. A career move.

Jean Burgoyne was an attractive Englishwoman whose vitality had appealed to de Forge when he met her at a government reception in Paris. He always felt need of her when he had made a speech.

As Lamy drove him to the villa the Chief of Intelligence glanced at his chief. De Forge was staring ahead, presenting his famous profile to his subordinate.

'That reference, General, to friends in Paris was a clever remark. Most confidence-inspiring. And true.'

'What would not have been clever would have been a reference to an even stronger ally. General Lapointe, next to myself the most important member of the *Cercle Noir*.'

'Lapointe is vital,' Lamy agreed.

French military power rested on the *force de frappe*, the formidable group of long-distance rockets deep in silos on a plateau to the east. And the rockets were armed with nuclear warheads.

One of the soldiers who had listened most closely to de Forge's address did not immediately return to barracks with his comrades. Lieutenant Berthier, protected against the Siberian cold, walked by himself across the parade ground.

As he strode along Berthier repeated to himself the speech he had listened to word by word. He had an excellent memory but wished to be sure every sentence was imprinted on his brain. When the time came for him to report the contents of the speech he wanted to be word perfect.

Tweed moved fast the following morning. Paula found herself sitting next to him aboard Flight SR951 – bound from Geneva for Basle, the Swiss city at the north-west tip of the country where the French border meets the German frontier.

The flight took off promptly at 7.10 a.m., was due to touch down at 7.55. Paula glanced behind them, saw the seats were empty, as were the seats in front. No damn wonder: they'd had to get up at five in the morning. She still kept her voice low.

'Now will you tell me why – instead of flying direct to Paris to see Lasalle of the DST – we're first meeting Victor Rosewater in Basle?'

'Because he was Karin's husband.'

Paula gritted her teeth. The previous night she had phoned Rosewater at his apartment in Freiburg, asking if she could meet him in Basle, that maybe he'd like to hear from her exactly what had happened to his dead wife as she'd been with Karin. Rosewater had agreed at once and they'd arranged to see each other at the Hotel Drei Könige. Now, from Tweed's terse reply, she realized he was going to tell her nothing more after instructing her to make the call the previous evening. What was Tweed playing at?

'After we've seen Rosewater we'll fly straight on to Paris,' Tweed remarked. 'When you'd fixed up this meeting with Rosewater I called René Lasalle in Paris. He seemed very anxious to see me at the earliest possible moment. Events appear to be moving out of control. Confirming Kuhlmann's worst fears. The momentum of events is gathering pace.'

'What events?'

Tweed handed her a copy of the *Journal de Genève* he had bought at the airport. The headline in large type jumped at her. She read it in French but thought of it in English.

SERIOUS RIOTS IN BORDEAUX. 1,000 CASUALTIES.

She read the article below. Large groups of men wearing Balaclava helmets had gone berserk, attacking pedestrians, wrecking shops near the Gare St Jean, painting anti-Semitic slogans on walls. The odd result had been no arrests were made: the police had been taken completely by surprise.

She glanced down out of the window. The aircraft had flown half-way along Lake Geneva, had now swung north-west overland. Below they were crossing the Jura mountains behind Geneva. The range was like a whaleback and its summits were crested with snow. She shivered, handed back the paper.

'What is behind it all?' she asked.

'You should have asked "Who" – and I have no idea.'

She didn't believe him but said nothing. They'd be landing at Basle soon and she was bracing herself for talking to Karin's widower. What on earth could he tell Tweed?

At the isolated villa east of Third Corps GHQ, de Forge, wearing only pyjama trousers, jumped out of bed and ran to the shower. He turned on the cold water tap and stood quite still as ice-cold water sprayed his slim body.

Jean Burgoyne climbed out of the king-size bed more slowly, wrapped a towel round her nude body, opened the door and picked up the newspaper the maid had left on the floor. She perched on the edge of the rumpled bed as she read the headline, looked up as de Forge reappeared, dried himself, swiftly dressed in his uniform. She stood up, still holding the towel with one hand, the newspaper in the other.

Jean Burgoyne was five feet seven, about the same height as de Forge, had blond hair, good bone structure, long well-shaped legs. Her face was also longish with a firm chin and a flawless complexion which owed nothing to make-up. She handed the paper to de Forge. The headline was about the Bordeaux riots.

'Charles, this wouldn't have anything to do with you, would it?' she asked, her glance shrewd.

De Forge glanced at the paper. He dropped it on the deep wall-to-wall carpet. His right arm rose and he struck her across the face with the back of his hand. She reeled backwards under the blow, fell across the bed. The towel dropped, exposing her well-moulded figure. Her eyes stared at his as she reached for the towel, wrapped it round herself again, stood up.

Her voice calm. She even managed a wicked smile.

'Charles, don't ever do that again. You may be a great man, but I doubt whether de Gaulle ever struck a woman in his life. Maybe,' she continued, 'this is why your wife, Josette, wants so little to do with you.'

He took a step forward, his eyes glowing with anger. She raised one warning finger, her voice now little more than a whisper.

'I said never again. I mean it. Now, that creep, Major Lamy, will be freezing outside. Duty calls, *mon Général*.'

He hesitated, unsure whether she was mocking him. Then, turning on his heel, he walked to the door and paused before opening it to leave.

'Jean, I will phone you again when I am available.'

'As you wish . . .'

But de Forge had gone. Outside the balustraded two-storey stone villa surrounded with evergreens a de luxe Citroën stood parked. Major Lamy was walking up and down, swinging his arms round his body, slapping his gloved hands against his greatcoat. It was even colder than the night before. De Forge glanced at the sky which was a low ceiling of sullen cloud. It looked like a threat of snow coming.

De Forge took the wheel: he loved driving at speed. Lamy sat by his side as de Forge sped down the twisting drive, spurting up showers of gravel until he emerged on to the road. He pressed his foot down as he queried with Lamy the general situation. He was still smarting from Jean's first remark: women were for only one purpose. They should bloody well never ask serious – even dangerous – questions.

'Exercise General Ali is ready to start as soon as you reach GHQ,' Lamy informed his chief.

'That's routine. I see we've started in Bordeaux.'

'Only the beginning.' Lamy smiled, twisting his lips. 'More is on the way. Toulon, Marseilles, Toulouse.'

'Then Lyons,' de Forge continued. 'Make it look like the start of an uprising, a revolution. After that,' he said with satisfaction, 'the big one. Paris . . .'

Back at the Villa Forban Jean Burgoyne sat in front of her dressing table, using a pad of cottonwool dipped wychhazel to apply to where de Forge had struck her. She didn't think there would be a bruise but it was best to take precautions.

'And I think a brief holiday back home in England would be a good tactic,' she mused aloud. 'Charles can fret for me for a while. And I can spend a few days at my uncle's house in Aldeburgh . . .'

At 8.45 a.m. exactly Tweed hurried inside the Drei Könige – the Three Kings Hotel – in Basle. Carrying both cases with Paula at his heels, he handed them to the waiting porter, gave him a generous tip, asked him to store them safely.

'Victor's here already,' Paula whispered.

Facing the reception counter inside the main entrance was a well-furnished sitting-room area. A tall, well-built man wearing a German sporting jacket and slacks stood up from a deep leather armchair, came forward to greet Paula, hugged her, gave her a kiss on the cheek.

Tweed studied the Englishman, who had spoken in German, one of the several languages both Tweed and Paula spoke fluently. Tweed guessed Victor Rosewater was maintaining some kind of cover even in Switzerland.

In his thirties, Tweed estimated, Rosewater had an easy manner, was clean-shaven with the weather-beaten complexion of a man who spent a lot of time outdoors. He had a strong nose, shrewd brown eyes under dark eyebrows and a well-brushed thatch of thick hair. A good-looking man with a powerful personality.

'This is Tweed,' Paula introduced in German. 'He is in security,' she continued, following her chief's earlier instructions. 'Also a good friend.'

'Security?'

Rosewater's eyebrows rose a fraction, asking for further enlightenment.

'Security,' Tweed repeated and left it at that as he shook hands.

Rosewater had large hands, a strong grip. He smiled warmly and nodded, pressing Tweed no further. A natural probe on the part of a man engaged in undercover military intelligence, Tweed thought.

'They have a pleasant dining room overlooking the Rhine,' Rosewater suggested. 'Maybe you would like to take breakfast with me? I drove down the autobahn from Freiburg. It was no distance at all, but I skipped any nourishment. Personally, I'm as hungry as a horse . . .'

Tweed knew the room, had stayed at the hotel before,

but he made no reference to this. Rosewater led the way to a table by one of the large windows overlooking a closed verandah where in summer the wealthy met for drinks and dinner.

Beyond the verandah the Rhine flowed swiftly, a muddy colour compared with the Rhône at Geneva. A barge train hauled by a stubby tug ploughed slowly upriver against the current. Rosewater sat facing his two guests, made the remark to Paula after breakfast had been ordered.

'I'm coming to terms with Karin's demise.' He glanced at the barge train. 'At least I kid myself I am. I suspect, frankly, I'm still in a state of shock.'

'Do you really want to hear about it now?' Paula asked.

'I think it would help me. My work is putting me under great pressure at the moment . . .' He looked at Tweed briefly. 'Not entirely divorced from your world of security. I can't make up my mind whether that's helping me or not.' He looked at Paula. 'Just tell me how it happened. What shook me most was when you used the word murder on the phone. Why Karin?'

'That's what we would like to know,' Tweed intervened brusquely and then went silent, eating some of the excellent bread on the table.

Paula had just started talking and then trailed off into silence. She sipped her coffee slowly and took her time spreading jam on a piece of bread. Rosewater had switched his gaze to the far side of the restaurant and Tweed looked quickly in the same direction.

An attractive brunette in her thirties sat by herself at a table by the wall. She had crossed her shapely legs, her skirt sliding above her knees, stroking her tilted leg slowly with one hand as she looked straight at Rosewater. He watched her for a moment with an expressionless face, then stared at

Tweed. He gave a broad grin to disguise from the brunette what he was saying.

'I've seen that woman before somewhere. I think I've been tagged, and God knows I'm careful.'

'Maybe she just likes you,' Paula teased him.

Rosewater, she realized, had a personality appealing to many women. He exuded good nature and a sense of fun. Rosewater's voice remained serious.

'I would doubt that. Once is a chance encounter – twice is a danger signal. I don't know whether Paula told you, Tweed, but I'm Military Intelligence.'

'She mentioned it in passing. You don't have to worry. In my job I have to be very discreet. Also at times I have a shocking memory.'

He sipped coffee, leaving the field to Paula. She was in a better position to ask questions. Rosewater persisted in addressing Tweed.

'You said your job was security?'

'Security,' Tweed agreed, and again left it at that.

'Would this be a good moment to tell you what happened in Suffolk?' Paula intervened. 'Or would you sooner not have the details?'

'Tell me everything. I'll feel better for knowing . . .'

He turned to her, listened with an intent expression as she gave him an edited version, leaving out any reference to Park Crescent, as she had with Chief Inspector Buchanan in London. Rosewater, ignoring his breakfast, watched her until she'd concluded.

'. . . so the police arrived and took charge. Eventually I drove back home to try and get my mind off the whole experience.'

'Did you see the murderer – even though I suppose he wore one of these Balaclavas?' Rosewater asked.

'I had a good view from the treetop. I'm not sure. I was busy trying to hide myself from the men with guns.'

'I see.' He broke a roll, automatically piled butter and marmalade on a chunk, chewed it with a thoughtful expression. 'I think I'll visit Aldeburgh as soon as I can,' he said eventually. 'I was appalled I couldn't attend her funeral. I was involved in a very important check on a possible suspect – a saboteur, I'll call him. That was inside Germany.'

'I was there,' Paula said quietly. 'I laid a wreath for you. Do you want to see her grave?'

'No!' Rosewater showed emotion for the first time. 'I don't think I could bear that. I want to remember Karin as she was. Are the police anywhere near tracking down the swine who killed her?'

'Nowhere near, as far as we know,' Tweed commented. 'I was wondering how you could visit Suffolk, tied down as you are in Germany. You could take leave, I suppose?'

Rosewater dabbed at his strong mouth with his napkin as he glanced across the room at the brunette and looked away. She was still staring at him, tilting her crossed leg provocatively up and down.

'I have a strange job, Tweed. You could call it a roving commission. To locate the people I'm after I can travel anywhere in Europe, often incognito, as now. I shall make it my business to visit Aldeburgh as soon as I can.'

'When you do, Victor,' Paula suggested, 'call me before you leave Germany at this number.' She scribbled on a notepad she'd extracted from her shoulder bag. 'If I'm not in leave a message on the answerphone. If you want me to – but only if – I'll come with you to Aldeburgh.'

'Thank you.' He put his arm round her shoulder. 'I'd appreciate your company on such a trip. I will phone before I come.' He looked at Tweed. 'And where are you off to, now? Or does that question come under the heading of indiscreet?'

'Not at all. London,' Tweed lied smoothly. 'You say you travel all over Europe. What do you think of the trouble building up in France? Specifically, in Bordeaux?'

'Yes, Europe is my playground,' Rosewater agreed. 'A battlefield more than a playground. Germany is mainly my theatre of operation. As to Bordeaux, I haven't had time to read any papers.' He checked his watch. 'Soon I'll have to leave.'

'Just before we go,' Tweed said, leaning over the table, keeping his voice down. 'In my job I have recently heard rumours of an ace assassin operating on the continent. Name of Kalmar.'

Rosewater used one hand to scoop crumbs off the table into the other. He dropped them on to his plate and studied Tweed.

'So you've heard of him. They call him the Ghost in the Shadows. No one knows his nationality, where he's come from, where he's based – if anywhere. He reminds me of a moving target. I've a funny feeling that some time during my work I may encounter Kalmar. Twice I've just missed him by a whisker. Provided with an address, I go there and find the bird has already flown.'

'Interesting.' Tweed stood up, insisted on paying the bill.

'You've left your lighter,' Paula said as they began leaving. She picked it up.

'Observant lady, and thank you,' responded Rosewater, pocketing the lighter.

It was, thought Paula, the only outward sign that he had been upset by her story. He wasn't the kind of man who normally overlooked anything, she felt certain.

As they walked out of the restaurant Tweed glanced at the brunette who still sat smoking a cigarette with a cup of

91

coffee in front of her. She stared boldly at Rosewater as they left. Certainly an attractive woman, Tweed thought.

The taxi he had ordered for the airport was waiting. They said goodbye to Rosewater, who hugged Paula and thanked her for her help. While the driver was walking round to his seat after opening the rear door, Paula glanced out at Rosewater. He was standing outside the entrance, tall and handsome. Tweed followed her gaze as Rosewater waved and she waved back, then the taxi was moving. Paula looked at the expression on Tweed's face.

'You're thinking what I am. Victor would make a good recruit for Park Crescent.'

'You will persist in believing you can read my mind,' he chided her. 'But he's bright. The way he dodged my question about Bordeaux. What you'd expect from a top flight Military Intelligence officer. I should know.'

'I wonder what he is really doing?'

'From the little he said, infiltrating the IRA cells operating against British bases in Germany. Now, we should find out what is really happening. Within a couple of hours we'll be in Paris. With Lasalle – I called him briefly from the airport after we landed from Geneva.'

'And I wonder how Bob Newman is faring,' Paula mused.

Chapter Eight

At Arcachon, about thirty miles west of Bordeaux, the anchorage, triangular in shape, is almost entirely closed off from the fury of the Atlantic by a narrow peninsula which forms a barrier. The only entrance, to the south, is a narrow opening between the tip of the peninsula and an island.

Isabelle was well muffled against the piercing wind, clad in a heavy knee-length trench coat and a hood pulled over her head. By her side walked Newman, wearing the new clothes he had purchased at several local shops. He wore a black beret, a dark French overcoat, and training shoes. They walked past the Casino de la Plage and out on to the exposed promenade. It was deserted and the gale beat at them with full force. Isabelle pointed to a jetty.

'The Jetée d'Eyrac. That's where in summer the boats leave for Cap-Ferret. Further along to the east is the port. You can see the boats sheltering there.'

Newman stared into the distance where a forest of masts swayed drunkenly under the blast of the wind. The previous night Isabelle had guided him to a small hotel near the Gare, had then been driven to her sister's apartment behind the front.

'Do you have to leave today, Bob?' she asked wistfully.

'Definitely. There are things I have to find out. I rely on you to stay here until I contact you at your sister's. On no account go anywhere near Bordeaux.'

'If you say so.' She jutted her chin at the wind to show

93

her disappointment. 'In summer you wouldn't recognize the place. Luxurious yachts from all over the world come here with their rich owners. There is even one strange ship with its hull cut in two.'

'Cut in two?' Newman was instantly alert. 'Can you describe it more clearly?'

'I don't know much about ships. All I can say is it's a big luxurious job.'

'Name?'

'No idea.'

'How often does it come in here?' Newman persisted.

'I don't know. But I can tell you that unlike most of the millionaire-type private ships it doesn't just arrive in the summer season. I've seen it heading for the port at various times of the year. Including now – in November.'

'And that's unusual?'

'Very. Millionaire yachts turn up here in the summer. There's the right atmosphere. Topless girls on the beach – sometimes bottomless, too. The Casino is booming. And the night club, the Etoile. I went there once at my sister's insistence. Never again.'

'What happened?'

'An English lord made a heavy pass at me. Wouldn't take no. Seemed to think every French girl was just dying to get laid by his Lordship. I should be able to remember his name.'

They moved closer inland as waves began to hurl themselves against the promenade, splashing spume over the wall. Their force was so great Newman could have sworn the promenade shuddered when a storm wave hit.

'It's not usually like this,' Isabelle commented. 'I think we ought to get back.'

'I'm going to my car now. I have to move on. Stay in

Arcachon, Isabelle.' He decided to drive home his plea regardless of her feelings. 'Remember what happened to Henri in Bordeaux. And they know you exist.'

'Lord Dane Dawlish,' she said suddenly. 'That was the man who made a pass at me at the Etoile.'

Newman drove back to Bordeaux at speed under a sky heavy as lead. The low clouds scudded east like drifts of grey smoke. Before leaving his Arcachon hotel he had phoned the airport, booked a flight to Paris on his open ticket. He had also booked a flight from Paris to Heathrow. First, he'd call at the Pullman Hotel to pick up his case. He wasn't worried about the old second-hand case he'd left at the *pension*: also he had paid for his miserable room for a fortnight in advance.

He was approaching the Gare St Jean when he ran into a traffic jam. Vehicles, bumper to bumper, were not moving. He checked his watch. Reasonable time yet to catch his Air Inter flight to Paris. The driver of a car next to him leaned out of his window to speak to Newman.

'Don't go into the centre. A lot of trouble there.'

'What kind of trouble?'

The traffic was moving before the other driver could reply. Newman shrugged. Trouble was becoming a way of life in France. He had passed the Place de la Victoire when he saw there was no traffic ahead. Instead the street was filled with a sinister-looking mob. He swung his wheel, drove down a side street and parked his Citroën well away from the main street.

Locking the Citroën, he ran back the way he had come, peered out, saw the mob seemed even larger. A sign advertised a bar on the first floor. He ran up the steps, entered a crowded room, ordered a Pernod to have a glass in his hand, slithered between men and women chattering excitedly until he reached a window overlooking the main street.

Below a mob of Balaclava-masked men waving clubs and bottles were shouting slogans. *Pour France . . . Pour France . . . Pour France? Oui! . . . Juif? Non!!!*

The inflamatory chant went on. *For France? Yes. The Jew? No!!!* Holding his glass, Newman went on watching. He had the distinct impression the chant was organized. The riot became more savage. Men stormed into a restaurant, tore down the lace curtains, upturned chairs with customers, throwing them to the floor. Men and women: it made no difference. Terror was loose on the streets.

Having wrecked the interior the rioters flooded out, seeking a fresh target. One man with an aerosol paint canister sprayed a word across the window from the street. In huge red letters the word *Juif!* disfigured the glass. On the fascia above was the owner's name. Bronstein.

Newman estimated over two hundred Balaclava-masked men were prowling the street when he saw the CRS van stop further up the street. The paramilitary had arrived to quell the berserk mob. Berserk? What followed was extraordinary.

The apparently wild mob moved into a series of separate units. Somewhere a bell like a strident alarm was bellowing its clangour non-stop. A warning? A signal? Instead of retreating, units of the mob ran towards the van where CRS men clad in black coats and visored helmets were emerging with clubs. Seven men in the mob produced stubby wide-barrelled pistols, aimed at the van.

The CRS troops were about to advance when the projectiles from the pistols hit the cobbles in front of them, sending up clouds of tear gas. The CRS men stumbled, coughing, some ramming their hands to their injured eyes. A second unit, also armed with similar pistols, aimed for the no man's land of deserted street between the CRS and the mob. More projectiles hit the area accurately. Black smoke billowed. Smoke bombs.

Below the bar inside which Newman stood a TV man with a camera was grabbed by two men, held as a third took the camera he hadn't yet used. The lens was aimed away from the mob, swivelled slowly across the wreck of shops, restaurants, bars. No pictures of the mob.

When he had finished using the camera, one of the thugs holding the TV cameraman clubbed the back of his head. The TV reporter was perched on the edge of the kerb. He slumped into the gutter. The camera was dumped into his lap.

The strident alarm bell had stopped ringing. The mob moved in ordered groups, like troops on an exercise, some vanishing down side streets. Others climbed inside large tradesmen's vans which had appeared from the direction of the Gare St Jean. The vehicles sped out of the area.

Suddenly the street was deserted. The CRS men, recovering from the tear gas onslaught, appeared through the curtain of smoke to find their targets gone. Newman opened the window cautiously, heard the boots of the CRS trampling across heaps of shattered glass. It looked like the aftermath of a battlefield.

There was a hush inside the bar as Newman sidled his way through the crowd, ran down the steps before the CRS arrived. He continued running up the side street, reached his Citroën, unlocked it, dived inside, drove away from the main street, heading for the airport.

*

He had intended calling at the Pullman Hotel to collect his few belongings. Now he decided to forget it. His one aim was to leave Bordeaux alive.

He doubted whether this was the only riot which was in full swing in the city. What he had seen had all the hallmarks of a carefully organized campaign of terror. Objectives: to scare the population witless. To demoralize them into a state where they would welcome any force which could bring strong government, law and order. Anything which would allow them to live their normal lives in peace. It was a diabolical strategy.

He approached the airport cautiously, certain there would be watchers – even phoney DST men. And they'd probably have the registration number of his Citroën, which had to be handed back to car hire. Slowing down, he let traffic catch up with him. As he drove into the airport a queue of cars was ahead of him, disgorging passengers. Newman switched off, took out the keys, looked round.

Close by, a man in uniform stood waiting by an empty limousine. His cap band carried the name of a hotel. Newman reached for his case, climbed out, approached the chauffeur, speaking rapidly, a five-hundred franc note between his fingers.

'Excuse me, can you help? I'm going to miss my Lyons flight. I have to hand in that Citroën to the car hire people up there. Could you hand it in for me?' He winked. 'Trouble is I have the most accommodating girl waiting for me. She won't wait for the next flight . . .'

'What about payment?' the chauffeur demanded, eyeing the banknote.

'Nothing to pay. Paid in advance as usual . . .'

'Petrol?'

'I've used a lot less than I've already paid for.'

Newman extended the folded note.

98

'It's a lot but the smallest I've got. And what is waiting for me in Lyons is worth it.'

'My pleasure, sir . . .'

The banknote vanished inside the chauffeur's clothing. He ran to the Citroën and Newman hurried into the airport, then slowed down. Two men in trenchcoats with hats stood erect by a café. Stood too erect, more a military stance. With his beret pulled well down, Newman strolled to the counter, had his ticket verified, left his case at the check-in counter, walked to the departure point for his Paris flight.

He only relaxed when the Air Inter machine took off. And he had no intention of lingering in Paris. A flight straight back to London at the earliest possible moment. As the ground receded, a flat plain of green and grey segments, he hoped to God Isabelle would be safe in Arcachon.

Chapter Nine

The Paris headquarters of French counter-espionage – the DST – is located in an obscure side street few tourists ever notice. This is despite the fact that the rue des Saussaies, a narrow winding street off the rue du Faubourg St Honoré, is close to the Elysée Palace, residence of the President of France.

The entrance is a stone archway leading to a cobbled yard with only two uniformed policemen giving a clue that this building is the key to the protection of the French Republic.

Tweed and Paula were seated in the cramped office of the chief of the DST, who was standing while he poured coffee. René Lasalle was a tall, heavily-built man in his forties. A dynamo of energy, he placed the cups in front of his guests, darted round his desk to sit behind it. He studied Tweed from under thick brows through horn-rimmed spectacles, his eyes alert and quick-moving. 'A man for all seasons,' Tweed had once described him, 'and especially in a major crisis.'

'I'm glad you brought Paula with you,' Lasalle began. He gave her a half-smile. 'An experienced woman can detect something vital a man might miss.'

'What is the situation?' asked Tweed, determined to hear his host's comments before he made any of his own.

'Critical. Soon to be catastrophic. For France – and maybe for the whole of Europe.'

'You're not usually so melodramatic.'

'First tell me where you two have been,' Lasalle suggested.

'Geneva, then Basle. From Basle straight here.'

'So Robert Newman is operating on his own in Bordeaux.'

Tweed was rarely taken aback. Even now his expression gave nothing away. Paula was equally staggered and tried to keep her own expression neutral as she crossed her shapely legs.

'Is Newman all right?' Tweed asked quietly.

'I would say he is now. Two of my men spotted him as he boarded a plane at Bordeaux airport for Paris . . .'

He excused himself as the phone rang. Listening for a moment he said, '*Merci*,' and replaced the receiver.

'Newman is moving fast. I sent men to meet his aircraft here at Orly. He took a cab to Charles de Gaulle Airport and is aboard a flight for London.'

'You said *now* a few moments ago, referring to Newman. Why?' asked Tweed.

'When he arrived at Bordeaux Airport he was dressed like a Frenchman. My operative who spotted Newman had once met him. His clothing suggests to my suspicious mind he was evading pursuit by someone. Possible?'

'He flew to Bordeaux with a commission from the German news magazine, *Der Spiegel*. To interview General Charles de Forge.'

Lasalle raised his eyebrows. 'Our Mr Newman is a brave man. France is about to experience an earthquake. And I'm convinced the man organizing it is General Charles de Forge, who sees himself as the new de Gaulle. I would say a pseudo-de Gaulle.'

'Can you explain that in more detail?' Tweed asked. 'And did you find out why my agent, operating under the name Henri Bayle, was arrested by the DST?'

'One question at a time, please. Excuse me...' He answered the phone again, then spoke rapidly in French. Paula got the gist of it. Lasalle was ordering a new team of twenty DST men to leave for Bordeaux at once.

'You're reinforcing your people in Bordeaux,' Paula commented. 'Sorry if I sound interfering, but I couldn't help hearing what you said.'

Lasalle smiled at her. 'Of course, the pressure is such I'd forgotten for a moment your French is better than my English.'

'Nothing wrong with your English. Again, my apologies.'

'Not necessary.' Lasalle waved his hands. 'Now your questions, Tweed. First, when Bayle was taken from the Bar Miami and later murdered at the Gare St Jean there was not one single genuine DST operative in the Bordeaux area. I should know – I'm aware of the location of every DST man under my command. The men who took Bayle were impersonators.' A bite came into his normally soft tone. 'I do not find that amusing – which is one reason why I am flooding that city with my men.'

'And the other reason?' Tweed enquired.

'May I come to that later. I have been in touch myself with the Prefect of Bordeaux. The police there have come up with nothing so far. But he told me a curious story. He had an anonymous phone call. It reported a Berliet truck of the type used by the CRS would be found at the bottom of a gorge well outside Bordeaux. With bodies inside. A rough indication of the location was given by the caller.'

'Curious, as you say,' Tweed agreed. 'They found it?'

'No! No truck, no bodies. But they located the bridge described...' He arched his hand in a hump-back. 'The police found the bridge, partly collapsed and one wall in the gorge.' He paused. 'They also found traces of a very heavy tracked vehicle. The type of vehicle used by the Army. To be specific, by the Engineering Section of the Third Corps. Only such a machine would be able to lift and transport away a Berliet truck.'

'You're checking with General de Forge?' Tweed pressed.

'Why? I have no solid evidence. No witnesses. So it becomes merely another mysterious incident added to my dossier on de Forge.' He looked at Paula. 'Another fact in that dossier is the existence of de Forge's English mistress at the Villa Forban near Third Corps' GHQ. A Jean Burgoyne. Comes from some nowhere place I'd never heard of in East Anglia.' He checked the dossier. 'Here it is – Aldeburgh.'

Paula forced herself not to stiffen. She began reciting a catalogue of facts.

'Jean Burgoyne. A blonde beauty. Comes from landed gentry in Lincolnshire. Walked out of the London season because she said "London society is such a bloody bore." I quote her. Reputed to have a very high IQ. A bit wild and independent-minded. Likes adventurous living.'

'The Villa Forban,' Lasalle repeated. 'Owned by de Forge, used as a secret hideaway for meetings with the infamous *Cercle Noir*.'

'What's that?' Tweed enquired. 'And it sounds to me you have an informant planted in de Forge's camp.'

'Did I say so?' Lasalle raised his eyebrows. 'Now, we will take some lunch at a Swiss restaurant near the edge of the Place de la Madeleine. Afterwards I will tell you about the Black Circle . . .'

In her bedroom at the Villa Forban Jean Burgoyne sat in front of her dressing table, clad in only a silk dressing gown, unbelted at her slim waist. De Forge, she guessed, was about to engage in some frenetic activity.

It was only midday and his second visit to her bed in

twelve hours – always a sign that something big was under way. It was as though he felt the need for her in times of crisis. On a drum table by the window lay his leather dispatch case.

De Forge emerged from the shower, completed towelling his lean frame. He dressed quickly in his uniform and then his eyes fell on the dispatch case. He froze for a second, then completed his dressing.

Normally he handed the dispatch case to Major Lamy before entering the villa. But it had started snowing when he arrived this time and he'd hurried inside, depositing the case on the table. He walked slowly to the dressing table, his hypnotic eyes staring at hers in the mirror. She ignored his gaze after a second, continued applying face cream. His hands gripped her shoulders, slithered the gown off them, exposing her well-rounded breasts as the cloth slipped to her lap.

'Not again, Charles,' she said in her slightly husky voice. 'Time you went. And I'm flying home for a few days in England. Today.'

The grip on her shapely shoulders tightened. Jean never showed any fear of de Forge, a quality she suspected added to her attraction for him. His voice was dangerously quiet.

'I left my dispatch case on the table over there. It is not exactly in the position I left it. I have an eye for detail . . .'

'Your eye must be slipping.'

The grip tightened more, his fingers pressing through the white flesh to the bone.

'You looked at the papers inside while I was in the shower.'

'Take your hands off me, you fool,' she replied with equal quiet. 'You think I'm interested in your stuffy papers? You're becoming bloody paranoid – spies everywhere. And,' she continued calmly, 'if you hit me again I'll sock you with this brush...' Her right hand grasped the handle. 'Now push off with that creep, Lamy, and play your silly war games.'

'Why are you flying to England?' he demanded as he released his grip, stood back away from her.

'Because I want to, Charles.'

This time she had insisted on using the shower first. Now she pulled on her tights, dropped a slip over her head, put on a black form-hugging knee-length dress, tucked her small feet into court shoes, fastened a string of pearls round her neck. All in record time.

'Why do you want to go back to England?' de Forge persisted. 'You're always flying off somewhere – like a dragonfly. I may need you here.'

'Because I like to visit my uncle, to see my home. You will just have to contain your desire. If you're desperate you could pay Josette a visit. How long is it since you've seen your wife? And when you do go to her apartment do you take that damned dispatch case there, darling?'

De Forge's mouth tightened. He moved towards her with a deliberate step. Again, she held up a minatory finger.

'Remember what I said when you struck me last time. I meant it. And why do you always choose women whose names begin with the letter "J"?'

De Forge asserted his natural will-power, refused to respond to her mockery. He was putting on his képi when someone rapped quietly on the door.

'Come in,' Jean called out to show who was in control.

The door opened slowly and Lieutenant André Berthier, fair haired and good looking, his képi tucked respectfully under his arm, stepped into the room, careful to look straight at de Forge.

'Excuse me, General, but Major Lamy sent me in as you asked to be reminded of the time.'

'Maybe the lieutenant would like a glass of champagne?' Jean suggested, moving towards the ice bucket beside the rumpled bed.

'He would not,' de Forge replied in a cold voice. 'He is on duty.'

'You do have some handsome men on your staff, Charles,' Jean whispered.

She stroked her blond hair across a shoulder, staring at Berthier. She studied his build, his strong young face. Berthier, aware of her scrutiny, stared at the wall.

'Competence is the only qualification for my choice,' de Forge responded in the same chilly tone.

He marched to the door, picked up the dispatch case. Her remark about taking his dispatch case to Josette's apartment in Bordeaux had alerted him: he *did* take the case with him on his occasional visits.

Jean watched him leave with grim amusement. Always arouse a little jealousy when your lover was departing – it kept you in his thoughts. Hearing the outer door close, she ran to the bedroom door, opened it a fraction. Yes, they had gone. She went to the phone, dialled a number.

Outside it was arctic cold as snowflakes drifted down. Standing by the bullet-proof limousine, Major Lamy reached out to open the rear door. It seemed to have iced up. His large strong hand gave it a powerful twist, the door opened, de Forge brushed flakes off his uniform, sat inside. Lamy closed the door as Berthier sat in the front passenger seat next to the chauffeur, ran round the back, climbed in beside de Forge. The limousine sped down the drive, the wheels spurting up gravel.

De Forge glanced at Lamy. The Intelligence Chief often reminded the General of a fox with his long face, his expression, his pointed jaw. De Forge closed the sliding glass panel, shutting them off from the front compartment so Berthier could not hear him.

'Why do you choose Berthier as bodyguard?'

'Because,' Lamy explained, 'he is an expert with machine-pistols. He has one now by his side. He scores higher than anyone else on the range.'

'Kalmar did a good job with that spy, Henri Bayle,' de Forge commented, switching the subject suddenly – a favourite tactic to keep his officers off balance. 'I wonder who he really is. You must have some idea.'

'No idea.' Lamy gazed out of the window where the snow had become a white curtain. 'He keeps his identity a close secret. Communication only by phone – between two public call boxes. Payment in Swiss banknotes. Inside an envelope placed inside a small leather pouch. Always a different drop for the pouch. Always at a remote spot in the country – a location which can be watched for miles all round.'

'You'd almost think he had military training,' de Forge decided. 'Still, he does a perfect job. That's all that matters.'

'I have a different problem you might wish to consider,' Lamy said quickly, changing the subject. 'We are running low on the secret projects fund. And we need more of the special missiles – and the nerve gas they are armed with.'

'Don't worry. I have received a coded signal from our supplier. More funds are on the way, more missiles, more nerve gas.'

'When will the ship arrive?'

'Soon. I will tell you when I have a definite date.'

'And the pick-up point is Arcachon? As before?'

'Yes, Lamy, it is. There is one more task calling for immediate action. I want Jean Burgoyne followed when she leaves the villa. Reports on where she goes, who she meets.

107

A complete rundown. Berthier is fluent in English. Stop the car, give him my orders.'

'Why now, General? How can Berthier follow her in his uniform? She will recognize him.'

'Your brain is getting duller, Lamy . . .'

De Forge glanced behind the limo where outriders in uniform had joined the cavalcade to bring up the rear. More outriders preceded the car. They had taken up station as soon as de Forge's limo emerged from the entrance to the Villa Forban. Jean Burgoyne had complained she didn't want a lot of rowdy motorcyclists on the property.

'She is leaving soon for the airport,' de Forge continued. 'Send one outrider back to stay under cover, watch the villa gates, and follow her discreetly if she drives away. He can use his radio to contact Berthier. What happens to Berthier? He takes over one of the motorcycles, rides like hell to GHQ, changes into civilian clothes. I've seen him in mufti. He wears a hat which hides his fair hair, sports tinted glasses. Give him some money. Stop the car. *Now*, Lamy . . .!'

The major alighted from the car after telling Berthier to get out. He spoke rapidly to the lieutenant. With his back to de Forge, he took out his wallet, extracted three 1,000-Swiss franc notes. The equivalent of well over £1,000.

'That's dealt with,' he reported as he sank back into his seat, his face raw from the brief exposure to the elements.

The car with its outrider escort began to move again. De Forge was thinking he'd also have to arrange to have his wife, Josette, put under surveillance. In case Paris had infiltrated Third Corps the answer was more spies.

Chapter Ten

'General Charles de Forge is the most sinister political figure France has seen this century,' said Lasalle.

Paula look at Tweed, merely nodded, encouraging the DST chief to continue. They had returned from the restaurant and again sat in Lasalle's cramped office.

Paula had grasped Tweed's tactics. He was still at the stage of gathering data before returning to London, before deciding how to deploy his forces. A phase now familiar to her.

'He is inflaming French public opinion against Germany,' Lasalle went on. 'Dubois, head of the *Pour France* party, is his puppet, the ventriloquist's dummy. It is de Forge who supplies the angle for Dubois to take. It is outrageous – Germany is the most peace-loving nation in all Europe. De Forge is whipping up artificial fear of the new unified Germany.'

'Why?' Tweed asked. 'What is de Forge's objective?'

'To become the next President of France . . .'

'Has he a hope in hell? A general?'

Lasalle gave his wry smile. 'There is a precedent – General de Gaulle . . .'

'Who took power at a time of national emergency when the government became desperate.'

'Which is precisely the scenario de Forge is successfully recreating. Disorder, fighting in the streets. Clearly you have not grasped the significance of what has happened in Bordeaux.'

'Why Bordeaux?'

'Ah, Bordeaux! There you put your finger on it. You see, Bordeaux was the city which witnessed three French crises – and two humiliating defeats at the hands of Germany. In 1871 when Bismarck's armies destroyed us, annexed Alsace-Lorraine. In 1914 when the Paris government panicked, fled to Bordeaux temporarily. Above all, in 1940 when, as you know, the premier, Paul Reynaud, fled – again to Bordeaux – with his government. And surrendered to Hitler.'

'I still don't see why de Forge should launch his campaign from there.'

'He asked to be transferred to the command of the Third Corps, partly because it was based close to that city. De Forge is using Bordeaux as the symbol of French humiliation. What better city to launch a revenge campaign from? To make France the most powerful nation on the continent?'

'You said "partly". What was the other reason?'

'Because there he is close to his friend and ally, General Lapointe, commander of the *force de frappe* – France's atomic strike force.'

'And his request for this transfer was accepted?'

'Another ally is the Minister of Defence, Louis Janin. De Forge has Janin in his pocket.'

'Surely the President could do something, must know what is going on?'

'Ah, the Elysée!' Again the wry smile. 'The President is treading carefully. He cannot yet believe that a mere general would challenge him. And *Pour France* is worrying him with its growing popularity. Throw out the Algerians, the Arabs, Dubois thunders.'

'It has hardly become a national emergency,' Tweed insisted, determined to make Lasalle prove his case.

'We are close to it. The riots in Bordeaux. I hear that down there people . . .' He broke off as an aide rushed in, laid a long sheet of paper in front of Lasalle while apologizing for the intrusion, then rushed out after glancing at his chief's visitors. Lasalle's normally relaxed expression became grim. He looked at Tweed.

'You said there was no national emergency. This decoded fax has just come in. There have been major riots in Lyons. First reports indicate over one thousand five hundred casualties and the centre wrecked. Rioters were wearing Balaclava masks and not a single one has been arrested. The CRS were held back with tear gas, smoke bombs. Every hour it is coming closer to Paris.'

'So the plan is working.'

'Yes, Tweed. *De Forge*'s plan is working. He is destabilizing France, creating conditions for revolution. Who will save France? I give you one guess.'

'Tell me about the *Cercle Noir* you mentioned earlier.'

'The Black Circle.' Lasalle threw out both hands in a gesture of helplessness. 'A strong rumour that it is a small club planning all this. My investigations suggest – no proof – that its members are General de Forge, General Masson, Army Chief of Staff, General Lapointe, Louis Janin – Minister of Defence here in Paris. And Emile Dubois.'

'Any other members?' Tweed enquired.

'Perhaps one more. They have codenamed him *Oiseau* . . .'

'Bird?' Paula interjected. 'A curious codename.'

'We believe he comes and goes, that he is not only providing de Forge with funds to finance his campaign – but also secretly transporting to him advanced weapons not in his official armoury. Perhaps even lethal nerve gas.'

'Any idea who Bird could be?' Tweed pressed.

'None at all. Incidentally, do not mention any of our conversation to anyone – including a Cabinet Minister or a member of my staff. De Forge has spies everywhere.'

Tweed was stunned. He'd never heard the DST chief talk like this before. Paula reacted crisply.

'So, de Forge has a bandwagon rolling and a lot of people are climbing aboard?'

'You express it well,' Lasalle agreed. 'Let us hope it is not already too late.'

'On the other hand,' Paula suggested, 'I expect you also have your informants well placed. Otherwise how would you know so much about what is happening inside de Forge's camp?'

'I do have informants,' Lasalle replied cautiously. 'But it is not only the situation here which worries me. Strange developments are taking place inside Germany. An extreme right-wing group, *Siegfried*, is operating underground across the Rhine. This helps de Forge to portray the new Germany as a threat.'

'Is there no one – apart from the President – high up you can trust?' Tweed enquired.

'One strong man. Pierre Navarre, Minister of the Interior, and ultimately my boss. He detests de Forge. His attitude has one disadvantage. The President, I know, feels all will be well so long as Navarre is in the Cabinet to counter Louis Janin, who tells the President there is no danger of a coup.'

'So inertia rules?'

'Exactly. Before I come to a delicate subject, is there anything else you wish to know?'

'Yes,' Paula said promptly. 'Can you give us data on de Forge's personal life? That could be his weak point.'

Lasalle stood up, opened a wooden cupboard behind him attached to the wall, revealed a safe. Turning the combination dial from a code he carried in his head, he swung open the metal door, took out a thick green dossier, placed it on his desk.

'You've been busy,' Tweed observed as Lasalle opened the dossier.

'De Forge is becoming an obsession with me,' Lasalle admitted.

Paula glanced round the office on the first floor as the Frenchman searched the file. The furniture was ancient – a cheap wooden desk, the surface well worn; all the cupboards were also shabby wood; the windows could do with a clean, the curtains hadn't seen a laundry for a long time. Yet when they had entered the old building she'd glimpsed through an open door on the ground floor a room full of computers, fax machines, shimmering green screens. DST was an odd mix of the old and advanced technology.

Lasalle addressed himself to Paula as he began speaking. 'De Forge has been married for ten years to Jossette, a Parisienne society woman. She has an apartment in Bordeaux, another here in Passy. She was left a fortune by her father, who was Minister of Defence when de Forge married her. Her picture . . .'

Paula studied the photograph of an elegant brunette, seated on a sofa, wearing a short skirt with her superb legs crossed. A lady who knew how to display her assets.

'Attractive, intelligent, knows what she wants,' she hazarded.'

'An excellent character analysis,' Lasalle replied, impressed. 'And she wishes to be the wife of the President of France, her husband.'

'Is he faithful to her?'

'My God! No! De Forge has an insatiable appetite for the good things of life. At the head of the list he places women. He has an English mistress, as I mentioned before lunch. She spends time at the Villa Forban, near Third Corps GHQ. May I introduce you to Jean Burgoyne . . .'

Paula studied the photo he had extracted from the dossier. She recognized the glamorous girl with long blonde hair. Seated in a canvas chair on a lawn with a backdrop of dense evergreens, Jean Burgoyne wore a tight-fitting blue sweater which revealed her enticing figure and her wide mouth was smiling, a smile of wicked amusement.

'The picture is a bit blurred,' Paula commented.

'Taken secretly with a telescopic lens.'

'And I suppose Josette doesn't know she exists?' Paula remarked, phrasing her point carefully.

'You believe that!' Lasalle gave a mocking laugh, relaxing briefly for the first time since they'd met. 'I have proof Josette is well aware of de Forge's many little peccadilloes. Is that the word?'

'That's the word, René,' Paula said and chuckled. 'She puts up with them?'

'She ignores them. I told you – she wishes to remain the wife of the man who will become President of France. A most ambitious woman. She also has her affairs – and always with men who could be useful to de Forge.'

'Quite a lady, if that's the word,' Paula commented.

Lasalle extracted a fresh photo. 'And this is Major Jules Lamy, Chief of Intelligence to de Forge. Some say he is de Forge's *éminence grise*, his evil genius. Lamy is a keep fit fanatic. They say he runs ten miles every day, no matter what the weather.'

Tweed leaned towards Paula to look at the picture. A foxy-faced man, strong features, staring eyes. Paula grimaced, handed back the photo.

'Don't like the look of him at all. Wouldn't like to bump into him on a dark night.'

'Finally, this is Sergeant Rey. I have two copies – take one. If the formidable Robert Newman is thinking of returning to Bordeaux, best he knows about Rey.'

'What is his function?' Tweed asked as Paula leaned to look at the photo.

Rey wore the uniform and emblems of a sergeant. He had a gnome-like face, was of uncertain age, but his eyes were cunning and cruel. Again the picture was slightly blurred.

'He is officially de Forge's batman,' Lasalle said, his tone grim. 'The important thing to remember is that he is a genius at constructing booby-traps. Inventive as the devil.'

'De Forge sounds to specialize in devils,' Tweed commented half-humorously to lighten the atmosphere.

He handed the photo to Paula who tucked it carefully inside a compartment in her shoulder bag. Lasalle slowly drummed his fingers on the desk, staring at Tweed.

'Now I come to the delicate subject. I know how much you value and look after your agents. Henri Bayle who was murdered in Bordeaux. He was taken from a place he worked at called the Bar Miami by two fake DST officers. The autopsy report has come through by fax. A detailed report.'

'What does it tell us?' Tweed asked quietly.

'That he was strangled. The aspect I find intriguing about the report . . .' He paused, glanced at Paula. 'I hope I don't sound cold-blooded?'

'Not in the least,' Paula said briskly. 'We need all the data we can get.'

'The pathologist,' Lasalle continued, 'records in his report that the strangler was a professional. An odd word to use but he goes on to explain. The act of strangulation was swift and very efficient. Thumbs were pressed against Bayle's wind-pipe and held there until he expired. After death – and this is curious – the murderer savagely bruised the neck. Sounds like a sadist, even a psychopath.'

'More likely an attempt to cover his professional expertise,' Tweed responded.

'It is rumoured – no more – that the killer was a man we have heard of. Kalmar.'

'Where did the rumours come from?'

'We think Kalmar himself advertises his existence – to increase his reputation, and therefore his fees, for such assignments.'

'Origins?'

'Shrouded in mystery.' Lasalle waved his hands again. 'Some say he is a Mittel-European. Others that he has come from the East – the Balkans. Like Interpol, we have no description, no clue as to his nationality – but he is alleged to be fluent in several languages. Again, which ones we don't know.'

'In other words, René,' Tweed smiled, 'we know damn-all about Kalmar so far.'

'He will make a mistake sooner or later.'

'After creating more corpses,' Paula suggested.

Tweed glanced at his watch, reached for his overcoat.

'We have a flight to catch. Back to London. For your help, for the information, many thanks, René. We must keep in close touch. We shall be working on this day and night. It is just possible the solution to what is going on lies in England . . .'

Chapter Eleven

On a stormy November night all roads led to Aldeburgh, the strange old town on the Suffolk coast of Britain.

Tweed and Paula had landed at London Airport, hurried to their flats for a change of clothes, had met up again at Park Crescent. From his office Tweed made a series of quick phone calls, told Monica to hold the fort, then left the building with Paula, each carrying a suitcase. Getting into his Ford Escort, he drove them out of the city, across the flatlands of Essex in the dark and on into Suffolk. They arrived at the Brudenell Hotel on the front to find the place almost deserted of guests at that time of the year.

Paula had found it a weird experience to return to the scene of her terrifying experience with her dead friend, Karin Rosewater. Tweed had been so active she had kept quiet until he invited her to his large room on the first floor. He had summoned what he called a 'council of war' and they drank coffee while they waited for the others to arrive.

Newman had been phoned, back from Bordeaux and Paris for only a few hours. Marler was on the way, bringing with him in their own cars two more SIS men – Harry Butler and Pete Nield, who often worked in tandem. Paula asked the question as they waited.

'Why did you tell Lasalle the solution might lie here in England?'

'One interesting and deadly – literally – fact. Your friend, Karin, was strangled by someone the Suffolk pathologist described as a professional. Remember what the autopsy report said?'

'How can I ever forget it?'

'Sorry, I put that too bluntly. Then in Paris René Lasalle gives us the gist of the Bordeaux pathologist's comments on how Francis Carey was murdered at the Gare St Jean. He used the same word – professional. He even went on to give almost precisely the same description of how Carey's murder was enacted.'

'I did actually notice,' Paula admitted, 'but I thought it must be a coincidence. You're not suggesting that . . .'

'The strangler in Suffolk is the same strangler in Bordeaux? I'm suggesting just that.'

Tweed reached into his breast pocket. He brought out a current British Airways timetable, opened it at a page with the corner turned down.

'I collected this before we left Park Crescent. The murder of Karin Rosewater took place in the evening. In the evening of the *following* day Francis Carey was murdered in exactly the same way in Bordeaux. This timetable shows a BA flight leaving Heathrow at 10.55, arriving Bordeaux 12.25. There's also another direct flight via Air France – leaves a little later but gets to Bordeaux mid-afternoon.'

'Aren't you letting your imagination run away with you?'

'The facts I've given have nothing to do with imagination – allied to two different pathologists' identical descriptions of the murder technique used.'

'Kalmar?' she ventured.

'A top assassin can move fast. Operating in Europe he'll know all the routes, flight times. It's part of his stock-in-trade.'

'Kalmar,' she repeated. 'A strange name.'

'Chosen deliberately to conceal his real identity, his real

118

nationality. One fact common to both pathologists' reports –
the strangler has large hands.'

He broke off as the phone rang. Paula answered it, said
come up now, put down the receiver.

'Newman has arrived. And so have Marler, Butler, and
Nield. Good job you asked for extra chairs . . .'

The spacious bedroom had a wide bay window overlooking the North Sea. The curtains were drawn against the
night but Paula could hear beyond the windows the insidious surge of the sea, the thump of waves hitting the beach
with the incoming tide. When the four men had entered the
room, found themselves seats, she poured coffee. Character-
istically, Marler refused a chair, leaning against a wall while
he lit a king-size cigarette.

Tweed wasted no time. He sketched in briefly what was
happening in France and Germany, gave them the data
supplied by Lasalle and Kuhlmann.

'We have to take action urgently,' he went on. 'I had a
quick call from Lasalle after I'd arrived back at Park Crescent.
More details of the Lyons riots had reached him. He said
events were assuming the character of an insurrection. I
suspect de Forge is only waiting for the trigger – some new
event which will give him the excuse to move on Paris. Now,
Bob, you learned something while you were in Bordeaux?'

'I learned a lot – all of which confirms what you've just
said . . .'

Tersely, he described the hazards of his experience of his
stay in Bordeaux. His interview with de Forge, the punishment well, his narrow escape when pursued by the Berliet
truck. And Isabelle's ordeals.

'That's it,' he concluded.

'This Isabelle,' Paula asked, curious about the way he
had described her, 'she's attractive?'

'I suppose she is,' Newman replied and said no more.

He fancies her, Paula thought. She sounds to be quite a girl. And she probably likes Bob, too.

'That riot you witnessed in Bordeaux,' Tweed said in a business-like tone. 'You conjured up a picture of a disciplined force – not a mob of hotheads. The way they outmanoeuvred the CRS, a skilled paramilitary force. Almost sounds as though they were well-trained troops under those damned Balaclavas.'

'Which was exactly the impression I got, watching from that upstairs bar,' Newman confirmed. 'I was about to make the same comment.'

'Anything else?'

'Some of the smaller rioters are probably members of *Pour France* – farmers, peasants, shopkeepers. But the big stuff, I'm convinced – after what I saw in Bordeaux – are de Forge's men disguised with those Balaclavas.'

'Then the situation is more than dangerous, it is explosive. And we have very little time left.'

Marler spoke for the first time, in his off-hand drawl. 'Then why, may I ask, are we all assembled here out in the backwoods of England?'

'Because this is where it all started – the murder of Karin Rosewater, the attempt to kill both women. Why? Because they had been caught exploring underwater off Dunwich. Something is going on up there.'

'Might be able to give you a start point,' Marler continued. 'While you were all gallivanting abroad I drove around up here – as far as Dunwich and then up a bit further north to Southold. Visiting pubs. The people who frequent local pubs know things.'

'So what did you discover?'

'That the man financing the new underwater exploration

of that sunken village, Dunwich, is a certain Lord Dane Dawlish.'

'A millionaire several times over,' Tweed mused after digesting Marler's information. 'And someone must be financing de Forge – Lasalle made that point. He'll need money to pay his men extra for creating the riots, to smooth palms liberally high up in Paris. It's a long shot – we need a link between Aldeburgh and Bordeaux. And we haven't got one – except for the similarity between the two murders. We need far more.'

'So it's probably helpful,' Marler remarked, 'that I wangled an invitation to a shooting party on Dawlish's estate at Grenville Grange.'

'How did you work that one?' Tweed asked.

'I was having a quick lunch at the Cross Keys – a very good pub further along the front from here. Behind the Moot Hall. At the next table was a bunch of tough-looking individuals, smartly dressed. Gabbing about a clay pigeon shoot at Dawlish's place. I got talking to them, put on an act, told them I was a stockbroker on holiday, that I could shoot clay pigeons out of the sky. They took the bait – a heavy type called Brand laid a bet with me. Five hundred quid, as he put it.'

'What do you do to win?' Newman asked. 'And maybe I could join the party.'

'I have to blast all my clay pigeons out of the sky. I'm going to lose. No point in letting them know about my marksmanship. You can come – if you insist. Brand said bring friends if I wanted to. Dawlish, I gather, is very sociable. Likes big parties.'

'When?' Newman asked.

'Tomorrow. Turning up at Grenville Grange about eleven in the morning. They think I'm Peter Wood. I've a stockbroker pal in the City of that name. I phoned, asked him to cover for me. If they check, his secretary will confirm her boss, Wood, is away in Suffolk.'

Tweed leaned forward. 'Why such careful precautions?'

'Something phoney about them. Except for Brand, they don't look comfortable in their fancy country gear. An athletic gang, in their late twenties, early thirties.'

Tweed took from his breast pocket the well-filled wallet he always carried. Extracting ten fifty-pound notes he handed them to Marler.

'Your lost bet. I think you're wise to conceal your marksmanship. It's another long shot – Dawlish. But there is a link there. Dawlish involved in underwater exploration at Dunwich. And those scuba divers who tried to kill both Paula and Karin.'

'And I'll join you,' Newman decided. 'Under my own name.'

'If you must,' Marler agreed, shrugging his shoulders.

'That's what I like.' Newman grinned. 'Enthusiasm.'

'I'd like to come, too,' Paula suggested. 'The editor of *Woman's Eye* is a friend of mine. And they'd like an interview for their feature *Men of Distinction*.'

'That would be overdoing it,' Newman objected.

'And,' Tweed warned her, 'supposing some of the thugs who pursued you from Dunwich in dinghies turned out to be among the group of characters Marler met at the Cross Keys? You could be recognized.'

'Don't agree,' Paula insisted. 'They only saw us under murky water with our masks on. Impossible to recognize anyone wearing one of those.'

'But while you were changing out of your wetsuits on

the beach,' Tweed recalled, 'you said those killers in the dinghies were approaching the shore.'

'Too far away to recognize me. It was dusk, too. I'd turn up quite on my own,' she informed Newman. 'So I won't know either of you. And,' she pounded on, 'you are getting there at eleven. I'll phone Dawlish and make an appointment for midday.'

'If you can . . .'

'Men are vain. Successful men are very vain, love to get their names in quality magazines. Bet I pull it off.'

'Under those circumstances,' Tweed decided reluctantly, 'I suppose it might be a good idea. We're so short of time the sooner we cross Dawlish off the list of suspects the better.'

'I'd say he fits like a glove,' Marler observed. 'You quoted Lasalle a few minutes ago as saying someone was secretly supplying nice General de Forge with arms. Dawlish has armaments factories. One of them could be in the woods between Snape Maltings and Orford.'

'How do you know that?' Tweed asked sharply.

'Because, as I told you, I drove round up here. On my way to Orford I passed a track leading up into the woods off a lonely road. The area was fenced off with an eight-foot high wire fence, electrified. Plates attached to the fence with a friendly warning. "Keep Out! Danger!" Plus skull and crossbones. The lot.'

'That's a long way from France – especially Bordeaux.'

Tweed blinked, gazed into the distance. Something he had heard Paula say on another occasion. What was it? Maybe it would come back to him.

'You're looking for a French link?' Newman enquired. 'Could be one downstairs inside this hotel. When I was approaching the elevator a youngish chap stubbed his toe

123

on a step. I distinctly heard him mutter *Merde!* under his breath. He then asked me the way to the lounge in perfect English.'

'Describe him.'

'Late twenties, early thirties. Clean shaven. Walks very erect. Struck me as a military type. Wearing dark glasses – Lord knows why at this time of the year.' He glanced at Paula with a dry smile. 'Some women would describe him as handsome.'

'I must visit the bar,' Paula said promptly. 'Bet he finds his way there. After I call *Woman's Eye* for tomorrow.'

'I suppose we could have come to the right place,' Tweed thought aloud.

'You don't know how right you are,' Marler needled him. 'Chief Inspector Buchanan and Sergeant Warden are staying here. I had a brief encounter with Buchanan yesterday.'

'Why are they still here?'

'The Chief Constable has asked Buchanan to continue his investigations into Karin Rosewater's murder. The whole of Aldeburgh knows about him.'

'We can't let him get in the way.' Tweed stood up. 'The exact nature of de Forge's threat to Germany is vague – so even more menacing. We can't do much this evening. All of you have rooms I reserved for you from London. I want action tomorrow.'

'Where do we fit in?' asked the heavily-built Butler.

As usual, he had remained silent with his partner, Pete Nield. But both men had memorized every single word said.

'I was coming to you,' Tweed replied. 'Are you armed as I suggested?'

'Nice to know he can't tell,' the more extrovert Nield remarked, fingering his moustache.

Both men were clad in clean denims and windcheaters. Butler nodded, produced from his hip holster under his windcheater a 7.65mm Walther automatic. Nield showed his own Walther.

'Good,' Tweed approved. 'Because tomorrow I want you to follow Newman and Marler discreetly to this Grenville place. You are to act as guards, back-up in case of trouble.'

'We expect trouble from a man like Dawlish?' queried Marler sceptically.

'Monica drew up a dossier on him while we were away. I skipped through it before I drove out with Paula. He built up his empire from nothing – and used some dubious methods on the way. Exercise the utmost caution. Paula, see if you can find out who Newman's Frenchman is. It is the first whiff of the French we've had in Suffolk.'

Paula, wearing a Chanel-style blue suit with a white blouse and a pussy bow, walked into the bar as a tall slim girl with a mane of blonde hair turned, a glass of champagne in her hand, and collided with her.

Paula jumped aside and the spilt champagne just missed her suit. Jean Burgoyne stared at the suit with horror. Paula smiled reassuringly.

'It is all right. It went on the floor.'

'My God! I'm so sorry. How simply dreadfully clumsy of me. Are you sure it isn't spoilt? That's Chanel, isn't it? You look stunning.'

'You don't look so bad yourself. And this isn't an original, I'm sorry to say. I made it myself.'

Jean Burgoyne did look stunning in a light green form-fitting sheath dress which displayed her excellent figure to full advantage. Two slim straps supported it over her bare, well-shaped shoulders. Her greenish eyes studied Paula, her wide mouth smiled.

'I'm Jean Burgoyne . . .'

'I'm Paula Grey, a freelance journalist on *Woman's Eye* . . .'

Thinking quickly, Paula had decided it was best to stick to the same story. In a small place like Aldeburgh you never knew who knew who. She had instantly recognized the glamorous blonde and hoped she was on her own.

'I buy every issue,' Jean told her. 'The least I can do is get you a glass of champagne. That is, if like me, you're on your own.'

'As it happens, I am. I wasn't looking forward to a solitary evening . . .'

Paula took Jean Borgoyne's glass to a quiet corner table. She was puzzled. What was Burgoyne doing in this part of the world? Another French link: de Forge's mistress in Aldeburgh. And she was quite a girl, Paula thought. She moved gracefully and every man in the bar was watching her.

As she brought more champagne to the table Paula spotted the Frenchman with tinted glasses Newman had identified. He ordered a drink and sat alone, erect in his chair. He looked briefly at Burgoyne and then turned away. Burgoyne had sat next to Paula, raised her glass.

'Cheers! Paula! May I call you Paula? I'm Jean.'

'Please do. I'm ready for this.'

'Join the club.' She drank half the contents. 'I'm just back from France. Bordeaux, actually. I have a friend there. My uncle, who brought me up, lives in one of the houses at the back of Aldeburgh – he likes the seclusion of the place . . .'

She went on talking in her low husky voice, used a hand to throw her mane back over her shoulder. 'My parents were killed in a road smash when I was six. He took over. He's eighty now. My father – Uncle's brother – would have been eighty-two. I was born late. All hell is breaking loose in France. I was telling my uncle about it. He's still got all his

marbles. Used to be a Brigadier. In Military Intelligence.'
She smiled roguishly. 'Sorry, I'm rattling on about myself.
You will be thinking I'm trying to manoeuvre you into
interviewing me.'

'Honestly, the thought hadn't crossed my mind. But
you'd be a perfect subject.'

'Not me, Paula.' The roguish smile again. 'When I came
down from Oxford I trained to be a barrister, then never
practised at the Bar. A perfect subject? Not for *Woman's Eye*.
I like men too much – I think you'd find my life a bit too
spicy.'

'I do have a commission,' Paula explained. 'Tomorrow I
interview Lord Dane Dawlish. I phoned him a few minutes
ago. He sounded enthusiastic.'

Jean gave Paula an odd appraising look, drank out of her
half-empty glass, put it down with equal care. Paula kept
silent: she felt sure she'd by chance pressed a button.

'I was at a party at Grenville Grange when I met my
French friend,' Jean said slowly. 'You'll have to watch
Dawlish. You're attractive. He'll make a pass at you.'

'That was your experience?'

'You can say that again. Talk about having to fight off a
wolf. Good luck. Put on plenty of clothes.'

Paula was trying to keep her face expressionless while
she watched a tall handsome man enter the bar. It was
Victor Rosewater.

All roads led to Aldeburgh . . .

Chapter Twelve

Grenville Grange was perched on a peninsula projecting into the river Alde several miles inland from Aldeburgh. Near Iken Church, all the lights were on that evening as Lord Dane Dawlish sat in his study behind a Queen Anne desk talking to Joseph Brand.

Dawlish was of medium height, a powerfully built man in his late fifties. He had a bull neck and a squarish head. Thick grey sideburns curled beside his ears and he was clean shaven. His nose and jowly jaw were pugnacious. His brown eyes had a challenging expression. He radiated physical energy and his manner was aggressive.

'I didn't get where I have by being polite to people who stood in my way,' was one of his favourite maxims.

'You checked out this Peter Wood who's joining us for the shoot tomorrow?' he demanded.

'Phoned his London office. His secretary said her chief wasn't available, was away in Suffolk.'

'So he could be pukka.'

Brand pursed his thick lips. A small man, wide-shouldered, weighing sixteen stone, he regarded everyone as a potential enemy. One of his large hands drummed silently on his knee below the desk as he sat facing his boss. In his late forties, he had a pear-shaped head, terminating in a full chin below a wide thin mouth.

'How much more information do we need?' Brand asked.

'As much as we can get. He's a stranger who struck up an

acquaintance with you in that pub. I like to know who's prowling under my roof. And a five hundred bet is throwing money around. His entrance fee?'

'Stockbrokers make a lot of money,' Brand protested. 'Christ! I should know. They live off commissions.'

'And off suckers like you who play the markets which I don't.'

Caught on the raw, Brand forgot his position. The words were out of his mouth even as he knew he'd blundered.

'At least I don't waste money on women right, left, and centre . . .'

Dawlish drummed the hairy knuckles of his right hand on the desk slowly. He smiled, not a pleasant smile. His eyes stared straight at Brand's.

'You've overlooked something. I get a lot back for my money. And I think you've overlooked who you're talking to. You can easily be replaced, Brand. Your sort come ten a penny.'

'I'm tired, sir. I've been working since five in the morning . . .'

'And what have you got to show for it?' Dawlish demanded brutally.

'My informant at the Brudenell reports a lot of new arrivals today. And this is November. One of them is Robert Newman, the foreign correspondent . . .'

'Who this Peter Wood phoned me about. On the excuse of thanking me in advance for having him at my shoot. What he really called about was to ask if he could bring Newman. As I told you earlier . . .'

'Which is someone else I checked on for you,' Brand said hastily.

'Don't bloody well interrupt me. A lot of people seem to be taking a sudden interest in me – and this is a critical time. In case you've forgotten.'

'Could be a coincidence . . .'

'I've survived by not believing in coincidences. On top of those people, a Paula Grey is coming to interview me. She sounded sexy on the phone. Could be a bonus for me there.' Dawlish added and grinned coarsely. 'Is the weapons consignment nearly ready?'

'Half the delivery is ready. The balance will be at the collection point soon.'

'And you're keeping a close eye on the met forecasts for the Bay of Biscay? The voyage to Arcachon can be a real bastard.'

'I record them hourly,' Brand assured his boss, relieved that he seemed in a more amiable mood.

'And the Cat will have completed its overhaul?'

'I checked with the skipper today. The Cat will be in good shape.'

'It had better be.'

Dawlish stood up, walked to the large window behind his desk. He stood with his back to Brand, gazing out across the lawn sloping to the landing stage at the edge of the Alde. A moonlit night showed storm clouds scudding in from the east, from the North Sea.

Silhouetted against the light from the room Dawlish stood so still on his thick legs he looked like a Buddha. Brand had never met another man who could remain motionless for long periods. Dawlish had no fear of hostile action from the grounds. For one thing they were patrolled by wolfhounds. For another the windows were made of bullet-proof glass. Brand risked disturbing his thoughts, wanting to demonstrate his thoroughness.

'Another arrival in Aldeburgh – seen in the bar of the Brudenell – is Jean Burgoyne.'

Dawlish's reaction was different from what Brand had expected. He swung round, his eyes glowing, his manner explosive.

'What the bloody hell is she doing back here? All this

happening when we're approaching what I told you was a critical time. The biggest delivery yet. Plus a wad of money for our friends in France.'

'Burgoyne has an uncle in Aldeburgh,' Brand pointed out in a conciliatory tone. 'She does visit him occasionally . . .'

'Bloody hell, have you lost the few marbles you've got left? Jean Burgoyne's uncle Brigadier was Military Intelligence. Goddamnit! Another coincidence – and with this other lot arriving . . .'

Dawlish strode swiftly to the luxurious cocktail cabinet concealed behind a floor-to ceiling bookcase, pressed a button which operated a sliding case, exposing the cabinet. He poured a large Scotch, drank the whole glass, and didn't offer anything to Brand.

'The uncle is eighty . . .' Brand ventured.

'And a perfect conduit back to the Ministry of Defence. I'm getting the feeling I'm being crowded. Always before that feeling has meant trouble.' He handed the glass to Brand. 'Get me another. A large one. We're going to have to take precautions tomorrow. Arrange to have men ready to take up the chopper. Both men to be armed. I may want someone followed, maybe dealt with.'

'That could be dangerous,' Brand warned, handing back the refilled glass. 'Another death after what happened to Karin Rosewater.'

'To succeed in this world you have to take risks.'

'One other thing I found out today. Someone else is staying at the Brudenell . . .'

'Don't play with me, Brand. Who?'

'Chief Inspector Buchanan of the CID and his sidekick, Sergeant Warden.'

'So, if we sense danger there may be a fatal accident during the shooting party. With the blame manipulated to one of the guests,' Dawlish concluded and drank the rest of his Scotch.

Chapter Thirteen

In the bar at the Brudenell Jean Burgoyne had said she'd better get home. She gave Paula her address and a phone number before she left.

'I've found our conversation frantically relaxing,' she said warmly. 'Please promise that we'll meet for another chat soon. There may be some problems I'd like to talk over with you. That's if you don't find me a crashing bore,' she added hastily.

'Anything but,' Paula responded. 'I'm not sure how long I'll be here but I'll call you. We'll meet.'

'I'm simply *not* after an interview,' Jean stressed anxiously. 'Please don't think that.'

'I know. We'll meet,' Paula repeated.

As soon as Jean had gone Victor Rosewater walked over to Paula. Again she thought he was a handsome-looking man and he was smartly dressed in a check sports jacket and well-creased grey slacks. But his face was drawn, his smile forced as she invited him to sit beside her. He put a glass of orange juice on the table.

'I said I would come here,' he began, 'but the last person I expected to be lucky enough to meet was you.'

'Why didn't you phone me? You've got some leave?'

'I was going to call you from here. It was a rush catching the flight from Europe. And as I told you in Basle, I've a roving commission. I came here because this is where Karin died.'

'You think that's a good idea?' she asked quietly.

'No power on earth can stop me finding out who murdered her. The solution must be here. Why? How? Who?'

His expression and tone were grim and determined. He smiled again, drank some orange juice as the wind hammered the windows as though trying to break through the glass. Rosewater put down his tumbler.

'It must have been a night like this when her life was ended.'

'Something like this,' she said, wondering what he was thinking.

'Do you mind walking in the dark with this wind blowing?'

He was gazing into the distance, staring past her, not aware of the other customers drinking and chattering. Revenge was the most potent of all driving forces, she thought as she watched him.

'What do you want to do?' she asked eventually.

'Please say no if you don't like the idea. But I want to go and see where it happened, under the conditions it happened. There may be something the police have overlooked. No one knew Karin like I did. She could have left a clue.'

She was about to say there were clever men from Scotland Yard who had been all over the ground, when Newman walked in. He paused when he saw Paula was not alone. She beckoned him over.

'Bob, this is Victor Rosewater.' She gave him a warning look. 'He was Karin's husband. Tweed and I met him in Basle, as you know. Victor, this is Robert Newman.'

'The foreign correspondent . . .'

Rosewater stood up, shook hands. Newman's arrival seemed to help him. He had recovered his normal poise. Newman joined them, looked at Rosewater's glass, asked if he was drinking orange juice.

'As a matter of fact, I am.'

'You're teetotal?'

'Good God, no!'

'Then maybe something a little stronger would help on a cold night like this. How about a Scotch?'

'Thank you, but no.' Rosewater looked embarrassed. 'I just don't think alcohol is a good idea, feeling as I do at the moment.'

'Victor wanted to be shown where the tragedy happened,' Paula told Newman. 'He thinks he might just find something the police overlooked.'

'You mean now?' Newman queried, a hint of surprise in his tone.

'Yes,' Paula continued. 'Under the same conditions of weather there were that night. And I think the storm has blown itself out. I can't hear the wind.'

'And it would be about this time, wouldn't it?' Rosewater asked, checking his watch.

'Yes, it would,' Paula agreed. 'Within an hour or so, anyway.' She looked at Newman. 'I'm quite prepared to go out for a walk after I've wrapped up well.'

'Then I'll come with you,' Newman decided.

'That would be a great relief to me,' Rosewater said. 'The two of you coming with me – if it's not a great imposition, which I suppose it is.'

'Nonsense.' Newman stood up. 'Let's get on with it. I'll get my things. Meet you both in the lobby a few minute from now . . .'

Aldeburgh was dead. The streets were deserted as Paula, Newman and Rosewater left the Brudenell by the entrance away from the front. They left the town behind when they entered the public car park. The wind had dropped as quickly as it had risen. Paula had a creepy feeling as her feet crunched the pebbled ground of the car park.

It was moonlit and she could remember the exact spot where she'd parked her car when she'd arrived with Karin. The car Butler had later driven back to London for her after Newman had taken her home in his Mercedes. They walked out of the car park on the gravel road leading to Slaughden Sailing Club in the distance. As they passed the old barn-like structure with a sign reading *Boat Storage* a cloud blotted out the moon and it was pitch dark.

'Which way now?' asked Rosewater, walking alongside Paula.

'A bit further along this awful road and then we turn down a footpath leading across the marshes.'

She had switched on her flashlight at the same moment as Rosewater turned on a more powerful beam. Behind them Newman walked slowly, glancing all round, his own flashlight switched on. Paula turned off the road, led the way down the steep bank and followed the footpath over the marshes below the gravel road. Rosewater caught her up, slowed down when he realized his long legs were making it difficult for her to keep pace.

'How long to get there?' he asked.

'About ten minutes from here . . .'

Despite the lack of wind it was very cold. Paula was muffled in a fur-lined coat, its hood pulled over her head. On her feet she wore gumboots. The two men were also clad in gumboots as they squelched over the soggy ground.

They came to the point where the footpath forked – one fork leading back up to the road, the other up to the dyke. Paula slipped on a patch of mud, nearly fell. Rosewater grabbed her waist, kept her erect, hauled her up on the dyke. Behind them Newman paused: his acute hearing had caught the sound of the engine of a distant vehicle which seemed to be growing louder although still some distance away. Sound carried a long way in the menacing silence which hung over the marshes. He could still hear the surge of the sea.

Rosewater trod along the narrow path atop the dyke, the marshes below him on the right, the anchorage beyond a mess of grassy creeks to his left. Paula was following close behind him and Newman brought up the rear, wishing he'd brought a weapon. He could still hear the sound of the vehicle approaching across the marshes.

Paula was trembling – and not with the cold. The nearer she approached the location where Karin had been found the worse she felt. The dark didn't help. She couldn't even see the distant copse of firs where she had sheltered while Karin was being strangled.

'Stop, Victor,' she called out.

She stood still, made herself play the flashlight down the side of the dyke, along a small creek filled with stagnant water. She froze. By the light of her beam she saw the small craft, rotting, the staves showing like the bowed ribs of a disturbed skeleton. It was just as she had seen it with Karin's corpse laid out inside it. She gritted her teeth, forcing herself to speak.

'She was found inside that wreck of a boat . . .'

Rosewater flashed his own beam on the craft, ran, slithered down the grassy bank. Crouching down, he examined its interior. Then, laying the lighted flash on a grassy tuft, he grasped hold of the craft, heaved it over upside down with manic energy, hauling it on to the grassy tufts. Paula slipped a hand over her mouth to stop crying out. Newman's hand gently held her arm.

'Let him get it out of his system,' he whispered.

Rosewater had picked up the flashlight again, was now

feverishly searching the grass, the muddy clefts, feeling the ground with his free hand. The moving hand stopped suddenly. Paula stiffened. Rosewater moved the beam very slowly over a patch of grass. Moments earlier he had been acting like a man in a frenzy. Now he was moving his hand slowly and systematically. The hand stopped again, the fingers closed over something. He opened his palm, shone his flashlight on an object, tucked the torch under his arm and used his gloved hand to rub it, to clean it.

He scrambled back up the bank, his bare hand clenched tightly. Facing Paula, he opened the hand, shone the beam on it. She stared at the gold ring which bore an insignia. Picking it off his palm, she showed it to Newman who glanced at it, then at Rosewater.

'Karin's?'

'No. Look at the size of the diameter. Karin had a small hand, slim fingers. Recognize the symbol on the signet?'

'The Cross of Lorraine. French. De Gaulle's symbol for the Free French during World War II.'

'And because of the size,' Rosewater pointed out, 'it was probably dropped by the murderer. Find the owner and we've found the strangler . . .'

'Put it in your pocket! Quickly!' Newman ordered.

The sound of the engine was suddenly much louder as a vehicle approached rapidly across the marshes. Newman was about to urge them both down the far side of the bank away from the marshes when a blinding glare of light silhouetted the three figures perched on the dyke.

'Stay exactly where you are,' commanded a familiar voice. 'There is nowhere to run. I repeat, stay on the dyke . . .'

Newman threw up a hand to shield his eyes against the fierce glare. He shone his torch down on to the track below the dyke bordering the marshes. The vehicle was a buggy with enormous tyres – the only type of vehicle which could have crossed the treacherous ground.

'Turn off that damned light, Buchanan,' Newman shouted back. 'We've as much right out here as you have. You hear, Buchanan?'

'*Chief Inspector* Buchanan, if you please,' Warden shouted back from behind the vehicle's wheel.

'Don't be ridiculous, Warden,' Buchanan whispered.

It was the first time Newman had heard the stolid Warden give voice to speech. He turned to Paula and Rosewater, commenting at the top of his voice.

'Miracles happen. It can actually speak!'

'All right, that's enough, Newman,' Buchanan called out. 'I'm coming up there.'

'Then tell that driver to douse his bloody light.'

The searchlight, mounted on top of the buggy, went out. Buchanan climbed agilely up the bank, produced his own torch, shone it on the upturned craft.

'That could come under the offence of tampering with evidence,' he said mildly.

'Come off it,' Newman snapped. 'You've had the markers and tapes which undoubtedly cordoned it off removed. So anyone could have played about with that boat.'

'I still need to talk to all of you. Would you prefer the police station or the Brudenell where I'm staying?'

'You can't take us to the police station,' Newman continued, keeping up his aggressive attitude. 'And you know it. But yes to the Brudenell. Provided you give us a lift back in that buggy . . .'

Chapter Fourteen

'So,' Buchanan continued, addressing Rosewater, 'you came here to see where your wife was strangled?'

They were assembled in Buchanan's bedroom which over-looked the street, on the opposite side to Tweed's much more spacious room on the floor below. It was cramped with so many people – Newman, Paula, and Warden – in addition to the Chief Inspector and Rosewater. Newman had a grim look, disliking Buchanan's brutal approach.

'That's right,' Rosewater replied. 'A rather natural reaction, wouldn't you say?'

'And you're a captain in Military Intelligence?'

'With the BAOR – British Army of the Rhine.'

'You're on leave then? Compassionate?'

'No.' As tall as Buchanan, Rosewater stared straight back at his interrogator. 'I can go where I like, when I like.'

'Unusual for a British officer. What permits you such freedom of movement?'

'My job. I told you. Military Intelligence.'

'Care to enlighten me a little further?' Buchanan suggested.

'No. Security. You have no authority to ask such a question.'

Buchanan sighed. 'May I remind you, Captain Rosewater, this is a murder investigation I'm engaged on?'

'No reminder necessary,' Rosewater told him tersely. 'May I remind you it my wife who was murdered?'

'Did you find anything interesting when you were messing around with that boat?' Buchanan persisted.

'Not a thing,' Rosewater lied promptly.

'Haven't you pushed this interrogation far enough?' Newman interjected.

He was seated on the bed alongside Paula. Rosewater and Warden occupied the only chairs. Buchanan kept strolling round the room, jingling change in his pocket. He stopped in front of Paula, looked down at her.

'And why were you out on the marshes, Miss Grey?'

'To guide Captain Rosewater to where it happened.'

'Really?' In one word Buchanan expressed his scepticism. 'How did you happen to meet this officer stationed in Germany?'

'Purely by chance. I knew Karin. So once I met her husband while I was on holiday over there. In Germany, to be precise,' she added acidly.

'And Newman, you're here by chance?'

'No. On purpose. Occasionally I still interview prominent people. Just to keep my hand in.'

'Even though that book you wrote, *Kruger: The Computer That Failed*, became an international bestseller, made you financially independent for life?'

'Your memory is slipping. I just told you – to keep my hand in. I don't enjoy hanging about doing nothing all the time.'

'From my previous experience of you that's something you rarely do.'

'If you say so.'

Buchanan glanced at Rosewater, at Paula, at Newman, his expression cynical. He looked at his watch, put both hands back in his trouser pockets.

'You can all go now. And while I remember, thank you for your close co-operation . . .'

'Sarcastic bastard, that Buchanan!' Paula burst out to Newman as they walked along the corridor and down the staircase to the next floor.

'Oh, he's just doing his job,' Newman glanced back at the man behind them. 'And he's good at it. I must say you handled him well. Just answered his questions, adding nothing.'

Rosewater, following them down, smiled. 'It wasn't too difficult. I've been on the other end often enough – interrogating suspects. Care to join me in the bar. I think maybe I could do with that Scotch now. Freezing out on the marshes. I hope you didn't catch a chill, Paula.'

'No, I was well wrapped up.'

Paula paused as they reached the lower floor. 'Bob, I want to go and see someone. Why don't you and Victor have a chat on your own?'

'We'll do that. See you for dinner.'

'But we will miss your company,' Rosewater assured her.

Paula waited, fiddling with the folded coat she'd worn for the trek to the dyke. As Rosewater passed her he handed her something. When they were gone she opened her hand.

It was holding the ring Rosewater had dug out of the mud. She hurried to report to Tweed in his room.

Earlier, lieutenant André Berthier of Third Corps had waited patiently while Jean Burgoyne sat chatting with the attractive raven-haired girl. Two beauties – one brunette, one blonde. He wouldn't mind a more intimate acquaintance with either. Both would be even better. He dreamed a little to pass the time but never for a moment did his alertness desert him. Reminding himself of the role he was playing as an Englishman, he ordered another gin and tonic because it was such a British drink. Sipping it, his mind went back to the orders he'd been given in France . . .

Outside the car which de Forge had been travelling in – leaving the Villa Forban – the instructions had been explicit. Major Lamy was not noted for wasting words.

'You follow the Burgoyne woman wherever she goes. I want a detailed report on where she does go. Above all, who she meets. Names, addresses. Here is some money to finance the trip. She's flying back home to Britain. Take that motorcycle, drive like hell to GHQ, change into civilian clothes – your English ones. Be back at the Villa Forban in half an hour . . .'

Berthier had used the same forged passport and driving licence he'd used on previous trips to Britain. Following Burgoyne aboard her flight to Paris, then her flight to London Airport, he'd collected the Ford Sierra ordered by phone during his wait at Charles de Gaulle Airport for the London flight.

For some reason he couldn't fathom Burgoyne had driven in a car waiting for her straight to the Brudenell Hotel in Aldeburgh. He had registered in the name of James Sanders, wearing his tinted glasses and a trilby hat to conceal his fair hair. If anyone joshed him about wearing dark glasses in November he had his explanation ready.

'I've weak eyes. Strong light hurts them . . .'

Lamy had trained his protégé well. Immediately he'd arrived in his room Berthier had locked the door. Moving as swiftly as he could, he'd taken the bottle of hair colourant from his case, had gone into the bathroom and applied the liquid carefully. He used a drier attached to the wall, checked his appearance in the mirror, hurried downstairs.

His fear that Burgoyne would have gone mounted when he couldn't see her in the lounge. He strolled into the bar and she was standing at the counter, collecting glasses of champagne, taking them to the table where the attractive raven-haired girl sat. Berthier had ordered his first gin and tonic, sat at a corner table. The two women chatted a while like old friends.

Berthier was confident Burgoyne wouldn't recognize him. Despite the fact he had stood in her room at the Villa while he'd waited to escort de Forge to his car.

The colourant transformed his appearance. The tinted glasses completed the masquerade. Besides, Burgoyne had seen him in uniform before. Wearing civilian gear could make the same man unrecognizable. He had just finished his gin and tonic when Burgoyne put on her coat and walked out of the bar.

Berthier followed her as she left by the steps leading to the back entrance on to the street behind the hotel. Her car, a Jaguar, was parked further up the street. He ran to the Ford Sierra, slotted in next to the entrance. As she drove off Berthier was a discreet distance behind her.

No other traffic was about as she turned left in the cold night down a narrow side street, then right into the equally deserted High Street for a very short distance before turning left again and climbing a curving hill. Here it was all gloom and high walls and the odd glimpse of lights in a large house down a drive. The part of Aldeburgh where the well-off lived.

Berthier slowed, driving only with his sidelights on. The Jaguar abruptly swung left off the road, vanished. On this side of the road Berthier saw there was a wide grass verge with here and there occasional trees. He swung his Ford on to the verge, switched off his sidelights, the engine, got out of the car.

The bitter cold of the November night hit him. As he walked slowly to where the Jaguar had disappeared he turned up the collar of his English jacket, shoved his hands

143

inside his pockets. On either side of the gap she had driven through stood stone pillars, topped with lead decorations of old sailing ships. The imposing residence was called Admiralty House.

Berthier peered round a pillar up the gravel drive and saw a small Georgian mansion. The lights were on behind the uncurtained windows of a room to the right of the front door. Berthier saw an elderly man with wisps of white hair pouring something from a bottle, standing very erect. The Burgoyne woman appeared, closed the curtains. Just before she shut out the view Berthier saw the lights from a chandelier gleaming on her mane of blonde hair.

He went back to his car, treading on damp turf. Seated behind the wheel, he tried to puzzle it out. Lamy had obviously expected she would go to meet a lover. Berthier doubted whether the old boy fitted that category.

He sat clasping his strong hands, began squeezing the middle finger of his left hand, massaging the knuckle absent-mindedly. When, after half an hour, it seemed obvious she wasn't going anywhere else that night, he drove back to the Brudenell, descending from the highest point in Aldeburgh.

Paula described tersely the visit to the scene of the crime before producing the ring. Taking out a handkerchief, she unwrapped it carefully and presented the ring to Tweed.

They were alone in his bedroom. He had had coffee and sandwiches sent up and sipped from his cup as he held the ring in the palm of his hand. Putting the cup down, he slipped the signet ring on his middle finger. It slithered off.

'You see,' Paula repeated, 'it links up with what the

pathologist said. The strangler has large hands. That ring can only fit a man with large hands.'

'The Cross of Lorraine. Interesting,' Tweed commented, using a paper napkin to clean off more mud. 'It could be significant. On the other hand . . .'

'A link with France,' Paula insisted. 'So why do you sound sceptical? I've told you where it was found and how.'

'At this stage I'm keeping an open mind. We have a lot of data, quite a few pieces of the jigsaw, but some are still missing.'

'Well, what have we got so far?' Paula demanded.

'Briefly, Lasalle's belief that an insurrection is imminent in France. Organized by the infamous *Cercle Noir*, with the driving force possibly General de Forge. That theory may be backed up by Newman's riot experience in Bordeaux.'

'You sound very sceptical,' she repeated.

'Too early to interpret the data positively. I could be wrong. Then we have Kuhlmann warning us about the *Siegfried* underground movement in Germany. That *could* be linked with events in France. And don't forget the mysterious Kalmar, possibly the strangler of Karin and Francis Carey. I have the strongest feeling he is the key. Locate, identify Kalmar, and we'd know what was really going on.' He switched topics, his mind moving swiftly. 'I'll take this signet ring. You realize it must be handed over to Buchanan soon? We can't hide evidence in a murder case.'

'I could give it to Buchanan now . . .'

'No. I want the Engine Room at Park Crescent to make a perfect copy. Then it must be given to Buchanan. Does he know I'm here?'

'I'm sure he doesn't.'

'We'll keep it that way. I'll stay in my room tonight. Then leave early in the morning. I'll drive back to London in my own car. I must get back to Park Crescent. But first I'd better talk to Victor Rosewater, warn him that I'll be giving this ring to the CID. He'll have time to prepare his story.'

'I'd better go and fetch him now. Before he goes in to dinner with Bob.'

'I agree. In a minute.' Tweed studied the signet ring again. 'I have the oddest feeling I've seen this somewhere recently. No idea where. It may come back to me. And, Paula, exercise the greatest care when you interview Lord Dane Dawlish tomorrow.'

'Newman and Marler will be there, too – at the shoot.'

'You must still take great care,' he repeated. 'Monica has now completed her dossier on Dawlish.'

'Why?'

'Because he's armaments. Because he lives in the area where Karin was murdered. Probably he's nothing to do with what we're after. Just checking. One more thing I'd like you to do.' He gazed at the wall. 'And again proceed with caution.'

'Understood. What is it?'

'There's that Frenchman here – if Newman heard what he muttered under his breath when he stubbed his toe. So don't forget to meet him if you can. Find out what he is doing here. Now, wheel up Captain Victor Rosewater. Tell him I'm security chief with an insurance outfit.'

'So the best thing, I'm sure, is for me to tell Chief Inspector Buchanan I discovered the signet ring,' Rosewater said firmly.

He had just listened to Tweed's suggestion and reacted positively. Tweed studied Rosewater, remembering Paula had remarked he'd make excellent material as a new member of the SIS. Certainly he was very quick in grasping a situation, Tweed thought, as Rosewater continued.

'I'll tell him neither Paula nor Newman knew I'd found it. I shoved it straight into my pocket so I could study it later. After all, it was my wife who was murdered. I have an obvious interest in identifying the man who killed poor Karin.'

'Buchanan will give you hell,' Tweed warned. 'Suppressing evidence and all that.'

'I can handle him. Remember, I've had some experience at interrogation. You're giving me the ring now?'

'It's locked away in a safe place. And I think it would be better if we let a few days elapse before Buchanan confronts you. I may decide to be present myself.'

Rosewater settled himself more comfortably in his chair. He watched Tweed for a whole minute before he put the question.

'Paula said you were with an insurance outfit. Security doesn't seem to go with that, if you don't mind my saying so.'

'Not at all.' Tweed smiled cryptically. 'We specialize in insuring wealthy targets against kidnapping,' he lied easily. 'That's confidential. On occasions we have to negotiate with kidnappers who have snatched a client – a tricky operation.'

'So I can imagine.'

'Our territory is the whole of Western Europe. The active areas are France and Germany. So I travel a lot. Certain German industrialists are especially nervous about this mysterious *Siegfried* organization which has sprung up.'

'You mean they might try to get funds that way?'

'Exactly. Again, very confidential. Even more so as you travel a lot.'

'My job teaches me to keep my mouth shut. Going back

to that signet ring, will I get warning when the police are going to be informed?'

Tweed produced his calling card showing him as Chief Claims Investigator, General & Cumbria Assurance, with only the telephone number. Tweed watched him as he slid the card into a wallet.

'You'll be staying here for the next few days I assume?' Tweed enquired. 'So I know I can reach you?'

Rosewater grinned for the first time. 'I'll be available. I plan to mosey round this strange old town a bit. Now I'd better get downstairs for dinner with Bob Newman.'

When Paula left Tweed she paid a brief visit to her room to check on her appearance. Downstairs she found the youngish man with tinted glasses Newman had described in the bar. He occupied a corner table by himself, a glass in front of him. It was then Paula remembered he'd been sitting at the same table when she'd been talking to Jean Burgoyne.

She wandered in, looked round as though unsure where to perch, then chose an empty table near Tinted Glasses. Sitting down facing him, she crossed her shapely legs. Tinted Glasses noticed her immediately. He hardly hesitated. Getting up, he walked slowly across to her, the glass in his hand.

'Excuse me. If I'm intruding I'll go away at once. I am on my own and I wondered if we could chat. That is, unless you're expecting someone.'

She smiled. 'I'm expecting no one. And we are fellow guests. Do sit down.'

'After I've got you a drink.' He put his glass down. 'What do you fancy?'

'Would a glass of champers be in order? I prefer to stay with the same drink . . .'

She had listened carefully and caught no trace of accent. He brought the glass of champagne back, sat next to her, raised his own glass.

'Cheers! Here's to a memorable evening.'

'Cheers!' Paula responded. 'I'm afraid I don't have the whole evening though. I spent too much time talking to Jean Burgoyne a little while ago. In this bar.'

'Really? Who is Jean Burgoyne?'

'She's a well-known society girl. Gets her picture in the top magazines a lot. And sometimes in the gossip columns in the newspapers. She's just returned from France. Do you know France at all?'

'Excuse me. My manners must be slipping. I'm James Sanders . . .'

'Paula Grey. You don't know France, then?'

Berthier adjusted his glasses, pushed them up the bridge of his strong aquiline nose. He turned to face her. It bothered her that she couldn't see his eyes clearly.

'As a matter of fact, I've just returned from Paris . . .' Always stick as close to the truth as you can, Lamy had trained him. 'A waste of time,' he went on. 'Business at this time of the year is dead.'

'What business is that? I'm sorry, that was rather personal.'

'Selling marine equipment. Wholesale and retail to private buyers. Boaty people. Which is why I'm here. Loads of boaty types in Aldeburgh.'

She nodded. Was he piling on the English colloquialisms a little too heavily? She couldn't be sure.

'Isn't business pretty dead here. At this time of year?'

He swallowed half his drink. 'I hope to make contacts for

the spring. My business is seasonal. Out of season you can often meet a lot of chaps who'll be interested when winter is just a bad memory.' He still faced her, the tinted lenses like soulless eyes.

'*Vous en voulez un autre?*' Paula asked suddenly.

She spoke very rapidly the way a Frenchwoman would, enquiring whether he'd like another drink. He moved, as though about to get up, then shifted his position, settling himself more comfortably. For a second she could have sworn his face froze.

'I'm sorry,' she went on, 'I assumed you'd speak French. Seeing as you have to do business in France.'

He grinned, waving his strong hands. 'I know I should but I don't. Usual British attitude – damned foreigners are expected to speak English. As a matter of fact, they do – the few people I deal with in Paris. And mostly I'm showing them marine spare parts in a catalogue. So it's easy. What did you say, actually?'

'I asked if you'd like another drink.'

'I'm the host,' he replied. 'How about another glass of champers?'

'I've had enough. But I was suggesting I bought you one this time.'

'I think I've had enough too.' He adjusted his glasses again. 'You're sure you can't join me for dinner?'

'I'd love to. But I've already arranged to have dinner with two friends.' She looked at her watch. 'And if you don't mind, Mr Sanders . . .'

'James . . .'

'If you don't mind I'm expected in the dining room. It's been nice talking to you. Good luck with making useful contacts.'

She stood up and he stood with her, pulling his chair out of the way. He cleared his throat as though unsure whether to say more. Then he came out with the invitation she was expecting.

'Maybe tomorrow I could take you out for a drive round the countryside? We should be able to find somewhere up-market for lunch.'

She smiled. 'That's nice of you. But tomorrow's out of the question. I have an appointment. Maybe some other day. If we're still both here . . .'

He was walking back towards the bar counter when she left. A couple were walking out of the elevator and she dived inside, pressed the button for the first floor. Tapping on Tweed's door in a certain way, she waited until the door was opened.

Tweed was dabbing his mouth with a napkin and he had a visitor. Marler, immaculately clad in a sports jacket and well-pressed slacks, wearing hand-made shoes which gleamed like glass, gave her a mock salute.

'I suspect the clever lady has been busy,' he drawled as Tweed re-locked the door.

'Another helping of sandwiches?' Paula asked, eyeing the plate on the table alongside a pot of coffee.

'You know I'm always hungry when I've reached the stage of deploying forces.' Tweed sat down at the table. 'I've just been giving Marler some very special instructions.' He indicated sheets of papers with names scrawled, some listed in groups encircled with loops. Dotted lines joined certain groups together. Tweed looked at Paula.

'Any luck with Newman's pseudo-Englishman? If he is.'

'Name, James Sanders. So he said,' She wrinkled her brows. 'The devil of it is I can't be sure. He almost talks like a foreigner with an excellent command of English, but peppers his conversation with colloquialisms in a way I'm not certain a genuine Englishman would. I threw a question at him in French – would he like another drink? He seemed to start getting out of his chair, but the movement was so slight again I couldn't swear he was French. Verdict? Not proven. Now I must get down to join Bob and Rosewater for dinner, leaving you two to plot.'

'Tomorrow...' Tweed's expression was grave. 'Be extremely cautious at Grenville Grange. I have a sixth sense there could be danger inside that place.'

Chapter Fifteen

A Gothic horror.

Paula had stopped her car – borrowed from Nield – in front of the closed wrought-iron gates which guarded Grenville Grange. At the end of a long curving drive she saw the grotesque mansion. Victorian architecture at its most hideous: a grey, three-storey pile with a projecting wing at either end; small turrets foresting from the roof; huge gargoyles silhouetted against the clear wintry sky.

She had driven out of Aldeburgh, turning left, speeding along the A1094 past the golf course on her right. The rolling green had been covered with heavy frost the colour of *crème de menthe*. Turning left near Snape, she had driven on past the famous Maltings, turning left once more along a narrow country road to Iken. Frequently she checked the road map open on the seat beside her. One more left turn and she was out in the wilds with a view down to a wide loop of the river Alde which looked like a sheet of blue ice. Now this . . .

She pressed her horn several times, a large figure dressed like a countryman appeared, holding a savage-looking wolfhound on a leash which leapt towards her, snarling. Welcome to Grenville Grange.

'What do you want?' the big man asked. 'Private property.'

'Pretty obvious,' Paula called back. 'Paula Grey. I have an appointment with Lord Dane Dawlish. At noon.'

'Show some identification.'

'Come out and damn well look for yourself,' she shouted back. 'And keep that silly pup away from me. Or, alternatively, call up his Lordship and tell him you have stopped me driving in . . .'

Glaring, the guard unlocked the gates, opened one, shortened the leash, walked towards her. Paula noticed all his clothes looked brand new. Not what she would have expected from a guard.

She showed him the press card, one of several cards produced for her in the Engine Room basement at Park Crescent. She hung on to a corner while he examined it.

'You'd better drive in,' he said grudgingly.

'So you did know I was coming?'

She smiled at his flushed face as he went back, pushed open the other gate, then jumped back as she rammed her foot down, scattering gravel over the wolfhound as she raced up to the house. A wide semicircle gave plenty of parking space below a wide balustraded terrace with steps leading to the entrance.

She switched off the engine and immediately heard the *cr-a-a-ck* of shotguns firing. The shoot was in progress somewhere behind the looming pile. She noted Newman's Mercedes 280E was parked at the edge of two rows of cars. About twenty vehicles with a number of BMWs, a Ferrari and a Lamborghini. Dawlish liked money at his shooting parties. She checked the time. 11.50 a.m. Ten minutes early. She liked to throw strangers she was visiting off balance. Sometimes you found out something they wished to conceal.

Locking the car, she avoided the steps up to the entrance, wandered round the left-hand side of the mansion. At the rear a vast lawn bordered on two sides by walls of firs ran down to a large landing-stage projecting into the Alde.

She counted about thirty guns, men of different ages, all

smartly – even foppishly – dressed. It was still barely above freezing point and she wore a knee-length suede coat and a silk scarf. The shooters were ignoring the black pottery shards raining down on the lawn as the shotgun-wielding men spaced round the edge of the lawn took it in turn with their twelve-bores. She saw Marler take aim as five more targets flew above the lawn. He missed three out of the five and in a brief silence she heard his drawling voice.

'Can't hit the damned things . . .'

Like hell, you can't, she thought. If you wanted to you'd shoot the lot out of the sky.

She looked up as she heard a chopper flying low. Skimming the treetops, it hovered, then flew on over the roof of the mansion out of sight. Paula, thinking for a moment it might be a Coastguard machine, tried to catch its identification markings. As far as she could see, it didn't have any. Staring straight up the side of the house, she saw a satyrlike gargoyle leering down at her.

'Chap up there on the roof seems quite keen on you,' an upper-crust voice suggested.

She swung round and a young chinless wonder was eyeing her with open interest. He had his shotgun perched over his shoulder at an affected angle.

'You must be one of his Lordship's harem of fillies,' he continued. 'He's over there . . .' He jerked his head. 'Waiting for you, I'm sure – all eager beaver and able.'

Paula stared straight back. 'I've got another suggestion,' she said coldly. 'Why don't you drop dead?'

'Be like that.'

The young fop strolled off and Paula looked in the direction he'd indicated. Newman was talking to a heavily built man of medium height clad in riding gear. Dawlish was listening with a grim look and suddenly there was a hush among the crowd spread round the lawn, sensing that something dramatic was happening. Marler stood behind Newman, lighting a king-size cigarette. Paula heard the exchange clearly.

'What was that question you asked?' Dawlish rumbled.

'I hear you have an armaments factory not far from here. I gather that's one of your main sources of income. The end of the Cold War will have to make you find customers for weapons elsewhere. Or maybe you're glad we just may have peace on earth – even if it eliminates profits from wars?'

'You were invited here as a guest at my shooting party,' Dawlish rasped, one hand tucked in the pocket of his jodhpurs. 'Now you're trying to get an interview out of me, Newman. For *Der Spiegel*, you said . . .'

'Don't you want publicity for some reason?' Newman went on amiably. 'As one of the leading industrialists in the Western world? They say you can sell guns to peoples and places no one else can. You must have contacts at the very top . . .'

'The exit is that way,' Dawlish broke in, jerked a thumb towards the car park. 'If you're not off the property in two minutes I can have you escorted.'

'Save your manpower,' Newman suggested jocularly. 'Your hired thugs probably have other dirty work to do . . .'

'Thugs?'

Dawlish took one pace closer to Newman. He looked choleric. High blood pressure? Paula wondered.

'Your so called gamekeepers and beaters,' Newman continued, 'in their fancy new gear. Dressed up to look like countrymen. Professional security guards would be my guess. Kicked out of respectable security firms?'

'*Two minutes* . . .'

Dawlish turned away, looked round, beckoned to a heav-ily-built man with dark hair, who came running. Paula realized Dawlish didn't miss much: he was heading straight for her as the other man joined him. She caught the first part of Dawlish's instructions.

'Radio the chopper. Tell them to follow Newman. He has an old blue Merc. Big job. If necessary, they teach him a lesson. I've been warned about Newman . . .'

He lowered his voice and even though they were coming closer to her she couldn't catch the rest of what Dawlish said. She saw Newman hand his gun to a guard, Marler hand his weapon to the same man and the two of them wandered towards the car park without a glance in her direction. She was worried: on her way to Grenville Grange she'd seen no sign of Butler and Nield, recalling that Tweed had told them to act as protectors. Then it struck her that wherever Butler and Nield were waiting she'd never have seen them: they were professionals.

'Get on with it now, Brand. They're leaving . . .'

She heard Dawlish's last order to the heavy-set man who hurried away as the owner of Grenville Grange approached her with a broad grin. He whipped off his hard hat.

'Paula Grey? You're early . . .'

'I like to be prompt.'

Brown eyes like bullets swept over her. A strong hand gripped her right arm as he guided her up steps, across the rear steps, opened a French window, ushered her inside, locked the door, adjusted the heavy net curtains.

'Let me take your coat, my dear . . .'

As he helped her off with the coat his fingers lingered a few seconds too long on her well-shaped shoulders. He gestured towards a large deep couch with cushions as he took her coat, opened a cupboard, slipped it on a hanger and left it on a hook.

Paula looked round for a single armchair but Dawlish had organized the room well for her reception. Each armchair was occupied with a pile of leather-bound tomes. Which left no alternative but to set herself on the couch at one end. Dawlish offered her Scotch or wine but she chose coffee. He pressed a button in the wall. A manservant clad in black opened a door in the rear of the large room.

'Coffee for my guest, Walters. A large Scotch for me. And next time knock before you come in. Get on with it . . .'

Which seemed to be his favourite phrase Paula thought as she glanced round the room while extracting her note-book from her shoulder bag. Except for the windows over-looking the lawn, the other three walls were oak-panelled from floor to ceiling with bookcases inset at intervals. In the wall facing her a log fire crackled inside a deep-arched alcove. The atmosphere was overpoweringly warm as Dawlish stripped off his riding boots, dumped them in the hearth, slipped his large feet into a pair of handmade brogues.

'Mind if I strip off my jacket?'

He was doing so while his eyes roamed over her coatless figure. He sat on the couch close to her, laid a hand on the right knee of her crossed legs, squeezed it.

'Where do we start?' he asked with a broad smile.

Dawlish emanated an aura of great physical energy and, despite his bulk, his movements were swift. Like sitting next to a sexual powerhouse, Paula thought before she replied.

'We start by your removing your hand off my person.'

'But such an alluring person . . .'

The nails of her right hand hovered over the hand. She had very tough nails. They dug gently into the back of his hairy hand when he didn't move.

'I'm quite capable of drawing blood, scratching so you will be scarred for weeks. Then I'll leave at once – in other words, go to hell.'

'Spirited. I like that.'

But he took his hand away from her knee. Leaning back against the cushions, he fingered the sideburn closest to her, studying her as though seeing her for the first time.

'I'm at your service,' he said eventually.

'I understand you're interested in conservation. Also underwater exploration. I hear you're financing the new expedition to explore the sunken village of Dunwich.'

'The Cat is a dream for that job.'

'The cat?'

Paula, puzzled, stared at Dawlish as there was a knock on the door. Dawlish, looking pleased with the effect he'd created, bawled out, 'Come on in . . .' They waited while Walters put down a silver tray, poured coffee for Paula, handed Dawlish a cut-glass tumbler of neat Scotch and left the room.

'Down the hatch!' Dawlish said, swallowed half the drink.

'I'm all at sea,' Paula commented after sipping coffee.

'*All at sea!*'

Dawlish repeated her words, roared a deep belly laugh. Before she knew what was happening he looped an arm round her slim waist, hoisted her to her feet, led her across the room to a section of wall to the right of the huge fireplace. He pressed another button.

There was a whirring sound of unseen machinery operating. A large section of panelling slid upwards, revealed what looked to Paula like one of the dioramas she'd seen in military museums. She was gazing at a huge sheet of plateglass shaped like a porthole. Beyond, a strange model of a vessel perched on a stretch of blue sea. Dawlish pressed the button again. The weird vessel sailed through waves which suddenly rose up ahead of its prow.

Paula was still carrying her notebook and pen. For a

moment her expression froze. Dawlish watched her with amusement, mistaking her fear for astonishment. Paula was gazing at a model replica of the weird vessel which she'd seen with Karin when they'd surfaced off Dunwich, clambered aboard their dinghy, had fled for their lives from the scuba divers with knives between their teeth. To cover her reaction she scribbled indecipherable shorthand in her book.

'The Cat,' Dawlish said with an expression of overweening pride. 'Short for a great marine technological advance. The twin-hulled catamaran. Instead of bouncing over waves – like previous vessels – it *pierces* waves, cuts through them. Top speed forty-two knots. I call mine *Steel Vulture*. The for'ard view – aft or port – seen from another vessel, looks like a vulture slicing the waves.'

Paula watched, trembling inside, as Dawlish pressed a different button. The model reversed back to its previous position on the left. Dawlish set it moving again. More waves heaved on the 'sea'. The *Steel Vulture* sailed across to the right.

'Its beam is very wide,' she remarked quietly.

'It can carry over one hundred people,' Dawlish rambled on proudly. 'Plus a number of heavy vehicles. It's like a car ferry. They have a bigger one in operation on the ferry run from Portsmouth to Cherbourg. But the *Vulture*, built in Norway, has more advanced refinements.'

Almost hypnotized, Paula watched the twin wakes slushing from the stern. She forced herself to go on talking.

'Where do you berth such a vessel?'

'Down at Harwich when she's not at sea.'

'And you said you use it for the Dunwich exploration?'

'Frequently. She's the mother ship for the divers who go down to map the town beneath the sea. Maybe you'd like a trip aboard my latest toy?'

'Yes, I think I could use that in my article,' Paula agreed

automatically. 'You could get me by calling the editor of *Women's Eye*. I rove around a lot.'

'So you'll make my underwater exploration the theme of your piece? The last time Dunwich was investigated under the sea was by some aqua clubs in 1979. I'm doing the job on a much larger scale. I can afford the equipment . . .'

As he rattled on enthusiastically Dawlish pressed the buttons, returned the model to its original start point, closed down the sliding panelling which concealed the mobile diorama. Paula walked back to the couch, sat down, said something which transformed the previous friendly atmosphere.

'Apart from the underwater thing, which *costs* you a lot of money, I'm sure, I gather you *make* a fortune out of your armaments factories. Does that ever bother you? Being a merchant of death?'

He strode across the room, dropped his weight next to her, grasped her wrist with one hand in a grip which felt like a steel handcuff. His expression was ugly.

'What the hell made you ask that question?'

Paula wondered where Newman and Marler were, wished to God they hadn't left so early.

Chapter Sixteen

Newman had driven away from the Iken peninsula at speed. Beside him sat Marler as they drove along a hedge-lined road with fields beyond still crusted with a white coating of frost. The sun was a blurred disc and white mist like a slow-moving curtain drifted among the trees.

'Care to take a shufti at Dawlish's armaments set-up in the forest on the way to Orford?' Marler drawled.

'How do you know it is armaments?'

'What would be your guess? Out in the wilds. Closed off with a high wire fence – electrified. Guards with dogs patrolling behind the wire. Think he's running a marshmallow factory, chum?'

'If you're that keen, why not?' Newman agreed. Guide me.'

'Left at the top here, then later left again when you hit the main road to Snape Maltings. Then a country road to Orford.'

'We're being followed.'

'I know. Saw it in the wing mirror. Ford Sierra – I didn't even see where Butler and Nield sneaked out after us.'

'So they're pros. How do you think the party went – and you're one lousy shot when you want to be.'

'I wanted to be,' Marler commented. 'And you lit some fuse under Dawlish. Did you have to stir him up quite so much?'

'That was the general idea. When a man gets uptight he sometimes gives away more than he intends.'

'Far as I could see, the only thing he gave away was us. Push off or be escorted.'

'I achieved my objective. I rattled him. To prepare the way for Paula. You saw her arrive, of course. And after Dawlish told us to get to hell out of it he eager-beavered his way towards her. He'll run into a wildcat if he tries pawing her.'

'But you could have queered her pitch,' Marler protested. 'He'd be in a bad mood.'

'Which she'll spot and play on skilfully. Bet she gets back with some intriguing data.'

'Just so long as she does get back . . .'

Five minutes later Newman had negotiated an awkward turn left and they were driving through even lonelier country towards distant Orford. It was incredibly silent and still when Newman paused, parked for a minute, switching off his engine. On both sides forests of evergreens – firs and pines – spread away across rolling heathland. They had already passed one sandy track leading off the road into the wilderness, the track vanished round a curve. Marler lit a cigarette.

'The entrance to skull-and-crossbones is just beyond two more bends,' he remarked.

'And how do you know this place is anything to do with Dawlish?'

'Because I'd make a good detective.' Marler smiled cynically. 'At the bottom of one of the warning plates attached to the fence there's printing in small letters. *Dawlish Conservation Ltd.* Some kind of conservation project with all the defences I've told you about.'

'I heard the sound of an engine in the sky just now.'

'Sounded like a chopper floating around. Unlikely to be Traffic Patrol out here. Could be a Coastguard machine.'

'Could be something else.' Newman started up his engine. 'Let's get moving and see what happens.'

'Out here? I'd say nothing ever happens out here in broad daylight.'

Newman was suddenly very conscious of the fact that they carried no weapons to defend themselves. Was it the atmosphere of brooding menace which seemed to hang over the wilderness? The utter solitude of this part of the world? They hadn't seen a vehicle since leaving Iken.

He found himself crawling along the winding road, glancing at the undergrowth bordering the road on both sides. Newman had a hemmed-in feeling. They rounded the first bend and another stretch of deserted road opened up, disappearing round another bend a hundred yards away.

'Might as well get out and walk,' commented Marler who seemed oblivious to any danger.

'Who is behind the wheel?' Newman snapped. 'And we're pretty close now, aren't we?'

'One more bend and Dawlish's private little world is on our left . . .'

Newman continued to let the Merc crawl. He frowned, pressed the switch which slid back the roof above their heads. Marler tapped ash from his cigarette into the ash tray.

'Want us to freeze? It's damn cold in these woods . . .'

'Shut up! Listen!'

Newman could hear the sound distinctly now. The chug-chug of the helicopter coming back from a different direction. They drove round the second bend. The road now stretched straight as a ruler for some distance and the forest had retreated on either side with a band of open heath beyond the low hedges. To their left a high wire fence appeared with metal plates attached to it at shoulder height.

The fence was about two hundred yards long and in the

middle was a double gate, also constructed of wire. Beyond the gate a wide gravel track ran away towards copses of trees. Just visible were single-storey buildings constructed of concrete and without windows. Newman found it sinister that there was no sign of the guards, the dogs, Marler had described earlier when he had driven past this outlandish place.

He parked opposite the closed gates, leaving his engine running. Marler jumped out, walked up to the gate, then paced methodically back the way they had come until he'd reached a concrete post. He strolled back to the car. Above the open roof Newman could hear the chopper much closer. It sounded to be circling the area out of view.

'What the devil were you playing at?' he asked as Marler sank back into his seat.

'Checking the place to fuse the electrified fence with a wooden-handled screwdriver in the dark.'

'Why, if I may ask?'

'You just did, old boy. Answer, in case I decide to come back and take a closer look at that establishment by night.'

'I wouldn't advise it. Not on your own . . .'

Newman was staring up the track. Its surface was rutted where heavy vehicles with wide tyres had driven over it. He still didn't like the lack of any sign of human life. It was as though someone had sent an order for all the guards to withdraw out of sight. And he couldn't rid himself of the feeling that unseen eyes were observing them.

'Finding it all a bit creepy?' Marler enquired.

'Well, it's not the place I'd choose for a picnic.'

'Ever thought Dawlish could have taken away the guards to reinforce Grenville Grange? There was quite a pack of visitors there this morning.'

'I don't think that's the explanation,' Newman said

slowly, looking everywhere. 'Dawlish is a millionaire. He has the funds to employ as many security men as he wishes . . .'

He broke off as the silence was murdered by the onset of a deafening roar. For a minute or so the chug-chug of the helicopter had faded. Now it sounded to be on top of them. Newman pressed the switch which closed the roof, released the brake, sped forward. At that moment men with shotguns rose out of the gullies which had concealed them behind the wire. A hail of buckshot peppered the road in front of, behind, the Mercedes. Newman noticed nothing hit the car. They were being encouraged to move forward along the straight stretch of road.

'Ahead of us . . .' Marler warned.

Something darted across the road twenty yards in front of the car. A fox, startled by the roar, was taking cover. Beyond it the grey chopper suddenly appeared, skimming the treetops. The pilot changed course, flew towards them, immediately above the road. As it hurtled forward something dropped from the machine, landed on the road. There was a brilliant burst of blinding light. Newman screwed up his eyes, swung the wheel, just avoided the blaze. The machine swept over them.

'Magnesium flare,' Newman said tersely. 'One of those hits us, or I drive over it, and the petrol tank goes up.'

'He'll be back,' Marler replied, twisting round in his seat. 'And next time could be bull's-eye . . .'

Newman pressed his foot down further, wishing to heaven now that the road was winding. The endless straight stretch made them a perfect target, the pilot able to calculate their likely position in advance.

'It's gone,' Marler reported.

'Ready for another run,' Newman foresaw.

He had hardly finished speaking when they saw the chopper appear again well ahead of them, flying along the avenue of death towards the Mercedes. That was when Newman saw in his rear-view mirror the Ford Sierra racing up behind them full tilt.

Nield was behind the wheel in the Ford. Beside him Butler had wound down his window, unfastened his seat belt. Now he was leaning out of the window, back pressed against his seat, both hands gripping his Walther. The road surface was good which helped him hold the gun steady.

The chopper was approaching Newman's vehicle ahead of the Ford. This time there was no magnesium flare. Instead smoke, turgid black smoke, began to streak from the rear of the machine. The smoke drifted down swiftly, heavily. The helicopter was still about three hundred yards away from Newman's Merc. Like a crop sprayer, it jetted the smoke along the road surface. Newman's mouth tightened. He slowed down, reduced speed more and more.

'What the hell are you playing at?' Marler demanded.

In the Ford Butler aimed his Walther for the pilot's cabin. It would be a chance in a million if he scored a direct hit but it was the only chance he had. Pressing the trigger, he emptied the magazine, his knuckles white with the strain of holding the weapon on target.

A different kind of smoke began to drift out of the helicopter. Whereas previously it had held an arrowlike course the machine began to quiver, wobbling. Suddenly it veered away from the road, flame flared, it vanished over the treetops. The shockwave of a distant *boom*! shuddered both cars. A column of oily smoke climbed above the forest, then there was silence as Newman stopped his car short of the eddying smoke. Behind him Nield slowed, stopped close to the Mercedes. Another fox darted out, started to run through the fringe of the smoke. Abruptly it stopped running, reared up almost vertically, flopped on to the road and lay still.

'And that,' said Newman, 'was why I slowed . . .'

He got out of his car, followed by Marler and Butler, who had reloaded. Newman approached the animal slowly, waited for the smoke to dissipate. Only then did he go close to the animal. The fox sprawled on its side, its long brush tail flat and still as the body. Its eyes were starting out of its head, its jaws wide open. Newman touched it with his foot. It was like touching a rock: the corpse was stiff, unyielding.

'I want to take this back in the boot for expert examination.'

'What on earth for?' Marler enquired.

'Because that was no ordinary smoke that chopper sprayed – tried to spray us with. It contained some element which, as you see, was lethal . . .'

He went back to his car, explained briefly to Butler, and took a roll of hessian cloth from the boot. Then he put on a pair of old sheepskin gloves. They walked back to where the dead fox lay.

Butler, who was wearing gloves, helped him to place the fox on the cloth they had spread across the road, to roll up the corpse and carry it back to the car. When it was safely stacked in the boot Newman stripped off his gloves, tossed them on top of the bundle.

'I'd advise you to do the same,' he told Butler.

He shut the boot when both pairs of gloves had been dropped inside. Then he clapped a hand briefly on Butler's shoulder.

'Thanks for saving us, Harry. We'd be like that fox now but for you.'

'Part of the job,' Butler replied typically. 'Where to now?'

'Back to the Brudenell. Tweed left early this morning so

we'll probably settle our bills, get back to London.' He looked at Marler who was standing close by. 'Well, it worked.'

'What did?'

'My stirring up Lord Dane Dawlish. That chopper attack was a blunder, a major giveaway. Tweed will be interested.'

Chapter Seventeen

During his morning drive back to Park Crescent in the Ford Escort Tweed was worried. Too many people were descending on Lord Dawlish for his shooting party. And besides Newman and Marler, Paula had chosen the same morning for her interview with the millionaire.

His anxiety grew as he drove into London. By the time he parked close to his HQ he'd decided what to do. Hurrying up the stairs to his office, he opened the door and spoke to Monica before even taking off his coat.

'Urgent.' He checked his watch. 12.30 p.m. And Paula's appointment had been for noon. 'Very urgent. Look up the number of Lord Dane Dawlish at Grenville Grange near Aldeburgh. Write it down and give it to me quickly.'

He opened a file after taking off his coat and sitting behind his desk. He hardly saw the papers he was looking at. Monica was having trouble obtaining the unlisted number. After speaking to the operator she broke the connection, called a friend of Tweed's in Special Branch.

A few minutes later she slammed the phone down, scribbled on a sheet of paper, tore it off the notepad, and took it to Tweed.

'Sorry it took so long . . .'

'I've got it. That's the main thing. I'll dial the number myself. I may have to crash through a screen of underlings . . .'

*

Paula had shown cool outrage when Dawlish grabbed her by the wrist.

'If you don't let go of me I'll walk out on you now. And you won't like the article. Headline? *Lord Dawlish Manhandles Women.* Won't do your image a power of good, I'd have thought.'

Dawlish released his grip. Still red-faced he repeated his question more quietly.

'Who the hell put you up to asking that question about armaments? Someone else threw me the same sidewinder not ten minutes ago.'

'I'm not someone else. For your information I happen to operate independently. And it was rather an obvious subject to bring up – you do control armament factories. I do my homework before I interview anyone. Or would you prefer to dodge the issue?'

'No issue to dodge, as you put it. I also control whole chains of supermarket stores in North America. Which is my main source of income.' He leaned towards her. 'I feed people. Armaments is a sideline. I suppose, like all reporters you're looking for a sensational angle,' he sneered.

'A balanced report is what I aim at. You have a really wide spread of activities. That's the way the article will read. Supermarkets, financing underwater exploration of a sunken village. I think I'll concentrate on the latter. It's unusual.'

'Do I have your word on that?' Dawlish barked.

'Look, are you deaf? I've already told you once what I'm going to do.'

'I like a girl with guts.' Dawlish became amiable. 'I spend half my time pushing thickheads into carrying out my instructions correctly. Only way I've got where I have. You're very intelligent. Shouldn't have lost my temper. There was an incident outside just before I met you. My apologies.' He grinned. 'Why not join me in a glass of wine to show no hard feelings? Then later I can show you round the house. Some interesting pictures upstairs.'

Upstairs? Bedrooms. Here we go again, Paula thought as she shook her head. 'If you don't mind I'll stay with coffee.'

'Coffee can be served upstairs,' Dawlish persisted. 'I have a Rubens up there. That would be something for your article.'

'Don't like Rubens.'

'What were your sources for discovering one of my minor activities is armaments?' Dawlish suddenly shot at her.

Paula paused. She sensed the situation could turn ugly. Dawlish was not a man accustomed to being turned down by females. His attitude and expression had become aggressive. The phone rang. Dawlish pursed his thick lips with annoyance, picked up the instrument off a table.

'What the devil is it? Who did you say was calling? I see. Hell, you'd better put him on.'

'Dawlish here . . .'

'Chief Inspector Buchanan speaking,' a voice interrupted him. 'I know you have a Paula Grey visiting you,' Tweed continued. 'I want her to drive back at once to the Brudenell Hotel for questioning. When I say at once I mean now.'

'It's not convenient just at this moment . . .'

'Make it convenient, I'm investigating a murder case – that takes priority over everyone's convenience. Put her on the line, Dawlish. *Now!*'

Dawlish looked grim. He put his hand over the mouthpiece. He decided to try once more to delay his guest's departure.

'She could leave within about an hour . . .'

'And I could send a patrol car over there to fetch her. I'm beginning to wonder about your reluctance to co-operate,' Tweed continued.

'Just a moment.'

Dawlish shoved the phone at Paula. His tone was brittle. He raised his voice so it would carry along the line.

'Chief Inspector Plod insists on speaking to you. He'll give you his own message.'

'Miss Grey?' Tweed went on speaking quickly. 'This is Chief Inspector Buchanan. Would you kindly drive back to the Brudenell Hotel immediately. I have further information I need from you . . .' Tweed dropped to a whisper, using his normal voice. 'Get out of there at once. I don't like the sound of Dawlish's mood.'

Paula managed to keep her expression blank.. Earlier it had sounded exactly like Buchanan.

'Very well, Chief Inspector. I can't imagine how I can help, but as you insist I'm leaving now. I should be with you inside half an hour. Goodbye.'

Handing back the receiver, she put her notebook and pen inside her shoulder bag. Standing up, she walked swiftly to the cupboard, slipped on her coat before Dawlish could reach her, turned round.

'I'm sure I have enough for my *Woman's Eye* piece. I would like to thank you for your courtesy in agreeing to see me.'

Dawlish shoved a hand into the pocket of his jodhpurs. He looked grim and highly unsatisfied. He stood like a wooden statue as he asked the question.

'What was all that about? Are you in trouble?'

'I discovered the body of a girl who was strangled on the marshes near Aldeburgh not so long ago.'

'I read about it. Karin . . .' He snapped the thick fingers of his other hand. 'Somebody-or-Other.'

'Rosewater.' She watched his eyes, which were like bullets again. 'She was German with an English husband. No one can work out why she was murdered.'

'Some psychopath probably. You'd better go and meet Mr Flatfoot. I just wonder how he knew you were here.'

'He knows I'm staying at the Brudenell. He only had to make enquiries – I asked some of the staff how to get to Grenville Grange.' Paula lied easily.

'Don't forget my invitation to join me for a trip aboard the Cat,' Dawlish reminded her as he escorted her to the spacious entrance hall and the front door. 'Here is my card with my ex-directory number. Don't print that, for God's sake.'

'I promise,' Paula said, taking the gold-edged embossed card.

'Just call me when you're available,' Dawlish urged her affably, one hand on her arm. 'I'll give you several dates.'

Paula turned her head suddenly as he opened one of the double doors. Leading into the hall was a single door to her right and it had been open about a foot. In the gap she caught a glimpse of a man watching her and then it closed.

'Drive carefully,' Dawlish advised jovially as she left, running down the terrace steps and across to her car.

She sank into the seat behind the wheel, sighing with relief. Dawlish had an overwhelming personality and she'd exhausted herself fighting him off. She switched on the ignition and spoke to herself as she drove down the gravel drive towards the gates which were opening automatically.

'Thank God for Tweed . . .'

Inside Grenville Grange Dawlish walked to the door in the right-hand wall, opened it and glared at the man waiting inside.

'I just hope to hell she didn't see you, idiot. Now follow me and report, Lieutenant Berthier.'

*

At Park Crescent Monica gazed in astonishment at Tweed. He had just completed his call to Grenville Grange.

'In all the years I've known you,' Monica began, 'I'd no idea you were such a good mimic. You really sounded just like Chief Inspector Buchanan.'

'Oh, I have hidden talents.' Tweed smiled wrily and polished his glasses on his handkerchief. 'Now, we must move fast. Get me René Lasalle . . .'

'I'm on scrambler, René,' Tweed warned when the call came through.

'So am I. The situation here is grim . . .'

'I'm working on it,' Tweed assured him. 'So is most of my team. Round the clock. I need certain items urgently . . .'

'Which are?'

'When Paula and I met you in Paris you showed us some photos from a certain gentleman's dossier. Can you send me quickly copies of photos of the following – Josette. You know who I mean?'

'Yes. Who else?'

'Major Lamy, de Forge, and Jean Burgoyne.'

'I'll make copies from the negatives myself, send them to you by personal courier. Code-name Versailles. I will also send you one of someone else. A Lieutenant André Berthier. On Lamy's staff. Could be a key liaison officer – and something else. That's it?'

'For the moment. Keep in touch . . .'

'Who is Josette?' Monica enquired.

'General de Forge's wife. When Newman goes back into France he'll need to be able to identify the main players.'

'Won't that be dangerous – after what happened when he was there recently?'

'Very dangerous, but knowing Bob he'll insist on going back. He was worried about that girl, Isabelle, who is hiding away in Arcachon. And something else intriguing cropped up in my conversation with Lasalle . . .'

He repeated Lasalle's comment about Lieutenant Berthier, telling her a photograph was on the way.

'That was a cryptic remark,' Monica commented. 'What do you think he meant?'

'No idea,' Tweed said quickly, too quickly. 'Talking about Newman going back to France reminds me.' Unlocking a drawer, he took out the photograph of Sergeant Rey handed to him by Lasalle in Paris. 'Come and look at this specimen.'

'Don't like the look of him one little bit,' Monica decided after studying the photograph.

'Sergeant Rey. I think his rank is deceptive, maybe a cover. He's de Forge's expert on boobytraps. Have the Engine Room make six copies. Newman must have one – and I may send him back-up when the time comes. Anyone who goes near Third Corps – or Bordeaux, for that matter – needs a copy of that reptile.'

'I'll get it done now . . .'

'No. First, get me Chief Inspector Kuhlmann on the line. Let's hope he's at his Wiesbaden HQ.'

'You really are moving,' Monica remarked as she went back to her desk and began dialling the number from memory.

'I don't think we have much time left . . .'

'Kuhlmann here,' a familiar growly voice introduced himself on the phone. 'On scrambler. And you'd damn well better be.'

'I am, Otto. Something has happened from your tone of voice.'

'I'm on the track of this *Siegfried* movement. Imported terrorists planning to create all hell over here.'

'Any leads?' Tweed asked quietly.

'Yes. I got a tip-off. From an Englishman. We raided an

address in Freiburg, found a small cache of arms and explosives. To be precise, six Kalashnikov rifles, five pounds of Semtex explosive, timers, and other devices for making half a dozen bombs.'

'And how many *Siegfried* terrorists?'

'None. The birds had flown. Not even a fingerprint in the apartment. They'd cleaned up so well I think they must have had a woman with them. Any luck at your end?'

'We're trying. I may have news soon. Patience, Otto. Is that friend of yours, Stahl, still at the same address you gave me?'

'Affirmative.'

'Incidentally, that tip-off from an Englishman. Would it have anything to do with *The Name of the Rose*?' Tweed asked, quoting the title of a famous novel.

'Yes, it would. Let's leave it at that. And I may fly to London soon. Even scramblers can be intercepted . . .'

Tweed put down the phone, disturbed. The same sinister atmosphere seemed to prevail in Wiesbaden as in Paris. A diabolical air of nervousness and mistrust among men at the top about their staffs. First Lasalle, now Kuhlmann.

'Who is Stahl?' Monica asked.

'Give me one of the top secret cards. Thanks. Stahl is an agent of Kuhlmann's operating under cover inside Bordeaux . . .' He was writing on the card as he spoke. 'This gives the address, phone number – and the French name he's using. I want an envelope for Newman kept in the safe.' He handed back the card. 'That goes in Newman's envelope. Add to it the copy of the photo of the evil gnome-like Sergeant Rey when you've got it from the Engine Room.'

'Will do. What was that business about *The Name of The Rose*?'

'Kuhlmann had a tip-off about one of the safe houses

used by *Siegfried*. The tip-off came from Captain Victor Rosewater. I told you about our meeting him with Paula in Basle. Paula thinks he'd make good material for us.'

'Sounds as though Paula could be right.'

At Grenville Grange Dawlish had taken a long phone call from New York as soon as he entered the living room with Lieutenant Berthier. The Frenchman stood staring down the lawn to the landing stage. Beyond, in the wide loop of the river Alde, a luxurious yacht was moored to a buoy. He watched as a motorboat left the yacht with three men aboard. They headed the craft for the landing stage, jumped ashore, ran up the edge of the lawn and disappeared round the side of the mansion. They were a tough-looking crew: well-built men in their thirties, who moved with athletic strides.

'All right, Berthier,' Dawlish called out. 'Get to it. What news do you bring?'

Berthier, erect, swung round on his heel, felt for his tinted glasses, pressed them deeper into his top pocket. Dawlish's manner was abrupt, his tone brusque.

'I was ordered to ask you when the next consignment would arrive.'

'Consignment of what?'

Dawlish watched Berthier's reaction closely. His visitor's eyes were blank, unblinking.

'I have no idea, sir. The message was exactly as I have phrased it.'

'But you could make a guess?' Dawlish persisted.

'I could not, sir. My orders were to transmit certain questions to you. Then I take the answers back to my superiors.'

'What unit are you attached to, Lieutenant? You are just a lieutenant? Or maybe that covers a higher rank?'

'Just a lieutenant, sir. And I'm attached to the engineers. Bridge-building. That sort of work.'

'I see.'

Dawlish was careful not to show it but he was impressed. Security was as tight as a closed hatch.

'The next consignment will be delivered within roughly three weeks from now. That answers your question?'

'It does. Thank you, sir.'

'Relax, man.' Dawlish became amiable. 'You're not on duty. Pour yourself a drink. You press the button in that bookcase – next to the volume of *Pilgrim's Progress*.'

'I never drink when on duty, sir.'

'Then bloody well pour me one. A large Scotch.'

Dawlish turned at the Frenchman's pedantic adherence to duty. He had never been able to break down the cold mask Berthier habitually displayed. Give him an order and he'd do anything. Dawlish found it disconcerting that he couldn't penetrate the armour Berthier seemed to surround himself with. Frightened of few men, Dawlish had always found Berthier's presence unsettling. He took the glass of Scotch without a word, drank half the contents.

'There is another question I was asked to transmit,' Berthier continued. 'Where will the consignment be landed?'

'Arcachon . . .'

Dawlish nearly added, 'as on previous occasions,' but stopped himself just in time. Possibly Berthier did know as little about the operation as appeared to be the case.

'And a signal confirming the exact arrival date and time will be sent by the usual route twenty-four hours earlier?'

'Yes.'

Dawlish left it at that. Again he studied Berthier. Six feet tall, strong face, good build, large hands hanging close to his sides. Almost as though standing to attention. On parade. The eyes were blue and ice-cold. The prototype of a well-trained machine.

'You're leaving when?' Dawlish demanded.

'I have been ordered to stay for a short time to explore for certain information. I am staying locally.'

Dawlish would like to have asked where 'locally' was but doubted whether he'd be told. Rather than risk a rebuff from a man whose reactions he was unsure of, Dawlish simply nodded. He drank the rest of his Scotch, stood up.

'Walters will show you out . . .'

He paced the room when Berthier had gone. People left an atmosphere behind them when they had intruded and gone. Dawlish felt that Death had just paid a visit to Grenville Grange.

Chapter Eighteen

Still furious with the way Dawlish had tried to paw her, Paula was very glad to see the man walking down the steps of the Brudenell as she left her parked car. Victor Rosewater, clad in a British warm, came forward to greet her, gave her a strong bear hug.

'You look strained,' he commented. 'Had a bad experience?'

'Actually, it was a trifle unpleasant . . .'

She was surprised and pleased at how perceptive he was. And he made no attempt to question her at that moment – instead he said just the right thing.

'I was on my way for a walk through Aldeburgh. That can wait. I suspect you could do with a drink. I'll wait in the bar while you divest yourself of your coat . . .'

In her room, Paula took a couple of minutes to check her make-up. She chose her favourite brooch to pin to the lapel of her suit, combed, brushed her raven-black hair and sprayed it.

'Champers?' Rosewater suggested when she perched by the counter.

'Lovely. I need it.'

'Let's go sit in a quiet corner,' Rosewater suggested as he carried two glasses of champagne.

Again she appreciated his consideration. Intuitively he had guessed she might want to talk where no one could overhear them. As she faced him she looked at his gear. A smart small-check sports jacket, corduroy trousers to ward off the cold outside, a cream shirt and a pale blue tie. He looked very fit. He raised his glass.

'Cheers! Do you want to talk about your experience or shall we avoid the subject?'

'I'd like to get it out of my system.' She felt a little odd getting on such warm terms with the man who had been Karin's husband. But Rosewater was not only good-looking: more important, he had an easy manner with women. He sat patient and attentive as Paula went on.

'I do a bit of journalism on the side,' she said, shading the truth. 'I've just come back from interviewing Lord Dane Dawlish for *Woman's Eye*. It turned out to be an ordeal. He couldn't keep his hands off me.'

'Nothing serious – really serious – happened?' he asked quietly.

'No. I fended him off. I should have scratched his face.'

'Probably just as well you didn't. Dawlish has a reputation for playing rough with women who don't accommodate him.'

'How do you know that?' she asked curious.

'It's part of my job to know all about the main players in the international game.'

'Game, Victor?'

'Wrong word. British understatement. It's anything but a game – a deadly struggle for power, for money. You don't become a Lord Dane Dawlish abiding by the Queensberry Rules.'

'My research showed up that Dawlish is heavily involved in the armaments trade.'

'You mentioned that to him?' Rosewater asked casually.

'Yes I did. And he got very uptight.'

'Probably because he's running down that side of his

business. End of the Cold War, and all that. He's still got plenty of other golden eggs in his basket.'

'Like his underwater exploration of the sunken village up at Dunwich?' Paula suggested.

Rosewater sipped at his champagne, took his time over reacting to her sudden change of subject. He put down his glass, fingered the stem. Then he shook his head and smiled as he looked at her, his eyes moving up from her slim waist to her eyes.

'He's losing money on that, I'm sure. It helps his image as a man mad keen on conservation. Who knows, perhaps he is just that. Must make a change from business and the wheeling and dealing he's devoted his career to.'

'I suppose you're right.' Paula checked her watch. 'After a quick lunch I have to get back to town. Are you staying on – still trying to find out who murdered poor Karin?'

'I'll be coming to London myself in a few days. Tell Tweed he can get me at Brown's Hotel if he needs me. Prior to that, here at the Brudenell. Now, before you go and leave me all alone maybe we could have a quick lunch together.'

'There's a very good pub up the High Street called the Cross Keys.'

'Let's eat here. I need something substantial to keep me going. Must be the cold weather . . .'

As he escorted her to the dining room Paula had the odd feeling Rosewater had given her a clue. She was damned if she could recall at the moment what it had been.

Newman and Marler had a ploughman's lunch at the Cross Keys when they drove back from the forest where the chopper had attacked them. Butler and Nield followed them in, took another table as though they were on their own. Their normal procedure when they were guarding someone.

'We have company,' Newman whispered after he'd ordered. 'Large table on our right. Five of them. The ugly-looking customer who seems to be the boss is Brand. I heard Dawlish call him that after he left us.'

'Oh, I've made the acquaintance of Mr Brand already,' Marler replied, talking in a normal tone. 'He's the chappie who bet me I couldn't shoot clay pigeons out of the sky.'

The burly man who sat with his back to them, his shaggy hair touching his collar, turned slowly round, his chair scraping the floor. Under thick eyebrows he stared at Marler and grinned unpleasantly.

'And took five hundred nicker off you, you lousy shot.'

'Didn't quite score a hundred per cent, did I?' Marler agreed, quite unruffled by Brand's aggressive manner.

'A hundred per cent?' Brand swept a large hand to draw his four rough-looking companions into the argument. 'This ponce couldn't hit a barn door from six feet away.'

Newman caught on to the situation. Marler had first encountered this tribe of thugs at the Cross Keys. They had undoubtedly heard of the fiasco with the chopper, had come here on the off-chance they'd see Marler again. They wanted revenge. Time to intervene.

'One thing, Brand, I could hit you from a distance of six feet, which is about the distance between us now.'

'Is that so, creep?'

Brand shoved his chair back, stood up slowly. There was movement among his companions who started to get out of their chairs. Butler stood up, hoisted the rubber cosh he kept in a special pocket in his raincoat. Walking to the table, he tapped one thug on the shoulder with the cosh.

'Anyone here who wants his skull cracked? All he has to do is try and stand up. Better stay sat down, gentlemen.

Leave it between the two of them. Fair's fair. Don't you agree?'

There was something menacing in the way Butler stood, six feet tall, well built, slapping the cosh into the palm of his left hand. He was smiling as he kept looking round the table. Movement ceased. Brand edged towards Newman.

Newman remained seated, elbows on the table, hands clasped under his chin. Brand's right hand whipped forward, grabbed his plate of half-eaten food, tipped it on to the floor. He grinned unpleasantly again.

'Now you'll have to eat off the floor. Expect you're used to it. Most dogs are.'

'That remark is a trifle provocative,' Marler commented.

Brand's right hand clenched, he aimed a piledriver blow at Newman's jaw. There was a blur of movement. Newman was standing, his chair thrown back on the floor. Brand's fist had missed its target. Newman's stiffened left hand hammered down on the bridge of Brand's prominent nose. He staggered back, eyes filled with tears of pain.

Newman followed him, slammed his right fist into the exposed jaw. Brand hurtled backwards, hit the counter, collapsed in a heap below it, motionless. The man sitting to the right of Brand's empty chair started to get up. Newman's hand pressed his shoulder, forced him back into his seat.

'If you want trouble you can have it. But I'm ex-SAS. I'll try not to kill you, but accidents happen . . .'

Which was true, Marler thought. Newman had survived an SAS course when writing an article on the unit. The thug subsided, muttered something but remained seated. At the far side of Brand's table another man started to get up. Nield shoved him down, hauled the chair from under him. As the thug toppled backwards Butler's right forearm struck him in the face, increasing the momentum. The back of the

185

man's head hit the floor and he lay still. Nield checked his neck pulse.

'Still breathing. He may have a headache when he wakes up . . .'

A waitress came rushing out, horrified. Newman took a banknote from his wallet, handed it to her.

'As you saw, they started it. Here's something to cover any damage. Sorry about the food on the floor. A decent tip out of that should make you feel a bit better.'

'Thank you,' the waitress said, glancing at the size of the banknote. 'They're regular. I'd never have believed it.'

'I should ban them in future,' Newman advised. 'Their table manners leave something to be desired . . .'

Accompanied by Marler, he walked out of the rear door across a small garden to where they had parked his car. Beyond the promenade a nor'easter was blowing up. The grey sea heaved and rolled with huge waves working themselves up into turbulence. Butler and Nield had melted out of sight through the front door.

Newman pulled up the collar of his trenchcoat, stared along the deserted front. Aldeburgh was strange and quaint. To his right old houses joined together lined the front, rooftops stepping up and down. At the crest of the shingle beach were several winches – used to haul in the few fishing boats which still operated out of Aldeburgh. No harbour.

'You chose the Cross Keys hoping for a roughhouse?' Marler suggested.

'Not really,' Newman replied as they settled themselves in the front of the Mercedes. 'But I was curious to see whether Brand and his henchmen did turn up – since you'd told me that was where you first met the ugly ape.'

'They did turn up.'

'Which is significant. Dawlish has just made his second blunder. First, when he sent the chopper to attack us in the forest. Second when he sent them to beat the hell out of us back there – to discourage us from coming back.'

'I think I can guess the significance.'

'The fact that we were seen outside that armaments factory hidden away in the forest. Something secret and weird is going on there. Dawlish has shown his hand.'

'So I check out the place again – at closer quarters – on another occasion.'

'*We* check out the place later.' Newman was driving away from the front, turning into the High Street, heading out of town. 'Right now we're returning to London.'

'I prefer operating on my own,' Marier insisted.

'We'll let Tweed decide. The next priority is to talk to him, report in detail what has happened. He might fit some of it into other data he's keeping inside that brainbox head. And don't forget the fox we have in the boot. It won't last for ever and I want an expert analysis of what killed it . . .'

Isabelle Thomas was thinking of Newman as she drove her Deux Chevaux through Bordeaux in the early afternoon of the same day. She slowed down as she approached the apartment of her mother, looking everywhere at all the parked cars. She was looking for a vehicle with a man – or men – sitting in it.

Now she had disobeyed Newman's firm warning to keep out of Bordeaux she kept seeing the Englishman in her mind. She thought he'd be furious at what would seem a trivial reason for taking this risk. But she'd remembered the brooch she had left behind in the apartment, the precious brooch given to her by Joseph, her dead fiancé.

Poor Joseph. He had committed suicide, jumping into the river Gironde with weights attached to his ankles, and all because he thought he was deformed, a cripple with horribly stretched thumbs after hanging in de Forge's punishment well.

I'd like to kill de Forge, she thought. Slowly . . . agonizingly.

She knew Joseph had saved up about half a year's pay to buy her that brooch. Her only memory of the man she had expected to spend the rest of her life with. Taking one last look round, she swung into the alley and parked her car out of sight round the corner at the end in the small yard. Just as Bob Newman had done. He'd give her hell if he knew about her trip back into the city.

She unlocked the back door, slipped quietly inside, shut and locked it. The building seemed horribly quiet as she slipped up the stairs, paused outside the apartment door. Before inserting the key she pressed her ear to the solid panel, listening. Could they be waiting for her inside?

Taking out a pencil flash from her handbag, she shielded it with the palm of her other hand, switched it on and examined the lock. No sign that anyone had tampered with the lock. I'm paranoid, she thought. Inserting the key she opened the well-oiled door silently, closed it with care, slipped on the security chain. Now she was safe.

To ease the tension she leaned against the door, pushed her mane of titian hair back over the knee-length green coat she was wearing against the bitter cold. The apartment felt like a morgue. Not a happy analogy, she told herself. Show some guts.

Without switching on any lights she moved across the gloomy room to the tall windows overlooking the street one floor down. Mid-afternoon and it was almost dark outside. The sky was a sheet of lead pressing down on the shabby city. Bloody November.

Isabelle studied the street. She watched the doorway where the two DST men had hidden when she had last been here with Newman. No sign of anyone. The temperature outside was close to freezing. A woman shopper hurried along the street, stoop-shouldered, huddled against the cold, carrying two plastic bags. No one else. Yes, she had got away with it.

She walked back across the living room to her bedroom, switched on the light after drawing the curtains. It took her only a minute to burrow under a drawer of her under-clothes, to find the precious brooch. Wrapping it in a slip, she noticed the door to the living room was ajar a foot, so the light would be shining through into the uncurtained living room. Pushing the brooch inside her coat pocket, she ran across the room, closed the door, switched off the light.

She stood with her back leant against it, waiting for her eyes to become accustomed to the gloom. Really she should have brought some kind of weapon to defend herself. She waited a little longer, opened the door and made her way into the bathroom. Taking a canister of hair spray off the glass ledge, she removed the cap, slipped it into her pocket, glad she was leaving. In her ears rang Newman's warning.

She was approaching the door out of the apartment when someone knocked on the door. She froze. Her mother had nothing to do with the neighbours, didn't speak to anyone else in the building. The knocking was repeated more vig-orously, urgently. She stiffened herself, took a deep breath.

'Who is it?' she called out.

'Plumber. One of your radiators is leaking, flooding the apartment below.'

'Not from this one,' she called back, giving herself time to think.

'Oh yes, it is,' the voice insisted. 'A plumber can trace the source of a leak. It's in your apartment. Water is pouring down the walls below.'

It had happened once before, a long time ago. When she

was a little girl. She remembered watching the plumber working. And she couldn't go round to check. That would mean switching on all the lights. Which would be a give away to anyone watching the apartment from outside.

She inserted the key very quietly, turning the lock. She hesitated before removing the chain, then decided to get it over with. She stood back a short distance from the door, the flashlight in her left hand, forced herself to call out.

'The door's unlocked . . .'

It opened slowly until it was wide open. She switched on her flashlight. Two men in trench coats stood framed in the doorway. The two DST men who had taken Henri away from the Bar Miami. The two fake DST men – as Newman had warned her – who had been involved in Henri's murder at the Gare St Jean. She went ice-cold with hate. The taller man held up a hand to shield his eyes from the flashlight and grinned.

'We thought you'd be back. You're coming with us. We are DST . . .'

She aimed the spray she was holding in her right hand, pressed the button, moved it in a swift arc, spraying both of them in the eyes. The taller one swore foully, clawed at his eyes. Isabelle lowered her head, jumped forward, butted him in the chest with all her strength. He staggered backwards as she kept on charging him like a bull. His back broke the banister rail. The impetus of her enraged charge toppled him over. He screamed as he fell down the drop two floors to the concrete basement.

Isabelle swung round. The other smaller man still had his hands over his eyes. She grabbed a handful of his hair, pulled his head forward. Instinctively he jerked backwards a fraction, which was what she was expecting. She changed her tactics, pushed with all her force, smashing his skull against the hard edge of the door frame. The sound of bone meeting wood was loud. He slumped to the floor. She thrust the canister and her flashlight into her pockets, stood, took hold of his inert heels, dragged him to the gap in the banister, heaved his legs over the edge, levered his body after them. He made no sound as he followed his companion. She heard a distant thud.

Locking the door, she left the building by the rear staircase. Settling herself behind the wheel of her car, she sucked in deep breaths. She must drive normally. Near the Gare St Jean she saw an empty parking slot, a public phone booth near by. She drove into the slot, locked the car, walked quickly to the booth. Inside she used her flashlight to check the number of the Prefecture in Bordeaux. When the police operator answered she spoke forcefully.

'I have to report a very serious crime – attempted murder. It has just taken place. Put me through to the Prefect at once. I will speak to no one else. If you keep me waiting I'll ring off. It concerns the DST . . .'

In his first-floor office in the old grey stone building with two wings flanking a central courtyard, only a short walk from the Mériadeck Centre Commercial, the Prefect frowned at the mention of the DST, told the operator to put the caller through. Using his foot, he slammed his office door shut.

In the phone booth Isabelle had covered the mouthpiece with the end of her silk scarf to muffle her voice.

'This is the Prefect. Who is calling?'

'Take this address do – immediately . . . You've got it? Good. On the staircase you'll find two fake DST men if you send a patrol car now. *Now!* There was a struggle. On the staircase. Both men are unconscious – and they were involved in the murder of Henri Bayle . . .'

'Who is this?' the Prefect demanded.

But the phone had gone dead. A short stocky man in a grey business suit, the Prefect had been chosen for his ability to take quick decisions. Fake DST? But the name which really alerted him was Henri Bayle – the man murdered recently at the Gare St Jean.

He locked his office door. Picking up the phone he asked the operator to give him an outside line. And he warned the man that if he listened in he'd be dismissed instantly. Then he dialled the number of René Lasalle, Chief of the DST in Paris. He got straight through.

'Prefect of Bordeaux here. We have spoken before, as you'll recall. I've just had an anonymous call about two false DST men at a Bordeaux address. The caller, who I think was a woman – voice blurred – said they were involved in the murder of Henri Bayle . . .'

He kept the call brief. Breaking the connection, he picked up the phone again, ordered two patrol cars to the address.

'Urgently. Break into the building if necessary. And the men should be armed with automatic weapons . . .'

Isabelle drove at speed through the night along the N650, the same route Newman had driven her on their way to Arcachon. Close to the sea she pulled in by the side of the highway in the middle of open country outside the village of Facture. Across the fields she saw an old barn, half-burnt out, the rafters exposed like human ribs.

Reaction set in. She shuddered uncontrollably as though she had a bad chill. She felt frozen. Nerves. Gradually she regained control, taking deep breaths of the icy air coming in through the window she had opened.

It was only a short distance to Arcachon now. She would stay there from now on. And in the morning she would call Bob Newman and tell him what had happened. Maybe it was important.

Chapter Nineteen

The following day at Park Crescent Tweed spent a lot of time listening to verbal reports of what had happened at Aldeburgh, later questioning all the people assembled in his crowded office closely.

Crowded into the room were Paula, Newman, Marler, Butler, and Nield. Monica occupied her desk, quietly taking notes. They had just finished their reports when Newman spoke again.

'I've just remembered something I'd completely forgotten to tell you. It concerns Isabelle . . .'

'The beautiful titian-haired Isabelle,' Paula teased him.

'I merely described her,' Newman rapped back, irked.

'It was the way you described her.' Paula purred.

'I'd now like to say something important without interruption. It was your description, Paula, of Lord Dawlish's catamaran, *Steel Vulture*. A while ago, when you told us about your grim experience when Karin Rosewater was killed, you said when you both surfaced off Dunwich there was a strange ship, its prow cut in two . . .'

'That's right.' Paula leaned forward, serious again.

'Well, when I was walking along the Arcachon front with Isabelle she described a strange vessel which sails in there – a ship "with its prow cut in two". Something very close to that. It sounds exactly like the *Steel Vulture*.'

'That is interesting,' Tweed interjected. 'Maybe now we have a link between Suffolk and France.'

'And,' Newman went on, 'she also told me a Lord Dane Dawlish turned up at some party and made a heavy pass at her, which she rebuffed.'

'That's dear Dawlish,' Paula commented. 'And surely we now have another connection between Aldeburgh and France?'

'We have what may be a vital one,' Tweed agreed. 'Between Aldeburgh and Arcachon – which is close to Bordeaux. And Dawlish is armaments. And Lasalle told me some unknown organization was supplying General de Forge with arms and money. It could be fiendishly clever.'

'What could be?' asked Paula.

'Landing arms at Arcachon instead of direct to the port of Bordeaux where the watch on incoming cargoes will be stricter. Bless Isabelle – and you, Paula.'

'But at what a price,' Paula said nostalgically. 'The price of Karin's life.'

'Victor Rosewater is available then if we need him?' Tweed asked, changing the subject.

'Yes. He may even track Karin's murderer. He's a tough character.'

'Describe again to me, Bob, how this signet ring came to be found.' Tweed bent back in his swivel chair and watched Newman. 'Start from the beginning. Every minute detail . . .'

He unlocked a drawer half-way through Newman's recall of what had happened on that dark night on the marshes with Paula and Rosewater. Tweed took a large silk handkerchief from the drawer, screwed up into a ball, laid it on his desk.

When Newman had finished, ending with their trip in the marsh buggy with Buchanan and Warden to the Brudenell, he congratulated him on his total recall. Opening the handkerchief he took out two signet rings, pushed them across the desk to Paula.

'Which one is the ring Rosewater found under the boat?'

Paula examined them carefully. She slipped both squarely on her middle finger. Both were far too large to stay on. Puzzled, she looked at them again, shook her head, stared at Tweed.

'I don't understand. They're identical.'

'Not quite. There's a tiny scratch on the inside of one ring. That's the original. The Engine Room worked for thirty-six hours – including through the night – creating the twin. You see, I have to hand the original to Chief Inspector Buchanan – but I wanted a copy. Find the finger that wore it and we may have found our murderer.'

'Why *may*?' Newman asked aggressively.

'Because nothing is conclusive. Just as we can't assume yet that Dawlish is linked to de Forge. We need more solid evidence – and urgently. Which is why, Marler, I think you should get moving on that special mission in France I described to you.' He held up a hand, looked round his audience. 'No, only Marler and I know about it.'

'First things first,' Marler entered the conversation for the first time. 'I have to explore that factory in the forest on the road to Orford . . .'

'And I go with him,' Newman said firmly.

'Nothing doing,' Marler said emphatically.

'Hold it, both of you,' said Tweed. 'You both just survived your previous trip into that area. No argument. You explore that factory together. Armed. Then, Bob, we'll turn our attention to France, launch a major expedition to find out what de Forge is really up to – and what this *Siegfried* business is about in Germany. It will be dangerous.'

'What about my fox?' Newman asked.

'Collected for immediate delivery to the top veterinary pathologist in the country, Robles. Hours ago. And I gave them the keys to your car because Robles wanted to examine the boot too. Now, I think we ought to go to lunch in small groups. Maybe there will have been developments even by the time we get back . . .'

Tweed realized Monica was excited as soon as he returned to his office with Paula, Newman, and Marler. She waited until he had taken off his coat and settled himself behind his desk. Outside there was a cold November drizzle, a raw biting wind.

'The courier arrived from Lasalle with the photos you asked for. He left them and went straight back to Heathrow to board a flight for Paris.'

'And?'

Newman sat in the armchair close to his desk and Paula perched herself on one arm. Marler adopted his usual stance, leaning against a wall. Monica brought over an envelope, placed it in front of Tweed with a smile of smug satisfaction.

'You're going to be interested.'

'Sounds as though I'd better be.'

Tweed extracted the glossy prints. He laid them out across his desk. There were three copies of each print. On their backs Lasalle had written names in his own neat writing. Josette de Forge. De Forge himself. Major Lamy. Lieutenant Berthier. Jean Burgoyne.

Tweed handed a set of copies to Paula, another set to Newman. He began examining them himself. Glancing up at Monica, now behind her own desk, he saw her watching him with anticipation. He went on looking at the pictures, then stopped and reached for his magnifying glass. He looked up at the others.

'I thought I'd seen that signet ring before.'

196

He held up the photograph he had been studying. In Paris he had spotted the ring without the aid of a glass. He was holding up a photo of de Forge's Chief of Intelligence, Major Lamy.

'So,' Newman said after an interval of silence, 'we've found Kalmar, the assassin. Nice work.'

'Not necessarily,' Tweed warned.

'But it's conclusive,' Newman protested. 'His ring was found under the boat where Karin was strangled.'

'And how do you think a man like Major Lamy flew here, stayed somewhere, and was available for murdering her? Bearing in mind his job, the danger of being recognized in England. Also does anyone know he speaks English fluently?'

'He might. He might be able to slip over here, back again without being spotted.'

'"Might" isn't good enough,' Tweed rapped back. 'It remains a possibility – no more at this stage.'

'He looked like a nasty piece of work when I met him,' Newman said and relapsed into silence.

'You're forgetting earlier events,' Tweed said cryptically. He picked up a sheet of paper with Monica's handwritten notes. 'But this is conclusive, may well interest both you and Marler. We know how your fox died. Ready?'

'Very.'

'Robles phoned a preliminary report to Monica while we were out at lunch. He suspects the fox was killed by some type of nerve gas mixed with the smoke that helicopter ejected.'

'Nerve gas?' Marler was startled out of his normal coolness. 'So if Newman and I had breathed in any of that smoke . . .'

'You'd be as dead as the fox,' Tweed completed his sentence. 'Nerve gas. That really is sinister.'

'And,' Monica interjected, 'my researches turned up the fact that Dawlish Chemicals has a high security laboratory in the factory complex on the road to Orford.'

'Robles,' Tweed went on, 'is taking the carcase in a refrigerated truck to a friend of his who works at Porton Down, the chemical warfare establishment. Then he'll be able to tell us the precise type of nerve gas used.'

'We'd better get back to Suffolk fast – Marler and myself. Time we took a closer look at Dawlish's conservation activities,' Newman suggested.

'Agreed,' said Tweed. 'The sooner the better – Marler has to go to France. But take great care.'

'We do know now we're not dealing with pussycats,' Newman retorted. He left the room with Marler.

The phone rang. Tweed waited while Monica took the call. She asked someone to wait just one moment, nodded to Tweed's phone.

'It's Lasalle in Paris. Wants to talk to you urgently.'

'More problems, René?' Tweed enquired. 'Yes, I'm on scrambler . . .'

'I've had a call from the Prefect of Bordeaux, a man I can rely on,' Lasalle stressed. 'He had an anonymous phone call – thinks it was from a girl – who gave him the address of an apartment block here in Bordeaux. Told him he'd find the two fake DST men who were involved in the murder of Henri Bayle. Your agent found at the Gare St Jean. He went to the address himself. Incidentally, the girl said he'd find the two men unconscious. He found them all right. Dead. Both of them.'

'How did they die?'

'Hard to say, apparently. Both had fallen two floors. His men found traces of blood on the door frame of the apartment occupied by Isabelle Thomas and her mother. Both women have disappeared. But their descriptions fit what witnesses at the Bar Miami said about the two men who took Bayle away – after a little arm-twisting. I'm flying to Bordeaux to interview General de Forge. With this I can shake him, rattle his cage. He's had it all his own way too long . . .'

'Take care,' Tweed warned. 'You're not going down there alone?'

'Yes, I am.' He paused. 'Maybe with a little back-up.'

'One more thing before you go. Do you know if Major Lamy is fluent in English?'

'Speaks your language like a native. An English native.'

In his cramped office Lasalle put down the phone, checked the time. He had an appointment with Navarre, Minister of the Interior. Throwing on his coat and hat – it was sleeting outside – he left the building, walked into the rue du Faubourg St Honoré, turning to the right away from the Elysée Palace.

Normally mild-mannered but tenacious, Lasalle strode along briskly with a grim expression. Reaching the entrance to the Ministry in the Place Beauveau, he expected the guards, who knew him well, to usher him straight past the gates. A guard barred his way.

'Identification, sir.'

'You know me by now . . .'

'Orders, sir. Identification, please.'

Lasalle produced his special identity pass, handed it to the guard. After examining it, the guard returned the pass, waved him on with a salute. So Navarre had stepped up security, Lasalle thought, hurrying across the spacious yard in front of the ministry building: that's good.

The minister's office is on the first floor, overlooks the front courtyard. Its occupant rose from behind his desk as Lasalle was ushered inside. Pierre Navarre was a short stocky individual with dark hair, thick brows and impatient eyes. Like General de Forge, he came from Lorraine. He shook hands with the DST chief, told him to sit down and, holding a document in one hand, hauled a chair close to Lasalle's. He handed him the document which Lasalle read quickly. Scrawled at the bottom of the letter was Navarre's strong, swift signature.

'That should do it, Minister,' Lasalle said.

'Time we put pressure on that bastard,' Navarre remarked savagely. 'When do you fly to Bordeaux?'

'Within the hour . . .'

'Report to me what happens. I will be working here a little late . . .'

A little late. The phrase echoed in Lasalle's mind as he hurried back to his office. Navarre was noted for the hours he kept – often eighteen hours a day. In his office he phoned a Bordeaux number, gave certain orders, slammed down the phone and ran to the car waiting in the courtyard to take him to the airport.

Arriving at Bordeaux Airport late in the afternoon under a murky sky he was met by a DST officer who led him to a bullet-proof Citroën. Lasalle jumped inside, followed by the officer. The driver, who had the engine running, raced away from the airport.

'What about the reserves?' Lasalle asked the officer beside him in the rear.

'Assembled and hidden in a field near Third Corps HQ. General de Forge expects you to come alone?'

'Yes. He's not the only tactician in France . . .'

Out in the country well away from Bordeaux the driver slowed, pulled up alongside a gated field. A man in a blue raincoat opened the gate, lifted his arm in a signal, then waved Lasalle's vehicle on. Lasalle glanced back through the rear window as they raced along a straight stretch of road. Behind followed a convoy of eight cars, filled with armed DST men. Behind them followed CRS motorcyclists, clad in black leather coats, automatic weapons slung over shoulders. The huge convoy pulled up in front of the entrance to Third Corps.

A uniformed lieutenant approached the Citroën, frowning. As Lasalle pressed the button which lowered the window he peered inside. Lasalle wasted no time.

'Open the damn gate.' He flashed his identity card. 'Lasalle of DST, Paris. General de Forge is expecting me. I phoned Major Lamy early this morning.'

'You were expected alone . . .'

'Don't argue with me. Open the gate.'

'I'll have to fetch Major Lamy . . .'

'He has two minutes to get here. I said *two minutes*. Move, man. Things seem sloppy round here . . .'

Within a minute a car drove up behind the gate. Major Lamy emerged, walked through the pedestrian gate. He stared along the road at the endless convoy.

'What is that white vehicle?'

'An ambulance. Now, General de Forge is expecting me, so open the gates or we'll drive through them.'

Lamy looked at the four CRS outriders who had drawn up alongside Lasalle's Citroën. Wearing black crash helmets, the CRS riders stared back at him through their sinister goggles.

'If you insist,' Lamy decided. 'But this is a military establishment . . .'

'I didn't think it was a holiday camp,' Lasalle interrupted him. 'The gates . . .'

'Only your vehicle can enter . . .'

'Then the rest will smash down the gates and follow me. Give the order . . .'

Lasalle pressed the button again and the window shut in Lamy's face. He turned, nodded, the gates opened, and Lamy had to run to dive into his car which led the way to General de Forge's quarters. Behind them the convoy streamed through the entrance, nose to tail. They proceeded down a long concrete avenue lined with single-storey military buildings. Lasalle noticed that at the beginning of each side road a large tank was stationed, each huge gun barrel aimed at a low angle, its tank commander standing in the turret. De Forge was emphasizing his power.

Lamy's car eventually stopped outside a building indistinguishable from the others. Lasalle jumped out of his own car, clutching the brief case he had held on to since leaving Paris. Lamy escorted him into a large room with a woodblock floor gleaming like glass. At the far end General de Forge waited, seated behind a large desk.

Lamy marched forward while Lasalle strolled, taking his time, glancing curiously round the room. Hanging from the right-hand wall was a huge banner carrying the symbol of the Cross of Lorraine, de Gaulle's symbol when he formed the Free French during World War II.

'Welcome to Third Corps GHQ,' de Forge said in a stiff voice as he remained seated.

Lasalle sat in the hard-backed chair on the far side of the desk, facing the General across the acre or so of desk. No papers. Three phones of differing colours. A blotter framed in leather.

'Does he have to remain?' Lasalle enquired, nodding his head towards Lamy as though he were the Army's mascot. Lamy, standing erect, hands clasped behind his back, stiffened even more. He looked at his master.

'It is the custom,' de Forge informed him, 'for Major Lamy to be present, even for meetings of minor importance.'

Lasalle nodded, ignoring the insult. Unfastening his brief case, he extracted a folded sheet of paper and laid it in his lap. He stared straight at de Forge, his expression giving no clue as to his mood. But his tone of voice was like a whiplash.

'This is a serious matter which brings me here. May I remind you that under the Constitution the military is entirely subordinate to – the servant of – the civil power? I represent that civil power. Let us be very clear on that before I proceed.'

'Proceed, then,' de Forge ordered, his face bleak.

'We have had several cases – even numerous instances – of unauthorized personnel impersonating DST officers. I don't have to remind you that is a grave offence, I take it.'

'I have no idea what the hell you are talking about.'

'Give me just a minute more and all will be clear. I have outside two examples of men who impersonated DST officers.' Lasalle stood up. 'Could you please accompany me.'

'Why should I?'

'Because I am ordering you to, General.'

'You have no power to order me to do anything!' de Forge roared in his parade ground voice.

Lasalle made no reply. He leaned over the desk, handed the folded sheet to de Forge. The General glanced at Lamy, looked back at Lasalle, who remained staring back coldly. De Forge slowly opened the sheet. His eyes saw the printed logo at the top, realized it was a sheet of the personal stationery of the Minister of the Interior. He read the instruction. *You will co-operate with my emissary, René Lasalle, Chief of the Direction de la Surveillance du Territoire. You will accede to any request he may make. He has plenipotentiary powers.*

'Now perhaps you will come outside with me,' Lasalle said quietly.

Lasalle walked more briskly back down the long room than his pace on entering. Half-way to the door, he paused, looked back. De Forge was following, his riding boots as brilliantly polished as the floor. Lamy remained by the desk.

'Major Lamy,' Lasalle called out, taking command, 'you will come too.'

He resumed his brisk trot to the door, opened it, looked outside. His orders had been obeyed. Escort cars had moved to the far side along with his own vehicle. The ambulance stood backed up to the entrance, doors still shut, two men in white coats standing by the step. Lasalle stood aside, watched.

General de Forge emerged from his office, stood stock still, taking in the long convoy at a glance. His thin lips tightened.

'This is an invasion.'

'You could call it that,' Lasalle agreed. 'DST officers, real ones, all armed. Also CRS, again armed, as you can see.'

'This is an outrage . . .'

'I call it a precaution,' Lasalle replied mildly.

'What impertinence have you called me out here for?' He saw some soldiers standing, gazing at the spectacle. He turned to Lamy. 'Major, send all those men immediately for a run over the obstacle course in full battle order.'

'That can wait,' Lasalle said firmly. 'Major Lamy may also be interested to see this.'

He nodded to the two white-coated men, descended the steps to join them, followed by de Forge and Lamy. Opening the rear doors, the two men stood on the step. A blast of icy air rushed out of the interior. De Forge and Lamy stared at the interior. Large metal drawers were stacked inside. A drawer at floor level was opened. The white-coated men stood back, Lasalle waved a hand.

'I told you I had brought two men who impersonated DST officers in Bordeaux.'

The white-coated couple opened another drawer. In each drawer a half-clothed corpse was stretched out, its head perched on a wooden block. Icy air from the refrigerated mobile morgue continued to flow out.

'Those men are dead,' Lamy burst out.

'You are most observant,' Lasalle commented. 'They are soldiers – presumably from the Third Corps since they were found in Bordeaux.'

'How on earth do you know that?' de Forge asked contemptuously.

'Oh, they carried no identification except the fake DST credentials. They were dressed in civilian clothes – but one point was overlooked. Those underclothes are Army issue. That point is certain.'

De Forge looked at Lamy. The Chief of Intelligence went closer to the corpses. He swung on his heel, addressing the General.

'I recognize both men now, sir. They are deserters – disappeared from their unit weeks ago.'

Lamy could think fast. Lasalle privately paid him that compliment. But he did not let go so easily.

'Posted officially as deserters?'

'Major Lamy,' de Forge intervened, catching on, 'go and fetch the records so we can show the gentleman from Paris.'

He walked back into the building as Lamy ran round the corner of the building and disappeared. Lasalle nodded before following de Forge. The white-coated men closed the drawers with their grisly contents: both bodies were badly damaged round the skulls. He followed de Forge back into the building.

'Both men were involved in a brutal murder,' Lasalle informed de Forge as they waited for Lamy: de Forge seated at his desk while Lasalle wandered back and forth in front of it. His restlessness irked de Forge but the General sat immobile as a statue.

'Deserters are scum,' de Forge eventually responded.

'If they were deserters.' Lasalle phrased his comment carefully. 'Someone clever was giving them orders . . .'

He broke off as Major Lamy marched towards the desk, a file under his arm, ignoring Lasalle. He placed the file in front of the General.

'Privates Gillet and Ferron,' he reported. 'Deserted five weeks ago. Not seen since.'

'There you are.'

De Forge waved towards the two sheets he had glanced at. He made no move to hand them to Lasalle. The DST chief reached across the desk swiftly, grabbed the sheets, looked at them.

'Those copies are our property,' de Forge warned.

Lasalle was holding the sheets up to the light. He turned each sheet in turn to different angles. Then he slipped them inside his briefcase, snapped it shut.

'Must I remind you I am conducting a murder investigation? These records represent vital evidence. A spectroscope examination will prove whether these so called records were, as I suspect, produced within the past five minutes.'

'I deeply resent your implication,' Lamy snapped.

'All part of my work. The civil power takes precedence over the military.' He stood up. 'Thank you for your cooperation. I will be back . . .'

De Forge waited until he heard the convoy moving off. He then gave Lamy the order. 'Organize really ferocious riots in Lyons. We must move fast.'

Chapter Twenty

Newman heard the phone ringing when he opened the door of his ground-floor flat at Beresforde Road, South Ken. He ran, sure it would cease ringing just as he reached the instrument in the large living room. Grabbing the receiver, he gave his number – but omitted his name. It was Tweed.

'Bob, I thought you ought to know. Lasalle has called me from Bordeaux. The two phoney DST men who took Francis Carey from the Bar Miami before he was murdered have been found at the apartment of Isabelle Thomas's mother . . .'

'Found? What does that mean?'

'Curb your anxiety. I haven't finished. The Prefect of Bordeaux received an anonymous call – from a girl, he believes – who reported the presence of the two men. She said they were unconscious. In the basement. The police found them. Both men were dead.'

'Oh, God! How had they died?'

'Very curious. No one is certain. But they had fallen two floors, their skulls crushed. Do you think Isabelle could have done that?'

'Not deliberately. Seems unlikely she'd have coped with two of them – although she's exceptionally strong. Swims every day in a leisure club. You say Lasalle called from Bordeaux?'

'Yes. Flew there. Made an audacious move. Fixed up to see de Forge, took the bodies in a refrigerated truck, showed them to him. Identified as soldiers by their Army-issue underclothes. They always forget something. He's shaken de Forge.'

'Is that good?'

'It may provoke him into a wrong move. We need the trigger to make him show his hand. Trouble is, I don't know what that trigger will be. Must go now. You're leaving soon for your return trip?'

'Just waiting for Marler. He's due in about half an hour.'

'Don't push it to the limit . . .'

Newman had hardly replaced the receiver when the phone rang again. Marler? Warning him he'd be late? He picked up the phone, again gave only the number.

'That's you, Bob, isn't it? I recognize your voice.' Isabelle. All in a rush. He told her to slow down. 'You're going to be very mad with me. I was a fool to ignore your warning . . .'

'Slow down, Isabelle,' he repeated, alarmed. 'Are you in danger? And where are you calling from?'

'It's all right, it's safe, I'm calling from my sister's apartment in Arcachon, she's not here, I'm alone . . .'

'For Pete's sake then, slow down. Now, nice and easy.'

'I went back to my mother's flat in Bordeaux, Bob . . .'

Without more interruption he listened grimly to her experience. She was talking at normal speed now, giving him a terse but detailed report of everything that had happened. She concluded by telling him about how she'd called the Prefect of Bordeaux before driving like hell back to Arcachon.

'Maybe you were followed,' he suggested.

'Not possible. I kept an eye on my rear-view mirror. There was hardly any traffic at that hour. And I stopped for a few minutes in the country outside Arcachon. No vehicle of any kind appeared.'

'Then that's all right.' Newman hesitated, decided he had

to ensure she stayed in Arcachon by frightening the life out of her. 'There's one detail in what you told me you got wrong.'

'What was that?'

'You said the two fake DST men were unconscious. Both of them were – are – *dead*.'

'Are you sure? How do you know that, Bob?'

She sounded as cool as the proverbial cucumber when he'd expected hysterics. Almost a note of satisfaction.

'I assure you they're both dead as a doornail. I know, Isabelle. For a certainty. I have my contacts.'

'So the men who led poor Henri to his death are dead now themselves.'

'As dead as you can get,' he stressed.

'I didn't waste time going down to look at them. Bob, are you mad with me for going back to Bordeaux, for disobeying you?'

She sounded as though that possibility worried her far more than the news he'd given her.

'Will you be going back to Bordeaux again?' he asked.

'No! I promise you, I know I promised you before but this time I'll keep my word. Bob, you do believe me, don't you? Say you believe me. Please say it . . .'

Her metabolism was all revved up again. The words tumbled over each other like some river roaring down over rapids.

'I believe you,' Newman assured her. 'A lot of people will be looking for you. Are you certain no one in the city knows about your mother having a place in Arcachon?'

'I'm absolutely sure, certain, positive. I told you, she doesn't like anyone in Bordeaux, she's never let anyone know about her apartment here. So no one would dream of looking for me here. When will I see you again?'

'I'll contact you as soon as I can. Meantime read some of

those books I saw in your apartment. Go out for a walk after nightfall. And push your hair up under some kind of headgear. A beret. A scarf. Anything . . .'

'I promise, Bob. I'll tie up my hair, then hide it under a scarf. And I'll wear trousers. I have a pair. I never normally wear them because I don't think they look feminine. No one even here will recognize me. I will see you soon?'

'As soon as I can make it. Someone is at the door. Must go. Chin up . . .'

Newman peered round the side bay window through the heavy net curtains which gave him a view of the entrance. It was almost dark already. November dark. Marler stood at the entrance, carrying a long holdall. That meant he was bringing his dismantled Armalite rifle. He must be expecting trouble at the Dawlish factory on the road to Orford.

Marler's new Volvo station wagon was parked in a slot further down the road. They'd be travelling in that, Newman thought as he went to the lobby to operate the button which opened the front door. His Mercedes 280E was still in the hands of the veterinary pathologist.

'You'll need some insulation,' Marler said as he entered the apartment. 'It's cold enough out there to freeze the whatnots off a monkey.'

Marler was wearing his sheepskin, collar turned up. Newman thought the intense cold – met forecast had said it would be below freezing point – might help them. Guards didn't like patrolling too thoroughly on cold nights. At least he hoped he was right in his assumption.

In his Park Crescent office Tweed knew Paula was excited about something as soon as she entered. She put down the cardboard-backed envelope she had been carrying on her desk, took off her suede coat, one of her few extravagances.

Taking one of Lasalle's photos from the envelope, she laid it on her desk. As she asked the question she covered the print with one hand.

'Is it all right if I play around with this print with my felt tip pen? It's one of the photos Lasalle sent us.'

'Go ahead. The Engine Room made up a large number of copies of all the photos.'

Tweed showed no curiosity, writing out a list of names on his pad. Monica, in contrast, surreptitiously was watching Paula as she used her felt tip pen. Paula put down the pen, lifted up the photo, held it at a distance.

'It's him,' she announced. 'I thought it was when I was looking at the photos in my flat.'

'Who?' Tweed enquired.

'Lieutenant Berthier, on the staff of Major Lamy, is here in this country. To be precise he's probably still staying at the Brudenell Hotel in Aldeburgh.'

She took the photo to Tweed, placed it in front of him. She had used the pen to sketch in a pair of tinted glasses over the eyes, to darken his hair. Tweed looked at what she had sketched, then at her.

'Clever,' he said. 'You are right. I saw this man leaving the bar at the Brudenell when I was on my way out for a night walk over the marshes.'

'He's the man Newman thought he heard swear in French when he stubbed his toe, as you'll recall. He's the man,' Paula continued, 'you asked me to chat up, which I did, as you know. I spoke to him suddenly in French, asked him if he'd like another drink. Remember? He started to get up from his chair to fetch more drinks himself, then stopped in time and pretended to be settling himself more comfortably in his chair. I *thought* he knew what I'd said. Now I know I'm right.'

'So,' Tweed remarked, 'we have another French link

211

between Suffolk and France. Berthier. There is something very serious going on near Aldeburgh. This is one coincidence too many.'

'He told me his name was James Sanders,' Paula recalled thoughtfully, 'that he was a salesman dealing in marine spare parts, that he'd just returned from Paris.'

'Another possible link,' Tweed said immediately. 'An officer on Lamy's staff, posing as a salesman of marine parts, would have a legitimate reason for contacting Dawlish. Because of the Cat, the *Steel Vulture*. More pieces of the jigsaw are coming to light, fitting into an insidious pattern.'

'I think I'll return to Aldeburgh,' Paula suggested. 'I could use the excuse of visiting Jean Burgoyne.'

'Except we know Burgoyne is de Forge's mistress. Tricky. We don't know at this stage who we can trust – if anyone.'

'I still think I should go back, especially as we know Berthier is there. He might let something slip if I play up to him.'

'I don't like the idea,' Tweed told her. 'I have in front of me a list of names – any of which could be the highly professional assassin, Kalmar.'

'Can we see the list?' Monica interjected.

'No. Not yet. I want to be more sure of my ground – I still need more data . . .'

'Which I might obtain if I go to Aldeburgh,' Paula insisted. 'And both Newman and Marler are on their way there. Newman is bound to phone you – you could tell him I'll be at the Brudenell.'

'You can go only if you wait at the hotel until Newman has contacted you. That's an order.'

'I'm on my way.' Paula jumped up before Tweed could change his mind. 'I'll pick up my ready-packed case at my flat, then drive up to Suffolk . . .'

'Do you think that was wise?' Monica queried when they

were alone. 'She's going back to where one murder has been committed. The murderer could still be in the area.'

'What baffles me,' said Tweed, his mind elsewhere, 'is *if*, by a longshot, it's Dawlish who is supplying arms to the Third Corps secretly how does he transport them there?'

'Aboard that catamaran,' Monica said promptly. 'Dawlish himself told Paula the size of the vessel – that it can carry over a hundred people and a number of heavy vehicles. And Newman's friend, Isabelle, told him she'd seen a vessel which fits the *Steel Vulture*'s description dock frequently in Arcachon.'

'You don't get my point. Dawlish also said the vessel is berthed at Harwich. I happen to know they've tightened security at Harwich. They found a large drug consignment aboard a ship bound for Rotterdam – a reverse ploy of the drug traffickers. Drugs brought in here by some other route are then sent *out* to the continent. With that kind of security would Dawlish risk a search? I think not.'

'Then what's the solution?'

'No idea. He may not be involved at all. But that has stimulated a different line of investigation. I'm calling Heathcoate, Harbour Master at Harwich. He owes me.'

Tweed unlocked a drawer, checked through an address book, found the number, dialled it himself, gave his name, asked to be put through to the Harbour Master.

'Is that you, Heathcoate? How are you? Yes, I want a favour. A ship called the *Steel Vulture*, a twin-hulled catamaran . . .'

'Owned by millionaire Lord Dawlish. A very advanced design, the ship of the future. He berths it here. It is moored here now. What about it?'

'Ever search it? The drugs business.'

Heathcoate chuckled. 'You think millionaires are outside the law? Because they're not. Answer, yes. We searched it twice over the past six months. Clean as a whistle. You think we missed something?' Heathcoate enquired. 'That we should keep an eye on that ship?'

'Waste of time. And it's not drugs I was thinking of. Don't ask me what. Top secret.'

'You expect me to talk and then you clam up,' Heathcoate grumbled with mock seriousness.

'Buy you a Scotch next time we meet. Thanks anyway . . .'

'No good,' Tweed told Monica. 'Heathcoate searched the catamaran twice in six months. Nothing. Dawlish is too smart to risk being caught. Looks like a dead end. But someone told me something which might be the loophole and I'm damned if I can recall it.'

'You didn't hear a word I said a few minutes ago,' Monica chided him. 'I said one murder has already been committed where Paula is going back to. The murderer could still be in the area.'

'I don't think that's at all likely.'

It was a remark Tweed was to regret in the near future.

The *Cercle Noir* was holding an emergency meeting at the Villa Forban near Third Corps GHQ. It had been called by General de Forge during Jean Burgoyne's absence from the villa. He sat at the head of a table in the living room with the curtains closed. Outside it was dark.

Seated round the table were Louis Janin, Minister of Defence; General Masson, Chief of the Army Staff; General Lapointe, commander of the atomic *force de frappe*; Emile Dubois, leader of the new political party, *Pour France*; and the man known as *Oiseau* – Bird.

Janin was a short, heavily built man with slicked-back dark hair who wore rimless spectacles. He had the air of an intellectual. Nominally de Forge's superior, he was awed by the General's charismatic personality. General Lapointe was made of sterner stuff: a small lean-faced man, he believed only Charles de Forge could save France from domination by an all-powerful Germany now unification had taken place. Emile Dubois was squat and a natural orator. Given to waving his arms to stress a point, he hoped one day to become Premier under the Presidency of de Forge. General Masson was a second-rate soldier, greatly conscious of the dignity of his post.

'We have reached a crossroads in history,' de Forge began. 'Now there is a growing state of turbulence in this country there can be no turning back. There will be new and more terrible riots in Lyons. Then the target is Paris itself.'

'Are we moving too fast?' Janin queried.

De Forge held intellectuals in contempt. 'We must move ahead faster now the momentum has built up. Caution is the reaction of faint-hearts and cowards.'

'Navarre has the ear of the President more and more,' Janin warned, nettled by the implication.

'Navarre may have to go,' de Forge informed him.

'Surely you do not mean Kalmar?' Janin protested.

'The General made no suggestion at all in that direction,' Lapointe said severely.

'My members are travelling *en masse* to Lyons,' Dubois assured de Forge. 'We shall be there to play our part.'

'I had a visit from a lackey of Navarre,' de Forge reported. 'Lasalle of the DST. He is trying to build up a case against us. He will fail, of course. But when we take power he will be the first to be hurled into the street. We need men of strong patriotic fibre in all key positions. I need your agreement that in Lyons we light a furnace, ignite a beacon which will be seen in Paris. And we must send advance contingents inside the capital secretly.' He hammered a clenched fist on the table. 'From this second on the momentum must be accelerated non-stop. All agreed, hammer their fists on this table . . .'

Five fists hammered the table with varying degrees of conviction. Janin's, de Forge noted, was the feeblest response. And now the Minister of Defence raised the objections which were worrying him.

'As before, I still do not like the fact that one member of the *Cercle* remains unknown to us.'

Oiseau sat at the far end of the oblong table, facing de Forge, his head concealed beneath a Balaclava mask. He was the one man who never spoke a word at the secret meetings. Now he turned and gazed at Janin without saying a word. De Forge exploded.

'I have told you before, Janin, time and again, *Oiseau* supplies us with the extra arms we need. More important still, he supplies us with finance from his own funds – finance which is untraceable back to its source. Without that finance *Pour France*, our vital civil arm, could never have been built up. His identity is of no concern to you. And I noticed his fist hammered the table with much greater force than yours.'

'I feel it is dangerous to make a major move until we know the reaction of the President,' Janin persisted.

'So we don't make a major move until we see how he reacts to the new Lyons riots.' De Forge's mood became mocking. 'You like discussion, Janin. It is decision that worries you. Just keep me informed about the Elysée . . .'

The meeting continued for another quarter of an hour. Most of it was occupied by de Forge reinforcing morale, working up a sensation of enthusiasm, a conviction that victory lay just round the next corner.

As always, the members of the *Cercle Noir* left the Villa

Forban one by one, with a five-minute interval between each departure. *Oiseau* was the first to depart. He bowed briefly to de Forge, collected his coat himself from the cupboard in the hall, walked out into the bitter night where a limousine waited to whisk him to the executive jet at Bordeaux Airport. Only when the driver, Brand, dressed in a chauffeur's uniform, drove out between the villa gates did his passenger, *Oiseau*, remove his Balaclava helmet.

Inside the villa de Forge waited until the other members had left. Then he opened the door into the next room and closed it. Seated in the study Major Lamy was working on papers at a desk while a cassette played Stravinsky's *Rite of Spring* softly. Lamy switched off the machine and looked up.

'Are there any notepads I could use? I've checked the desk – except the deep bottom drawer I can't open. I see it has a special lock.'

'That is the drawer where Jean keeps her jewellery,' de Forge told him. 'She has the only key. God save me from some of those cretins who have just left.'

'Anyone in particular?'

'Janin. I suggest Navarre might have to be removed – Janin mentions Kalmar. Can't he remember Lapointe thinks Kalmar is merely a thug who roughs up people causing us trouble?'

'Lapointe would not approve of Kalmar's real talent.'

'Of course not. He'd leave the *Cercle* immediately.'

'Janin is a weak sister,' Lamy agreed. 'But there is nothing to worry about – he's clever at playing up to the President. Flattering him.'

'The President is the main stumbling block to our plan. I can't forecast which way he will jump. We'd better leave now. Back to Third Corps . . .'

'I shall be away for about thirty-six hours from now on,' Lamy informed his chief while they sat in the rear of the limousine moving off down the drive.

'So long – to organize Lyons?' de Forge, ever supicious, queried.

'You ordered that Lyons should be turned into an inferno. I must check our contingent is in place, we cannot rely on that Dubois with his amateurs. Also, our contact inside Lasalle's HQ has reported a Paula Grey has met and talked to Lasalle recently. My contact thinks she is a British agent. He is providing me with a photograph he took of her secretly.'

Lamy was staring out of the window away from de Forge as he spoke.

'A job for Kalmar? The decision is yours. And you know,' de Forge went on cynically. 'I think we can cope, however long you are away.'

Chapter Twenty-One

At Park Crescent, Tweed was checking through sheets of data prior to arranging for teams to leave for France. Most of it was in his head but, meticulous, he relied on written records in case he missed one detail. He looked up at Monica. It was late at night.

'This man, Brand, seen by Newman and Paula at Grenville Grange. Later involved with Newman in that brawl at the Aldeburgh pub. Find out everything you can about him fast. I think he's Dawlish's right-hand man.'

'Needed yesterday, of course,' Monica commented.

'Or the day before that . . .'

Marler parked his Volvo station wagon beyond a bend in the country road before he reached the entrance to Dawlish's factory. As a precaution for a quick getaway he had executed a three-point turn so the Volvo faced the way they had come.

'At least the moon has gone behind clouds,' Newman remarked as he followed Marler out of the car. 'Let's hope it doesn't reappear at the wrong moment . . .'

Both men were armed. Newman carried a .38 Smith Wesson in a hip holster. Marler was relying on his Armalite rifle. Both men carried duvets folded over their left arms as, in rubber-soled shoes, they walked slowly along the road. They paused at the bend, listening, watching what they could see of the fence which guarded the establishment. No sounds, no sign of guards patrolling with dogs.

'They won't expect us to try anything twice,' Newman whispered.

'You hope,' Marler said drily.

They approached the fence and again paused, to listen, to look. There was no wind. The silence of the forest in the night was oppressive, nerve-rattling. Newman took the decision.

'Let's get on with it,' he whispered. 'Your move.'

Marler took a wooden-handled screwdriver from his pocket, walked to the gate, turned, paced out the same distance he had estimated on their previous visit. Reaching up, he pressed the metal end against wires protruding from a white plastic tube. There was a brief flash.

'Electrified wire fused,' he said to Newman, standing behind him. 'Let's hope it doesn't set off an alarm.'

'We'll soon know. Don't give them time to react . . .'

Inside the folded duvets each of them also carried an extending metal ladder, attached to the duvet over a plastic hook. Newman unhooked his ladder, extended it to its full length, perched the top rubber-covered rung halfway up the wire. Marler mounted the ladder, flung his duvet higher up over the wire. Still carrying his own duvet, he swung over the duvet-covered wire, dropped to the ground inside.

Swiftly he erected his own ladder, perched it against the inside for an easy retreat later, climbed back up, swung his own duvet over Newman's. The reporter was heavier than the slim Marler. Within seconds Newman was standing beside him. They were both inside enemy territory.

*

'Watch where you tread,' Newman warned. 'I'll lead. I have a funny feeling about this place. The lack of guards isn't natural . . .'

Part of his mind was going back to a memory over the years. When he had trained with the SAS to write an authorized article on that legendary élite of soldiers. Somehow he had survived the course. He heard the voice of the SAS trainer he only knew as Sarge. *Approaching any security area never forget the ground your feet are treading on may be the greatest danger . . .*

Newman shone his pencil flashlight, shielded with the palm of his hand, downwards where he would tread next. Behind him Marler, notorious for going his own way, was carefully placing his feet where Newman had just placed his own. Damp mushy ground with here and there a rock half-embedded. The slow trudge uphill continued. Marler wanted to call out 'For Christ's sake get a move on.' He kept his mouth shut, deterred by Newman's slow, methodical progress.

Frequently Marler glanced up, skimmed his gaze round the deserted wilderness – deserted except for one of the single-storey concrete blockhouse-like buildings. All in darkness. No sign of movement, no sound. The sheer silence was uncanny, disturbing. They were within thirty feet of one of the morgue-like buildings and this one had windows facing them like black slit-eyes. Were they being watched? Would the first indication that they had walked into a trap be a hail of bullets?

Newman held up his other hand. Marler, eyes accustomed to the dark, saw the gesture, halted. Newman was crouching down, flashlight in one hand, his other hand, also gloveless – you couldn't fire a weapon wearing gloves – feeling something on the ground. His fingers were frozen to the bone but he continued his probing as Marler crouched behind him.

'Trouble?' Marler whispered.

'Could be lethal,' Newman responded calmly.

'What is it?'

Newman patted the ground to his right gently, poked at the clumps of heather. He gestured for Marler to come forward to that piece of ground. Now they crouched along-side each other. Marler glanced at Newman, saw his expression was grim.

'Look at these,' Newman whispered.

He moved his flashlight slowly. In the beam Marler saw metal prongs protruding from tufts of grass. As the beam continued moving he counted seven prongs, protruding no more than half an inch. The metal was new. It gleamed in the glow of the flashlight.

'Anti-personnel mines,' Newman said tersely. 'Tread on one and if they're explosive you lose a leg. Maybe both legs. It's too dangerous to move any closer. We are dealing with right bastards.'

'So?'

'We go back exactly the same way we came. Again, let me lead.'

'Can we wait for thirty seconds? Before I left London the Engine Room boffins gave me a new camera. Infra-red lens and zoom. Miniaturized. I want to photograph the windows in that building . . .'

'What are you waiting for? Thirty seconds. And I'll be counting . . .'

Marler took a small oblong plastic box from his pocket, aimed the lens at the windows of the building one by one, taking six shots of each. They'd said the thing adjusted itself to light conditions – even pitch dark. Just aim, press the button. He did so.

'Finish as soon as you can,' Newman warned. 'The clicks are loud. They could have installed sensors. This lot is capable of any devilry . . .'

'Ready, Commander.'

Marler gave a mock salute after he'd slipped the camera back into his pocket. The way back seemed even more of an ordeal than their way in. Newman again checked with his flashlight – with even more care now he'd seen those sinister prongs. Marler suppressed a sigh of relief as they arrived at the fence. Newman went over first. As he followed Marler paused, stomach looped over the duvet, reached down the inner side of the fence, grabbed hold of the metal ladder. As he landed on the road side Newman, the taller, stretched up an arm, hauled down the duvets. Carrying both ladders, they walked through the silence of the night back to where the Volvo was parked.

'We didn't achieve much,' Newman mused. 'Can't win them all.'

'We won't know that until the boffins in the Engine Room have developed this film,' Marler pointed out.

They had stowed everything in the rear, were sitting in the front. Newman, who liked driving, had asked Marler if he could take over the wheel.

'Be my guest . . .'

'Listen!'

Somewhere close behind them they heard a vehicle rumbling over rough ground. The sound came from inside the fenced off area: had it been driving along the road behind them it wouldn't be making such heavy weather as they listened to its slow progress.

'We *were* spotted,' Marler remarked.

'I don't think so. We checked the car thoroughly before we got into it. No sign of someone fooling around with the engine, no bombs attached underneath. And they'd have come after us inside the wire. I'm driving off now to find a place we can hide. That vehicle will be coming this way.'

'Not the other?'

'Which leads only to Orford, a dead end? I think not. . . .'

With headlights undimmed he drove on round two bends, the beams sweeping over motionless trees. Then he swung off the road to the right up a track into the forest, made a U-turn, parked behind several trees with a view of the road between them, switched off, waited.

A heavy truck, lights undimmed, drove past the entrance to the track, heading for Snape Maltings. Newman drove after it without any headlights at all, keeping his distance without losing sight of the red tail-lights. He turned effortlessly round a bend. Marler grunted.

'Without even side lights you'll end up in the ditch.'

'No I won't. You're forgetting – I drove the Merc on this very road not long ago. I can remember.'

Marler was partially reassured. He remembered Newman had only to drive along a strange route once to be able to return along the same route without missing his way once. With the Armalite perched across his lap, he settled more comfortably.

The truck turned right along the deserted road at Tunstall, still heading for the Maltings. Beyond the collection of ancient warehouses which stages Benjamin Britten concerts in summer the truck continued through the lonely countryside towards Snape village.

'Marler, I think there's only the driver with that vehicle. I'm going to overtake, then stop him. You get out, pretend you're some kind of authority, search his truck.'

'If you say so.'

Newman switched on his headlights full, pressed down his foot, raced past the truck for a short distance. Then he slowed down, swung the wheel, positioned the Volvo across the road as a barrier, his headlights blazing. He told Marler to leave his door open so the courtesy light added to the illumination. Marler nodded, climbed out, walked back, stood on the grass verge.

The truck came on, moving at a fairish speed. Its own headlights showed up the obstacle. The truck slowed, stopped close to the Volvo. The driver was opening the door of his cab when Marler jerked it open further. He caught the driver who was falling out. Shock tactics often worked.

'Bloody 'ell! What the 'ell do you think you're up to?'

He was a runt of a man, weatherbeaten face, aged between forty and sixty, eyes bloodshot. He wore a padded windcheater, brand new. Dawlish seemed to be a stickler for his staff being well-fitted out. Marler smelt alcohol on his breath. Cognac? He waved his General & Cumbria Assurance identity card quickly in the runt's face.

'Ipswich CID. I want to look in the back of this truck. You can refuse – but then I'll report you for driving under the influence. My colleague already has your registration number.'

Marler saw a look of fear in the bloodshot eyes. Dawlish must come down heavy on staff who needed disciplining. The driver led the way to the rear. As he walked behind him Marler noticed the legend painted along the vehicle. *Dawlish Conservation.*

He further noticed as the driver took out a bunch of keys that the rear doors were fastened with two new padlocks. He waited as the driver had trouble unlocking them, then opened one door, stood back.

'You won't find no drugs if that's what you're after.'

'Just wait here. Don't try and lock me in – my colleague will make mincemeat of you . . .'

Switching on his flashlight he swept it over the contents. Stack upon stack of neatly piled canvas sacks. Each one tied up with a simple metal clasp. He removed one, shone his torch inside. It was full of Balaclava helmets. Not what he'd expected. He examined a number of other sacks at random. All full of Balaclavas. Odd. Most odd.

'What are the Balaclavas for?' he asked as he jumped to the road.

'Big fancy dress party at Christmas . . .'

Marler grabbed him by the shirt collar exposed under the windcheater. 'Don't fool with me. You could find yourself occupying a cell at Ipswich police HQ.'

'It's Gawd's truth, mate. Christmas is coming. Didn't you know? We deliver early. A big order. A palais do would be my guess. Don't know who you're dancin' with until the great moment comes. Midnight. Everyone takes off 'is or 'er mask.'

He was talking too much, giving too much detail. Marler waved a hand, waited while the driver attended to the padlocks.

'And your destination is?'

'. . . Lowestoft.'

There had been a brief hesitation before this question was answered. First, he talked too much, then he only uttered one word. As he walked back with the driver to his cab Marler slapped him on the rump. As he expected his hand hit something hard in the driver's rear trouser pocket. A flask of cognac.

'Just watch your driving,' he warned. 'And switch off those damned lights. They're blinding my colleague . . .'

Newman manoeuvred the car swiftly once Marler slipped into the passenger seat. He moved off before the truck driver could turn on his lights again. Marler lit a king-size.

'That was smart,' Newman commented. 'Getting him to

switch off his lights. That way he didn't get our registration number.'

'Which was the idea, chum. Care to guess what he is transporting at this hour?'

'Don't like guessing games.'

'You'd lose, anyway. Loads of sacks crammed with Bala-clava helmets. Just that. From the middle to the cab they were piled up to the ceiling. I estimated there were hundreds, could be thousands. Told me a cock-and-bull story – they're for a Christmas bash. And he lied about his destination. Said it was Lowestoft. Maybe we should find out just where he *is* going?'

'For once I agree with you. The next turn-off is the crossroads at Snape. A tenner to a fiver he takes the right turning along the A1094 to Aldeburgh.'

'No takers.' Marler looked thoughtful. 'Yes, the number of Balaclavas aboard that truck must run into thousands. Some fancy dress party . . .'

Well ahead of the truck, at the lonely crossroads Newman swung the Volvo on to a wide area of grass, drew in by a hedge, switched off lights, engine, waited. Marler put out his cigarette, lowered his window a fraction so he could hear.

In the silence of the dark which seemed to press down on them they heard the truck coming a long way off. Marler checked his watch by the illuminated hands. It was 1.30 a.m. A funny time to be making a delivery.

They sat very still as the truck came closer. Reaching the crossroads, headlights dipped, the driver didn't hesitate. He turned on to the A1094. But he had turned *left* – away from Aldeburgh. Newman switched on lights, started the engine, followed, his lights dimmed.

'I should have agreed that bet,' Marler said.

Once through the small village of Snape, Newman drove with only his sidelights on. The red lights of the truck were sufficient guide, and their short wait at the crossroads had brought back his night vision. The truck turned right on the A12, increased speed, proceeding north. There was no other traffic at all on the road.

'Looks as though maybe Drunky was telling the truth when he said Lowestoft,' Marler observed. 'But I'd have sworn he was lying.'

'And with things like that you have been known to be right.'

'Thanks for the unreserved vote of confidence.'

Marler found the steady drive along the main highway hypnotic as Newman drove on and on. The occasional car was appearing now, two blazing eyes rushing towards them. Newman felt it safer to switch on his own headlights dimmed. The cars rushing past them had no such consideration. Several times Newman reacted.

'Dip your headlights, you swine . . .'

The truck was moving at high speed, eating up the miles. Newman pressed his own foot down to keep up, but maintained a decent distance between the two vehicles so the truck driver wouldn't suspect he was being followed. Marler checked his watch again.

'Lord knows what time we'll arrive at the Brudenell – or whether they'll let us in at this hour.'

'I coaxed a front door key out of the girl when I registered before we set out for the factory.'

'I'm surprised *you* were able to charm her to that extent.'

'We'd stayed there recently. She now regards us as trustworthy types.'

'Oh, very trustworthy. Breaking into private property.'

He was about to light another king-size when he paused. The truck was slowing down. Still a good distance from

Lowestoft. And in the middle of nowhere. Newman also reduced speed. The truck's right-hand indicator light was flashing, warning it was about to turn off the highway. Newman slowed even more, glanced in his rear-view mirror. Nothing behind him for miles. The truck turned down a side road leading east towards the sea.

Newman pulled in to the side. His face was like stone as he leaned forward, staring at the signpost pointing to the truck's destination. Just one word.

Dunwich.

Chapter Twenty-Two

The following day at the Brudenell, Paula was restless and impatient. She felt she had to keep her word to Tweed – not to stray until she had contacted Newman. Easier said than done. The receptionist had told her they were staying at the hotel, had discreetly given her their room numbers. After all, she had seen them together during their recent visit: Newman and Marler.

Paula took the elevator to both rooms. And met the same message hanging from the door handles of both rooms. *Please Do Not Disturb.* Frustrated, she went to her own room, put on her suede coat and a cashmere scarf. It was a raw, bitter day outside but she felt trapped indoors. The first person she encountered when she stepped out of the elevator on the ground floor was Lieutenant Berthier, masquerading as James Sanders, dark-haired and complete with tinted glasses. He wore a windcheater, heavy grey slacks, and a polo-necked sweater. His feet were shod in trainers.

'Hello, Mr Sanders,' she said quickly. 'Making any contacts you might sell marine parts to?'

'The weather doesn't help – most people are keeping their heads down. You're going for a walk? I'm after a bite of fresh air myself. Along the promenade?'

'That will be bracing.'

She stepped out of the door he opened for her leading direct to the promenade. Berthier might let something slip and it was something to do until Newman decided to rise and shine. She almost made a reference to his use of the word 'bite', certain he had meant 'bit', but the first word was perfect for the weather. She decided not to say anything – he might think she'd spotted an error in his English.

'Later I could drive you somewhere nice for lunch,' he suggested.

'That's generous of you, but I have to stay near the hotel for a phone message,' she lied easily.

Berthier walked on the seaward side, protecting her from the storm which was blowing up. Mountainous waves heaved their bulk against the front, splashing spume on to the promenade. Paula noticed several of the ancient terrace houses had shutters closed over their basement windows. In some cases the windows had been blocked up. When the North Sea really raged it must inundate the promenade, lapping against the basements. She walked leaning into the force of the wind. Berthier took her arm.

'Don't want you blown over.'

'Why don't you try to contact Lord Dane Dawlish?'

She felt his grip on her arm tighten for a second when she'd asked the question. He relaxed his hold quickly.

'Why should I get in touch with him?' he asked.

'I'd have thought your research would have turned up the fact he's a likely prospect. He has a huge catamaran called the *Steel Vulture*. He might be a good customer.'

'I'll think about it.'

'Do more than that,' she pressed him. 'He lives not far away. At Iken.'

'Where's that?'

All the wrong answers, she thought. In his role as a salesman she felt sure his research would be meticulous. He'd hardly have missed Dawlish.

'Up the River Alde on the way to Snape Maltings. You know the strange course the river follows,' she prodded.

'I'm a Yellow Pages man myself. Let's call in at the Cross Keys for some coffee. It's the nicest pub in the town.'

'Good idea.'

She answered automatically. Once she had liked Aldeburgh as a comfortable refuge away from the world. Now her main image of the place was a night of horror when masked men with rifles, hardly human, had pursued Karin and herself like a pack of wolves hunting their prey. She recalled what they – one of them – had done to Karin. *Stop it!* she told herself.

'We're nearly there.'

Berthier checked his watch as he led her away from the promenade into the garden leading to the rear entrance.

Paula was relieved to get away from the front. She had been lucky: no ruinous salt water had splashed on her precious suede coat.

'This table suit you?' Berthier suggested. 'It's near the serving counter. Just coffee?'

He ushered her to a chair, went over to the counter to give his order. It was less cold in the Cross Keys but Paula kept her coat on. She had just noticed who was sitting at the large table close to hers.

Five tough-looking men wearing pea-jackets. Half-facing her was the wide-shouldered heavy-set Brand. She looked away, saw the waitress behind the counter staring at him. Brand turned, stared back at the girl. She took a deep breath, spoke sharply.

'I thought I told you not to come back.'

'It's all right, he's with me . . .'

Lord Dawlish appeared round a corner from the room at the front. Hatless, he was clad in a British warm, the collar turned up. He joined the five men, sitting in a chair which Paula guessed had been kept for him. She was beginning to worry: the atmosphere had become menacing.

No one was speaking at the table occupied by Dawlish. The seamen-types were watching her. She tilted her chin defiantly, looked up at the low oak-beamed ceiling, which seemed to press down on her. Dark oak. The tables, uncovered, were made of the same dark oak. She remembered the pub on a previous trip as a comfortable welcoming place. It was the occupants who had changed the atmosphere.

Berthier returned to her table, the waitress served the coffee. She looked at Berthier who sat facing her. He was gazing straight at her, saying nothing, eyes invisible behind the tinted lenses. He wasn't helping at all; she thought as she sipped the excellent coffee. He just kept looking at her, damn him.

Then she remembered he'd checked his watch before they'd entered the place. Was this a prearranged rendezvous? Before going up to her room at the Brudenell to fetch her coat she'd called out to the receptionist that she was going for a walk. Berthier could have been within earshot.

'Not the weather for a trip on the Cat,' Dawlish called out to her. 'You haven't forgotten my offer, my dear?'

One of the men at his table sniggered. She placed her cup carefully back in the saucer, her expression frozen. She stared at Dawlish.

'I may have the time, I may not,' she said abruptly.

Dawlish tossed back half the double Scotch he'd ordered. He held on to the glass as he spoke in a mocking tone.

'It would be a unique experience. A day – and a night – aboard the Cat.'

One of the men gave a braying laugh, cut it short when Dawlish glanced at him. Paula was convinced she was being subjected to calculated pressure. To run her out of Aldeburgh? Berthier, immobile as a statue, continued to stare at her from behind his bloody glasses. A man walked slowly into the pub from the rear entrance.

Tall, so tall his hatless head almost touched the beams, he wore a trench coat, which showed damp patches. He must have walked along the promenade from the Brudenell. He wore no gloves on his large hands.

Victor Rosewater paused, looked at Paula, Berthier, and then at the nearby table, his strong face showing no particular expression. But now there was complete silence as he remained standing there.

'Paula, you look as though you've had enough of this place. Care to come for a stroll?'

'Who asked you to interfere . . .' Brand began.

Rosewater turned his gaze on the heavy-set man. He said nothing and Brand subsided in mid-sentence. No one seemed anxious to argue any more, to mix it with the newcomer.

'Yes, Victor,' Paula said quickly, standing up. 'I have had enough of it. I'd welcome a stroll.' She looked at Berthier. 'Thank you for the coffee . . .'

Rosewater escorted her through the pub to the front exit on to the street away from the front. They began walking back along narrow streets parallel to the front and lined with quaint houses.

'This way,' Rosewater remarked, 'you won't get that lovely suede coat splashed by salt water. As you can see from my trench coat the waves are now crashing over on to the prom.'

'Thank you.'

And he was showing consideration which never entered the head of Berthier, she thought. She looked up at him curiously.

'How did you know I just wanted to get to hell out of that place?'

He smiled. 'I'm a bit sensitive to atmospheres. Seemed you were uncomfortable. That the reason could have been the people in the place. A rum bunch, I thought. And the chap you were with didn't seem to be helping all that much.'

'He says that he's a salesman of marine spare parts – that his name is James Sanders.'

She felt it might be important to put Rosewater on his guard against Berthier. She'd thought about it for a split second before saying anything. Rosewater was on to it instantly.

'*Says?* You sound as though you don't believe his name or his way of earning a living.'

Rosewater had slowed down. Paula had long legs but he had much longer: he had realized she was hurrying to keep up. Not only did he seem to have all his marbles: he was considerate in little ways.

'I don't,' she replied. 'I suspect he's some kind of con man. I could be completely wrong.'

Despite the rapport between them, Paula had no intention of revealing information which Tweed would regard as highly confidential. They walked in silence for a minute and neither seemed to feel compelled to talk. Rosewater took hold of her elbow, guided her down a narrow thoroughfare into the High Street.

'Where are we going?' she asked.

'You can get quite a good lunch at a place called the Captain's Table. It's quiet – at this time of the year – the service is good, the food quite edible.'

'Sounds a marvellous idea . . .'

Anything to get away from the atmosphere which had hung like a dark cloud over the Cross Keys. Somehow she equated it with the dreadful night when Karin had died. Why? She wasn't sure.

The Captain's Table was a small restaurant, an oblong room with just a few tables beautifully laid for lunch. Paula

235

thought it was more like a room in someone's home than a restaurant. A distinguished-looking man welcomed them, escorted them to a window table overlooking the High Street, handed them menus and left them alone.

'That man in a British warm,' Rosewater began, 'isn't he Lord Dawlish? I've seen his pictures in the magazines.'

'Yes. Lord Dane Dawlish. Millionaire. Supermarket and armaments king.'

'He was talking to you when I came in. Said something about a cat. You know him?'

'Yes . . .' She explained how she had interviewed Dawlish, how he had shown her the extraordinary diorama, that the Cat was a catamaran, a big job. She left out any reference to the presence of Newman and Marler at the shoot, to the fact the Dawlish had come on strong with her.

'And those men with him,' Rosewater went on as he closed the menu, 'a bunch of roughnecks if ever I saw one. Who are they?'

'I recognized two of them from my visit to Grenville Grange. They're members of Dawlish's staff.'

'Crewmen from the *Steel Vulture*?' Rosewater suggested. 'Incidentally, I'm having the roast lamb. I had it the other day and it was good.'

'I'm having the same.' She paused, smiled. 'How come you turned up at the Cross Keys at just the right moment?'

'I followed you and that chap from the hotel,' he said frankly. 'I didn't too much like the look of him. I'd seen him the night before in the bar. Why does he wear those dark glasses all the time?'

'He says he has weak eyes, that daylight hurts them. I think that was very sweet of you – to act as my protector. And your mind must still be full of Karin,' she said gently. 'Is that why you're still here? In the hope of finding a clue as to who did it?'

'Something like that,' he said in his reserved manner. He gave Paula the impression of a man under iron self-control. Almost superhuman endurance. Like a bloodhound, she thought, following the scent.

'These interviews you do for women's magazines,' he said after their meal had been served. 'Is it a sideline? Is your main work with Tweed's company?'

'Yes, Tweed is my boss. I'm his personal assistant – I do a lot of the confidential research for insurance cases,' she chattered on blithely. 'That's my main line of work. It's confidential, so I can't talk about it much.'

After a satisfying meal washed down with a bottle of Chablis – Rosewater found out she didn't like red wine – he escorted her back to the hotel. There was no rain but an army of low clouds like grey smoke was scudding inland, seeming to skim the rooftops. The wind had increased in force, hurtling down the High Street like air through a wind tunnel. Paula felt she might be swept off her feet. As though guessing her state of anxiety, Rosewater slipped a firm arm round her waist.

'We don't want you blown out to sea,' he joked. 'And the met forecast is for worse to come. Gales up to eighty miles an hour tonight . . .'

He still had his arm round her waist as they went inside the hotel, climbed the stairs, ran smack into Newman and Marler in the hall. Rosewater released her, said he'd enjoyed her company, and vanished inside the elevator.

'So you haven't been lonely,' Newman observed, his expression grim.

'You object?' Paula flared up, mistaking the reason for his expression.

'No. We have something to tell you. *Dunwich* . . .'

*

Major Lamy left the British Airways aircraft which had flown him from Charles de Gaulle Airport in Paris to Heathrow.

He had checked that the troops were in place in Lyons. From there he had flown to Paris by Air Inter. Waiting for his flight to London, he had phoned an obscure British car hire firm, ordered a Rover in the name of William Prendergast. The forged passport in the same name was the one he presented to Passport Control. With a strong following tail wind the flight had taken only forty-five minutes.

Carrying the small case he had taken aboard the plane, Lamy left Passport Control behind and walked towards the Customs exit. He wore a British business suit under a Burberry raincoat and his shoes were also British. He was the archetype of an Englishman back from abroad.

Lamy didn't notice in the crowd of passengers a tall, fair-haired man standing watching the flight arrivals. Jim Corcoran, a friend of Tweed's and Chief Security Officer, checked one of the small photos rushed to him from Park Crescent by motorcycle courier. He looked at the back of the photo. Major Jules Lamy.

Corcoran followed Lamy, keeping a certain distance behind him. He noticed Lamy bypassed the carousels where passengers were already waiting resignedly for their suitcases to appear one day. He followed Lamy through the *Nothing To Declare* Customs aisle.

Lamy increased his pace as he left the Customs area. Several drivers stood behind a barrier holding up cards with names. *William Prendergast.* Lamy went up to the girl holding up that name. Corcoran could have stopped him immediately, charged him with travelling on a false passport – unless he'd used his real name at Passport Control. But the request made by Tweed's assistant, Monica, had been specific.

Corcoran followed Lamy and the girl to the short-term car park. Up the ramp, across the bridge, inside the park. He took out his own car keys, twirling them as he followed the couple. The car Lamy climbed inside was a Rover – after he had paid the girl with a sheaf of banknotes and dealt with the formalities. Corcoran memorized the registration number, tried to follow the girl, who wasn't wearing a uniform, but she vanished.

When the Rover had driven off Corcoran ran back to his office. Locking the door, he dialled Monica's number, hoping to speak to Tweed.

'He's not here, Jim,' Monica said quickly. 'He had to dash off somewhere. Have you any news?'

'Sounds like Tweed – dashing off. Yes, one of your subjects in the photos just arrived aboard a BA flight from Paris. Travelling under the name William Prendergast in a hired Rover, registration . . . Major Lamy.'

Monica thanked him, broke the connection, was working non-stop for the next hour. She phoned a contact at Vehicle Registration, Swansea, gave him the number and the code confirming she was SIS. Vehicle Registration reacted with almost unique speed, phoning her back in ten minutes, giving her the name and address of the car hire firm in London. She didn't make the mistake of calling the company direct. Instead she phoned another contact at Special Branch, gave him the data, stressed how urgent it was. Inside three-quarters of an hour Special Branch called her back.

'A William Prendergast hired the Rover, phoned early this afternoon. He had to give the destination he was taking it to.'

'Go on, don't tease me, Martin,' Monica pleaded.

'Aldeburgh, Suffolk . . .'

*

'Look, Brand, you've got to handle this job right. No slip-ups,' Dawlish snapped.

'Have I slipped up yet?' growled Brand, stirring his bulk in the carver chair in the living room of Grenville Grange. 'I am your right-hand man, remember?'

'At the moment,' Dawlish rapped back. 'But there's always a first time for a slip-up. Make sure this isn't it.'

'The job will be handled professionally,' Brand told him curtly.

'Make sure it is. Tonight.'

Approaching Aldeburgh, Major Lamy slowed down. He had lost count of the number of times he had checked to make sure he was not being followed. In mid-afternoon the traffic had been light once he had left London behind, which had helped.

He had kept within all the speed limits: he couldn't afford the risk of being stopped by a police patrol car. Once again he checked in his rear-view mirror. Nothing. Shortly afterwards he drove into the courtyard of a hotel on the outskirts of Aldeburgh.

Carrying his small case, he entered the hotel, registered as William Prendergast with a fictitious London address. He had also phoned the hotel from Paris to make the reservation with no reference to where he was calling from.

He sneezed several times behind the scarf pulled up over his face. He wore a deerstalker hat pulled down across his forehead.

'Your room is ready, Mr Prendergast,' the receptionist informed him. 'One night, I think you said?'

'Yes. I'll pay in advance now for the room and breakfast,' Lamy said. 'I may have to leave early tomorrow morning,' he continued, in English.

He paid in cash and she handed him the receipted bill. He sneezed again as he stooped to pick up his case.

'You seem to have a bad cold, sir,' she sympathized.

Inside his bedroom he whipped off the scarf, no longer bothering to fake a sneeze. He checked his watch. He was a careful organizer. Plenty of time to do a recce of the area. He took from his breast pocket an envelope, extracted from it the photograph he had been handed at Charles de Gaulle Airport. The envelope had been passed to him by his informant inside Lasalle's Paris HQ in rue des Saussaies. It was a photo of Paula Grey.

Chapter Twenty-Three

Kalmar sat in the car in the public car park close to the Brudenell Hotel. No other vehicle was in sight. It was supposed to be daylight but the low storm clouds sweeping across the sky made it seem more like night.

He could hear the *thump*! of giant waves against the high rampart extending south along the coast beyond the hotel. No work was going on but huge cranes and Portacabins showed the artificial sea defences were being strengthened. He clasped his gloved hands as he saw spray rising like mist above the rampart, carried over to the marshes by the fury of the gale.

He flexed his strong fingers. You just couldn't afford to leave a witness alive. And there had been one witness to the strangling of Karin Rosewater. He thought about the witness, about her walking, talking, remembering. Then *talking* . . .

The grip of his fingers tightened. He imagined grasping her by the throat, carefully pressing his thumbs into her wind-pipe. Her eyes starting out of her head as he was the last person she'd ever see in this world.

He had decided. At the earliest opportunity. Tonight. He wouldn't be paid a Swiss franc on top of the fat fee he'd already collected for the Karin job. But you just couldn't afford to leave a witness alive.

*

Paula sat in her room with Newman and Marler. Newman had been giving her a terse account of the trip to the armaments factory in the middle of the night. He went on to describe how they had followed the truck after Marler had discovered its contents. She made her first comment.

'Who would need thousands of Balaclavas?'

'You heard what I told you about my Bordeaux trip,' he snapped. Perched on her bed she stared at him, hurt by his brusque rejoinder. He seemed edgy. 'Remember that riot I watched,' Newman went on. 'It was pretty savage stuff. And the mob was pretty well organized. *And* I didn't see one without a Balaclava mask to avoid identification. Now there's been a much bigger riot in Lyons. Haven't you seen the pictures in the papers? Every man taking part in that orgy of violence is wearing a Balaclava. My bet is to hide the fact they're troops from de Forge's Corps.'

'I still don't follow this Dunwich puzzle,' she protested. 'Just supposing they are de Forge's men, he could obtain Balaclavas in France . . .'

'And be sure the supplier – or one of his workers – wouldn't report the delivery to the DST? The police?'

'Oh, you mean . . .'

'I mean,' he overrode her, 'that with the mobs growing larger they may need a lot more Balaclavas. It would be more secure if they brought them in from abroad in secrecy. Hence that truck on the way to Dunwich. You saw the *Steel Vulture* off Dunwich the day you and Karin went scuba diving.'

'So the *Vulture* could be the means of transporting the Balaclavas to de Forge – via Arcachon?'

Newman grinned. 'Now you're catching on.'

'Why didn't the two of you follow the truck all the way to Dunwich, see where it stopped?'

'Because,' Newman explained, 'we hadn't alerted their

driver up to that point. You know the side road to Dunwich is a narrow country road. I didn't want us to risk being spotted. So we came back here.'

'I see.' Paula put her hands on her hips, stretched. 'Bob, you seem irked with me, irritable. Why?'

'Because you're back here again. Where Karin was murdered. I don't like it. Someone might think of you as a witness. The killer could still be hanging around in the vicinity.'

'I doubt that's at all feasible. He'll be long gone.'

Newman shrugged. 'Please yourself.'

'I usually do – like you. Listen to who's talking.'

Marler, sensing the start of verbal warfare, broke in for the first time. He had been leaning against a wall, watching and listening.

'If I could get a word in edgeways, I think I'd like to leave, get back to Park Crescent. I'm anxious for the little men in the Engine Room to develop that film I took of the laboratory at Dawlish's factory in the forest. You don't mind if I drive my own Volvo back, do you, Newman?'

'And how am I supposed to get back tomorrow? Swim? In case you didn't know, the trains stopped coming here quite a few years ago.'

'You can drive me back, Bob,' Paula said quickly. 'I came in Tweed's Escort.'

She was beginning to feel contrite. Newman had been brusque only because he was worried about her. Marler waved a hand – as much as to say, 'You've got transport, chum,' and left the room.

'I think I'm going for a walk,' Newman said when they were alone. 'You're right, I am edgy. Maybe it's the storm they predicted for tonight. Want to come with me?'

'I'd love to, but I'm feeling bushed. Mind if I cry off and have a bath instead?'

'I could stay and scrub your back for you, but maybe I'll take that walk instead. Wallow . . .'

Left on her own, Paula went into the bathroom, turned on the taps. Her excuse had been a bit of a white lie. Earlier she had phoned Jean Burgoyne and they'd agreed to have drinks together that evening at the home of Jean's uncle, Admiralty House. Jean had proved her efficiency: while Paula was enduring the unpleasantness at the Cross Keys she had left an envelope at reception with a local map marking the position of the house perched on the hill behind the main part of the town.

Paula had liked Jean when they'd chatted in the bar at the Brudenell during her previous visit. During that short conversation a friendship had sprung up between the two women.

But that wasn't Paula's real motive in contacting her. She had not forgotten that Burgoyne was General de Forge's mistress. She hoped to guide the subject round to that delicate subject in the hope of extracting information for Tweed.

She followed Newman's advice and wallowed in her bath, gradually feeling the tension drain out of her body. In her mind she played with the problem of what to wear for the occasion. Eventually she decided on a fine wool print dress with a mandarin collar and a wide belt. She favoured wide belts: they emphasized her slim waist.

'So that's settled,' she said to herself as she stood up and towelled herself vigorously. 'And combined with my suede coat I should be warm.'

The temperature was dropping outside rapidly according to the weather forecast. A good job it was only a short drive. Jean had offered to collect her but she'd evaded the offer. Paula, independent, liked to have her own transport.

Dressed for the occasion, she went down in the elevator to see the receptionist.

COLIN FORBES

'I'll be going out about six,' she told her. 'I expect to be back about eight. Could you let the dining room know? I'll be as hungry as a horse when I return. The weather . . .'

'And it's going to get worse,' a man's voice said behind her. She recognized Berthier's husky tone. 'Winds up to eighty miles an hour.'

'Sounds lovely,' she replied. 'Excuse me, I'm expecting a phone call.'

She slipped into the elevator, pressed the button, sighed with relief as it moved upwards. She'd had enough of Berthier for one day. Damn it, she reminded herself, I must get into the mental habit of thinking of him as *James Sanders*. Otherwise I'm going to put my foot in it.

She locked her bedroom door, kicked off her high-heeled shoes, reminded herself of something else – to wear sensible shoes when she was driving to Admiralty House. She was expecting no phone call and she sat in a chair, picked up her paperback of Tolstoy's *War and Peace*, determined to finish the huge tome. She had about half an hour before it would be time to leave to visit Jean.

In the bar on the ground floor Brand glanced at his watch. He was drinking Scotch with water – he needed a clear head tonight. From where he sat he had seen Paula enter the elevator. He guessed from her dress that she could be going out somewhere for the evening.

Of course she could be dining in the hotel, but Brand didn't think so. Despite his coarse manner Brand was surprisingly sensitive to social nuances. He'd have bet a month's fat salary that within the hour she'd leave the hotel.

Unlike his working clothes worn during the morning at the Cross Keys, he was now dressed in a smart, heavy grey suit tailored to allow his thick arms easy movement. On a

246

chair next to his he'd placed his motoring gloves. The last thing he needed tonight was company at this moment.

Tweed was moving at high speed across Suffolk behind the wheel of Newman's Mercedes 280E, headlights sweeping in the night over hedges lining the road. The wind battered the side of the one and a half tons of car, threatening to blow it off the road.

Tweed kept a firm grip on the wheel, indifferent to the grim weather conditions, driving automatically, his mind full of anxiety. He was heading for Aldeburgh, Monica had phoned the Brudenell to book him a room, and he was determined to get there as fast as possible.

He had Paula on his mind. His instinct that she was in danger was strong. He couldn't have explained why his earlier doubts had surfaced into fear – but he did know that when he'd had this instinctive feeling of trouble before it had always proved to be right.

He had tried to reach her on the phone at lunchtime but the receptionist at the Brudenell had told him she was out somewhere. He had decided against leaving a message: he might be alarming her for nothing.

Then Newman's car had been returned by one of Robles' staff. The veterinary pathologist had phoned him the report from Porton Down – and that had not made reassuring news. The worst possible case, had been the verdict.

It was the return of Newman's car which had made Tweed take one of his lightning decisions – that he would drive it to Aldeburgh himself. Before leaving London Newman had phoned from his flat, had told Tweed he'd be staying at the Brudenell for two days and nights.

There another reason for Tweed's urgent flight from London. He wanted to see for himself the scene of the crime where Karin Rosewater had been murdered. You could listen to other people's detailed accounts of the landscape, but there was nothing like checking it for yourself. He looked at the clock on the dashboard, calculated he'd arrive in time to explore the marshes at about the same hour when the murder had been committed. After making sure Paula was all right . . .

Paula, wearing her suede coat, her scarf wrapped round her head against the wind, stepped out of the elevator, handed her key to the receptionist, told her she was driving to see a friend in Aldeburgh.

It was black as pitch outside the front entrance. She walked quickly to the Ford Escort, parked in a slot up against the hotel wall. Climbing behind the wheel, she slipped her key into the ignition, turned it. Nothing happened. Just a discouraging grunt. She tried again and again to start the engine. Nothing. She looked up as a shadowy figure appeared beyond her side window. Lieutenant Berth . . . No, *James Sanders*.

'Won't she behave?' he asked. 'Let me try.'

She hesitated, thought: I'm just outside the hotel. Getting out, she stood while he slipped behind the wheel and fiddled with the ignition. He tried six times and shook his head.

'Probably the battery is dead. You were going for a long drive?'

'No, only local. To an address in Aldeburgh.'

She wished she hadn't reacted so quickly as he climbed out. He'd wound up the window and now he closed the door.

'That's my Saab parked next to your car. I'll drive you wherever you want to go. Nothing else to do.'

Again she hesitated. She had tapped on Newman's door before coming down. No reply. Obviously he was still out walking: he could walk for miles when in the mood. And Marler had gone back to London. Paula made a virtue of punctuality and it was only a short drive.

'I have a map showing where I'm going. Admiralty House is the name. It's marked with a cross . . .'

Berthier took the map as he sat behind the wheel, left his door open, pretended to study the map. He knew damn well where he was going. Only recently he'd been outside Admiralty House when he'd followed Jean Burgoyne.

Paula again hesitated before getting into the front passenger seat. I can cope with him if I have to, she thought, and slipped into the seat. Berthier handed back the map.

'I've got the route. As you said, it's very local . . .'

She fastened her seat belt and he drove off. She adjusted her shoulder bag, wished she was carrying her .32 Browning automatic, but she wasn't. Relax, for Pete's sake.

He drove along the deserted High Street, turned left up the curving hill past houses which seemed to have no lights. Paula was surprised as they ascended how dark the back road was. Expensive houses at the end of long drives but not the sort of place she'd want to live.

Close to the entrance to Admiralty House, where the road levelled out at the summit, Berthier swung the car on to the grass verge. He switched off the engine, turned to her.

'I've admired you ever since we met,' he began. 'You're a very attractive woman.'

'Thank you . . .'

She unfastened her seat belt quickly. His strong left hand wrapped itself round her neck, his right hand slipped under her coat, felt the dress, slipped under that. He'd released his own safety belt and was leaning over to her, pulling her towards him. She raised her right hand, free of the glove she'd slipped off, reached for his face with her hard nails.

'Leave me alone or I'll mark you for life . . .'

'Gutsy? I like that in a girl.'

His grip increased on the back of her neck. Her nails dug into his face without drawing blood. Suddenly her hand left his face, she rammed the point of her elbow against his Adam's apple. He spluttered, released the grip on her neck, his other hand sliding out from under her coat. Her left hand opened the door, her right grabbed the loose glove, she jumped out on to the mushy grass. She spoke quickly before slamming the door shut, her tone contemptuous.

'Thank you so much for the lift, Mr Sanders. I won't be needing transport back . . .'

Hurrying along the verge, she turned into the entrance to Admiralty House. Walking along the drive she saw the curtains were pulled back from an inviting living room well illuminated. Jean Burgoyne saw her coming, met her at the door.

'Welcome to the Brigadier's den . . .'

Paula went inside. She'd already decided not to say anything about the episode with Berthier. Later she would walk home. It wasn't all that far.

Chapter Twenty-Four

Tweed found two car slots available up against the wall of the Brudenell when he arrived. Plenty of space to park Newman's large Mercedes. He collected his small case off the front passenger seat, the special walking stick devised for him by the Engine Room, got out into the icy night, locked the car, walked into the hotel.

'Yes, Mr Tweed, we have a room reserved for you. The same room you occupied recently,' the receptionist assured him. 'And a number for you to phone urgently as soon as you arrive.'

'Thank you. I'll make the call from my room . . .'

Inside the large room with windows overlooking the front he threw his Burberry on to the bed. The North Sea was making more noise than it had last time. The windows were closed but he could hear the crash of countless tons of water against the promenade.

Dumping his case on the floor, propping the stick by the wall, he opened the folded slip. Monica's number. Something had happened. He picked up the phone, dialled.

'Tweed here, Monica. I am speaking from my hotel room,' he said rapidly, warning her.

'I understand.' A brief pause. 'The *brand* product was originally used in diving operations – from a North Sea oil rig. It was found to be defective – its use was discontinued under a cloud. Later it was used by bodyguards employed by two security firms. Again it was thought to be defective

– nothing proved. It was then taken up by a firm of qualified accountants. Latest development, held in high regard by a firm at Dawlish Warren in Devon. End story.'

'Thank you for doing such a good job.'

'Don't go. There's more. Rather sensitive, could be urgent.'

'Something affecting my business trip here . . .?' Tweed was talking rapidly. He raised his voice suddenly. 'Operator! This is a bad line. Can you do something about it?' He listened for the click telling him someone was listening in. No click. His acute hearing waited for a sharp intake of breath. Nothing. No one was listening in. 'Go ahead, Monica.'

'Lasalle called. He's worried.'

'About what?'

'His informant at Third Corps tells him Sergeant Rey has disappeared. Lasalle thinks it might be an ominous development.'

'Lasalle is right.'

'There's more. Corcoran phoned from Heathrow. Major Lamy flew in a few hours ago – just after you left. No doubt about it. Travelling as William Prendergast. You won't believe this.'

'Try me.'

'He left Heathrow in a hired car he drove himself, a Rover. On his way to Aldeburgh. I tracked him myself. That's all.'

'It's enough,' Tweed said grimly. 'Thanks again. Don't hesitate to call me with any more news. Get some rest . . .'

Tweed put down the phone, began pacing the room. Brand, Dawlish's right-hand man, had originally been a diver for an oil rig. It sounded as though he'd been mixed up in something shady. Sabotage? Later he'd been a bodyguard for two separate firms – and dismissed from both. Had he already become a spy for Dawlish? And Monica's reference to the tiny coastal resort of Dawlish Warren had been clever. She was telling him he'd moved from the two security firms straight into Dawlish's employ. The reference to qualified accountant was strange – it sounded as though Brand had been one, which meant he was far more than just a thug running other thugs. Tweed continued pacing, thinking about the Lasalle data.

Sergeant Rey, de Forge's boobytrap specialist, had vanished from Third Corps GHQ. Where could Rey be? What mission might he be engaged on? Of course, he could be on leave. But Tweed didn't think so. De Forge wouldn't be sending anyone on leave now the momentum of his campaign was building up.

Even more intriguing – possibly more ominous – Lamy secretly visiting Aldeburgh. That *was* another positive link between Suffolk and France. One Tweed didn't like at all.

He decided he must find Paula at once. Throwing on his Burberry, picking up his walking stick, he left the room, avoided the elevator, ran down the staircase, went to Reception.

'I'm looking for my friend, Paula Grey,' he told the girl behind the desk.

'Oh, she drove off a little while ago. She is visiting someone in Aldeburgh.'

'Go by herself?'

'Yes . . .'

'Do you know where she went? I have to get in touch with her urgently because of that phone message,' he improvised.

'I'm sorry, I have no idea . . .'

'Are Newman and Marler in the hotel?'

'No.' The girl was surprised by the bombardment, by the sense of urgency Tweed generated. 'Mr Marler left to go back to London. Mr Newman is out for a walk.'

'Thank you.'

Tweed decided he'd do the job he'd come to do – to take his mind off his anxiety. He walked out of the back entrance, passed Newman's Merc, hurried across the car park on to the gravel road. He carried the stick in his right hand, a flashlight in his left hand. It was so dark he needed the beam to find his way.

Tweed had total recall of important conversations. He was able to remember exactly the route Paula, Newman, and Rosewater had followed when the latter had unearthed the signet ring. Major Lamy's? Apparently.

Passing an old shed set back from the gravel road he noted the sign. *Boat Storage.* He was close to where the path led down off the road on to the marshes. The powerful beam focused on a narrow footpath leading away from the road, down on to the marshes. This was it. He slithered agilely down it on to level, soggy ground. The wind blew his hair all over the place but he didn't notice: he was totally concentrating on following the same route.

The beam showed him the footpath running parallel to the gravel road above. He walked rapidly, holding the stick as a soldier might hold a rifle midway along its length. He switched off the flashlight and stood still, waiting for his night vision to return. Ahead he saw the dark silhouette of a high bank. The dyke which ran alongside the harbour.

Switching on the flashlight again he came to the point where the footpath forked – one fork leading back up to the road, the other up to the dyke. He paused. Easy to go wrong here. He climbed the path to the ridge of the dyke, saw where the footpath followed the crest of the dyke east. The harbour below it on his left, the marshes below him on his right. This was correct.

He moved rapidly along the tricky path. Stopping for a moment, he swivelled his beam across the harbour, saw boats swathed in blue plastic covers like huge blue eggs. Their masts rocked wildly, then moved more slowly. The wind had dropped suddenly. He heard a strange noise. He changed his grip on the stick so he held it by the handle.

The walking stick was a weapon. The tip was weighted. One blow could crack a man's skull. But there was more to it. Under the handle was a button. Press the button and a two-inch steel spike projected. It was *not* a sword stick, but one jab and an attacker would be injured. It was not Tweed's habit to carry weapons but Aldeburgh was becoming a dangerous place – the marshes possibly even more dangerous. To retract the spike he only had to press the button a second time. Now he recognized the weird sound. The twanging of metal wires against the metal masts of boats. He walked on.

He was aiming his flashlight down the slope to his left now. He must be near the place where the trio had discovered the relic of the craft where Karin Rosewater had died. The beam swept over a creek of stagnant water, swept back a fraction.

The craft, staves showing like ribs of some animal, was lying upside down at the edge of the creek. This was where the signet ring had been discovered. Tweed made his way down the awkward slope, keeping his balance easily. He stood on a firm tuft of grass encircled with ooze, slowly played his torch over the area inch by inch. For a minute he crouched down, examining carefully the messy terrain. His gloved hand poked at the grass, felt its sogginess give way under his pressure.

He sighed, stood up, scrambled back to the summit of

the dyke. It had all been as he expected to find it – down to the last detail.

Stooping against the wind which blew up suddenly with greater force he hurried back along the dyke, followed the same route back to the Brudenell. Inside, he made himself speak casually to the receptionist.

'Has Miss Grey returned yet?'

'Not yet.'

Tweed returned to his room, full of foreboding.

Jean Burgoyne was a lively hostess. Dressed in a form-fitting green dress, she also wore a wide belt round her slim waist. Her dress stopped just above her knees, revealing her shapely legs clad in dark green tights. Her long thick mane of golden hair glistened under the lights of the chandeliers in the living room. Quite a girl, Paula thought.

She was seated in a comfortable armchair close to a blazing log fire. Jean sat in a hard-backed chair next to her, legs crossed, one high heel dangling. Both women were holding glasses of champagne.

'Paula, this is my uncle, Brigadier Burgoyne,' she introduced as a man entered the room.

The Brigadier was small, well-padded under his velvet smoking-jacket. His head was egg-shaped, bald on top with strands of white hair brushed carefully on either side. He had a ruddy complexion and looked more like a man in his mid sixties than eighty.

'Pleased to meet you, Miss Grey,' he said formally, bending to shake her hand. 'Jean has told me quite a lot about you. But I can see with my own eyes you're a woman of resource. Like that . . .'

He had walked briskly to a sideboard, pouring himself a

glass of port from a decanter, when Paula asked the question. For a fraction of a second he stopped pouring – so briefly only Paula's sharp eyes caught it.

'I understand, Brigadier, you were with Military Intelligence.'

'Oh, all that's long behind me . . .' He glanced swiftly at Jean, switched his gaze to Paula, raised his glass. 'Your good health.' He sipped the port, remained standing by the sideboard.

'You must miss that work,' Paula continued, determined to stay with the subject. 'Especially as there is so much scope for it now. France is a good example. We need to know exactly what is going on over there – at the Third Corps particularly.'

The Brigadier stood quite still. His eyes blinked once. Like an owl. He looked rather like an owl, Paula was thinking.

'I'm rather out of touch these days.' Burgoyne was looking vague, which he hadn't before. 'I wonder if you'd think me very rude if I went to my study upstairs? I've work on some legal papers which need my attention. Just came down to say how do you do. Hope you'll come back to see us again. Don't mind my absence. Jean stays up all hours . . .'

He shuffled out of the room. A very different movement from the quick tread when he'd entered. You're acting, you sly old thing, Paula thought.

'He tires quickly,' Jean explained. 'He liked you – I could tell.'

'But *you* know Third Corps, don't you?'

Jean drank the rest of her champagne quickly, offered more to Paula, who refused, then filled her own glass again. She pushed a wave of blonde hair back over her shoulder, watched Paula over the rim of her glass as she spoke.

'You seem to be very well informed.'

'Don't mind me, I'm a journalist. It's my job. And I promised – no interview.'

'I do know General de Forge,' Jean said slowly after drinking more champagne. Her sleeve touched the ice bucket standing by her side. She jerked it away. 'It is cold.' She chuckled, a pleasant lilting sound. 'I regard him as a friend. Very dynamic, very stimulating. One of the most important men in Western Europe. Holds strong views, which is refreshing.'

'On deporting all foreigners from France? Especially Algerians and Negroes?'

'He has a lot of support for his views. Support which is growing by the hour.' Jean drank more champagne, refilled her glass. She was certainly knocking it back, Paula noted. 'Some people think de Forge is a second General de Gaulle,' Jean went on. Her tone was neutral.

'Do you?' Paula asked.

'De Gaulle was a great statesman. De Forge is only a soldier. How could he ever become a statesman?'

'Maybe the first stage would be to create chaos.'

Jean had long fair lashes. She studied Paula through them, her eyes half-closed. Reaching for a silver box, she raised the lid, took out a cigarette, lit it with a gold lighter she also took from the box. Paula hadn't seen her smoke before during their short acquaintance. Jean blew a smoke ring, spoke as she watched it float to the ceiling.

'You really are a professional newshound to your finger-tips,' she commented dreamily.

There was no criticism, no irritation in her manner. It was a statement of fact. She stroked her cheekbone with the index finger of her left hand. Her bone structure was perfect. She really was a beautiful woman, Paula was thinking. The kind of woman who would drive a lot of men mad with desire.

'I'm just interested in what is going on in the world,' Paula fenced.

'You're right, of course. A lot is going on in France.' Jean seemed to be speaking in a trance. 'And no one can predict where it will all end.'

'Where do you think it will end?'

'At the gates of hell . . .'

She chuckled again, but this time there was a bitter note. She switched the conversation to Aldeburgh.

'Aldeburgh is rather unreal. Haven't you noticed? It's inhabited mostly by retired people – diplomats, soldiers like my uncle. They were brought here as children for their holidays by their parents. When they came home from abroad for good this was the only place they knew. There's nothing much in the way of jobs for youngsters. Except as shop assistants. Most of the work is in Ipswich, which is quite a distance. The other residents are second-homers. They've bought some of the houses on the front for summer visits . . .'

They chatted for quite a while longer. At one stage Jean left Paula alone for a few minutes to go to the bathroom. Paula lifted the lid of the cigarette box, took out the gold lighter. Engraved on it was the same symbol which was engraved on the signet ring Victor Rosewater had recovered on the marshes. The Cross of Lorraine . . .

'I'd better get back to the Brudenell,' Paula decided a little later. 'Thank you so much for such a relaxing evening.'

'I'd like it to go on all night long. If you're ever near Bordeaux, phone this number. It's the Villa Forban. I'll come and collect you in the car.'

She handed the sheet she'd scribbled on to Paula, escorted her to the front door. Opening it, Jean peered out.

'It's a foul night. You have transport? If not I'll drive you . . .'

'I have transport,' Paula lied.

She wanted to walk back, to absorb impressions she'd stored up of the Brigadier, of her conversation with Jean. Muffled against the raw cold inside her suede coat, her head protected with her scarf, she walked down the drive, waved to Jean who stood in the doorway, turned to the right to walk back down the hill.

She was treading her away across the damp grass verge when she heard something. She was about to look back when a thick brown paper bag was shoved over her head, rammed down hard. A pair of large hands grasped her round the neck, swung her through a hundred and eighty degrees, so she faced her attacker. Strong thumbs pressed against her windpipe. She couldn't breathe.

She might have panicked but her first reaction was that this was the bastard who had strangled Karin. She resisted the instinct to claw futilely at the lethal hands. She jerked her hands up to the bag, to roughly the point where it covered her mouth. Her hard nails tore furiously at the material. For a moment she thought it was too tough to penetrate. Then, as the hands tightened their grip, her finger nails ripped open a large slit. She clenched her fist, hit with all her force, as low down the body of the invisible man as she could, hoping for the kidneys. She heard a grunt. For a few seconds the hands loosened their grip. She opened her mouth, pressed to the hole, let out an ear-splitting scream.

'A-a-a-a-a-a-a-r-r-g-h . . .!'

Chapter Twenty-Five

Paula was hurled backwards as she heard what sounded like the firing of a high-powered handgun four times in rapid succession. Fortunately she was still on the grass verge, but she lay there winded. She heard a fresh sound. A car's engine starting up. She made the effort, pulled the bag off her head, forced herself up on her elbows – in time to see the red tail-lights of a car retreating in the opposite direction she'd travelled when driven there by Berthier.

Jean Burgoyne came rushing out of the entrance to Admiralty House. She stopped, gazing up and down the deserted road.

'Over here,' Paula called out feebly.

She was clambering to her feet, staggering, when Jean had reached her. She flicked at her coat with her hands to brush off rubbish.

'My best coat – suede . . .'

A sudden gust of wind funnelled down the road, nearly blew her off her feet again. Jean grabbed her by the arm, led her back slowly to the drive, along it, into the house. Only then did Paula see she was carrying a large revolver.

'My uncle's service revolver,' Jean said, seeing her looking at the weapon. 'What on earth happened out there? Are you all right? Would you like a drink? More champagne, coffee, tea? Something with brandy in it?'

'Nothing. Really. Thank you . . .'

She took off her coat, examined it, standing in the living room. She decided it had survived without serious damage.

'It will have to go to the cleaners.' She felt dazed. 'Did you fire that revolver?'

'You bet I did. Into the air. I heard you screaming – sounded like a banshee going full throttle. Feel like telling me what happened?'

Paula did so, tersely, pausing to give her throat a rest, to drink some lime juice. She was careful to give an edited version, pretending she'd been subjected to an attempted sexual assault.

When she'd finished she agreed that Jean should drive her back to the Brudenell, but first she insisted on a brief search outside with a flashlight Jean produced for the paper bag which had been thrust over her head. It might be important evidence.

They searched fruitlessly along the verge, in the road, for five minutes, and then Jean insisted that they got into her car and drove straight back to the hotel. Paula was still holding up well, worried she might say too much to Jean. She was also worried about Newman. When he had heard what happened he would give her hell.

They arrived outside and as she stepped out of the car Paula checked the other vehicles. Berthier's Saab was parked next to Newman's Mercedes. What the devil was the Merc doing here? Jean accompanied her inside and they ran into Newman pacing up and down the lobby.

Jean introduced herself, not realizing it was unnecessary – Newman recognized her immediately from the photo Lasalle had sent by courier to Park Crescent. Paula thanked Jean effusively, said she wouldn't forget her invitation if she ever found herself in Bordeaux. Something made her call out as Jean was leaving.

'And, please, be very careful to take care of yourself. It's a dangerous world we're living in . . .'

'As you have good reason to know. Bye.'

'Tweed is here,' Newman told her as they rode up alone in the elevator. 'We'll go to his room, if that's all right. You look all shook up. White as a sheet. Has something happened?'

'Better tell you while Tweed can listen too . . .'

Settled in an armchair in Tweed's room, sipping frequently at a cup of the sweetened tea she'd asked for, she told them about her experience. Tweed sat in another armchair, close to her, leaning forward, hands clasped.

He was in two minds whether to let her go on as she had insisted on doing. Her request for sweetened tea, when normally she never touched sugar, suggested to him she was in a state of shock. He'd voiced the suspicion but she had denied it. Tweed was still wondering whether he ought to pack her off to bed. On the other hand, if she *was* up to describing what had happened now she was more likely to recall small details, any of which might be important.

Paula had the thirst of the devil. She paused again to sip the tea. The truth was she was in shock, but concealing it by asserting her strong willpower. As she went on speaking she kept herself under control by moving two fingers slowly up and down the shoulder strap of her bag. She had come to the point when Jean said she would drive her back and they got into her car. Newman spoke for the first time.

'Didn't anyone think of calling the police?'

'Oh, yes. Jean was very determined to do just that but I dissuaded her.' She looked at Tweed. 'You've had enough trouble with Buchanan and I suspected it would get back to him. He might have asked awkward questions you don't want raised at this moment.'

'You could be right,' Tweed agreed. 'Good thinking.'

'I don't agree!' Newman burst out. 'If they'd put out an all-points bulletin they might have stopped the car.'

'What car?' Paula asked him. 'All I saw were two red tail-lights disappearing. No idea of the make – even of the size of the car.'

'They might have set up roadblocks,' Newman persisted.

'Probably no point,' Tweed objected. 'Supposing the man who attacked Paula is staying in Aldeburgh? Which I suspect is likely. His car will be parked in a garage.'

'And that occurred to me,' Paula agreed. 'I studied a map of the town – the road where Jean Burgoyne's uncle lives is a kind of horseshoe. He could have driven back into the High Street from the opposite direction to the way Berthier brought me. He might have his car parked outside this hotel. I did notice Berthier's Saab was parked back in the same slot we took it from.'

'Did you feel the radiator to see if the engine was still warm?' Newman asked.

'Oddly enough,' she flared up, 'I didn't think of it. After you've just escaped being strangled it's easy to forget something.

'In any case,' Tweed pointed out, 'on a night like this an engine would cool quickly.' He looked at Paula. 'You have slight bruising on your neck . . .'

'Which I noticed in the mirror when I slipped into my own room for a wash before Bob brought me along here.' She felt her throat. 'It's very slight – probably my scarf saved me a worse bruising.'

'I was going to say,' Tweed continued, 'maybe we ought to get a doctor to examine it.'

'No doctor,' Paula said as she stood up, stifling a yawn. 'If you don't mind I think I'd like to get some sleep. I was going to have a bath . . .'

'Don't,' Newman warned. 'You could fall asleep in it.'
He grinned. 'Unless you'd like me to come and help you into the bath.'

She smiled gratefully, realizing he was introducing an element of humour to soothe her nerves, shook her head. When she reached the door she paused, her mind racing as she turned to speak to them before leaving.

'I told you every word that was said at Admiralty House. There's something odd about Brigadier Burgoyne. He was spry as a five-year old when I arrived – physically and mentally. When I started talking about Third Corps in France he dried up.'

Tweed leaned forward, a gleam in his eye. 'How do you mean?' he asked quickly.

'Prior to that he had all his marbles. He suddenly went vague on me. I had the distinct feeling he was acting out his old man routine. He even shuffled out of the room. When he entered you'd have thought he wasn't a day over sixty.'

'Interesting,' said Tweed, gazing into the distance.

'And there's something strange about Jean Burgoyne,' Paula went on.

'Strange?' Tweed probed. 'In what way?'

'I don't know. Yet. She invited me to the Villa Forban if I was ever in the Bordeaux area. I think I'd like to go there if ever the opportunity crops up.'

'No point in thinking about that now. Get to bed as soon as you can,' Tweed urged her.

Paula seemed reluctant to go. 'Do you think that the murderer could be a woman?' she asked suddenly.

'Why do you think that?' Tweed, surprised, queried.

'I don't know that either, yet. Sleep well, both of you . . .'

*

'Kalmar is somewhere here in Aldeburgh,' Tweed said as soon as they were alone. 'I'm convinced of it. I was careful not to say that while Paula was here. She's gone through enough for one day. Kalmar's identity is the key to this whole European riddle – to what is happening in France. In Germany.'

'And there are plenty of candidates for the role of assassin here in Aldeburgh at the moment,' Newman commented. He had been told by Tweed of the conversation with Monica as they had waited for Paula's return. 'Major Lamy, Sergeant Rey, Lieutenant Berthier – and Brand.'

'So your first priority in the morning is to drive Paula back to London in your Merc. That's an order.'

'Which I'm happy to carry out . . .'

'She musn't linger here a moment longer,' Tweed stressed. 'You must remove her from the zone of danger – Aldeburgh.'

'And then, I suppose,' Newman said cynically, 'she'll want to move into a zone of even greater danger when she hears where I'm going. France.'

Chapter Twenty-Six

SECOND LYONS RIOT. FRENCH SITUATION WORSENS.

In his Park Crescent office next day Tweed read the text below the alarming headline. Monica had obtained the copy of the leading Paris newspaper, *Le Monde*, during his absence.

Over 2,000 casualties... more than 400 killed ... Lyons in a state of chaos ... The President may visit city ... martial law considered ...

He skip-read the account in French quickly, glanced at Paula who sat behind her desk. She was looking more normal. A good night's sleep in Aldeburgh before Newman had driven her back had done her a world of good. Earlier, Newman had repaired Tweed's Escort.

'I read it,' she said. 'Could it be General de Forge stepping up the pressure?'

'Someone is,' Tweed replied cautiously. 'I'm flying to Paris later today to consult with Lasalle. He doesn't seem to trust the phone. That's after I've seen Chief Inspector Kuhlmann.'

'Here? He's flying to London?'

'Yes, expected any moment. Monica took the call before I arrived back. Someone else who doesn't trust phones. It worries me – the atmosphere of intrigue at the very top. While in Paris, I'm meeting Pierre Navarre, Minister of the Interior – the only strong man in the government.'

'We've come back from a troubled time in Aldeburgh to an inferno.'

'I suspect the inferno is still to come.' He noted her understatement – 'a troubled time' – which covered a near-successful attempt to strangle her. Paula was very resilient. 'On top of all this,' he told her, 'we have Chief Inspector Buchanan descending on us later. At my request, admittedly, and Victor Rosewater will join us. I must give Buchanan that signet ring and both of us – Rosewater and myself – will have to take a few salvoes from our friend, Buchanan. I expect we'll survive . . .'

As he was speaking the phone rang, Monica answered it, said could he wait just a minute. She put her hand over the mouthpiece.

'It's started. Otto Kuhlmann is downstairs.'

'Wheel him up . . .'

The German walked in, wearing a dark business suit, an unlit cigar clamped tightly between his teeth. He looked grim but went over to Paula, put his arm round her shoulders, gave her a hug. He stared at the scarf tucked in above her form-fitting powder blue sweater. The scarf had slipped. Kuhlmann's sharp eyes missed nothing.

'Your throat,' he rasped. 'You've been in the wars?'

'You could say that,' Tweed intervened as Paula adjusted the scarf. 'Tell you about it in a minute. Sit down. Welcome to London. Coffee?'

'Please. Black as sin.'

Kulhmann sat in an armchair, shifted his bulk, staring again at Paula. He twiddled his cigar as he watched her.

'Do light your cigar,' Paula urged. 'I like the aroma of a Havana.'

Monica had hurried from the room to make coffee. Kuhlmann lit his cigar, looked at Tweed, waved the cigar towards Paula.

'Her throat,' he persisted.

Tweed gave a terse account of their trip to Aldeburgh, expressed his certainty that Kalmar had been in the area. He gave the German a list of his suspects, told him he'd not reached the stage where the finger pointed at one man.

'Any idea where he comes from, his nationality?' Kuhlmann asked. 'I also have been trying to get a grip on him. All I hear from my contacts is he's from somewhere in the East. That covers quite a lot of territory. Not a hint of his age, his description.'

'The shadow of a shadow,' Tweed remarked. 'Rather curious. Possibly even significant. But that isn't why you flew to see me, Otto.'

He waited while Monica poured a large cup of black, steaming coffee. Kuhlmann thanked her, drank half the cup in one steady stream.

'*Siegfried*,' he began. 'Rosewater rang me again from somewhere. I didn't ask him from where. He is Military Intelligence. Gave me another address he'd just obtained from an informant. An apartment in Munich. We raided it, found another arms cache. Twelve Kalashnikov rifles, spare mags, six grenades, and two kilos of Semtex.'

Tweed leaned forward. 'And terrorists?'

Kuhlmann waved his hands like a swimmer. 'I think the local police fumbled it. Patrol cars approached with sirens screaming. No terrorists. No one in the apartment. And again, not one single fingerprint. Another woman at work, I'm sure. A man would have missed something.'

'So *Siegfried* is in place,' Tweed commented.

'Our own informants in the criminal underground say they are – and they know what's going on. Upwards of a hundred trained saboteurs and assassins. Likely targets: leading members of the government, including the Chancellor himself. Apparently they're waiting for a signal from abroad. Then they start to destabilize Germany. What I'm really worried about is the growing campaign in certain parts of the French press against Germany.'

'All of which is orchestrated. Every responsible person knows Germany is the most peace-loving nation on the continent,' Tweed continued. 'Certain elements in France are whipping up anti-German feeling for their own sinister ambitions. To cover up the fact that all they're interested in is seizing power in Paris. The *Cercle Noir*.'

'The Black Circle.' Kuhlmann waved his cigar. 'And we've heard rumours about them. They're anti-Semitic, anti-American, anti-British. The trouble is we don't know who they are. But they wield a hell of a lot of clout. And if I can't smoke out the *Siegfried* terrorists before they break loose they'll justify what the yellow Paris press is saying about us.'

'Which is the whole idea, the core of the plan.'

'On top of this the criminal underworld reports they expect huge reinforcements to arrive soon. From where? If it's from the East – like Kalmar – they'll get through.'

'You have any good men at Wiesbaden who speak French?' Tweed asked.

'Yes, why?'

'Send them undercover into Geneva. Spread the word they are trying to contact Kalmar for a big job. Fee – three million marks. No, make that Swiss francs.'

'If you say so . . .'

'And send more undercover men, German-speaking, into Basle. Same message.'

'You know something?'

Kuhlmann watched Tweed through blue cigar smoke. Then he drank the rest of his coffee and Monica refilled his cup.

'Just do it. What about Stahl, your agent posing as a Frenchman in Bordeaux? Any news?'

Kuhlmann hesitated. 'Hell! You've been frank with me. He's still there. The trouble is you warned me that he shouldn't use his transmitter. His last signal said he had a load of information – that he'd bring it out as soon as he could. A very brief signal. You're operating in France?'

Kuhlmann looked at the ceiling as he asked the question casually.

'On a large scale.'

'That's really why I came. It's difficult for German agents to operate inside France. The Chancellor has put a veto on the idea.'

'Why?'

'As you know, he has a good relationship with the President of France. If the Paris press could get hold of a story that we have agents inside French territory they'd have a field day.'

'What about Stahl then?'

Kuhlmann looked up at the ceiling again. Paula knew he was working out his answer.

'That's my secret,' Kuhlmann said eventually. 'And if the fact ever came to light, I sent in Stahl before the Chancellor said there was a veto. And now it be difficult for Stahl to get out quickly. That Black Circle may have done just that – put a circle round Bordeaux.'

'They have.' Tweed recalled Newman's evading action when he'd slipped past the watchers at Bordeaux Airport. 'The airport is a trap,' he warned. 'And my guess is they're also watching the rail stations, maybe even have check-points outside the city for motorists.

'So Stahl is trapped.'

'We might be able to reach him. No guarantees. So, we

are on your side, Otto. All you can do is to go back, hope, and pray . . .'

Tweed checked his watch when Kuhlmann had said good-bye, had left for Heathrow. Monica guessed what was on his mind.

'Yes, Victor Rosewater is due very shortly . . .' She picked up the phone which had started ringing. As she listened her expression changed. 'You mean all three of them have arrived together? That they're here now?'

Her expression was a mixture of puzzlement and annoyance. She looked at Tweed.

'I don't think you're going to like this. The idea was Rosewater arrived for a half hour's quiet chat with you before Buchanan grilled him.'

'What's gone wrong?'

'They're all waiting downstairs. Rosewater, Buchanan, and his sidekick, Sergeant Warden.'

'Very odd. Oh, now I get it.' He raised his eyebrows at Paula. 'Send them all up, Monica . . .'

Rosewater entered the room first. Wearing a trenchcoat, hands thrust in his pockets, he looked at Paula, winked. His manner was cool and poised as always. Behind him a wooden-faced Chief Inspector Buchanan followed with Warden, also wooden faced, as always, bringing up the rear.

'Coats off, gentlemen,' Tweed said breezily. He looked at Buchanan. 'And you're half an hour early.'

'I like to be in good time,' Buchanan said as he handed his coat to Monica. 'We bumped into Mr Rosewater as we were walking up and down outside. It seemed a good idea to get on with it.'

Tweed had already caught on to Buchanan's tactics. With

Warden he had deliberately turned up very early, hoping to see Rosewater arrive. That way there would be no time for Tweed to prime the Intelligence officer.

With his guests seated, Tweed wasted no time. Leaning into the back of his chair he explained how Rosewater, Newman, and Paula had found the signet ring on the marshes. He unlocked a drawer, took out the copy of the original ring, handed it to Buchanan.

'This comes under the heading of suppressing evidence in a murder . . .' Buchanan began, staring at Rosewater.

Tweed's clenched fist crashed down on his desk. 'Now you listen to me – and don't forget where you are. You have been given the ring. Voluntarily. In case you've forgotten, you're at the headquarters of the SIS. And, in case you've overlooked it, Captain Rosewater is a member of Military Intelligence. I happen to know that he is involved in a matter of the utmost importance to national security. There will be no questions asked, no accusations made, without my agreement. I will not have you adopting an overbearing manner in my office.'

He sank back in his chair, his expression furious and his mouth tight-lipped. Paula was staring at him.

'So that's the way you're going to play it,' Buchanan observed calmly, stretching out his legs, crossing his ankles.

'I'm not *playing*, as you put it!' Tweed leaned forward again. 'Men have died outside this room. One of them my agent. Abroad. Where you have no jurisdiction. I can and do operate abroad,' he snapped. 'If you want information which may help you in *your* investigation, then you will cease and desist. Now!'

'My main concern is who murdered this gentleman's wife, strangled her in cold blood on those marshes where this ring was found.'

Buchanan's manner was still mild. He might have been conducting a friendly conversation in a pub. In contrast Tweed still appeared to be in a controlled rage.

'You've got the ring. You've heard the circumstances under which it was found.' His voice rose. 'But I am concerned with the cauldron boiling up in Europe, a situation which is worsening by the hour. In case you don't know what I'm talking about, read the papers.'

'I realize you have grave responsibilities. Perhaps it would be better if we came back when you are less fraught. And I would like to ask Captain Rosewater a question . . .'

'No!' Tweed stood up. 'Captain Rosewater is directly involved in what is happening in Europe. I know you will not think me impolite if I say I do not have the time to prolong this discussion. I'm under pressure. A major conflagration is building up in Europe.'

'I think I have what I came for.' Buchanan stood up, the signet ring held in his hand covered with a surgical glove he had slipped on before accepting it. He dropped it inside a plastic bag Sergeant Warden held out. 'But I may need to see Captain Rosewater at the Yard . . .'

'Sorry, Chief Inspector,' Rosewater interjected, 'but I expect my job to take me back to Germany today. Where I'm based.'

'But you'll have time to come and make a statement.'

'I'm afraid not. Tweed has described what happened very precisely. I'll be on the first available flight.'

'*Bon voyage,*' Buchanan replied ironically and left the room.

'You saved me a tough inquisition,' Rosewater said as soon as they were on their own. 'That Chief Inspector is one bright cookie.'

'I didn't want him trying to penetrate your role in France and Germany. You'll be based in Freiburg if I need to contact you?'

'Mostly.' He looked at Paula. 'If you can coax your boss into being generous, maybe you'd come and visit me. I gave you the address.'

'I may be waiting on your doorstep,' Paula joked.

Rosewater stood up. 'I meant what I said to Buchanan. I'm leaving for the continent now. If you can't get me in Freiburg, contact Kuhlmann. He may be able to reach me. We're keeping in close touch.'

'Take care,' Tweed warned, watching him, '*Siegfried* is deadly. I gather you're having trouble tracking them.'

'They've organized themselves into independent cells, each with a mission when the balloon goes up in Germany. Sabotage and assassination on a large scale. That much I have learned. Strictly between these walls I'm trying to infiltrate agents inside *Siegfried*. It's a race against time – before their controller gives the signal. He could be Kalmar . . .'

'Why,' asked Paula when Rosewater had gone, 'haven't you told Buchanan about Major Lamy and Lieutenant Berthier? Both were in Aldeburgh. Even Sergeant Rey?'

'Because,' Tweed explained, 'I'm letting them run on a loose rein, giving them plenty of rope. Meantime you and I are leaving for Paris. You have your usual case packed here for emergency take-offs? Good. Monica has booked three seats on the Paris flight today.'

'Three?'

'I'm expecting Newman to arrive here any moment. He's going in via Paris. The Bordeaux Airport is closely watched. And you'd better ask Lasalle for a weapon – we're moving into the cauldron.'

Chapter Twenty-Seven

Major Lamy, wearing his normal French civilian clothes, disembarked from the Air Inter Flight at Bordeaux Airport. He did not know it but later that same day Tweed would fly to Paris. Lamy was met by a chauffeur in a civilian uniform, escorted to the waiting Citroën.

Half an hour later he entered the large room where General de Forge was studying the newspaper accounts of the devastation caused by the fresh Lyons riots. De Forge neatly folded the paper he was reading, added it to the pile, waved to Lamy to sit opposite him.

'Did you get *Oiseau* to agree?' he demanded.

'Mission accomplished.' Lamy sat erect, aware this was a formal interview. '*Oiseau* agreed to supply double the original number of missiles with nerve gas warheads.'

'*When?*' De Forge fired back at him.

'He said he would send a signal from the transmitter aboard the *Steel Vulture* giving the delivery date. I had the impression it would be soon.'

'*Soon? Oiseau* wants to learn military precision. We may need those weapons within one week from now. Have you heard the President is thinking of travelling to Lyons to inspect the damage? Because he dislikes flying he'll go there aboard the TGV?'

Lamy's expression showed no sign of his surprise, that he hadn't known: de Forge expected you to know everthing that was going on. The TGV – the *Train de Grande Vitesse* – famous for its bullet-like speed of up to 150 m.p.h.

'That concerns us?' he enquired.

'I will give you orders soon. Urgent orders. This may be our opportunity. Have you also heard the Prefect of Paris – the man who might have got in our way when we focus on Paris – has been assassinated?'

Lamy nodded. 'Kalmar has delivered again . . .'

'Kalmar! Are you sure you know it was him? I had a phone call on my private number from a man calling himself by the codename *Manteau*.'

He watched Lamy closely as the Intelligence chief stared back, sitting more erect. Lamy found himself still thinking in English, a mental habit he'd easily slipped into during his trip to Aldeburgh. *Manteau* meant *Cloak*.

'What did this *Manteau* say?' Lamy asked.

He hardly had the words out of his mouth before de Forge exploded.

'He said he had shot the Prefect. He gave me a detailed description of how and where and when – which has not appeared in the press yet. I ordered Berthier to phone our contact inside Lasalle's DST. He gave exactly the same details of the assassination. *Manteau* has asked for a fee of half a million Swiss francs. He said that if I refused that was all right, but he would expect my next commission.'

'How the devil could he know we wanted the Prefect eliminated?' wondered Lamy.

'Because there has to be a leak inside my own GHQ,' de Forge shouted back. 'You had better discover that leak fast. Whoever it is must be shot in the Landes. His body disposed of in the usual way.'

De Forge was gazing closely at Lamy as he spoke. Aware of the scrutiny, Lamy gazed back without blinking. Then he changed the subject quickly, opening the briefcase in his lap.

'I will carry out the investigation myself.' He took a large fat envelope out of the case. '*Oiseau* has supplied the funds requested. Three million Swiss francs. He gave them to me without hesitation.' He placed the envelope on the desk.

'Why aren't you already conducting that investigation?' de Forge stormed.

Lamy was hurrying out of the long room to change into his uniform when de Forge called out for him to wait a moment. His voice was dangerously quiet. Lamy was well accustomed to his chief's unpredictable changes of mood, knew he was treading on tricky ground. He turned.

'Yes, my General?'

'Did you organize that Ku Klux Klan-style attack on the Jews in the south before leaving for England?'

'Yes. It was to take place last night. I'm sure you'll hear news of it today. And a reporter with a gun in his back and a camera in his hand will have recorded it.'

Tweed, Paula, and Newman met a grim Lasalle when they had arrived at rue des Saussaies in Paris. The Frenchman greeted them courteously, ordered an aide to bring coffee, waited until the four of them were alone.

'What's happened now, René?' Tweed asked quietly as he sat down, sensing his host's disquiet.

'This newspaper has just been flown to me by courier from Bordeaux by the chief of my team in the city. It is the most hideous atrocity.'

He spread the newspaper over his desk facing them, said nothing, knowing they could all read French. The front page carried a huge picture, one of the most sinister Paula had ever seen. The headline screamed:

'ANTI-SEMITES GO BERSERK AT TARBES. TWENTY JEWS BURN.

The photograph was weird, macabre. Figures clad in what appeared to be white sheets from head to toe carried blazing torches. The sheets were shaped so they rose to the point of a triangle above the invisible heads with slits for the eyes. Each figure carried a flaming torch in one hand, a long knife in the other. The group of roughly forty men was formed into a triangular formation. At the apex – in front of the white-sheeted figures – the leader carried the Cross of Lorraine blazing with fire.

It was not the only thing blazing. Men, mostly bare headed in the night, were running as flames enveloped them. One desperate fugitive wore a skull cap. Tweed turned to the next page which was covered with photos. Corpses burnt to a cinder littered the ground. Paula swallowed, stiffened herself.

'This happened last night?' Tweed asked.

'Yes,' Lasalle explained. 'Apparently there is some old castle where a Jewish group gathered to discuss the scriptures. I gather it was some kind of club – that they attended meetings regularly. So the fiends who did this knew when their victims would be there.'

'It's horrific,' Paula whispered. 'Why?

'Obvious, I'd have thought,' Newman commented. 'We all know there's anti-Semitism below the surface in many countries. Someone in France is working up the population – that part of it which is anti-Jewish.'

'But this is a massacre,' Paula protested.

'Exactly,' said Newman. 'A vicious atrocity to work up more chaos. The man behind this is a monster.'

'Dubois, I'm sure,' Lasalle said. 'His speeches are vitriolic against all foreign elements, as he terms them. Especially the Jews.'

'What about the reporter?' Newman probed.

'My DST chief who is in charge in Bordeaux says he was

kidnapped at gunpoint. Then he was forced to take these foul pictures. The President is appalled. The trouble is he's just about to leave on the TGV for Lyons.'

'Today, you mean?' Tweed queried.

'Yes. And he's taking the Prime Minister with him. The security problem is a nightmare. Still, that's simply something else to pigeonhole in my mind. As Churchill once said, my mental culvert is almost overflowing – something like that. What I'm about to tell you now is top secret.'

'Understood,' said Newman, knowing he was the visitor Lasalle was bothered about.

'The Prefect of Paris was assassinated last night.'

'Oh, my God!' Paula burst out. 'He was one of the few strong men you could rely on in an emergency.'

'Which was why he was a target. Now, listen, we have decided to keep it quiet, away from the public and the press.'

'How on earth can you do that?' Newman protested.

'By saying he has gone on holiday. He was due for some leave. I'd cancelled it but no one knows that. There was a witness to the killing. The disturbing thing is I had a phone call from a Frenchman calling himself *Manteau*. He claimed he had shot the Prefect. We have been hearing rumours about this new professional assassin, *Manteau*. A professional. So now we have two to cope with – Kalmar and *Manteau*.'

'Unless,' Tweed said quietly, '*Manteau* is Kalmar. He could be cleverly confusing the search for him.'

Lasalle stared at Tweed. 'I had never thought of that. It fits in with the pattern of mounting chaos. I've kept the witness downstairs. You might like to question her. With your skill at interrogation you might extract something I've missed . . .'

He spoke into his intercom. Paula watched the door,

curious to see who was the witness. Tweed accepted Lasalle's offer to sit in the chair behind his desk, sat with his hands clasped. The door opened and a DST officer ushered inside the last type of witness Paula had expected.

A short overweight bag lady shuffled into the office. She clutched a large bundle held together with a piece of soiled cloth. Glaring at the DST officer she spoke to Tweed, assuming he was the boss, that Lasalle must be an underling.

'They tried to take my bundle. All my possessions in the world are inside it. Never let it out of my sight. I sleep under one of the Seine bridges. The *flics* keep moving me on. Say I'm not nice for the tourists. Who gives a monkey's cuss for the tourists?'

'Please sit down, Madame,' Tweed said in French. 'And I will personally ensure no one touches your possessions.'

'You'd better if you want to ask me questions. And I'd like more money first.'

Lasalle, standing to one side, brought out his hands from behind his back. He riffled through the wad of banknotes he was holding.

'You get these later. But only if my chief is satisfied with your answers.'

'I've already told *you*,' she went on grumbling. 'Why don't you tell him?'

'Because,' Tweed intervened in a sympathetic tone, 'it's important I hear what happened to the Prefect from you. You strike me as a woman who keeps her eyes open.'

'Don't miss much, I can tell you,' the bag lady replied, mollified by Tweed's manner.

'So tell me, please, what you saw.'

'I was crossing the Île de la Cité on my way to doss down. It was one o'clock in the morning. I know that because I'd looked at a clock. The Prefecture is on the Île de la Cité. But you know that. I know the Prefect by sight. I should do. In the past he's given me a few francs. More than any *flic* would do.'

'So tell me what you saw last night.'

Paula was studying the bag lady's clothing. She was wrapped in a khaki-coloured army blanket, fastened at the neck with a huge safety-pin. Round her head she wore a large scarf, the colours faded, wisps of grey hair protruding. Newspaper projected from the worn pair of man's shoes encasing her large feet. But her bare red hands looked strong and her jaw jutted as she began, staring at Tweed.

'I was a distance away from the entrance to the Prefect's building. A car was parked on the opposite side of the street, the side I was on. A man was crouched behind the car, seemed to be doing up his shoe lace. I recognized the Prefect as soon as he came down the steps towards his car . . .'

Her previous rasping tone had sunk to a monotone, like a woman reciting by rote. Of course, Paula thought, she's told this same story before to Lasalle.

'The man crouched behind the car stood up. He was holding what looked like a rifle. He steadied it on the roof of his car, took aim, fired. The Prefect stopped halfway down the steps, then collapsed.'

'And the assassin?' Tweed coaxed.

'Jumped into his car, didn't he, and drove off like hell. Don't ask me the make of the car. I don't know them. Never owned a car.'

'What did the assassin look like? Height? Weight? Was he bare-headed? What colour of hair if he was . . .'

'Stop! Stop! For God's sake . . .'

'Sorry. Take your time.' Tweed spoke very slowly. 'I expect you noticed how he was dressed?'

'Wore a cloak, didn't he? A dark cloak. Dark like his hat.

Don't see them much these days. Cloaks. Except sometimes when the toffs are going into the Opéra.' Her mouth clamped shut.

'You probably noticed something else about – the Cloak.'

'That's it. All happened so quickly. I wouldn't know him if I saw him again. Then the police came running out of the building, waving their guns. Too late, as usual. That's it. Except they grabbed me. What about my money?'

Tweed nodded. Lasalle held out the wad of banknotes, then withdrew it as she reached out. His voice was harsh.

'You remember the conditions. You don't talk about this to the press, the radio, to anyone on God's earth. If you do you lose the bigger sum I'll give you later.'

'Bigger? How much?' Quick as a flash.

'That you'll find out when I decide you've earned it. I'm having you watched twenty-four hours a day.'

He gave her the banknotes. Without checking the amount she stuffed them somewhere under her blanket, glared at Tweed, stood, picked up her bundle, refusing help from Lasalle who opened the door. The DST officer was waiting in the corridor, escorted her away. Lasalle closed the door and looked at his three visitors with raised eyebrows.

'I know that *Manteau* isn't Kalmar,' Newman said flatly.

They all stared at him. Newman shrugged, rubbed one eye and spoke again.

'I didn't phrase that well. I was up half the night. I don't believe *Manteau* is Kalmar.'

'Why not?' Lasalle enquired, his tone soft.

'The *modus operandi*. Kalmar strangles his victims. Carey in Bordeaux at the Gare St Jean. Karin Rosewater in Aldeburgh. *Manteau* shot the Prefect.

'The assassin would have had trouble getting close enough to the Prefect to strangle him,' Tweed pointed out.

283

'As you learned from your SAS training, Bob, there's more than one way of killing – and men skilled with different techniques.'

Lasalle waved an impatient hand. 'There was also a witness to that hideous massacre of the Jews near Tarbes. He's waiting downstairs. I think you ought to meet him. The head of the discussion group. Moshe Stein . . .'

Moshe Stein was a heavily built man of medium height with a tough face and a gentle smile. Above his beaky nose, dark alert eyes took in everyone in the room. His thick black hair was neatly brushed back from a high forehead. He wore a well-pressed dark blue business suit and above the firm mouth was a bushy moustache. Lasalle introduced his other guests as 'members of a top security organization'. He spoke in English and as Stein responded in the same language he smiled warmly.

'Moshe Stein,' Lasalle explained, 'is the sole survivor of the Tarbes massacre.'

'I am afraid I am a coward,' Stein said to Paula, settling in his chair. 'I saw this horrific attack from our HQ, the chateau. Very old but very small. I realized I couldn't help – there were too many of the killers. I felt someone should live to tell the authorities. So I hid in a secret cellar. When they had gone I walked to the local station, took a train to where I could board the Paris Express. I feel ashamed and guilty.'

'Nonsense,' Paula said robustly. 'You did the sensible thing. You may even end up avenging your friends . . .'

Stein talked in his quiet voice, recalling the arrival of the assault force. He thought they'd imitated the American Ku Klux Klan which, he understood, had revived in a small way in the deep South of the States. He looked at Newman.

284

'I'm going back to my small villa in the Landes. That is a beautiful area of France. Great forests of firs and pines spread a great distance until the Atlantic stops them. Even the beach is beautiful – great sand dunes rear up, concealing the endless cold blue water beyond.'

Paula thought Stein was rather poetic: as he spoke a dreamy look came over his weatherbeaten face. Again he looked at Newman.

'There is something mysterious going on in the Landes. You are a newspaper reporter. I thought we'd travel together. That is, if you think there may be a story.'

'I agree,' Newman said at once. 'Providing we can leave today. Also, providing we can call in at Arcachon.'

'We take the Paris–Bordeaux Express,' Stein suggested.

'Yes. But we must leave it at an intermediate station before Bordeaux. I have a reason. Trust me.'

'I do. I have been watching you. We could leave the express at Angoulême, hire a car, drive the rest of the way. First to Arcachon, then on to the Landes.'

Newman took out a map of France he'd brought with him, located Angoulême and agreed. He didn't say it was far enough north of Bordeaux not to have watchers.

'That was quick,' Lasalle said when the two men had left his office. 'Newman is decisive, Tweed.'

'Newman is pretty good at assessing character. Clearly he liked what he saw. We meet Navarre now? Good.'

'And I've decided I'm going to visit Jean Burgoyne at the Villa Forban,' Paula announced. 'She told me she was going back there before she drove me to the Brudenell from Admiralty House.'

'Wait here in Paris,' Tweed ordered. 'Phone Monica when you've got a hotel room, give her the name and address and phone number. If I decide to let you go you'll be accompanied – by Butler and Nield.'

'If you insist. Don't look so worried.'

'I am.' Tweed stood up as Lasalle checked his watch. They were due at the Ministry of the Interior. 'I am worried,' Tweed stressed. 'I'm convinced General de Forge is waiting for a trigger to set Europe ablaze. I just don't know what that trigger will be.'

Part Two

Trigger of Death

Chapter Twenty-Eight

The President of France walked down the six steps which lead from the entrance to the Elysée Palace to the waiting motorcade in the courtyard.

He stepped into the rear of his Citroën as his *chef de cabinet* held open the door. Closing the door the *chef* ran round the rear of the vehicle to join the President. The chauffeur and armed guard in civilian clothes waited until both rear doors were closed, then slipped into the front.

There were eight Citroëns comprising the motorcade drawn up in the courtyard behind the grille gates fronting on the rue du Faubourg St Honoré. The Prime Minister got quickly into the car behind the President's. Staff members and armed guards climbed into the other vehicles.

Uniformed armed guards carrying automatic weapons patrolled the street immediately outside the Elysée. Traffic had been diverted. In the distance curious crowds were held well back by uniformed police. At a signal the gates were opened, the President's limousine was driven out, proceeded at speed towards the Gare de Lyon with the rest of the motorcade streaming close behind.

Armed motorcycle outriders kept pace with the vehicles. Four more outriders formed a group ahead of the President's limousine. A further group of outriders brought up the rear behind the last vehicle.

The President held himself erect, knowing that despite the speed, residents of Paris were lining the pavements, gazing with excitement as the motorcade raced past them. Only when they were close to the Gare de Lyon did the President's driver slow down. He turned into the station, pulled up precisely alongside a red carpet leading to the presidential coach.

Stepping out of his car, the President inspected the guard of honour drawn up, uniforms immaculate. He nodded his approval to their commander, boarded the train. A white-coated steward, spotless, bowed, led the way to his armchair seat in the luxurious coach. Aware now that the permitted TV cameras were focused on him, the President, small and stocky, sat with his profile tilted at the correct angle. He took a leather folder handed to him by an aide and pretended to be reading a file.

The presidential coach was immediately behind the huge locomotive which would transport him to Lyons. The *Train de Grande Vitesse*, the pride of French Railways, sat in the Gare like a long sleek polished bullet.

When it had left Paris behind it would move like a bullet, travelling at speeds up to 150 m.p.h. There was a pause while the rest of the President's entourage boarded the express. The Prime Minister's coach was behind the President's and he also had a large entourage.

The rear coaches were reserved for the press, radio, and TV personnel. They would record the President's tour of devastated Lyons. His political aim was to show France how much he cared for the victims of the outrage.

There was no signal to warn of the TGV's departure. One moment it was standing in the Gare de Lyon, the next moment the magnificent train was gliding out into the cold sunlight of a bitter November day.

For the first time the President spoke to his *chef de cabinet*.

'Is everything arranged for my arrival at Lyons? I need a car for the first part of the tour.'

'A bulletproof limousine will be waiting at the staton.'

'Later, I shall leave the car at an appropriate moment when the crowds are massed. I will walk and mingle with them, express sympathy, shake many hands . . .'

'The chief of security was worried that might be what you intended. Lasalle has warned there is a professional assassin, Kalmar, operating. He has already killed at least two people. He would prefer you to remain in your car.'

'Lasalle fusses. The President of the French Republic must show himself to the people in their hour of need. That is what you will tell security . . .'

The President busied himself with state papers, rarely looking out of the window. The amount of paperwork which crossed his desk at the Elysée was formidable. He was paying close attention to detailed reports of the unrest in the south. He really had no idea how to placate the disturbing growth of terror.

In the open countryside farmers and workers heard the express coming. They paused to watch as it passed them in the distance. A blur of movement – incredible movement for a train. In the large cab of the locomotive an engineer checked his watch, looked at a colleague.

'We shall be there soon. Keep up maximum speed. The President will expect it . . .'

South of Roanne the line crossed a high viaduct spanning a river far below. The TGV was approaching at top speed as it neared the viaduct. This was normal procedure. The Chief Engineer peered through a window, saw the viaduct rushing towards him. He tucked a Gauloise between his thick lips, decided not to light it yet.

The locomotive reached the viaduct, began crossing it, hauling the coaches behind as though they were made of plastic. In the distance, not more than half a mile away, a large village was perched on a hill. France spread away . . .

The whole length of the TGV train was crossing the viaduct when the explosion occurred ahead of it near the end of the viaduct. A large stretch of track was hurled skywards. The TGV thundered forward, the wheels encountered the gap. The locomotive swept sideways, rammed the stone wall as though it were constructed of paper. The TGV continued its onward rush – into space. It shot forward like a torpedo, dragging the coaches with it. Then it curved downwards, plunging at hellish speed into the ravine. The locomotive swivelled in mid-air. The Chief Engineer bit clean through his unlit Gauloise. They found his decapitated head later, half the cigarette inside his mouth.

The locomotive hit the bottom of the ravine like a bomb detonating. A tumble of coaches smashed down on top of it, behind it, in front. No one survived in the President's coach. No one survived in the Prime Minister's coach. Many died instantly in the other coaches, some were terribly injured.

At the edge of the village a middle-aged man in tattered clothes had been waiting for the express, staring through a pair of old binoculars. He focused on the viaduct. The gap in the wall reminded him of a gap in a man's teeth.

Chapter Twenty-Nine

General de Forge's limousine pulled up outside the Villa Forban. He didn't wait for the chauffeur, he opened the door and dived out as soon as the car had stopped. He had the keys to the two locks on the front door in his hand, inserted them one by one, pushed open the heavy door, walked inside, slammed it behind him, and stopped.

'What are you doing here?'

Jean Burgoyne, wearing a green form-fitting sweater and a mini-skirt, pushed a wave of blond hair over her shoulder. She waved her shapely hands in a gesture of surprise.

'Aren't you glad to see me, Charles?'

'You didn't inform me you were coming back so soon,' he responded stiffly.

'You think I am your serf? That I should report all my movements to you?'

Her voice was soft and husky, showed no sign of annoyance. She took a gold cigarette case from her handbag, selected a cigarette, placed it between her lips, lit it with her gold lighter. The one engraved with the Cross of Lorraine.

De Forge strode up to her, snatched the cigarette out of her mouth, threw it on the polished wood-block floor.

'That will burn the nice flooring,' she remarked.

'So pick it up.'

'No, darling, you put it there, you pick it up.'

His lips tightened. He moved a few paces, crushed the burning cigarette under the heel of his riding boot. Jean was intrigued by his rage. She walked to one of the bullet-proof windows flanking the door, peered out. Only the chauffeur stood by the limousine.

'Where is your friend, Major Lamy? And your guard, Lieutenant Berthier? They always come with you.'

'I've told you before. Don't ask questions about military affairs.'

She made a moue. 'I'm only thinking of your protection. You do have enemies. Would you like some coffee?'

'Might as well . . .'

When she had disappeared he walked into the living room, paced restlessly. She had touched a raw nerve mentioning the two officers.

Much earlier Lamy had contacted Kalmar through the cut-out telephone the assassin used. A woman's voice had told Lamy which public phone box to go to, the time Kalmar would call the phone box number. So Lamy had reported, confirming that he'd passed on de Forge's new request. All this after Lamy had phoned their informant inside Lasalle's HQ at rue des Saussaies. Lamy had then driven to Bordeaux where he'd caught an early Air Inter flight to Lyons.

Berthier, as instructed, had been flown to Lyons aboard a Third Corps helicopter. Neither man knew of the other's movements. He continued pacing, checking his watch. He should get news by lunchtime.

Another thing which irked de Forge was finding Jean at the Villa Forban. In her assumed absence he had come there to search her possessions, to go through the place with a fine-tooth comb. He checked his watch again. Would it work – his masterstroke?

In his large office overlooking the courtyard and the Place Beauveau beyond, Pierre Navarre, Minister of the Interior, got down to business without any formality. Tweed was impressed by the drive and determination of the lean-faced dark-haired Frenchman. *Formidable* – as the French said.

'Your plan is working, Tweed,' Navarre began. 'As I imagine you already know.'

Navarre looked at Lasalle, raised his dark brows, and Lasalle nodded agreement. Three people sat in chairs arranged in a crescent round the Minister's desk. Paula sat to one side, Tweed faced Navarre across the desk, Lasalle occupied a chair on Tweed's right. Paula risked a question.

'Minister, why is France so suddenly in a ferment? I have always regarded your country as stable. Now we have riots, this horrible eruption of the Ku-Klux-Klan mob attacking the Jews.'

'A good question.' Navarre leaned forward in his chair behind the Louis-Quinze desk, his piercing dark eyes fixed on hers. 'Under the surface France is desperate to become itself again. Certain elements hanker for the time of de Gaulle – when France bestrode Europe like a colossus. The unification of Germany has increased this hankering. De Forge is exploiting this nostalgia to the full, putting himself forward as a new de Gaulle. It is naked ambition.'

'Surely he can't get away with it,' Paula persisted.

Navarre made a Gallic gesture, spreading his hands.

'I don't think he can. But he is cleverly appealing to this unspoken desire on the part of certain Frenchmen – for France to make a great *impact* on Europe, on the whole world later.'

'I'm still not sure,' Tweed intervened, 'why you've asked for my support.'

'Simple!' Navarre made the same gesture. 'We are submerged in the situation. So perhaps we do not see it as clearly as we should. You are insular – no criticism intended, rather the reverse. But you therefore see the crisis through detached eyes. What you have already suggested may confuse the enemy. General Charles de Forge.'

'I am fearful,' Tweed responded. 'I sense de Forge is just waiting for what I call the trigger. An event which will give him an excuse to act.'

'The President of France stands between de Forge and chaos,' Navarre replied in his rapid French. 'He may hesitate. He listens too closely to that poodle of de Forge's – Janin, the Minister of Defence. But the second riot in Lyons has, I know, stiffened the President's determination. And soon I expect another visitor who will give us the German point of view. Chief Inspector Otto Kuhlmann is flying here at my request. With the full authority of the Chancellor of Germany . . .'

General de Forge, an expert tactician, a man not liking to waste time, had decided he might as well take advantage of his visit to the Villa Forban he could no longer search. He went to the bathroom as Jean Burgoyne, clad only in a short slip, perched on the rumpled bed and slid on her tights.

She was again fully dressed when de Forge emerged, buttoning up his uniform. It seemed a good moment to chat to him as she brushed her mane of golden hair.

'Who is really behind all these terrible riots, Charles?'

'How would I know?'

'Major Lamy should have been able to tell you. That is what Chiefs of Intelligence are for.'

'The French people are getting fed up with the foreigners who infest France, who take their jobs, who pollute the streets by their very presence.'

'And yet I saw a report in *Le Monde* that the so-called mobs operate with military precision. And if they were ordinary people why wear these Balaclavas? It seems to be very important not a single person is identified?'

'I suppose they're worried the police might be able to pick them up if they knew who they were.'

De Forge spoke in an off-hand manner as he studied his appearance in a wall mirror. Jean knew that manner, that tone of voice: he was covering up. He'd just enjoyed himself so maybe he'd talk.

'You haven't convinced me, Charles. And what about that horrible massacre of the Jews near Tarbes? The killers wore Ku-Klux-Klan robes. Again, masked men – and again the reporter they temporarily kidnapped to witness the horror used the phrase "an assult carried out with military precision".'

De Forge adjusted his képi, turned slowly to face her. His hands were on his hips as he stared at her with his hypnotic eyes. She stared back. His voice was quiet, menacing

'What are you suggesting, Jean?'

'I'm not suggesting anything. But I am waiting for you to suggest an explanation for strange, sinister events.'

'The people are rising up to express their fury – their fear – at the emergence of an all-powerful Germany.'

'I see.' She sounded quite unconvinced, switched to a different topic. 'Is your wife, Josette, still indifferent to our friendship?'

'Josette remains loyal to me – to my position as the leading soldier in France,' de Forge said cynically. 'She has gone back to our apartment at Passy in Paris. She feels the time has come to hold some more of her famous salons. A lot of influential people attend them.'

'I also get the impression,' Jean remarked, 'that you are waiting for some important news. I felt that while we were in bed.'

De Forge shrugged, another giveaway gesture. 'You have too lively an imagination.'

All de Forge's instincts of danger close to him surfaced.

He was careful not to look at Jean. She had a way of inveigling herself into his mind. Had he told her too much? She was very curious about his activities, his future plans, had recently asked some dangerous questions.

'I must go.'

He hugged her tightly. Out of her line of sight his eyes were ice-cold. Had the time come to take precautions? Perhaps she was another assignment for Kalmar?

Or for *Manteau*?

The phone began ringing insistently.

The Paris–Bordeaux Express had stopped at Angoulême, well north of Bordeaux. Newman and Moshe Stein had alighted, were moving fast. While Stein went to collect the hired car Newman found a public phone, called Lasalle's office in rue de Saussaies.

He was told Lasalle was not available. Newman used all his powers of persuasion to convince the man at the other end that Lasalle was expecting his call. He was asked to give his number, to wait . . .

Moshe Stein drove up in a Renault, parked on the opposite side of the street, pretended not to see Newman. It was late afternoon, the sky was a storm of low dark clouds. It would soon be night and they still had a long drive to Stein's villa in the Landes. After they had visited Arcachon *en route*.

Before leaving Paris Newman had purchased a complete outfit of new clothes. He wore a beret, a French windcheater, French trousers and shoes. He fretted as he waited. Would anyone ever call him back? The phone began ringing . . .

Lasalle, still in Navarre's office with the three English visitors, answered, grasped that Newman was in a call box, put Tweed on the line.

'We've reached Angoulême,' Newman reported, speaking fast. 'I'm running out of coins. Arcachon next stop. Then on to the Landes with Moshe.' He was careful not to use the name Stein. 'In an emergency you can leave a message with Isabelle. I forgot to give you her number. It is – . Moshe has told me things which make me suspect we may be a target. Strange things happen in the Landes. Nearest small place to his villa is St Girons. He gave us a false address in Paris. Villa is close to the sea. St Girons is on the D42 – which cuts off west from the N10. Phone number . . .'

'Got it,' Tweed replied. 'Paula is coming south – may need a bolthole. Have you one more minute? I'll put her on the line . . .'

'Do it.'

'Bob . . .' Paula spoke clearly, quickly. 'Don't say too much. Could Isabelle be my bolthole?'

'Yes. I'll warn her you're coming. "Gruyère cheese" is your password . . .'

'Thanks, Bob. That's all.'

'Paula! Don't come. Moshe has told me things during our trip so far. Down here is a greater danger zone than round the Brudenell.'

'Then take care. Won't hold you.'

The connection was broken before he could protest any further. He stood in the box for a minute longer, thinking. God! There was a mistrust, danger everywhere. Moshe had given a false address inside the DST! A second before Lasalle had answered Newman had heard a girl operator say 'Ministry of the Interior . . .' Even in that stronghold of French security Tweed had listened, had said very little. Paula had said *Don't say too much*. She had used Isabelle's first name but not her surname. And his call had passed through the Ministry's switchboard.

Had he said anything directly linking Isabelle with Arcachon? He recalled his conversation. No, he hadn't. It all amounted to something quite terrifying – treason, treachery, paid informants in the highest places.

He left the box as it began to drizzle, a cold, raw drizzle of rain like a mist. Walking swiftly across the street he got into the passenger seat beside Stein. His suitcase was in the back. Stein, who knew the way, was behind the wheel.

'Let's move, Moshe . . .'

A long way south Newman saw in the night, in open country in the middle of nowhere, a petrol station illuminated like a glowing torch. He asked Moshe to stop for petrol.

'We're still well-tanked.'

'Stop for petrol,' Newman insisted.

He got out with Moshe and wandered round the inside of the cabinlike shop attached while Moshe had the Renault filled to the brim. Newman had seen plenty of Second World War photos and on a shelf he recognized an old German jerrican with a capacity for many litres.

The old boy who ran the station stared as Newman strolled out, holding the jerrican. Newman grinned.

'Wartime souvenir?'

'I have several,' the old boy responded as he held the nozzle from the pump. 'A truck driver threw them out when he was fleeing back to Germany.'

'Mind filling it up? So we have a spare supply? I'll pay whatever you want for the souvenir.'

The old boy, having filled up the car's tank, carefully filled the jerrican, Newman handed over the agreed price, placed it carefully in the back of the car under a rug after making sure the cap was well screwed down.

'We need that?' Moshe enquired as he drove off.

'We might. Keep moving at high speed, but just inside the limit. And avoid Bordeaux like the plague. Straight to Arcachon.

Earlier in Navarre's office in Paris the phone had rung again soon after Paula had spoken to Newman. She was just about to leave but waited on a gesture from Tweed.

Navarre took the call, spoke briefly, asked a couple of questions, again held out the instrument to Tweed.

'It's for you. Your butler is calling,' he said with a blank expression.

'Tweed here . . .'

'Thank God!' It was clearly Harry Butler's unmistakable voice. 'We flew in about an hour ago as you'd asked. I've had a helluva job at rue de Saussaies to persuade them to put me through to you. Had to show my card, describe what you looked like. Pete is with me, again as requested. What now?'

'Go to the Swiss Restaurant in the street leading off rue St Honoré direct up to Place de la Madeleine. It's on the first floor.'

'I remember. We met there once before. Then?'

'Both of you wait for someone to turn up. Stick to that someone like glue. Take instructions from the person you're guarding.'

'Got it. We need ironmongery?'

He meant weapons – handguns with plenty of spare ammo. Tweed assured him that they would be supplied. He put down the phone, looked at Paula who was lingering near the door. She had plenty of time to catch her Air Inter flight to Bordeaux.

'When you've been back to rue de Saussaies,' he told her,

'you walk straight to that Swiss restaurant – I'm sure you heard what I said on the phone. First floor.' He switched his gaze to Lasalle. 'Can you help again? I'd like Paula to go back with you now to rue de Saussaies. She needs two 7.65mm Walther automatics and plenty of spare mags.'

'And also,' Paula added, 'I need a .32 Browning – with extra mags . . .'

Navarre stood up when they had gone and he was alone in the large office with Tweed. He paced slowly, hands behind his back.

'What is the ultimate objective of this devious plan you have set moving?'

'De Forge is trying to destabilize France,' Tweed replied. 'I am going to destabilize de Forge. Apart from the fact that he was responsible for the murder of one of my agents – something I won't forget – it is essential we have a stable Europe to face whatever might confront us from the East . . .'

He stopped talking as Navarre answered the buzzing of his intercom. The dark-haired, agile Frenchman listened to the message Tweed couldn't catch, told them to send him up, switched off, and faced Tweed.

'Otto Kuhlmann has arrived. He will be with us in a moment. We are keeping in close touch with Germany . . .'

The door opened, Kuhlmann entered, his expression grim. He shook hands with Navarre, with Tweed, settled his bulk into a chair, studied his unlit cigar and then began speaking.

'I've come to hear whether there have been any further developments. The German press is full of the riots in Lyons, the anti-American and anti-German slogans which were shouted.'

'Don't worry,' Navarre reassured him. 'We are all working together. Tweed has a plan. I can't reveal the details. Tell us the present situation in Germany.'

'Germany is very uneasy, uncertain of itself. Suddenly we are the most powerful country in Europe with unification. It worries thoughtful men and women. Gorbachev took the lid off Russia – but I'm not sure he realized he was also taking the lid off Germany. He may have opened the gate to dark forces. To *Siegfried*. What scares me is *Siegfried* could be the weapon of the extreme Right. I just hope to God the members of *Siegfried* are imported terrorists. If so, our dragnet must locate them sooner or later . . .'

Kuhlmann talked on while Tweed sat thinking of Newman and Paula. Each of them by now well on their way to the south, to the Bordeaux region – de Forge's territory. He was still pondering the future when the phone rang once more.

Navarre ran behind his desk, picked up the phone, listened. It was a long call with the caller doing most of the talking. Watching him both Tweed and Kuhlmann were aware of a rising sense of tension. Navarre sat up straighter, leaned forward, his facial muscles taut. He put down the phone slowly, looked at his visitors.

'A catastrophe has occurred. That call was from Lyons – from the DST chief there.' He took a deep breath before continuing. 'The President of France is dead. The Prime Minister is dead. A saboteur blew up the track ahead of the TGV they were aboard. The whole train plunged into a deep ravine. Huge casualties.'

'The trigger,' said Tweed. 'The trigger General Charles De Forge was waiting for. France is about to erupt like a volcano.

Chapter Thirty

As they approached Arcachon at reduced speed Newman watched Moshe's headlights sweeping over the fringes of the *bassin* – the almost landlocked harbour. In the beams he saw beyond the country road a marsh-like area, small creeks of stagnant water with an oily gleam. In the near distance the lights of Arcachon came closer in the dark.

'I have to visit someone,' Newman said. 'Probably for no more than an hour, maybe longer. Do you mind staying at a small hotel until I come for you?'

'Of course not, my friend. I know a small hotel near the station. Why don't we drive there first, then you can take over the car?'

'It would be a help,' Newman admitted.

He felt a sense of relief. He was tired and the idea of walking to Isabelle's apartment did not appeal. Earlier, from a public call box in a village he had called her to warn he was coming. She had sounded wild with excitement, which worried him.

Moshe pulled up in front of a small hotel, got out with his case, wished Newman luck and ran inside. The cold was intense as a bitter wind scoured the resort. Ten minutes later Newman was inside Isabelle's apartment. Dressed in a warm two-piece blue suit she flung her arms round him.

'Oh, my God! You have no idea how glad I am to see you. Have you heard the news, Bob? It's terrible . . .' Again the words came tumbling out. 'The President is dead, has been assassinated. The TGV he was aboard on his way to Lyons was blown up. And, Bob, the Prime Minister is also dead. He was aboard the same express . . .'

'Slow down, slow down, Isabelle.'

'I'll make you some nice hot coffee. You feel cold. You must be in this weather. Milk but no sugar. You see, I remember . . . Come and make yourself comfortable in the living room. There is a log fire. Then we can talk . . .'

Newman welcomed the log fire crackling away as he sat by himself on a couch in the cosy room. Not only for the warmth after the arctic conditions outside – but also it helped him to marshal his thoughts.

The President of France dead – and the Prime Minister. When interviewing de Forge he'd sensed the General straining at the leash – the partial straitjacket of Presidential authority which had restrained him – to some extent. Now de Forge was free to act in any way he wished. There would be confusion – chaos – in Paris.

And all this, he thought grimly, meant that Moshe Stein and himself, too, would be in far greater danger in the Landes. What Moshe had told him had previously alerted him to the risks they were taking. Now those risks were tripled.

'Coffee . . .' Isabelle placed a tray on a small table and poured. 'Isn't the news frightful? It's so good to have you here. With me. The two of us alone again.'

She had splayed her long legs like a cat underneath her as she sat on the floor, leaning against his knees, sipping her coffee. He asked the question bothering him.

'Where is your sister? Any risk of her coming back?'

'No.' A catlike smile. 'After your phone call Lucille called me from Stockholm at her boyfriend's place. She is staying there longer. She's very understanding about us.'

'If she now? She knows my name?'

'Of course not!' Her back stiffened. 'I'm careful about your safety, even though I trust Lucille. But you know – pillow talk with her boyfriend. All she can tell him is a friend is with me. You look very French in your gear.'

'That's the idea.' Newman had removed his beret and raincoat. He made the effort before the warmth – and Isabelle – overcame him. 'I'll have to leave soon.' Her hand gently fondled his knee. Much more of this and he'd be spending the night with her.

'Bob, were you furious with me when I told you on the phone about my trip back to my mother's apartment in Bordeaux?'

'No, just concerned. And relieved that you escaped from those two phoney DST thugs. They'd have murdered you – like they did Henri at the Gare St Jean.'

'Instead I murdered them.'

'You defended yourself with great courage and ingenuity. It was an accident they deserved.'

'I have another confession to make . . .'

'I'm not a priest.'

'I know that.' She smiled wickedly. 'Anyone less like a priest I can't imagine.' Her hand moved up to his thigh, rested there. He clamped his own hand on top of hers, squeezed it to encourage her. And to prevent her hand wandering too much.

'Henri kept a notebook. He had filled it up and was going to record things in a fresh one. He gave me the old notebook to keep, said I should guard it. I promised not to look inside – he said that would be dangerous – and I kept my promise. I hid it among my underclothes in the Bordeaux apartment. It's still there.'

'Why didn't you give it to me?' Newman asked quietly.

'I forgot. I know it sounds crazy but so many things –

awful things – happened. Henri's murder. Then when we were at the apartment we spotted those men watching. I was concentrating on doing what you told me so we could get away safely.'

'And during your second visit – to get Henri's brooch?'

'For God's sake!' she flared up. 'Those men knocked on the door. You know what happened afterwards. I forgot the notebook again. Can you wonder I did?'

So Henri Bayle – alias Francis Carey, Tweed's agent – had left some kind of record of what he'd discovered in the Bordeaux region. Maybe he hadn't died in vain – an outcome Newman knew Tweed would live with for the rest of his time on earth unless Carey's mission had produced something vital. And maybe there was vital data in that hidden notebook. It could be even more important now France was sliding into anarchy after the brutal removal of the President and his Prime Minister.

'Isabelle, you have a key to the apartment in Bordeaux?' he asked casually.

'Of course. It's in the drawer of that escritoire.'

'Mind if I borrow it for a few hours?'

'*Why?*' Her eyes blazed with anxiety. 'What are you up to now?'

'Fetch me the key and I'll tell you.'

'I'm coming with you.'

She threw the remark over her shoulder as she jumped up and ran to the drawer. Newman was thinking it was fortunate he'd warned Moshe Stein he might be a while before he picked him up at the hotel – even more fortunate that Moshe had loaned him the hired Renault. Isabelle came back, holding the key in her hand behind her back. She knelt in front of Newman.

'You can't have the key until you tell me why you need it.'

'To get hold of Henri's note book. We need to know where to look before we go.'

She took his statement as agreement that she could come with him. She explained exactly which drawer in the bedroom contained the notebook, buried deep among her underclothes. Newman nodded, leaned forward, pulled her towards him. She came willingly as he hugged her, reaching one hand behind her shapely back. She kissed him greedily, felt to be devouring his mouth. His right hand grasped hers, forced the fingers apart, felt metal, took the key.

She wrenched herself free, a flaming fury. Standing up she looked down at him.

'You tricked me! Damn you! You're going by yourself.'

'Supposing we went together,' Newman said calmly, pocketing the key. 'The apartment may still be watched. You come with me. Half my attention is concentrated on protecting you, making sure no harm comes to you. When all my attention should be concentrated on guarding myself. Taking care of you, we could both get killed. My chance of survival is enormously increased if I'm on my own.'

She stood with her arms folded. Her flash of rage had subsided. Newman was counting on her intelligenec to grasp the sense of his argument. She smiled suddenly.

'I do understand, Bob. I liked your use of the word "protecting". You realize that is the back door key?'

'I was going to ask you that. Much easier to slip in and out that way.'

'And you'll be coming back here afterwards?'

'Your mother has a key to the Bordeaux apartment?'

'Yes . . .' The word was out of her mouth before she realized the implications of what he'd said. 'You mean you won't be coming back here? Then how will I know you are safe? I *must* know that, Bob.'

'I'll phone you when I can. Can't promise when that will be, but I can promise I'll phone.' He hesitated, knowing the next topic could be sensitive. 'Isabelle, an important girl who works for another man may come to see you . . .'

'Important to you?' Her eyes gleamed.

'I've just told you, she works for someone else – a man who is a close ally of mine. Her name is Paula. She'll identify herself by using the phrase Gruyère cheese.'

'I will look after her,' Isabelle promised, mollified to some extent.

Newman wondered what would happen if the strong-minded Paula did meet the equally strong-willed Isabelle. Maybe it hadn't been too good an idea giving Paula the French girl's address and phone number back in London. Too late now. He stood up.

'Would you by any chance have a few empty bottles? Wine, whatever?'

'It just happens that I was about to throw out a whole collection of empty mineral water bottles. I drink a lot of mineral water.' She looped her arm through his. 'I'm a thirsty soul – and not only for you. They're in the kitchen.'

They walked through a swing door and Newman noted everything was spotless, well organized, in the kitchen, which had a pleasant light blue colour scheme for the cupboards and working surfaces. Isabelle opened a cupboard, dragged out a strong plastic bag.

'There are twenty inside here – empty but with the caps on. I know, I counted as I dumped them. I do things like that. What are you looking at?'

On a shelf were stacked a series of aluminium funnels. Newman picked up a funnel, dived into the bag as she held it open for him, took out a bottle, removed the cap, inserted the end of the funnel. It fitted inside the neck of the bottle perfectly.

'Could I have this too? Unless it's your favourite?' he asked.

'Funny man.' She smiled. 'Drop it inside the bag. You are most welcome . . .'

He hugged her before he left, had trouble disentangling himself from her octopuslike embrace, walked through the deserted streets to where he'd parked the Renault, hid the plastic sack under a travelling rug in the back. He was driving slowly through Arcachon when he thought he recognized a lone French officer in uniform. The beams played over him for only seconds, then the solitary man merged with the shadows. Despite the uniform, the kepi pulled well down over the forehead, Newman could have sworn he'd just seen Lieutenant Berthier.

Something about the way he held himself, moved. Newman recalled his encounter in the lobby of the Brudenell – when the man posing as James Sanders, salesman of marine spare parts, had stubbed his toe and muttered *Merde!* It was an added worry as he drove out of Arcachon along the N650 to Bordeaux.

The first thing Newman noticed on entering the centre of the city was that there were far more troops in uniform walking in groups. Even at this late hour. He had decided to drive to the Bar Miami where Henri Bayle had been kidnapped by the phoney DST men before being murdered.

He knew the address from something Isabelle had told him on his previous visit. Doubtful whether the bar would still be open at this time of night, he parked close to it, walked the rest of the way.

Newman was confident that in his French clothes, his beret worn at a jaunty angle, he would pass unnoticed among the few couples hurrying to get out of the cold. The Bar Miami was still open.

He walked inside slowly, staring round to check whether there were any French officers among the patrons. They appeared to be mostly civilians – the hardened drinkers still clustered at a few tables. The head barman, described by Isabelle, was polishing the counter.

'Pernod,' Newman ordered.

'We'll be closing soon,' the heavy-set barman said as he took the money.

'Isabelle Thomas,' Newman whispered. 'Can't find her at her apartment. We're like that.' He showed two fingers entwined, winked. 'Any idea where she could have gone?'

The barman was about to shrug: Newman sensed the beginning of the negative gesture. Then the barman saw the two hundred-franc notes peering out from between Newman's fingers. His hand polishing the bar moved more slowly, he took a swift look round, leaned forward.

'I can't give you an exact address.'

'A location would help. Somewhere to start.'

'The other . . .' The barman stopped in mid-sentence and mentally Newman completed what he'd been on the verge of saying. *The other man said almost the same thing* . . . He couldn't take his eyes off the banknotes just out of his reach.

'Arcachon,' he whispered. 'That's the best I can do.'

'I need to know how *you* know that,' Newman persisted.

'The girl was in here some time ago – with her boyfriend. The one who got mugged down at Gare St Jean. I heard him tell her he'd visit her when she was in Arcachon. That's it.'

'Somewhere to start,' Newman repeated.

With a sleight of hand he passed over the banknotes. The barman began polishing furiously as though regretting his

311

indiscretion. Newman drank his Pernod, left the bar, hurried to his car.

He sat behind the wheel with the engine running for a few minutes. The news was the worst possible. If the barman would betray Isabelle to him, a stranger, for a handful of banknotes, then he'd clearly done the same before. It looked very much as though Isabelle was being traced by de Forge's men. And he couldn't get out of his mind the instinct that it *was* Berthier he'd seen in his headlights. He'd have to warn her at the earliest possible moment.

But the next job was to try and recover Bayle's – Francis Carey's – notebook. He drove away as men began to drift out of the Bar Miami. From now on he had to be careful.

Chapter Thirty-One

Newman drove slowly as he came close to the apartment building. He planned to park the Renault in a side street about a hundred yards beyond the alley where he'd parked during his visit with Isabelle. Far enough away not to arouse the suspicion of any watchers; close enough to run for it if he had to.

The street was fairly deserted. It was dark except for the glow from an illuminated shop window opposite the entrance to the apartment block and the murky glimmer of the street lights.

No one lingered outside the entrance but a group of men in heavy overcoats were crouched on the pavement outside the illuminated shop. They were playing some game with dice. In this bitter cold? As he cruised past them he glanced at the motley gathering. Inwardly he stiffened but he maintained the same speed.

A hundred yards or so beyond them he turned left into a narrow cobbled side street, parked with two wheels on the sidewalk. Grim-faced, he sat behind the wheel, his engine still running.

One of the group of dice-players had looked up as he'd passed them. Clad in his old heavy overcoat, collar turned up, the man also wore a fur hat. For a brief second Newman had had a clear view of the face beneath the hat. A face he'd seen before in a photograph.

An evil, grinning face. Like a gnome. A dangerous

gnome. Sergeant Rey of the Third Corps. De Forge's booby-trap genius. A man rumoured to carry far more clout than his rank of sergeant would suggest.

So why was he sitting crouched on the pavement opposite the apartment block in the freezing cold night? And grinning? As though in anticipation of some professional delight.

Newman adopted a slouching walk as he left the side street and moved towards the alley with the back entrance. A few couples also slouched along the street, huddled together, even pausing for an embrace.

Newman was recalling something Isabelle had told him. The staircase they had come down from her mother's first-floor apartment – the staircase down which the two fake DST men who tried to attack Isabelle had ended up dead – led only to her mother's apartment, which was peculiar. Round the back another rear staircase led to the other apartments.

So anyone investigating that staircase by picking the lock would realize the same fact. Someone like Sergeant Rey. Expert at rigging up boobytraps.

Out of the corner of his eye he was watching the group of dice-players who seemed absorbed in their game. As he drew level with the alley Newman was collided into by a couple absorbed in their own company.

'*Pardon!*' said the youth automatically.

When they had moved on Newman was inside the wide alley. Parked at the end of the alley before it turned the L-shaped corner to the rear of the apartment was a battered old van. By the glow from a low-powered wall light Newman read the legend *Ramoneur*. Chimney sweep.

He walked alongside the wall of the next building beyond the apartment block, his rubber-soled shoes making no sound on the cobbles. He was watching the closed door which led to the staircase, the door to which he had the key in his pocket. It was pure fancy – maybe nerves – he told himself, but the closed door had a sinister look.

He was also watching the van as he came closer, wondering if the chimney sweep was behind the wheel, smoking a cigarette before he went home to his nagging wife. He came up to the front, peered inside. Empty. Parked for the night. Probably the sweep had the nicest wife in all Bordeaux. He looked back at the closed door.

The idea came to him suddenly. Brought on by his certainty that it was Sergeant Rey he had seen with the dice-players. He took a bunch of keys from his pocket, selected the pick-lock given to him by a small-time villain in the East End of London. It all depended on whether the sweep was using old-fashioned equipment still favoured by some housewives – especially out in the countryside, the type of brush with a long handle composed of bamboo lengths inserted into each other – as opposed to a vacuum sweep.

It took him less than a minute to fiddle open the rear door. Shielding the beam with his hand, he examined the interior with his pencil flash. Thank God! The old-fashioned type.

Newman worked quickly, assembling the long handle. When he had the handle ready he attached the brush. Leaving the van, he looked round the alley, towards the main street at the end, listened. Nothing. No sign of life anywhere.

Holding the long, supple handle, he approached the rear door to the apartment block at an angle. Extending the brush in front of himself, he crouched low, moved the brush over the door. He covered the upper half, ran it slowly round the framework, then he pressed the brush as hard as he could against the area of the lock and the door handle.

The explosion was a muffled boom. The whole door flew

out, shattered into several pieces. The brush and handle were ripped out of his hands. Dust drifted from the inside of the apartment block. Had he attempted to open the door he would have been blown to pieces.

Newman ran towards the devastated entrance, ran inside. Holding his breath against the cloud of dust, he raced upstairs, pencil flash in one hand, key to the apartment door in the other.

If he moved swiftly he had no worry about the other inhabitants reacting quickly. They'd be in a state of shock, would stir themselves slowly. He opened the drawer in the bedroom, searched among Isabelle's underclothes trying not to leave a mess. The notebook was wrapped inside a slip. Francis Carey's note book. Small, slim, and bound in blue leather. He slipped it into his pocket, ran out of the apartment, closing the door before he hurtled down the staircase. He glanced over the banister which remained intact – opposite Isabelle's apartment a large chunk had been torn away. Looking down into the well he saw a dim light on the concrete basement floor. No wonder the two DST men had ended up dead – plunging down that drop.

He peered out into the alley before leaving the building. Deserted. But sooner or later the police would arrive. He walked swiftly towards the entrance, keeping close to the wall. He had just reached the corner when a man in a heavy overcoat walked round it. Sergeant Rey.

Newman reacted instantly, reinforced by his SAS training. Rey also reacted swiftly, shoving his right hand inside his coat. Newman's stiffened edge of his right hand struck Rey a vicious blow on the side of the neck. Rey slumped to the cobbles, began moaning and wriggling. Newman had hoped to kill the bastard. No time to hang about.

He ran towards his parked car after glancing over his shoulder. The dice-playing group was still watching the front entrance. He was halfway to the side street before they saw him, began clambering to their feet.

Newman's feet hardly touched the ground as he rushed to the Renault, dived inside, started the engine, drove off in the opposite direction from the main street behind him. At the bottom he turned into another side street. A second before he turned he glanced in his rear-view mirror. No sign of the dice-players. Slow on the uptake. And they hadn't seen his make of car.

He drove out of Bordeaux just inside the speed limit, headed along the lonely road back to Arcachon.

Moshe Stein opened his bedroom door in the small hotel on the third tap from Newman. Fully dressed, he ushered him inside, pointed to the rumpled bed.

'I slept in my clothes. I'm ready to drive through the night to my villa if that suits you. But maybe *you* need sleep. And your windcheater is covered with dust. Also, I repeat, I'm happy to go there by myself.'

'Don't talk rubbish. Give me time to make one phone call. Get ready for that instant departure . . .'

Newman used the bedside phone to call Isabelle. She spoke on the second ring: Newman guessed she'd been sitting by her phone.

'It's Bob,' he said. 'Now listen, I haven't much time. The sneak of a chief barman at the Bar Miami heard Henri mention Arcachon when you were talking one night. Just one bribe and he passed on to me what I'm sure he's also passed on earlier to others less friendly . . .'

'I will be very careful, Bob. Wonderful to hear from you. Where are you speaking from?'

'A long way off,' he lied. 'Now *listen*! I think when I was driving out of Arcachon I saw a certain Lieutenant Berthier. Got the name? Good. He's one of General de Forge's inner circle of confidants. Description . . . Got it? He's in uniform but he might change into civvy clothes. Which is why I emphasized his physical appearance. Stay indoors as much as you can . . .'

'I have to go out shopping some time.'

'Go out early – as soon as the shops open. Avoid crowds. Wear a scarf round your head. Stay indoors as much as you can. I may phone you again in the not very distant future.'

'When? *When*, Bob?'

'As soon as I can. Must go.'

He put down the phone before she could protest. He had been careful not to mention her name. He trusted Moshe implicitly – but how much torture can any man resist? After what had happened in the alley in Bordeaux he was beginning to think de Forge had become a monster. It could have been Isabelle – even her mother – who had tried to open that rear door. Their bodies would have been shattered into a bloody pulp.

'I'm ready when you are,' Moshe's voice said behind him. 'That is, if you still insist on coming. They know they missed one man during the massacre at Tarbes. A list of the members of the reading group and their addresses was left behind in the visitors' book everyone signed. I'm known to be an outspoken opponent of de Forge. I – we – will be targets.'

'I'm ready now,' Newman replied.

Half an hour later they were driving well south of Arcachon through the night towards the Landes.

*

Paula disembarked from the Air Inter flight at Bordeaux well after dark. Behind her, but apparently on his own, Harry Butler followed, dressed in casual clothes and wearing a leather jacket. He carried his suitcase in his left hand and he glanced all round the concourse.

Only a few passengers had come off the flight but there were quite a few uniformed French soldiers strolling round, carrying automatic weapons. Behind Harry Butler, also appearing to be on his own, walked Pete Nield, clad in a smart business suit and looking like a salesman.

It was Butler who spotted the girl in the uniform of a stewardess filming the new arrivals. He hurried on past Paula, walked into the raw cold of the night and found the waiting hired car he'd phoned for before leaving Paris. The courier girl was holding a card. *Pierre Blanc.* A nice common name and the Engine Room back at Park Crescent had provided all the necessary papers in that name.

Butler shoved his bag in the back, leaving a seat vacant, paid the girl in cash. Paula, carrying her small case, was walking away from the airport. Butler got behind the wheel, took his time settling himself, drove away and caught up with her. He stopped briefly, she jumped into the back, he drove off towards Bordeaux.

Behind them Pete Nield, who spoke fluent French, had joined the taxi queue. Paula stacked her case alongside Butler's, stretched – stiff from the flight – then relaxed, gazing out at the lights of the night.

'Well, Harry, we managed that well.'

'No, we didn't. A fat little man smoking a cheroot is on our tail in a Fiat. He saw me pick you up.'

'That's a problem.'

'Not really.' The burly Butler shrugged. 'The plan is we go first to the Pullman Hotel in the Mériadeck area, book in, pay in advance with cash, leave a few things in our rooms, then take off.'

'So? The fat little man with the cheroot?'

'We don't drive straight to Archacon when we leave the Pullman tonight. I've studied a map of the area. First we drive south. That Fiat has a very advanced-looking radio aerial. Cheroot may make regular reports. There is a country road I'll take, again heading south. Later we double back, make for Archachon and the delectable Isabelle. Newman's description, not mine.'

'And Cheroot?'

'Will no longer be with us . . .'

Paula had phoned Jean Burgoyne at the Villa Forban from Paris. Jean had told her tomorrow afternoon would be a good time for her visit: she would be *alone* at the villa. Paula had decided it would be a good chance to go and see Isabelle Thomas at Arcachon in the morning.

It was Harry Butler who had worked out the strategy on the assumption they were spotted by so-called 'DST' agents. They arrived at the modernistic Pullman, registered for one week, paid for two rooms in advance in cash. The hotel reminded Paula of a concrete bee-hive, especially when she looked round her room on the floor entitled *Privilège* – which meant their expensive accommodation.

The solid double-glazed window was shaped like a cell in a bee-hive, was difficult to look out from at that height. She moved quickly, lifted the lid of her case, took out a large plastic bag. Inside were a few clothes she'd been on the verge of throwing out.

She hung several things in the small cupboard. In the bathroom she put a half-used tube of toothpaste in a glass, tucked a worn toothbrush beside it and added one canister of talcum powder. Anyone secretly entering the room would conclude she was returning there shortly. Checking her watch, she closed her suitcase, waited exactly thirty minutes, and took the elevator back to the lobby.

Butler, having furnished his own room in a similar fashion with articles he never wanted to see again, was waiting behind the wheel of the Renault. Pete Nield sat in the back: arriving later by taxi from the airport he'd furnished his room with similar unwanted articles.

'Arcachon, here we come,' whispered Paula, sitting next to Butler.

'Not yet. Cheroot and his Fiat are parked up the road. First south out of Bordeaux into the countryside . . .'

Half an hour later they were driving along a traffic-free country road. Free except for their Renault and the headlights of a car some distance behind them. As they drove on Paula began talking.

'I wonder what's happened to Marler? He seems to have vanished off the face of the earth.'

'He's over here somewhere,' Butler responded. 'Don't ask me where because I haven't a clue.'

'Tweed had some very special mission for him. Love to know what it is. Most mysterious.'

'Why not ask Tweed when you next see him?'

'I suppose he's still in Paris. I got the impression he intends to stay there for a while to maintain contact with Navarre. We really have arrived at a historic time. The President and the Prime Minister killed in that TGV crash.'

Paula had first heard the news from a Frenchman she'd chatted to aboard the flight to Bordeaux. The few passengers were all talking about it excitedly. She also thought she had detected signs of alarm.

'I suppose I could ask Tweed,' she said with a poker face.

'And get a flea in your ear,' Butler grinned. 'And I'm

willing to bet Marler – wherever he is – doesn't have any idea where we are. Tweed is playing this one very close to his chest.'

He stiffened as the car crested a hill, glanced quickly in his rear-view mirror. Nothing behind except Cheroot and his Fiat. They descended a long straight slope. Nothing on the road ahead as far as they could see by moonlight. Butler slowed at the bottom of the hill, paused, manoeuvred his car so it blocked the narrow road broadside on.

'As good a place as any,' he said in his matter-of-fact manner.

'For what?' Paula asked.

'Wait and see.'

Butler checked the Walther in his hip holster, the weapon Paula had handed to him in a briefcase in the Swiss restaurant in Paris. Lasalle had been very accommodating and Paula was carrying a .32 Browning in her shoulder bag. Similarly, Nield was armed with another Walther. Butler took a map from the door pocket, got out of the car, leaving his headlights full on.

He walked a short distance back the way they had come and then stood in the road, holding up the gloved hand gripping the road map. The Fiat crested the hill, came rushing down towards him, slowed, crawled cautiously as Butler waved.

The Fiat stopped. Only the driver, Cheroot, behind the wheel. Butler walked confidently forward, displaying the map in the car's headlights. He came up on the side of the driver who had lowered the window, was gazing at him suspiciously. Butler began to gabble in French.

'We have lost our way. I don't even know where we are. This map is no help. Maybe you could . . .'

The fat little man, wearing a dark suit, kept the smoking cheroot clamped between his thick lips as he listened. Butler's right hand, encased in a motoring glove, struck like a snake. His clenched fist smashed into the Frenchman's jaw. There was a click as though something had been dislocated. The driver sagged behind his wheel.

Butler opened the door, felt around inside his overcoat, hauled out a .32 Browning. He hurled it over a hedge into a field, then followed it with the mag he'd first extracted.

Continuing his search, Butler found an Army identity card in his breast pocket. *Caporal Jean Millet*. He skimmed the card after the weapon into the field. A soldier who loses his identity gets into a helluva lot of trouble. Butler then noticed Millet had bitten right through his cheroot, leaving half of it presumably in his mouth – the other half lay burning on the floor. Maybe it would set the Fiat ablaze. With luck.

Butler ripped out the microphone apparatus attached to the dashboard, reached up and broke the aerial off the roof. Next he drew the key out of the ignition, hurled that into the night. His last act was to open the bonnet, feel around with his gloved hand, ripping up wires. As he walked back to the Renault he decided he could assume the Fiat had been immobilized. He got in behind the wheel.

'Trouble?' enquired Paula.

'For Corporal Jean Millet, yes. Now we can double back to Arcachon. Let's hope the natives are more friendly there.'

Chapter Thirty-Two

General Charles de Forge was alone in his office at GHQ, Third Corps, when the phone rang. Expecting Lamy, he lifted the receiver, announced himself in a brusque tone.

'*Manteau* speaking,' a voice said in perfect French. 'I did the job for you. Not bad. The President *and* the Prime Minister with one bomb. Which is what you wanted, I know ...'

'Who the hell are you?'

'*Manteau*. I just said so. Wrecking the TGV should come cheap to you for two million Swiss francs. I'd advise you to pay up this time, General. You don't want me to turn my attention to Third Corps GHQ, do you?'

'I need proof ...'

'Which you will get shortly. When you are convinced I'll tell you how to make the payment. In high-denomination banknotes. I hope the serial numbers don't run in sequence. I wouldn't like that.'

'Are you threatening me?'

'No, of course not. I never threaten. I act. Take it as a piece of life-saving advice. Goodbye ...'

The connection was broken. Stunned by the audacity of the call, de Forge sat still. Where the hell was Lamy? A knock on the door jerked him out of his state of momentary confusion. He called out in a barrack-room tone.

'Enter!'

The door opened and Lieutenant Berthier, immaculate as

always in his uniform, walked in holding a sheaf of papers in his left hand. His hair was still browner than normal: the result of the colourant he'd used before travelling to Aldeburgh. Just in time he remembered to salute.

'Well? Is it important? I'm expecting someone else.'

'Major Lamy phoned on his way here. I told him about the Reuters reports we'd just received and he said you would wish to see them at once.'

'Then put them on my desk.' De Forge prided himself on his ability to think of three things at once. 'You were sent to Arcachon to locate Isabelle Thomas, the mistress of the spy, Henri Bayle. You succeeded?'

'Not yet, General. She is not in the phone directory . . .'

'Phone directory!' De Forge's fist crashed on his desk. 'I send you there to find someone. You have her description from that barman at the Miami dive. And all you can do is to check the phone directory?'

'I did more, I assure you. I made discreet enquiries – no shopkeeper in Arcachon I was able to contact had any knowledge of her. I walked the streets in the hope of seeing her. Walked the streets all night . . .'

'Then go back and walk the streets all day. She could be dangerous. We do not know what Bayle told her. Return to Arcachon at once!'

'Yes, General . . .'

During the conversation de Forge realized the marked map of Paris was spread open on his desk. He folded it while he gave Berthier his dressing down. Alone, he began to read the reports with growing amazement. An hour later he was staring into space when there was another knock. This time it was Major Lamy.

'Where the hell have you been?' de Forge demanded 'You have been absent for many hours.'

'I have just returned from Lyons. My return flight was

delayed because of what happened. Have you read those reports?'

'I have read them.' De Forge sat very upright in his high-backed chair. 'It says here some old man in a village near the viaduct was train-watching through binoculars. Some damned stupid hobby of his. He says he saw just a few minutes before the TGV arrived a man in a cloak on the viaduct. *Manteau!* Later, DST officers searched the village, found a grey cloak stuffed in a litter bin. I don't understand any of this. Kalmar was supposed to . . .'

'Kalmar was assigned the mission . . .'

'Don't interrupt me! While you were taking for ever to return from Lyons I had a phone call. Guess who from?'

'Kalmar?' Lamy suggested.

'No! From *Manteau!* How the devil would he get hold of my private number? *Manteau* said he had wrecked the TGV. I didn't believe him. Now I read these reports. That idiot of an old man couldn't have invented his story – no one had heard of *Manteau*. On the phone he demands two million Swiss francs for destroying the TGV. You'll have to handle him when he calls again.'

'You don't mean we pay that enormous sum?' Lamy queried.

'Tell me, Lamy, just how much have we paid out to the unknown Kalmar so far?'

'Three million Swiss francs. That is for various jobs.'

'I know that!' De Forge stared down his subordinate. 'I have handed over three million for you to pass on to the ghost man, Kalmar. *Someone* has a lot of money in their Swiss bank account. Haven't they, Major?'

'General!' Lamy protested, shaken. 'I have told you how Kalmar operates. I phone a number, a girl answers, tells me the public phone box I have to go to, its number. Or, frequently, she asks me for names – the *targets*. Then she tells me the remote phone box I must go to. I wait for Kalmar to call me at that box at the agreed time. I give him more detailed instructions about the target – or targets. He speaks to me in English but with an accent I can't identify. I leave the money in a cloth bag behind the box. Every time be warns me he is watching – that if I attempt to identify him when he collects he'll kill me.'

'All very convenient,' de Forge sneered. 'Now we will turn our attention to Operation Austerlitz. The organization of panic in Paris. The sabotage units are moving into place?'

'All is going according to plan . . .'

'The famous phrase which means everything is going wrong. What is your view of Berthier?'

'One of my most trusted men,' Lamy replied emphatically.

'Those are the ones to watch,' de Forge observed cynically. 'A successful traitor is the man everyone has the utmost confidence in.' He unfolded the map of Paris which was marked with the positions of the saboteur cells moving into the capital. 'I had Berthier here an hour ago and I noticed he was studying this battle map upside down.'

'He is a member of the inner circle – the selected few who make up the top security section of Intelligence. I would expect him to be interested in all that is going on.'

'If you say so.' De Forge sounded unconvinced. 'The main thing is we must time Austerlitz carefully. It is too early to strike yet. The explosion must precede our march on Paris – to restore order when the present system is on the verge of collapse.'

'Our men will await the agreed signal.'

'See that they do. It could be soon now. Meantime step up security in the Landes. Do it now.'

'And Kalmar? When he calls?'

'Stall him. Although it is my bet this *Manteau* will call

you first. Insist on finding out how he knew our next requirement.' De Forge stared grimly at Lamy. 'My main worry is still this Kalmar–*Manteau* mystery. Is it the same man or are there two of them? But that is your problem. And don't forget,' he repeated. 'I want security in the Landes tighter than a steel drum.'

In Paris the lights were burning late in the Ministry of the Interior. Navarre had ordered food and drink to be brought in for himself, Tweed, Lasalle, and Kuhlmann.

The German police chief had been frequently on the phone to his Chancellor. The news of the catastrophe of the TGV wreck had reached Germany. Navarre also spoke to the Chancellor, assuring him that the crisis was coming under control, that all anti-German and anti-US demonstrations had been banned, that they represented only a tiny fraction of fanatics, which was the truth.

'Your plan is working, Tweed?' he asked during a brief interval of peace.

'My people are in place,' Tweed replied. 'They know what they have to do. We have moved with extraordinary speed. But what are your plans now France is without a President, a Prime Minister?'

'I have called an emergency meeting of the surviving cabinet for two this morning.'

'Why that unearthly hour?'

Navarre grinned. 'I plan to take control. Someone has to. I have great stamina. I am an owl – the night hours are my friend. If necessary I will exhaust the others until they agree to my appointment as temporary Prime Minister. But I will also retain control of the Ministry of the Interior.'

'A key post,' Tweed observed.

'Exactly. I am already mobilizing large numbers of heav-

ily armed CRS units ready to move south. I have comman-
deered a large fleet of helicopters. We may need them in the
Landes.'

'Why the Landes?' Tweed asked.

'Because General de Forge's strength, his support, is in
the south. Reports are coming in of civilians buying up
carbines and ammunition. Ostensibly for hunting. But I
know they fear the Algerians. Dubois of the *Pour France*,
backed by de Forge, will do everything he can to add fuel
to the flames. He is already making speeches saying the
Muslim element must be deported before North Africa goes
up in flames.'

'Going back to your taking over the Premiership,' Tweed
pointed out, 'won't your appointment have to be confirmed
by the National Assembly deputies?'

Navarre grinned again. 'Quite true. But there is a precedent. In 1958 de Gaulle was called back, confirmed by the
Assembly to form a government. The deputies were scared
witless, desperate for strong leadership, fearing a paratroop
landing in Paris by French troops from Algeria. A similar
situation prevails now. The deputies are again scared out of
their wits, desperate for strong leadership. De Forge hopes
to put himself forward – but I'm pre-empting him. Tonight.
At 2 a.m.'

They were eating when a further phone call came
through for Kuhlmann. He listened, said very little, asked
to be kept constantly informed, put down the phone.

'My informant has located another *Siegfried* cell. This time
in Hamburg. Armed police stormed the building they were
holed up in.'

'They?' Tweed queried. 'You mean this time you trapped
some terrorists?'

'Three men and a very small cache of explosives and
arms. Early interrogation indicates the men captured are

small fry from Alsace. Which makes sense since they speak both French and German in that French province near Switzerland.'

'The same informant who put you on to the other places, the one in Freiburg?' Tweed asked quietly.

'Yes. Why?'

'I just wondered. And now I am also wondering how Newman is getting on. Heading straight into the Landes.'

After bypassing the city, Moshe drove on and on along the N10 over a hundred kilometres south of Bordeaux. It was the middle of the night but Moshe seemed tireless, refusing to let Newman share the driving as be overtook long-distance truck after truck. The road surface was excellent and they were now deep in the Landes.

On both sides dense stands of black fir trees walled in the road, an endless land of trees. Newman noticed that some of the juggernauts they overtook had names. A reminder of how far south they were, that Spain was not so far away. Newman was becoming hypnotized by watching twin glaring eyes approaching from the opposite direction, speeding past. Then the traffic thinned. Moshe began talking to keep himself alert.

'One incident during the Tarbes massacre I forgot to tell you. All the other Jews were burnt to death, as you already know. Two of us decided we would escape by a rear exit. My friend went ahead of me to open the door while I searched for a weapon. When he opened the door it blew up in his face, threw his mangled body against the wall opposite.'

'I guess that would be an acquaintance of mine. Sergeant Rey. De Forge's boobytrap specialist. I met him but when I left him he had trouble with his jaw. How did you get away?'

'After seeing what happened to the door, I scrambled out of a window, dropped into a narrow gully concealed by dead ferns. I crawled to safety. There is a similar escape route from the Villa Jaune, where we are going. I will show you. I will also introduce you to an old woman who knows how de Forge uses the Landes near the sea. As a burial ground . . .'

It sounded macabre, but Moshe would tell him more when the time came. Moshe had now swung off the main highway to Biarritz on to the more countrified D42. The signpost had carried the legend ST GIRONS. With what Moshe had just told him Newman was recalling Tweed's precise instructions before he left Paris.

'It is the south which is de Forge's domain. Bordeaux is the symbol of defeat in 1871 and 1940 which he is exploiting to the full. This time, victory and power for France will come from Bordeaux, or so he is saying.'

'How do you know that?' Newman had asked.

'Lasalle has planted at least one informant inside de Forge's camp. I've no idea who it is, but Lasalle receives regular reports. So that is why I'm pleased you're going south. Find out what that devil is up to. Above all, if you can, find evidence which will bring him down. We are supporting Germany as well as France in this endeavour. And when you can, maybe you'd like to contact Kuhlmann's secret agent in Bordeaux – Stahl. You have his details . . .'

Tweed, Newman remembered, had been unusually emphatic and forceful, stressing his points with chops of his hand. All indications that under his calm, detached manner Tweed was more worried than he'd ever been.

'Moshe, this Villa Jaune we're going to. Describe for me its location.'

'West of St Girons. Hidden in the forests of the Landes. But very close to the sea. At night especially you can hear the waves crashing on the nearby beach. And during the day, often, if it is a heavy sea. The dunes run for miles. It was an idyllic spot before the murders began.'

'What murders?'

'Better that you see for yourself. One demonstration, they say, is worth a thousand words. And there is someone who can show you maybe better than I can.'

'Describe the layout of the villa. Inside.'

'A single-storey old building built of wood. On the side facing the sea there is a verandah running along the front. Inside two bedrooms, one living-dining room, a kitchen, a toilet. That's it.'

'The entrances and exits,' Newman persisted.

'A heavy wooden front door leading to the verandah, windows at the front and on both sides. None at the back – except for one low down, almost level with the ground, which has bars. The window opens close to another deep gully similar to the one which saved my life at Tarbes. There is a rear door to one side. Also a cellar – with no way out.'

'I've got the picture,' Newman replied.

He said nothing more as they drove on through the night, passed through St Girons, which had no lights, and some distance beyond Moshe swung on to a track leading through the fir forest.

Newman checked his watch. It would be dawn in about two hours' time. Assaults were often launched at dawn.

In Arcachon, by chance, Butler chose the same small hotel Newman and Moshe Stein had used earlier as temporary accommodation for Stein. They walked in as planned during the middle of the night. Paula hanging on to Butler's arm, pressing herself close to him.

Butler wasted no time dealing with the sneaky-looking night clerk who studied the couple and Nield bringing up the rear with the cases. In his hand Butler held folded French banknotes, asked for three rooms alongside each other speaking in French.

'That might be difficult.' The clerk peered over his half-moon glasses. 'We are almost full up.'

'In late November? Come off it. We've had a long drive from the Côte d'Azur. I said three rooms, alongside each other. Of course, if you can't manage it . . .'

The banknotes began to disappear inside his pocket. The action galvanized the deal. He made a brief performance of studying the register.

'Pardon me. It so happens we have three such rooms on the first floor. Even in the middle of the night . . .' He named an excessive price.

'You think I'm a raving lunatic?' Butler continued in French. 'Take this for all three rooms for the night.'

'I will see you are not disturbed.'

The clerk leered. He was convinced the three rooms were a ploy – that Paula would be sharing a bed with Butler. Which was exactly the impression they wished to create.

Butler carried Paula's case into the middle room, so she would be flanked by Nield and himself in the other two rooms. He was leaving the cramped room when Paula spoke.

'Thank you, Harry. For looking after me.'

'Which reminds me,' Butler responded. 'No slipping away without us.'

'I promise. In the morning I'll phone Isabelle and hope I can go see her with my two escorts. Then in the afternoon we'll drive to the Villa Forban so I can renew my acquaintance with Jean Burgoyne. After phoning her first.'

'Should be OK. Just so long as we remember we're right in the danger zone. Anything could happen. Goodnight . . .'

In a small apartment near the rue du Bac on the left bank in Paris, Marler sat up in bed smoking a king-size. He was fully dressed in French denims and a French shirt, and his only concession to brief relaxation was his open-necked collar.

By his side was one of the most sophisticated mobile telephones in the world, engineered by the basement crew at Park Crescent. It was equipped with a powerful transmitter and a very long aerial which extended at the press of a button. He was in frequent communication with Tweed at Navarre's Ministry of Defence. But its potential range was far greater.

Inside a ready-packed suitcase was an assortment of items apart from a change of clothes. Marler was posing as a cosmetics salesman: inside the small case were 'samples' of his trade – certain articles of equipment disguised by the Engine Room at Park Crescent to look like cosmetics.

Inside a large hold-all under a woollen scarf was a dismantled Armalite rifle complete with sniperscope and ammo. The weapon had been delivered to him inside the hold-all by one of Lasalle's trusted couriers in a dubious Montmartre club. Marler had then travelled aboard the Metro to return to his base. The only person in the world who knew his whereabouts was Tweed.

Marler was also carrying a very large sum of money and a collection of open-booking Air Inter tickets. Some had already been used. Checking the time, Marler closed his eyes and fell asleep. He had the ability to catnap at any hour. The mobile phone tucked on the pillow close to his ear. He'd hear the beep instantly. He was expecting fresh instructions.

Chapter Thirty-Three

'Here we are. My little home in the forest,' said Moshe.

Newman stared grimly at the Villa Jaune. It was large –
but little more than an old wooden cabin. Located in a
clearing, it was encircled by a dense palisade of firs which
seemed about to advance on it in the night, to swallow it
up. Where the hell the 'Jaune' – the 'Yellow' – came in was
more than Newman could fathom, but he felt disinclined to
ask Moshe.

He checked his watch. Well over an hour to dawn yet.
As Moshe carried both cases to the verandah and opened
the heavy front door, Newman gathered his own load. He
took the sack containing twenty empty mineral water
bottles, Isabelle's metal funnel, and the jerrican of spare
petrol out of the car.

The vehicle was parked near the side of the 'villa', and
was partly concealed by the bank of undergrowth Moshe
had driven it into. Newman arrived on the verandah as
Moshe switched on lights. Dumping his load, Newman
called out: 'Moshe, I'm going to take a look round the
outside. Be back in a minute.'

'A glass of wine will be waiting . . .'

A high wind was blowing spasmodically. As Newman
prowled round the area he heard a sound like the surge of
the sea, realized it was the wind in the treetops. The wind
dropped suddenly and a similar sound continued. A crashing of breakers on the nearby shore.

Newman studied all the approaches. He went to the rear of the cabin, found the deep gully Moshe had told him about. Masked by last autumn's dead bracken, it ran a distance away from the back of the Villa Jaune. A man crawling along it would be completely concealed from anyone standing at ground level. Halfway along it ran through a culvert, then continued on the other side.

Newman found the atmosphere of the Landes claustrophobic. He felt hemmed in as he moved silently over the spongy ground, his Smith & Wesson in his hand. He felt a need to get into the open and walked towards the sea.

The forest ended abruptly. Ahead of him was the vastness of the Atlantic, huge rollers sweeping in slowly, thumping down on the shore, spreading a carpet of surf on the beach. His night vision was good and he was aware suddenly of movement on the beach.

He was perched up where he stood and between where he waited and the beach was an area of Saharalike sand dunes. Further south the dunes rose to a great height. The figure crouched by the shore, picking up something, was an old woman wrapped in a black shawl.

He moved back into the forest slowly, then walked rapidly to the cabin. Easy to find – from a distance it was a beacon of lights. Was Moshe crazy? He opened the front door and his companion was sitting in front of a large wooden table, sipping from a glass of wine. He gestured to a second glass.

'That is for you.'

'Are you mad? This place is lit up like a Christmas tree. If they are coming for you, you're making it so damned easy for them.'

'If they're coming, I am ready.'

'Well, I'm not. And there's a weird old woman fooling around on the beach. At this hour.'

'Good!' Moshe jumped up. 'Old Martine. She is the one who will tell you what has been happening here. We go to her now . . .'

'After you've switched off the bloody lights and locked the door . . .'

Together they hurried to the sea. Newman had trouble keeping his balance as he plunged after a more sure-footed Moshe down the sand dunes. Moshe called out to the old woman, then warned Newman.

'Old Martine is suspicious of strangers. She has reason to be, as you'll hear. I will introduce you as a security agent from Britain – which in a way you are. She thinks all French security personnel are in league with de Forge.'

Newman now saw what the crone had been doing. Close to where the surf carpet covered the sand she was collecting brushwood washed ashore. Her lined face with a beaky nose and a strong jaw peered out at Newman from under the shawl as Moshe made the introduction.

'I am here on an official mission,' Newman told her frankly in French. 'To investigate the crimes of General de Forge.'

Her alert eyes studied him. 'Your French is very good for an Englishman,' she observed.

'I have been told that I can pass for a Frenchman . . .'

Newman spoke the words slowly in English, waited a moment, then reverted to French.

'You have information which would be useful to help me bring him to justice?'

The dam broke. She spoke rapidly, brandishing her sheaf of brushwood like a weapon. Her eyes glittered with hatred.

'My nephew was in the Third Corps. De Forge had him shot as a spy. Just as he had many others shot here. This is

338

de Forge's cemetery – the Landes. Come with me. Come! I will show you. Come!'

Her free gnarled hand grasped Newman's arm. He was surprised at the strength of her grip as she hurried him back to the sand dunes, released her grasp, scrambled in front of him up the dunes with great agility. The wind had dropped and as she led them into the forest away from the surge of the Atlantic an eerie silence closed in on the group.

She was heading towards the Villa Jaune and then turned south away from it, following a path between the trunks of the giant firs. Newman checked his watch. He hoped this wouldn't take long. He was anxious to return to the cabin. As they'd passed through sleepy St Girons he'd noticed a car parked in a side lane with two men inside. He had the strongest instinct the maximum danger hour was close to dawn.

The crone led them down a shallow slope into a clearing littered with low humps shrouded with dead undergrowth and rotting bracken. Old Martine brandished her brushwood like a wand.

'De Forge's burial ground.' She peered up at Newman. 'You have strong nerves, sir?'

'I've seen some grim things in my time.'

'Then use your foot to dig into one of those humps. If you like, use your gloved hands – although you may not like what you find . . .'

Newman crouched over the nearest hump, thrust aside a deep mass of matted bracken, swept soil damp from recent rain to one side. His hand encountered something hard. He dug deeper, stopped. He was staring at a skull, part of a skeleton stretched out and which, he guessed, must have lain there for at least two years.

But what fixed his gaze was the third eye in the skull. A

339

hole which could only have been made by a bullet. No trace of clothes. Removing his gloves, he took out the small camera supplied by Park Crescent, pressed the button for night shots, took three. Putting on his gloves, he then replaced the soil, hauled the undergrowth back in roughly its original position.

'Now here!'

The crone had taken charge. She stood, erect now, her bony finger pointed at another hump which showed signs of recent disturbance. He walked over to it, crouched again, gritted his teeth, removed the covering of bracken and soil. Underneath lay the body of a French soldier in the early stages of decomposition. This time there was no doubt that he had been dispatched by a bullet fired into the forehead. Newman knew he was a French soldier because he still wore his uniform of a private.

He used his camera to take ten shots of this corpse. It was the body of a young man who had joined up to serve the Army and this was his fate. Newman then forced himself to search the corpse's pockets but all traces of identification had been removed. He looked at the man before he rebuilt the grave. The victim gave a macabre impression of being asleep.

'Now here!'

The crone again. The bony finger pointing at death, at another hump. Newman was experiencing a feeling of nausea. He shook his head, glanced slowly round the clearing, counted twenty makeshift graves. A horrific crime.

'Why?' he asked the crone.

Martine spat on the ground. 'De Forge eliminates those who do not support him. I told you about my nephew . . .'

'Yes. Suspected of being a spy. But what about all the others? They can't all have been spies.'

'Some objected to digging the graves. They were shot.'

'How do you know that?' Newman pressed.

'I saw, heard one man throw down his shovel, protest to his officer. He was shot immediately.'

'How could you see them without their seeing you?' Newman demanded, still unconvinced.

'I sat in the undergrowth at night when I heard activity. You don't believe Old Martine? Watch.'

She moved away, dressed in black, suddenly vanished into thin air. Newman had been watching her and was disconcerted. He looked round carefully, then called out.

'Martine, where are you?'

'Over here.'

Newman, followed by Moshe, walked in the direction her voice had come from. He damned near stumbled over the huddled form crouched at the foot of a thick tree trunk. He was convinced. He told Moshe he was going down to the beach for a moment. Newman was not taking any chance of infection after messing about with corpses. He threw his gloves out to sea: the tide was receding. Bending down, he washed his hands thoroughly in the surf.

When he was making his way back to Moshe he saw Martine in the distance, moving north up the beach, gathering more brushwood.

'We must hurry back to the villa,' he told Moshe. 'You know where Martine lives?'

'In a tiny abandoned villa on the outskirts of St Girons. She keeps herself warm with brushwood fires and logs from the forest. She sells the excess, uses the money to feed herself.'

'How some people live.'

'At least she is alive.' Moshe waved a hand towards the hideous burial ground. 'Troops from de Forge's army land

341

in rubber dinghies from the sea. I sometimes heard the
crackle of rifle fire. I thought it was target practice. I never
dreamt I was hearing firing squads.'

'Talking about survival, we have to make certain preparations as soon as we reach the villa. This is what we will
do . . .'

The attack came a little earlier than Newman had expected.
They were settled inside the cabin with only lights switched
on illuminating the verandah when they heard the distant
chant coming closer.

'Death to all Jews! Death to all . . .!'

Since returning to Moshe's home both men had been
working non-stop. Moshe had oiled the rear barred widow
so it slid open noiselessly. Newman had obtained cleaning
cloths from Moshe, had torn them into strips. Then he
attended to the mineral bottles he'd obtained from Isabelle.
He divided them up – ten for himself, ten for Moshe. The
bottles, caps screwed on, were distributed in the pockets of
Newman's trenchcoat, tucked down inside his belt. Moshe
wore a jacket with large pockets, similarly stuffed with
bottles; more inside his own belt. Newman gave him his
spare lighter as the chant grew in volume. They were very
close now.

'I still think you should leave,' Moshe began arguing. 'If
you go now you could probably escape.'

'It's my war as well as yours. My job is to help stop de
Forge. Those are his men coming to get you. I'll bet ten
thousand pounds on it.'

'I think you ought to leave,' Moshe persisted. 'I wish I
had never agreed to let you come.'

'Don't you want vengeance? Isn't that the same chant

you heard at Tarbes just before your friends were all incinerated?'

'The very same chant . . .'

'So it could be some of the same men. Don't you want revenge?' Newman repeated.

'We cannot just lie down and die again as once we did.'

'So what the hell are you grumbling about?'

'I wasn't grumbling,' Moshe protested.

Newman grinned in the dark. 'You were giving a very good imitation of it . . .'

He stopped speaking as he heard the chanting increasing in venom. They sounded to be inside the clearing which surrounded the villa now. He crept to a window as a glow of light lit up the interior of the cabin, creating sinister shadows on the walls. He sucked in his breath.

The leader of the attacking group holding aloft a cross of fire – the Cross of Lorraine adopted by General de Gaulle during the Second World War. Newman stared at this ghastly perversion of a sacred symbol. The leader was flanked by four men spread out like a military wing on either side, advancing on the cabin. All nine men wore terrifying white sheets which came to a peak at the tops of their invisible heads. All the flankers carried flaming torches as they chanted the same dirge over and over. It was pure Ku Klux Klan.

'You must go now, Bob,' Moshe whispered.

'Two of us will leave here alive – or two of us will be left here dead,' Newman said calmly. 'You know the plan.'

'Yes, I can do it. Is it time?'

'Let them get a little closer. The bastards are enjoying themselves, want to make the terror last a little longer.'

'They will burn the villa to the ground.'

'That is *their* plan. Now we operate ours . . .'

They left the villa by the rear window, closing it behind them. Newman led the way, crawling swiftly along the gully below the level of the surrounding ground. He had already made one trip earlier to make sure they could ease their way swiftly through the culvert pipe. He emerged from the end of the stuffy gully and smelt the aroma of pines. Moshe clambered out behind him. As planned, Newman moved to the right of the villa, Moshe to the left.

Newman had a bottle in his hand, uncapped it and the pine aroma was replaced by the stench of the bottle full of petrol from the jerrican – fed inside with the aid of Isabelle's funnel. He pulled out a short length of the strip of cloth he had stuffed in the neck, came round the end of the villa to face the two outer flankers on his side. Using his lighter, he ignited the cloth, hurled the bottle. It landed between the flankers, exploded into flame. Greedily, the flame set light to the sheets of both men and they became human fireballs, screaming.

Newman lit a second fuse, threw it at the leader holding the obscene fiery cross. The bottle exploded at his feet, swept a sheet of flame over his strange clothing. The cross wobbled, fell on to the ground and the leader fell into the inferno, shrieking with terror. Newman threw a third bottle. It exploded just before it landed, firing the white sheets of two more attackers. They dropped the torches and this added to the conflagration.

Over to his left Moshe was hurling his own fire bottles. His aim was accurate. Four attackers were in flames, running a short distance as they shrieked, then collapsing. Hell that night was flames soaring into the night. The chanting was replaced with the shouts and shrieks of the men who had come to murder Moshe Stein, to burn him to death.

There was a sudden silence. The only sound was the dying crackle of fire burning itself out as an unpleasant stench began to drift through the Landes. Two men had rolled on the ground in a futile attempt to save themselves, and their action had extinguished the fire more quickly compared with the others now burnt to a cinder.

Newman walked over to these two dead men. The sheets had been destroyed but their clothes had miraculously survived as they lay motionless. Under the sheets they had been wearing French Army uniforms. Newman calmly took out his camera, recorded five photos of each corpse.

'It is horrible,' said Moshe, hurrying up behind Newman.

Hardened by his experiences a few years before behind the lines in East Germany during the days of the Cold War, Newman's hand was steady as a rock as he took his pictures. He put away the camera, emptied his pockets of unused bottles.

'It was them or us. Now I have evidence. I suggest we pack at once and drive straight back to Arcachon. I have to make contact with Paris . . .'

Chapter Thirty-Four

At 8.30 a.m. in Arcachon smoke-coloured clouds pressed down on the resort like a lid. It was bitingly cold as Paula stepped out of the Renault near the entrance to the apartment block where Isabelle Thomas lived.

Butler stepped out of the rear to escort her. Pete Nield remained at the wheel – to guard the car, to watch the entrance ahead of him. Both Butler and Nield carried small walkie-talkies. At any sign of danger approaching while they were inside, Nield would warn Butler.

Paula had phoned Isabelle from the hotel before they set out. The French girl had not sounded enthusiastic about the arrival of Paula, but had agreed to see her. Butler had insisted on accompanying Paula to the apartment.

Isabelle opened the door on a chain. She peered out and studied Paula.

'Yes?' she enquired.

'I'm Paula Grey. I wonder if you have any Gruyère cheese?'

'Who is the man with you?'

'My minder.' Paula smiled. 'A friend and a professional bodyguard. He has me on a tight leash.'

Isabelle released the chain, opened the door, closed and replaced the chain, locking the door when they were inside. She led them across the dining-living room to a sitting area. Butler said he wouldn't intrude, was there somewhere close by he could wait?

'You would like coffee?' Isabelle asked.

'Yes, please. Black, no sugar,' Paula responded.

Five minutes later Isabelle returned with coffee, leaving Butler in the kitchen. Again she studied Paula from tip to toe, unsmiling as she sat opposite her with the table between them. Paula sensed an underlying hostility and realized its source with Isabelle's next question.

'You are a very close friend of Bob Newman's?'

'I work for a security organization. Mr Newman helps us from time to time. He knows the world so well from his experiences as a foreign correspondent. *I* know him well but I wouldn't say he's a very close friend.'

Paula saw the relief in Isabelle's eyes she tried to conceal. So it was jealousy. She could understand Newman being attracted: Isabelle was not only an extremely good-looking girl, she was also very intelligent. It explained the enthusiasm with which Newman had described her. Paula charged the subject quickly.

'Do you feel safe here? You've suffered some ghastly experiences.

'There's something I should tell you, Paula. May I call you Paula?' Her mood had changed, had become animated. 'Good. I'm Isabelle. Bob told me to do any shopping early in the morning. To keep under cover here the rest of the time. I've done exactly as he said.'

'You're wise . . .'

'Wait! I heard something. A shopkeeper told me about a rumour that the peculiar ship from Britain with its hull split in two may arrive here soon. Bob was interested in that ship. And in a lecherous man called Lord Dane Dawlish.'

'He's expected?' Paula asked sharply.

'I don't know.'

'Have you any idea where this shopkeeper heard the rumour?'

'Yes!' Isabelle looked pleased. 'He told me he heard it in the Martinique Bar near the front.'

'Could you describe to me the location of this Martinque Bar?' Paula probed.

'Yes!' Isabelle seemed eager to help now. 'I can draw you a plan showing you how to get there from here. It will be open now. It's not really a very nice place. I'll get a pad . . .'

When she had drawn her diagram Paula noticed how neat and clear it was. Like her handwriting. She drank more coffee as the French girl made sure she understood the directions. Although like a coiled spring in her intensity, Isabelle moved with great gracefulness.

'Can I ask you a question?' she asked when Paula folded the diagram.

'Ask away.'

They had conversed in English ever since Paula's arrival. A feeling of warmth was developing between the two women.

'Have you any idea,' Isabelle began tentatively, 'when we may expect to see Bob back in Arcachon?'

'No idea at all. Most of the time he doesn't reveal to me his movements.'

'Paula!' Isabelle was intense again. 'I almost forgot. This may be something you should know. Bob phoned me some hours after he'd left. To warn me he felt sure he had seen an officer called Lieutenant Berthier when he was driving out of Arcachon late at night. He described him. He said I should be careful of this man.'

Paula was taken aback. Her mind flashed to the incident when he'd driven her to Jean Burgoyne at Admiralty House in Aldeburgh. When he'd attempted his amorous approach. Berthier – who had posed as James Sanders, who was a key member of General de Forge's inner circle. Arcachon was no longer the safe haven they had hoped for. She worded her reply carefully.

'I have heard of this Berthier. He is a dangerous man. Please do take Bob's advice and stay under cover. And now I must go.'

'You must be careful yourself,' Isabelle urged. 'If you need a safe place to hide, come here immediately.'

'I won't hesitate to take up your offer.' Paula hid her dismay at the news of Berthier's presence. 'And I will keep in touch with you.'

Butler emerged from the kitchen. 'Thank you for the cup of excellent coffee,' he said formally.

He waited until they reached the pavement after he had peered out in both directions. They walked towards where Nield appeared to be sleeping behind the wheel of the Renault.

'Do you trust her?' Butler asked.

'The only people I trust in this situation are Tweed's team. Berthier turning up here is a shock. We'll have to keep a lookout for him where we're going.'

'And where might that be?'

'To the Martinique Bar. That's where the rumour originated that Dawlish's *Steel Vulture* may be coming here. I shudder every time I think of that ship. It takes me back to when poor Karin and I were scuba-diving off Dunwich. When we surfaced we saw that evil-looking ship. Let's hope we can find out something at the Martinique.

It's not really a very nice place. Isabelle's description of the Martinique was pure British understatement. Paula, dressed in a trenchcoat, walked in by herself as Butler strolled in half a minute later, giving the impression Paula was on her own. This time Nield did not stay with the car: he wandered in shortly after Butler had entered.

A seamen's waterfront bar – even though not on the front. Paula walked straight up to the bar. She was aware of seamen in pea-jackets staring openly at her. One made an obscene suggestion in a loud voice. She ignored it.

'A dry Vermouth, please,' she asked the barman.

Perching herself on a stool, she chanced a tricky question when the barman, a rough-looking type with a cast in his right eye, brought her drink.

'I hear that British twin-hulled ship, the *Steel Vulture*, is due to arrive back in Arcachon soon. Is it?'

'I wouldn't know. My job is to make this place pay.' He glanced over Paula's shoulder. 'The customer you should ask is sitting at that table in the corner behind the door.'

Paula sipped her drink. It was too early in the day for any drink, but it would look funny if she just left the glass full. She looked round the bar which had pictures of nude girls in various poses on the walls. Then she had a bad shock. Sitting at the corner table was a heavily built man with wide shoulders, dressed in a clean pea-jacket. Brand.

She had last seen Dawlish's deputy at the shooting party held at Grenville Grange on the river Alde. The day she had interviewed Dawlish, repelled his advances. Brand was staring straight back at her. He said something to his two tough companions, stood up, made his way towards her. His large hand gripped her shoulder as he climbed on to the adjoining stool.

'Miss Paula Grey. Now what would a nice lady like you be doing in Arcachon – and in a bar like this?'

'If you want to talk to me will you kindly first remove your paw?'

'A choosy dame.' The hand left her shoulder. 'It's a small world, as they say.'

'As you just said – so what are you doing here far away from Aldeburgh?'

'Still the nosy investigative reporter. Always asking questions. One day that habit will get you into nasty trouble.'

'I happen to do the occasional interview. My main job is with an insurance company.'

Brand grinned unpleasantly. 'And you're practised at evading questions. I asked why you were here. In this bar. In Arcachon.'

Paula swivelled her stool, to face him, to make it easy to get away if necessary. She smiled icily.

'Brand, Ill make a deal with you. I'll answer you if you first answer me. Fair enough?'

'No, it isn't.' Brand's expression was ugly. 'Don't get clever-clever with me.' His hand reached out again, grasped her forearm, held it tight. Paula willed herself not to wince. He had the grip of an ape. 'The last woman who tried that is still bruised all over. I want an answer . . .'

'I can give you one.' Butler had come up behind Brand. His tone was as controlled as his expression. 'Miss Grey and I have an appointment to keep. And if you don't take your hand off her pronto I'll break your arm. Maybe both arms.'

Brand let go of Paula, dropped off his stool, swung round to face Butler who stood a good two inches higher. Brand bunched his huge fist, stared at Butler who stood quite still. Something about Butler's stance, his poker-faced expression, bothered Brand. He shrugged, turned to go.

'I could make mincemeat of you,' he growled.

'Try it,' Butler suggested.

Brand's bull-neck, his face, reddened. He turned back and measured up Butler again. His arm stiffened, ready to strike the first blow.

'You can have a brawl if you want to,' Butler went on calmly. 'Of course someone will call the police and I have

351

plenty of witnesses as to who started this. When you're lying poleaxed on the floor.'

'You'll be late for your bloody appointment.'

Brand marched off back to the corner table where his two companions waited. One of them had started to get up when he saw what was happening. Nield, who had wandered close to the table, pressed his left hand hard on the man's shoulder. He held him down as he spoke in French, his eyes flickering to the other man.

'DST. Make any trouble and I'll crack you on the skull.' His right hand was inside his coat, gripping the Walther. 'And then I'll haul you in for questioning as a suspected terrorist . . .'

Paula and Butler passed the table where Brand had just sat down again. Dawlish's right-hand man looked away from the group as it left.

Paula reacted as she settled herself beside Butler who was behind the wheel. Nield slipped into the back of the Renault.

'Thank you, Harry. That was getting grim. Did you see the size of his hand? He was really hurting me. But he backed off from you.'

'Which is interesting,' Butler commented. 'It was the mention of the police coming which scared him off. Of course, you know who he is.'

'Brand. Dawlish's close confidant, as far as we know. He got uptight when I asked him what he was doing in Arcachon. I'm wondering whether the *Steel Vulture* is expected. If that's why he's here.'

'Unless he has some other job in mind first. Where do we go now?'

'To the Villa Forban so so I can meet Jean Burgoyne. She is confident de Forge won't be there today. But we'd better be careful – very careful.'

'I thought that was why Pete and I were with you,' Butler remarked drily.

He'd studied the map Lasalle had provided Paula with showing the most solitary route to the villa. He was driving along the windswept front as Paula had suggested. She wanted to check that there no sign of the *Steel Vulture*. It was a dirty day for any fishing vessels out beyond the shelter of the *bassin*. Paula suddenly sat up very erect.

The front was almost deserted. A strip of folded canvas above the window of an ice-cream parlour was flapping furiously, trying to tear itself loose. Even inside the *bassin* waves were rolling in, high and surf crested. In the distance the clustered masts in the port were swaying madly. One man, dressed in a trenchcoat, his hair flying all over the place, was striding towards them. Paula felt sure she recognized the athletic stance, the swinging stride of the tall solitary walker.

'Harry, pull in when we reach that man coming this way.'

As he came closer Paula saw that it was Victor Rosewater. The last person she'd expected to see in Arcachon. She stepped out into the wind as Butler parked the car.

'Victor! What a wonderful surprise. I certainly never expected to see you down here.'

Rosewater gave her a bear hug, glanced into the car and looked a question at Paula. How like him she thought – not to pry directly.

'It's all right,' she assured him. 'They're Tweed's. So you can talk freely. What are you doing?'

'Tweed told me you were in this area when I phoned Monica. Careful lady, that. I had to give her a number where Tweed could call me back.'

'And why are you here, Victor? It's good to see you.'

'My immediate purpose was to find you. Which is why I was walking along the front. Can we talk?'

'Later in the day. I'm off to see someone. See the café down that side street? Could we meet there about four this afternoon?'

'I'll be there at three-thirty. If necessary I'll wait and wait and wait . . .'

'Who was that?' Butler asked as he drove down the side street away from the front, still heading for the port.

'Victor Rosewater, a Military Intelligence officer based at Freiburg in Germany. Has a roving commission . . .'

She told him how with Tweed she'd first met Rosewater at the Drei Könige Hotel in Basle, recalled the murder of his wife, Karin, which she had almost witnessed. Butler drove back to where the road continued along the *bassin* as she talked. They arrived at the port. No sign of the *Steel Vulture*.

'We'd better go straight to the Villa Forban,' Paula said, checking her watch. 'I wish I could tell Tweed about Brand being here.'

'I noticed a public call box on the way in,' Nield called out. 'You could contact him from there . . .'

Tweed, still in Paris, had spent the night at the Ministry of the Interior. Navarre had supplied himself and Kuhlmann with camp beds. The close co-operation between Britain, France, and Germany – between Tweed, Navarre, and Kuhlmann – was to become legendary in later years when it came to light.

Tweed was still stiff from his night on the camp bed when Paula phoned. He listened as she reported the presence of Brand in Arcachon, her meeting with Victor Rosewater.

'Yes, I told him he might find you in Arcachon,' Tweed confirmed. 'He's moving closer in to the enemy. Tell me what he says to you after you've met him later in the café.

He may have obtained fresh information. I need to be kept very up to date.'

'How is Bob Newman?' she asked.

'No word from him. I expect I'll hear what he's found out soon. Now listen, Paula. This visit to the Villa Forban is fraught with danger. France has no President, but Navarre was confirmed as Prime Minister early today by a narrow majority. This may activate de Forge to make his ultimate move. He's unpredictable. You could run into something pretty dangerous at the Villa Forban.'

'The coast is clear at the moment. It's a unique chance to discover something vital. Jean is very close to her friend.'

'You will have company?' Tweed pressed.

'The whole time. They're staying closer to me than one of those sticking plasters. Stop worrying. Must go. Bye.'

Tweed put down the phone with grave misgivings. He now wished he'd forbidden her to risk the trip.

General de Forge straightened a ruler so it was precisely parallel with the edge of his desk. Lamy thought it a typical gesture: de Forge was noted for his meticulous attention to detail. Some officers called it an obsession. The General looked at his subordinate, seated opposite in the large room, who had just reported on the arrival of more sabotage units in Paris.

'So,' Lamy concluded, 'Paris can now be destabilized at the moment you give the signal. Despite the appointment of Navarre as Prime Minister. He won't be able to control the situation.'

'I keep thinking of Jean Burgoyne,' de Forge remarked, staring into the distance. 'Whether I can trust her.'

'You'd decided not to see her today,' Lamy reminded him. 'There is a great deal requiring your attention.'

'Security is paramount,' De Forge continued as though he had not heard Lamy. 'It takes precedence over everything. Order the car.' Taking one of his instinctive decisions, he stood up and put on his kepi. 'We are driving immediately to the Villa Forban. With a heavily armed escort.'

'You are sure about this, General?' Lamy enquired.

'I am a very observant man.' De Forge's mouth tightened. 'I was at the villa recently and left my dispatch case on a table while I had a bath. Afterwards when I came to pick up the case I noticed it had been moved slightly, did not line up with the table's inlay design as I'd left it. I know we have a spy who is reporting to Lasalle. When we identify that spy he – or she – will pay the ultimate penalty. They will end up in the Landes with the others. My escort is to carry automatic weapons . . .'

Chapter Thirty-Five

Marler carried two holdalls as he disembarked from the Air Inter flight which had transported him from Paris. The fact that there were no security checks on internal flights was a huge advantage.

Dressed in denims, a windcheater, and trainers, he wore his beret down over his forehead at a jaunty angle. He strolled across the concourse at an easy pace, whistling a French tune. Slim and slight in build, no one could have picked him out from the average Frenchman.

The hired Peugeot he'd phoned ahead for from Paris was waiting for him. He showed the girl his false papers in a common French name, paid her in cash, winked at her and got behind the wheel.

Driving a few yards along the kerb, he paused, took out a map of the area. Checking his recollections of the route, he drove on. The call from Tweed giving him his fresh instructions had come through to his base in the apartment near the rue du Bac.

'Step up the pressure,' had been Tweed's final order.

At the Ministry of the Interior in Paris Tweed had been given his own small office by Navarre, a room equipped with a scrambler phone. It was mid-afternoon as he sat in his shirtsleeves, polishing his glasses on his handkerchief.

He was trying to work out how Lord Dawlish could

smuggle arms aboard the *Steel Vulture* – assuming his Lordship was doing just that. After all, he was in the international armaments business. But the *Vulture* had twice been subject to search at its base port, Harwich, for drugs. So would Dawlish risk using his unique vessel for transporting arms? At any time Heathcoate, the Habour Master, might order a third search. No, Dawlish was too shrewd to gamble on ruin, a heavy term of imprisonment. There was something at the back of Tweed's mind he couldn't bring to the fore. He dialled the number for Park Crescent, spoke to Monica.

'Paula dictated to you a statement of the events at Dunwich and Aldeburgh – on the day her friend, Karin Rosewater, was murdered. Could you read it back to me. Detail is what I'm after . . .'

He listened as Monica rapidly read the report back to him. Occasionally he made a note on the pad in front of him.

'That's it,' Monica said eventually. 'Any help?'

'I'm not sure. Something still eludes me, but I'm certain it's there. It will come back to me – I just hope it does in time. No further developments here . . .'

Earlier Tweed had called Monica, had given her details of his new temporary base. *No further developments* – that was not strictly speaking true. Navarre had been confirmed as Prime Minister by the National Assembly – by the most narrow of margins.

The door opened and the man he was thinking about walked in. Navarre had had only two hours' sleep but was full of energy. He perched on the edge of Tweed's desk, clasped his lean wiry hands.

'Well, my friend, I now have a problem. I was about to dispatch a large contingent of heavily armed CRS south together with a fleet of helicopters. Now Lasalle tells me a small army of saboteurs have infiltrated Paris, taking up position to start an insurrection. So do I concentrate on the north – here – or the south?' He waved a hand. 'I expect no answer. Only I can decide. But de Forge is close to making his big move, his masterstroke. The takeover of the French government.'

'What about the Chief of the Army Staff, General Masson, de Forge's superior? He could remove him.'

'I have already asked him to do so. He refused. Said if I insist he will resign. What would that do to public morale? The announcement that the Chief of the Army Staff had resigned. It would play straight into de Forge's hands. I now suspect Masson is a secret member of the *Cercle Noir*, that he is de Forge's creature.'

'You have a difficult decision – where to position the paramilitary CRS units,' Tweed observed.

'A decision I have to take within hours. Oh, Kuhlmann is wanting to see you . . .'

The German police chief came in almost as soon as Navarre had left. Smoking his inevitable cigar, he looked fresh, determined, aggressive. He sat in a chair, looked directly at Tweed as he spoke.

'I've decided to handle this *Siegfried* problem in my own way. Nearly every Kriminalpolizei officer has left Wiesbaden, covering most of Germany. They're putting maximum pressure on all known underworld informants to locate the hidden *Siegfried* cells. I've told them to use any method necessary to make people talk.'

'The Chancellor knows this?'

Kuhlmann clapped a hand to his broad forehead in a mock gesture of forgetfulness. He grinned.

'You know something? With all that's going on it never

crossed my mind to tell him. Now I think I'll wait for the results of this ruthless and intensive search. I'll keep you in touch . . .'

Alone again, Tweed read through Paula's report for the second time. Everything was becoming a race against time. Navarre's protection of Paris. Kuhlmann's offensive to locate *Siegfried*, and his own search for the way Dawlish might be smuggling huge reinforcements to de Forge. Paula's report that Brand was in Arcachon made it all the more urgent.

It was dusk as Lord Dane Dawlish walked down the beach at Dunwich to board the large waiting rubber dinghy with a powerful outboard motor. He had substituted for his hard riding hat a peaked naval cap. He also wore a blue blazer with gold buttons and dark blue trousers.

Dawlish believed in dressing for the role he was adopting at any given moment. He was now presenting his sailor image. It went with the occasion. And emphasized his reputation as a playboy. Of course, if he happened to meet a beautiful woman so much the better: he'd live up to his playboy image with her.

The *Steel Vulture*, which had sailed from Harwich early that morning, was anchored offshore. Even in the twilight scuba divers were going over the side, exploring the depths of the sunken village.

'Is the operation completed?' he asked the First Mate who had come to escort him as the crew manoeuvred the craft closer to the weird twin-hulled giant.

'It is still being carried out, sir.'

'Should have damned well been completed by now. Butts will be kicked if we're behind schedule.'

'I'm happy to report we're exactly on schedule, sir.'

'You may be happy. I'll only join your happiness when the skipper reports the cargo is aboard . . .'

Onshore a few villagers, well wrapped against the zero temperatures, were gazing through field-glasses at the *Steel Vulture*. They were fascinated with Dawlish's persistence in locating Dunwich under the sea. And it was good for business.

The local pub had been packed with customers – divers coming ashore for a break, slaking their thirst with a roll of banknotes. Dawlish was popular, Dawlish was good for business. No one suspected that anything sinister was taking place. They watched as Dawlish climbed on to the platform suspended just above a calm sea.

When the *Steel Vulture* had raced north from Harwich early in the morning it had swung through a hundred and eighty degrees before anchoring off Dunwich. It floated about a half-mile out from the coast and the activity visible from the beach was on the starboard side.

What could not be seen by the curious sightseers was the very different and furious activity on the port side facing out to sea. A squat mobile crane was operating a long chain suspended deep down. When not in use the crane was telescoped inside a huge cube of a deckhouse. Close to the stern was an advanced seaplane. It was not only equipped with floats for landing on water: it also had a retractable undercarriage which could lower wheels below the floats, enabling it to land on the ground.

The *Vulture*, specially designed in a Norwegian shipyard, had cost Dawlish forty million dollars with its various accessories. Dawlish went straight to the bridge and his mood was aggressive as he addressed the skipper, Santos.

'I presume we can sail for Arcachon tonight?'

Santos spread apologetic hands. 'I am not sure the load-ing will be completed for a few hours. We may have to sail tomorrow . . .'

'A few hours!' Dawlish was outraged. His bulletlike eyes glared at the skipper. 'I should have come here earlier to crack a few skulls together. Why the hell do I have to supervise everything myself to ensure the schedule is kept? Always the same story. I have to do every bloody thing myself.'

'It is dangerous work,' Santos pleaded. 'You would not wish us to have an accident with such a cargo.'

'Report to me every half-hour. The trucks loaded the vessel during the night?'

He was referring to the trucks which had brought their consignments from the factory in the forest on the road to Orford. The factory Newman and Marler had earlier tried to search, had been frustrated by their discovery of land mines which caused them to abandon the expedition.

The villagers in Dunwich were not surprised when trucks arrived in the middle of the night. Two divers who patron-ized the Ship Inn had casually mentioned the trucks were bringing in food supplies for the crew and high-tech equip-ment for the divers who were using new techniques to explore the sunken village.

Santos wished Dawlish would leave the bridge. His nationality was Panamanian and he was paid a larger salary than he'd get anywhere else in the world. Large enough for him to keep his mouth shut.

'Report to me on progress every half-hour!' Dawlish repeated, and stormed off to his luxurious cabin.

His quarters were also equipped with the latest com-munications technology. He had hardly closed the door, started to pour himself a large Scotch, when his private radio telephone rang.

'Hell and damnation.'

He put down the drink, sat in the armchair, picked up the phone. Brand's burring controlled voice came over the receiver from Arcachon as clear as a bell.

'There could be trouble here. Guess who I ran into in a local bar . . .'

'I don't like guessing games. Get to the point, for God's sake.'

'That cow, Paula Grey, who interviewed you. I tried to find out what she was doing here and got nowhere.'

'That is too much of a coincidence . . .'

Dawlish gave Brand precise instructions, coding them in language no one else would have understood. Aware of the British government's highly sophisticated listening system at Cheltenham, Dawlish took no risks with security. And during their conversation neither man had mentioned the other's name. As for Paula Grey, Dawlish didn't think her name would ring any bells.

Tweed had just returned from a brisk walk round Paris in the drizzle drifting down from a miserable overcast sky which blanketed the city. He had sensed a growing unease among the population.

Walking into a bar he had listened to some bargees chatting while he sipped at a cup of coffee. Their views struck him as alarming, considering they weren't among the élite of Paris society.

'We need General de Forge to take over,' one man had said.

'I reckon he could be a second de Gaulle,' his companion had agreed.

'A strong man to clear out these Arabs and other foreign trash,' a third bargee had said emphatically. 'I know exactly what I'd do. Round up the bastards and deport the whole tribe back to where they came from. De Forge is the man to do just that . . .'

Arriving back at the Ministry of the Interior, Tweed showed the pass Navarre had issued him with. He hurried back to his office and the phone was ringing. He grabbed for it.

'Yes? Who is this?'

'Monica. I have more news.' I hope you'll understand me. First, those films Marler took when he was on a fishing expedition with Newman. Are you with me?'

She was referring to the pictures Marler had taken of the laboratory-like building during their brief raid on Dawlish's factory in the forest on the road to Orford in the Aldeburgh area.

'Yes. They've taken the devil of a time to develop them and come up with a comment.'

'It's weird. I'll jump ahead a bit. When the data came back from Porton with their scientific report the Home Secretary authorized Special Branch to investigate the place. They were accompanied by experts from Porton. I have to tell you they came up with nothing.'

'Nothing?'

Tweed was taken aback. He recalled the veterinary pathologist's report on the dead fox Newman had brought back. Nerve gas.

'I don't understand,' he replied.

'Wait, please. I said I'd jump ahead a bit. The photos taken by Marler were subjected to intensive examination at Porton – using, I gather, new magnification techniques. It was the opinion of the experts that certain containers which showed up were just the type used for storing nerve gas. Hence their agreeing to travel all the way from Porton to join the Special Branch men.'

'So what the devil did they discover – or not discover – inside that laboratory?'

'The place was empty. Not a single container left. And they tested the whole place with special instruments. It was clean as a whistle. Almost too clean – that's a quote from one of the scientists. And no landmines.'

'Thank you, Monica. Keep in touch . . .'

Tweed felt depressed as he replaced the phone. He still felt certain he was missing something. He picked up the report of what Paula had said, began re-reading it again. Word by word.

Butler drove the Renault along the country road and stopped a hundred yards from the entrance to the Villa Forban. As agreed in advance, Paula stepped out and walked swiftly to the closed grille gates.

'I've got a bad feeling about this,' said Nield who sat in the rear.

'Join the club,' answered Butler. 'Which is why we are taking the precautions I thought up.'

Paula reached the gates, saw the entryphone Jean Burgoyne had told her to look for set into one of the pillars. She pressed the button, looking along the road which led to GHQ Third Corps.

'Yes? Who is it?'

Jean's distinctive voice speaking in French. Paula put her mouth close to the entryphone.

'Paula here. Are you alone?'

'Yes. Come in. I will operate . . .'

'*Don't* open the gates. We are coming in from the back of the estate. Please trust me. Leave a rear door open – I'll be there in about five minutes OK?'

'Anything you say. Looking forward very much to seeing you . . .'

Paula ran back to the car, jumped in beside Butler. She told them Jean was alone, that it was all right. Butler nodded, said nothing as he drove off the road up a very narrow side road. He'd studied a large-scale map before they had left Arcachon, had found this road led to the back of the villa. He'd also discovered that it forked, that another narrow route led across country before it rejoined the road they'd come along.

To their right was a high stone wall. This didn't worry Butler, who had cross-questioned Paula about the location of the villa the night before in Arcachon. Early that morning he had visited a ship's chandler, had purchased a length of strong rope and an iron grapple. They'd be able to scale the wall at the back.

It was mid-afternoon and the sky was like thick grey soup. No wind, but it was arctic cold. The met forecasts, which Butler monitored when he could, had talked of a heavy sea mist coming in. And they were later than they'd expected to be, which again worried Butler. They'd taken a wrong turn.

Following the road round the back of the walled estate Butler saw the rope and grapple wouldn't be needed. He positioned the car carefully under the branches of an overhanging tree which had its trunk on the far side of the wall.

'Think you're athletic enough to shin up that branch and climb down the other side of the tree, Paula?'

She gave him a dirty look, started to open her door to get out. Butler laid a hand on her arm.

'We do this my way. We're in enemy territory.'

'General de Forge's stronghold,' Nield commented. 'We must be crazy.'

'So,' Butler continued, 'I'm coming with you. If you

366

prefer to talk to Burgoyne on your own, OK. But I want to be in the next room. And I go up the tree first.'

'What about me?' asked Nield.

'You stay with the car – and turn it in the opposite direction for a quick getaway. This won't be any pleasure trip.'

'The other way?' Nield repeated. 'That means about an eight-point turn. Thanks a lot . . .'

Butler checked his Walther, got out of the car, gripped the strong branch, swung himself over, paused to view the estate. Trees forming a screen by the rear wall – useful. Through the bare branches he saw a few acres of lawn, the back of the villa. He scrambled down the tree.

Paula, dressed in denims, a windcheater and trainers under her trench coat, followed. First she took off the coat, folded it, threw it over the wall. Agilely she scaled the tree, dropped beside Butler who helped her on with the coat. The silence inside the wall was eerie, unsettling.

'I'll go ahead, check the ground,' Butler said.

'But Jean said she was alone . . .'

'And could have been speaking with a pistol held to her skull.'

Marler settled himself comfortably in position where he had a wide range of view. The Peugeot was concealed beneath a copse of evergreens: impossible for anyone to catch sight of it.

Crouching low on the knoll behind dead undergrowth he adjusted the focus of his field-glasses. Slowly he systematically swept the lenses searching for anyone – anything – he had missed. He spotted nothing.

It was very quiet. No birdsong. No wind. Dead silence. Patiently he waited – inactivity he was long accustomed to.

Chapter Thirty-Six

Tweed was seated at the desk in his temporary office in the Ministry of Defence when the phone rang. He recognized Monica's voice.

'Go ahead,' he urged.

'I told you I was going to try and get information on the structure of the *Steel Vulture* which was built at a Norwegian shipyard. Our Oslo contact has reported back. He apologizes for the delay. He wanted you to have the complete picture.'

'Which is?'

'Dramatic. The yard where the ship was built was burnt to the ground soon after they'd dispatched the *Vulture* to Britain. It was a catastrophe. The workers who had built the ship were celebrating in a shed with the doors closed. The building went up in flames and no one survived. The police suspected arson, but no one was ever arrested.'

'Deliberate, ruthless, and horrific . . .'

'I haven't finished yet. Our Oslo contact went to the office of the marine architect who designed *Vulture* – to get a copy of the plans. They'd had a break-in just about the time of the shipyard fire. A lot of plans had been stolen – including those of *Vulture.*'

'Naturally . . .'

'I'm still not finished. Our contact asked where the marine architect lived. He apparently skidded in his car on an icy road in the mountains – ended up at the bottom of a deep abyss. Dead.'

'Of course. Thank you very much, Monica. And do not hesitate to phone me again . . .'

Tweed put down the phone, leant back in his chair. He was now totally convinced there was something dangerously unorthodox about the *Steel Vulture*. So vital that it had to be kept secret at all costs. Even at the price of incinerating the whole workforce of a shipyard – and faking an accidental death of the marine architect who had designed her. Brutal murder.

He sat playing back in his mind from memory the report Paula had dictated of her horrific experience off Dunwich, followed by the equally terrifying pursuit across the Aldeburgh marshes, ending in the strangulation of Karin Rosewater. He wasn't going to leave it alone until the significant fact in her account sprang at him.

At the Villa Forban, Butler found the rear door unlocked. He opened it quietly but as he pushed it slowly open it creaked. He was holding the Walther in his hand while he pressed it wide open and stepped inside an ultra-modern kitchen. He found himself staring into the muzzle of a 7.63mm Mauser.

Behind the automatic pistol a woman with long blond hair stood, gripping the butt with both hands in a most professional manner. Butler spoke in English, whispering as his eyes swept the kitchen.

'Can I write a message on that pad?'

As he spoke he carefully laid down his Walther on top of a working surface. He had noticed the pad with a pen lying beside it. The woman, who was beautiful, nodded, still aiming the weapon. Butler tore a sheet from the pad, turned it over, placed the sheet on the cardboard back, wrote a quick message. He then held up the sheet so she could read it.

Are you alone in this place? Paula Grey is waiting at the bottom of the garden. I'm her escort.

'Thank God! I'm Jean Burgoyne.' She had lowered the gun. She looked badly shaken. 'I caught a glimpse of you through the window. A strange man with a gun. I thought de Forge had sent someone to kill me. Please ask Paula to come in. I'll make coffee. Do you take milk?' She managed a wan smile. 'Isn't it ridiculous? One moment I'm scared witless, the next I'm asking if you take milk. Do you? And sugar?'

'Black for me,' Butler replied calmly. 'And for Paula. Can I take my gun? Thanks. I'll fetch Paula . . .'

He went back outside and beckoned to Paula who came running from behind a tree trunk. He stopped her before she went inside, told her briefly what had happened. Following her into the villa, Butler inwardly felt the tension draining out of his system.

First, he'd thought maybe hidden men had forced Burgoyne to confront him. Second, he'd noticed how her finger was on the trigger: one squeeze and that would have been that. He needed the coffee.

'I'll watch the front of the villa while you two talk somewhere else,' he suggested. 'Then if anyone turns up unexpectedly we'll leave by the rear door. I'd just as soon you left it unlocked.'

'Gladly.' Jean gave him a warm smile. 'I'm so sorry I startled you. You must have had an awful shock.'

'All in a day's work . . .'

Butler left the kitchen, checked the layout of the ground floor, took up a position behind a curtain in the living room where he could watch the drive leading to the grille gates.

'. . . and I'm so glad to see you,' Jean went on as she poured coffee. 'I'm a bit jittery. We can talk in the study at the back after I've taken your escort his coffee.'

She was back very quickly and led the way to the study which overlooked the large garden at the back. Paula sat in an armchair, noticed Jean's hand shaking as she drank her coffee. This seemed a perfect moment to tackle her host on a dangerous topic, to try and get her to talk frankly.

'Jean,' she began, 'Harry told me you thought de Forge had sent someone to kill you. Why would he do that?'

Burgoyne seemed to close in on herself. Her mood became wary. She smoothed down her long thick hair. Paula kept up the barrage gently.

'You've reached the stage where you have to talk to someone about it. I sense that you've been under strain for months. And my job is actually security.'

'National security?' Jean enquired casually.

'It can impinge on that.'

Jean smiled. 'I think I told you my uncle in Aldeburgh was in Military Intelligence . . .'

'And still has contacts with the MOD?' Paula interjected.

'I didn't quite say that, did I?' Jean studied her cup. 'But after you'd been attacked and I'd driven you back to the Brudenell, what do you think he said when I got back?'

'I couldn't even guess.'

'Uncle said that girl is something to do with Intelligence. I always know, he went on.'

'So, let's suppose he wasn't a mile away from the truth. Pure supposition on my part, of course.'

'Of course.' Jean smiled her warm smile again. 'You may have guessed I've been de Forge's mistress for more months than I care to count. Not for the pleasure of it, either.'

'And what have you discovered? That man is a bloody menace to France – to the world,' Paula said vehemently.

'He plans to make himself President of France,' Jean said, staring at the wall. 'He is secretly co-operating with Dubois, the fanatic who heads the *Pour France* movement. He is plotting to create so much chaos the ordinary women and men will see him as a saviour.'

'But exactly how will he go about it?' Paula pressed.

'I don't know whether I should tell you.' Jean hestated, but only briefly. 'He left his dispatch case here one day for a short time on a table in the living room. While he had a bath I went through it – there were plans for a military coup. Details of the units to be used, the routes to be followed for a swoop by his Third Corps on Paris.'

'What details?'

'I memorized them at the time. After he'd gone I wrote them down. I'd give you the notes I made but it would put your life in danger.'

'Leave here now with me and my escort. Bring the notes with you.'

'Where are you staying?' Jean asked.

'In Arcachon.'

'It shouldn't be too difficult for me to drive there, to hand the notes to you. Here we are too close to the Third Corps GHQ. It's my responsibility. Where can I get in touch with you in Arcachon?'

Paula decided it would be useless to press her further to hand over the notes. Jean Burgoyne was a strong-willed woman. The exchange would have to take place in Arcachon.

'I'll be staying at a small hotel. The Atlantique. A silly name for such a small place, hardly more than a *pension* . . .'

She looked up as Butler walked swiftly into the room, grabbed her by the arm. Something had gone wrong. He hustled her towards the door, speaking quickly in a low voice to Jean.

'Trouble has arrived at the front. De Forge, I think. And a heavy escort . . .'

'See you in Arcachon,' Paula whispered.

They hurried to the back of the villa, out of the door which had been left unlocked. As Paula took off like a marathon runner for the rear wall Butler paused to shut the door quietly. He then tore after Paula. When he reached the wall Paula had already shinned up the tree, dropped out of sight on the far side. Butler paused again for a second astride the wall top, glanced back at the villa. No sign of life. He dropped to the ground from the overhanging branch, ran to the Renault.

Paula was already seated in the rear, Nield had the engine running. Butler dived into the front passenger seat and Nield drove off at a moderate speed: if he rammed his foot down he'd make more noise.

General de Forge had his keys ready to open the front door of the villa. He glanced over his shoulder to where Lamy waited in his limousine and the group of armed motorcycle riders sat astride their machines, weapons looped over their shoulders.

De Forge walked swiftly through the living room, opened the connecting door to the study. Jean Burgoyne was sitting reading a book. She looked surprised, closed the book, stood up.

'I thought you weren't coming today, Charles . . .'

'Exactly!'

As he spat the word at her he shoved her roughly back into the chair, made his way into the kitchen. He looked round, turned the handle of the rear door and it opened. Security at the villa was tight. All windows were bullet-proof. The rear door had a fish-eye spyhole. But it also had three bolts in addition to the lock. It was seeing the bolts drawn free which had attracted his attention.

Drawing his pistol, de Forge stepped outside, stared

down the full length of the garden. He saw nothing but he heard something – the faint sound of a car retreating in the distance.

He rushed back inside, locked the door, ran straight to the front door. Throwing it open he ran down the steps to the limousine. Lamy was outside the vehicle instantly, stood on the gravel.

'There's a road at the back of the villa leading across country, isn't there?'

'Yes. And very much a lonely country road . . .'

'Send an outrider along that road. If he overtakes a car he's to stop it – by force if necessary. Get someone on that road now.'

He walked back inside the villa as Lamy issued instructions. Alone in the study, Jean took the Mauser from a drawer. Should she shoot the bastard now? She hadn't had time to go and lock and throw the three bolts across on the rear door. She'd heard his key rattling in the front door and he might have caught her.

When de Forge walked into the study she was sitting in the same chair, staring at him with a cold look, the book closed on her lap. She'd decided against using the gun: Paula's escort had warned her de Forge was not alone. If she killed him she'd end up dead herself. She got her verbal blow in first.

'Have you gone mad? I'm not one of your slave privates you can knock about whenever the whim takes you. This time you have gone too far.'

'No!' De Forge gripped the top of her armchair, partly to regain self-control. '*You* have gone too far. The rear door was open. Who was with you? Who ran for it when I arrived unexpectedly?'

'No one,' she said quietly, laying her book on a table as she stood to face him. 'I went into the back garden for some fresh air. Then I heard your cavalcade arriving so I came quickly back because you expect me to be waiting for you. And I'm damned if I see why I have to explain all my movements. In fact, I'm not prepared to.'

De Forge had his fury under control. His brain was ice-cold and racing. He smiled, took her in his arms, kissed her. She stood there, letting him do it, without responding. He released her from his embrace.

'You're looking more beautiful than ever,' he commented. 'The fresh air did you good. I just called in *en route* – to make sure you were all right. I'll come tomorrow – in the evening. Until then . . .'

He was careful to walk quickly across the polished wood-block floor of the hall, so she would hear he was in a hurry. His expression changed as he sat in the limousine beside Major Lamy and the vehicle began moving. His voice was harsh.

'You sent an outrider to look for that car?'

'Immediately. He will stop it, identify the occupant. He will then use his radio to call me to say who it is, still detaining the car.'

'Good. There might well be an unfortunate shooting accident. A fatal one. Back to GHQ.'

'Press your foot down, Pete,' Butler ordered. 'If they did hear our car they may send someone to follow us. I want to be off this loop road, back on the main highway before anyone catches us up. Then we have no connection with the Villa Forban.'

'Hold on, Paula,' Nield warned and rammed his foot down.

The narrow winding country road was sunk in a gully which meant they were concealed from the main road they were looping round to join. Its surface was uneven and bumpy. Paula braced herself as Nield swung the wheel to the left, to the right and the car rocked at high speed.

Nield had been a racing car buff who earlier had driven at Brand's Hatch. Few drivers could have moved at his pace and kept the vehicle on the road. Paula watched the needle climbing on the speedometer and then decided she didn't want to know how fast they were travelling.

They were within a couple of miles of the highway when Paula glanced back. The road had straightened, was stretched ahead of them like a ruler. The rocking had stopped, the road surface had improved. Paula stared through the rear window, reached for her field-glasses inside her shoulder bag. She was now able to swivel round and aim the binoculars.

Behind them a dot had appeared, a dot which grew steadily larger. She focused on it and sucked in her breath. She patted Butler on the shoulder. He twisted round.

'Trouble?'

'I think so. There's a soldier coming up behind us like a bat out of hell. A tall aerial on his motorcycle. What looks like an automatic weapon looped over his back.'

'You could shoot him, Harry,' Nield suggested, checking his rear-view mirror.

'No,' said Butler. 'Killing one of de Forge's men with a bullet would raise all hell. As I keep reminding you, we're in enemy territory.'

'You've got a better idea?'

'I might have . . .'

Butler explained his suggested tactic – providing they had the right situation. Paula looked back again and the rider was closer, but not close enough yet to see him clearly. Butler glanced in his wing mirror for the third time. Then he gave the order to Paula.

'Get down out of sight. Huddle on the floor as far as you can. We don't want you seen.'

'Anything you say, sir.'

Paula squeezed herself as low as she could. She curled her long legs in a most uncomfortable posture. Thank God the road surface was smooth now.

Nield kept up his speed but the rider overtook them rapidly. The road was wider – wide enough for him to speed past them, then maintain the same pace ahead of the Renault. Butler saw the camouflage jacket. As the rider had flashed past he'd seen the sinister helmet, the goggles which made the rider seem eyeless, the tall aerial quivering with the speed, the automatic weapon across his back.

The rider held on to the handlebars with one hand – not a difficult feat since this stretch of road was so very straight – and used the other gloved hand to waggle it up and down. A signal. A command. *Stop your car!*

'Keep moving,' Butler ordered Nield, 'but gradually reduce your speed.'

'I don't see any chance of carrying out your tactic,' Nield commented.

'Just keep going,' Butler replied calmly. 'We could get lucky.'

'You're an optimist,' Nield chided him.

'Positive thinking, pal.'

'Anything happening?' Paula called out.

'Yes,' said Butler. 'You're to keep your head down.'

The motorcyclist suddenly increased speed, roared on ahead, then vanished from sight. Butler grunted with satisfaction when the rider didn't reappear in the distance. There was obviously a dip in the road. The motorcyclist was waiting for them out of sight. He looked at Nield, who nodded, reduced speed a little more. Butler twisted round to speak to Paula.

'Go on keeping your head down. There may be a little excitement in the next minute.'

Nield drove on and without warning the road sloped to a shallow dip. A hundred yards away the motorcyclist, his machine standing on its strut beside him, stood in the middle of the road. He held his automatic weapon in his hands. As the Renault appeared he began to raise it, prepared to aim it.

Nield reacted as Butler had suggested. He rammed down his foot, shot forward at high speed, driving point blank for the soldier who had almost aimed his weapon. When he saw the projectile hurtling towards him he hesitated, which was a mistake.

At the last moment he jumped to one side. The bumper of the Renault struck him a glancing blow. The rider hit the hard road surface like a sack of cement, lay still. The Renault also hammered into the motorcycle, toppled it on its side. Nield braked and Paula swore inwardly, but had cushioned her head with her shoulder bag. Butler looked back. The aerial on the motorcycle was a mangled wreck. No means of communication.

'You did a nice job, Pete,' he commented.

'Flattery will get you a long way.'

Nield drove on to join the highway, to proceed at speed towards Arcachon where Paula had an appointment with Victor Rosewater.

Chapter Thirty-Seven

General de Forge's limousine, preceded by outriders with a second group bringing up the rear, was travelling along the lonely road halfway back to GHQ. On both sides in the distance rose low hills, some topped with clumps of trees. Major Lamy sat beside him, studying a map of Paris.

The chauffeur braked suddenly. De Forge sat up more erect and stared forward. The leading outrider lay in the road, his machine sprawled beside him, the wheels still revolving slowly. Shakily, the rider clambered to his feet.

'What the hell!' de Forge snapped. 'Can't he even keep in the saddle . . .'

The crack of splintering glass stopped him. Something shot across the interior of the car. The window next to de Forge was crazed – like the window next to Lamy where the bullet had entered.

'Down!' Lamy shouted. He grabbed de Forge, forced him below window level. 'That was a bullet. Stay down and I'll investigate . . .'

'You bloody fool,' de Forge stormed. 'Tell the chauffeur to get moving. At speed . . .'

Lamy gave the order. The chauffeur drove the limousine round the fallen machine and its rider, scattering the rest of their escort. As they moved past Lamy looked out, saw the machine lying in the road. He stared at de Forge.

'They stopped us by firing a bullet into the front tyre of the lead machine. I saw it, ripped to shreds. And it must have been a special explosive bullet to penetrate the windows.'

'The bastards can't even shoot straight.'

De Forge was quoting almost exactly the words General de Gaulle had used after the abortive attempt to assassinate him on 22 August 1962. The General was fond of using similar language to that employed by the legendary de Gaulle.

To demonstrate his iron self-control, his ability to keep in mind different problems at the same moment, he switched the topic.

'I have decided Jean Burgoyne is a spy. She must be eliminated swiftly. Contact your woman agent, Yvette, at once. Tell her to drive immediately from GHQ back up this road, to take up a concealed position near the Villa Forban. If Burgoyne leaves she is to follow her and report back where she has gone to. She'll need a civilian radio car from the Transport Section.'

As the limousine drove at speed closer to GHQ, accompanied by several outriders who had caught up with them, Lamy picked up his mobile phone. He got hold of Yvette in her room immediately, repeated de Forge's instructions.

'I will leave at once, sir,' Yvette reported back.

Lamy put down the phone. He glanced at the bullet holes in the windows. Certainly a very special bullet must have been used to pierce the glass. And the bullet had passed within inches of de Forge's head. Yet the General appeared to have his mind on other things. He issued a fresh order.

'Lamy, just before I left I had a call from *Oiseau* in Britain. He told me his trusted confidant, Brand, had encountered a Paula Grey in Arcachon. She also sounds to be a spy. So Kalmar now has two targets. Inform him to act urgently . . .'

*

380

In Paris Tweed was talking from his temporary office on the phone to Pierre Loriot of Interpol, based in the same city. Loriot was replying to the question he had been asked.

'Tweed, I am afraid I have no concrete information on the assassin, Kalmar. Only unconfirmed rumours. That he has operated in Bucharest, Warsaw, and Berlin. That he comes from the East, whatever that means.'

'I'd like one solid fact,' Tweed insisted. 'Method of killing, any knowledge of explosives, a hint about what he looks like, his age. So far he's a ghost.'

'I was coming to two of those points. Only rumours, but fresh ones. That his favourite method of assassination is strangulation. That he has an expert knowledge of explosives.'

'I said one solid fact,' Tweed repeated.

'We're still searching for just that. I'll be in touch,' concluded Loriot.

Tweed was putting down the phone when Otto Kuhlmann came into the office with a bouncy tread. He waved his cigar.

'What are you concentrating on now?'

'What about yourself?' countered Tweed.

'We're turning Germany upside down tracking *Siegfried* – and we may be getting results. The pressure is so great their cells are beginning to move around to safer houses. We missed one gang of three men and a woman by one hour. In Dusseldorf. They left behind a large cache of guns, explosives. And fingerprints. This time they hadn't time to clean up the place.'

'And you've sent these fingerprints to Interpol?'

'Of course.' Kuhlmann made an impatient gesture. 'Do you think it significant that Interpol, after checking its records, reported they couldn't link them on their computers with any known terrorists?'

'Highly significant,' Tweed replied with satisfaction, certain that it confirmed a theory he held.

'And what are you concentrating on?' Kuhlmann repeated.

'The identity of Kalmar. I'm waiting for a few more pieces of the jigsaw I'm building up – you might call it an identikit of Kalmar. There's something very odd about that killer.'

The private phone began ringing almost as soon as de Forge had sat behind his desk in his office at GHQ. Lamy had gone to his own quarters to arrange arm's-length contact with Kalmar: to phone the girl who would give him a public call box to go to.

Placing his kepi carefully on his desk so the peak faced him, de Forge picked up the receiver. Maybe Lamy was calling to say he was on his way, driving to another remote public phone.

'Yes? What is it?'

'The bullet which penetrated your limousine was aimed to miss you by five centimetres precisely. Which it did. Next time it will go through the side of your skull.'

'Who the blazes is this?'

'You know perfectly well. *Manteau*. You owe me two million Swiss francs. Arrange for Lamy to make the payment. I will call Lamy at his private number five minutes from now.'

'How do I know you . . .'

'You can read the papers. I presume you can read?'

'You dare to insult me?' de Forge said in a clipped tone.

'I dare to kill you if I am not paid. Others have paid. Except one. He paid too – with his life.'

'I am heavily guarded,' de Forge continued in his icy tone.

'You were this afternoon. And travelling in a bulletproof limousine. That didn't save you. I know all your movements. If there is another job you require executing, let me know. Through Lamy. But only after you have paid up. In Swiss franc banknotes. As I said before, with the numbers out of sequence . . .'

'I must consider your proposition . . .'

De Forge realized he was talking into space. The Frenchman at the other end had broken the connection. De Forge sat quite still, then dialled Lamy's number.

'Come to my office immediately.'

'But General, I have to leave *immediately*. I have made contact.'

'My office. *Immediately*.'

De Forge slammed down the phone. It gave him brief satisfaction to do to his subordinate what *Manteau* had done to him. He aligned his notepad with the edge of his desk, his face grim. Lamy came in without knocking on the door, out of breath, and his chief ignored this breach of etiquette. He was working out how to conceal that he was in a totally irresolute mood.

'Is there an emergency, General?' asked Lamy.

'Sit down. Keep still. Concentrate while I talk. Do not interrupt . . .'

Tersely de Forge outlined the conversation he had just had with *Manteau*. As he spoke he watched his chief of Intelligence closely. There were beads of sweat on Lamy's high forehead. It could, of course, be the result of his rushing to reach his master's office.

'So that is the situation,' de Forge concluded. 'And he made a reference to reading the papers. I assume that *you*

383

are keeping up to date with developments – that you read the newspapers?'

He took hold of a tidy stack of piled newspapers. *Liberation*, *Figaro*, *Le Monde*. He threw them across his desk into his subordinate's lap.

'Read!'

The headline in large type jumped at Lamy. He had read them but it seemed discreet to do what he was told. He arranged the headlines one under each other.

'MANTEAU' KILLED PRESIDENT, PRIME MINISTER

'MANTEAU' ASSASSINATED PARIS PREFECT

'MANTEAU' MURDERS TOP STATESMEN

'*Manteau!* de Forge burst out. 'Nothing but this *Manteau*. So why are we paying Kalmar? Is he subcontracting the jobs to *Manteau*?'

'I doubt that very much,' Lamy ventured.

'Oh, you do! And not an hour ago *Manteau* carried out his threat. That bullet passed within centimetres of my head. And,' he continued sarcastically, 'in case you hadn't realized it, his attack was brilliantly organized. First he shoots the front tyre of the lead outrider to stop my car. He didn't shoot the outrider – although I'm damned sure he could have done just that. And *Manteau* is calling you on your private number in your office in five minutes. God knows how he obtains these numbers. But you'd better be in your office when *Manteau* calls.'

'What are your instructions, General?'

Lamy had stood up quickly. De Forge threw up his hands and looked at the ceiling, as though asking the Almighty for sympathy in coping with the idiots he was surrounded with.

'You pay him, of course. Two million Swiss francs. And make sure the numbers are not in sequence.'

'But I have to go to a phone box in the wilds to take the call from Kalmar. What do I say to him?'

'Can't you work that out?' de Forge grinned sardonically. 'I always have to plan everything. You give Kalmar the two targets. Jean Burgoyne and Paula Grey in Arcachon. When he asks for payment, tell him we're expecting huge new funds shortly. Which is true.'

'And *Manteau*? I just pay him, whatever way he wants?'

'You do that.' De Forge grinned again. 'And you give the new targets. Jean Burgoyne and Paula Grey. Let's see who does the jobs for us, who earns the money. Time you rushed back to your office . . .'

Alone, de Forge walked round his office, hands clasped behind his back. He was pleased with his devious ploy. Which of the assassins would succeed? It was clean-up time, the elimination of all spies before he made his bid. For the Presidency of France.

In Paris at the Ministry of Defence Tweed had also been reading the newspaper headlines and the text beneath them. He looked up as René Lasalle came into his office.

'Has Navarre decided where to concentrate his forces?' Tweed asked. 'In the north, here round Paris – or in the south close to de Forge's GHQ?'

'He is still waiting before he decides. He expects some new development which will point the way. He has heard that Josette, de Forge's wife, has arrived in Paris and is holding what she calls "salons" – afternoon parties at the de Forges' apartment in Passy. A lot of influential people attend these salons, including the press. She seems to be preparing the ground for her husband's arrival in Paris.'

'I see.' Tweed looked out of the window. The sky was still a leaden blanket. 'René, could you give me the address of the Passy apartment?'

Lasalle tore a sheet off Tweed's notepad, wrote an

address in his neat script. Folding the sheet, he handed it to Tweed.

'What are you up to now?'

'Time I went back into the field, saw for myself, This place is fraught with tension. It's becoming positively claustrophobic.'

'I have one more piece of information,' Lasalle continued. 'There is the foreign member of the notorious *Cercle Noir* who goes under the code name *Oiseau*. He is attending these conspiratorial meetings much more frequently.'

'How on earth do you obtain such information?'

'That's top secret. I have informants.'

'In the plural?' Tweed queried.

'You heard correctly. One bit of advice. If you do go to Passy, take care . . .'

By himself again, Tweed wrote the word *Oiseau* on his notepad. He added the English translation. Bird. Then he drew a vulture. It was all adding up. But who could be Lasalle's informants?

Yvette Mourlon, Lamy's woman agent, had received her orders from her chief. She was sitting in the battered Peugeot she had driven from Third Corps GHQ and was now in position to watch the Villa Forban. She had driven the vehicle with a souped-up engine into a field where she could see the grille gates but couldn't herself be seen.

Yvette was a plain-looking girl with sallow skin and poor legs. In addition she had a cruel mouth. Her loyalty to General de Forge was carried to the point of devotion. The General cleverly gave her small gifts from time to time, a compliment she'd never received from any other man. He was careful to keep her at a distance but her dedication to him was complete.

Her Peugeot had also been equipped with a high-powered transmitter which enabled her to communicate with Third Corps GHQ from long distances. Her great advantage was she was a girl no one ever looked at twice. She wore a crumpled raincoat and a pair of old, worn gloves.

She leaned forward as she saw the gates opening. Even from a distance she recognized the driver of the Rover as the car drove away to the north. Jean Burgoyne's long blond hair was unmistakable. Yvette waited, then turned on the ignition, drove out of the field and followed the Rover.

Jean Burgoyne had not been fooled by de Forge's apparent change of mood just before he left the villa. She had seen through his pretended amiability, and realized he no longer trusted her an inch.

She had always known this day would come – the day to run for her life. Packing quickly, she slipped the notes she'd made of Operation Marengo – after skip-reading the papers in de Forge's dispatch case – in a polythene bag. Using adhesive tape, she attached the bag to her body under her panties.

She had taken with her only the minimum selection of everyday clothes. Without a qualm she had left behind the mink cape, the silk underclothes de Forge had given her: she wanted to wear nothing which reminded her of their relationship. But she did slip the Mauser pistol into her handbag.

The devious country route to Arcachon was deserted as she drove through the late afternoon. She would go to the Atlantique Hotel in Arcachon, book a room, contact Paula. If Paula wasn't available soon she'd contact Paris.

*

The man known as Kalmar sat in his hotel room studying a photograph of Jean Burgoyne. He had no doubt the opportunity would soon present itself when he would strangle her.

He hadn't a photo of Paula Grey, but he didn't need one. After all, he'd met her. He didn't often get an assignment to eliminate two targets. He was rather looking forward to the double killing.

Lamy's instructions over the phone had been precise and simple. The odd thing was Lamy had given him no idea of the location of either target. That was most unusual. Sometimes Kalmar wondered about Major Jules Lamy. His pay as Chief of Intelligence would hardly amount to a fortune. And he was the only other man – apart from de Forge presumably – who knew the targets. Which might explain some strange events which had occurred.

Putting the photo back into an envelope, he tucked it inside his pocket. This looked like very easy money. The thought that the fee paid involved the murder of two women never crossed his mind.

Newman had slept for twenty-four hours in his bedroom at the Atlantique Hotel in Arcachon. Driving north from the Landes non-stop to Arcachon with Moshe Stein, he had arrived exhausted in the late afternoon.

And, like himself, Moshe had been flaked out, all reserves of energy used up. Both men had retired to their rooms. Newman had wanted to phone Tweed but when he lay on the bed after a quick wash he fell fast asleep.

It was a troubled sleep, crucified by nightmares. Firing squads on a lonely beach backed by the sand dunes with the forests of the Landes behind them. Stretcher parties carrying the dead victim up over the dunes into the forest, dumping a body whose face looked like his own into a hole in the ground. An old woman watching, cackling with obscene delight at the spectacle. A man wearing a Ku-Klux-Klan mask bending over him. The man removing the mask to reveal the grinning face of Major Lamy.

Eventually Newman woke, feeling his head was stuffed with cotton-wool. He forced himself out of bed, checked the time. It was almost dusk outside. Stripping to the waist, he sluiced himself with cold water, dried off. His brain was beginning to function.

He was shivering from the cold. The heating in the hotel was meagre. He threw on a few fresh clothes, the first ones he came to when throwing back the lid of his case.

Sitting on the edge of the bed, he dialled the special number at the Ministry of the Interior from memory. He had to be very forceful to get put through to someone in high authority, who turned out to be Lasalle.

'Need to speak urgently to Tweed.'

'I'm afraid he is not in the building just at the moment, Mr Newman. Can I help?'

'Only Tweed can. Thanks. Call you back,' Newman mumbled and put down the phone.

Only Tweed could be trusted with the information he had gathered. He went along the corridor to Moshe's room, knocked on the door. He had to knock several times before the door was opened on a chain. Moshe's bleary-eyed, unshaven face peered at him.

'Oh, it's you. Sorry, I was asleep.'

Moshe put the chain back on the door when Newman had entered. He ran a hand through his tousled hair.

'I feel as though the Eiffel Tower fell on me. What do we do now? I still think you should leave me here. Go north. Take the car. No reason why you should risk your life any more.'

'I'm sticking with you until you're safe in Paris. Meanwhile, I may have to go out. You have money? Good. Bribe the people here to send a decent meal to your room. Stay here until I knock on the door like this.'

Newman rapped his knuckles with a certain tattoo on the dressing table. Going back to his room, he had a quick shave, tidied himself up, put on a warm coat. It would be pretty raw outside.

First he'd enquire whether Paula was in the hotel. Accommodation in Arcachon was fairly limited in winter. He found she was registered but out. That would give him time to visit Isabelle. Maybe she had seen someone floating round Arcachon, someone he ought to know about.

Chapter Thirty-Eight

'I'm sorry I'm so late, Victor. I never expected you would wait.'

Rosewater grinned as Paula hurried up to him in the bar restaurant she'd earlier called a 'café'. Clad in a black leather jacket and heavy navy trousers with a razor sharp crease, he gave her a bear hug, asked her what she would like to drink as they sat at a table.

'Vermouth, please.'

'Are you hungry?' he enquired.

'Ravenous. Haven't eaten for hours.'

'There's the menu. What do you fancy?'

'Don't need to look. A huge mushroom omelette with lots of fried potatoes. Damn watching my figure this evening.

'I'll take pleasure watching it instead,' he assured her and summoned a waiter.

The restaurant was only half full. Butler wandered in as though on his own. He chose a small table by a window. Paula had said it was unnecessary for her two escorts to come, that she'd return to the Atlantique as soon as she'd finished her meal with Rosewater.

'You can go in on your own,' Butler had told her. 'Then I'll follow, merge with the wallpaper. But we're staying with you all the time. Tweed's strict orders.'

Outside Nield sat in the parked Renault where Butler could see him through the window. Nield was surveying

COLIN FORBES

his surroundings. What attracted his attention was a red Porsche, parked twenty yards or so further along the road.

Parked in the shadows, away from the nearest street lamp, it was difficult to tell whether there was anyone in the driver's seat. Nield slipped his Walther out of its holster and laid it on his lap. The Porsche bothered him.

Inside, Paula was sipping her vermouth, studying Rosewater. Even late in the day he looked as fresh as paint with his strong jaw, his handsome face, and pleasant smile. Paula liked men who smiled a lot.

'Tell me what you've been up to,' Rosewater invited.

'Oh, just visiting an old friend.'

'Man or woman?'

'Now you're prying.'

'I'm jealous . . .'

His gaze swivelled as a tall elegant Frenchwoman entered the restaurant. A waiter relieved her of her coat. She made a performance of the action. Slipping her arms out of the sleeves slowly, she raised her hands to smooth down her long sleek hair. The movement emphasized her well-built slim figure. Dressed in black, her breasts protruded against the tight dress. She was looking directly at Rosewater and gave a slow smile.

Paula followed Rosewater's fixed gaze. Across the room Butler chose the same moment to turn round, taking his time to lift a salt cellar from the empty table behind him. His eyes swiftly scanned the new arrival.

The waiter led her to a table by a window next to where Butler sat. He put down the salt cellar, which he had no intention of using.

'That woman . . .' Rosewater switched his gaze back to Paula. 'She's attractive so it's odd she's alone. She is just the sort of woman who could be one of de Forge's army of spies.'

392

'Let's forget her, enjoy our evening,' Paula suggested.

'So was it a man or a woman? I am jealous,' Rosewater repeated.

'You've increased my appetite no end. And what, may I ask, have you been occupying yourself with?'

'Driving all round the countryside, stopped at road-blocks, showing my papers. Not my real ones.'

'Roadblocks?' Paula was puzzled.

'Soldiers of the Third Army . . .'

'You mean the Third Corps.'

'No. I questioned that. They clearly said the Third Army. They seemed to be searching for someone. I tried to get them to talk but all they'd say was they were on military manoeuvres. Then they shut up like clams. You'd think it was a state of martial law.'

'Rather disturbing,' Paula probed.

'It's not going to disturb our meal . . .'

An hour later Paula felt her stomach. She had pigged it, but felt much better for the experience. Glancing at her watch, she grimaced.

'I'm afraid I must go now, Victor. Thank you for a wonderful evening. I've enjoyed every moment.'

'Hold on,' Rosewater protested. 'I thought we'd go for a drive. I know a club which will still be open. We could have a nightcap, maybe even a dance.'

'Sorry. I'd love to. But I'm tired. Give me a number where I can get in touch with you.'

Rosewater took out a notebook, scribbled a number. Handing over the sheet he'd torn out he put the same question to her.

'Where can I contact you?'

'You can't.' She smiled. 'I move around. My job.'

'Mysterious lady . . .'

The waiter brought her coat. Rosewater helped her on

with it. His hand squeezed her shoulder affectionately. As they walked to the door Butler, who had paid his bill strolled after them. He caught them up as they stood outside. Paula introduced him to Rosewater.

'This is my cousin, Harry.'

'Saw you in the restaurant,' Rosewater commented as they shook hands. 'You should have joined us,' he added without enthusiasm.

'I'm no gooseberry.' Butler's expression was blank.

'We're walking,' Paula explained. 'Where is your car?'

'Parked round the corner in a cul-de-sac off the front,' Rosewater replied. 'Let's keep in touch. Goodnight.'

He walked off towards the front. Butler touched Paula's elbow and she stayed where she was until Rosewater had disappeared round a corner. Then they walked to where Nield still sat patiently in the Renault. Paula thought of him sitting in the car while she had eaten a prince of meals. She dived into the back.

'Pete, when did you last eat?'

'Half an hour ago.' Nield twisted round, grinned at her, holding up something. 'Sandwiches from a cool bag. I always travel with rations. Plus a flask of coffee.'

'Get moving,' said Harry as he sat beside Nield. 'Back to the Atlantique. Drive slowly.'

'Not yet. Before we go I want to investigate that Porsche. It's been sitting there ever since we arrived. Back in a minute.'

He was out of the car before Butler could reply. Paula saw Nield was carrying his Walther in his right hand held down close to his side. Nield walked along the pavement on the opposite side of the road to where the Porsche stood like a tiger crouched to spring.

He strolled along like a local on his way home, collar turned up against the bitter night. No one else was in sight.

His rubber soled shoes made no sound as he came close to the car shrouded in the unnerving shadows.

With his left hand he pulled his collar tighter round his neck as he glanced across at the stationary vehicle. Paula felt moisture exuding from her palms as she saw Nield casually cross the road at a diagonal angle so he could see the driver's seat from the rear. Paula tensed herself for the sound of gunshots.

He circled the car from the rear, walked in front of it and back down the street. Climbing in behind the wheel of the Renault, he holstered his Walther.

'False alarm. No one there. So back to the Atlantique.'

'And drive slowly,' Butler repeated as they started to move.

'You said that before.'

'I'm hoping Jean Burgoyne will phone me,' Paula remarked. 'The sooner she gets away from that villa the better.'

'She'll have to look after herself,' Butler replied.

Nield stopped suddenly, swore, said he'd dropped his wallet. He left the engine running, hurried back the way they had come. He returned fairly quickly, saying he'd been lucky as he stuffed his wallet into his pocket. Paula thought his behaviour odd: Pete never lost anything. They cruised the streets of Arcachon on their way back to the Atlantique. Mostly the streets were deserted: the late hour, the subzero temperature, the time of year – November about to run into December. They turned a corner and Paula called out.

'Crawl, Pete.'

Ahead of them a man walked on the pavement on their side. Despite his heavy overcoat, his astrakhan hat, Paula recognized his way of holding himself, of walking with a deliberate tread like a man pacing out a specific distance.

'That's Lieutenant Berthier again.'

'Sure?' asked Butler.

'Certain. I should know. I spent time with him during my visit to Aldeburgh when he was posing as James Sanders.'

'Move just a bit faster, Pete,' Butler advised. 'He'll be suspicious if we crawl past him.'

Paula glanced quickly out of the window just before they came alongside Berthier, then ducked out of sight. Yes, it was definitely de Forge's man. They were approaching the Atlantique when Butler made his comment.

'It's a bit odd. Berthier prowling round the town. And we encountered polite Mr Brand, also in Arcachon. You would think something was about to happen in this neck of the woods.'

'Don't!' Paula protested. 'I'm worried about Jean Bugoyne. She could have called while I was out.'

'Soon know that,' Butler replied.

Yvette Mourlon, de Forge's agent, had followed the Rover driven by Jean Burgoyne without her quarry suspecting she had been followed. Yvette's beat-up Peugeot looked like so many other French cars involved in a collision.

Arriving at the Atlantique after dark, Jean went up to the desk clerk. She phrased her enquiry carefully.

'My friend, Paula Grey, said she was staying at a hotel in Arcachon. I hope I've got the right place.'

She rested on the counter her hand holding two banknotes. The clerk's hand straightened up the register and with the same movement he relieved her of the money.

'You've come to the right hotel. She's here.'

'Great! Could you give me her room number?'

'Wouldn't do you any good. She's out.'

'Have you any idea when she's expected back?' Jean pressed.

'None at all. She doesn't tell me her movements.' He hesitated, leaned over the counter. 'I had the impression she was going out for the evening. Had a man with her.'

'Thank you. Do you mind if I wait?' She glanced round the gloomy lobby. 'On that banquette over there?'

'Please yourself . . .'

The leather banquette had a slit in it and stuffing protruded. Not exactly the Ritz, Jean thought, as she settled down to wait. She sat there for quite a long time and then began to get nervous. De Forge might have returned to the villa. In which case men already be out looking for her. She felt very visible.

Opening her bag, she extracted a well-worn local map and studied it. The trouble was she going to have to leave it with the night clerk who was the nosy type – so she'd little doubt he'd find a way of opening a sealed envelope. The solution occurred to her and she marked three different locations on the map with crosses. Then she inserted a number inside a circle above each cross. One. Two. Three. She scribbled a note, put map and note in one of the large envelopes she always carried, wrote Paula Grey's name on it.

Taking it to the night clerk who sat reading a newspaper, she handed the envelope to him with two more banknotes.

'I have to go out. Could you please give this to Paula Grey as soon as she returns? And I expect you'll have a room for me at this time of the year?'

'Name?'

'Lisa Mason. No. I'm in a rush. I'll fill in the register when I get back . . .'

*

Earlier Yvette Mourlon had watched Burgoyne enter the Atlantique. She waited for a few minutes to see if she was coming out again. Convinced she was staying for the night, she drove a short distance further down the street, parking in the shadow of a high wall. She elevated her aerial and turned her transmitter to the right point on the waveband. She gave her codename when she had made contact and began talking.

'Yvette here. Subject at Hotel Atlantique in Arcachon at moment. Appears to be there for the night. Any orders?'

'Yes, Yvette. Keep subject's hotel under surveillance. Report immediately any fresh movement of subject. Follow if necessary. Repeat – immediately.'

'Understood . . .'

Yvette slammed the microphone back inside the concealed compartment. Arrogant bitch! And she found it strange that this uppity cow of a girl took certain messages – that Major Lamy, whom she normally spoke to, was absent sometimes. Always when someone died later.

Lieutenant Berthier was walking along a side street close to the front when his mobile phone beeped. He stepped inside the alcove of a doorway, pulled out the phone from under his coat, answered, listened.

He received exactly the same message which had been transmitted to Yvette except for the reference to continue surveillance. He was also told to phone back at fifteen-minute intervals.

Berthier closed down his aerial and began hurrying to the front where he'd left his means of transport.

*

Brand made the phone call from a cubicle in a corner of the bar. He listened, replied briefly, replaced the receiver. Leaving the money for his drink on the counter he hurried to where he'd parked his car.

Chapter Thirty-Nine

Paula took the envelope handed to her by the night clerk at the Atlantique. She was hurrying upstairs with Nield and Butler when the clerk called after her. His expression said worlds: all three together in one room?

'A man called to ask if you were in.'

'Leave a name?'

'Just puts down the phone on me when I say no.'

Inside her room Paula examined the envelope with Butler while Nield peered out between the curtains.

'This has been opened,' Paula decided. 'Then it has been crudely stuck down again.'

'Old Nosy behind the counter,' Butler remarked.

She opened up the envelope, took out the folded map and the note. The message was short. *A courier will come tonight with a number giving my location. 22.00 hours.*

'Jean is being very security-minded. I don't like this.'

She spread the map open on the only table in the cramped room. Number One was inscribed above a cross with 'Villa Rose' written in. Number Two had an inscription, 'Crossroads'. Number Three was inscribed 'Boathouse'. She gave the map to Butler, checked her watch, 9.45 p.m.

'Harry, you be navigator when the courier arrives with the rendezvous. I wish to God he'd hurry up. There isn't much time. The precautions she's taken – I wish I'd been here when she called in.'

'Let's just relax and see what happens,' Butler reassured

her. 'From what I saw and heard at the Villa Forban she's a resourceful woman.'

'I'll go downstairs and wait for this courier,' Nield said and left the room.

He was back within a minute, his manner urgent as he rushed into the room when Butler opened the door. Nield took hold of Paula's arm.

'He insists on handing it to you. Be quick. That clerk is kicking up about him being inside the hotel . . .'

Paula ran downstairs, closely followed by Nield as Butler leaned over the banister, his Walther held behind his back. A scruffy-looking man with a day's beard on his chin was glaring at the clerk. He turned, moved towards Paula, handed her an envelope.

'I was given your description,' he said in Provençal French. 'I had to give it to you personally. No other person.'

'Thank you. Can I give you something?'

'I've been well paid.'

The down-and-out tipped his soiled hat to Paula, glared again at the clerk, left the hotel. In her room Paula ripped open the envelope. A sheet of folded paper in the same handwriting as the previous note carried the terse message. *Number Three.*

'It's the boathouse,' Paula said. 'Between Gujan and Facture. Guide me, Harry,' she said as she was leaving the room.

'I'll drive,' Nield offered as they ran down the stairs.

'No, damnit! I'll drive,' Paula snapped as they reached the street. 'I don't like any of this one little bit.'

Jean Burgoyne stood on the verandah of the boathouse smoking a cigarette. She rarely smoked but her nerves were stretched to breaking point. She shielded the light of the cigarette with her left hand. Huddled in a sheepskin coat, she had found the interior claustrophobic. The only sound was the lapping of the water against the piles. At the end of the verandah was a creek, the shell of a small craft lying in the stagnant water.

The boathouse was perched close to the edge of the *bassin*. Abandoned, at one time a slipway had led across marshland to the water. Now only the outer struts of the slipway were left and all around was an air of decay.

The verandah had wooden steps leading up to it at either end. One flight from firm ground where Jean had mounted the verandah; the other at the far end leading down to the lonely creek. She had parked her Rover in a shallow bowl by the side of the wide track leading off the road to the boathouse. The quiet lapping of the water in the middle of the boathouse, where an inlet from the *bassin* reached it, would normally have been a soothing sound. At night, in this remote spot, it was getting on her nerves.

She had chosen this rendezvous because it was well away from any other habitation. She felt convinced that de Forge would have discovered her absence, that she was in danger. She was determined to hand to Paula the notes of Operation Marengo attached to her upper leg. It was an outrageous plan, a plot for a coup. It was vital the details reached Paris.

She heard a creak. Like a footstep on old wood. Flattening herself against the wall of the verandah, she held her cigarette cupped in the palm of her hand, listened, stared at the steps from firm ground. There was no repetition of the sound. She let out a sigh, straightened up. Old wood creaked by itself.

She had thought of waiting at the Atlantique, hoping Paula would appear at any moment. But she hadn't liked the way the leering night clerk had kept glancing at her surreptitiously. If she could bribe him so could anyone. And any search would start with the few hotels open in Arcachon. It had seemed safer to wait at an out of the way refuge.

She dropped her cigarette over the railing into the water. It fizzled, went out. She wasn't risking stubbing it out on the ancient planks beneath her feet. The last thing she wanted was for the place to go up in flames. Then she heard two other faint sounds. The noise of car engines. Probably passing on the main road. But the sounds stopped. Had she heard *two* cars? She wasn't sure: sound travelled a long distance at night. She shivered. It was horribly cold. But she was honest with herself: she had shivered with fear.

The strain of spending months at the Villa Forban had at last taken its toll. The strain of ministering to the needs of de Forge, of coaxing him into saying too much, of sending back secret reports to Paris. While it was going on the adrenalin had kept her cool and calculating. Now she'd left it behind she was suffering a reaction. God, she'd be glad to get back to Aldeburgh, to Admiralty House, to the peace and quiet of her uncle's home and his intelligent conversation – conversation she could listen to without memorizing every word.

The wood creaked again. She stiffened. The sound had been different, the creak stronger – as though under pressure from the tread of someone heavy. With her back against the wall she slithered towards the steps leading down to the creek. Then remained motionless. The slurp of the water reminded her of the movement of a shark. Absurd! Get a hold on yourself, girl. Then she saw the enormous shadow appearing above the steps from firm ground. The silhouette of a large figure. She couldn't see the face. That horrified her.

This was for real. The planks creaked ominously as the figure advanced towards her. Jean ran in the opposite direction. She reached the steps leading down to the creek. She hurried down them and heard the squelch of other feet in the soggy ground close behind her. She swung round, suddenly remembered the Mauser she'd tucked in her coat pocket. She grabbed at the butt, hauled out the weapon. She was terrified.

Her night vision was good. She saw why she hadn't seen a face. The man wore a Balaclava helmet. One large hand grasped her wrist, twisted it, nearly broke it and she dropped the Mauser. Two hands fastened themselves round her throat, two gloved hands, the thumbs pressing expertly against her windpipe. She stumbled back into the old boat and his weight pressed on top of her. Not for a second was the remorseless squeeze on her throat relaxed. Jean Burgoyne's last view of this world was the Balaclava helmet, the cold eyes staring down at her through the slits. The vision began blurring, then faded for ever.

The killer stood up, breathing heavily. He crouched to search her and heard the sound of approaching cars. He jumped up, made his way, crouched low, across the marsh, his rubber boots sinking into the mush. Later he reached the car he had parked some distance from the boathouse where an eerie silence had descended.

Yvette Mourlon had followed Jean Burgoyne when she'd left the Atlantique. When she saw her quarry making for the boathouse she'd elevated her aerial, reported the location. Then she had remained parked a good way off from the boathouse w nich, she suspected, was a killing ground.

Yvette had a crush on de Forge. What might occur inside the boatho e to the rich well-dressed woman concerned her not all. Yvette loved only one thing more than de F. Money.

404

Chapter Forty

'There's the boathouse. Pray to God we're in time.'

Paula spoke as she drove like hell along the road with her headlights undimmed. There was no other traffic at this hour, so what the devil did it matter. She had the bit between her teeth and, beside her, Butler was careful not to speak.

'Bleak-looking bloody spot,' Nield commented in the back.

Paula slowed, searching for the track leading off to the left. Her headlights picked it up and she swung on to the track, headlights blazing. A signal to Jean that she was coming, that help was very close and she wouldn't be alone much longer.

Jamming on the brakes in the lee of the boathouse, she reached for the handle of the door. Butler's restraining hand gripped her arm.

'Better leave me to go first . . .'

'Get your bloody hand off me! I'm in a hurry.'

Wrenching the door open, she jumped out, unzipping her shoulder bag, extracting her Browning .32. Her other hand hauled out a torch from her coat pocket. As she climbed the steps Butler was close behind her, Walther in his hand.

Paula slowed down when she arrived on the verandah, swivelling her torch beam. She tried the door into the boathouse half-way along the verandah, flashed the beam over an ancient yacht, its hull falling to pieces. Was Jean unsure who had arrived?

'Paula here. Jean, it's Paula with friends. Are you in there?'

Only when there was no answering reply did she proceed further along the verandah, aiming the beam ahead in case one of the planks was rotted. She didn't want to fall through, ending up in the lapping water. She arrived at the end of the verandah where another flight of steps led down.

Nield had stayed with the car. He heard another vehicle approaching, slipped out of the vehicle on the side furthest away from the road. He crouched low as headlights illuminated his car, gripped the Walther more firmly.

Paula's flashlight had also shown up smudged footprints of mud, large footprints, too large for Jean. She paused at the top of the steps, again aiming the beam. It stopped moving suddenly. She froze. Close behind her Butler whispered.

'What is it?'

'Oh, my God! Not again! Please! Not again . . .'

She ran down the steps and over the short stretch of the marsh. Stopping afresh, she held the torch steady with sheer will-power. The body sprawled on its back inside the wreck of a craft. The blond hair splayed over the stern. The creek with its oily surface, the ooze. It was Aldeburgh all over again. She gritted her teeth as Butler pushed past her, leant over the corpse, using his own flashlight.

'Stay where you are, Paula.'

She nearly jumped out of her skin as a hand grasped her arm. It was Newman's voice. She turned to face him, the last person she'd expected to meet during this horrific experience.

'Bob. Thank heaven. She's dead, isn't she?'

Even as she spoke she heard herself and thought it was a

stupid question. The ugly bruisings and swellings on Jean
Burgoyne's neck had been only too apparent in the beam of
her torch. She turned to follow Butler and Newman stopped
her.

'Wait here. Don't move an inch.'

'She was going to give me some valuable papers.'

'I told you not to move one inch. Pete is back-up at the
other end of the verandah.'

Newman joined Butler, treading over the spongy grass.
He bent alongside the other man. It was an ugly spectacle.
Burgoyne's eyes were starting out of her head. Her throat
was a brutalized mess. Mangled. But her mane of blond hair
was still beautiful. Pathetic was the word which occurred to
Newman.

The bottom of her sheepskin had been ripped open, a
button torn away. Gently he lifted the coat higher, exposing
her skirt, which had also been thrust up in her struggle for
life. Something was protruding below her panties. Delicately
he lifted the panties higher up her long slim leg. A polythene envelope was attached to her body with sticking
plaster. You're not supposed to fiddle around with a murder
victim, he thought. He pulled at the tape, released the
polythene envelope, pulled down her panties.

'I think the killer heard us coming,' he called up as he
approached Paula, his tone matter-of-fact. 'So he failed in
his search. She may not have died in vain.'

Putting arm round her, he led her back along the verandah. She walked like a zombie, remembered she was stll
holding the Browning. She slipped it back inside her
shoulder bag. He kept his arm round her as she descended
the steps, walked back to the car. Beyond, Newman's own
Renault was parked.

'I'm all right,' she said as they reached the car.

'You're damn well not.'

'No, I'm not! Oh, Bob, it was just like Karin at Aldeburgh. She was found strangled. She was left like some unwanted child's doll in an old boat. It's exactly the same nightmare all over again. If ever we find out who did these things I'll shoot him myself. I'll empty my whole bloody gun into his guts . . .'

Then, as Newman was hoping, she broke. Sobbing, she buried her head against his chest. He clasped his arms round her, hugged her to him, stroked the back of her neck, her hair. Gradually the shuddering left her body. Butler and Nield had tactfully stayed at a distance, both with guns in their hands, both surveying their surroundings. Paula tugged the handkerchief out of her shoulder bag, dried her eyes, looked up at Newman.

'I don't care what her relationship with de Forge was – she was a good woman. I was beginning to like her very much. I suspect she was very brave, that she had been spying on that swine.'

'You could be right.' Newman held up the envelope. 'We can look at this when we are well away from here. There could be reinforcements. And we don't want the locals in on this.'

'Legally, I suppose . . .'

'Damn the law. De Forge is the law here. This is a job for Lasalle. I'm phoning him from the hotel. And I'm getting you well clear of this area.'

Paula had recovered, was standing away from him, tidying up her coat. She shook her head.

'I'm not leaving here until Tweed orders me out. I came to do a job. Jean's dead, but I'm alive.'

'I'd like to keep it that way,' Newman told her and led her to his Renault.

*

'How on earth did you happen to turn up when you did?' Paula asked.

They were driving back to Arcachon with Butler and Nield in the other car close behind. Newman was moving fast as he explained.

'When Moshe and I arrived from the Landes we flopped out in the Atlantique for twenty-four hours. You were out when I surfaced. I decided to visit Isabelle, which I did. I was just arriving back at the Atlantique when I saw you diving into a car and driving off like a bat out of hell. I decided to follow to see what was up.'

'You saw. I hate leaving Jean like that. Seems awful.'

'So what was the alternative? We take the body away and then what? Inform the local gendarmes and we're up to our neck in trouble. Worse still, we could be immobilized. You think Tweed would like that – just when France is exploding? Now there have been anti-American and anti-Arab riots in Marseilles. It's spreading.'

'How do you know that?'

'Isabelle has been listening to the radio, watching TV. She said there have been a lot of casualties. And our old friends, the Balaclava mob egging things on.'

'You mentioned the Landes. How did you get on there?'

'Talk about that later,' Newman said grimly. 'Now I just hope we can reach Tweed and Lasalle. De Forge's world is closing in on us.'

In Paris, Tweed had experienced a disturbing evening. The courier Monica had sent with his forged press card had arrived. Lasalle had told him Josette de Forge was holding one of her 'salons' starting at eight o'clock.

Arriving by cab in Passy, Tweed had told the driver to drop him a few doors from the address he was making for.

As he walked up to the elegant terrace house facing a small park he saw limousines pulling up, disgorging the guests. Among them he recognized Louis Janin, Minister of Defence and catspaw of General de Forge. The flunkey at the door asked him if he had an invitation.

'Press,' said Tweed. 'Tell Madame de Forge I'm from the *Daily World*. And hurry it up. It's cold out here. If you're not back in three minutes I won't be here. But I'll make a phone call to Madame tomorrow – and I doubt whether you'll be on the staff any more. My card . . .'

As he waited other guests arrived in limousines, all wearing evening dress. Some of the women sported a fortune in jewels. Tweed, in his neat business suit, felt quite at ease. Why should he dress up for this nest of vipers?

The flunkey returned, hurrying, his manner very different. He ushered Tweed inside, took his coat, led the way across the red carpeted hall into a large room crammed with guests. The room was tastefully furnished and illuminated with glittering chandeliers. There were pictures on the wall and Tweed thought one was a Gauguin.

The flunkey had to edge his way through the chattering throng, their babble punctuated by the clink of champagne glasses. Tweed noticed a full general in uniform. Masson, Army Chief of Staff. He shouldn't have attended. Then he was ushered into the presence.

Josette de Forge was a tall, slim woman clad in a black velvet dress which showed to advantage her superb figure. A commanding woman who was also chic, her long sleek black hair was tied in a chignon. The dress was low-cut, exposing her excellent shoulders and held up more by hope than by gravity. Her dark eyes surveyed Tweed as she held his card and he quickly realized she was putting herself out to charm him.

'The *Daily World*, Mr Prentice. You are most welcome to

my little salon. Champagne?' She summoned a waiter and Tweed reluctantly took a glass. 'Come and sit with me so we can talk,' she continued in English. 'All these people. It really is simply too dreadful. But you ask one, you have to ask so many others. They so easily take offence if not invited ...'

As she prattled on she led him to an elegant couch next to the wall, waved a hand for him to join her, sat down crossing her long legs which were revealed by a deep slit in the dress. Tweed made a point of noticing them: he felt sure it was expected. He replied in English, concealing the fact that he spoke fluent French.

'You have a very distinguished gathering here, including General Masson. He gives you moral support in the present crisis?'

'It really is most intriguing, Mr Prentice, that now the British press is beginning to take an interest in France. Soon Paris will once again become the capital of Europe as it was in the time of Napoleon.'

'What about Germany?'

'They respect power.' She made a dismissive gesture with her free well-shaped hand. 'And soon we shall be recognized as the superpower of Europe. After all – ' she sipped at her champagne – 'we have the *force de frappe*, atomic weapons. There is General Lapointe over there, commander of the *force.*'

The eagles gather, Tweed thought, turning to look at the uniformed general she had indicated. Of medium height, slim, with a neat small black moustache, he was listening to a blonde beauty who gazed up at him with adoring eyes.

'He has divorced his wife,' Josette went on, 'so Lisette is hopeful. He may bed her but she will not become his second consort.'

'I gather Prime Minister Navarre has other ideas – that he approves close co-operation with the new Germany.'

'Navarre! *Pouf!*' She blew him into the wind. 'He will not last long once my husband arrives in Paris.'

'You are expecting him? With an army, you mean?'

Her magnetic black eyes narrowed. She studied Tweed before she replied. Then she looked round the room and her full red lips made a moue.

'We can't talk properly in this dreadful bedlam. Come with me. They'll have to do without me for a while.'

She made it sound like a deprivation as Tweed stopped a waiter topping up his drink and followed her. Opening a side door she went through into a smaller room which was mostly furnished with *chaise longues* wide enough to take two people lying down. Locking the door, she led the way to a *chaise longue* against the wall. As she arranged herself on it she patted it.

'Come and sit close to me so we can put the world right.'

Tweed perched on the edge, turned to face her while she lounged against the headrest. He took out a compact tape recorder from his pocket, placed it on a small coffee table, pressed the start button and there was a whirring sound.

'I hope you don't mind,' he suggested.

She reached forward, used her pink-varnished index finger to press the stop button. The whirring sound ceased. She smiled languidly, her bare arms clasped behind her swanlike neck.

'You might not want a recording of all we say to each other. In any case, I don't like those machines.'

'As you wish.' He took out a notebook and pen. 'You won't mind if I make notes? Good. Perhaps you'd say again what you told me in the other room? I couldn't catch all you did say,' he lied.

412

'Of course . . .' She repeated what she had said, drawing up her knees and leaning on them as she watched him.

Her movement again exposed her long legs. Tweed scribbled as she spoke.

'And,' he coaxed her when she was silent, 'you said you were expecting your husband to arrive in Paris with an army.'

'You newspaper men are wicked.' She gently slapped his knee, let her hand linger. 'You asked me that question. I hadn't answered.'

'And your answer?'

'He will come to Paris, of course. At the right moment. When France is crying out for a strong man to save her. And maybe an army will come with him – he inspires great loyalty and may not be able to prevent them following him.'

Which was a pretty damned devious approach, Tweed thought as he went on scribbling. He could see now how the coup could be justified. Her revelation had already made his visit worthwhile. Immensely so. Her hand began to wander. He clamped his own hand on hers. He was finding her the most dangerously attractive woman. He decided to face her with it.

'Supposing your husband walked in and found us like this now?'

'The door is locked.'

'You know what I mean.'

'Oh, Charles finds his amusement elsewhere. He has a long-term mistress. English, as it happens. Then he has other feminine sources of relaxation. Don't you ever relax?'

She had turned over her hand under his, entwining their fingers together. She tugged gently to draw him closer. Tweed asserted his considerable will-power. He reminded himself that de Forge was probably responsible for the cold-blooded murder of his agent, Francis Carey, in Bordeaux. And was she just feeling playful – or did she see this as a golden opportunity to spread de Forge's propaganda across the Channel? He took a deep breath.

'If we don't continue this interview I could lose my job.'

'Fire away, Mr Prentice. Then we can relax later.'

'I have heard rumours of some kind of high-level club which is planning to take over France. Even a rumour that one of the club's members is a foreign armaments manufacturer who is secretly supplying General de Forge with new weapons.'

He had shaken her, but she was a clever woman. Her reaction was unexpected. She stretched out her exposed leg and laid it across his lap. He perched his notebook on the leg, smiled, waited for her answer.

'I can't imagine where you heard such a melodramatic idea. Of course, as you will have seen from the guests outside, very influential people attend my salons. They wish to keep up with the latest developments. Events are close to a climax.' She wiggled her leg. 'Talking about climaxes . . .'

'Your weakness,' Tweed said brusquely, 'is you haven't any political support.'

'You think not!'

She removed her leg, jumped up. He had struck a nerve. Straightening her dress, she walked over to a wall mirror to make sure she was decent. Then she beckoned to him as she unlocked the door. Tweed followed her back into the salon. Josette took his arm, used her other hand to point to a man talking non-stop to a small brunette, chopping a hand up and down to emphasize what he was saying.

'There,' Josette said, 'is your – our – political support. Emile Dubois. Leader of the *Pour France* party. Thousands flock to his banner every day.'

Tweed studied Dubois. Of medium build, running to fat, he would be in his fifties. He had a mass of shaggy hair, a straggly moustache above thick lips. With his dinner jacket he wore an ordinary white tie which looked a trifle soiled. A thoroughly unsavoury-looking character who reminded Tweed of pictures he had seen of Pierre Laval, wartime collaborator.

'You certainly have the big guns on your side,' Tweed remarked, wishing to leave Josette in a satisfied frame of mind.

'And the big guns always win. Why don't you come to see me tomorrow evening? I have no salon and will be alone. Let me give you my card. Phone me to say when you will arrive so I can be ready for you . . .'

Josette opened the drawer of an escritoire standing by the wall. She took out an engraved card with a red rose above the lettering. Her smile was inviting as she gave it to him.

'My personal card, my private number. Given only to a few.'

Tweed thanked her, said good-night and the flunkey brought his coat. As he left the building Tweed patted his jacket pocket to check the small tape recorder was safe. He had been careful to collect that off the table before moving back into the salon.

'There is a taxi waiting across the road, Mr Prentice,' the flunkey advised him, ever-helpful now.

Prentice. It was the cover name Monica had chosen before having the card printed, and she had told Tweed's close friend, the editor of *Daily World*, that this was the name Tweed would be using. Inside the cab Tweed took out the tape recorder, looked at it and smiled to himself.

*

You think not!

Josette de Forge's voice came clearly out of the recorder as Tweed stood up, switched it off, looked at Lasalle in Navarre's office at the Ministry of the Interior. Navarre, who had retained the portfolio of the ministry when he became Prime Minister, was spending time in another building. Lasalle had just listened to Josette's whole conversation with Tweed.

'How did you manage it?' he asked. 'You said that she switched off the recorder.'

'She thought she had. The Engine Room at Park Cresecnt are ingenious. They structured it so the stop button starts it, and the start button simply creates a whirring noise as though the tape is running – when it isn't. When the tape is really running it's completely silent.'

'But supposing she'd agreed to your using it and hadn't stopped it?'

'I'd have said it didn't sound right, fiddled with it, and operated a concealed lever which starts the tape running.'

'We could use a few of those ourselves. But the critical result of your visit is her vague reference to de Forge arriving in Paris with an army. That is vital data. You have heard that de Forge has been appointed temporary commander of the Third *Army*?'

'No. Navarre approved that?'

'Didn't get the chance. General Masson announced the appointment publicly without reference to him. Navarre's only remedy would be to dismiss both his Army Chief of Staff and General de Forge. That could provoke an uprising. He can't do it.'

At that moment Navarre himself strode into the office with a brisk step. His lean face was grim and determined. Lasalle explained about Tweed's visit and Navarre asked to listen to the recording.

He sat behind his desk, quite relaxed. He stared at the tape recorder, listening intently as it played back all Tweed's conversation with Josette. As he switched it off Tweed made his observation.

'I'm very glad you retained the portfolio of the Ministry of the Interior when you became Prime Minister.'

Navarre grinned. 'My trump card. Control of the DST, the police, above all of the CRS, our paramilitary units. The question is when to play that trump card. I need hard evidence of de Forge's treachery.'

The phone rang, Navarre listened, handed it to Tweed.

'Robert Newman for you . . .'

Chapter Forty-One

General de Forge was also up late, pacing his office at GHQ as he listened to Major Lamy reporting the success of Kalmar. Lamy found it disconcerting to have his chief prowling round, often behind him as he spoke. It was a psychological trick de Forge was fond of – to put a visitor at a disadvantage. He interrupted Lamy's flow of words.

'The bottom of your coat and your shoes are caked with mud.'

'It's muddy in the countryside.'

'Even so, before you come to see me you should clean up. You are expected to give an example of smartness at all times to any soldier who may see you.'

'My apologies. I was anxious to let you know what Kalmar confirmed over the phone. Jean Burgoyne is dead.'

'One spy eliminated. And I'm considering developing the present manoeuvres into Operation Marengo – the march on Paris. After you've activated Operation Austerlitz – to throw Paris into chaos. And the cross of fire must appear everywhere from now on.'

While talking another part of de Forge's mind considered his conviction that there was a traitor at GHQ. Paris was being fed information – the informant at the DST in the rue des Saussaies had confirmed this. It had to be a member of his inner circle. Lieutenant Berthier? Major Lamy himself? He had to be detected quickly, liquidated. An essential condition before he ordered Austerlitz and then Marengo.

'The cross of fire was used both in the Marseilles and Toulon riots,' Lamy assured him hastily. 'The newspapers will be full of pictures tomorrow. You wish me to set in motion Austerlitz?'

'Not just yet. Timing is everything in a successful campaign. You said Berthier phoned you, that he was sure he caught a glimpse of Paula Grey inside a car with two men in Arcachon. She is Kalmar's next target. He must finish her off within the next twenty-four hours.'

'That doesn't give Kalmar much time. He's a meticulous planner.'

'Then he'll have to speed up his meticulous planning. I am equally concerned with your contact with the mysterious *Manteau*.'

'He phoned me, told me to put the two million Swiss francs in a cloth bag, to deposit the bag behind an isolated telephone box outside a village south of Bordeaux. I did so. Then drove away.'

'But what else did he say?' de Forge asked over Lamy's left shoulder.

The General was a devil, Lamy thought. How could he have guessed there was more?

'*Manteau* told me I was to drive back towards GHQ for half an hour, then I could return. That if I felt inclined to return earlier that was all right by him, but I'd be shot through the head.'

Yes, de Forge ruminated, that sounded like typical *Manteau* language. Not a bit like Kalmar.

'Anything else?' he rapped out.

'Yes. He said he'd deal with Paula Grey. And any other people you needed extinguished. The very word he used.'

Well, at least the payment should stop any further attempts on his own life, de Forge decided. He felt relieved:

the bullet which had penetrated his limousine had come rather too close for comfort.

'Send a yellow signal to the Austerlitz units in Paris,' he decided suddenly. 'Immediately . . .'

When Lamy had left he checked his watch. The next and final signal would be red: the signal for the saboteur units to set Paris aflame. He must strike soon before Navarre established his hold on the government.

Navarre and Lasalle watched Tweed as he took the call from Newman but could read nothing from his expression. Tweed made brief notes, asked a question now and then, eventually told Newman to hold on. He looked at the two Frenchmen.

'He's calling from a hotel in Arcachon. Should be a safe line – he has Butler watching the clerk who operates the switchboard – but I want quick decisions.'

'Tell us the problem,' Navarre said crisply.

'Newman has photographic evidence of atrocities committed by de Forge's men . . .' Tersely he told them about the burial ground in the Landes, the attack on Moshe Stein's villa by men masked as Ku Klux Klan.

'Let me speak to him,' Lasalle said.

'Lasalle here. I'll be brief. You have the film? Good. Do you know the airfield just north of the Etang de Cazaux, to the west of the N652?'

'Yes. I noticed it when Moshe and I were driving up here from the Landes.'

'An Alouette chopper will land there at daybreak. Give the pilot the films. Codename Valmy for the pilot.'

'I'll be there.'

'Tweed is gesturing, hold for a moment . . .'

Tweed had been thinking of Newman's shorthand

420

description of the discovery of Jean Burgoyne's body by Paula. He'd decided to pull her out of the area. He told Lasalle quickly about the murder. Lasalle clapped a hand to his head.

'My God! Jean Burgoyne was one of my agents I told you I had in the area. This is terrible. Now I only have one left . . .'

'Give me the damned phone,' Tweed snapped. 'Bob, where is Paula? With you. Put her on quickly . . . Paula, I'm sorry about Jean Burgoyne – it must have been a shock. A great shock . . . Yes. I can see how it brought Aldeburgh back to you. Now listen, I'm pulling you out. Bob knows Lasalle is sending a chopper. You're to board it, come back to Paris.'

'No. I'm staying on to try and find this killer. Up to now he's strangled two of my friends – Karin Rosewater and Jean Burgoyne.'

'Paula.' Tweed's tone was grim. 'This isn't a request, it's an order. You're to fly back in the Alouette.'

'No,' she repeated with the same firmness, 'I'm staying here. There's Bob with me – as well as Harry and Pete.'

'I don't think you heard me,' Tweed rasped. 'I am giving you an order . . .'

'Which I'm disobeying. You don't like it, you can sack me later.'

'You're an obstinate woman . . .'

'When I want to be. And I want to be now. How is everything there?'

'Put Newman back on the line. Now!'

'Tweed, I'm here,' Newman responded after taking the phone.

'Paula is being difficult, as you doubtless realize now. So I want her aboard that Alouette – even if you have to carry her into the machine physically.'

421

'Can't do that,' Newman said laconically. 'You're making a mistake. She'd feel she was running away. Can't say that I disagree with you in one way. But she's a fully paid up member of the team. Don't forget that.'

'If you say so.' Tweed's tone was abrupt. 'I'm hoping that evidence you're providing will give us a powerful lever to neutralize the enemy. Of course, a witness would have made all the difference.'

'There is a witness,' Newman told him, thinking of Martine, the old woman who collected brushwood by the shore. 'Getting on a bit, but still with all the marbles there. And could be very impressive on TV.'

'We want that witness.'

'It means my going back to the Landes. But I can see that it's important, could tilt the scales.'

'The Landes?' Tweed was alarmed. 'I can't ask you to do that.'

'You didn't. I've just decided myself I'm going soon as I can.'

'Bob, before you leave promise me you will let me know – or get one of the others to do it.'

'OK. Promise. Take care.'

'*You* take care.' Tweed's tone was urgent. 'I'd better warn you we have reason to believe that all hell is about to break loose. Prepare yourself . . .'

As Tweed put down the phone he reflected this was the critical point in the titanic struggle to save France. After laying out the situation, Navarre had stood as though gazing into the fog of an uncertain future while he listened to Tweed's phone call. Tweed looked at him first, caught his expression, guessed his thoughts, then studied Lasalle.

The DST chief was edgy and also unsure. Should he

launch his battalions – the DST, the paramilitary CRS and other forces under his control? If so, in which direction? To the south where de Forge was organizing controlled chaos? Or should he dig in round Paris?

Only Tweed was certain what was needed. A foreigner in a foreign capital, he seemed as relaxed as if he were behind his desk at Park Crescent. He spoke decisively.

'I know what we must do, but first bring me up to date on the present situation as you see it.'

It was Navarre who answered, still forceful even at this late hour.

'As you know, Masson has bypassed me, has announced publicly the appointment of General de Forge as temporary commander of the Third Army. That army is now manoeuvring over the whole of the south of France. Pretended objective of the so-called exercise? To repel an invasion force landing at Marseilles, Toulon, and Bordeaux from the sea and the air. The fictitious enemy is a General Ali, a dictator based in North Africa – coming to the aid of his persecuted Arabs in France. Which fits in with the anti-Arab propaganda of Dubois.'

'And the real objective?' Tweed asked.

'It gives de Forge the perfect excuse to move his army over a huge area in any direction.'

'We must strike now,' Tweed insisted. 'Without pause, without mercy. These are evil forces we confront – racist, anti-Arab, anti-German, anti-American.'

He had stood up when Chief Inspector Otto Kuhlmann hurried into the room. His teeth were clamped tightly on his unlit cigar. He held a folded sheet of paper in his hand.

'I've just returned from a lightning trip to Germany,' he informed Navarre. 'May I continue?'

'By all means.'

'Tweed,' Kuhlmann began, 'early in the crisis you

advised me to send undercover police to Basle and Geneva.
You said that was where Kalmar passed on instructions for
the next phase. In neutral Switzerland. And where he got
orders.'

'So what has happened?' Tweed enquired.

'Four people we know are involved in this business
visited either Basle or Geneva – or both – recently. Here is a
list of their names and destinations.'

Tweed unfolded the sheet. He glanced down the list,
handed it back to Kuhlmann.

'The man we know as Kalmar is on that list. I just can't
prove it. Yet.'

Tweed went straight to his own office, closed the door and
sat at his desk. There were urgent phone calls he wanted to
make without anyone overhearing him, specific instructions
for action he wanted to give.

His first call was to Marler.

His second call was to Newman and he spoke to him for
some time. Then he asked to speak to Butler. His orders
were brief. He asked to speak to Pete Nield. Again the
orders were brief.

He asked Nield to put Paula on the line. Again it was a
long conversation – far warmer than his previous call to her.
He had just put down the phone when Kuhlmann came in.

'Take a seat, Otto. No, I'm not identifying Kalmar. My
strategy is that the assassin should feel he's safe,
unsuspected.'

'OK by me. I came to talk to you alone. While in Germany
I had a brief radio signal from Stahl. Remember him?'

'Of course. The Hotel des Bergues in Geneva – seems
ages ago. You told Paula and me about him. Your agent

posing as a Frenchman inside Bordeaux. You gave me the assumed name, his address, his phone number.'

'I said the signal was brief. It was also encouraging – and disturbing. He has valuable information but can't get out of Bordeaux. Can you help?'

'I think so. I have people in the area. The codeword for identification was Gamelin.'

'Correct. And thank you for your help.'

'I can promise nothing, Otto,' Tweed warned, and the German left the room.

Tweed reached for the phone, dialled the number of the Atlantique Newman had given him. He was going to make it very clear to Newman that it was up to him whether he ventured into Bordeaux again to rescue Stahl. Newman had had more than his fair share of ordeals so far.

When Tweed had phoned Marler earlier the slim Englishman was perched on the edge of his bed in the apartment near the rue du Bac in Paris. Smoking a king-size, he had a large-scale map of France spread out and was studying it. When the phone rang he picked it up and careful not to give any name.

'Yes? Who is it?'

'Tweed. Another mission. Urgent. Of course. I want to step up the pressure, screw it down tight. We're launching full-scale psychological warfare. At least, I am. Any ideas?'

'Give me a sec to think.'

Marler blew a smoke ring, watched it float up to the cobwebbed ceiling of the small scruffy room. The ring dissolved.

'I've thought of something. Pure psychological warfare. It means I'll be away from here for a while.'

'Good luck . . .'

Marler put down the mobile phone inside his small open case on a chair. He checked his open-flight Air Inter tickets. He'd used several but there were plenty left. Selecting a container of face powder with a yellow undertone, he walked over to the wall mirror and applied some.

It was an innocuous item among his samples. After all he was posing as a cosmetics salesman. The powder gave his skin the sallow tinge which is common to certain Frenchmen. He studied himself in the mirror, adjusted his beret to a jaunty angle.

He wore washed-out blue denims and a windcheater. He had days before tested out his appearance, walking into a bar, ordering a drink. He had lingered over the one drink the way Frenchmen in bars do. He had chatted to the barman, to several customers, complaining about how bad business was. They had all agreed. More important, they had all accepted him as one of them.

'Time to go out and do your thing,' he told his mirror image.

He was aware he was talking to himself. It was a habit he occasionally indulged in when on his own for long periods. He looked forward to leaving the rundown apartment on the Left Bank where the heating was nil.

At the Atlantique in Arcachon Newman also had a map spread out on his bed, but this was a large-scale map of Bordeaux. In the room with him were Paula, Butler, and Nield.

'I have to go back into the city to haul out Stähl, a German agent in hiding,' he explained. 'I'm going in tonight. Best chance after dark.'

'You're crazy,' Paula burst out. 'First, you were lucky

when you went there before. And all the news reports far more security now than there was earlier. Look at the papers . . .'

They, too, were spread over Newman's bed. All showed pictures of the riots in Marseilles and Toulon. The most prominent feature of the photographs was of men in Balaclavas with the Cross of Lorraine – the crosses blazing with fire in the night. The atmosphere of insurrection was growing by the hour.

'Second,' Paula hammered away, 'you'll have no sleep if you go to Bordeaux. And you have to meet that helicopter near the *étang* at dawn tomorrow. Your reflexes won't be so good if you run into something, which you probably will.'

'Thanks for the vote of confidence,' Newman snapped back.

'I'm just thinking of your safety, you cretin.'

'Let's cool it.' Newman grinned. 'I'd grasped that and I am grateful, touched.'

'Obstinate bastard,' she chaffed him, her good humour returning with his infectious grin.

They hugged each other. Pete Nield winked behind them at Butler. There always came a moment like this during an operation. A situation of continuing danger. Too little sleep. Fatigue. Nerves frayed.

'I can't find Stahl's address on the map,' Newman admitted as he released Paula. 'The Passage Emile Zola. Before I head for Bordeaux I'll visit Isabelle. She should know.'

Paula grinned wickedly. 'Mind she doesn't keep you there all night in her apartment.'

He slapped her on the rump, looked at Butler and Nield.

'You two take good care of her while I'm away.'

'But you have to come back here before . . . you drive down to meet the Alouette,' Butler said.

He'd been on the verge of saying *before you drive down to*

the Landes. But he guessed Newman had omitted to tell her about that dangerous expedition. And Newman's instruction about her had been superfluous: on the phone Tweed had told Butler and Nield separately that he held them personally responsible for Paula's safety, that she was in grave danger.

Chapter Forty-Two

Victor Rosewater was a long way from Arcachon. He sat in the living room of his ultra-modern flat in the Konvikstrasse in Freiburg – on the edge of the Black Forest in Germany. He checked his watch. 4 a.m. Helmut should arrive shortly.

Rosewater had been flown by a private plane from Bordeaux Airport to Basle in the middle of the night. After paying the pilot the substantial sum agreed, Rosewater had driven his car parked near the airport across the Swiss border up the autobahn to Freiburg.

The weather was lousy. Heavy snow smothered the ancient rooftops of the University city. Rosewater got up, walked into his kitchen which had every up to date appliance. He poured himself another cup of coffee from the percolator, went back to his chair in the living room. As he sipped coffee he stared at the photograph of Paula Grey he had secretly taken. The print was propped up against an old silver jug he had bought in an antique shop. Silver was his hobby and he had quite a collection.

Paula was a very attractive girl, he thought. And, unlike so many attractive women, she had a vibrant personality. 'You've got everything going for you,' he mused.

Helmut Schneider: his mind switched to the German he had flown to Freiburg to meet. Helmut was an extrordinary man. He had a network of informants through the whole of Germany, a number of them unsavoury characters. Among the more respectable were barmen, hotel commissionaires and concierges, cab and bus drivers – all people who noticed what was going on round them, who heard unguarded conversations.

Among the less savoury were brothel keepers, unlicensed arms merchants and dubious night club bouncers. It was a world the public had no idea existed.

Until recently Helmut had told them to inform him, for a price, about any strangers patronizing these establishments with Irish accents, their modes of transport. By using these sources Rosewater had tracked down several IRA cells before they'd had time to become active.

He had recently given Helmut a new instruction. To search for clues as to the whereabouts of *Siegfried* units. Now he waited to hear if Helmut had had any luck.

The weird thing was Helmut rarely left his cheap apartment in Frankfurt. All communication was carried out over the phone. But Helmut was a man of cunning. He took short-term leases on an apartment, rarely using the same phone number for more than two months.

He would then move on to another part of Frankfurt. This involved calling a host of informants to give them his new number. But Helmut had a strong instinct for survival. Staying in one place for long was risky, could easily be a lethal mistake.

A tapping on the knocker of the front door interrupted the mind-wanderings of Rosewater. He jumped up, hauled from his holster a 7.65mm pistol, went to the solid front door, and peered through the spyhole before drawing bolts and unlocking the door.

Outside crouched a bizarre figure. Dressed in black from head to foot, the man wore black glasses and carried the white cane of a blind man. It took Rosewater a moment to recognize Helmut Schneider.

'Shake the snow off your coat,' he ordered. 'And maybe you'd be considerate enough to remove your boots.'

The apartment had fitted carpet wall to wall. Meticulous in his dress, Rosewater kept the luxurious apartment clean as a new pin. He closed the door after Schneider had removed the soft snow from his coat, divested himself of his boots and walked into the warmth of the hall. Rosewater gestured towards the living room, took coat and boots to the kitchen, hung up the coat behind a door and dumped the worn boots in the sink. He poured another cup of coffee and handed it to Schneider, who had seated himself in an armchair, feet in socks stretched out towards a radiator, in the living room.

'Any results?' About *Siegfried*?' Rosewater greeted his guest.

'A clever girl has infiltrated their High Command. Won't tell you who she is.' Schneider grinned, exposing two missing teeth. 'She has personal reasons to hate the guts of shit like that. She has brains – and she's got guts.'

Schneider had removed his dark glasses and his cunning eyes gleamed with satisfaction. Arriving at the apartment he'd looked like a down-and-out: now he was alert, erect, and watchful. Like a clever ferret.

'But actual results?' Rosewater demanded impatiently.

'Contain yourself,' Schneider reproved him, continuing in German, the language both men were speaking. 'It's warmer in here. Like bloody Siberia out there.'

'Why the elaborate disguise?' Rosewater asked, suddenly anxious. 'You weren't followed?'

'I was.'

'You mean to here? For God's sake . . .'

'Contain yourself,' Schneider repeated, pleased that he had shaken the normally cool Englishman. 'You really think

I can't spot a shadow? Two of them, moving separately. I lost them in Heidelberg. Then I changed cars at a friend's place. Then I put on this gear when I'd left the second car on the outskirts of your patch.'

'Very professional.' Rosewater forced himself to mask his growing irritation. 'And the results?'

'*Siegfried* is in Hamburg, Dortmund, Berlin, Hanover, Düsseldorf, Frankfurt, Karlsruhe, Munich, and Stuttgart. It's a big operation.'

While talking Schneider extracted an old wallet from beneath three layers of clothing: two woollen pullovers and a jacket. He unzipped a concealed compartment, took out a grubby, folded sheet of A4 paper, handed it over to Rosewater. Then he spread his feet a little closer to the radiator.

Rosewater looked down the list of detailed addresses and recognized several. He looked at Schneider who had removed his mittens, was holding the cup in both hands to warm himself.

'This is the lot?' he asked.

'By no means.' Schneider finished his coffee, placed the cup on the hearth. 'I expect to have another long list very shortly. I'll phone the number you gave me so they can contact you.'

'Good.'

Rosewater was thinking Schneider was ideal for the job. A social outcast, a man able to mingle with, to haggle with the shabby half-world which was his network. And there was no danger he'd try to pre-empt Rosewater by handing to the police this information. The police were his enemy.

Schneider, a pickpocket, had served five short sentences in German prisons. One more misdemeanour and he'd go down for a very long sentence.

'Time you left,' Rosewater suggested.

Schneider made the universal gesture asking for money

– rubbing thumb against middle finger. Rosewater made it a matter of policy to wait until he asked for money: it discouraged the German from thinking there was a bottom-less pit available.

Taking four five-hundred Deutschmark banknotes from his pocket he handed them over. The equivalent roughly of seven hundred pounds. But Helmut's expenses came high. The German looked dubious.

'Not enough to cover what I'll have to pay out. Double this might just manage it.'

'I haven't got that to spare.' The usual haggling which Schneider expected. 'You'll have to get by with this. Not a Deutschmark more.'

He produced two more five-hundred Deutschmark notes, dropped them on the table. Schneider scooped them up as Rosewater went into the kitchen, collected the coat and boots. He banged the latter to get rid of the snow which hadn't melted in the warmth of the central heating. He was anxious to get Schneider out of the apartment.

The German put on his disguise before leaving. Adjusting his dark glasses, he adopted a stooped posture, tapping the white cane against the walls to accustom himself again to his role of blind man.

Rosewater was glad to see the back of him. He was anxious to drive to Basle Airport. There he would catch the first flight to Bordeaux via Geneva, driving on to Arcachon. Rosewater had overheard in the Bar Martinque a man with a distinct Irish accent. Discreet enquiries had confirmed the Irishman frequented the bar. And also he wanted to meet Paula Grey again.

Twelve hours earlier during the previous evening Newman had driven to Isabelle's apartment from the Atlantique. As he moved along the front the *bassin* was a seething mass of heaving waves, reminding him of Aldeburgh.

He was also thinking of the notes he'd extracted from the polythene envelope attached to poor Jean Burgoyne's lifeless body. Reading them alone in his room he had been startled to find he was looking at plans for an army movement on Paris. The details gave the route to be followed north by a lightning thrust of de Forge's armoured divisions. Their objective was Paris.

Could the information be genuine? Newman thought so: Jean had given map references, used language which sounded to have been extracted from military dispatches. His dilemma was whether to entrust such vital data to an Alouette which might crash before it arrived in Paris. How else could he get the notes into the hands of Tweed?

Parking in a side street a short distance from her apartment, well away now from the front, he stepped out. Before he approached the entrance he stood banging his gloved hands round his body while he made sure he had not been followed.

He had phoned Isabelle just before leaving the Atlantique. When he pressed the bell beside her apartment door she had it thrown wide open in seconds. She was talking while she locked and bolted the door.

'It has been so long since I've seen you, Bob. You will stay the night? If you don't want to make love we'll sit and chat. Perhaps I shouldn't have said that. But I've been thinking of you. Have you been thinking of me?'

All in one breath. She snuggled up against him. Her body pressed against his. She was moaning with pleasure, hands clutching at him. I have a problem here, he thought. He grasped both her shoulders, gently pushed her to arm's length, and she stood staring at him, quivering, her eyes huge.

'Isabella, I need your help. I have to leave almost at once. To go to Bordeaux again . . .'

'No! Not Bordeaux! You don't know what it's like now. Friends have told me. There are army patrols in all the main streets . . .'

'I don't want a main street. I want the Passage Emile Zola. Ever heard of it?'

Releasing her, he took out his street map of the city and spread it over the living-room table. She stood next to him, her hair brushing his face, a pen in her hand. She had it poised to make a mark when he stopped her.

'No. Marked maps are dangerous. You do know where it is?'

'Yes. It is very difficult to find. You can walk past it a dozen times without seeing it. But I can take you there.'

'Nothing doing. This is one trip I make on my own.'

'Really?' She pulled at strands of her hair. 'Which way will you drive in to Bordeaux? I suppose you will follow the same route we used?'

'It seems sensible, since I know it.'

'Very sensible. When the Passage Emile Zola is on this side of the city.'

She pointed to the eastern area, furthest from Arcachon and on the way to the airport. He looked at the area she had vaguely indicated and couldn't see the passage. In any case, it wasn't included in the map's index. His tone changed, became rough.

'Look, stop fooling around, Isabelle. Someone's life is at stake. Without making a mark just damn well show me where this passage is.'

'There.' She retracted her pen tip and lightly touched the map. 'And to have any chance of surviving the army patrols we'd take a roundabout route and approach it from the east. I can guide you.'

435

'Thanks. I won't risk you coming again.'

'Excuse me. I must turn off the coffee percolator.'

She disappeared through the swing door into the kitchen, was absent for no more than thirty seconds, then came back with a coat over her arm, a canvas bag in her hand. Newman said goodnight after swiftly folding the map. He went to the door, threw back the bolt, turned the key, and left the apartment.

He had unlocked the door of his car, was easing himself behind the wheel of the Renault, when the passenger door opened and Isabelle, wearing the coat, slid in beside him, closing her door. She moved like a cat. He'd not heard a footstep. Her arrival had been so sudden he'd slipped his hand inside his sheepskin to grip the butt of his Smith & Wesson.

'Give me the map,' she said calmly. 'You said someone's life was at stake. That makes two of you. Without my local knowledge you'd never make it. Hadn't we better get moving?'

'Manteau here.'

General de Forge, alone in his GHQ office, froze. Only two words but they'd had an extraordinarily sinister ring over the phone.

'Yes, what the hell is it now? You've been paid.'

'Trickery. My God, you do take chances. Don't you want to go on living?'

'Just hold it there.' De Forge had a grip on himself now. 'I would appreciate an explanation of that cryptic remark.'

'The money, General.'

'What about it? The amount was as agreed.'

De Forge was puzzled. Lamy had delivered it as

instructed – or was his Chief of Intelligence going into business for himself? Was Lamy the rotten apple of the inner circle?

'The amount was as agreed,' *Manteau* repeated. 'But three-quarters of it is counterfeit. The remaining quarter has bills in numbered sequence. That was a grave mistake, General. Maybe even suicidal.'

The voice was so deadly calm it was unnerving. As though discussing a perfectly normal business transaction. The man was like ice. And de Forge was appalled at what he had been told, hardly knew how to react.

'I'll investigate,' he said brusquely. 'I handed over the money to the emissary myself. It was as requested at that moment.'

'So you say. So you would say, of course. I'm going to have to provide one last demonstration. Incidentally, I have left the cloth bag containing what was inside behind the same phone box. Have it collected. Just in case you are telling the truth. Which I very much doubt.'

'What demonstration are you talking about . . .'

De Forge realized he was talking into a dead line. Shaken, he put down the phone, thought for a moment, picked up the phone again, ordered Major Lamy to come at once. He next called Lieutenant Berthier's quarters, found the officer had just returned, told him he wanted to see him, to wait outside his office when he arrived. De Forge was standing with his back to the huge silhouette of General de Gaulle when Lamy entered. Which meant Lamy had to remain standing.

De Forge told him about the *Manteau* call. He watched Lamy closely as he spoke, his manner grim. The Chief of Intelligence was careful to wait until his commander had finished, his face devoid of expression.

'So what have you to say?' de Forge demanded.

'This is crazy,' Lamy protested. 'I delivered the money as arranged. Counterfeit? Impossible.'

'Unless someone is stashing away a nest egg for himself,' de Forge remarked coldly.

'Is that an accusation, General?'

'Rather call it a suggestion. There's one way to discover the truth. As I told you, he has left the cloth bag behind the phone box. Go and bring it back to me immediately.'

'Now? At this hour of night?'

'Have you gone deaf? I said immediately. And take with you an escort. Lieutenant Berthier will be waiting outside. Take him with you – and one other officer.'

'What about Kalmar, General? He has just phoned me and asked for his fee. For eliminating Jean Burgoyne . . .'

He stopped speaking as the phone rang. De Forge looked Lamy up and down with a chilling expression he was famous for. He lifted the receiver.

'De Forge. I'm busy. Who the hell is it now?'

'*Manteau* reporting, General. During my previous call I omitted to tell you I have extinguished Jean Burgoyne. That will cost you one million Swiss francs. Tell Lamy he'll receive instructions how to make payment. This time in real money, if you please.'

'Listen to me . . .' Again the line went dead.

De Forge replaced the phone carefully as though it might explode in his face. He looked at Lamy again for almost a minute before he told him about this latest call. Lamy listened, his mind racing over how to respond.

'I don't know how he could possibly have known where she was. Jean Burgoyne chose a very remote rendezvous. And without Yvette following her no one would have known.'

'But someone did know,' de Forge said softly. 'You knew – or that girl who took the call here from Yvette knew. She passed the information to you over the radio and you *said* you'd phoned Kalmar at an agreed number.'

'What do you suggest?' Lamy asked stiffly.

'That you carry out my order – collect that bag with the money from behind the phone box.'

Lamy turned to go. Then he decided to risk more protest. De Forge didn't seem to realize what he was asking.

'If *Manteau* is in the area, watching that isolated phone box, he'll think it's a trap – when he sees my escort in the car with me.'

'It's a risk you'll have to take,' de Forge told him brutally. 'Send in Lieutenant Berthier and wait outside for him . . .'

Berthier stood rigidly to attention as de Forge studied him. The General was watching for any signs of nervousness, of sweat appearing on his forehead – as he had with Lamy.

'Paula Grey,' de Forge snapped. 'Any news by now?'

'Yes, General. She is staying at the Hotel Atlantique in Arcachon. The night clerk showed me her signature in the register. The problem is she's protected by two bodyguards. Professionals, by the way they behave. Never let her out of their sight.'

'Thank you, Berthier. You have done well.' De Forge had become amiable. He made it a point never to be at odds with more than one officer at a time. 'I may send you back to Arcachon. At the moment Major Lamy has a job for you and is waiting outside . . .'

Alone, de Forge sat at his desk, drawing Crosses of Lorraine on fire on a pad while he thought. Kalmar. *Manteau*. Could they be the same man? Or were both an invention of Major Lamy's?

Lamy was an expert marksman. Lamy had always been the go-between separating de Forge from the unknown killer. It was an arrangement which suited de Forge: no one could ever link him with the assassin. Lamy had suggested the idea. Lamy always took the huge sums paid to the assassin when someone had to be eliminated. The President and the Prime Minister, for example. And before transferring to Intelligence Lamy had been an explosives technician with the Engineers. Was Lamy accumulating a fortune at the expense of the Army?

De Forge was irritated and confused. He should be concentrating all his brainpower on Operations Austerlitz and Marengo. The mystery of the assassins – if there were two of them – was taking up valuable time. I should know the solution when they return with the money, he decided. And the problem of Paula Grey should also soon be solved.

Chapter Forty-Three

Major Jules Lamy was a loner. He intensely disliked his
escort and had sat both officers in the rear of the car. In the
middle of the night his headlight beams, undimmed, swung
over a bleak landscape of deserted fields with not a single
habitation in sight.

He was within two miles of the small village which had
the phone box on its southern outskirts. The advantage was
he could search round the box for the canvas bag containing
the money without risk of being seen by any villager. That
was, assuming the money was there.

In the rear Berthier sat beside the other lieutenant and
behind the empty front passenger seat. His Service revolver
was resting in his lap, his hand holding the butt. He had
removed it from his holster surreptitiously, certain that
Lamy would object if he had known about the gun.

Neither of the lieutenants had spoken a word during the
long drive from GHQ. Both knew Lamy wished them in hell
and were careful not to break the silence. Berthier was on
edge. He mistrusted this drive through the darkness without
a motorcycle outrider escort. They were a sitting target, in
Berthier's opinion.

The thought had just passed through his mind when
Lamy slowed as he negotiated a sharp and dangerous bend.
He was crawling when their silence was broken. A shatter-
ing *crack* stunned the three occupants. Berthier was the first
to realize it was a bullet.

The *crack* was followed instantly by a splattering of breaking glass. The officer next to Berthier was showered with glass splinters. Berthier saw a hole in the window on his side also. He took off his kepi and the brim had disappeared.

'Move!' he shouted at Lamy. 'We're under fire. That was a bullet . . .'

At the moment he spoke Lamy pressed his foot down on the accelerator. He saw a straight stretch of road and zig-zagged along it at speed. He was careful not to keep up a predictable rhythm: his zigzagging was erratic and proved Lamy was a skilled driver. He also asserted his authority as he drove.

'Anyone hurt back there?'

'Our colleague is cut about the face,' Berthier reported. 'But I think he'll live.'

Berthier had escaped any injury. The bullet had scattered shards of glass over his companion when it entered, but had blasted the glass outwards on Berthier's side. Siberian air sheered into the interior through the two holes. Descending into a deep gully beyond the straight stretch, Lamy slowed, stopped, gave the order.

'When I'm searching round the phone box you take up position – away from the car and well separated. Can you manage that, Lieutenant Chabert?'

'I think so sir . . .'

'Think isn't good enough.'

'I can, sir,' Chabert replied hastily.

Using a large handkerchief he was mopping blood off his face. As the car started up again he examined his face with his fingers but there were no shards of glass embedded in the skin. The two officers prepared to leave the car as Lamy pulled up a few yards from the phone box.

Wasting no time, Lamy jumped out, crouched low, gun

442

in hand, peered inside the box with his pencil flash. Empty. He found the cloth bag where *Manteau* had said it would be: behind the box. The same bag – Lamy recognized a dirty mark – but the cord tying it had been unfastened and retied with a different knot. Lamy dumped it on the front passenger seat, the lieutenants dived into the rear, Lamy turned the car round and drove back towards GHQ. What they would find inside the bag was his great concern. And fear of another bullet.

After listening to Lamy's report de Forge walked out of his office into the icy night without bothering to don his greatcoat. He stood, hands on his hips, looking at the bullet-holes in the car. He gestured with his head to lieutenants Berthier and Chabert.

'Get into the rear of the car and remember exactly how you were sitting when the bullet struck.'

Berthier, still wearing his képi minus the brim, leaned forward beyond Chabert as he had been doing, about to say something to Lamy. De Forge studied their positions, recalling his own experience when a bullet had penetrated his limousine. He waved for the two officers to get out.

'You'll have to draw a new képi from the quartermaster,' he observed to Berthier.

'He nearly got me, General.'

'No, he aimed to miss by centimetres again.' He looked at Lamy. 'We've had the demonstration we were promised. Back to your quarters,' he ordered the two lieutenants. 'Berthier, leave for Arcachon as soon as you've put on civilian clothes. Check on that girl, then report back to Major Lamy immediately . . .'

He marched back into his office with Lamy following him. The cloth bag lay on his desk. De Forge waved a hand.

'Open it up. Check the money.'

Another major from the Paymaster's Office, summoned by de Forge, entered while Lamy was examining the packages. The Paymaster officer had been a banking official before joining the Army and de Forge handed him a Swiss thousand-franc bill.

'Would you say that was genuine?'

De Forge wandered restlessly while the officer took out a magnifying glass. Switching on de Forge's desk lamp he examined the banknote carefully, left his glass on the desk, gave his verdict.

'It's a counterfeit. A very good one. But definitely a counterfeit.'

De Forge picked up two more of the notes Lamy was checking. He handed them to the Paymaster officer without a word. Again the process of careful examination was repeated before the officer returned them to de Forge.

'Also counterfeit. No doubt about it.'

'Would these be supplied by a bank in error?' de Forge enquired.

'Absolutely not. They are high denomination notes. No bank would be fooled. One note, possibly – although it would be most unusual. Three? Never.'

'Thank you. Major, you may go now. And not one word about this to anyone. There may be a scandal I have to investigate.

'Well, Major Lamy?' de Forge asked softly when they were alone.

Lamy looked disturbed, puzzled. He held up a stack of notes.

'The numbers are all in sequence. They weren't when I delivered them.'

'You think our English friend, *Oiseau*, has been swindling us?'

It was a trap question. De Forge waited for an answer as Lamy considered his reply. He pursed his thin lips.

'I don't think so for a moment. He is buying friendship – yours – for future arms deals with countries France has close relations with.'

'Take the lot away and put them in the safe. Now!'

When Lamy had gone de Forge's confidence in *Manteau* had risen in direct relationship to his loss of confidence in Lamy. Now he must concentrate on Operation Marengo.

About the same time, early that morning when de Forge was watching the checking of the money, Helmut Schneider sat eating breakfast at a truck drivers' café on the outskirts of Karlsruhe.

After leaving Victor Rosewater in Freiburg he had driven north along the autobahn. It was a very different Helmut in appearance. Prior to getting into his car he had discarded the dark glasses, the white cane, the disreputable overcoat and boots, stowing them into a holdall which he hid at the back of the boot of his car.

In the café he wore a clean windcheater, his denims, and a peaked cap of the type German students used to wear. He drank his steaming coffee slowly, took his time over consuming a hamburger. Frequently he checked his watch.

As soon as the main Post Office was open he parked close to it in Karlsruhe, centre of the German judicial system. Walking the rest of the way, he entered the Post Office, glanced at the few early customers, slipped inside one of the phone booths.

Dialling a number inside Germany, he spent several minutes transmitting a coded message which, to an eavesdropper, would have sounded like a normal business conversation. Replacing the receiver, he walked back to his car and resumed his journey back to his apartment in Frankfurt.

To reach the Passage Emile Zola, Isabelle had guided Newman along a devious route round the southern fringes of Bordeaux. Her idea was they would enter the city from the east to avoid any idea they had come from Arcachon.

Newman also had had an idea before they drove off. They went back into her apartment and raided the wine store, carrying a dozen bottles of Beaujolais to the car. At Newman's suggestion Isabelle had borrowed a white scarf from her sister's wardrobe. She wrapped it round her head. White – the colour of 'just married'.

The roundabout route took a long time and it was early morning but still dark as they entered the city. Newman drove in from the direction of Bergerac along the N136. They had seen large numbers of mechanized vehicles manoeuvring in the distance but had encountered no trouble so far.

'We are approaching the Pont de Pierre,' Isabelle warned him. 'That is where there could be a checkpoint.'

She proved to be right. Coming up to the bridge over the river Garonne, Newman saw in his headlights troops with automatic weapons standing in the road. Behind them a wooden barrier with gates barred the way. His headlights were blurred in a mist rising off the river.

'Get ready to go into our act,' he reminded her.

With the white scarf concealing her hair and draped over her shoulders, she snuggled up close to him, holding a bottle of wine in her hand. Newman lowered his window and with her free hand she lowered hers. Newman stopped the car, left the engine running, grabbed a bottle of wine and began rolling in his seat as troops crowded in round the vehicle. In a drunken voice Newman began singing the *Marseillaise*.

'The new Beaujolais,' he shouted and tossed a bottle out of the window.

He had thrown it over the heads of the troops near the car and there was a mad scramble as one soldier caught it in mid-air. Newman was again singing and the refrain was taken up by the soldiers who a moment earlier had been shivering in the icy mist, bored to tears with the task of manning the checkpoint.

Isabelle threw her bottle. She flashed a smile at the men near her. They stared at her lecherously and then jostled to grab the bottle. She picked up another as Newman hurled a fresh one well clear of the car.

'The new Beaujolais!' he roared in drunken tones.

'It's a bit late in the season this year,' Isabelle whispered and giggled nervously.

Newman threw another bottle, repeating the well-known slogan and Isabelle hurled a bottle from her side. The troops were standing further back to have a chance of catching the bottles. Newman, grinning drunkenly, began honking his horn for them to remove the barrier so he could drive on.

'We're in a hurry,' he shouted good-humouredly.

'You won't be a virgin much longer,' a soldier shouted at Isabelle.

'Obscene lout,' she muttered, smiled, threw out another bottle.

Newman kept his hand on the horn, leaned out of the window, hurled a bottle at a soldier close to the gates. The soldier caught it in mid-air. Several soldiers were already drinking the wine, passing bottles round. The soldier close to the gate opened it, waved them on, bottle in his his hand. Newman grinned, saluted, sped across the bridge to the far side and Isabelle guided him through side streets.

He began to recognize where he was – in the vicinity of the Mériadeck office and shopping complex. A concrete horror which was more like a fortress. He checked his rear-view mirror and saw an Army jeep with four soldiers following him. He told Isabelle. Then told her the mist had blotted it out.

'Turn right!' she said.

He swung into a narrow side street. In the murk Bordeaux looked even more dreadful. Wrecks of old buildings, with Cinzano posters on the end walls, smeared with grime and peeling at the edges. Again he had the impression of a city which had been bombed.

'Turn left quickly!'

He found himself in a narrow street with battered cars parked on both pavements. Isabelle was leaning forward staring through the gloom. Newman looked in the mirror. No sign of the jeep.

'Grab that slot! We're nearly there.'

Newman swung the Renault on to the pavement, swivelled the wheel, crawling, straightened up an inch from the car parked in front. He backed a few inches, stopped, switched off the engine. Even in London no one would have regarded the space he occupied as a feasible slot.

He'd noticed the Citroën backing down the street towards him as he'd swung in so swiftly. The car stopped as he stepped out and nearly slipped on a patch of solid ice. The air on his face was cold as the Arctic. A smartly dressed woman jumped out of the Citroën, came up to him, her face distorted with fury.

'That was my slot. Didn't you see me backing? I want that slot,' she raved.

Newman reopened his door, reached in, brought out the only vintage bottle of Beaujolais. He bowed, presented it to her with a flourish.

'We've just got married. A present to celebrate our happiness. Please.'

She grabbed the bottle, turned it round, peered at the vintage. Glancing at Isabelle who stood on the pavement, she tossed her head.

'I suppose it is some compensation. God knows where I'll get another slot. The bloody troops have surrounded a building just up the street. Their jeeps have five slots. It's disgusting . . .'

Without a word of thanks she returned to her car, backed it past the Renault. The vehicle disappeared into grey mist. Newman looked at Isabelle, spread his hands in a gesture of resignation.

'I thought it best to keep her quiet.'

'She'll keep quiet, the greedy harridan. While she was telling you about the troops I saw the gleam in her eye. It was the vintage, wasn't it?'

'Yes. And she may have done us a favour. I don't like the sound of those troops surrounding a building. How far is it to the passage?'

'About a hundred yards further along this street.'

Newman put his arm round her and they walked slowly, more interested in each other apparently than where they were going. He thanked God he'd taken the precaution. As the mist drifted away they saw ahead the military jeeps parked either side of the street on the pavements. Two cars, which had presumably occupied slots the Army needed, lay on their sides in the middle of the street.

Newman sidled them into the deep alcove of a doorway. On both sides troops with automatic weapons were stationed. All were staring at the building on the same side as Newman and Isabelle. A familiar figure was crouched by the entrance, packing something against the base of the door. Newman recognized the evil gnomelike Sergeant Rey.

'Could that be the building we're going to?' he asked
Isabelle.

'Yes, it is. The Passage Emile Zola is just a few yards
from here. It runs down the side of the building.'

'The troops are preparing to assault it. De Forge's boobytrap expert is packing what I imagine is explosive by the
door to blow it open.'

'We've arrived in the nick of time.'

'Or just too late,' Newman replied, thinking of the poor
devil, Stahl, holed up inside.

Chapter Forty-Four

Tweed took the call from Paula in his office at the Ministry of the Interior. His first concern was to ask whether it was a safe line.

'Quite safe,' she assured him. 'I've taken precautions. I've had time to think about your request for me to return to see you.'

'I'm listening,' Tweed coaxed her when she paused.

'I've read certain documents Jean Burgoyne was carrying. I think I should bring them to you at once aboard the chopper Lasalle is sending. Jean risked her life – ' she gulped – 'lost her life to get these to me. And they're really important. That's one thing.'

'And the other?' Tweed enquired concealing his relief.

'I think it's awful the way Jean is lying out you know where. Out in the cold and the damp. I know it doesn't make any difference to her . . .'

'Stop worrying,' Tweed interjected. 'A team of DST men was dispatched by Lasalle from Bordeaux to take her away, fly the body back to Paris. The machine bringing her is already in the air.'

'Thank God. There's one more thing.'

'Which is?'

'I'm only returning to Paris on the understanding I can come back here very quickly. You know who I have to locate.'

Kalmar, Tweed thought. He was careful not to tell her

Lasalle was very upset about the murder of Burgoyne. He was thinking quickly about her request.

'I agree to your suggestion,' he decided.

'And the condition laid down?'

'The request you made,' Tweed corrected her.

'Of course, I'm sorry. It was a request.'

'I agree.'

'And that DST team,' she persisted. 'They did know where to find her?'

'Newman was very specific when he phoned me earlier. About the location. I repeat, she is already in mid-air. We look forward to seeing you. Now please put Butler on the line . . .'

He had put down the phone when Kuhlmann came into the office. In his hand he held a folded fax sheet. He handed it over to Tweed.

'Just came in from Wiesbaden. You were right. Damn it, you always are.'

At the Atlantique they had devised a simple system of making sure the duty clerk – who also handled the small switchboard – didn't listen in while someone was making a call. Nield had made friends with the day and night clerks.

Both smoked. The day clerk favoured Gitanes, the night man Gauloises. Nield always had a spare pack to give them, plus a generous tip for services like sending up sandwiches and coffee.

He made it a habit to stroll down and engage them in conversation whenever a call was being made. So they wouldn't suspect his intention he also stopped by for a chat when a call was being made.

When Butler had finished speaking to Tweed, Paula

asked him what had been said. Butler punched her arm gently.

'If you must know everything, Pete and I have to accompany you to the dawn chopper, see you safely aboard. When you come back from Paris we're not to let you out of sight for a second. Tweed was pretty ferocious about that.'

'I have the feeling Tweed knows a lot more than he's telling us. It's almost as though I'm a target and he knows that,' Paula mused.

'Tweed knows what he's doing.' Butler checked his watch. 'You've had no sleep and you have to meet that Alouette at dawn. How about some kip?'

'You're right.' She sat perched on the edge of her bed with a worried look. 'I suppose I ought to flop out now.'

'You look bothered about something.'

'Recently I've remembered something very weird that happened in Aldeburgh. Don't ask me what – I need to think it through. And I wonder how Bob is getting on in Bordeaux?'

'There may be a rear entrance to that building in the Emile Zola passage,' Isabelle said. 'Like there is to my mother's apartment here.'

'Then I'd better risk it,' Newman decided. 'Before those troops storm the building.'

'*We* had better risk it,' Isabelle said firmly. 'Using a different version of the trick which came off at the Pont de Pierre. Don't argue. I know that passage.'

She gripped his arm, pressed herself against him after making sure her white scarf was draped over her shoulders, gazed up at him with adoring eyes. They walked slowly and when a soldier turned to look at them Isabelle pulled

Newman's head down and kissed him full on the mouth. The soldier grinned, turned away as they drew level with the entrance to the passage.

They slipped inside the narrow alley unchallenged. There was a smell of rancid rubbish, Isabelle wrinkled her nose as she hurried Newman to a door near the end of the alley. He noticed that at one time there must have been an exit at the other end but the outline of an arch was blocked up. Pity. No alternative escape route. Isabelle aimed a pencil flash Newman had lent her. The light showed the name plate below the entryphone, the grille smeared and rusty.

Jean Picot. 3ème.

'That's the name Stahl is hiding under?' Isabelle whispered.

'Yes.' Newman looked round the end of the alley. No sign of any life. 'It's strange there are no troops here.'

'Don't you see? They missed this alley. You nearly walked past it yourself. I dragged you in.'

'True.' Newman was looking up the sheer wall. 'He's at the top of the building according to that name plate. So here goes.'

He pressed the button on the entryphone, pressed his ear close to the shoddy grille. Was the damned instrument still in working order? A voice spoke in French.

'Who is it? I'm just going to bed.'

'Gamelin.' Newman repeated the codeword. 'Gamelin.'

'Come up quickly.'

Isabelle pushed the door when the buzzer went. Newman pulled her back when it was open an inch or so, his foot keeping it that way. He took the pencil flash off her, swiftly ran the beam all round the door frame. No wires. No indication of a boobytrap. Was it possible that the troops didn't know about this entrance?

'Is this passage marked on any map?' he asked quickly.

'None that I've ever seen. Shouldn't we hurry?'

She nearly slipped on the ice before dashing inside as Newman aimed the flashlight ahead of her, showing an old iron-railed staircase. Despite the large canvas bag she had hung over her shoulder she ran up the stairs with great agility as Newman, annoyed at her impetuous act, followed and guided the way, shining the beam in front of her.

He had pushed the door to the alley shut with his foot.

Isabelle was flying up the stairs, flight by flight, the bag swaying against her hip. At any moment Newman expected to hear the muffled explosion of the front entrance being blown in. Had they walked into a trap? What kept him going was the thought of Stahl, the agent of Kuhlmann who had stayed under cover for so long. He must have a lot of guts.

Pounding up the worn bleak concrete steps, the treads worn in the middle by God knew how many thousands of footsteps which had naturally moved up the centre. The whole place had a musty smell – bleak was the word. The atmosphere of one of the many abandoned-looking buildings which infested Bordeaux. They reached the top landing.

Newman raised the beam, saw alongside the closed door a similar name plate to the one in the alley. No entryphone. Just a button to press the bell. He pushed his thumb against it, held it there. They had so little time left.

The door opened a few inches still on a chain. The face which peered out was not what Newman had expected. Round and with a bushy mop of hair and a bushy moustache. Eyes behind horn-rim glasses peered at them.

'Gamelin,' Newman repeated quickly. 'Troops are surrounding the building. We've got to get out of here fast.'

'English?'

The query was put in the same language, not French this time. Newman felt brief annoyance. Everyone else had accepted him as a Frenchman. He reverted to English.

'Yes. Do you want to escape or don't you? We've risked our own lives to . . .'

'Come in.'

The door closed for a second, the chain was released, and they were inside as Stahl closed and bolted the door with one hand. In the other he held a grenade. Newman stared at it, then at Stahl. The German was small, tubby, and exuded energy. His eyes studied Newman, then Isabelle. He moved close to Newman.

'I recognize you from pictures in the papers. Kuhlmann has talked about you. But who is this girl?' he whispered.

'Isabelle Thomas. She's proved herself.'

Isabelle's hearing was more acute than Stahl had anticipated. She glared at him.

'I have already killed two of de Forge's men. How many more would you like me to dispatch before you're happy?'

'I have to check,' the German said sharply. 'That's how I've survived so far.'

This conversation was quick-fire. But Newman was anxious to get out of the building. Just assuming that was possible.

'We have to leave here fast,' he told Stahl. 'Back down the staircase we came up and into the passage?'

'Too dangerous.' Stahl shook his head. 'Show me the soles of your shoes,' he ordered Isabelle. She perched on one leg like a steady stork, showed him the sole of her trainer studded with rubber. He nodded, turned to Newman, who swiftly performed the same action. Why was Stahl wasting valuable time? He was wearing rubber-soled shoes with the surface hardly worn. Again Stahl nodded.

'It's very dangerous – going out over the rooftops. They

456

are covered with ice. But more dangerous to risk that staircase.' As though to confirm his opinion they heard somewhere way below them the muffled thud of an explosion.

'Rey has blown open the front door,' Newman warned. 'Have you collected information?'

He was asking the question as Stahl, clad in a leather jacket and corduroy trousers, moved quickly to a door, opened it, revealing a narrow staircase going upwards to a skylight. Stahl darted up the staircase, pulling on a pair of thick gloves. He answered as he reached the top tread and raised a hand to the skylight window. Over his shoulder was a leather bag similar to the canvas bag Isabelle was carrying as she rushed up the staircase behind Newman after closing the door at the bottom.

'A lot of information,' Stahl replied. 'In a book in my pocket. The grenade was in case it was soldiers outside the door when you arrived. I'd have threatened to blow myself up with them. Remember, the roofs are like a skating rink, I go up first, then you. We'll haul Isabelle up after us.'

Earlier he had dropped the grenade inside his bag. While talking he had pushed back the skylight on to the roof and icy air flooded down the staircase. Agilely, Stahl hauled himself on to the roof, spread his body flat and extended a hand to Newman.

Moving cautiously, Newman emerged into the bitter air of the Siberian night. The roof had a steep pitch and he saw it was above the street where the troops were assembled for the storming of the building. They must already be on their way up. On one landing Newman had noticed when they were racing up to Stahl's apartment another staircase. At this point the troops could run straight up to Stahl's apartment.

By the light of a sputtering neon sign on the far side of

the street Newman saw the sinister gleam of pack ice on the tiled roof. He sprawled alongside Stahl, one foot dug into a hole where a tile had disappeared. He heard below a splintering crash from inside Stahl's apartment. They had already broken down the door. He was reaching down for Isabelle, had grabbed her under her left armpit when he heard the thud of Army boots coming up the staircase. He tried to haul her up, but she wouldn't budge. She stared up at him, her expression grim.

'He's got hold of my leg. Hang on to me, Bob. Don't touch my right arm . . .'

It flashed across his mind what a wide range of moods she had: excitable when he'd arrived at her apartment in Arcachon. Now with her life at stake she was cold, calculating. Her right hand fiddled inside her bag, came out holding a kitchen knife with a wide blade. Taking a firm grip on the handle, she looked down, saw the soldier staring up at her, holding her leg in an iron grip. She raised the knife, aimed for the side of his neck, plunged it in deep, still gripping the handle. He emitted a horrible gurgle, let go of her leg as blood spurted, collapsed into the staircase.

Newman hauled her on to the roof. She sprawled beside him, her left hand gripping the rim of the skylight frame, her right hand wiping the mess off the knife before she dropped it back inside her bag. Newman used his left foot to kick ice off the roof. Three tiles scuttered down with the ice, exposing rotting rafters. He jammed his foot inside the exposed hole and Isabelle rammed her left foot into the hole he'd left for her. Newman was holding on to the skylight frame as he glanced round. Stahl was perched on top of the roof, legs astride each side as he beckoned them to join him.

'We go this way,' he called out, still speaking English.

Newman was about to help Isabelle to join him when she slipped. Appalled, he watched her sliding down the icy slope to the brink. Her feet dug into the metal gutter below the roof. Her gloved hands clawed the roof for better purchase, found none. Only the gutter was saving her. Newman let go of the skylight frame, slithered towards her. His gloved hands grasped one of the exposed rafters. Holding on, he swivelled himself through one hundred and eighty degrees, let go, hoping one foot would embed itself in the same hole. Both feet slid into the hole, were held by the cross beam below the rafters. He stretched out a hand as Isabelle stretched hers and he had her round the wrist. He was on the verge of hauling her up when she jolted, the full weight of her body jerking in his hand, but he held on. The bloody gutter had given way, falling into the street. Which he should have expected. This was Bordeaux.

He hauled her slowly up over the glistening surface and now the ice helped her body to move smoothly. Lying alongside him, she jammed her feet into the large hole, managed a wan smile. He looked up at the ridge of the roof where Stahl had moved further along like someone astride a vaulting horse in a gymnasium. Stahl beckoned again for them to join him.

'We go this way,' he called out.

Newman had one arm round Isabelle's waist as his other hand hammered at the ice, dislodged more rotten tiles, found purchase to haul them higher. It seemed slow progress but the skylight was close to the ridge and Newman had hauled both of them to the summit. Isabelle was closer to the skylight as Stahl shouted a warning. Glancing over her shoulder, Newman's arm still holding her firm round the waist, she saw a soldier gripping an automatic weapon emerging. Newman was heaving her up to the ridge when she spoke.

'Hold my right arm,' she commanded.

Perched on the ridge, he did what she had told him to,

leaning down to grip her arm as she deliberately let her body slide a foot or so. Drawing up her left knee, she shot out her leg as the soldier, now on the roof, fumbled with his weapon. Her trainer hammered into the face of the sprawled soldier. He lost the grip his left hand had had on the skylight frame. They watched as he began to slide. Desperately his hands clawed at the roof as the weapon slithered out of view. His feet dug into the ice, loosened a large slab. The slab skated over the edge. High up Newman could almost see to street level. The soldier's momentum increased. He followed the ice slab over the brink, his arms windmilling as he screamed, an ear-splitting yell of terror, while his body plummeted downwards. The yell stopped abruptly as his body hit the iron-hard cobbles four storeys down.

Newman had hauled Isabelle on to the ridge, they were easing themselves along the ice-cold rounded tiles when the head of another soldier appeared above the fanlight opening. Stahl took a grenade out of his bag, removed the pin, tossed it carefully. The grenade disappeared down the fanlight opening. A sharp *crack!* The soldier's head disappeared. There was one further sound – the tumbling of bodies down the staircase. Then a sudden silence. Newman and Isabelle worked their way along the ridge. He was worried by the sudden disappearance of Stahl who had dropped out of sight. Literally. He was aching from the effort of straddling the ridge top when he reached the end. Looking down he saw why Stahl had vanished.

Six feet or so below the end of the ridge was a railed metal platform. Stahl stood looking up with a beaming smile. The German had nerves of steel. Newman glanced over his shoulder, saw Isabelle was close behind him and there were no signs of activity from the distant skylight. He dropped to the platform, his body loose, his knees bending to cushion the drop.

Turning round, he was just in time to grab hold of Isabelle by the waist, breaking the force of her fall. She was breathing heavily, had removed her white scarf and stuffed it inside her bag. She smoothed his hair.

'Where to now?' Newman asked.

Stahl put a finger to his lips, ushered Newman to the rear of the platform, leaned forward and pointed down. Newman leaned over and saw he was looking down into the Passage Emile Zola. It was crowded with troops who carried automatic weapons. Presumably they'd found their way down from the landing where the two staircases met inside the building. He moved away as Stahl tugged at his sleeve.

'Is there any way out?' Newman asked. 'I don't fancy any more rooftop climbing – we might not be so lucky next time.'

'How did you get here?' Stahl asked.

'By car. A hired Renault. Left it parked the other side of the entrance to the passage. About twenty yards from it. We'll never be able to reach it without being spotted.'

'I think we might,' Stahl replied. 'They won't expect us in that street. They'll be sending troops all over the rooftops. We go down this fire escape first. I suggest I lead the way with Isabelle . . .'

Newman noticed for the first time a flight of metal steps leading down the side of the building from the platform. He followed as Stahl descended, one hand on the side rail, the other round Isabelle's waist. It was a gesture she resented.

Inwardly her nerves were screaming but outwardly she was composed. They descended one flight, reached a landing, turned down a fresh flight. Stahl kept glancing into the well below them. Then both Isabelle's feet slid from under her and she'd have crashed down the flight but for Stahl's tight grip, holding her against him until she recovered her balance.

'These metal treads are coated with solid ice,' he explained. 'It really is no time to practise skating.'

She looked at him and he grinned impishly. From that moment she liked Stahl. And she felt that with these two men looking after her there was a chance they'd escape from the hell that Bordeaux had become.

On the first floor Stahl led the way across a treacherous metal bridge where the ice was solid underfoot from rail to rail. At ground level he led them through a labyrinth of alleyways on what seemed to Newman to be a circular route. They emerged into the street where the Renault was parked only fifty yards away.

The street was deserted. Stahl's prediction had come true: the troops were scaling the world of the rooftops. At Newman's suggestion the German slipped into the back, hid himself under a travelling rug. Poking out his bushy head, his moustache frosted with ice mist, he joked.

'I've found a bottle of Beaujolais. May I imbibe? My excuse is that if we're stopped you're taking a drunken friend home. Me!'

Isabelle guided Newman through the ice mist along a new route. The grey vapour made Bordeaux even more shabby and derelict, if possible. There was a checkpoint and a barrier on the far side of the Pont Saint Jean, but Newman was in no mood for further encounters with de Forge's troops. He had also noticed the mist was very thick by the river – more like a fog. In his undimmed headlights he saw shadowed figures drifting as though in a nightmare and beyond another of the flimsy barriers they'd seen on the Pont de Pierre.

'We're not stopping,' he warned his passengers.

Isabelle was puzzled. Approaching the western end of the bridge Newman dimmed his headlights, reduced speed to a crawl as though pulling up. Suddenly, driving on to the bridge, he pressed his thumb on the horn and kept it at a blaring howl. Switching his headlights full on, he pressed his foot down, roaring over the bridge, smashing through the barrier. The drifting shadows jumped out of his way to both sides. He increased speed, thought he heard a rifle shot, then they were way beyond the bridge.

'Turn right now!' Isabelle shouted, straining against her seat belt to see where they were.

He swung the wheel, his horn silent, the tyres screeching at the wildness of his driving. He slowed down as they came to a sharp corner in a narrow street. Isabelle guided him through a complex labyrinth which seemed to go on and on for ever. Without warning they were clear of the suburbs, free of even a hint of ice mist, driving through open country along a deserted road.

'How long to Arcachon?' Newman asked.

'We'll be there well before dawn.'

'We have to be.'

Newman was almost exhausted, flaked out with two endless drives, the tension of rescuing Stahl. And ahead of him was a drive to meet the Alouette near the *étang*. After that a long drive south to the Landes, to pick up their witness. Martine, the crone who collected brushwood on the Atlantic shore. Could he last out? And if he ran into trouble, would his reflexes be fast enough?

Chapter Forty-Five

The tension which grows in the early hours under pressure was showing itself inside the Ministry of the Interior in Paris. Tweed, unshaven, sat behind his desk as Navarre came in from an emergency Cabinet meeting. Lasalle, also short of sleep like the others, was pacing restlessly. Only Kuhlmann, seated in a leather armchair was, like Tweed, relaxed and alert.

'Any news?' Navarre demanded, looking at Lasalle as he perched his buttocks on Tweed's desk.

'A whole fleet of CRS trucks is speeding down to Bordeaux, may already have reached the city. They're being parked round the Prefecture.'

'More psychological warfare,' Tweed said quietly.

'Psychological warfare?' Navarre queried.

'The Berliet trucks have no CRS inside them,' Lasalle explained. 'Only a driver and one other man in the cab. Their arrival will be reported within minutes to de Forge. With luck they'll have to wake him to tell him – ruin his night's sleep. Tweed wants to wear him down.'

'But how will you transport the huge number of CRS when it comes to the final confrontation?' Navarre asked brusquely.

'I have secretly assembled a whole armada of helicopters at airfields on the outskirts of Paris. When we strike we do it from the air.'

'I like the idea,' Navarre decided. 'I have recorded a TV

address to the nation. I hammer home the point that the civil power takes precedence over the military in democracy.'

'The Cabinet was told this?' Lasalle, alarmed, enquired.

Navarre smiled grimly. 'No, Louis Janin, our so-loyal Minister of Defence, would have informed de Forge at once. I have a feeling we are close to that final confrontation.' He took a cassette from his jacket pocket, handed it to Lasalle. 'That is the recording of my address to the nation. Lock it in your personal safe at rue des Saussaies. Please remain available there or here. It's only a short walk to your HQ.'

'When do you expect de Forge to make his move?' Kuhlmann asked.

'I suspect it has already begun. This dangerous exercise General Masson has sanctioned – with the so-called assumption that they're repelling a North African invasion by the fictitious General Ali. I have just heard that some of de Forge's advanced motorcycle patrols have reached Angoulême.'

'A long way north of Bordeaux and closer to Paris,' Tweed observed.

'Exactly,' Navarre agreed. 'And now, gentleman, I must snatch a few hours' sleep.'

The others agreed it was a sound idea and Tweed was left alone. Opening a map he studied the position of Angoulême, shook his head. He was folding the map when the phone rang. It was Monica at Park Crescent, still at her desk in the early hours.

'Howard has returned from his extended trip to the States,' she told him. 'He wants to see you over here for consultation at the earliest moment. He's just come from a visit to the PM.'

'Tell him I'll catch the first available scheduled flight this morning. Also tell him I'm flying back to Paris before the evening.'

'I don't think that's quite what he had in mind,' Monica warned.

'Then I'll put it in his mind when I get there. All you need to confirm is that I'm coming. And I may want to drive to Aldeburgh while I'm in Britain. Again a quick trip. Back in town in time to catch a Paris flight.'

'Should I have your car ready?'

'The Ford Escort,' Tweed replied. 'Very reliable but not too noticeable. Also check on the present whereabouts of Lord Dane Dawlish and his catamaran, the *Steel Vulture*. Heathcoate, the Harwich Harbour Master, might help.'

'I'd already thought of him. Look forward to seeing you.'

Tweed frowned as he put down the receiver. Howard was the Director, his only superior in the SIS. What on earth was this urgent summons all about? And what had passed between Howard and the new PM, a man of very decided views? He'd interviewed Tweed before the journey to Paris, listened to what Tweed had to say, had agreed his mission was vital.

He picked up the phone after checking his watch, dialled the number of the Atlantique in Arcachon. When the duty clerk answered he phrased his request carefully. No name.

'I wish to speak to Mr Harry Butler who is staying with you. Tell him it's a friend – he's expecting my call . . .'

'Butler here. I'm glad you called. Please hang on just a sec . . .'

Butler put his hand over the mouthpiece, called out to Nield who was catnapping on the bed with his clothes on.

'Pete, a call's come through.'

'I'll get down fast.'

Nield slipped on his shoes, checked his jacket as he ran to the door to make sure he had a packet of the Gauloises favoured by the night clerk. When he reached the lobby the clerk hastily put down his phone as Nield asked for a cup of coffee, explaining he couldn't sleep.

'Go ahead,' Butler said in the bedroom.

'I have to leave for London by the first flight. I'll be back late this evening. Warn Paula. That's it.'

'Will do.'

In Paris Tweed picked up the phone again to call the airport – to ask them to hold a return ticket to London for him. He had no inkling of the consequences which would follow his call to Arcachon.

At the Atlantique in her bedroom Paula was wakened by the alarm clock she'd set for 4 a.m. She wanted to be ready in good time to board the Alouette.

She showered, dressed quickly, applied make-up in three minutes. She snapped shut the lid of the case she had packed the night before and at that moment she heard the agreed tattoo tapping on her locked door. Even so, she took the Browning automatic from her shoulder bag before opening the door on the chain. It was Butler.

'Come in, Harry. I'm ready for the trip. Is Bob back?' she asked anxiously.

'Not yet. Not to worry. It was one hell of a roundabout route they were taking.'

'I hope nothing's gone wrong,' she said as she closed and locked the door. 'I didn't like the idea of his going back to Bordeaux again one little bit.'

There was a note of concern verging on affection in her tone, Butler noticed. He smiled reassuringly.

'Bob can look after himself. What I came to tell you is I've decided we ought to move out of here. It's dangerous to stay in one place for long.'

'But where to?'

'I can't find another suitable hotel. I'm going to ask Bob whether we could move for a few days to Isabelle's apartment. Difficult for anyone to trace us there.'

'Isabelle?' Paula sounded doubtful. 'I can get on with her but I'm not so sure it would work the other way.'

'Bob will fix that . . .'

He looked at the door where the correct tattoo rapping had been repeated. Extracting the Walther he opened the door on the chain, saw Newman standing outside with a bushy-haired stranger. He let them inside and Newman introduced them by first names only to Stahl. Paula took an immediate liking to the amiable German who looked her straight in the eye as they shook hands. Newman was determined to check the bona fides of Egon Stahl.

'Egon wants to put through a call to Kuhlmann,' he said. 'I'll get the number.' He looked at Butler. 'I see Nield is still downstairs, playing poker with the night clerk . . .'

Butler nodded. In fact Nield had been unable to sleep, so he had gone down into the lobby to play cards. An expert card sharp, Nield was just about to deal when he saw Butler peer over the banister very soon after Newman had returned with the jolly bushy-moustached man. Butler was signalling they were about to make a call. Nield shuffled the pack again, dealt the clerk a winning Royal Flush. That should keep his mind on the game while the call was being made.

In Paula's room Newman dialled the Ministry of the Interior, gave the code word Tweed had suggested, asked to speak to him. After a pause Lasalle, sounding fogged with sleep, came on the line. He listened to Newman before telling him his boss had just left for the airport.

'Actually we want to speak to Otto Kuhlmann,' Newman explained.

A far more alert Kuhlmann came to the phone quickly

and Newman handed the instrument to Stahl. He had concealed from the German that he spoke his language as fluently as he spoke French.

Listening to Stahl he heard a reference to *Kapitan* Fischer. The emphasis on *Kapitan* told him this was Stahl's identification word. Stahl reported that he had obtained vital data, that he would keep it until he met Kuhlmann. From the rest of the conversation Newman gathered Stahl's chief had told him that his rescuer was totally reliable, that he could tell him everything.

Paula was watching Newman as he sagged on her bed, checked his watch. She thought Newman looked at the end of his tether, desperately short of sleep, haggard, and with a drawn face. He leaned towards her, whispered hoarsely as Stahl ended his conversation.

'Tweed is no longer in Paris. Lasalle told me he was on his way to the airport.'

'He was expecting me,' Paula protested. 'Aboard the Alouette.'

Butler had joined them. He listened for a moment, then lowered his voice while Stahl was washing his hands. The sound of the water running into the basin muffled their conversation.

'Tweed said he wouldn't be back from London until some time this evening.'

'Then there's no point in my flying to Paris aboard the chopper,' Paula decided, still watching Newman who had stifled a yawn. 'Harry, you'd better call Lasalle and tell him to send the chopper to land at dawn twenty-four hours later.'

'I *have* to drive to the *Landes*,' Newman commented, spacing out his words, talking with an effort.

'Like hell,' Paula snapped. 'You're flaked out. Anyone can see that. You'll end up driving the car into some ditch.'

'Have to collect the witness . . . Martine . . .'

'Yes, we do,' Paula continued briskly. 'So I'll share the driving with Harry and Pete. You can sleep in the back. Then you'll be fresh enough to guide us when we get close to the witness.'

She used the last word because Stahl, adjusting his glasses and smiling, had come close to them. He stared at Newman, then at Paula.

'I'm OK,' Newman growled. He propped himself against the headboard to stop falling asleep. 'You stay here, Paula. The Landes . . . dangerous.'

'It would be for you,' she snapped and stamped her foot. 'You say you're OK, you haven't slept for ages, and you can't even keep your eyes open now.'

'And,' Butler reminded him, 'Pete and I have to stay next to Paula. Remember?'

Stahl intervened. 'You have a problem? Maybe I could help? I slept during the day and I'm fresh.'

'You wouldn't have a weapon of sorts?' Butler enquired.

'Would these help? Give you confidence?' Stahl replied.

In his eager beaver manner he unzipped his leather bag. Butler stared as he produced a Heckler and Koch sub-machine-gun. Newman recognized the type used by the SAS that had a collapsible stock. As he went on talking Stahl was careful to aim the muzzle at the ceiling.

'This 9mm sub-machine-gun has a rate of fire of six hundred and fifty rounds a minute, a range of almost five hundred feet. I have a lot of spare mags, as you see. Also I have grenades, a lot of them. Like this one.'

'You're carting around a ruddy armoury,' Butler commented.

'But I was trapped in that building before Mr Newman and the girl, Isabelle, brought me out. I couldn't have tried to escape without transport. The patrols in the streets keep stopping people at night – especially those on foot. I could come with you.'

'You're hired for the duration,' Paula decided without consulting anyone. Newman blinked at her.

'You've taken charge?' he enquired.

'Yes. Someone has to until you're fresh. I just elected myself. Harry, you'd better call Lasalle now, turn back that Alouette.'

Butler told Newman they were moving base to Isabelle's apartment before they left, went to the phone. Newman raised a hand, dropped it.

'I'd better tell Isabelle that . . . ask her, I mean.'

'No!' Paula's tone was firm. 'I'll talk to her briefly before we set out for the Landes. Won't tell her where we're going, but I'll check to see whether she can cope with this lot. I can handle her.'

'Still don't think you should come with us to the Landes, it could – will be – a damned dangerous undertaking,' Newman protested again.

'It's decided,' Paula told him. 'And try not to go to sleep before we carry you into the back of the car. It will be a full house,' she added, glancing at Stahl, 'but we'll manage. And both of you should have a shave. If you don't mind.'

Victor Rosewater, clad in a British warm camel-hair, arriving on the flight from Switzerland at Bordeaux Airport, walked across the concourse. Stopped by an army patrol, he waved a pass at them.

'Get out of my way, I'm in a hurry.'

He hastened to where he'd left his car parked. Two minutes later he was roaring away confidently. His destination was Arcachon and, as usual, he wanted to get to where he was going quickly.

To avoid registering at a hotel he had hired a small cabin cruiser moored at the edge of the *bassin*. He bought food from a supermarket, cooked it himself in the cruiser's galley, or ate out at restaurants. Rosewater was expert at evading a country's regulations designed to record who had arrived from abroad.

When he'd checked his vessel his first call was planned for the Bar Martinique. He was determined to trace the movements of the talkative Irishman who frequented the bar. Then he hoped to meet Paula Grey again, even if it meant exercising patience.

Carrying his holdall, Marler disembarked from the Air Inter flight at Orly, Paris. Once again he avoided the waiting taxis: cab drivers had good memories.

He used the anonymous Metro to reach the station nearest his shoddy apartment close to the rue du Bac. On his way up to his room, the key in his pocket, he doled out more francs to the reception clerk – enough for another two weeks' stay.

'Business good?' the clerk enquired, accepting the tip.

'So, so . . .'

Inside his room Marler checked for any indication that it had been searched. If so, he'd move to the other apartment he'd reserved a few streets away. There was no sign of any intrusion.

Taking off his trainers, he sat on his made-up bed and took the mobile phone from his holdall. Dialling the Ministry of the Interior, he asked for Tweed by using a codename. After a delay Lasalle came on the phone, told him the man he wanted was abroad for the whole day.

'Thank you. I'll call him later, René.'

Chapter Forty-Six

Tweed was on the warpath at Park Crescent. Arriving on the first flight from Paris, he had found Howard waiting for him in his own office. Monica greeted him, looked grim, then buried her head in a file.

'You bought yourself a new suit in the States?' Tweed suggested with a straight face.

'You must be joking.' Howard indignant. 'This came from Harrods. Chester Barrie. The best money can buy off the peg.'

Plump faced, his complexion pink, clean shaven, six feet tall and with a well-fed look, the Director was at his most pompous. He stood by Tweed's desk, shot his cuffs to expose jewelled links and smoothed one of the lapels of his dark grey suit with a thin chalk stripe. The trousers had the fashionable turnups. He placed a hand on his right hip.

'I called you back to find out what was going on in France. And I've had an interview with the PM since I returned. I understand that, like his predecessor, he gave you one of those damned personal directives.'

'Yes, he did,' Tweed said tersely, seating himself behind his desk.

'Well, did he tell you that he's working on a twin-track basis?'

'What does twin-track mean?' Tweed enquired, polishing his glasses on the corner of his handkerchief.

'It means . . .' Howard paused, took up his favourite pose,

473

sprawling in the armchair with one leg propped over the arm. His black leather shoes gleamed like glass. 'It means,' he repeated, 'that the PM has another unit in the field of which we have no knowledge.'

Of which . . . Typical of the Director's liking for pedantic phraseology. Tweed began drumming his fingers slowly on the desk, a sign that he was in a mood of cold fury. Monica looked up, intrigued at the prospect of battle.

'Doesn't he realize,' Tweed demanded, 'that a manoeuvre like that can cause total disaster? Two different units stumbling around on the same territory without any idea of the other's existence? Didn't you point out that it could lead to a catastrophe?'

'Well . . .' Howard adjusted the display handkerchief in his breast pocket. 'He is the new boy. We need his support so we have to give him some licence.'

'In other words you're telling me you didn't have the guts to object,' Tweed growled.

'I deeply resent your insubordinate language.'

'Resent away.' Tweed showed no contrition. 'Did he by any chance give you a hint as to who the other unit is?'

'None at all.' Howard's manner was stiff. 'And I most certainly didn't ask him. We are talking about the new PM. He has a right to his own ideas.'

'He struck me as a man who appreciates straight talk.' Tweed was disgusted. 'He was waiting to see if you'd press him, insist on being given the information.'

'You weren't there . . .'

'He was testing you,' Tweed insisted.

'My dear chap.' Howard ran a manicured hand over his perfectly brushed dark hair. '*We* are the ones who are on trial. My guess is he's simply not relying on one organization. The situation is serious. By the way, how serious is it?'

Tersely, Tweed brought him up to date. He concluded by revealing he'd made a quick call from a London Airport public phone to Lasalle – that Lasalle had received a late call from Butler saying they were moving south to bring back a witness.

'South?' Howard sounded appalled. 'South from Acachon? My God! Straight into the jaws of the lion's den. The den of General Charles de Forge. Whereabouts exactly are they going to?'

'The Landes, I expect.'

'Heavens, man! Are you crazy?' Howard swung his leg on the floor, jumped up, buttoned his jacket. 'You've just told me about this hideous burial ground of de Forge's. In the Landes. How could you let our people venture near there again?'

'I let my people in the field have wide latitude as to how they react in an emergency. You know that,' Tweed said quietly. 'They took the decision themselves and I am backing them to the hilt. If you think you can run an operation from an armchair here, then you've spent too long in the States.'

The quiet vehemence of Tweed's attack threw Howard off balance. He pursed his lips, looked at Monica, who looked back at him.

'What are your next plans?' Howard added eventually in a reasonable tone. 'I mean you personally.'

'Before I return to Paris tonight I am driving to Aldeburgh. That's where it all started – with the murder of Karin Rosewater. If Lord Dawlish is at home I'm calling on him.'

'For what purpose, if I may ask?'

'You may. He's up to his neck in this thing, I'm sure now. I want to rattle his cage.'

'I insist you take protection. No, hear me out.' He held up his hand as Tweed opened his mouth to protest. 'What

475

about Fred Hamilton? Be good experience for him. And he scored tops on the target range I understand.'

'He's very promising,' Tweed admitted.

'Then that's settled.' Howard beamed his broad smile. 'I shall feel far less worried as you're going there with Hamilton by your side. Must get on. Piles waiting for me to deal with . . .'

Monica stared at Howard's back as he left the room. She looked furious and burst out as soon as she judged Howard was well clear.

'Piles, indeed! I dealt with everything that came in for him while he was away. All he has to look at are copies of my replies.' She calmed down. 'Still, you could have knocked me down with a feather when he insisted Hamilton accompanied you. He sounded really concerned.'

'He was,' Tweed agreed. 'And it will take him time to learn to cope with the different style of the new PM.'

'What are you doing in France to cope with de Forge?' she asked.

'I'll tell you.'

Tweed clasped his hands behind his neck, stared at the ceiling after checking his watch. He began to talk.

'In my temporary office in the Ministry of the Interior I have pinned a photograph of de Forge Lasalle found for me on the wall. It faces my desk. I study my enemy, try to put myself in his shoes.'

'I read that General Montgomery did that – had a picture of Rommel pinned up in his caravan so *he* could get inside the mind of his opponent.'

'That very much over-dramatizes what I'm doing. Maybe there is a similarity – I wouldn't know. To get down to brass tacks. I'm convinced de Forge has set the stage for a *coup d'état* to make himself President of France. All the riots, the absurd – but highly effective – use of men in Ku-Klux-Klan garb. I'm convinced he's waiting for just one more development before he makes his move.'

'Which is?'

'The arrival of more funds – and especially sophisticated weaponry – from Lord Dawlish, armaments king. In short, the berthing of the *Steel Vulture* at Arcachon. Brand, his deputy, is already there.'

'Where is the *Steel Vulture* now? Can't it be stopped?'

'Answer One, I'm driving up to Aldeburgh to shake Dawlish. Then on to Dunwich to try and trace the vessel. Answer Two, no we can't stop the vessel. We have no proof it's carrying arms.'

'You mean General de Forge is going to start a war?'

'Definitely not,' Tweed replied. 'He's going to try and use the threat of overwhelming force to subdue Paris and the present government. I predict there will be rumours that his troops are armed with nerve gas.'

'And what are you doing to stop him?'

'Two things at the same time. Rattle him by using psychological warfare tactics – to cause him delay. Rather unusual techniques. The second thing is to get evidence which will discredit him before he strikes.'

'This is serious, then.'

'The worst threat to the stability of Western Europe since the Berlin Wall collapsed. A military dictator in Paris would upset the whole of Europe. Now I must get moving. There's not much time left for me to drive to Aldeburgh and Dunwich, then drive back in time to catch a late flight to Paris.'

As he stood up Monica brought to his desk a copy of the *Daily Mail*. She laid it down flat and pointed to the headline and the main story.

MANTEAU – 'THE CLOAK' – MASTER ASSASSIN

As he put on his Burberry, Tweed glanced at the story which had now crossed the Channel. *Manteau* was 'credited' with having killed the Prefect of Paris, with the assassination of the President and the Prime Minister by blowing up the TGV Express, and also with the killing of an Englishwoman, Jean Burgoyne.

In each instance, the article continued, the assassin had left behind his trademark. The Cloak. In the case of the Paris Prefect a cloak had been found stuffed in a nearby litter bin. When the TGV Express was wrecked DST men had found another cloak in a nearby village. And now, with the strangulation of Burgoyne, DST men had discovered a discarded cloak inside the boathouse in the vicinity of Arcachon.

'This *Manteau* is very sinister,' Monica observed.

'And mysterious,' Tweed agreed impatiently. 'Hamilton is waiting with the car?'

'Yes. Have a care. Kalmar may still be in the Aldeburgh area.'

'Or do you mean *Manteau*?' Tweed commented as he left.

Fred Hamilton sat behind the wheel of the Ford Escort. Marler mockingly had nicknamed the new member of the team the RSM: he thought Fred took life desperately seriously.

'I'll take the wheel,' Tweed said brusquely.

Hamilton transferred his tall figure to the front passenger seat. Twenty-eight years old, he sat like a ramrod, glancing round as they moved through the London traffic to check whether they were being followed. He was clean shaven with brown hair trimmed short and an aquiline nose. They were well clear of London, driving through Essex when

Tweed asked his question after glancing at Hamilton's trenchcoat.

'You're carrying a handgun, aren't you?'

'A Colt .455 automatic pistol. Magazine capacity seven rounds. Plus spare mags.'

'I don't think you'll need that.'

'Mr Howard insisted. And, with respect, sir, it's when you don't expect to need a firearm that you find it saves your life.'

'No need to call me "sir". Just Tweed will do . . .'

He drove like the clappers across Suffolk, just inside the speed limit. Ignoring Aldeburgh, he slowed down as they passed Snape Maltings, turned on to the country road for Grenville Manor. He was on the point of turning left down the last stretch to Iken, the river Alde a calm lagoon below them, when a car parked on the grass verge started up, followed them, with the Volvo's horn tooting.

Hamilton slipped his hand inside his trenchcoat. Tweed looking in the wing mirror, shook his head, swore inwardly, pulled up, and the Volvo parked behind them.

'I know these people. The Yard,' Tweed warned Hamilton.

It was, of course, Chief Inspector Buchanan and Sergeant Warden. Tweed sat gazing ahead as Buchanan got out and strolled up to his window.

'A small world, Tweed,' he said, his grey eyes glancing at Hamilton. The tall man had bodyguard written all over him. 'We were taking a rest,' Buchanan continued genially, 'before keeping an appointment to interrogate Lord Dawlish.'

'My intention too,' Tweed replied stiffly.

'Then why don't we combine our visit? What colours are you sailing under this time?'

'Special Branch.'

'Then together we could possibly exert more pressure on his Lordship. I'm sure you'll have no objection . . .'

It was a grey weepy day. Inside Grenville Grange, Lord Dawlish gazed out of the windows down over the lawn to the landing stage. Over the lawn where once – it seemed a hundred years ago – he'd held his shooting party. His yacht, *Wavecrest V*, moored to the landing stage, rested motionless in the still water. Rain streaks slashed the windows, speckled the turgid surface of the Alde.

Dawlish was in a blazing fury. He had recently returned from the *Steel Vulture*, still stationed off Dunwich, and he could have strangled the skipper, Santos. Arriving on the bridge he'd asked the vital question.

'When can we sail? I want a straight answer. Now!'

'The loading – ' the swarthy-faced Santos had spread his hands – 'it is still proceeding.'

'For God's sake, man, how long is it going to take?'

'Señor, it is a dangerous cargo we are loading. A very large cargo – the largest yet. You would wish us not to risk an accident which might damage vessel.'

'I'm interested in results. Conditions are ideal. A calm sea – and the met forecasts for the Bay of Biscay are good. How long do you expect that to last?'

'My first consideration is the safety of your beautiful ship, Señor . . .'

'It's not a cruise liner. Of course I'm concerned for its safety.' Dawlish waved a thick forefinger under Santos' nose. 'But I'm also seriously behind schedule. Put more men on the job, you cretin.'

'All available divers are working round the clock. Is that right – round the . . .'

'I don't give a damn for your fractured English. Give me a straight answer,' Dawlish had stormed. 'When will we be ready to sail?'

'The night after this night we will be ready. You will see . . .'

'That's a deadline,' Dawlish had raged. 'And if not kept maybe you'll be dead.'

He had attended to two more things before leaving. Rushing to his cabin, he had coded a message. It was phrased carefully.

Expected cargo will be delivered agreed destination within seventy-two hours. My next signal will be the last, will give ETA. Oiseau.

After taking it himself to the radio op. room he went on deck aft of the bridge. The specially designed aircraft which could land on ground or water – equipped with floats it also had a retractable undercarriage fitted with wheels – sat on the pad.

'I want to see you take off and land again on this vessel,' he had ordered the pilot.

Constructed as an adapted miniature version of the Harrier jump jet, the machine's jets began building up power. He watched it as the pilot lifted off vertically, hovered above the vessel, then landed with pinpoint precision on the pad. Satisfied with that at least, he had returned to Grenville Grange. Only to find a message waiting for him that Chief Inspector Buchanan of Homicide would be calling later in the morning.

'What the hell could this flatfoot want?' he asked himself aloud as he stared across the lawn.

Dawlish had convinced himself they had given up investigating the murder of Karin Rosewater. Someone tapped nervously on the panelled door. Dawlish bawled out for the intruder on his thoughts to come in. A manservant entered.

'A Chief Inspector Buchanan and a Sergeant Warden have arrived. They say they have an appointment.'

Dawlish told him to stay where he was. Opening up the cocktail cabinet, he poured himself a stiff neat whisky. He downed the drink in two long gulps, licked his thick lips, closed the cabinet.

'Send the bastards in.'

Entering the room Buchanan noted that Dawlish favoured an outfit of riding kit, which seemed bizarre at the end of November. He even wore a hard hat as he stood with his back to a large brick alcove fireplace where a log fire crackled. In one hand he held a coiled riding whip. He used it to gesture.

'Kindly sit there.'

Buchanan smiled to himself as he sat on a couch facing the light from the window and Warden perched uncomfortably beside him. An old trick: stand in the shadow yourself and plant your visitors with the light on their faces.

Dawlish frowned as a third man entered, paused, looking carefully round the room. He seemed to be examining every piece of furniture – everything except the owner.

'Who the blazes are you?' Dawlish snapped. 'I was told two men from Scotland Yard would be coming.'

'Special Branch.'

Tweed held up a card forged by the experts in the Engine Room at Park Crescent. He took his time putting the card back in his wallet before replying.

'Obviously the message was garbled. But it is important that I ask you some questions later. Chief Inspector Buchanan takes precedence.'

'I don't understand any of this. Sit down. There.'

The whip gestured towards the large couch where there

was space for a third visitor. Tweed ignored the suggestion. Walking to a carver chair placed against the same wall as the fireplace, he sat down. It placed him sideways on to Dawlish, who had to turn round to observe him. Buchanan smiled to himself again, guessing the reason for Tweed's manoeuvre.

'I prefer a hard chair,' Tweed said neutrally. 'I now leave the floor to the Chief Inspector.'

'Who has not yet shown any identification,' Dawlish snapped.

Buchanan saw his chance. Standing up, he strolled over to Dawlish, showed him his identity card, remained where he was, leaning an elbow on the mantelpiece, several inches taller than his host. He produced a photograph.

'Do you recognize her?'

'No.'

'Come, Lord Dawlish? the photo is a trifle blurred and you hardly glanced at it. I repeat, do you recognize this lady?'

'Who is she?' Dawlish asked, studying the print handed to him.

'You tell me. You seem to be having trouble answering the question. She is familiar then?'

'I've never seen her in my life. What is this about?'

Dawlish thrust the photo back at Buchanan. He glanced at Tweed who sat, knees together, hands clasped in his lap as he watched Dawlish. His Lordship seemed unsure whether to move away from the two men flanking him. He threw the whip on to a table, tossed his hard hat after it, thrust his large hands into the pockets of his jodhpurs.

'This,' Buchanan informed him in the same level tone, 'is about the brutal murder of Karin Rosewater on the marshes at Aldeburgh. Not so far from here.'

'So why come to me?'

'Because a witness to the murder of Rosewater, Paula Grey, saw at least five heavily built men wearing Balaclavas, armed with rifles, pursuing them after following the two girls in a dinghy from Dunwich. You have divers aboard the *Steel Vulture*, I understand, Lord Dawlish,' Buchanan added conversationally.

'That's what my philanthropic project is all about – using divers to explore the sunken village overwhelmed by the sea years ago.'

'So, you admit you employ divers.' Buchanan made it sound like an accusation. 'My problem is to find the members of the murderous gang who chased the two girls, one of whom was brutally strangled.'

'I still don't follow why you're bothering me.'

Dawlish's tone had become aggressive. Ostentatiously he checked his Rolex watch.

'Because,' Buchanan continued in the same calm manner, 'I am having trouble locating men who could have formed that gang. You check your divers' background before you hire them?'

'Meticulously.' Dawlish found Tweed's unblinking stare irritating, turned to face him. 'What do you want to know?'

'In addition to your *philanthropic* activities you made your fortune out of armament deals. You supply arms to France?'

'France has its own armaments industry,' Dawlish barked.

'You haven't answered my question. Does your ship the *Steel Vulture* ever visit French ports?'

Dawlish rounded on Tweed. 'Look, I've had enough of this. A man with my interests – which, incidentally, are mainly supermarkets – needs some relaxation. That may surprise you,' he said sarcastically. 'But I cruise all over the world in the *Vulture*.'

'A dual-purpose vessel, then,' Tweed remarked.

Dawlish froze. His hard black eyes gazed at Tweed with vehemence. If looks could kill Tweed would have dropped dead.

'What the hell do you mean by that?' he demanded.

'Did I touch a raw nerve?' Tweed enquired innocently. 'I referred to the fact that the *Vulture* is used to explore your sunken village. Also for jolly trips off to foreign parts.'

Buchanan intervened, handing his card to Dawlish.

'I'd like a complete list of your divers sent to me at the address on my card. I could, of course, investigate their backgrounds in other ways. Thank you for giving us some of your valuable time, Lord Dawlish. I think that's all. For now at any rate. Tweed?'

Merely nodding, Tweed stood up and followed Buchanan and Warden. They were leaving the room when Tweed paused, turned round in the doorway to address Dawlish.

'I've heard that Brand is always with you. A kind of Siamese twins act. He's abroad on his hols?'

Dawlish aimed a stubby finger at Tweed's chest like a gun.

'The front door is behind you.'

Chapter Forty-Seven

Running up the wide staircase, Dawlish went into a front
bedroom and watched the two cars leaving together – the
Volvo in front – watched them until they vanished round a
curve in the drive. He walked down to his room overlooking
the lawn more slowly. Opening his cocktail cabinet, he
poured himself another neat double Scotch.

Settling his bulk in an armchair, he swallowed half the
Scotch, put the glass down on a table. He didn't give a damn
for the lofty Chief Inspector from the Yard. It was the enig-
matic intruder from Special Branch which had shaken him.

First, his reference to France, to French ports. Second, his
ambiguous phrase 'dual purpose' about the *Steel Vulture*.
And third, that last question about Brand. The way his eyes
had studied Dawlish's when he mentioned the name.

'May he rot in hell,' Dawlish said aloud.

He drank the rest of his Scotch in one quick gulp.

Tweed followed Buchanan's Volvo until they reached the
A12. Here Buchanan turned south for London. Tweed
swung right, accelerated along the highway. North for
Dunwich.

'Satisfactory, sir?' Hamilton asked when they had driven
many miles.

'I think so.'

Tweed said no more, concentrating on maintaining the

maximum speed along the highway which was compara-
tively free of other traffic. Impatiently, he had to slow down
when he turned off east along the country road to Dunwich.
Arriving at the coast, he left his Escort in the car park next
to the Ship Inn.

Getting out of the car, Tweed took a deerstalker hat from
the rear seat, crammed it on his head. He looped a pair of
binoculars round his neck. It gave him the appearance of a
man on holiday, probably a birdwatcher. He looked at
Hamilton.

'Try and look more relaxed. We're tourists.'

Hamilton's reluctant concession to Tweed's request was
to shove both hands inside the pockets of his trenchcoat. He
liked his right hand free to grab for the Colt. Tweed led the
way out of the car park, turned right and made his way up
a steep winding path past a signpost. *Cliff Path.*

'You've been here before, sir?' Hamilton enquired.

'A long time ago. It's one of the few places which never
changes.'

Tweed hustled up the difficult path, emerged on to a
grassy plateau on top of the cliffs. A wooden seat stood
facing the rippled grey of the calm sea, as though waiting
for someone to sit on it. Tweed saw what he wanted to see
without binoculars, but he pressed the lenses to his eyes,
focused them.

The *Steel Vulture* came up clear as described by Paula,
motionless about half a mile out. Tweed swept the vessel with
his glasses. A lighter was moored to the platform suspended
just above the water – presumably for carrying supplies. A
large dinghy with an outboard motor was attached to the
lighter. Was it the dinghy which had carried men in Balaclavas
in their cold-blooded pursuit of Paula and Karin? He pressed
the lenses closer to his eyes, adjusted the focus with care.

Aft of the bridge was a strange-looking aircraft. No one

had reported that. So, once aboard, Dawlish had great mobility. Tweed saw several men descending into the dinghy, probably prior to coming ashore.

'We'll get away from here fast . . .'

He had hardly completed the brief instruction before he was hurrying back down the winding path back to Dunwich. Hamilton had trouble keeping up with him. Tweed already had the car engine started as he dived into the passenger seat beside him. Taking one last look at the anchored vessel beyond fields spreading down a slope towards the beach, Tweed drove off.

He was speeding back down the A12 when he suddenly slowed, turned on to a wide grass verge and stopped, leaving the engine running. He sat like a man in a trance, hands quite still on the wheel. Hamilton glanced at him, saw his glazed look, was careful to keep quiet.

Butler had once warned Hamilton that if he was with Tweed when this happened he should keep quiet. It meant that something of great significance had struck him.

Twin-track.

That was the phrase Howard had quoted the PM as using in their conversation. Two different units in the field – and Tweed hadn't been told which other unit was operating. It simply confirmed to Tweed that he had been right about the identity of Kalmar, the assassin.

He resumed the drive to London at top speed.

'Have you had anything to eat?' Monica asked the moment Tweed entered his office. 'I thought not,' she said as he shook his head. 'Ham sandwiches on your desk and a flask of freshly made coffee.'

'Thank you. Most considerate.'

Tweed checked the time as he sat at his desk. Half an hour

before he had to leave to catch his flight back to Paris. Unwrapping the foil, he bit into a ham sandwich and realized he was ravenous. Monica came over, poured coffee from the flask into a mug.

'You're going to stay in Paris until it's over one way or the other?' she asked.

'No. To Paris first, yes. Then I fly south to Arcachon to take charge at this critical moment.'

'Porton Down phoned again,' she said grimly. 'They did find one flask among some rubbish. Their top expert returned from holiday. He says the flask shows positive traces of nerve gas. From Dawlish's factory near Oxford.'

'Which makes my visit to Arcachon even more vital.'

'Won't it be dangerous?' Monica pressed.

Tweed devoured another sandwich. 'Probably. But my team is in the danger zone. I must be there with them.'

'You know something you're not telling me,' she accused.

'If I do, I haven't told anyone else. Don't feel out of it.'

'General de Forge is about to move, isn't he?'

'Within the next two or three days. He's waiting for one more development. I want to be there when that development happens.'

The phone rang. Annoyed, Monica ran to her desk, picked up the phone, listened, said she'd see if he was still in the building.

'Chief Inspector Buchanan on the phone . . .'

'Tweed here.'

'I think we make a good team. I detected signs of alarm in his Lordship. I'm tracing those divers.'

'Good idea. A better one would be to check all the hotel registers in Aldeburgh for the night Karin Rosewater was murdered. Concentrate on the names of the people involved in this thing. Should lead you to the murderer. Sorry, must go now . . .'

Part Three

Cross of Fire

Chapter Forty-Eight

'Operation Marengo – the seizure of Paris – has begun.'

General Charles de Forge had taken his decision in the middle of the night. He was poring over a large-scale map of France spread over his desk. By his side stood Major Lamy.

'The advance elements of the First Armoured Division are approaching the outskirts of Angoulême,' Lamy reported. 'They are moving at speed under the cover of darkness. Motorcycle patrols have already reached the outskirts of Angoulême. The Divison will then proceed north tomorrow night – to outflank Paris and move on the capital from the north. According to plan.'

'No!' de Forge contradicted. 'That is the official plan. There is a spy in our midst who has to be caught.' He glanced at Lamy. 'From Angoulême the Division, followed up by heavy reinforcements, will turn north-east, racing via Argenton for Chateauroux and beyond up the N20.'

'The plan has been changed?' Lamy asked in surprise.

'No! The plan I have distributed is a cover plan. If rumours of our movements leak to Paris they will think we are going to keep west of Paris until we can swoop on it from the north.'

'And the real plan?'

'Has been handed as sealed orders to each commander – orders to be opened and acted on only on receiving a personal signal from me. I have sent the signal.'

'Should I now activate Austerlitz in Paris?'

'Not yet. What you can do, Major, is to contact Kalmar and tell him to finish the job. Paula Grey. She has to be a spy. That's it.'

'But Kalmar is pressing for payment – pressing hard.'

'Then pay him.' De Forge's tone was silky. 'I am sure you can lay your hands on the necessary funds.'

Lamy left the presence, his mind in a whirl of calculation. De Forge had refused to reveal to his Chief of Intelligence the real Marengo plan. And only on rare occasions did he address his subordinate by his rank – instead of by name. De Forge was distancing himself.

In his office the General continued to study the detailed map. The sealed plans ordered his commanders to continue north up the N20 – to head point blank for Paris by the most direct route. The last strategy Navarre would expect from a general noted for his devious manoeuvres. He would be in Paris before the government woke in their beds.

And Austerlitz, the infiltration operation, would throw the government into a panic when commando groups started to take over key centres of authority – only hours before de Forge's advance units entered Paris.

Paula was behind the wheel well south of Bordeaux, heading for the Landes, when the catastrophe occurred in deserted open countryside. At a garage they had exchanged temporarily the Renault for a much more spacious Renault Espace, leaving the original vehicle and a large sum of French francs as collateral.

Butler sat beside her, navigating. Immediately behind them were seated Nield and Stahl. Newman was sprawled at the back of the car, fast asleep. At the entrance to an abandoned farm with a large barn the car stopped.

Paula repeatedly turned on the ignition, used the accelerator. It was no use: the engine refused to come alive. Butler got out to the examine the engine and Stahl followed him.

'I don't know much about these engines,' Butler remarked.

'That's great,' said Paula, who had also got out.

'But I do,' Stahl told them eagerly. 'I have spent much time in France. I have driven one of these. Let me take a look . . .'

They waited half an hour while Stahl checked the engine. Paula looked round, was conscious of how exposed they were on the deserted country road. Apparently Stahl had the same thought.

When the half-hour was up he raised a hand, indicating they should stay where they were. He trotted off up the short track leading to the farmhouse which had a crumbling roof, exposing the rafters where tiles had slid away.

The barn was made of stern stuff. The roof was intact and the huge doors swung outward, held firmly on hinges, as Stahl opened the barn, investigated the interior briefly, ran back to the road.

'We must push the Espace into that barn so I can work on the engine. Paula, you handle the wheel. Get out, everyone.'

'Why?' Paula demanded.

'Because,' Stahl explained patiently, 'I can see it will take me several hours to repair the engine. I must dismantle, then put it together again. We were sold a pup. Is that right?'

'Yes,' Paula snapped impatiently. 'Are you sure you can get it going?'

'Absolutely. But I need the time. And we are in a very exposed position here. We have already seen tanks in the distance. Please! We all push.'

Nield was already standing beside Butler but Newman was unaware of anything. He flopped fast asleep, exhausted. Paula climbed behind the wheel while Stahl, Butler and Nield pushed the vehicle up the level track inside the huge empty barn, its floor deep with straw. The glass of windows on three sides was coated with a thick layer of grime. At the back a ladder led to a loft with an equally grimy skylight. Stahl closed one door, Butler the other. While Nield held a pencil flashlight, Stahl began work on the engine.

'Do you really think you can manage it?' Paula persisted.

Stahl grinned. 'I used to be a mechanic before I took up my present occupation. But please do not expect quick results . . .'

During all this activity Newman had not moved an inch – let alone opened an eye. He was in a very deep sleep. At lunchtime Paula collected the basket with sandwiches wrapped in foil and two flasks of coffee. When she had visited Isabelle just before they left Arcachon the French girl had asked Paula how many people there were, how long they would be away.

'Four people,' she lied, omitting Stahl. 'And two or three days,' she lied again.

'Then you'll need food and drink to see you on your way.'

Isabelle had insisted, had prepared sandwiches in a few minutes, her knife flashing while Paula prepared coffee. At the time Paula had cursed the delay: now she blessed Isabelle's consideration. Handing round sandwiches after unwrapping the silver foil, she then poured coffee and they shared the same makeshift cup – the top of the flask. Newman slept on.

While Nield held the new flashlight provided by Paula, Stahl, arms and hands covered with oil and muck, worked away. Half the engine seemed to be on the floor and Paula wondered whether he'd ever assemble it again. The alarm came in the early afternoon.

Butler had made it his business to keep a watch through the windows, resisting the temptation to clean a hole in the grime. At other times he climbed the ladder and peered over the countryside through the skylight. He was in the loft, Paula was scrunching restlessly over the straw, trying to ignore the rising dust, when Stahl waved the screwdriver he'd found in the vehicle's toolkit.

'It's OK. It will go first time. I promise you . . .'

'Trouble. Big trouble. And coming this way fast.'

It was Butler interrupting the German. Paula stiffened as Butler scrambled down the ladder. For a brief second she'd half-believed Stahl: he spoke with such assurance. Now her hopes that they could get away fom this musty-smelling barn were dashed. Whatever the situation Butler usually kept his cool, but there had been urgency in his warning. She glanced at Newman in the back of the vehicle. Still out cold.

'What is it, Harry?' she asked.

'See for yourself. Through this window. Tanks. De Forge's tanks. A whole squadron of them . . .'

She peered through the window from the side with Butler staring over her shoulder. Coming over a low ridge towards them were three large tanks, gun barrels elevated. She tightened her lips. Of all the bloody bad luck. Butler gripped her arm.

'Come with me. Take a better look.'

He shinned back up the ladder to the loft and she followed him. Heaps of straw in the loft. Dry as a bone. The barn was pretty waterproof. He took her to the skylight, stood back so she could look out. From that height she had a much better view – a panoramic sweep – over the low-lying countryside. A spread of fields as far as the eye could see. No trees. And a horde of tanks advancing in the direction of the farm.

'Doesn't look too good,' she commented.

'They are on manoeuvres.' It was Stahl speaking. He'd followed them up the ladder. 'We are at least under cover. Maybe they will change direction before they get here.'

Paula's stomach muscles tightened as she watched. Here and there veils of cold grey mist floated across the landscape, drifting over the ground. The tanks slid though the veils, emerging like landbound sharks seeking prey. Stahl, as always, was for action.

'The Espace will go now,' he pressed. 'Let us drive to the north, back the way we came.'

'Better take a look to the north,' Butler advised.

Stahl and Paula turned their heads. More tanks were advancing from that direction. They all seemed to be making for the farm from three points of the compass. West, south, and north. Only the east was clear. And the road ran roughly north to south.

Butler ran down the ladder, followed by the others. He peered out of the window which looked on to the separate farm building. About thirty feet divided the barn from the wreck of a farmhouse. As he turned round there was movement from inside the vehicle. Newman had at long last woken.

He staggered out, stared down as his feet crunched straw, shook his head as dust rose. Staring round with heavy eyes, his gaze fixed on Butler.

'What the hell is happening?' He looked at his watch. 'It's mid-afternoon. We should be in the Landes . . .'

Paula poured him lukewarm coffee. He swallowed it greedily, held out the container for a refill as Butler tersely explained what had happened, their present situation. The report galvanized Newman.

Handing the container to Paula, he shinned up the ladder to the loft to see for himself. Butler and Stahl followed him. On the barn floor Nield stood alongside Paula as they stared at the incoming tanks which now looked like leviathans. Mobile power at its most terrifying.

'We stay put,' Newman decided. 'Nothing else we can do. Try to make a run for it and they'll use us for target practice.'

'If it comes to it we can take some of them with us. The tank commanders are exposed in their turrets,' Stahl observed.

As he spoke he extracted the Heckler and Koch sub-machine-gun from his bag. He had cleaned his arms and hands on cloths found in the rear of the Espace.

'Put that away,' Newman snapped. 'We can only wait and hope for the best.'

'Or the worst,' Butler added under his breath.

Paula had run up the ladder to join them. She stared at the tanks as though hypnotized. A unit of three large machines was heading straight for them. Suddenly the lead tank increased speed, rumbled forward. She could hear the grind and clatter of its caterpillar tracks rumbling over the stony field.

'Oh, my God!' she gasped.

She could see clearly in the turret of the lead tank a sergeant wearing a helmet, waving his arms ecstatically, in his early twenties. The tank forged remorselessly on, slowed as it reached the farmhouse, mounted a wall. The wall collapsed, the entire farmhouse fell inwards under the impact as the caterpillar tracks ground over the rubble of the wreckage. The young tank commander swept his gloved hand in a sideways gesture, shouting into his microphone. Paula heard the command clearly.

'Now the barn. Flatten it . . .'

Her last thought was that she had made a brief call from Isabelle's apartment, telling Lasalle they were driving south, giving him the apartment's number and its occupant. She'd seized the chance to make the whispered call while Isabelle was preparing the sandwiches.

Tweed had arrived back at the Ministry of the Interior in the early hours of the morning when Newman and his team had left Arcachon for the Landes. He had been delayed for hours at Heathrow due to a bomb scare. His flight had left five hours after scheduled take-off.

Lasalle, just returned from rue des Saussaies, sat in his office. He was studying his map when Tweed walked in, his manner urgent as he took off his Burberry.

'Navarre,' Tweed said immediately. 'Where is he?'

'At an emergency Cabinet meeting. Impossible to get to him. Why?'

'I estimate he has a maximum of sixty hours before de Forge launches his bid for power. I heard at the airport here that Dubois addressed a huge rally in Bordeaux yesterday evening, that he said what he called "the people" would soon be in power. Which means himself as Prime Minister, I assume.'

'I have heard about that ominous speech. Why no more than sixty hours?'

'Because de Forge is waiting for a delivery of weapons – nerve gas missiles I suspect – before he strikes. The weapons will come aboard the armament manufacturer Lord Dawlish's vessel, the *Steel Vulture* . . .'

'The catamaran you told me about before leaving for London?'

'Exactly. I think I know where the weapons are hidden.

Something Paula told me eventually came back. It all links up with Kalmar, as I've always thought.'

'Where is this vessel now?'

'Anchored off a nowhere place called Dunwich on our east coast.'

'Then why not impound – search – the vessel?'

'Because I have no proof of my theory.' Pacing restlessly, Tweed thought that must sound strange to Lasalle. 'The trouble is the catamaran is based at Harwich. While there at different times recently it was searched – for drugs. Nothing was found. Dawlish has clout in high places, contributes large sums to party funds. I know I'm right but, as I said, I can't prove it.'

'We could send aircfaft to patrol offshore. If we knew which areas to concentrate on.'

The approaches to Arcachon. The Bay of Biscay,' Tweed said promptly.

'I will put the idea to Navarre as soon as I can. I do not have the authority. You mentioned Paula. She called a few minutes before you arrived . . .'

He paused as Otto Kuhlmann, in shirt sleeves, looking rumpled, appeared. The German held an unlit cigar in his hand as though he felt lost without it. Lasalle waved to a chair, continued.

'I was telling Tweed that Paula Grey called from Arcachon just before he got here. She was speaking in a low voice as though not wishing to be overheard. She said the team, including Egon, was driving south . . .'

'That damn bomb hoax,' Tweed burst out. 'Where was she calling from?'

'Isabelle Thomas's apartment. She repeated the number.'

'Get it for me, please. Urgently, René,' Tweed requested. 'I might catch them before they leave.'

501

'Stahl will be an asset,' Kuhlmann reassured Tweed.

'I'm sure he will. But we need the information Jean Burgoyne obtained. More urgently now . . .'

He took a deep breath as Lasalle handed him the phone. He was deciding how to talk to Isabelle if she had come on the line. She had. Odd, Tweed thought, to be answering the phone so quickly in the early hours.

'Is Paula there?' he asked.

'Paula? Who is that? And who are you?'

'A close friend – an associate – of Robert Newman's.'

'I have seen Newman's picture in the papers – if you refer to the foreign correspondent. You have not given me your name. Can you describe Mr Newman? Very accurately.'

Tweed swore to himself, but was impressed by Isabelle's caution. He could be anybody. She'd had enough trauma with phoney DST men. He gave her a detailed description of Newman but she hadn't finished with him yet.

'Let us assume he is carrying a weapon for self-protection. What weapon would that be?'

'A Smith & Wesson .38 Special,' Tweed said quickly.

'I'm sorry to question you so closely but I had to be certain of your claim to be an associate. Paula Grey is no longer here. No one is except myself. They drove off about half an hour ago.'

'I see.' Tweed was careful not to alarm her. 'They have been staying at a hotel,' he said, testing her.

'I know. The Atlantique. But when they return they will stay here. In two or three days' time. You have my number, so do not hesitate to call me again.'

'May I suggest you stay in your apartment as much as you can?'

'Bob – Mr Newman – has already told me that. Please do not hesitate to call me again,' she repeated.

'We are going to have to do something drastic, René,' Tweed said as he put down the phone. 'I'm alarmed – very alarmed. Because my whole team is heading for the Landes. Tell me, that map you're studying. It's festooned with crosses. Do they indicate areas where de Forge's troops are manoeuvring?'

'Exactly. From reports received so far . . .'

'And there are crosses in the Landes region.'

'You can read upside down. Ah! I see your point. Your people are moving straight into the danger zone. I am afraid so.'

'I repeat, we are going to have to do something drastic. I have another idea. Are the drivers of French petrol tankers likely to be sympathetic to de Forge?'

'My God, no! They're an independent gang. Very tough. They didn't even like de Gaulle. They loathe de Forge. Any breath of military rule is their idea of hell.'

'And the farmers,' Tweed went on. 'The farmers in the centre and north of France. Do they think de Forge is a saviour of France – like their compatriots in the south?'

'No. They deeply mistrust the Army. De Forge has successfully cultivated the farmers in the south by helping them to bring in their harvest. Farmers further north would chase a soldier off their land with a pitchfork. Why? Ideas seem to be tumbling out of your head.'

'I'm an owl,' Tweed said with a dry smile. 'Are you still worried that de Forge has a network of informants here in Paris reporting back to him?'

'Yes. I told you. I know he has. I just can't locate his network.'

'Then tomorrow I will accept Josette de Forge's invitation to see her again.'

'And your references to petrol tankers, to farmers?'

'This is what I suggest you do with lightning speed . . .'

503

Chapter Forty-Nine

'Get down the ladder quick!' Newman ordered.

Paula almost slid down it from the loft, followed by Stahl and Newman. The loft would hardly be the safest place when the tank crashed into the barn. They ran to the side window overlooking the carnage which had been a farmhouse. Paula kept to one side of the window with Newman, Stahl stayed on the other side.

Like the others, Paula felt she had to see what was happening before they ran for it. Ran where? She had a horrible vision of the walls toppling from a great height, caving in and burying them. They heard someone shouting in French as the young tank tearaway aimed his metallic monster at the barn.

A second tank appeared, broadside on, almost scraping the wall of the barn. Peering up, Paula saw the tank commander, a lieutenant. He had torn off his headset, was roaring at the top of his voice, waving his clenched fist. Through the glass of the window they could hear every word he said:

'I'll have you up on a charge. No! It will be a court martial. You crazy idiot! You have wantonly destroyed a farmer's property. We need the farmers on our side. You will also be accused of attempting to smash down the barn. You are relieved of command of your tank, Sergeant! My own NCO will take control. Get down immediately. You will be a prisoner in my tank . . .'

The engines of both machines had stopped. Inside the barn they froze, gazed at each other in disbelief. Outside they heard the sound of boots descending – presumably the sergeant leaving for the other tank. Newman gestured and they withdrew from a window, sliding back along the roughened wall.

Paula looked at Nield who had remained at the other side of the barn, cool as a cucumber, holding his handgun. With his other hand he gave her the thumbs-up sign and winked. She managed a smile.

The roar of the tanks' engines was resumed, the grinding clatter of their caterpillar tracks. Newman held up a warning hand to ensure everyone kept still. He waited until the sounds had receded some distance, then dived back up the ladder with Paula at his heels.

From a skylight he surveyed the landscape. It was not encouraging. The tanks were coming together in compact formations, manoeuvring across the distant terrain, conducting some mock battle. He shook his head.

'We're not out of the woods yet.'

'So how long do you think we may have to stay here?'

'Until we're very sure the coast is clear. And I see Pete is munching a sandwich. I hope you kept some for me . . .'

In the late morning of the same day Tweed arrived at the Passy home of Josette de Forge. He had phoned in advance, using the same pseudonym, Prentice of the *Daily World*, explaining that his editor was enthusiastic for more information.

'*Information*, Mr Prentice?' she had purred, giving the word an ambiguous inflexion. 'If you come now I shall be available for you . . .'

Available? When she opened the door herself she wore a

fluffy housecoat, open at the front, and underneath a flimsy chiffon slip which was very revealing. As she led him upstairs her housecoat swung wider while she mounted the curving steps, exposing a magnificent long leg. Tweed was relieved when she led him into a bedroom at the front. She turned to face him, taking his Burberry, her dark eyes peering at him through long lashes. She looked towards a large canopy bed draped with the most expensive and laced-edged linen.

'I thought we would be more comfortable up here. And we shall not be bothered by the servants. Just a pleasant tête-à-tête.'

'I do have some questions to ask,' Tweed insisted.

He walked over to a *chaise longue* and perched at one end. Not the piece of furniture he would have chosen but there was no chair in the elaborately furnished room. Hanging his Burberry in a dressing room, she came and sat close to him, crossing her legs.

'Do we have to waste time on boring questions? And when will your long article on my husband appear in your so respected paper?'

'Soon. That is a very fine bust over there.'

In case she was tempted to interpret the word 'bust' in another way he pointed. On a half-round table against one wall was a head-and-shoulders bust of Napoleon. He thought, apart from other factors, his visit had been worthwhile to observe the presence of the bust. He waited for her reaction.

'Charles brought that here. Maybe at the moment he is only Bonaparte, but in the future . . .'

'I heard a rumour that General de Forge's army is nearing Paris. Will Navarre permit that?'

'A delicious question, *chéri*. Navarre is a nobody who will be swept aside by the tidal wave of history.'

'You mean you expect your husband to occupy the Elysée?'

She patted his right cheek. 'Now, I did not say that.'

'But he is a clever man. I hear he has extraordinary Intelligence sources here in Paris. When I was last in this house for your salon I observed some influential guests. General Masson, for example. It occurred to me that your salons would be ideal occasions for passing Intelligence from GHQ Third Army to Paris, and the other way round.'

She was inserting a cigarette into an ivory holder as he spoke. Her hand slipped, broke the end of the cigarette. Her full lips tightened and for a moment she didn't look at him while she recovered her poise.

'You do have a lively imagination,' she retorted with an edge to her voice.

'Have I? Most of your important guests have been linked with de Forge's views.'

'It was a mixed gathering. Artists, intellectuals . . .'

'Together with generals and other key officers.'

'My salons are artistic gatherings . . .'

'Which would be excellent camouflage for Intelligence-gathering operations.'

'You are not putting these lies in your paper, I hope?'

'Only the truth, Madame de Forge,' Tweed replied.

'We are wasting time.' She dropped a fresh cigarette and the holder into a crystal ashtray. Turning to him, she leaned forward and he caught the aroma of expensive perfume as she wrapped her long bare arms round his shoulders.

He smiled, reached up, removed her hands just before she embraced him. Standing up, he walked to the front windows, draped with heavy net curtains. He moved one as though peering into the street, let it drop.

'What is it?' Josette asked, her expression bleak and cold.

'No one is watching this house, if that is what worries you. I thought I'd told you. My husband has his own dalliances. So why shouldn't I?'

She had left the door slightly ajar and suddenly there was a continuous ringing of the bell accompanied by non-stop hammering of the bronze knocker. Tweed went swiftly to the door.

'Excuse me, Madame.'

He ran down the staircase as a woman wearing a black shawl over her head and a black dress which draped her ankles appeared in the hall. The housekeeper. Brushing past her, he turned the security handle as he had observed Josette close it, flung open the door. There were six men in business suits and open trenchcoats outside. Beyond them two black limousines were parked at the kerb.

'The front bedroom upstairs,' Tweed said.

Lasalle and three men rushed up the staircase. As he entered the room Lasalle saw Josette holding an old-fashioned gold telephone to her ear, working the cradle up and down furiously. He placed a hand on her arm.

'DST. You have to come with us. And the phone wire has been cut. Please, we must leave at once, even if we have to carry you. Which would be undignified.'

They hustled her down the stairs, protesting. In the marble-floored hall two more men stood by the house-keeper. Lasalle walked up to her, excused himself politely, removed her black shawl. Turning, he wrapped it round Josette's head.

'What are you doing, you shit?' she screamed.

'Treating you like a lady. You wouldn't want scandal, the neighbours talking. You will leave as though you are the housekeeper. We are taking you to a comfortable residence well outside Paris. No, Madame. You have no say in the matter. Treason is an offence that carries a heavy penalty.

Make a scene,' Lasalle continued genially as they escorted her to a limousine, 'and I will give the papers a list of twelve of your lovers – eight of them married men. There is bound to be one wife who will shriek her head off in public, which would be a shame. Spoiling your eminent position in Parisian society . . .'

Holding her arm, he had seen her into the limousine where two men joined her. He closed the door, bowed for the benefit of any prying eyes. Josette had preserved – for her – a rare silence. The limousine moved off.

Tweed, who had watched, was full of admiration for Lasalle's skilled performance. Only a Frenchman could have pulled it off. He walked to the other limousine, climbed in the back as Lasalle joined him and the chauffeur pulled away.

'I have left men inside the place to search it,' Lasalle informed him. 'She will simply disappear. You see, I also know how to practise psychological warfare. Imagine the effect on de Forge.'

'Very good,' Tweed agreed. 'I had a nasty moment when I thought she might take me into a back bedroom. You saw my signal with the curtain, of course.'

'We left our cars the moment we saw the curtain move. I think you handled your part well.'

'I saw something which tells me the route de Forge will adopt to march on Paris – if it ever comes to that. Now we must launch Phase Two.'

'What did you see in that apartment?'

'A favourite bust of de Forge's. Of Napoleon. Remember Waterloo,' Tweed ended cryptically.

At Arcachon Victor Rosewater stood on the deck of his cabin cruiser, scanning the front with binoculars. He switched his survey to the craft in the port where the masts of a cluster of vessels swayed slowly under the gentle swell entering the *bassin* from the Atlantic.

Dressed in a polo-necked sweater under an oilskin he looked the typical sailor. A fine drizzle of rain was falling. The sky was like grey porridge. Everything looked grey. Satisfied that he was not observed, he ran down the companionway into a large cabin.

Throwing off the oilskin, he pressed a secret button. A section of the galley wall slid back, revealing a radio telephone and a transmitter. He pressed another button and on deck a tall aerial elevated alongside the mast.

Within minutes he was speaking to his contact, Oscar, at Kriminalpolizei HQ in Wiesbaden. They exchanged code words and Rosewater gave his message.

'Soon I will be able to supply a list of the addresses where our friends are staying in the Federal Republic. That is all . . .'

In Wiesbaden Oscar immediately transmitted the signal to Kuhlmann in Paris.

Despite Rosewater's careful surveillance of the *bassin* he had overlooked a broad-shouldered man dressed in a pea-jacket. Brand was crouched behind the wheelhouse of a smaller cabin cruiser moored in the port.

He was also using binoculars and had seen Rosewater scanning the anchorage. He continued watching as the Englishman disappeared inside the cabin. Through his binoculars he saw the elevation of the aerial. He stood up, stepped ashore and strolled along the waterfront to a public callbox. Shoulders hunched, a cap pulled down over his forehead, he appeared to be just an ordinary seaman. He entered the callbox, dialled the number from memory, announced himself as Bird Two. It was fortunate the girl who came on the line spoke English.

'Is that you, Yvette? Listen. You know where I am. There's a British spy ship in the harbour. The Red Ensign at the mast. Cabin cruiser. The *Typhoon IV*. Got that? Repeat the name. Yes, that's it . . .'

General de Forge was in a rage. Summoned to his presence, Major Lamy found him in a storming mood, unable to keep still. He looked at his subordinate with a piercing stare.

'You know what's happened now? I can't contact Josette. The operator says the line has been disconnected. My main pipeline into Paris has been cut. Just as we are about to launch Austerlitz within hours. Find out what the hell is going on. Why are you still standing there?'

'Yvette has reported a call from *Oiseau Deuxième* . . .'

Reluctantly he gave de Forge more bad news. As he feared, it did not improve the General's temper. De Forge hammered his fist on the desk.

'Send a team to clean out Arcachon. You know how important the place is. First this Paula Grey, who is still on the loose. Now this new spy. Include in the team Sergeant Rey. A boobytrap may be the answer for this cabin cruiser, *Typhoon IV*. And Kalmar has to liquidate the Grey woman at the earliest opportunity.'

'There is our problem of paying Kalmar . . .'

'*Your* problem! Flood Arcachon with men posing as DST. And don't forget Isabelle Thomas, mistress to Henri Bayle. Wipe the lot out. One more thing. I have a report from the Landes that the attempt to kill Moshe Stein misfired. Find him. There has been no report from Paris of his arrival – and if he had got there they would have put him on TV to moan on about the so called Tarbes massacre. I'm worried about the Landes. Dispatch another team by sea to remove the remains of the criminal elements from the graveyard in body bags. Take them out to sea, weight the body bags, and throw them into the Atlantic.'

'You don't wish me to be involved in this?' Lamy protested.

'No. Put Lieutenant Berthier in charge of the team. And tell him to wait until Sergeant Rey is available to join the unit. It may be easier and more effective to blow up the relics well out at sea. Act now . . .'

De Forge waited for a few minutes, then summoned Sergeant Rey to come and see him. When the gnomelike boobytrap expert appeared, képi under his arm, head bent respectfully, de Forge greeted him warmly by his real rank.

'Sit down, Captain. Recently I had a telephone engineer in our pay come and tap the phones of every officer among our inner circle. I have discovered the traitor who has informed Paris of some of my plans. I will play the tape in a moment.'

'Every officer?' Rey enquired.

His nominal role of sergeant enabled him to mix with the troops, to inform de Forge of what they were saying. Guile was one of the General's favourite weapons.

'Yes. Yourself included.' De Forge smiled cynically. 'I am noted for thoroughness. Now, this is what I want you to do . . .'

Newman and his team were still trapped inside the barn. It was early evening, a grey dusk was descending over the surrounding landscape. From the skylight window in the loft Newman watched distant tanks lining up behind each other in columns. They had their rear lights on but no headlights, and they were moving very close together. It reminded Newman of accounts he'd read of General Guderian's panzer breakthrough into France during World War II. His tanks had moved through the defiles of the Luxembourg Ardennes at night nose to tail, each German tank commander following the vehicle ahead by watching its rear lights. He descended the ladder.

'Are we still stuck here?' Paula enquired.

'I'm afraid so. Let's hope the manoeuvres don't go on all night. You look worried.'

'I was thinking of Moshe Stein. Where is he?'

'Still in his room at the Atlantique. He has food sent up and I warned him not to venture outdoors. As soon as we can, one of us must escort him to Paris.'

'Will he do that? Just stay in a cramped room?'

'He once spent six months in a cellar as a boy during the Second World War. Somewhere in the Balkans. He'll stay put.'

'Thank heavens,' Paula said with feeling. 'Then he will be quite safe.'

Chapter Fifty

France was ablaze. In Toulouse, in Marseilles, in Toulon, in Bordeaux, men in Balaclavas marched holding aloft slow-burning Crosses of Lorraine. They were joined by aggressive youths, small shopkeepers, market stall holders. The same chant built up to a crescendo, started by the hooded men in Balaclavas.

Pour France! Pour France! Au Pouvoir! Au Pouvoir!

For France! For France! To Power! To Power!

The conflagration was spreading to smaller towns, caught up in the frenzy. It was dark now and the symbolic crosses burned like menacing daggers.

On the hillsides bonfires were lit. Great beacons seen from miles away. Spreading the message further and further north. In Bordeaux Dubois was addressing an assembly of massed people crowding to listen as he orated at the Place de la Victoire.

'Frenchmen! Your hour has struck. The little people will at long last have their say. We will sweep aside the vested interests which have for so long used you as serfs. You will become the pride of all Europe. Paris will be cleansed of the filthy exploiters, the corrupt ministers, the men who buy you for a miserable handful of francs . . .'

'*Pour France . . .!*'

Not everyone joined in the manic orgy of mob violence. Some stayed indoors, the shutters firmly closed. In one

514

apartment a lawyer turned to his wife, his voice full of foreboding.

'Louise. This reminds me of what I've read of the early days of the Revolution in 1789. The prelude to the Reign of Terror . . .'

In central France and towards the north rather different scenes were taking place. Farmers were working in the night, hauling out of storage bales of hay. Their wives were helping too – helping to carry the bales to open trucks waiting to receive the loads.

DST officers were overseeing the operation. They were carefully listing the quantity and numbers of the bales, preparing records for future compensation by the government.

Many of the bales were ripped open once aboard a truck. Once a vehicle was full, tough young farmers armed with pitchforks jumped inside the truck, resting on the hay as the vehicle moved off to its pre-arranged destination.

Close to the main highways groups of petrol tankers were parked in laagers. Often as many as half a dozen. The drivers were content to sit in their cabs: they were being paid full wages without the stress of driving their mammoth loads through the night. Each driver had concealed in his cab a long coiled stretch of hosepipe. And each man had been supplied with a walkie-talkie and instructions by DST officers.

Wherever possible they were laagered inside evergreen woods. This meant they were invisible to observation from aircraft. It was now a matter of waiting for the orders to come over the walkie-talkies.

News of the fiery crosses burning in the south, of the crowds massing and chanting had reached Paris. Lights were burning late in the Ministry of the Interior which Navarre had now made his emergency HQ.

For one thing, the ministry was heavily guarded. For another it was equipped with the most sophisticated communication facilities in France. Navarre, in his shirt sleeves, had called a meeting in his large office. Round the table sat Tweed, Kuhlmann, and Lasalle. The only men he could fully trust.

'I have,' Navarre began, 'informed the Cabinet it will meet next in three days' time.'

'Why?' asked Lasalle.

Navarre smiled grimly. 'It is a trick. Within three days the crisis will be settled. One way or the other. I am sure de Forge has already heard the news. He will think we believe we have plenty of time, that no action will be taken against him in the meantime.'

'Are the measures we talked about being activated?' Tweed asked.

'The measures *you* suggested,' Navarre corrected him. 'Yes. Both with the farmers and the drivers of a whole fleet of petrol tankers. The trouble is we need to know the route de Forge's forces will take.'

'The N20,' Tweed said. 'The direct route to Paris. But I emphasize that is my educated guess. We need the data Stahl compiled, the data Jean Burgoyne obtained. And my people, who have the documents, are on their way to the Landes. That was a mistake, but I can't blame them. I'm sure they want to give us a complete package – including a witness we can put on TV.'

'Time is running out,' Lasalle said quietly.

'You still have an informant inside de Forge's camp?' Tweed enquired. 'Even after the murder of Jean Burgoyne?'

'That murder I mourn,' Lasalle replied. 'She was a brave woman. To answer your question, yes I still have one informant. I received a brief message early this afternoon. The *Cercle Noir* is holding one final meeting just after dusk today. That is why I say time is running out.'

'I think we must do something about that,' Navarre decided. 'At the Cabinet meeting General Masson said he would be away from Paris visiting a unit.'

'I think I would suggest that we do two things if you are agreeable. A double-pronged attack. Plus more psychological warfare. The first prong of the offensive should be . . .' Tweed elaborated.

Arriving in Arcachon, Sergeant Rey worked quickly. He had little time before he had to join Lieutenant Berthier's seaborne landing in the far south.

Rey dressed as a fisherman. He wore an oilskin with the hood pulled well down over his face. He trudged in a mist of drizzle, plodding in his gumboots, carrying a fishing rod. Over his shoulder was slung a canvas bag, presumably for his catch. Inside the bag was the time bomb.

He had earlier sat on a stone jetty, fishing line in the water dappled with the rain, watching the *Typhoon IV*. He saw no sign of activity and the curtains were drawn over the cabin windows. The owner was undoubtedly enjoying an afternoon nap.

Rey made no sound as he stepped from the shore on to the wet deck. He took one final look round to make sure he was not observed. Extracting the limpet-shaped bomb, he pressed a button, activating the magnetic legs. Crouching down, he attached it to a band of metal running round the outside of the cabin. He pressed a second button. The timer was now operating, the silent clock ticking away. Rey had five minutes to get clear.

He walked rapidly to his car as though fed up with the

drizzle which had developed into steady rain. Dumping his fishing rod with the canvas bag on the back seat, he climbed behind the wheel, started his engine, waited.

He had parked his car in a position where he could see *Typhoon IV*, moored by itself. He was several hundred yards away from his target. He checked his watch. One more minute . . .

The explosion was muffled by the rain but still loud. The *Typhoon IV* was ripped apart. The hull soared above the *bassin*. It shattered into pieces which fell back into the water, some pieces causing huge eruptions of water like fountains. Smoke rose from the portion of the hull still at the mooring point. Flame flared briefly, was quenched as the remains of the vessel disappeared.

'Another job dealt with,' Rey muttered to himself callously.

He drove off to the rendezvous with Berthier at a lonely point on the coast south of Arcachon. They should reach the Landes by mid-afternoon.

Aboard another cabin cruiser, his reserve base, Rosewater saw the explosion. He had expected something like this. All essential equipment had been moved to the cruiser he watched from through binoculars.

Earlier, while transmitting his brief message to Oscar in Wiesbaden, he had watched through the net curtains masking the windows of his cabin. He had seen Brand appear suddenly, hurrying along the waterfront. Too suddenly after Rosewater had scanned the area for any sign of activity.

It could have been a coincidence, but Rosewater had survived so far by never believing coincidences. And wherever he was stationed even for a few days he always had a second secret base. As the fountains of water vanished he shrugged his shoulders. He was not disturbed – his occupation assumed risks all the time.

Newman was driving the Renault Espace through the night. Paula sat beside him, checking her map. Behind them were seated Stahl and Nield. And in the back, staring constantly through the rear window, was Butler.

Taking a risk – because they had lost so much time – Newman was racing down the N10, the main highway towards the Spanish border. He had stopped at a truck drivers' café earlier to check the situation. Strategically situated by the side of the N10, the eating place was filled with the smoke of cheap cigarettes; so much so he paused inside the entrance of the long cabinlike structure to get used to the blue haze, the stench of overcooked food mingling with beer fumes.

Drivers from the trucks parked outside occupied all the tables. Others were standing. He pushed his way to the bar, ordered a Pernod, started chatting to a burly driver in French.

'We're on our way to the border from Paris on holiday. I'm wondering whether to turn back. Bloody Army seems to be everywhere.'

'Keep going south,' the driver advised. 'I'm up from San Sebastian. The tanks have all gone north. You'll meet nothing. You think this Dubois is any good? Don't believe a word he says. He's after a fat job in the Cabinet – to keep him quiet. That's politics for you.' He spat on the straw-covered floor. 'You take your holiday, mate . . .'

They drove on, reached the Landes, the sinister walls of the forest closed in on both sides. Here and there a massacre had taken place. Trees chopped down, the headlights of the Espace swept over vast clearings with ugly tree stumps left like the amputated limbs of giants.

Dawn was not so far away when, guided by Paula, Newman turned off the N10, swung west on to the D42 at Castets. Soon they reached St Girons, the village where their witness, Martine, lived. It took them a while to locate her tiny cottage on the edge of the village as Moshe Stein had described. Newman was disturbed to see lights in every window of the dwelling.

The first grey streaks of dawn filtered from the east as he took Paula with him and pressed the ancient bell. He heard nothing inside so he hammered on the woodwork. A shuffling sound like someone walking in clogs approached the door. It was opened on a heavy chain. Martine, fully dressed, peered out.

'Remember me?' Newman asked quietly. 'This is Marie. We have other friends outside.'

'Are you armed?'

The question shook Newman, unsure which answer would reassure her. Then he realized she was frightened.

'Yes we are . . .'

'Come in!' She couldn't open the door quickly enough and talked non-stop in an urgent gabble. 'You may be in time. You may be too late. Can you remember the way to the graveyard? They are going to kill another one . . . They landed from the sea . . . I was collecting brushwood when I saw them coming.'

'Saw who coming?' Newman asked.

Paula looked round the living room-cum-kitchen. It was spotless. An ancient stove stood against one wall and a welcome glow of heat met her. It was freezing outside.

'Their rubber boats with engines . . .' Martine clutching Newman's arm. 'One man had his hands tied behind his back. It's another firing squad. The swines are going to murder another one, then bury him. Hurry! You might be in time. I have just got back. They were just coming in to land when I hurried back . . .'

'We'll go immediately.'

Newman had to abandon the Espace after driving a short distance when he came to where the path leading into the forest was too narrow. The light was growing stronger but it was still not dawn as they ran flat-footed among the trees to prevent stumbling on the soggy earth.

They were very close to the sea: they could hear a surge of incoming waves slapping on a beach and the tang of salt air was strong in their nostrils. This was mixed with the aroma of pine and fir and, normally, Paula would have revelled in the scent. Now she was only hoping they would not be too late.

There had been a brief argument outside the cottage when Newman had told Paula to stay with Martine and she had insisted on coming. Newman had made a mistake in how he worded his suggestion.

'It might be better if someone stayed to guard Martine – and in any case it would be much safer if you waited for us here.'

'Safer!' she flared up. 'You think I'm just a passenger? Someone you can drop off the train as soon as the journey looks tricky? You're damn well wasting time – and I am coming with you . . .'

Newman found he could remember the way along the path he had previously trod and led the way. Behind him Paula followed and behind her Stahl, nursing his submachine-gun. Butler and Nield completed the small column. They had reached firmer ground, were threading their

521

course through the immense tree trunks towering above, when Newman held up a hand to stop them.

'We have reached the graveyard.'

'Is it those humps?' Paula asked, gritting her teeth.

'Yes. I think I heard someone over to the right. A voice, I'm sure.'

'Then whoever it is must be on the beach,' Paula commented. 'We'd better not waste a second . . .'

They crept forward through the trees, Newman in the middle, Paula on his left, Stahl on his right. Behind followed Butler and Nield. All held their weapons in their hands. The forest ended suddenly. They were out in the open and below the leaden sea stretched away, its surface ruffled with the endless waves rolling in.

Paula almost gasped with horror, clapped her left hand to her mouth. They were on an elevated bank of fine sand. Beyond, dunes spread away to the south, those in the distance rising to a considerable height. The tide was out and a belt of freshly washed sand edged the swirling surf from the gentle waves. It was the scene on the beach below which had startled Paula.

A lieutenant stood erect, blindfolded, facing north, his hands tied behind his back to a wooden stake rammed into the beach. Twenty feet away from him, facing south, were ten soldiers holding rifles. Well back, and midway between the target and the men with rifles, stood a hunched figure, also in uniform, a pistol in his hand by his side.

'My God!' Paula whispered. 'It's a firing squad. They're going to shoot Lieutenant Berthier.'

'And that creep with his back to me is familiar. Sergeant Rey. He's going to administer the *coup-de-grâce*. After that squad has shot him.'

'Can't we stop them?'

As she spoke Rey raised his weaselly voice, attempting to assume a commanding posture.

'Take aim . . .'

The rifles were rising when Newman's voice bellowed out. At the same moment Stahl aimed his sub-machine-gun.

'Don't move, Sergeant Rey! We can shoot you all down in seconds. Here is a demonstration . . .'

Stahl pressed the trigger and the sub-machine-gun spattered the beach, spraying close to the feet of the squad.

Fine sand spurted up in the soldiers' faces. In the act of raising their rifles they froze. It was like a waxwork tableau. Newman bellowed again.

'Sergeant Rey! Order them to drop their rifles. Now!'

Stahl aimed his sub-machine-gun again. Bullets sprayed the beach a few feet in front of Rey. He stiffened and gave the order. Ten rifles fell to the beach. For the third time Newman shouted an order.

'Sergeant Rey! Drop your pistol. Now!'

Still not daring to turn round, Rey obeyed. Newman gave him a fresh instruction.

'Order your soldiers to lie on their stomachs in the shape of a fan. A wheel – like the spokes of a wheel. One man facing outwards, the next towards the hub. Get on with it.'

Rey gave the order. The soldiers had to be told three times what was wanted. Newman's tactic was to have the face of one man between the boots of his companions. No communication could then be passed between them.

'Get rid of their weapons, Pete,' Newman whispered to Nield. 'And keep well clear of Stahl's line of fire – just in case someone gets lively.'

Nield collected Rey's automatic pistol first, ejected the magazine, fired the bullet up the spout towards the sea. He then gathered up the rifles, piling them away from the spreadeagled soldiers and near the surf line. Picking up each rifle, he extracted the cartridges, used a piece of hard wood he'd found among the brushwood littering the sand. He used it to damage the breeches. Then, one by one, he hurled each weapon as far out to sea as he could.

'Check Rey for other weapons,' Newman called out.

'Clean,' Nield reported after checking the gnome whose face twisted with hatred.

'Rey,' Newman ordered, 'you will now release Lieutenant Berthier from that barbaric stake. Nield, accompany him and keep your gun at the ready.'

As the two men reached the prisoner a strange silence fell over the scene, broken only by the peaceful sound of the surge of the sea. Freed, Berthier eased the ache out of his hands, flexing them, stretched his arms and walked with surprising firmness to Newman.

'Keep Rey where he is,' Newman ordered Nield.

He couldn't understand the furtive expression which had come over Rey's evil face. As though he were waiting for something. Berthier stood in front of Newman.

'Thank God! You saved my life. They turned on me when I was in one of the dinghies. They've dragged them into the undergrowth to avoid surveillance from the air. I managed to phone Paris,' he continued in a low voice, 'just before we embarked. Said I was calling my girlfriend. Then I delayed the passage of the dinghies down here before they grabbed me. I kept pretending to see lights of vessels – which meant we had to put out our lights and stop.'

'You phoned Paris? Who did you contact . . .'

Newman got no further. Rey shouted at the top of his voice.

'Don't move. Drop your weapons or you'll be shot down like the trash you are.'

As he completed his threat Rey dropped flat to the beach.

Newman glanced behind them. Twelve more French soldiers had emerged from the forest, most of them carrying automatic weapons aimed point blank at Newman's team. Two had shovels sloped over their shoulders.

Stahl stiffened, Newman warned him quickly.

'Don't, Egon. We'll be cut down. Drop it. We're outgunned.'

Newman was cursing himself for carelessness. As they'd hurried across the graveyard he'd noticed signs of recent disturbance of the humps. He had hardly registered the fact, so urgently had he wanted to reach the beach.

Obviously – now – another section of troops had been beginning to remove the evidence when they had heard Newman's team approaching. They must have retreated into the forest to observe who was coming. And Rey was now wearing the uniform of a captain. The gnome swaggered after Nield who joined the others with his hands in the air. Rey was grinning, exposing bad teeth, as he stared at Paula.

'We'll have some fun with you before six more corpses are sunk at sea. Your death, Berthier, may be prolonged.'

At the Atlantique in Arcachon Moshe Stein's bedroom door flew open and two grim-looking men in trenchcoats stared at him. The smaller man had a Luger pistol aimed at Stein's chest. The taller, more heavily-built man seemed to be in charge.

'DST. Moshe Stein? You're wanted for questioning.'

'Where? And why, if I may ask?'

'You may not.' The taller man strode forward and hit him across the face with his clenched fist. The ring on his finger cut Moshe's lip. 'You just come with us, you filthy Jew, and keep your dirty mouth shut.'

Both men gripped an arm, hauled him to the door and down the staircase. The staircase was narrow so the tall man went first, keeping hold of one arm, while his companion followed, also gripping an arm at an awkward angle. The descent was painful. No duty clerk behind the desk, Moshe noted. They frog-marched him into the street towards a waiting car.

Chapter Fifty-One

In Dunwich no one would have recognized the well-known figure of Lord Dawlish as he walked along the beach at half the pace of his normal vigorous stride. He wore gumboots, a pea-jacket underneath his oilskin with the hood pulled over his head.

He had disguised himself as a seaman on his way to the waiting large dinghy hauled up on the sand. No local would realize he was going on board, as he often did before the departure of the *Steel Vulture*.

Seeing his expression, none of the crew aboard the dinghy spoke to him as he settled himself at the stern. The outboard was started after several hefty seamen had pushed the dinghy into the sea and jumped aboard.

The dinghy purred across the calm surface while drizzle continued to fall. The atmosphere was so murky it was several minutes before the catamaran hove into view – weather conditions which gave Dawlish great satisfaction. After dark the *Vulture*, sailing illegally without navigation lights, could depart without anyone in Dunwich realizing it had left its station.

He summoned Captain Santos to his cabin as soon as he went on board. Taking off his dripping oilskin, he thrust it at the skipper.

'Take that and get it dried off. You will be ready to sail tonight? By God, the answer had better be yes this time.'

'Señor, I am most happy to report the loading is almost complete . . .'

'*Almost?*'

'That it will be complete by this evening. Most definitely, Señior. I give you my word . . .'

'And I'll give you the destination when at long last you've got your act together. Get out of here and kick a few backsides to make them work faster . . .'

Alone when Santos had hurried away, he opened the wall safe. Stripping off the pea-jacket, he removed the fat money belt strapped round his waist. He began taking out French and Swiss banknotes in stacks, all high-denomination bills. When he closed the safe it was holding a fortune.

He next took from his wallet the message he had already encoded before leaving Grenville Grange. Making himself comfortable in front of the transmitter, he sent the signal which passed from the aerial alongside the complex radar above the bridge. Decoded, the message was simple.

Expected consignment will arrive agreed destination tomorrow positively. Equipment and finance. ETA 0800 hours. Oiseau.

'Just in time for breakfast in Arcachon,' Dawlish said to himself.

At his GHQ General de Forge read the decoded signal Lamy had just handed him from *Oiseau*. He folded his strong hands and stared at his Chief of Intelligence without speaking. Lamy forced himself not to shift about in his chair. It was another favourite tactic of de Forge's – to use silence to intimidate his subordinates. He had a maxim he sometimes liked to utter at meetings of the *Cercle Noir*. And the final meeting would take place this evening. The maxim was typical of the General: 'There are two ways of ruling men. Through love or fear. I prefer fear.'

'Lamy,' he said eventually, 'you'll have to reply with our own signal. Warn him that we have observed French aircraft patrolling offshore. He should make a broad sweep well out in the Bay of Biscay. We move tomorrow.'

Newman was in a cold fury. The troops were eyeing Paula in anticipation. Rey saw his expression and grinned again, his eyes glowing with lecherous malevolence. He tapped Newman on the arm.

'You can watch. Before we shoot you. Then her.'

Newman glanced at Berthier and almost frowned. Rey was deciding which soldier should take Paula first. Berthier had glanced surreptitiously at his watch. Then his expression went blank.

It was at this moment when Newman's acute hearing caught the sound of engines approaching at high speed. Within seconds the surge of the sea was drowned with the roaring chug-chug of a whole fleet of helicopters. The Alouettes appeared over the treetops like a cloud of metal birds. Several vanished out of sight, descending into a clearing, Newman assumed.

More choppers were flying south parallel to the beach. They came in very low. Then they were landing on the sand, spilling out droves of CRS men in leather coats and armed with automatic weapons.

From the nearest machine a swivel-mounted machine-gun fired a warning burst, coughing up bursts of sand. A familiar figure jumped out, ran with an escort of CRS men to where the group was lined up. Lasalle.

'Surrender!' His order was a piercing shout. 'Drop your weapons or every one of you will be shot down.'

Rey suddenly broke away, screened by his recent prisoners, running into the forest. Newman followed him. His feet pounded the earth, surprised at how fleet of foot the horrific gnome was. Ahead other troops were fleeing.

They stopped abruptly. From behind every massive tree trunk – or so it seemed to Newman – appeared a CRS man, aiming his automatic rifle. The soldiers froze in their tracks. Rey slowed, stopped, staring round desperately for an avenue of escape. There wasn't one.

Rey heard the pounding of Newman's feet, turned. He reached for the pistol, which was no longer in his holster. Newman's fist smashed with tremendous force into the side of his jaw, breaking it. Rey sagged against a tree trunk.

'You'd do that to a woman!' Newman was beside himself. He grabbed Rey by the throat, began to strangle him as Rey's fists beat futilely against his chest. Lasalle and Paula caught up with them. CRS men grabbed hold of Newman, pulled him away from Rey, who collapsed.

'He's not worth creating a storm about,' Paula said in a chilling voice. 'You've done enough.'

Berthier appeared at Paula's elbow. He shook hands with Lasalle, thanking him.

'What happened?' Newman asked, breathing heavily.

He remembered then that ages ago he had given Paris the map reference of the graveyard. Berthier shook Newman's hand.

'I told you I called Paris. I warned Lasalle they were going to destroy the evidence of the killing ground.'

'And luckily saved yourself – and us,' Newman commented, rubbing blood off his knuckles with his handkerchief.

'You must have smashed the bone,' Paula observed, staring down at the unconscious Rey.

'All of them, I hope,' Newman said with vehemence.

'We must round up the rest of these killers'' Lasalle said. 'And where is your witness?'

'Give us ten minutes and we'll give you the witness.'

'Tell me where.'

'St Girons . . .'

'So we fly you there in one of the Alouettes. It will pick up your witness and fly you on to Paris.'

'I want to go straight back to Arcachon with my team,' Newman said firmly.

'So,' Lasalle spread his hands, 'the Alouette flies you to St Giron, the witness is put aboard, the Alouette flies you to Arcachon, then proceeds to Paris with the witness Navarre needs so badly.'

'Agreed.' Newman pointed to the sagging figure of Rey who was beginning to stir, groaning. 'What do we do with that? He was going to kill Berthier, was directing a firing squad when we arrived just in time.'

'He will be flown to Paris for intensive interrogation. He'll crack. That sort always does. Follow me . . .'

He led the way back to the beach. They passed CRS men handcuffing the hands of soldiers behind their backs. Paula was relieved to get on to the clean air of the beach. Stahl had collected their weapons, handed them back to their owners, including Paula's Browning.

Lasalle ushered them to the Alouette behind the lead machine he had travelled aboard. He shook the hand of each man as he climbed into the machine – Berthier, Newman, Stahl, Butler, and Nield. He had kept Paula to the last and hugged her before she joined the others.

'You have had an appalling ordeal,' he told her.

'It was a bit tense,' she admitted.

He felt her trembling as she smiled. Reaction was setting in. She took one last look south to where the high dunes

531

rose, where the sea glided in, retreated before another wave rolled in. An idyllic scene – to hide so much horror. As soon as she was inside the door was closed, the rotors began to whirl, the machine ascended.

Outside the Atlantique Moshe Stein had been hustled to the waiting car on the far side of the road. A man inside threw open the rear door. The taller captor took hold of Moshe by the scruff of the neck, prepared to hurl him inside.

There was a sudden screech of burning rubber, of cars braking violently. Four Citroëns were parked in a military-style manoeuvre – one car blocking off the car Moshe was about to enter, a second blocking the rear. Two more cars stopped on the far side of the road and men in civilian clothes holding automatics dived out. A tall, thin man with a streak of a moustache and without a gun, hands in his raincoat pockets, called out as he approached the trapped car.

'DST. Don't move. My men have orders to use their weapons at the first sign of resistance.'

'*We* are DST,' protested the man who had hit Moshe.

The thin man glanced at the coat lapel of the protester. He grinned without humour as the man produced his papers. Glancing at them, he held them up to the grey light, shook his head.

'Forgeries. And that is another offence.' He looked at Moshe's mouth where blood seeped. 'Who hit you?'

'Does it matter? Violence is the only language these people understand.'

'You're Moshe Stein? Good. And I agree with your remark. Come with me, please.'

Taking him out of earshot of the fake DST trio, he led

him to the second car on the far side of the road. He opened the rear door, stopped Moshe as he was about to get inside.

'You will be flown to Paris under protective guard. I understand they need you there urgently as a witness to atrocities. Talking about atrocities, I insist you tell me who struck you.'

Moshe shrugged. 'Since you insist, it was the tall one. And perhaps I shouldn't ask but I'm curious. How did you know those men were not genuine DST?'

'As you're going to Paris, I will tell you. It was the idea of my chief based in Paris. Knowing there were a number of men posing as DST he told us all to wear blue pins in our lapels.'

'Clever.' For the first time Moshe saw the blue pin.

The thin man closed the door, the car drove off. He beckoned to the tall man, opened the rear door of the first car. The prisoner glared at him viciously, bent his head to step inside. The thin man grabbed his collar, pulled him back, then slammed him forward so his face smashed into the top of the car. The prisoner yelped with pain. He had blood all over his mouth and chin, had lost three teeth.

'Tsk, tsk!' the thin man said sympathetically. He moved a foot over the wet street. 'It is very slippery. You should be more careful . . .'

Marler, carrying his holdall, had disembarked from the internal flight from Paris. He was walking across the concourse when he saw a group of soldiers stopping two scruffily dressed youths. He immediately changed direction, went to a bookstall, bought a newspaper.

He joined a crowd heading for a departure lounge, trailing in their wake. Looking back he saw the soldiers escorting the youths to a bench where their duffle bags were deposited prior to search. The troops were absorbed in their task.

Adjusting his beret, he turned round again, strolled out of the concourse. The car he had ordered from Paris was waiting for him. A Peugeot. He showed his papers to the girl, paid her a generous sum as though needing the vehicle for a few days, drove away.

Earlier, waiting in his room near the rue du Bac, he had received further instructions from Tweed over his mobile phone.

'Increase the pressure to the maximum. We have not much time left.'

'Don't worry. I have a new idea,' Marler had assured his chief. 'A very tight turn of the screw . . .'

Kalmar sat in his camper concealed in woods outside Arcachon drinking coffee. He was studying a map of the port. The coffee was black and strong and helped him recover his nerve. He had just experienced a frustrating shock.

He had traced Moshe Stein to the Atlantique and had been on his way to strangle the Jew. Arriving a short distance from the hotel, he had carefully parked his motorcycle inside a small alley. Always station your means of escape within easy walking distance of the target's home or temporary residence. But not so close that it might be seen and remembered by a passer-by.

He drew on his Gauloise, recalling the incident. He had been very close to the hotel, wearing the sort of trenchcoat favoured by the fake DST men crawling round the town. He had seen his target, Moshe Stein, being dragged from the hotel and had stopped, bending down as he pretended to tie an imaginary loose shoe lace. Then the other cars had arrived, other men had dived out of them.

Kalmar was a professional, so very observant. Before he turned away his sharp eyes caught the glitter of a blue pinhead in the lapel of one of the new arrivals. No similar pinhead in the lapels of the men who had hauled Stein out, who appeared to be arrested by the newcomers.

Kalmar had walked away. He knew exactly the right shop which sold embroidery equipment. Sure enough, they had a selection of blue pinheads. He had purchased half a dozen. He was wearing one now in the lapel of his trenchcoat. Taking another drag at his Gauloise, he folded up the map. His next target was Paula Grey, who had disappeared from Arcachon. His instinct told him she would soon return.

Chapter Fifty-Two

Navarre was holding a battle conference in his office at the Ministry of the Interior. Also present were Tweed and Kuhlmann. The three men were taking final decisions.

'Lasalle has signalled me,' Navarre informed his two confidants. 'He was brief. The graveyard has been discovered and soldiers were there on the verge of removing the corpses. The two witnesss, Moshe Stein and the old woman, Martine, are on their way here.'

'Old woman?' Kuhlmann queried. 'Will she make a convincing witness?'

'Lasalle says she is fiercely anti-de Forge and has all her marbles.'

'What about my people?' Tweed asked quietly.

Navarre ran a hand through his dark hair. His lean face radiated dynamic energy and determination.

'My apologies. I should have told you first. Newman, Paula Grey, and the rest of your team are safe. They are returning to Arcachon. They seem to think something crucial is going to happen there.'

'It is,' Tweed agreed. 'And the air patrols over the Bay of Biscay?'

'Are flying non-stop.' Navarre turned to Kuhlmann. 'I should have told you that your agent, Stahl, also is safe. He has joined Newman's team.'

'Not such a brief signal,' Tweed observed.

'Ah! Lasalle has a shorthand method of communication.

He can convey much with few words. Have you news yet of *Siegfried*, Kuhlmann?'

The German smiled cynically at Tweed. 'My informant has reported he will soon have the locations. Soon.'

'And the saboteurs de Forge has infiltrated inside Paris?' Tweed queried. 'Were you able to obtain Balaclavas?'

'Yes,' Navarre replied. 'We now have mobile CRS in small groups stationed near likely targets. That was a clever idea of yours, Tweed. The Balaclavas.'

'I simply pinched the brilliant idea Lasalle had of using blue pinheads to distinguish between real and fake DST.'

'The whole key to victory against de Forge,' Navarre went on, staring at Kuhlmann, 'is the timing of two strikes. Ours against the Paris saboteurs and yours against this *Siegfried* underground organization in Germany.'

'The strike against *Siegfried* should take place first,' Tweed warned. 'Preferably by only a few hours. So the timing will be hair-raising.'

'I'm ready. And I agree,' said Kuhlmann.

'So now we can only wait for news of Lasalle's attack on the *Cercle Noir*,' Navarre stated. 'The precision timing – in the correct sequence – is, as you say, Tweed, hair-raising.'

They were speaking in the common language they all understood: English. Tweed rose from the table, glanced at the clock on the wall.

'I am not waiting for anything. I gather a chopper is standing by to fly me to Arcachon. I propose to leave immediately. Events at that port will decide whether we win or lose . . .'

General de Forge was pacing up and down behind his desk. Lamy watched him. It was unusual for the General to be so edgy. Normally he was cool as ice. He guessed that the communications from *Manteau* were getting on his nerves.

'I have been waiting for you, Lamy,' de Forge said grimly. 'I was actually standing at the entrance to this building, wondering where the hell you were when I saw you arrive at the main gate on a motorcycle.'

'I had another urgent message from Kalmar's woman. I had to ride like blazes to a call box in a remote village in the hills. The phone started ringing just as I arrived.'

'What did he want?'

'Money. Of course. He is going ahead with the assignment to eliminate Paula Grey as soon as he locates her. But he was very aggressive in his demand for payment.'

'I expect large funds to reach me tomorrow.'

De Forge left it at that. He was not ready yet to tell anyone else the *Steel Vulture* was berthing at Arcachon at eight in the morning the following day.

'Kalmar also said *Siegfried* is now in place all over Germany . . .'

'So I hope you stressed we will be ordering him to send the signal for action within hours?'

'As you instructed me to do when he next contacted me. He will be available for me to contact him through the cut-out number of the woman.'

'So,' de Forge mused, 'we shall then have the spectacle of Germany reeling under car bomb explosions. Then when the world's attention is fixed on Germany we act. It will be a model campaign, Lamy.'

'And all planned by yourself months ago. Even down to the Ku-Klux-Klan-style demonstrations, the Cross of Fire riots in major southern cities. Not only a model campaign, a unique campaign.'

'You would be flattering me for some reason . . .?'

General de Forge stopped speaking as he heard thudding

feet approaching outside. Someone hammered in a frenzy on the door. De Forge nodded and Lamy went to the door and opened it. The sergeant of the guard stood there, fearful and gasping for breath.

The incident had occurred minutes earlier. On the orders of de Forge himself the guard at the main entrance gate had been doubled. Six soldiers on foot patrolled outside the gates, each armed with an automatic weapon carried ready for action in his hands.

On the grass verge a tank had been stationed, the barrel of its long gun aimed up the road to Bordeaux. As zero-hour came close the General had felt it wise to protect GHQ more strongly.

It was an unusually bright afternoon for the time of the year. Across the road from the gates the ground had been cleared of all undergrowth. Trees had been chopped down and taken away with the remnants of their trunks. The flat countryside now spread away for a long distance and made it impossible for anyone to approach without being seen.

Here and there low hills studded with boulders rose up and broke the flatness of the plain running towards the horizon. Behind the hills the landscape was criss-crossed with a series of gullies, often with shallow streams running along their beds. It was a scene of serenity and peace.

The first *cr-a-a-ck* of a rifle shot shattered the silence. A soldier dropped his weapon, stared at his hand streaked with blood. Followed by another *cr-a-a-ck*. A second soldier lost his weapon, gazed down at his own blood-smeared knuckles. *Cr-a-a-ck!* A third weapon hit the road. The soldier fainted with shock.

*

After listening to the NCO's report of the incident de Forge walked out, made straight for the main gates despite the sergeant's warning. 'You could be a target, General . . .'

De Forge never lacked courage. Ignoring the protests, he marched up to the gates, waved a hand for them to be opened, walked out into the road.

He examined the hands of the three men who had been hit, including the soldier who had fainted and had, fortunately, regained consciousness and stood up before the General's arrival. De Forge turned to Lamy who had followed him.

'More marksmanship shooting. Like the bullet which missed me in the car by five centimetres.'

'I don't understand . . .'

De Forge led him aside so they could not be overheard. 'You are stupid. In all three cases these men's knuckles have been grazed – sufficient to make them drop their weapons. Quite remarkable. I wish we had men who could shoot like that . . .'

He stopped speaking, stared at the distant landscape, at the boulder-studded hills. De Forge was reputed to have sharper eyes than any man under his command. In the windless sky a rope of smoke rose from one of the boulder-strewn hilltops. De Forge pointed.

'That's where he fired from. Lamy, go and investigate.'

'Yes, General. I think I'll get an armoured carrier and take an escort.'

'That's right, Lamy.' De Forge grinned. 'Play it safe . . .'

An hour later de Forge was poring over a battle plan for his advance on Paris. He folded it quickly, put it in a safe when Lamy entered.

'So, you survived,' de Forge remarked, sitting in his chair.

'The fire was caused by someone who had collected

bracken and wood. We also explored the area. We found tracks of a motorcycle in one of the gullies. And I've found this.'

Lamy produced something from behind his back, laid it on the desk and sat down. It was a large rumpled piece of cloth. De Forge opened it, spread it across his desk. It was a grey cloak. He felt a tingle of apprehension as he gazed at it.

When the phone rang de Forge knew who it was before he picked it up. His expression was blank as he asked who was on the line.

'*Manteau* speaking, General. Recently I shot three of your guards. I aimed to scrape their hands, make them drop their weapons. I think I succeeded.'

'You did.'

'So, General,' the voice continued respectfully' 'it was a last reminder that I'm short of one million Swiss francs for the killing of Jean Burgoyne. I called Major Lamy to give him instructions and he slammed the phone down on me. I dislike bad manners. I dislike people who don't pay up. You have three hours to remedy the situation. I will call Lamy one more time. After that, you are the target.'

The connection was broken. De Forge replaced the received, relayed the gist of the conversation to Lamy.

'That was more than a crime, it was a blunder, as Talleyrand once said – slamming down the phone on him.'

'Kalmar is the man we deal with,' Lamy insisted obstinately. 'He is the man we paid three million francs to for organizing *Siegfried*.'

'Which, in retrospect, may have been a mistake. Handing that task to a man whose identity I have no idea of. I suggest that when *Manteau* calls again you pay him.'

'We haven't the money,' Lamy protested. 'Only enough to pay the troops. And pay-day is today. At this moment we can't afford not to pay them. So what do we do?'

'What do *you* do?' de Forge corrected him with a dreamy look as he stared over his subordinate's shoulder.

'Kalmar has always delivered,' Lamy said with renewed obstinacy.

'Whoever Kalmar may be.' De Forge gave Lamy a piercing stare. 'Have you heard yet from Captain Rey? The traitor, Berthier, should be dead by now. The graveyard cleaned out.'

'No news so far, General. But Rey may be careful about sending even coded signals concerning such a matter. He could be waiting until he returns here to report personally.'

'If you say so.' De Forge rose and his action indicated dismissal. 'And find the money for *Manteau*.'

'There is nowhere I can . . .'

Lamy stopped in mid-sentence. De Forge was leaving the room to inspect the troops.

Brand came out of the phone box on the windswept front at Arcachon. The weather had changed suddenly and the *bassin* was a heaving mass of turbulence as waves crashed on to the promenade. Brand threw away his cigarette.

Today he had dispensed with the seaman's outfit he had previously worn. Now he sported a blue blazer with gold buttons and knife-creased grey slacks under his trenchcoat. On his head he wore a naval cap rammed down over his forehead. He looked the typical British yachtsman abroad.

He hurried round a corner to where he had parked his motorcycle. He had been using it to search Arcachon with great thoroughness. Settling himself in the saddle, he tucked his trouser ends inside his leather boots, pressed the starter button, and rode off to continue his search.

The Alouette transporting Newman, Paula, Berthier and the other passengers, including their witness, Martine, descended to the almost deserted airfield near the *étang* south of Arcachon. The waters of the lake were seething as the wind increased in ferocity. The pilot showed great skill in landing them. Paula breathed a sigh of relief as the skids touched firm ground.

'We haven't seen a sign of de Forge's troops,' she said to Newman as the rotors slowed to a stop.

'That's because he's massing his forces to the north,' Newman replied grimly.

'It's wonderful to get away from the horrible Landes,' she commented.

The door was opened, cold air flooded inside the machine, the exit ladder was lowered. Approaching the airfield Newman had observed the Renault Espace parked at the edge of the perimeter. Once airborne above St Girons, he had remembered they'd need transport. The co-pilot had radioed his request to Lasalle who received the signal inside his own radio-equipped Alouette on the beach.

'What type of transport most desired?' he had radioed back.

'Preferably a Renault Espace. But any vehicle large enough to take us all.'

He had been surprised to see it *was* an Espace waiting for them. Lasalle must have made a great effort to provide him with what he needed. The driver stood outside the vehicle, waving a welcome as they landed.

Newman had joined Berthier at the open door when he stiffened. From their concealed positions a troop of soldiers was running towards the helicopter. One man aimed an automatic weapon at the pilot's cabin. Paula, gazing over Newman's shoulder, trembled.

'Oh, my God! Just when I thought we were safe. De Forge's men . . .'

Major Lamy drove into Arcachon in the middle of the afternoon. He drove the Citroën slowly along the front, stopping frequently while he scanned the ships at their moorings swaying under the impact of the large waves sweeping inside the anchorage.

He wore the same clothes he had dressed in when visiting Aldeburgh. A shabby Aquascutum raincoat with a well-worn buckle and underneath an English sports jacket and trousers. His suede shoes were English, as was his tie and his striped shirt. Lamy was a thorough man.

After exploring the front and the port area he drove out of Arcachon to where a road edged the *bassin*, close to the boathouse where Jean Burgoyne had been strangled. A fleet of camouflaged canvas trucks, large vehicles, was parked near a wide slipway leading across the marshes to the edge of the *bassin*. He stopped again. A moment later two soldiers carrying rifles appeared on either side of his car.

'You can proceed no further,' the soldier next to his window said in French.

'I am English,' Lamy drawled in that language. 'Sorry, but I do not understand French. *Anglais*.'

'No go. No go,' the soldier ordered in heavily accented English.

'No go where?' asked Lamy.

'Back.' The soldier waved a hand away from the boat-house. 'You go. *Zone militaire*.'

'I'm frightfully sorry.' Lamy smiled from under his deer-stalker hat. 'I go back? OK?'

'OK. *Maintenant!*'

Lamy reversed his car up the track he had driven down to the road. Waving to the soldier, who did not respond, he drove back to Arcachon. He began driving round the town slowly, patiently criss-crossing Arcachon, slowing even more when he passed a pedestrian.

On the bridge of the *Steel Vulture*, anchored off Dunwich, Dawlish was consulting Captain Santos. In his pocket he had the signal warning him of air patrols.

'Santos, I have reason to believe there will be French aircraft patrolling off the coast, searching for us. We must elude them.'

'Elude, Señor?'

'Make sure they don't find us, you damned fool.'

'In that case we do two things. We change course, sail further out to sea. And we sail through night, reaching Arcachon sometime after dawn, I think. Please wait.'

Santos sloped over with his seaman's roll to his chart-room. Dawlish followed impatiently. Surely he could calculate a thing like that in his thick head. Santos would not be hurried. He used a ruler to take measurements on his chart, grunted, tapped the chart with the ruler.

'Yes, but it has to be a rough estimate. We can probably arrive a few hours after dawn.'

'See that we do.'

Furious with the delay, Dawlish returned to his cabin to compose a further signal, to code it, to transmit it.

*

De Forge swore inwardly when he read the fresh signal from *Oiseau* handed to him by the unattractive Yvette. But his expression showed no reaction. He might have to delay sending the order to his commanders to open their sealed orders, might have to delay Austerlitz. Decide at the last moment he told himself. Looking at Yvette, he had an idea.

'That night you followed Jean Burgoyne to the boathouse. I recall you said you saw a man and a woman in the headlights of their car?'

'Yes, General. The man Robert Newman, the foreign correspondent. I recognized him at once from pictures I have seen in newspapers. And I had a good look at the woman.'

'Good enough so you'd recognize both again?'

'Absolutely.' Yvette spoke proudly. 'I have a perfect memory for faces. I would recognize both of them.'

'Then take your old car and drive round Arcachon. Keep on driving, looking for them. If you spot either – or both – call me over your radio telephone.' He smiled and she glowed. 'I am relying on you, Yvette.'

Standing at the open door of the Alouette, gazing down at the soldiers surrounding the machine, Lieutenant Berthier whispered to Newman.

'Leave this to me. I think I can handle them. With a bit of luck.'

Straightening his képi, his expression stern, Berthier descended the ladder slowly. The unit's commander, a sergeant, looked uncertain as he held his automatic weapon still pointed at the officer.

'You normally point your weapon at an officer?' Berthier asked quietly. 'If you do not lower the gun at once I'll have you in the guardhouse, prior to demotion to corporal, maybe private.'

'Sir, we have been instructed to guard this airfield. To escort anyone landing here to GHQ,' he added nervously.

Berthier decided on the big bluff. He doubted whether de Forge had spread the news that he was due to be shot by firing squad.

'You mentioned GHQ,' he went on in the same even tone. 'You have heard of Major Lamy?'

'Oh yes, sir. He is . . .'

'Chief of Intelligence,' Berthier completed for him. 'I am Lieutenant Berthier, Major Lamy's aide. I have with me several very important people I am accompanying to Arcachon. A secret mission for GHQ. And you are running counter to orders from the very top.'

'We were not told . . .'

'Of course not, cretin.' Berthier's tone was harsh. 'I have just told you this is a secret mission. Why do you think the Espace is stationed over there waiting for us? There are checkpoints on the way to Arcachon.'

He made the last statement sound as though it could be an assertion or a question.

'As you say, sir, there are checkpoints.'

'So your unit, which is sloppily dressed, can serve GHQ some useful purpose. First, have you motorcycles?'

'Yes, sir . . .'

'Then four of your unit can act as outriders to escort the Espace through the checkpoints. You will be one of them. Once we have passed through the last checkpoint you turn round and ride back here. Meantime, withdraw all your men out of sight. The passengers aboard are so important they must not be seen. Now, get moving. We are late . . .'

When all the soldiers had disappeared Berthier beckoned

to the Espace. It drove to the foot of the ladder and the driver looked scared. The passengers filed down the ladder, entered the vehicle. Berthier sat in front beside the driver, told him to make for Arcachon at high speed. The four outriders joined them as they left the airfield – two in front, two bringing up the rear.

'I wonder why I am sweating,' Berthier remarked.

Kalmar sat astride the saddle of his motorcycle parked by the kerb on a quiet street near the front in Arcachon. He wore a black leather jacket and a Martianlike helmet. Adjusting his goggles, he prepared to continue his search of the town.

He had been cruising the streets for an hour and had stopped for a rest. A farm tractor crawled along the front. At the same low speed a Renault Espace followed it, the driver obviously waiting for the moment to overtake.

Through his goggles Kalmar stared hard. As the Espace crawled along he saw a woman peer out of the window midway along the vehicle. Paula Grey. He left the kerb, turned on to the front, keeping well back. The tractor proceeded further along the front, the Espace turned into a side street.

Kalmar could hardly believe his luck. Once again his instinct had proved right: Paula Grey had returned. When the Espace turned again into another side street he overtook it, careful not to glance at the windows. In his wing mirror he saw it pull up. He slowed down.

Newman jumped out first, helped Paula down, ran to the entrance to the apartment, inserted the key Isabelle had loaned him, threw open the door into the lobby. The other passengers jumped out, filed inside quickly. Newman went back to the driver who had also jumped out. Locking the

Espace, the driver handed the keys to Newman, walked away towards the front.

Kalmar watched all this in his wing mirror, counted up five men, including Newman. One had bushy hair and another, to his surprise, appeared to wear the uniform of a French officer.

Newman closed the door as the others climbed to the first floor. To the side of the lobby the door to the ground-floor apartment was open a few inches. A woman with sharp eyes and a beaky nose closed it. She opened it a few minutes later when someone pressed the bell. A man in a black leather jacket, holding his helmet under his arm and a package in one hand, showed her a cutting from a newspaper of Newman. He explained he had to deliver the package to Mr Newman. Which floor?

'Floor One,' Beaky-Nose replied. 'Now she's got five men up there.' She smirked. 'If you see what I mean.'

Kalmar began to mount the stairs, pulling his helmet back over his head. The moment he heard her close the door he slipped quietly back to the lobby, the skeleton key he'd used to open the front door in his pocket.

He closed the outer door quietly. Again he couldn't credit his luck. He had located where his target was staying. Paula Grey wouldn't have much longer to live.

Chapter Fifty-Three

The telephone van pulled up outside the apartment block. Four men in boiler suits jumped out, walked to the front door. One of them had a bunch of keys in his hand. The third key fitted, he opened the door and went inside the lobby. A short heavily built man, he immediately spotted the apartment door open a few inches, the beady eyes and beaky nose of the woman staring at them. He went to the door.

'You want a good man, you old bag? Better still, a bad one?'

'How dare you . . .'

She slammed the door in his grinning face. They ran up the staircase and the second, slim man, knocked on the door of Isabelle's apartment. Newman opened it a crack, his right hand concealing his Smith & Wesson. He stared at the thin man in the boiler suit. Lasalle.

'Are you going to be like Old Nosy downstairs?' Lasalle joked in English.

Newman let the four men in. Lasalle introduced his companions as DST officers. They had blue pinheads stuck in their boiler suits. Lasalle smiled at the surprise on Paula's face.

'I know what you're wondering. I've dispatched Martine and Moshe Stein by air to Paris. Rey and the rest of the thugs called soldiers are also on their way there for interrogation. We landed on the island in the *bassin* where a boat was waiting to bring us ashore. The telephone van was waiting. Precision organization. This town is crawling with de Forge's troops.'

'Quite takes my breath away,' Paula said with a grin.

'Now, no time to waste. You have those papers taken off poor Jean Burgoyne's body?'

'Here in my bag. They appear to be notes of dispatches outlining a military campaign. There you are.'

'Thank you.' He turned to Stahl. 'Kuhlmann told me you have vital information. Otto is in Paris where I go now.'

Stahl produced a small notebook from somewhere under his jacket. He handed it to Lasalle.

'I disguised myself as a DST officer,' he said in English. 'I got inside GHQ, then inside de Forge's office. He had rushed out during some emergency – leaving on his desk the order of battle. For an attack on Paris. The notebook has the details.'

'Thank you. A remarkable feat. Kuhlmann – and others – will be relieved to lay their hands on this.' Lasalle looked at Berthier. 'I am glad to see you escaped from de Forge. You have done wonders for your country. We can talk properly when you return to Paris.' His voice became casual. 'Is Isabelle about?'

'In the kitchen,' Newman said. 'I'll bring her out if that's what you want?'

'Please. A remarkable woman, from what you've told me. Just tell her we are from the DST. But hurry!'

'First, this is Henri Bayle's notebook. Inside is a list of de Forge's units he identified in Bordeaux.' After handing over the notebook for which Francis Carey had died, Newman brought Isabelle out after she'd hastily whipped off her apron. She had been preparing a pile of sandwiches. She shook hands with Lasalle. He gazed at her with a quizzical expression Newman found odd. Then the DST team were gone.

Berthier began speaking as they all sat round the large table, devouring the sandwiches. Isabelle frequently stood up with the coffee pot to refill cups. Paula had tried to help her in the kitchen but she had refused politely. Newman had told the others they could trust Isabelle, had recalled how she had accidentally killed two of de Forge's fake DST men – and had come with him on his dangerous mission to bring out Stahl.

'I was working for Lasalle for many months,' Berthier told them, 'once I realized de Forge was a menace to France. As an Intelligence officer, working under Major Lamy, I pretended to de Forge that I was fooling Lasalle, *pretending* to work for the DST. If you follow my meaning. Lasalle provided me with misleading information to hand on to GHQ. He also gave me a listening device I could attach to the wall of my office, next door to Lamy's. I overheard many phone conversations. When I called Lasalle I used a public call box in different nearby villages.'

'So what went wrong?' Newman asked. 'They were going to shoot you on that beach.'

'Later on no one was allowed to leave barracks at GHQ. I made the mistake of using an internal phone to report something vital to Lasalle. That bastard de Forge had had all phones tapped. I was overheard. Captain Rey took delight in telling me that on the beach.'

'But what were you doing in Aldeburgh,' Paula asked him, 'posing as James Sanders, salesman of marine spares?'

'General de Forge sent me with a message to Lord Dawlish. That is another evil man.' He looked at Newman. 'His only ambition is to establish close relations with the

French High Command so he can sell arms to certain middle eastern countries. Especially those where arms sales are officially banned. That is my story.'

Newman looked at Paula who had left her seat to gaze out of the window. It was the second time she had done so.

'What are you nervous about, Paula?'

'Shortly after we arrived I looked out of this window. A man on a motorcycle was riding down the street. He wore a helmet and was hunched over the handlebars. I am sure I know that man. Something about his movements as he turned the corner. It will come back to me.'

'Get on with your meal. Then I want to drive round Arcachon. I have the feeling something important is about to happen here.'

General Charles de Forge stood erect in the turret of his tank. Before him on the vast parade ground at GHQ were drawn up line upon line of tanks of the Second Armoured Division. Their commanders and crews stood at ease beside their leviathans, gazing at the General as he began his hypnotic speech.

'Soldiers of France! Zero hour is close! It is your duty to save the Republic from the corrupt politicians in Paris. Mob rule is rampant in Toulon, in Marseilles, in Toulouse, in Bordeaux itself, in Lyons, in half a dozen other cities. How long before Paris collapses into chaos?

'Soldiers! Who is behind this anarchy? There are three and a half million Arabs in France. Arabs! They have raped our French women, have wrecked shops, have set fire to French homes. The Jews are also rising – seeing their chance to take control. Algerians! Go home to where you came from! The slums of Africa, riddled with disease they bring here.

'Soldiers, *you* will be the saviours of France! Hordes of refugees threaten to overwhelm Europe from the East. France must resume its rightful role. Only France has the will to stem this tide of aliens. Are you ready?'

A storm of cheering broke out. A thunderous shouting of men whipped to hysteria.

'De Forge to Paris! To Paris! De Forge to the Elysée!'

As the roar eventually began to die down a captain turned to a lieutenant.

'What a great orator. He makes Dubois look like some amateur . . .'

De Forge waved, acknowledged the acclamation. Jumping from his tank he marched swiftly along the front line, shaking the hands of officers, of private soldiers. They were ready.

Chapter Fifty-Four

Tweed had arrived in Arcachon. It was now December.

The Alouette which had brought him from Paris was descending over the triangular-shaped *bassin* – prior to landing on the beach at the tip of the Île aux Oiseaux, the island north of Arcachon. A second Alouette was stationary on the sand. The flight had been timed for low tide. Tweed spoke to the pilot through his headset microphone.

'Could you please cruise over the front at a low altitude. I want to get my bearings.'

'What's the idea?' asked Fred Hamilton, sitting next to him.

Back at Park Crescent Howard had insisted that Hamilton should accompany Tweed as bodyguard. Reluctantly, Tweed had agreed.

The Alouette lost more height, changed course. It flew south almost to Cap-Ferret, located on the peninsula which blocked off the full fury of the Atlantic. A short distance further south was the narrow entrance to the *bassin* from the ocean – the entrance the *Steel Vulture* would have to pass through before berthing at the port.

'The idea,' Tweed said as the machine began to approach the front, 'is to see if I can recognize anyone.'

He had lifted a powerful pair of field-glasses and scanned the front, the boats moored offshore. He adjusted the focus on a man swabbing down the deck of a cabin cruiser. Victor Rosewater. Always present at the new trouble spot.

Near the port he frowned, focused afresh. A man wearing a naval cap was stepping ashore from a vessel, walking towards a motorcycle. Dawlish's right-hand man. Brand. Tweed had rather expected he would be in the area. His mouth tightened as he watched Brand exchange the naval cap for a yellow helmet, start up his machine, riding away from the shore into the town. He gave the pilot a fresh order.

'Please follow that motorcycle – without him realizing what we're doing if you can. Even if it means gaining some altitude.'

The Alouette climbed a little higher. The pilot showed great skill keeping his target in sight from a distance. Using his field-glasses, Tweed was struck by the intricate network of streets making up the town.

Brand was threading his way in and out of the maze. He seemed to have no particular destination. Then it dawned on Tweed the rider was searching the town. Looking for what? A few minutes later he saw the second motorcyclist.

He was riding down a street in a different part of the town from Brand. Tweed adjusted the focus as the rider turned into an alley, stopped, swung his machine round. From the way he took off his helmet, stretched his neck, Tweed guessed he was taking a breather.

In a town like Arcachon a motorcycle was a good way to get about but it seemed odd to spot two in such a short space of time. Tweed adjusted the focus while the rider was stretching aching muscles. A familiar face jumped into his lenses, a face Tweed recognized from one of the photos Lasalle had shown him. The face of Major Lamy.

Receiving a fresh instruction from Tweed, the pilot followed a new course along the southern and eastern shores of the *bassin*. They had left the town behind, marshes were stretching down to the water's edge, when Tweed saw military checkpoints on the roads inland. De Forge had the port sewn up tight.

He pressed the glasses close to his eyes as he saw the oblong of a slipway slanting down from firm ground into the water. Behind the slipway a fleet of camouflaged trucks. He frowned, swept the whole area. It had manned checkpoints guarding every approach road.

Tweed nodded to himself, lowered his glasses, ordered the pilot to land on the island immediately.

'You've seen something, sir?' Hamilton enquired.

'Yes. I have been surveying the coming battlefield.'

A boat was being drawn up on the beach as Tweed descended the ladder agilely from his Alouette. He was in a hurry. A slim man in a telephone company's boiler suit came towards him.

'Welcome to the Île aux Oiseaux,' said Lasalle.

Tweed came out immediately with what was on his mind while they shook hands. He described tersely the slipway across the marshes, the waiting fleet of army trucks, the checkpoints.

'Hamilton, my aide here,' he went on, 'visited Dunwich before he joined me at Heathrow *en route* to Paris. It was misty, he couldn't even see the *Steel Vulture*. I'm convinced that vessel – which moves at high speed – will be arriving here to deliver weapons to de Forge. Within hours. Maybe in the middle of the night. Or at dawn.'

'Not in the middle of the night,' Lasalle objected. 'It is a difficult passage into the *bassin*. The skipper will need daylight. It is a problem – the whole area is infested with his troops.'

'Then the *Steel Vulture* must never land. Contact Navarre. He has the authority . . .'

'To do what?'

'To issue a warning that mines from the Second World War are floating off Arcachon. No vessel must approach within ten miles.'

'That will stop Dawlish?'

'Having met him, I doubt it. He'll think it's a bluff. So get aircraft to drop real sea mines. I hear there is a type which has a beeper signal – makes them easy to locate, pick up afterwards.'

'That is so. You are ruthless,' Lasalle commented with a wry smile.

'So is General de Forge. I know the enemy now. I wish I could see him, face to face.'

'It might be arranged, with a safe conduct. But I would have to be present.'

'Then arrange it. I see you have another boat concealed in the undergrowth. Can I use it to visit Arcachon?'

'You have sharp eyes.' Lasalle smiled again. 'It is supposed to be concealed. But it cannot be seen from the air . . .'

'Where are Paula, Newman, and the others?' Tweed hurried on.

Lasalle explained that they'd returned from the Landes, their experience there, that they had moved from the Atlantique to Isabelle Thomas's apartment. Tweed shook his head.

'That so-called safe house could be traced. They simply must move at once. But where to?'

'I can help there,' Lasalle assured him. 'I have hired a large cabin cruiser, *L'Orage V* . . .'

'"The Storm". Appropriate for what is coming,' Tweed commented.

'It is berthed at the edge of the *bassin* away from other craft.' As he spoke Lasalle took out a map, marking a position with a cross. 'It is the HQ of my DST team operating in the town. Also well away from any checkpoint. There would be plenty of room for all of you.'

'Then get me ashore fast.'

Newman had just arrived back at Isabelle's apartment. He had driven the Espace round Arcachon, had decided he was taking too many chances. As soon as he came near the outskirts he saw a checkpoint manned with troops. He parked the Espace further up the quiet side street. They had stayed with one vehicle too long.

Tweed arrived a few minutes later, riding a bicycle provided by Lasalle from several stored beneath the undergrowth on the island. He had also marked Isabelle's address on the map.

'A man on a cycle is never noticed,' he had remarked.

Tweed had to press the bell. After a minute a large woman with a beaky nose and inquisitive eyes opened the door.

'I have to visit someone on the first floor,' he explained in French.

'The stamina of that girl,' the woman sneered. 'She has five men up there already. I expect she'll cope with you.'

'Would you repeat that comment?' Tweed demanded.

She wilted under his icy stare. Contemptuously, he pushed past her ample form into the lobby, ran up the stairs. Newman opened the door to him, unable to hide his surprise.

'All of you have to get out of here,' Tweed announced without ceremony as he entered the room. 'Immediately!'

He took in Butler, Nield, Berthier, Stahl, and Paula with a quick glance. His gaze rested longer on Isabelle, introduced to him without a name as a friend by Newman.

'Just why do we have to leave so quickly?' she demanded, her chin tilted, her eyes studying him.

'Because the town has practically been taken over by de Forge. I can give you five minutes to clear up, collect some things. Less would be better.'

'We have been safe so far,' she persisted and he realized she was challenging him, which he found intriguing. 'Kalmar, a top professional assassin, is in Arcachon. He strangled a girl in England. He has since strangled another woman not three miles from here. He seems to specialize in strangling attractive women. I think you're on his list. So is Paula. Pack your things. Quickly . . .'

L'Orage V was a very large cabin cruiser. It was moored part way up a creek outside Arcachon, shielded from the mainland by a copse of pine trees. Leaving the Espace, which Newman had parked inside the copse, Tweed insisted on exploring the apparently deserted vessel alone.

Walking gingerly along the gangplank, he stepped on to the deck. The *bassin* was still calm, its surface hardly ruffled by wavelets, but approaching from the ocean was an army of low black clouds.

The *Orage* had the wheelhouse for'ard, a companionway leading down to a saloon. Tweed's first warning that someone was aboard was as he stepped into the large saloon equipped with a long table. A hard object like the barrel of a gun was rammed into his spine. He stood quite still.

'Pierre?' he enquired.

'Who the devil are you?' a harsh voice rapped back.

Tweed held up the folded letter of introduction Lasalle

had given him. A hand snatched it over his shoulder. The gun stayed pressed into his spine. Then the invisible man spoke in French again.

'Stand quite still while I check you.'

'Check away. I rarely carry a weapon,' Tweed said in French.

A hand expertly patted him in all the right places. He felt the gun leave his back, turned round cautiously. A six foot tall, well-built man in his thirties faced him. Fair-haired, with humorous eyes, he wore a trenchcoat with a blue pinhead in the lapel.

'I was expecting you,' he greeted Tweed. 'Can't be too careful. De Forge's men are everywhere. I have to leave now you've got here. A job to do. How many of you in the Espace?'

'Five men and two women, excluding myself.'

'You should be all right. There are eight decent bunk beds in the foc'sle. A well-equipped galley, a ton of food, and plenty to drink.'

'Before you go, could I have a glass of water?'

Tweed had a horror of ships and the sea. Everything was always moving unpredictably. Even inside the creek he didn't trust the cruiser: the *bassin* was tidal. Before bringing the others aboard he swallowed a Dramamine with some water. Better be safe than sorry . . .

Five minutes later Pierre had gone, after telling Tweed he had sole use of the vessel. Tweed had hustled his team aboard with their kit and they were settled in. Paula offered Isabelle the lower bunk at the end of the sleeping quarters but Isabelle insisted she would take the upper one. They hurried into the galley, together checked the food supplies, the cooking arrangements. Newman noticed how well they were getting on together. Tweed then summoned them into the saloon, asking Nield to keep guard on deck and seating

561

the others at the long table. He sat at the head, his expression grim.

'There are rules. One, no one leaves this vessel without my permission. Two, I will establish a guard roster . . .'

'Which will include us.'

Isabelle and Paula had spoken together. Tweed glared.

'I'll decide that later. Lasalle will be coming to take me somewhere just before dusk. Newman will come with me. In our absence Egon Stahl will be in charge. Three, we take meals at regular hours . . .'

'We shall want to know the times in advance,' Isabelle said firmly.

'Well in advance if we're cooking,' Paula agreed.

'Why,' Newman asked, 'have you assembled us all together here?'

'Because the time has come for me to have complete control. And Isabelle's apartment had been used long enough.'

'Those are the only reasons?' enquired Stahl.

It was a shrewd question. Tweed had swiftly summed up the German as capable and resourceful. He must be to have survived in Bordeaux so long. Before Tweed could answer Newman put a question which had been intriguing him to Stahl.

'How on earth did you penetrate de Forge's GHQ?'

'Planning.' Stahl gave his infectious smile. 'I travelled inside the van which delivers daily bread to the officers. Hid inside the back, unknown to the driver. Locating where he loaded up took some research, but forget that. While he was delivering I left the van. Earlier in Bordeaux I picked the pocket of a fake DST officer who was checking my papers. I took his identity card.'

'Where did you learn to pick pockets?' Paula asked.

'Oh, that's how I started out in life.'

It took Paula a moment to realize he was joking. Stahl patted her hand, went on.

'I was stopped by a sergeant behind a cabin. I showed him the DST card, knocked him out, tied him up with rope, hid him in a large rubbish bin, which seemed appropriate. Then I waited a long time near General Charles de Forge's office. When he rushed out I marched inside. I told you the rest.'

'Interesting,' said Tweed.

'And you haven't answered my question,' Stahl reminded him. 'The other reason why you brought us all here?'

Tweed paused. He looked all round the table. He wanted his reply to have the desired effect: to make them more alert.

'Because when I was flying over Arcachon in the Alouette which brought me from Paris I saw Kalmar.'

Chapter Fifty-Five

Lasalle arrived in a large powerboat half an hour before dusk. The craft edged its way up the creek, filling with the incoming tide, bumped against the hull of *L'Orage V*. There were already several DST men aboard, armed with automatic weapons. Lasalle was impatient.

'Join us quickly,' he called up to Tweed. 'We are on a tight time schedule. Berthier, you come too . . .'

'Newman is coming as well,' Tweed told him.

The powerboat turned round beneath the hull of the cabin cruiser, raced out of the creek. Paula was standing on deck, anxiously watching the wake of the craft heading for the Île aux Oiseaux. Butler took her by the arm.

'Below decks. Now. You're a target out here.'

'I sense it's a dangerous mission they're going on.'

'Probably.' Butler followed her down the companionway. 'But surely you always realized when it came to a climax it would be just that. Dangerous . . .'

Thanking heaven that he'd taken Dramamine, Tweed hung on to the rail as the powerboat whipped over the waves which were now rolling in. A storm was imminent.

Reaching the island, Lasalle bundled them aboard a waiting Alouette. It took off almost before they had time to fasten their seat belts, put on their headsets. The machine headed east – inland and away from Arcachon.

'Is this when I meet de Forge?' Tweed asked.

'That's part of the idea,' Lasalle replied. 'In fact you're going to meet the whole of the *Cercle Noir* – now assembled for its final meeting at the Villa Forban.'

'How do you know that?'

'Berthier informed me.'

'From a phone inside GHQ?' Tweed queried.

'No. He phoned from a call box in a small village. That last call which nearly cost him his life told me de Forge was massing his Second Armoured Division at GHQ. This raid will be a complete surprise. We grab the lot . . .'

As they flew at top speed further inland Tweed, peering out of the window, saw other Alouettes rising up out of small clearings in woods, from inside huge barns. Beyond his window a whole fleet of Alouettes was flying at the same height. Another small armada could be seen through a window on the other side.

'Who is aboard those machines?' Tweed asked.

'Heavily armed, reliable units of the CRS. De Forge will be thinking any CRS are still stationed in the trucks at the Bordeaux Prefecture. In fact they were all flown down in Alouettes which made the trip one by one, landing in preselected sites chosen by a DST deputy who knows the area. I think I can see the lights of the Villa Forban.'

Dusk, a smoky grey dusk, had descended. The Alouettes were circling. Ahead Tweed could see a walled estate, a winding drive leading to a large villa with lights on. As they drew closer he saw limousines drawn up in front of the villa. Where poor Jean Burgoyne had spied.

The swoop from the sky had been well organized. Tweed watched large numbers of the choppers moving ahead of their machine, landing on all sides of the estate. The *Cercle Noir* was surrounded.

*

'No one can escape this cordon,' Newman remarked.

'And they've neutralized the guard at the gate,' Tweed pointed out.

As their machine flew below tree-top height he had seen guards – uniformed soldiers – holding up their hands at the entrance. An Alouette equipped with a swivel-mounted machine-gun had touched down on the grass verge opposite the closed gates.

Lasalle's Alouette landed in front of the villa next to the parked limousines. Pistol in one hand, keys in the other, he was the first out of the machine, followed by several CRS men in leather jackets who had sat at the rear of the chopper. Tweed, Newman, and Berthier jumped out and followed him to the door. Lasalle inserted and turned each key, nodded to the CRS.

'Where did he get those keys?' Tweed whispered.

'I gave him a bunch of keys I found in Jean Burgoyne's handbag,' Newman told him. 'Two were engraved with the Cross of Lorraine – like the emblem on the door . . .'

Lasalle had rushed inside the large hall. He seemed to know just where to go. Aiming his pistol he threw open a door to the left. Inside everything was confusion.

Tweed recognized General Masson, Chief of the Army Staff, hastily stuffing papers into a briefcase. General Lapointe, commander of the *force de frappe*, standing erect by a chair. Louis Janin, Minister of Defence, ashen-faced, sat petrified at the long table. Dubois, dressed again in a rumpled black suit, soiled white tie, shaggy hair awry, looked desperate.

But what attracted Tweed's attention was the chair at the head of the table, pushed back. And no sign of General Charles de Forge. Lasalle, standing at the near end of the table as CRS men crowded in, weapons aimed, addressed Masson.

'Where is de Forge?'

'General Charles de Forge, do you mean?'

Masson's manner was cold, brusque. He stared at Lasalle with undisguised contempt.

'I repeat, where is de Forge?' Lasalle snapped. 'You are all under arrest. The charge? High treason. And that applies to Charles de Forge – who was sitting in that chair. Where is he?'

'The General has never been here. Who are you? Address me as General . . .'

'Lasalle, Chief of the Paris DST . . .'

'You won't hold that job much longer!' Masson stormed. 'I will personally see you are thrown into the street . . .'

'You are a liar. Come with me this instant. All of you,' Lasalle ordered.

He went to a side door halfway along the room, opened it, walked into the next room which was furnished like a study with a large desk. Newman and Berthier watched as two CRS men had to grab Masson by the arms. He raged as they frog-marched him into the study.

General Lapointe, thin and grave-faced, needed no encouragement to do as he was told. With a certain dignity he moved into the study: he struck Newman as the most intelligent man in the *Cercle*. Dubois also offered no resistance. He pulled at his untidy moustache as he slouched after Masson with dropping shoulders. Lasalle was seated behind the desk, had used a key to open a deep bottom drawer. Newman glanced inside: it held a modern tape recorder. Lasalle had pressed the rewind button and the reels were spinning. The members of the *Cercle* were lined up against the wall as he pressed the play button, sat back, listened.

'Gentlemen, I will not waste words. Tomorrow we take Paris. I shall send the Austerlitz signal to destabilize the capital early in the morning . . .'

De Forge's crisp commanding voice. Unmistakably.

'Are you quite certain Austerlitz will work? Only that gives us the excuse that you are needed to restore order.'

Masson's voice, showing a trace of nervousness.

'Masson, you really must trust me. There can be only one commander of an operation. I, General de Forge, am that commander.'

Masson's normally ruddy face had lost colour. He stood like a frozen statue as the tape continued to relay the conversation.

'Of course we all accept you as commander of the operation, General. Soon I shall be addressing you as President. But how soon can we remove Navarre so I can take over his position?'

The oily voice of Dubois. His eyes shifted uncertainly from the CRS man on his left to the one on his right. Lasalle stopped the tape, stared at the three men.

'Do I have to play any more? I said high treason, Masson. You have only one alternative, not open to the others . . .'

While he had played the tape Newman had moved to the other side of the room, walled with glass-fronted bookcases. He noticed one case where the books inside had toppled. He ran his fingers down the hinges of the glass-fronted door. As he pressed one hinge there was a click. The edge of the bookcase slid an inch or so open all the way to the floor like a door. He hauled at it and the concealed door opened, exposing a flight of stone steps.

The Smith & Wesson was in his hand as he ran down the steps and down a long corridor under the house. He was stopped by a steel slab he couldn't shift. He ran back and Lasalle turned in his chair.

'De Forge got away through an escape tunnel,' Newman

reported. 'I've no doubt it comes out well beyond the walls round the estate. Probably had a car waiting for him.'

'Pity. Our troubles are not over.' Lasalle gave the order to one of the CRS men. 'Handcuff the prisoners, escort them to separate helicopters. They will be flown to Paris.'

'This is outrageous,' Dubois protested.

General Lapointe made no protest. He simply extended both hands, wrists close together. Lasalle shook his head as the DST man next to Lapointe produced handcuffs.

'No cuffs for General Lapointe. Simply escort him.'

Tweed had kept quiet up to now. This was, after all, Lasalle's affair, but he was curious about Lapointe. He asked his question as Masson was shown into another room and Dubois was taken away.

'General, your voice is on that tape?'

'Yes.' Lapointe smiled drily. 'You'll find you have the evidence you need on me.'

'You supported de Forge's plan?' Tweed pressed.

'He never told us his battle plan. He is a very careful man.' He paused. 'Oh, well, it is on the tape. I urged him to do nothing rash, to go and see Navarre to get his view. I still take full responsibility for my actions. Good evening, gentlemen . . .'

'Now for Masson,' Lasalle decided, jumping up.

'Before that how did you know about this tape recorder?' Tweed asked. 'You installed it yourself?'

'It was Jean Burgoyne's idea. A wire runs from the recorder under the carpet here.' Lasalle went to the wall adjoining the room where the *Cercle Noir* had always met. He pulled aside an escritoire. 'One of my technicians drilled a hole in the wall. A small powerful microphone was inserted – voice-activated. It picks up everything said in there. Jean always knew when they'd be meeting – de Forge would invent an excuse for her not to be here during the evening. She put on a fresh tape. Later she sent the tapes to me. One reason why I knew so much. Bless her. I came here earlier today with a new tape. Now for Masson . . .'

They entered the living room where Masson sat gazing at the wall. Lasalle drew up a chair, facing the general.

'You have two options. Proposed by Navarre. You will be guarded night and day in Paris – a rumour will be spread that *Manteau* has said he is going to kill you. You keep your present post until this problem is settled. You make only public statements sanctioned by Navarre. Later you retire – for reasons of ill health – on a full pension.'

Lasalle paused. He stared at Masson who gazed back with an icy expression.

'The other option,' Lasalle continued, 'is public disgrace, a court martial, maybe even a prison sentence.'

'I will co-operate,' Masson said immediately.

There was a strange gleam in his eyes. Lasalle smiled to himself: Masson had fallen for it. He was banking on de Forge winning. When Masson had been escorted from the room Lasalle turned to Tweed and Newman.

'Janin will be offered the same terms. He will accept. We are gambling. Nothing is solved. A great pity de Forge was able to escape. He will move fast. The final crisis is imminent. You had better fly back with me to Paris. Navarre has agreed to the laying of old mines.'

'Not yet,' said Tweed. 'We are staying in Arcachon for the moment. I want to see what Dawlish does. And I'd say now is the time for Kuhlmann to round up *Siegfried* – before they break loose.'

Kuhlmann's dragnet – spread out all over Germany – struck at 1 a.m. the following morning. Police units stormed into addresses in Hamburg, Frankfurt, Munich, and many other cities. The addresses supplied by Helmut Schneider, Rosewater's informant.

They surprised the *Siegfried* organization everywhere. By 3 a.m. in Paris Kuhlmann had received reports of several hundred pounds of Semtex, bombs with timer devices, large numbers of rocket launchers, and an armoury of weapons being seized.

'Enough to start a small war,' he remarked to Lasalle who had returned to Paris.

'And the men who were going to use this equipment?'

'Mostly from Alsace. Presumably because they can speak some German down there. Even members of a crank movement which wanted Alsace taken over by Germany. The media has no idea of what happened. A model operation.'

'Austerlitz in Paris will be different,' Lasalle commented grimly.

The *Steel Vulture* had sailed from Dunwich as soon as it was dark. Instead of riding the rollers in Biscay the twin hulls sliced through the waves like a knife through butter.

Dawlish was on the bridge as Santos – for the umpteenth time – checked the sophisticated radar himself. No sign of any vessel ahead. Earlier he had briefly registered aircraft flying out from the French coast but they had turned away, mere blips a long way off.

The *Vulture*, on Dawlish's direct orders, was completing its great sweep across the Atlantic without navigation lights. Santos had expressed reservations.

'I have never sailed without them before.'

'So it's time you learned to live dangerously,' Dawlish had snapped. 'We have radar. Best in the world.'

'No radar is foolproof . . .'

'Then make sure no fool is using it. Check yourself. That
is what a skipper is for. No more crap. That is, if you want
that promised bonus . . .'

Santos had shrugged. And he did want that large tax-free
bonus paid in cash. Now they were approaching Arcachon
and the first blood-red streaks of dawn were splashed across
the eastern sky. Santos stood alongside Dawlish on the
bridge when the wireless operator dashed up the companionway. He looked scared out of his wits, was waving a
piece of paper.

'Captain! I've just received this signal from the shore.
There are old wartime mines which have appeared! We are
ordered to turn round immediately before it is too late.'

'My God . . .!' began Santos.

'Bluff,' Dawlish barked. 'Sheer bluff. Mines, my foot. It's
a Navarre trick. Maintain your present course . . .'

'But if they are right . . .' Santos began again.

'I said *maintain your present course*, damn you!'

Aboard *L'Orage V* the tall DST officer they had met when
they arrived on the vessel stood crouched over a powerful
transceiver. Crowded behind him were Tweed, Newman,
Paula and the others. The DST man looked at Tweed.

'They've sent the warning signal repeatedly. No reply.'

'And there won't be,' Tweed replied. 'I know Dawlish.
He will try to bring in the *Vulture*. He'll think it's just a
trick. Nothing gets in the way of Dawlish. I'm going to take
a look . . .'

With binoculars looped round his neck he ran up the
companionway. On deck he climbed to the roof of the
wheelhouse, then mounted the ladder alongside the radar
mast. Below, Paula watched anxiously: Tweed had been
known to suffer from vertigo.

Perched at the top of the mast, Tweed could see beyond the entrance to the *bassin* the *Vulture* cutting through the waves with its twin hulls. He kept the night glasses pressed to his eyes. It really was an amazing vessel. Could it, with the luck the wicked so often possessed, dodge the mines and make its owner's landfall?

Dawlish walked to the port side of the bridge. He stared down. A metal sphere with protruding prongs was drifting a yard or so away from the hull. He left the bridge, ran to the small aircraft aft of the bridge where a pilot was always at the controls.

Climbing the ladder to the inside of the machine, he shouted his order. At the same time he pressed the button which automatically retracted the ladder, slammed the door shut.

'Lift off! Get this bloody toy in the air before we are blown to pieces. Course? I'll tell you later. Get her up now, for Christ's sake!'

Watching through his glasses, Tweed saw the *Vulture* slowing down prior to entering the *bassin*. He pursed his lips. It looked as though Dawlish was going to make it. Nerve gas in the hands of a man like de Forge. The mere threat would clear the way straight into Paris.

Then he saw the small aircraft appear, jumping clear off the deck, climbing vertically, and he guessed Dawlish was escaping. One hundred feet up, the machine hovered above the vessel below, ready to fly away.

Seconds later the *Vulture* detonated the mine. There was a dull thudding *b-o-o-m*! which echoed round the *bassin*. An immense geyser of water rocketed upwards to a great

COLIN FORBES

height, carrying with it huge chunks of metal debris. It
enveloped the hovering aircraft, which briefly vanished in
the dense spray cloud. The geyser sank back. The aircraft
sank with the geyser, toppling with a slow windmilling
motion. Below, one of the twin hulls split off, skidding
across the ocean surface. The other hull went down like a
high-speed elevator. As the tumbling aircraft hit the deck
the vessel fragmented. Massive pieces of the hull and bridge
were hurled out to sea. There was an ear-splitting dull roar
as the relics of the *Vulture* dived beneath the waves. The
missiles had exploded. A new eruption of water soared
upwards, a gigantic fountain infested with the wreckage of
what had been one of the most advanced vessels in the
world. Tweed consoled himself with the knowledge that
nerve gas would swiftly disperse in the ocean, would
become harmless. He braced himself and the shockwave
shook the mast. Then silence. He climbed down, looked at
his team.

'Dawlish is no more. The weapon delivery is destroyed. I
don't think for a minute this will stop de Forge.'

Chapter Fifty-Six

Marler had received his fresh instructions before Tweed had left Paris for Arcachon. For the first time he was not travelling Air Inter. He had waited for hours in the cabin of an Alouette parked on a small airfield outside Paris.

In the seat beside him rested his large holdall containing his Armalite rifle and sniperscope. He ate the meals brought to him by a girl who said little. Between meals he dozed quite a lot of the time. But when the pilot came to shake him awake he was instantly alert.

'News?' he asked abruptly.

'They're on the move. All hell has broken out in the streets of Paris. We're flying south now . . .'

All hell had broken loose in the streets of Paris. But the hell was being endured by the saboteurs infiltrated into the city and activated by Austerlitz.

A group wearing Balaclavas threw open the rear doors of a furniture van parked close to the main telephone exchange and spilled out gripping automatic weapons. As they approached the entrance other men clad in Balaclavas swarmed round them carrying rifles.

The leader of the attackers, bent on capturing the communications centre, was confused. Were these reinforcements he hadn't been told about? He was making up his mind when a rifle butt descended on the back of his head and he slumped to the ground.

With no leader, his troops were even more confused. The next surprise was when tear gas shells burst at their feet. None of the saboteurs noticed that the newcomers in Balaclavas wore a thin green band on their right arms.

The battle for the exchange was brief and rough. The CRS paramilitary troops – able to distinguish friend from foe by the green armbands – rounded up the Austerlitz attackers. They were bundled into waiting Berliet trucks hidden in side streets. Many of the defeated were carried aboard unconscious. The whole counter operation lasted exactly five minutes.

Similar scenes were taking place all over Paris. Lasalle had skilfully predicted the likely targets, had distributed CRS men disguised in Balaclavas close to every key objective.

The main assault was mounted against the Ministry of the Interior. A hundred Austerlitz troops surged out of various stolen tradesmen's vehicles. To their surprise and delight the gates were not locked leading into the courtyard from the Place Beauveau. Brushing aside the guards, they stormed into the courtyard, heading for the inside of the ministry. General de Forge had pinpointed this as the prime objective – on the advice of his wife, Josette, who had since disappeared.

They stopped suddenly as large forces of other men in Balaclavas appeared in front of them. Behind them the gates were closed and they were trapped. Before they could decide what was happening the CRS in Balaclavas were on them, wielding rifle butts, rubber truncheons, cracking skulls, felling the invaders. The CRS are not noted for their gentlemanly behaviour. Any man without a green armband was a target.

Navarre watched the violent mêlée from the window of

his office on the first floor. Again the vanquished attackers were carried, thrown into a fleet of Berliet trucks which edged their way through the opened gates.

An hour later the CRS unit commanders from all over the city had reported they'd done the job. Navarre acted immediately. Special CRS units had kept TV vans and reporters well away from the onslaughts. Navarre appeared on television. He briefly reported that 'terrorists' had been detained, that the city was now quiet.

General Charles de Forge was a resolute commander. When he received the call from Major Lamy in Arcachon he listened.

'It is a complete disaster, General!' Lamy sounded shaken. 'The *Steel Vulture* was almost inside the *bassin* when it blew up – exploded into the sky. It was reported that wartime mines had been seen floating offshore. I thought it was bluff. The extra weapons you were waiting for will never reach us . . .'

'Thank you, Lamy. Report back to GHQ.'

De Forge put down the phone. He stood up to address the officer awaiting instructions.

'We move now. Operation Marengo is launched. I intend to travel in the lead tank of an Armoured Division. I ordered the other commanders to open their sealed orders one hour ago. Victory will be ours – before the day is out . . .'

Aboard *L'Orage V* Tweed read the statement de Forge had issued the night before – timed to catch the next day's edition of *Le Monde*.

Exercise Marengo is being extended to Central France. The exercise will move no further north than Chateauroux. The population is warned to keep clear of where the exercise is taking place. Under certain conditions live ammunition may be used.

'What does it mean?' Paula asked.

Tweed looked out of the porthole. It was mid-afternoon and the cabin cruiser was swaying like a ballet dancer. He had taken another Dramamine.

'Note the use of the word "exercise",' he pointed out. 'Repeated twice. An attempt to confuse Navarre. And from Chateauroux the N20 runs due north to Paris. As I predicted that will be his route. Not a devious flanking movement to the west as they thought in Paris.'

'I am sure you are right,' said Berthier. 'He'll move at top speed through the night. When Paris wakes up de Forge's forces will be on the Champs-Elysées. He has won.'

'What made you predict his route up the N20?' Paula asked.

Tweed smiled drily. 'When I was visiting Josette in the Passy house I noticed a bust of Napoleon. One of de Forge's heroes. He'll have studied his campaigns. When Napleon was advancing against Wellington he drove his army at top speed direct for Brussels, surprising Wellington when his enemy reached Quatre Bras. Paris is de Forge's Brussels – the direct thrust by the shortest route.'

'And nothing to stand in his way,' Newman said grimly.

'Not a lot,' Tweed agreed. He looked at the DST officer in charge of the vessel. 'I think we should all return to Paris. There is an Alouette waiting for us on the island? Good . . .'

He paused as they heard someone crossing the gang-plank. Newman moved to the side of the bottom of the companionway, the Smith & Wesson in his hand. Footsteps clumped noisily down the wooden steps. Victor Rosewater stopped at the bottom, smiled at Paula and the others.

'I thought you'd be somewhere in Arcachon. Well, it's the big goodbye to Lord Dane Dawlish.'

'We're all drenched in tears,' said Newman.

Rosewater looked at Tweed. 'I thought you should know Major Lamy is still in Arcachon. Why isn't he with de Forge?' He glanced at Paula. 'Some unfinished business in Arcachon?'

Chapter Fifty-Seven

'I also saw Brand in a bar in Arcachon late this morning,'
Rosewater told Tweed.

'Brand. I've been wondering about him.'

Tweed said nothing more as he peered down out of the
window of the airborne Alouette. Aboard the machine were
Isabelle and Paula, chatting to each other, Stahl, Newman,
Butler, Nield, and Berthier. All on their way home via Paris.

Tweed, in a hurry, had been irked by the long delay on
the island. Some mechanical defect in the Alouette's engine
which had to be remedied. It was still daylight, but only
just, when they caught up with the Third Army beyond
Chateauroux.

Tweed asked the pilot to fly lower. First there were truck-
loads of infantry, armoured personnel carriers, motorcycle
outriders. Then they saw the endless columns of huge
mobile 155mm artillery. And ahead of the guns, also proceeding up route N20, more endless columns of heavy tanks.
Raising his field-glasses, Tweed focused on the lead tank
behind a swarm of motorcycle outriders.

General de Forge stood in the turret of his Le Clerc tank.
Disdaining a helmet, he wore his képi and slung round his
neck was a pair of field-glasses. Spotting the Alouette, he
raised his own glasses and Tweed had the oddest sensation
that they were staring at each other. Lowering the glasses,
de Forge gave a jaunty wave as his tank thundered on.

'He's now well north of the so-called exercise line,'

Tweed said coldly. 'The line he laid down. The exercise to be confined *south* of Chateauroux. And it is the N20. How on earth is he clearing the highway to give that army of steel through passage?'

'I've no doubt he'll find a way,' Rosewater replied. 'And what was Brand doing in Arcachon? Waiting for the *Steel Vulture*?'

'That, yes. And he may have had another objective. We have not seen the last of him.'

Marler stood behind the pilot in the chopper flying south over the N20. It was still daylight and a shaft of sunshine like a searchlight had broken through the high overcast.

'Here they come,' said the pilot in French.

'To liberate Paris,' Marler replied cynically in the same language.

Holding on to the back of the pilot's seat with one hand, he raised his binoculars. A group of outriders had stopped at an intersection. Behind them men were carrying signs from a civilian truck. Through the lenses Marler read the signs.

Diversion. Do not miss! Army manoeuvres!

'De Forge is taking over highway N20,' Marler commented. 'Keep following it. He can't be far behind.'

'And the bastard is marching on Paris . . .'

The pilot maintained the same low altitude. Marler was watching the light. Soon it would be dusk, then dark. Which would mean accomplishing his mission could turn out to be impossible. He raised his glasses, saw a clutch of outriders speeding up the highway. Behind them rolled the tanks.

Feet wide apart, bracing himself to keep steady, Marler refocused his glasses. He couldn't believe it. The erect figure of General de Forge was standing in the turret of the leading Le Clerc tank. Marler lowered the glasses, scanned the countryside. To the east of N20 a small hill rose. Mentally he checked the range.

'Can you land on that flat-topped hill?' he asked the pilot through the microphone slung below his headset.

'Perfect place to put down.'

'Don't stop the engine . . .'

The machine swooped away from the highway in an arc. As it hit the summit Marler, who had taken off his headset, grabbed his holdall, threw open the door, jumped to the ground, crouching below the whirling rotor. Running to a rock embedded in the earth, he dropped flat, hauled out the Armalite, screwed on his sniperscope, perched the weapon on the rock, adjusted the sniperscope when he had the leading Le Clerc tank in his crosshairs.

De Forge had a sensitive instinct for danger. He watched the chopper land. He turned once again and waved on the tanks coming up behind him with a confident gesture. He then gave the order to his gunner through his microphone.

'Target chopper just landed hilltop to the east. Fire when ready!'

The computer raced through its calculations at the speed of light. The huge barrel swivelled through ninety degrees. The elevation began lowering to bring it dead on target.

Marler pressed the trigger two seconds before the tank's gun sent a shell hurtling towards the chopper. The special explosive bullet blasted the front of de Forge's skull clean away. His body sagged down on to the crew below, fountaining blood, splashing into the eyes of the gunner who automatically pressed the button.

The shell curved a dozen feet above the chopper, landed on a farmhouse, killing the farmer, his wife, and three children, who were eating a meal.

Marler switched his aim, fired three times over the heads of the outriders who had sat stunned on their machines. They leapt out of the saddles, gripped their automatic weapons, began firing at random towards the chopper now climbing rapidly off the hilltop.

Inside the tank there was panic. De Forge, a grisly sight, was sprawled over them, still spraying blood. Five tanks behind the stationary vehicle, unaware that their General was dead, obeyed his last hand wave and trundled forward, their caterpillar tracks clanking and grinding like some huge stamping mill.

Immediately ahead was a copse of trees and behind them drivers of petrol tankers held hoses, were drenching the highway with petrol which spread like a lake. A farmer held a torch made of straw. He flung the burning brand, the petrol lake ignited, the five advancing tanks rolled towards a curtain of flame.

Confusion. Chaos. Tanks swivelling round, colliding with each other in their desperate flight from the wall of fire. Two tanks rumbled past either side of the tank where de Forge lay, crashed headlong into three Le Clercs moving up the highway. Soon the whole column ground to a halt, zigzagged across the highway. An army without a leader, without orders, with nowhere to go.

The Alouette carrying Marler back to Paris was a grey dot in a grey sky as dusk fell and a sheet of flame spread across the fields on either side where bales of hay soaked in petrol had ignited.

Chapter Fifty-Eight

'There is still the hunting down of Kalmar – identifying who Kalmar is,' Tweed said firmly.

It was twenty-five hours later and they were all assembled in Navarre's office at the Ministry of the Interior. Navarre had just spoken.

'We are cleaning up the mess rapidly,' he had announced. 'As you'll have seen from this morning's newspaper headlines, General Charles de Forge died tragically during an exercise when he insisted live ammunition should be used. We'll never know who accidentally shot him during that panic on route N20.'

'One of his own troops?' Marler suggested.

'That is the assumption,' Navarre had agreed. 'Then a large petrol tanker overturned, the petrol caught fire. As I said, a major tragedy.'

'Yes, indeed,' Lasalle said with a blank expression.

'The military exercise has been cancelled,' Navarre had continued. 'All troops have returned to barracks. There will be no reports of that mysterious graveyard Newman discovered in the Landes.'

'Just one of those things?' Newman had commented cynically.

'De Forge had earlier reported all the deceased as deserters. There's no point in upsetting the relatives. A logical outcome,' Navarre had remarked with typical Gallic realism. 'And the recordings for TV of the two witnesses, Martine and Moshe Stein, will never be relayed. The cassettes have been destroyed. The old lady, Martine, seems satisfied now she has heard of the death of de Forge. Moshe Stein is philosophical.'

'And the smashing of the *Siegfried* organization is completed,' Kohlmann commented. 'Which just about wraps it up.'

Which was the point at which Tweed had intervened.

'There is still the hunting down of Kalmar . . .'

'How would we know where to start?' Rosewater asked. 'We haven't a clue as to his identity.'

'I'm not so sure about that,' Tweed insisted. 'I made a phone call to Jim Corcoran, chief of security at Heathrow. He reported seeing Major Lamy arriving by direct flight from Bordeaux.'

'With a lot on his conscience,' Navarre rapped out.

'Corcoran followed him,' Tweed went on, 'got the number of the car he'd hired. I phoned the firm. Lamy was driving to Aldeburgh.'

'I want to go back there,' Paula told him.

'Too dangerous,' Tweed contradicted her. 'I also phoned Grenville Grange. Imagine who answered the call. Brand. He also is back in the Aldeburgh area.'

'I have leave due,' Paula persisted. 'I'll go there in my own time. I want to lay the ghost of what happened there.'

'Not a good idea,' Newman snapped.

'So I don't want you coming with me. It's a personal pilgrimage.'

'What about the trouble in the south of France?' enquired Tweed, changing the subject.

'Dubois was given two options,' Navarre explained. 'One, he could disband his vicious racist movement, *Pour France*. Two, he could stand trial for high treason as a member of the *Cercle Noir*. He was reminded we have that tape with his voice on it. Guess which option he chose.'

'He copped out,' Newman replied. 'That louse with the soiled tie has no guts.'

'You are right. He has agreed to dissolve his party. He will return to his old job of grocer in Provence, selling rotten fruit at extortionate prices. Without leadership the racists are impotent.'

'And we have to return to London,' Tweed said.

'Then I can visit Aldeburgh again,' Paula asserted.

It was late afternoon, a December afternoon, when Paula stood by the window of her bedroom at the Brudenell Hotel in Aldeburgh. Below her was the narrow Parade of the front. A storm of grey clouds was flooding in from the north east. Giant waves surged in, crashed against the sea wall, hurled spray as high as her window. A little wilder than the day when she had fled across the marshes with Karin but the atmosphere was similar. Time to go for her walk before it was completely dark.

She checked the contents of her shoulder bag, tightened the belt of her raincoat, tied a scarf round her head and left her room. Hardly anyone about downstairs. She smiled at the receptionist, ran down the stairs to the rear entrance, turned left and walked towards the bleak marshes.

Crossing the deserted public car park, her feet crunched the gravel of the road leading to the sea defences which were still being reinforced. At that hour the site was closed: all the workmen had gone home. Passing the Slaughden Boat Storage yard she turned down the steep grassy path on to the marshes.

The light was fading faster than she had anticipated. She found herself thinking of Kalmar, the brute who had strangled poor Karin. It seemed ages ago. The ground was more mushy than it had been the last time she had taken this walk. She reached the point where the path forked – left back up to the road, right up the steep path to the dyke overlooking the yacht anchorage.

She took the right-hand fork, picked her way along the narrow twisting footpath running along the ridge of the dyke. The tide was coming in, funelling its way up the narrow channel parallel to the coast from the opening to the sea almost twenty miles to the south. That was when she heard the steady tread of footsteps coming up behind her at speed.

Tweed parked his Ford Sierra in a slot by the wall of the Brudenell. Jumping out, he locked the car, ran to the entrance. Halfway up the stairs he stumbled, swore aloud. As he hauled himself up the rest of the steps, clinging to the banister rail, the receptionist appeared.

'Is there something wrong, sir? Oh, it's you, Mr Tweed.'

'I've twisted my bloody ankle. Sorry. Is Miss Paula Grey in the hotel?'

'She just left. Went for a walk over the marshes . . .'

'Not by herself, I hope?'

'Yes, no one was with her.'

Victor Rosewater appeared from the direction of the bar. He stared as Tweed collapsed into a chair, stretched out his right leg with the ankle turned at an awkward angle.

'Is there a problem?' he asked. 'Paula phoned me at my town flat to say she was coming here. Would I like to keep her company.'

'So why aren't you doing just that?'

'Because I didn't know she had arrived. I've been waiting for her in the bar.'

'Isn't Robert Newman here?' Tweed asked the receptionist. He appeared agitated. 'He told me he was coming here.'

'He arrived earlier, sir. He said he was driving over to Grenville Grange.'

'Oh, no!' Tweed looked at Rosewater. 'He's convinced Kalmar is back in Aldeburgh. He must have gone to Grenville Grange to tackle Brand. He'll find Brand isn't at the Grange.'

'What gave Newman that idea?' Rosewater pressed.

'Because both Major Lamy and Brand are back in Aldeburgh. Now Paula has gone gallivanting off across those marshes. I'm really worried. By herself. She's in great danger. And now all I can do is hobble a few feet.'

'I'll go and find her,' Rosewater assured him. He lowered his voice. 'And I have my Service revolver with me.'

'Then why the hell are you wasting time?' Tweed looked at the receptionist. 'Can you say how long ago she left here?'

'A good fifteen minutes ago . . .'

'I'll get after her now. You nurse your ankle.'

Rosewater had dashed down the stairs, clad in a trench coat, and had disappeared before Tweed could reply.

'Is she really in danger?' the receptionist asked. 'I am thinking of what happened on the marshes once before.'

'So am I. Pray God he's in time.'

Paula could hear the incoming water lapping across the marshes below the dyke. It was coming in like a flood. Yachts moored to buoys were rocking under its impact, their masts swaying back and forth. She turned as she heard the hurrying footsteps. It was Victor Rosewater.

'Thank God it's you, Victor. I wondered who it might be.

I felt I had to come and take one last look at where Karin died. A pilgrimage, as I said in Paris.'

Rosewater clenched his gloved hands together. He looked out across the anchorage where a yacht swathed in blue plastic for the winter was drifting in fast on the tide. It must have broken loose from its buoy and was now drifting through the reeds close to the dyke.

'Tweed has arrived at the Brudenell,' he told her. 'He's worried sick that you're out here on your own.'

Paula had one hand inside her shoulder bag. She smiled at him.

'But that suits you, doesn't it Kalmar?'

'What the hell are you talking about?' Rosewater demanded roughly.

'Oh, I should have known much earlier. Remember the night when we paid a second visit here with Newman – at your suggestion. You said you thought maybe the police had overlooked a clue. As we passed the Slaughden Boat Yard on the road you, said: "Which way now?" You made out you had no idea of the route here. Then when we came to where the path forks – one way back up to the road and the other less obvious path up to the dyke? I slipped. You were in the lead. You hoisted me *straight up on to the dyke*. I only realized what that meant recently. You knew where Karin's body had been found.'

'You, my dear, are a bit too clever for your own good. In any case, I've been worried you might have seen me strangling that silly bitch from your treetop view.'

'Silly bitch? Karin was your wife . . .'

'And getting very tiresome. Just like you . . .'

'Jean Burgoyne was a friend of mine. You choked her, you bastard. Choked her to death.'

'For a big, fat fee. That was a near run thing – at that remote boathouse outside Arcachon. But I'd done the job and got clear before your lot turned up.'

'You cold-blooded bastard. God knows what else you have done.'

'Organized *Siegfried* in Germany for one thing. As an Intelligence officer supposedly after IRA I had the contacts. For another big fee. Now you're the only one left. Isn't it ironic? You're going to die where your friend, Karin, did. Might give you some comfort . . .'

He moved closer to her. She had half dragged out from her shoulder bag the Browning automatic when his right hand grasped her wrist in a grip of steel, twisted it. The gun dropped to the path. His gloved hands shot up to her neck, thumbs aimed at her windpipe.

'You'll never get away with it,' she gasped.

'Why not? Tweed has two suspects in the area. Foxy Major Lamy and tough guy Brand. Say goodbye, Paula . . .'

The thumbs pressed hard into her windpipe. She tried to knee him in the groin, but the tall figure looming over her turned sideways. Her knee hammered futilely against the side of his leg. His image was becoming blurred.

The plastic cover over the nearby yacht had been ripped aside. Newman had jumped out, rushing over the ooze and clumps of grass, up the side of the dyke. He grasped a handful of Rosewater's hair, jerked savagely. Rosewater grunted, released Paula, swung round. The two men grappled, lost their balance, rolled together down the side of the dyke on top of the remnants of the craft where Karin had been found. Newman felt hands round his neck, used his shoulders as leverage to roll his body from under Rosewater, ending up on top of him. His own hands gripped Rosewater by the throat, forced his head down under the water below the wrecked boat. He held on. Rosewater's head was a dim silhouette under the surface. He opened his mouth to breathe and swallowed lungfuls of sea as he struggled to get free. Rosewater's head, hair matted to his skull, jerked above the surface. A hideous sight. Newman hung on, his hands squeezing tighter as he forced his antagonist deeper under the tide. Ignoring the desperate thrashing of the body, he held him down. Newman felt the hands round his own throat slacken, fall away. He relaxed his grip cautiously. The submerged body was lifeless.

Soaked to the skin, dripping water, Newman clambered unsteadily to his feet. He managed a little wave to Paula, staring down, one hand massaging her throat. He climbed Everest, hauling himself up the side of the dyke, stood by Paula who was now gazing over the marshes.

Newman heard the sound of an engine approaching. He saw a vehicle – a buggy with enormous tyres – bouncing towards them with blinding headlights. Shielding his eyes with his wet hand, he saw three men in the buggy as it stopped on the landward side of the dyke. Chief Inspector Buchanan, Tweed beside him, Sergeant Warden driving.

'Look . . . Bob,' Paula croaked.

She was pointing to the other side of the dyke. The tide was receding. Rosewater's body, his shoes protruding briefly above the water, was being sucked rapidly down the creek, into the anchorage with the debris of the wrecked craft. Relics of the boat floated rapidly south. Tweed, showing no signs of an injured ankle, was the first to stand beside them.

With his clothes clinging to him, Newman explained to the three men what had happened, kept it brief.

'We always thought it was Rosewater,' Buchanan told him. 'That business of discovering the ring with the Cross of Lorraine – pointing us away from Rosewater to France. Warden supervised an expert team searching the scene of the crime earlier. They would never have missed it. Problem was, no proof. But when a wife is murdered the first suspect is the husband.'

'I think we should get these two back to the Brudenell and a hot bath,' said Tweed. 'And a freak high tide was forecast. The body may be washed all the way into the North Sea.'

Epilogue

A week later Tweed gathered all his team into his office. The bruises on the throats of Newman and Paula – which had convinced Buchanan of the truth of their story – had healed. Marler stood against a wall, smoking a king-size. Butler and Nield perched on Paula's desk while Newman occupied the armchair.

'Who was *Manteau*?' Paula asked. 'I couldn't understand why there were two assassins.'

'There weren't,' Tweed said, leaning back in his chair. '*Marler* was *Manteau*. Only three people knew. Navarre, myself, and Lasalle . . .'

'But why?' Paula persisted.

'If you'll keep quiet I'll tell you. It was my idea – part of the psychological warfare against de Forge. We knew he was using Kalmar, so I invented another assassin to throw de Forge off balance. Berthier had supplied Lasalle with the private phone numbers of Lamy and de Forge. It was really very straightforward.'

'Straightforward? But *Manteau* was supposed to have engineered the wreck of the TGV express, the assassination of the President and the Prime Minister. And his trademark, a cloak, was found in a nearby village. A cloak was also found near the Paris Prefecture when the Prefect was murdered. And a third one near the boathouse when Jean Burgoyne was strangled. Marler couldn't have known those murders were going to take place.'

593

'Agreed.' Tweed smiled drily. 'So before *Manteau* came on the scene Lasalle purchased a number of cloaks from a theatrical costumier in Paris. Trusted DST officers were given the cloaks, stuffed one in a litter bin near the Paris incident. The Paris Prefect, incidentally, was never killed. He went on the holiday he'd planned under an assumed name to Martinique. Officially, he recovered from the bullet wound recently, resumed his duties. It was hours after the TGV tragedy that a cloak was found in the village. Plenty of time to fly one to Lyons. Then the DST bribed an old man in a nearby village to tell the press he'd seen a man in a cloak on the viaduct. Another cloak was flown to Arcachon. Marler, in the role of *Manteau*, kept phoning de Forge demanding large fees for doing the jobs. When a large sum was delivered we obtained Swiss francs from a Paris bank, many in numbered sequence, and a lot of them counterfeit seized by the Paris police months ago. Marler returned the money to confuse de Forge even more.'

'But who killed de Forge?' she asked.

'My dear,' Marler drawled, 'don't you read the papers? It was a random shot when de Forge's own troops panicked during the overturned petrol tanker incident.'

'Really?' she queried, and Marler nodded amiably.

'Berthier, Lasalle's spy inside de Forge's GHQ, played a vital part,' Tweed continued. 'With a listening device he overheard Lamy's phone calls with Kalmar's contact in the office next door. Including the new targets – which is how we knew *you* were a target.'

'Shivery,' she remarked. 'And for a while I liked Rosewater.'

'Which is why,' Tweed emphasized, 'Butler and Nield stayed by your side – with orders never to leave you alone.'

'When did you suspect Rosewater?' she asked.

'I wondered about him from the first. Remember when

we met him at the Hotel Drei Konige in Basle? He gazed with lecherous interest at an attractive woman in the dining room. To cover up, he suggested she was a spy. I'm sure Karin, working for Kuhlmann, began to suspect her own husband. He realized it, strangled her on the Aldeburgh marshes. From what he said to you he wanted to get rid of her anyway – so he could pursue his Casanova ways.'

'Hideous man. But just that? Looking at another woman?'

'No, far more. Newman caught on early. Remember he was with you that night the two of you took Rosewater across the marshes? Newman saw Rosewater hoist you on to the dyke without hesitation when you slipped – Rosewater who wasn't supposed to have a clue as to where Karin had been killed. He told me. From that moment you were guarded. The next thing which pointed the finger at Rosewater was Kuhlmann telling me his informant, Heinrich Schneider, had passed via Wiesbaden a list of addresses where *Siegfried* was based in Germany. But not a word from Rosewater even though Schneider had first told *him*. And when you came out of a restaurant in Arcachon after having dinner with Rosewater you later told me he'd suggested a ride in his car.'

'That's right,' Paula agreed. 'Butler stopped me going with him, thank God.'

'There was a red Porsche parked down the street. Rosewater turned away from it when Butler joined you. After you'd driven off Nield stopped the car so he could go back to find his wallet which he said he must have dropped . . .'

'I remember . . .'

'Nield went to the corner, saw Rosewater climbing behind the wheel of that Porsche. What captain in the Intelligence Corps can afford a Porsche on his pay? There were other strange coincidences.'

'Did they find Rosewater's body?' Paula asked.

'No, which was a relief to the MOD. Think of the scandal. They've just posted him as missing in Germany. His body is probably at the bottom of the North Sea.'

'You took a chance,' Marler remarked, 'using Paula for live bait.'

'I agreed,' Paula replied. 'Insisted when I caught on it was Rosewater. I'd been rather a fool about him. But Tweed had Butler and Nield concealed behind the dyke in case Newman didn't reach Rosewater.' She looked at Tweed. 'But how did Dawlish smuggle those missiles?'

'You told me, but only when I watched the *Vulture* coming into Arcachon was I able to recall it. At the beginning, describing your underwater swim with Karin at Dunwich, you said, "I thought I saw a great white whale." Unlikely in that part of the world.'

'Then what was it?'

'A dracoon – one of those very tough and large containers made of plastic they used to transport extra oil, dragging them on the surface behind tankers. Like a sausage. Dawlish was clever. The missiles, I guess, he brought in from a factory abroad, anchored off Dunwich, then stored the dracoons carrying missiles in the sunken village – hence his interest in underwater exploration. The *Vulture* could then sail safely into Harwich.'

'So all is well?'

'It is in France.' Tweed looked round the gathering. 'I think you all did very well. We helped to stop a military dictator taking power in Paris, which would have wrecked the new Europe. Major Lamy, who often supervised those hideous executions in the Landes, has been found dead in an Aldeburgh hotel. Shot himself. Captain Rey was found hanging in that horrible punishment well. Not popular with some of the troops, I assume. Now I think you'd all better go home.'

'I'd better call on Isabelle,' Newman said, standing up. 'Just to make sure she's settled in the temporary flat we've given her in South Ken.'

'Which is conveniently close to your pad,' Marler observed.

'Pure coincidence,' Newman snapped.

'And maybe Paula would like to join me for dinner,' Tweed suggested.

'What a lovely idea.' Paula jumped up. 'I'll just go and fix my face.' She walked past Newman without a glance in his direction.

Monica, who had said nothing from behind her desk, waited until everyone except Tweed had left.

'Isabelle might just be joining the SIS,' Tweed remarked. 'She was one of Lasalle's trained agents.'

'And your interview with the new PM before you opened the meeting here?' Monica enquired.

'He apologized handsomely and without reservation to me. You remember Howard was told the PM was experimenting with a twin-track policy? Testing us, so to speak? He left it to the MOD to choose someone from Military Intelligence. They chose Victor Rosewater! The PM won't do anything like that again. Now, I must go and freshen up.'

'Isabelle,' said Monica. 'That's dangerous. She may have the training – Lasalle is a pro. But Isabelle and Paula working together? Trouble.'

'They got on well enough in Arcachon. I saw it myself.'

'Men!' Monica cast her eyes heavenwards. 'That was for a brief time in a dangerous situation. You've a lot to learn, about women.'

'You're imagining it . . .'

'Am I? Didn't you see how Paula walked straight past Newman without so much as a goodnight? All right, bring in Isabelle. And watch the fur fly.'

WHIRLPOOL

For Jane

Contents

Prologue

Dawn came up like a warning.

Bob Newman, foreign correspondent, frowned as he drove his Mercedes 280E across the loneliness of Suffolk in February. Ploughed dark soil, crusted with frost, hemmed in the deserted road on either side. The weird light of dawn intensified his anxiety as his headlights now provided uncertain illumination. What was it his girl friend, Sandy Riverton, had said when she called him in the middle of the night?

'Bob, can we meet urgently? At the old church near Yoxford where we first met?'

He could have sworn her teeth were chattering with fear.

'Of course we can.' Stretched out in bed, he had suppressed a yawn. 'But why there? Is something wrong?'

'I can't explain over the phone. You *will* come? I've something I must tell you, something I should have told you before. It will help your investigation into INCUBUS. I must go. Can you make it there just after dawn? So no one will see us?'

'Sandy, what is this all about? Why that remote place – at that remote hour, for God's sake?'

'I can't linger. Do come, Bob. Please. I must go now. I will see you there?'

'Yes . . .' He had woken up. 'Where are you calling from?'

'Tell you when we meet. 'Bye . . .'

She had rung off before he could say another word. He

1

had jumped out of bed, washed, shaved, dressed very quickly. A correspondent learned to do that, even if he no longer needed to practise his profession – the best-selling book he had written years ago had given blessed financial independence.

There were no villages, no farms in sight as he slowed down, afraid that he might drive past the narrow track leading to the abandoned church and its separate bell tower. He had the heaters full on: it was a raw morning with a bitter wind blowing from the east, from the distant North Sea.

Not even a hamlet along this stretch of the road, he recalled. 'Near Yoxford' was an over-simplification of the position of the old church. It was in the middle of nowhere. So why would Sandy choose such a desolate rendezvous – at such a desolate hour? Because she was frightened, he thought grimly.

The cold bleak light was growing in the cloudless sky. Over to his left he caught a glimpse of a Georgian mansion huddled a quarter-mile off the main road. A deep central window was arched at the top. More Queen Anne than Georgian. And a curious coincidence – Livingstone Manor was the English country home of Franklin D. Hauser, President and Chief Executive of INCUBUS Inc., the giant American organization Sandy had worked for until recently.

He recalled another phone conversation with Sandy three weeks earlier. She had resigned from INCUBUS. No real reason given. When Newman had pressed her she had become vague.

'I just felt I was doing the same old thing, week after week, month after month. Time for a change, I suppose . . .'

She had left London without seeing Newman, telling him in a letter she was staying at her sister's place in Southwold further up the Suffolk coast. So why this mysterious meeting close to Hauser's lair?

Newman spotted the track leading off to the right and swung away from the main road. This was an area of sloping fields and the track mounted a gradual incline. The daylight was strong enough now for him to see the tower of the ancient stone church silhouetted against the horizon, perched on a ridge. The bell tower came into view, a square slim block of stone separated from the church by a dozen yards. He found his anxiety growing.

He had realized in January how very fond of Sandy he was, that he'd reached the stage where he might well ask her to marry him. She was so very different from his first wife, foully murdered during the old Cold War years in Estonia on the Baltic. He increased speed, impatient to reach his destination. The ton and a half of car rocked, driving over the ice-hardened ruts carved out by farm tractors in kinder weather.

He glanced automatically in his rear-view mirror, catching a glimpse of himself. In his forties, his hair was fair, he was clean-shaven and with a strong face. Normally his expression was droll, with a hint of humour about the mouth and eyes. Bob Newman was a man generally liked by both men and women. He breathed a sigh of relief as he bumped over the crest. Sandy's red Jaguar was parked behind a dense hedge, the twigs so close together they formed a visual barrier from a distance.

Parking his Mercedes alongside the Jaguar, he got out. His hand touched the Jag's radiator. Anxiety flooded back. The radiator was cold. She must have been waiting for some time. Where?

The only shelter he could see was the church, but it would be like an ice box inside. Slipping on his gloves, he saw out of the corner of his eye the sun rising above a belt of dark blue. The sea. A much smaller flash of light caught his attention. From the large arched window at Livingstone Manor.

The sun was reflecting off the window. In which case the reflection should still be there. It had vanished. Reaching into his car he hauled out the powerful pair of binoculars he always carried. Of medium height and build, he crouched behind the car, perched elbows on the roof, focused the binoculars. The window at Livingstone Manor came up close. A silhouette showed behind the net curtains, a silhouette aiming a pair of field glasses.

Probably an early-rising servant wondering who could be visiting the church at this hour. He laid the binoculars back on the passenger seat, turned to face the church. To reach the ancient Norman edifice with its pointed windows he had to pass through the bell tower, open to the world at both ends. Beyond, a curving path led uphill between gravestones to the church entrance. He turned up his coat collar, walked forward.

Both tower and church were sadly in need of repair. Doubtless at the time of the wool barons the church had a full congregation, but the economic tide had long ago receded from this part of the world. He walked inside the bell tower.

Afterwards he was haunted by the sound his footsteps had made in the brooding post-dawn silence, the crunch and crackle of his shoes breaking ice.

In one corner of the tower lay the bell which had fallen at some time in the past. During the great storm, the locals said. He was walking out of the tower when he glanced up, stopped, froze as he stared at the horror above his head.

Sandy was suspended by a rope attached to an old beam next to the ladder leading to the tower. The rope was knotted round her neck which hung sideways at a bizarre angle. Her lifeless eyes stared down at him, her tongue protruded from her mouth. Her neck was broken. Her

4

long gold hair hung down her back over her red wind-cheater. Her long legs were clad in denims. She looked like some grotesque statue in a pagan ritual.

Newman choked, grunted, then forced himself to move. He climbed the ladder, testing each rung carefully. Two of the rungs had been replaced by fresh wood. He stood near the top, alongside her corpse.

Reaching out he gently touched her pallid face. The skin was cold, felt like wax. The rope from which she hung was old. It was exactly like the remnant attached to the bell. He began talking out aloud, to himself.

'No. It's not possiblé. This is a mad dream. I don't believe it. I'm home in bed at my South Ken flat . . . This is a crazy nightmare . . .'

But he knew it was true. A part of his trained reporter's mind began to function, to observe. Could she have committed suicide? No. Why? Because she hated heights – she suffered from vertigo. He looked down at the yawning drop below. No!

He hated leaving her there but he descended the ladder because there was nothing else he could do. The odd thing was his first thought was her husband, Ed, must be told – Ed whom she was on the verge of divorcing. He must know.

Ed Riverton was a top executive in INCUBUS, the great American banking syndicate which was spreading its tentacles across Europe, investing in just about every type of company which existed. That was how Newman had met Sandy.

Travelling to Finland, he had interviewed Riverton in Helsinki. It had been a strange conversation: Riverton was nervous, evasive. Due to the fact that his marriage had been heading for the rocks? No, Newman had detected something he couldn't account for.

His mind returned to the dreadful present. Before he left the bell tower his eyes were drawn upwards. The view was hideous. She was swinging slowly from side to side, like a pendulum. Had he disturbed her rigid stance by touching her? Or was it the east wind blowing in through the open bell tower with renewed force?

What the hell did it matter? He had an awful premonition he would always remember her like this – that he'd never recall her cheerful buoyancy, her glowing smile when she had teased him. Yes, he'd always have this ghastly image imprinted on his mind – a grossly obscene caricature of the real Sandy.

He stumbled near the exit from the tower, recovered his balance. His mind was working on two levels. There was grief and shock, but another part of his brain was functioning – the reporter's. He forced himself to stare upwards again.

Above the beam round which the rope was tied was a platform where the top of the ladder rested. Carved in the platform was the hole through which the bell-rope had once hung. He calculated it was not possible for Sandy, kneeling on that platform, to reach down to the beam, impossible for her to have attached the rope from that perch. She stood – *hung* – five feet four inches high. Too short to have killed herself.

PART ONE

Profiles of Death

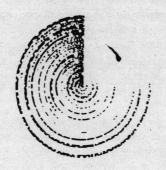

1

'Why – thank heaven – didn't you resign as you said you would?'

Monica asked Tweed the question while they waited for Newman to arrive. Tweed, Deputy Director of the SIS, stared out of the window of his first floor office at Park Crescent, London HQ of the Secret Service.

'Porridge-grey – and damn cold,' he commented on the weather.

Monica, middle-aged, her grey hair tied in a bun, his personal assistant for many years, leaned forward over her desk and studied Tweed. Of medium height and build, indeterminate age, he wore horn-rim glasses and was the man you passed in the street without noticing him. It was an impression which had often served him well. Clean shaven, his hair was still dark and behind the lenses his eyes were alert and penetrating.

'You haven't answered my question,' she prodded him. 'After seeing the PM you took a long leave and then came back. So what happened.'

'She wore me down,' Tweed admitted. 'When I did get back she had a very strange and dangerous problem which she dumped in my lap, assured me I was the only man she could trust to handle it. We talked for two hours and,' he threw out both hands in a gesture of surrender, 'at the end of it she, yes, wore me down.' His manner changed, became brisk. He walked behind his own desk, settled himself in his ancient swivel chair. 'I wonder what's worrying Bob Newman? When he phoned, asked if he

9

could come and see me, he sounded edgy and shaken. Not like him. Wouldn't give me a hint over the phone.'

'Well, we'll soon know. He's due any second. And what is the strange and dangerous problem?'

'INCUBUS is part of it. The International Continental Union Bank, US – United States. I do wish the Americans hadn't this love of trainloads of initial letters to designate an organization. You've heard of Franklin D. Hauser, President and Chief Executive? Who hasn't? They say he's as powerful as the President in Washington. An exaggeration, of course. It's the people he's employing who are worrying both Washington and Moscow. I can't go into details, but it's a curious situation.'

'Curious?'

Tweed paused. 'Can't tell you much. But I've been asked by the PM to co-operate with a special operative of the CIA. And an unknown member of the KGB. Now that I call curious.'

He gazed towards the window as the phone rang. Monica took the call, said to send him up right away, put down the receiver, looked at Tweed.

'Bob Newman has arrived. You did want to see him . . .'

'Yes. I'm curious about Bob, too . . .'

He broke off as Newman entered, closed the door, nodded to Monica and slumped into the chair in front of Tweed's desk.

'What on earth is wrong, Bob?'

Tweed was startled by Newman's appearance. Normally he was relaxed and had an easy-going manner. Now he looked haggard, grim faced.

'You look as though you haven't slept,' Tweed remarked.

'I haven't – not a lot. I was woken in the middle of the night by a phone call . . .'

Tersely, he recalled his experiences of the past few hours. He went on to explain his interview with the police as Monica slipped out to make him some coffee.

'They had a Scotland Yard man at Southwold Police Station. From Homicide. He just happened to be there after solving another case. All the senior police officers were down with flu – so the Chief Constable asked for his aid. A Chief Inspector Roy Buchanan. Very intelligent, very persistent. In his quiet way he really grilled me about Sandy.'

'I once met Buchanan,' Tweed said quietly. 'I agree with your description. A highly competent, dogged type . . .'

'Dogged is the word.' Newman paused as though unsure how to phrase his next words, then burst out: 'Buchanan thinks I murdered Sandy.'

Tweed waited, saying nothing, tapping a pencil as he watched Newman while the reporter drank black coffee from the large mug Monica had brought him. He drank the steaming liquid in gulps.

'Buchanan said that to you?' Tweed asked eventually.

'Not in so many words. But he made the point there were no signs that Sandy had struggled for her life, that she must have trusted her murderer. That thought had occurred to me before I was hauled off to Southwold police station for the interrogation. I could tell what he was thinking from the way he questioned me. Flicks at you verbally with a rapier.'

'Sounds like Buchanan.' Tweed stared at Newman. He had shaved, but it was a rough job: a piece of sticking plaster at the side of his face showed where he had cut himself. 'I see you cut yourself shaving?'

Newman's eyes blazed. 'Exactly the same question Buchanan asked me. He even suggested maybe I'd like to show him the cut. I ripped off the plaster. I suppose he hopes the pathologist who butchers her will find skin tissue under her nails. Mine.'

'Drink some more coffee,' Tweed advised.

'I have to make a call to Helsinki,' Newman snapped.

11

'Sandy was divorcing her husband, Ed. But the least I can do is to call him, let him know.'

'The phone is all yours.'

Tweed leant back in his chair, glanced at Monica while Newman checked his notebook, dialled a Helsinki number, waited and then stared at Tweed.

'It would help my concentration if you could stop tapping that blasted pencil.'

Tweed, still unruffled, nodded, placed the pencil on his desk, took out a handkerchief and began polishing his glasses.

Newman gripped the phone tightly, listening to the ringing tone. Would they never answer the bloody thing? A girl's voice came on the line, repeated the number in English.

'I need to speak to Edward Riverton urgently. I'm calling his home because he told me he was rarely in his office.'

'Who is this speaking?' A tremble in the girl's voice.

'Sorry, this is Bob Newman. I interviewed Mr Riverton in Helsinki a few weeks ago . . .'

Newman had a grip on himself now. His voice was perfectly normal, Tweed noted.

'Oh, God, Mr Newman,' the girl exploded. 'This is Evelyn, his sister-in-law. You know Sandy, I believe. She was talking about you on the phone recently. I've just had terrible news and I can't reach Sandy. Her phone rings in Southwold but no one answers.'

'Slow down, Evelyn.' Newman's tone was soothing, controlled. 'I remember you well. Especially that marvellous dinner you cooked. *Gravad lax*. Some of the best salmon I've ever tasted. Now, tell me the news.'

'It's unbelievable. They dragged Ed out of the North Harbour just after daylight twenty-four hours ago. I was at the Turku office and there was some delay in telling me . . . We only get four hours' daylight in winter . . . It's horribly cold. The harbour is packed solid with ice . . .'

She was babbling, on the verge of hysteria, even a nervous breakdown. Newman spoke slowly.

'Just take your time telling me. I'm a good listener. How did it happen?'

'The icebreaker *Otso* was clearing a passage for ships through the ice. One of the crew spotted Ed's body wedged inside a crevasse. They saw him just in time before the icebreaker crushed . . .' Her voice broke. Newman waited, heard her take in a deep breath. 'They took him to the mortuary and called me.'

'Who is "they", Evelyn? Give me the facts.'

'The Protection Police arrived and took him off the *Otso*. A man called Mauno Sarin phoned me. I knew there was something wrong from his voice. Can I get a drink of water?'

'I'll hold on.'

Newman looked at Tweed, sitting erect in his chair, while he held the phone to his ear, his other hand over the mouthpiece.

'There's the devil to pay about this business. Tell you in a minute . . . Yes, Evelyn, I'm still here. You said you could tell something was wrong from his voice. That was *before* he told you the news?'

'No, afterwards . . .'

She's gone over the edge, Newman thought. He cleared his throat. 'Just tell me what happened next.'

'I insisted on knowing everything. Sarin didn't want to tell me, then he said I'd know soon enough, and better from him than over the radio. Ed didn't slip into the harbour. For God's sake, Bob – he had been garrotted.' Her voice rose in pitch. 'With some kind of wire. The head was almost severed from the neck. Oh, God, Bob, how am I going to tell Sandy that?'

'Take another drink of water, a good big one, then we'll talk some more.'

Newman was ice cold in an emergency. How could he handle this? Tell Sandy's sister she was dead, hung by a rope inside an ancient bell tower? Horror piled on horror. But something was even more wrong than Sarin had realized. In the course of about twenty-four hours Ed Riverton had been brutally exterminated in Finland – and his wife had been eliminated with equal brutality in East Anglia, over a thousand miles away. He swallowed the rest of the coffee, managed to grin at Monica, then Evelyn was back on the line.

'I know you and Sandy are—' She broke off.

'Yes,' Newman replied in a monotone.

'I know I'm being a coward about this . . . should tell Sandy myself . . .' Babbling again. 'But I can't bring myself to do it now. Bob, could you possibly tell her yourself?'

Newman paused. Beads of moisture were forming on his forehead. Tweed was watching him closely, pencil gripped in his hand but motionless. How the hell can I tell her after what she's just been through, Newman asked himself. But someone had to.

'Evelyn, are you sitting down? With a full glass of water?'

'A jugful. Bob, what is it? I can tell from your tone something else is terribly wrong. Bob . . .' A deep intake of breath he clearly heard over a thousand miles away. 'Bob,' she repeated, 'I've got a grip on myself – and I am sitting down. Just tell me.' Calmer now, self-controlled. Temporarily.

'I've just had a similar shock, Evelyn. It's going to be a lot grimmer for you – on top of what you've just told me. And it is about Sandy. Like Ed, she's dead. It happened in the early hours of this morning.'

'I see.' Very controlled, too controlled, her voice dull. 'How did it happen, Bob? Car accident?'

'No. I said like Ed.' He paused, she burst out.

14

'Oh, my God! Not garrotted. Please, not that . . .'

'I phrased it badly. I mean like Ed she had been murdered. Want some more water?'

'No! No! How did she die? Tell me, damn you! I'm flying straight home. I'll just phone INCUBUS and say I'm leaving them . . . I had a job with them – *have* a job at the moment . . . Not in the same department as Ed . . .'

'Don't phone INCUBUS,' he warned. 'Just catch the first flight home. You have the phone number of my apartment in South Ken? Good. Phone details of your flight number and ETA. If I'm not there leave a message on the answerphone. Use a different name. Identify yourself as Jackie. OK?'

'How did Sandy die? You said she was murdered . . .'

'The details can wait till we meet. Don't forget to phone me that flight data.'

'Bob, I must go.' Suddenly there was a note of urgency in her voice. It alarmed Newman. 'I've got to get out of this place. While we were talking I was checking a timetable. I can just catch a flight if I rush. Have to pack. *Must* go now.'

'Evelyn . . .'

Newman slowly put down the receiver. She had broken the connection. There had been a note close to panic in her voice. As though she had seen something which disturbed her from the window of the apartment. He remembered the phone was perched on a window ledge in Riverton's Helsinki pad. He lit a cigarette, took a long drag. Tweed waited patiently.

'It's incredible – and sinister,' Newman began. He relayed to Tweed and Monica the gist of his conversation. Nothing in Tweed's expression betrayed his reaction as Newman concluded.

'Incredible,' he repeated. 'Two murders which took place within about twenty-four hours. One in Suffolk, one in Finland. The victims were man and wife. I know Sandy

15

was estranged from Ed, was thinking of divorcing him, but . . .'

'Were they still on speaking terms?' Tweed asked. 'Is there a chance Ed phoned Sandy and told her something important – something so important someone thought it was dangerous that she went on living?'

'Shouldn't have thought so.' Newman threw out a hand in a helpless gesture. 'Not impossible though. I really don't know.' He sounded at the end of his tether, all the adrenalin summoned up for his phone call now evaporated.

'And yet there's a common link,' Tweed pointed out. 'All three were working for INCUBUS – or had been until recently. Ed, Sandy – and *Evelyn*,' he added. Newman jerked upright, stared at Tweed, the picture of anxiety.

'So you think I was right?'

'Right about what?'

'To warn her not to tell INCUBUS she was leaving them?'

'There could just be an element of risk involved for her. Why, I have no idea, but the coincidence is very strange.' Tweed was doodling on his notepad as he spoke. He found he had drawn a noose, remembered how Sandy Riverton had died inside the old bell tower, scribbled it out before Newman could see it. 'What do you propose to do about it?' he enquired.

'Step up my investigation into the activities of INCUBUS and its chief, Hauser, in Europe. Incidentally, Hauser has his British residence in an old Georgian mansion not two miles from that bell tower.' He stifled a yawn. 'Checking into that organization may take months. I've decided to fly to New York – main HQ of INCUBUS, then on to Boston where they have another top secret outfit. Meantime I'm going back to my apartment to get some much needed kip, then I'll meet Evelyn at

16

Heathrow. She might just be the key to what I'm looking for . . .'

'Robert Newman is our only lead in our enquiries concerning the murder of Sandra Riverton.'

Chief Inspector Roy Buchanan made the statement to Tweed in the Park Crescent office. His tone was noncommittal, gave no indication as to his own suspicions. Six feet tall, in his forties, his manner was detached, his grey eyes watchful. He sat in the armchair recently occupied by Newman, his long legs crossed.

'What brought you to my doorstep?' Tweed asked amiably.

Monica watched the two men, fascinated. Under the surface of an everyday conversation a duel of two astute minds was taking place. Buchanan had balanced the cup of coffee Monica had provided on his crossed knees. He drank a little coffee before replying.

Seated in a hard-backed chair, Buchanan's assistant, Sergeant Warden, several years younger than his chief, watched in silence, his clean-shaven face devoid of all expression. Tweed had earlier asked him to pocket his notebook.

'You don't take notes here unless I request it,' he had informed Buchanan in an amiable tone.

'I had Newman followed here from Southwold,' Buchanan replied eventually. 'He said he was going back to his flat in South Kensington. I suppose it was discretion that led him to omit he was visiting General & Cumbria Assurance.'

A brief smile crossed his face as he repeated the cover name for the SIS engraved on the plate outside the entrance. And normally, Tweed thought, you'd never have got away with that. It confirmed the state of shock Newman was in – combined with no sleep.

'So, now you're here, how can I help you?' Tweed enquired.

'The Sandra Riverton murder has a macabre element.' Buchanan paused, hands inside his trouser pockets, very relaxed. 'I don't know whether Newman told you – the victim was hung from a rope inside an old bell tower. It suggests to me either an act of personal revenge or, alternatively, a demonstration to encourage the others, as the French say.'

'Really?' Tweed sounded only half interested. 'And who might be the others?'

'I wish I knew – always assuming that is the case.' A second pause. Tweed began to think the pauses were a Buchanan tactic – to emphasize what he said next. 'Newman did inform me that Riverton had recently been employed by the INCUBUS organization. They seem to be buying up half Europe . . .'

The observation seemed irrelevant, but Tweed doubted whether the man from the Yard ever said anything without a purpose. He kept silent, forcing Buchanan to continue. 'An odd coincidence is the fact that Franklin D. Hauser, chief executive of INCUBUS, has his English home in a mansion not two miles from that bell tower.'

'Probably just a coincidence,' Tweed remarked, 'as you suggested.'

'I paid a call at Livingstone Manor, Hauser's place. A butler, very English, the old school, told me Hauser was abroad. He showed great reluctance to reveal his where-abouts.'

'So you left without finding out?' Tweed's expression was so innocent Monica put up a hand to hide her smile.

'No.' Buchanan finished his coffee, twisted round to hand the cup and saucer to Monica. 'I enjoyed that coffee. Thank you.' He turned back to Tweed. 'I told him this was a murder investigation, that I'd adopt other

18

methods to trace his employer. That remark unsettled Jeeves. He then remembered Hauser was in Finland.'

'You didn't tell him that you have been asked to investigate INCUBUS. Never gave him the slightest hint.'

Monica made her comment to Tweed when Buchanan and Warden had left after a few more minutes' conversation. Paula Grey, a raven haired girl in her early thirties with strong bone structure, had just entered the office. She sat at her desk, crossed her shapely legs, rested her hands in her lap and listened. Tweed's close confidante, she often worked with him in the field.

'No, Monica, I didn't.' Tweed clasped his hands behind his neck. 'That's SIS business. Buchanan is clever. He was here on a fishing trip – trying to find out if Newman had told me something that might help his own investigations.'

'But Bob did just that. He told us that Ed Riverton, who had a top job with INCUBUS, was dragged out of Helsinki harbour,' she shuddered, 'after he had been garrotted.'

'In case everyone has forgotten, I'm still here,' Paula interjected. 'All this sounds a bit grim. Care to bring me up to date, anyone?'

Tweed swivelled to face her, gave a concise résumé of what had happened, including his own new directive from the PM and Newman's visit. Paula listened, watching Tweed, memorizing every detail.

'When do you start this weird co-operation with Washington and Moscow?' she demanded in her direct manner.

'This is very much under wraps.' He threw out his hands in a someday gesture. 'I don't even know who is coming from the States. Just one man – the personal representative of the President and operating entirely on

19

his own. Same with Moscow. The Soviet President's personal choice – also operating on his own. This is the tightest undercover programme ever devised.'

'And the time factor?' Paula pressed.

'Again unknown. Could be weeks, months away. I'll be contacted when the time comes.' Tweed frowned. 'I find the whole business mysterious. It has an almost ghost-like character.'

'But Bob Newman won't stand still,' Paula commented. 'Not after the horrific killing of his girl friend. *He'll* be investigating on his own account.'

'Which may prove invaluable to us,' Tweed pointed out. 'He is the free agent. If he feeds me the data he uncovers it might put us ahead in the game before the battle opens.'

'Would you let me help him?' Paula suggested.

'Have to think about that.' Tweed stood up, began pacing round the office. 'Let's face it – he may not want help of any sort. You know how he is – a lone wolf. That's what made him a successful foreign correspondent.'

'I might be able to persuade him . . .'

'And you might not,' Tweed warned. 'He's in a grim mood about the murder of Sandy Riverton . . .'

'Which may just be connected with the almost simultaneous murder of her husband in Helsinki,' Paula insisted. 'It really is stretching the long arm of coincidence to breaking point – a husband and wife, both recently employed by INCUBUS, both murdered within twenty-four hours of each other. What is Bob's first move?'

'To meet Evelyn, the sister, off the plane from Helsinki. She may just have vital information that will give Bob the lead he's looking for.'

'I can get in touch with Bob at his flat,' Paula said, reaching for her phone.

'No, you can't.' Tweed's tone was brisk. 'First, he

needs sleep. Second, what he's proposing is dangerous. I've got to think about whether I'm going to let you try to link up with him.'

'So I twiddle my thumbs, go through more files?'

Tweed smiled drily. 'No, you don't. You start building up a dossier on all known facts about the International Continental Union Bank, US. With special attention to the man who created that colossus – Franklin D. Hauser.'

2

The headquarters of INCUBUS Oy. in Finland was a new twenty-storey glass block on the western outskirts of Helsinki. The glass was a deep blue colour, opaque, so the outside world could see nothing of what went on inside the heavily guarded building.

On the top floor Franklin D. Hauser was addressing executives inside the large board room. Ten Americans and one Englishman sat on either side of a long gleaming wooden table. Hauser paced slowly back and forth at the far end behind his empty chair as he spoke.

'I have brought you folks here from all over Scandinavia because some of you are fresh from the States and this little old continent is different from back home. That doesn't mean you have to start over again. No, sirree. We're here to establish INCUBUS solid in Europe and we'll do it the American way . . .'

He paused to drink ice water. Swivelled round in his seat to the right of the empty chair, the Englishman, Adam Carver, tall, slim, in his late thirties, watched his chief's performance with concealed amusement.

Hauser, six feet tall and heavily built, in his fifties, wore the uniform of the American executive. A chalk grey suit, a new starched white shirt, a tie with diagonal stripes, the shirt with a button-down collar. Even Hauser's face was standard: plump, clean shaven, pink, smooth as a baby's. Only the ice-blue eyes betrayed the man's ruthless will. He was, Carver thought, in his most folksy mood. I could have written the script, he mused, as Hauser continued.

'But first I'd like to say a few words about myself. I have an estate in Arizona outside Phoenix with forty acres of land and a nice house. I have an apartment on Fifth in New York. I have a mansion and twenty acres in Suffolk, Britain. Wouldn't you say that was all a man needed?'

But you haven't got a wife any more, Carver observed to himself. She ran off with a younger film star. Hauser was talking again after removing his jacket, placing it carefully over the back of his chair.

'So why do I go on expanding the company instead of putting up my feet and shooting the breeze?'

Hauser stood still, arms folded across his powerful chest. Sunlight reflected from the snow outside flashed off his rimless pince-nez perched on the bridge of his strong nose. His executives sat bolt upright in their chairs, gazing at him, anxious to convey the impression they were hanging on his every word. There was not a man present who had not stepped over bodies of rivals to claw his way to his present position. One wrong move and all that in-fighting was on the line, would be thrown away.

'I'll tell you why,' Hauser continued, beaming his famous smile. 'I'm doing it for you people so one day you'll all have what I have. But you'll have to give it all you've got.' The tone had changed, there was an edge to his voice. 'If INCUBUS is going to become the biggest organization in Europe, you're going to have to hit it twenty-five hours a day. You'll have to sleep and dream INCUBUS. It's going to be a full-time job to drag Europe

22

into the twenty-first century. You people are going to do that job. Now I'm going to talk to you later, meantime you go down to Level Five and stay there until you've come up with a plan to infiltrate Finland. You'll have to be cunning, devious, smart. Already I've heard a Finnish businessman say in The Palace restaurant "Those God-damn Yanks are coming." He's behind the times. They're here. Work out a plan to convert this tiny country into a major base for our operation . . .'

His tone had been abrasive, challenging. He took off his pince-nez, perched them higher up his nose, looked down the table.

'Level Five. Get to it. Unless,' he ended in a decep-tively soft tone, 'there are any questions?'

There were no questions. The hard-bitten men round the table knew better than to make that mistake. They had been *told*. Carver watched as they gathered up their files, left the room in single file. Hauser's large hand descended on Carver's shoulder.

'You stay. We'll talk. You can go down later and whip up some action. Twelve hours in Level Five should con-centrate their minds, wouldn't you agree?'

Carver agreed. Level Five was underground. No view of the outside world. A labyrinth of rooms and corridors which had all the welcoming atmosphere of the interrog-ation centre in the Lubyanka in Moscow.

Hauser hunched his large body in his chair and gazed into the distance. His parents had named him after Franklin D. Roosevelt and he had carefully built up a similar outwardly benevolent image. It disarmed his opponents and the image impressed the outside world.

'I have a dream, Adam . . .'

He paused. Echoes of Martin Luther King, Carver thought, but not quite the same meaning to the stirring words. He waited, sensing his chief was in a reflective mood.

'I have a dream,' Hauser repeated, 'a vision of a world-wide homeland stretching from the Pacific coast of the States to the Urals. That politico, Gorbachev, is an amateur, a provincial hick who thinks he's made it big. And he talks of a European home from the Atlantic to the Urals. Well my vision is bigger than his. Adam, we're going to take over Europe and the Soviet Union. Dracon is working on the strategy.' He glanced at Carver. 'Frank Galvone is taking over from Ed Riverton.'

Hauser inserted a cigarcttc into an ivory holder, lit it. Carver, a good-looking man women fell over to meet, kept silent. He wasn't reacting to that ploy. Hauser thought the only way to keep his top men on their toes was to play one off against the other: to hint now and again someone else was after their job. Hence the reference to Galvone.

'A pity Riverton had that nasty accident,' Hauser continued. 'We'll all miss Ed.'

'That Finn, Mauno Sarin, you asked me to handle when he arrived here, said Ed had been garrotted before someone threw him into the harbour,' Carver commented.

'So crime is rearing its ugly head in little old Finland.' Hauser puffed at his cigarette. 'The penalty of growing affluence. Once upon a time the only crime in this neck of the woods was domestic. A jealous husband using an axe on his wife. Sometimes the wife used the axe. Times change. You satisfied this Sarin?' Hauser asked casually.

'He's chief of the Protection Police, so it's odd he was the one to come here. They're political – a small counter-espionage unit. Forty men, maybe a few more.'

'But you satisfied him?'

'I got rid of him. For the moment. I had the feeling he could be back. Don't underestimate him. Sarin is both cynical and shrewd.'

'So he comes back, you see him again. Take him out to dinner, pour champagne down his throat, and later in the

24

evening mention the little titbit that I'm friends with the Finnish President. If that doesn't turn the trick, offer him a nice car. Do it the American way.'

'That won't work with Sarin. He's incorruptible.'

'Adam.' Hauser laid a hand on Carver's arm. 'No one is incorruptible. With some you have to grease the wheels more liberally. And Evelyn Lennox has resigned, taken a walk. I had her followed to the airport. She took a flight for London. *Uno* has her address. Go and see her in a few days. By then our insurance outfit, Fraternal & Equality, will have visited her, offered her a big fat pension. Tied to the usual conditions, of course.'

'Who is going to see her?'

'Papa Grimwood will head the team.'

'Then why do I need to see her?'

'To make sure.' Hauser tilted his large jaw. Carver was familiar with the pose: borrowed from Roosevelt. 'To make sure she's accepted the pension – and the conditions. Her work was of a sensitive nature.' He gave another beaming smile. 'They don't call you The Charmer for nothing, Adam. You'll have her eating out of your hand.'

'What is Frank doing these days?' Carver enquired. 'Haven't seen him around here for a while. He used to spend most of his time in Finland.'

'I'm surprised at you.' Hauser's tone was mild but his dark thick eyebrows lifted. 'Asking questions outside your sphere of operations. And just after you've arrived back. Frank Galvone is still based with Dracon outside Boston.' He smiled again. 'But if you're anxious to see Frank he may be over here soon. It's time you two learned to get along. And now, I guess, you'll want to check up with *Uno* about the Lennox girl.' He opened the briefcase resting on his trouser leg, extracted a piece of plastic. 'There's the new combination. Let me have it back soonest.'

It was dismissal time. Carver took the plastic rectangle, nodded, left the room and headed for the elevator. *Uno* was the master computer located below ground level. It recorded every detail of past and present employees of INCUBUS. He was glad Mauno Sarin had no idea of its existence. And he hoped Papa Grimwood would handle the Lennox girl with finesse – assuming the old villain knew what the word meant.

Evelyn Lennox had checked flights to London. She found she could just catch a direct Finnair flight if she hurried. She packed a bag, looked at the phone, checked her watch. No time to call Newman: she would miss her flight. In the street outside her Helsinki apartment she hailed a cab.

'Airport, please. And could you hurry? I'm late for my flight.'

She was so absorbed with not missing the plane she didn't notice the pale faced girl with an aquiline nose and a scraped bone look. The girl started the engine of her Saab and followed the taxi. She was immediately behind Evelyn when the English girl bought her one-way ticket to London.

Aboard the plane as it climbed and headed out over the Gulf of Finland she sat in a daze. Earlier she had, despite Newman's warning, made a brief call to INCUBUS headquarters, leaving a message for her boss that she'd left for England.

Unlike her sister, Sandy, Evelyn was tall and had red hair. She wore a gaberdine suit of dark blue, a white blouse, and her sheepskin was tucked away inside the baggage compartment above her head. Staring down through the window, she gazed at the icefield which was the frozen Baltic. Not the best reason for flying home, but oh God, she was sick of the subzero temperatures, the

26

fact that the sun rose at ten in the morning and set at two in the afternoon. Endless dark which got to you, created a feeling of permanent depression.

Soon she fell fast asleep, worn out by the news Bob Newman had given her, by the earlier experience of the horrible death of Ed Riverton, by having to visit the mortuary to identify him, by the rush to the airport. She woke when the machine bumped something.

Staring out of the window she was astounded to realize she had arrived at Heathrow. She had slept for almost three hours. As the plane taxied along the runway she sighed with relief. No ice, no snow. It might be a sullen grey sky but it would be daylight for hours yet . . .

'That's the Lennox girl, Steve,' said Papa Grimwood, checking the photograph he had obtained from INCUBUS HQ in the West End. All British employees' details were on file. Evelyn was carrying her case to a waiting taxi.

'I have to collect the car from the multistorey,' Steve reminded him.

'So the timing is excellent,' replied Grimwood. 'We have her address in Wandsworth. We'll arrive on her doorstep within fifteen minutes of her getting there. Splendid timing,' he repeated, 'she'll be off balance from her extended flight. And very receptive to our methods of persuasion.'

Evelyn asked the cab driver to stop at the small supermarket near her house, bought the bare necessities for a drink of tea and something simple to eat. She had missed the meal served on the plane. The doorbell rang a few minutes after she had opened the lid of her case and returned downstairs to make herself a cup of tea. She frowned: no one knew she was back. Must be someone

27

selling something. She opened the door and stared at the grotesque couple.

'Mizz Evelyn Lennox?'

It was a gnome-like little man who asked the question after removing his trilby. His face was ruddy and lined and he had a nutcracker nose and chin. He stooped like a hunch-back. Difficult to guess his age – between forty and sixty. Wearing a new sports jacket and grey flannels under his open raincoat. He had squirrel eyes which darted about and he took a good look at her legs beneath her short skirt.

'What is it you want?' she asked, tired from the flight.

'Fraternal & Equality . . .' The gnome's companion showed a printed card, keeping a firm grip on it. 'We're going to make you safe for life, lady.'

'This is Steve,' the gnome introduced. 'I'm Papa Grimwood, senior representative of the company. If we could talk to you inside for a few minutes you won't regret it.'

She hesitated. Steve was six feet tall, heavily built and his clean-shaven pale face showed no expression. Grimwood was smiling in an oily manner. Evelyn had vaguely heard of the company, a subsidiary of INCUBUS. Grimwood edged forward, still smiling.

'We make arrangements for all ex-employees. Financial – for life.'

'Ex-employees of who?'

'INCUBUS.' Grimwood lowered his voice and she had the impression he revealed the information reluctantly. She was too exhausted to resist and showed them into the living room. They waited until she had sat down and then Grimwood hauled a chair closer to her, seated himself. Steve chose a chair to her left so she had to twist round to see him.

'First, we'd appreciate it if you'd sign this document – a small formality,' Grimwood assured her in his most Uriah Heep tone. 'Then you'll receive your pension from

Fraternal & Equality. Five hundred pounds a week in cash – for the rest of your life.'

'I don't sign documents without my solicitor checking them.'

As she said the words her mind was calculating. Five hundred a week was twenty-five thousand a year. Grimwood leaned closer. His accent was a peculiar mixture of Cockney and American. Midatlantic. Maybe he'd spent time in the States.

'There are conditions, of course,' Grimwood went on, ignoring her remark. 'You agree never to discuss your work for your recent employer with anyone. Never,' he repeated. 'With no one. Not a whisper.'

She drank more tea. She was damned if she was going to offer refreshment to them. She put down the cup, crossed her legs, clasped her hands on her knees.

'And supposing I did talk to someone about my job?'

'Oh, my dear...' Grimwood shook his head mournfully.

'I'm not your "dear",' she snapped.

'My profound apologies. As I was saying, that would certainly not be in your best interests.' Grimwood shook his head again. 'Dear me, no. Your very generous pension would stop at once.'

'And that would be the least of your problems.'

It was the first time Steve had spoken since they'd entered the house. His voice had been harsh, menacing. She swung round to face him.

'What does that mean?'

Steve spread his huge hands, strangler's hands – the thought flashed in Evelyn's mind. He stood up, walked towards her, leant his hands on the arms of her chair.

'Just a few people did make that mistake. They talked. It wasn't good for their health. To take one example, a man was killed in a car accident. Fraternal & Equality always take a great interest in the health of their clients.'

For a big man he had a curiously quiet voice, sibilant. He went back to his chair.

'Are you threatening me?' Evelyn asked.

She was frightened, but she was furious, and her brain was ticking over now. These people had turned up with uncanny speed. There had to be some link with Helsinki. Again she began to think about the murder of her brother-in-law.

'Gracious me!' Grimwood leaned closer. 'Papa is concerned about what you've said. Steve was just recalling a little history. Sign the document now and forget about it. Think instead of five hundred pounds – in cash – sent to you by special delivery every week. For the rest of your life . . .'

He broke off as the doorbell rang. Evelyn uncrossed her legs, got up slowly, began to walk to the living room door. Grimwood spoke quickly.

'Get rid of whoever it is. This is your only chance for a pension most people would give an arm and a leg for . . .' He was talking to himself. Evelyn was heading down the hall for the front door.

Newman slowed down as he approached 495 Greenway Gardens, Wandsworth. He thought the name singularly inappropriate: either side was lined with a wall of Victorian terrace villas. Bay windows on the ground and first floors, postage-stamp sized front gardens behind railings, nothing remotely green in sight. He parked a few doors from 495, walked the rest of the way, pushed open the black, freshly painted grille gate, noted the heavy net curtains masking the bay windows, stepped inside the quarry-tiled porch and pressed the bell.

The upper half of the front door was a stained glass window which seemed to emphasize the cloistered atmosphere of the deserted road. Within ten seconds he saw the silhouette of someone approaching beyond the glass. The door was opened and Evelyn stood framed against a long hallway.

Newman grinned and then frowned as a mixture of emotions flashed over her face. Surprise, fright, overwhelming relief. She put a finger to her lips and gestured inside.

'A spot of trouble?' he enquired in a whisper.

She nodded, reached out a hand to usher him inside. He was wearing a trench coat, military style with wide lapels, the collar turned up, belted. He slipped his gloves into his pockets as he followed her over the threshold and she shut the door.

'Two men. From the INCUBUS insurance outfit,' she whispered back. 'The tall one, Steve, threatened me if I refused to sign a document.'

'Let's take a look at them,' he suggested.

She ushered him into the living room, which overlooked the front street and had a large couch in the bay. Chintz furnishings, walls painted magnolia, decorated with framed pictures of water-colour landscapes. Newman's trained reporter's eye took all this in in a glance. He stopped in the centre of the room, staring at the two men.

The crouched gnome-like figure remained seated, gazing at the visitor. The tall heavy, dark-haired with thick brows too close together, stood up and balanced himself on the balls of his feet. A man ready for a fight. Evelyn waved a hand.

'Bob, these two gentlemen are from Fraternal & Equality, an insurance company. This is Mr Grimwood – apparently known as Papa. And this is Steve. No idea of his other name. And this is Robert Newman.'

'Ah!' Grimwood rose slowly to his feet, smiling his oily smile, extending a hand. 'Mr Robert Newman, the famous foreign correspondent. I recognize you from

31

pictures in the papers and news magazines. A pleasure to make your acquaintance, sir.'

Newman ignored the extended hand, looked at the man called Steve who had tucked his right hand inside the lapel of his buttoned jacket. He moved suddenly, took three paces forward. Steve began to slide out the hand holding something. Newman raised his own right hand in a diversionary gesture and whipped up his right foot. It connected savagely with Steve's kneecap. The tall man screamed with pain, slumping forward, Newman's hand came down, nails jabbing into the back of the half-withdrawn hand. Steve yelped and Newman grabbed the gun he was holding. He backed away, looked at Evelyn.

'A Walther PP., 7.65 mm automatic. Who are these people?'

'They are from Fraternal & Equality, the insurance subsidiary of INCUBUS.'

'Really?' Newman held the automatic in the palm of his hand. 'A new way of selling insurance?' he asked the gnome.

'I must apologize profoundly, sir.' Grimwood glanced venomously at Steve who was still doubled over, nursing his kneecap. 'My associate can be impetuous. I think he feared he was about to be attacked by you . . .'

'Answer the bloody question. Is this a new way of selling insurance?'

'I was about to explain, sir. You see, often I carry large sums of cash and need protection. Especially in these days of violence. If you read the papers . . .'

'Forget the papers. Evelyn, what happened before I arrived?'

'They tried to force me to sign that document . . .'

Grimwood grabbed for the bulky sheaf of printed paper but Newman had hold of it. 'Tsk! Tsk! Don't snatch – it's bad manners. The last thing an insurance salesman should display.'

'I'm not a salesman,' Grimwood bleated.

'And the only violence so far has been caused by your friend – pardon, your associate – Steve. I wonder if he has a certificate to carry a weapon? Maybe the police would be interested in checking that point? But first things first.' He turned to Evelyn. 'What is this document these two are so anxious you should sign?'

'That's company property . . .' Grimwood had hauled his bulk out of the chair, his manner quite different. 'I must ask you to hand that back to me.'

'And I must ask you to shut your gabby mouth. I was asking my friend here.'

'It's a big fat pension for life,' Grimwood persisted.

'With conditions,' Evelyn snapped.

'So I see.' Newman was skip-reading the second page which, like the first, contained clause after clause. He read one aloud. '"*If at any time the aforesaid beneficiary divulges to anyone details of her confidential employment with INCUBUS then the aforesaid beneficiary will forfeit all further claim to any pension rights hitherto granted whatsoever . . .*"'

Newman folded the document, put it in his pocket, looked at Grimwood. 'That's a new one on me. I don't think you're very nice people.'

'And,' Evelyn interjected, pointing at Steve, who had sagged into an armchair, hugging his knee, glaring at Newman, 'he threatened me. Talked about it not being good for my health if I refused to sign. He also told me about another ex-employee who'd had a fatal motor accident . . .'

'Steve didn't finish his story,' Grimwood whined. 'After the man involved died we paid a large lump sum to his—'

'I'm sure you did,' Newman said sarcastically. His voice changed. 'Get out! Both of you. Now!'

'My knee . . .' Steve began.

'Give you a helping hand,' Newman assured him

cheerfully. 'Open the front door, Evelyn.' He grabbed hold of Steve by the scruff of the neck, half lifted, half dragged him to the front door. At the entrance he shoved hard. Steve sprawled on to the pavement as Grimwood hurried down the hall.

'We shall complain. That is an act of violence.'

Newman pulled the Walther automatic out of his pocket, held it on his palm, closed his fingers when Grimwood reached for the weapon. He nodded towards the doorway.

'Shove it. Don't come back.'

3

As Evelyn closed and locked the front door Newman hurried back to the living room. He stood to one side of the bay window and watched beyond the net curtains. Grimwood was half supporting Steve who had clambered to his feet, making their way further along Greenway Gardens.

When they had passed the house he stood in the bay and watched their progress. A large grey Volkswagen van was parked about four houses along the street. Grimwood stopped by the van door, extracted keys, opened the door and helped Steve inside. Grimwood slipped behind the wheel, closed the door, started the engine and slowly moved off.

'They've gone.' Newman turned to Evelyn who stood white faced. She looked even more attractive, her wide mouth a slash of red lipstick, her good bone structure tapering to a pointed determined chin. Her thick red hair rested just below her shoulders on the blue gaberdine and her grey eyes stared back at him. Her expression was grave, so very different from Sandy.

'I could do with a tot of brandy,' she said. 'How about you, Bob?'

'No. Hot tea with a little sugar. You're in a mild state of shock. No wonder. And no alcohol.'

'You're right. Come into the kitchen with me while I brew up . . .'

The kitchen was a surprise. At the back of the house, overlooking a small garden with sour soil and moss-infested lawn, the kitchen was long and galley-like with all the latest equipment. Well laid out, so far as Newman could see while she made the tea. He perched on a stool before asking his question.

'You ignored my warning, didn't you? You phoned INCUBUS before you left Helsinki. And you didn't phone me.'

'I'm usually pretty sensible, but I panicked,' she admitted. 'I didn't have time to call you before catching a flight – but I felt I had to call INCUBUS. I couldn't just walk out on them after three years with the organization. At least that's how I felt then. Now I feel they can get stuffed . . .'

She recalled briefly what had happened after she arrived home. It was only after they had returned to the living room that she asked the question as she poured tea.

'How did Sandy die?'

'Drink some tea.' She was sitting down on the couch with Newman beside her. He waited until she had put down her cup and saucer. 'Sandy's murder was a shocking business. I'll tell you the details later . . .' She gripped his arm to protest but he was firm. 'I said *later*. What was it about your job in Finland which was confidential – to quote from this?' He pulled the sheaf of papers from his pocket.

35

Newman knew exactly what he was doing, that he was being ruthless – determined to extract information from her during her state of shock when she might talk more openly, when she was very hostile towards her previous employer after her recent experience.

She poured them more tea and he kept silent, anxious not to disturb her present mood. Drinking half her cup she put it down, twisted round to face him, her chin resting in her hand, and told him a strange story.

'As I told you when you came to dinner with Ed and me at his apartment in Helsinki, I'm a trained psychologist – like Sandy. I worked for what INCUBUS called the Profiles – Psychological Research Division. P–PRD. The Americans love initials. The key word is *Profiles*. Let me give you an example. There was an electronics outfit owned by a Finn in Turku, the second largest city. On the Baltic coast and the port where ships come in from Sweden. It was all very hush-hush – that was emphasized from the beginning.'

'What was significant about the electronics outfit?'

'INCUBUS's Finnish subsidiary – INCUBUS Oy. (or Ltd.) – was making a secret bid through another company to take it over. Most of its export trade is with Russia. High-tech stuff – they have Swedish high-flyer scientists working for them. A man called Timo Metsola owned the company outright. I was told to produce a complete profile of him.'

'What sort of profile?'

'The emphasis is on character.' She gazed into the distance and spoke as though reciting a lesson. 'The profile's strengths – strong will-power, physical endurance under pressure, reaction to intense pressure. Then his weaknesses – alcohol, drugs, any physical weakness such as being a diabetic. Any special fears such as vertigo, fear of drowning, dislike of flying, etc.'

'This is weird,' Newman commented. 'Didn't it strike you as a strange technique?'

'Gradually, it did. I eventually became worried and then frightened. I was told the data was needed for the Medical Division – among a host of other activities INCUBUS owns a number of pharmaceutical laboratories. The profiles of outstanding men who'd achieved a lot were supposed to give data for the development of new drugs. After studying Timo Metsola I began to think that was all eyewash – that the profiles had a more sinister purpose.'

'Why?'

'Because I learned by accident INCUBUS was trying to take over his company – and exactly the same thing had happened with another industrialist I'd been asked to draw up a profile for.'

'How on earth did you obtain this information? I realize you're a trained psychologist but give me some details.'

'By trickery and fraud and subversion. That was when I began to question to myself exactly what I was doing. Give you an example? INCUBUS also owns a big business magazine in the States called *Leaders of Mankind*. One of its features is a portrait of some top businessman anywhere in the world. When I first went to see Timo Metsola I had to represent myself as a reporter from that magazine. I had all the credentials.'

'When you first went to see him? You went more than once?'

'It was a series of interviews. Even these big men are flattered at the idea of a major profile in *Leaders*. I'd been trained by the P–PRD Division. What approach to use, which questions to ask, what to look for while I was conducting an interview. While I was talking to Metsola one day he swallowed some medicine. We had got to know each other pretty well by then. He said it was a preparation he had to take for diabetes. I noted that in the detailed report I handed in later.'

'Sounds weird, but hardly sinister.'

'But with the other Finn I interviewed there was something sinister.' Evelyn was playing with a lace handkerchief as she talked, plucking at it nervously. 'He was a shipbuilder – yachts. There's more than one of them in Finland.'

'Tell me about him,' Newman coaxed.

'Let me finish first about Timo. He had no intention of selling his company to anyone. Three months after I'd submitted my profile he sold out to INCUBUS. I built up the same sort of profile about the shipbuilder. And he didn't want to sell. But during the course of the interview it came out his brother was anxious to sell – he was addicted to gambling and owed a lot of money. Also he was the heir. Can you guess what's coming next?'

'Never guess,' Newman replied casually and lit a cigarette.

'Could I have one, please? I've given it up but I need one now.' She looked at him sideways. 'Light it for me.'

It was the first indication Newman had that she was interested in him. Watch it, he warned himself. He lit the cigarette, handed it to her. She took a deep drag, smiled at him, laid a hand on his arm.

'That tastes especially good.'

'What came next?' he asked brusquely.

'The yacht builder was killed in a supposed accident. He'd asked me to go and see him in the evening to continue the interview. There were lights on in all the windows.' She shuddered, took another drag. 'I found him. They'd had a huge fork lift truck on the roof where they stored materials. The truck had toppled off the roof just when he was walking underneath it. The two huge spikes were rammed into his body. They decided the brakes had been defective, that the high wind that night had tipped it over.'

'You believed that?'

'Yes. Until his brother took over the firm and promptly sold it to INCUBUS Oy. And his habit of arriving back late in the evening after dinner to do more work was recorded in my preliminary report. I began to wonder if I was creating profiles for murder. Sounds crazy?'

'Depends. Did you talk to anyone about this?'

'Yes, to the only man I could trust. Ed Riverton, Sandy's husband. He was on the banking side.' She moved closer to Newman.

'As you know, I interviewed Ed during my Helsinki trip – about the banking operations. I got the impression he was being evasive, which roused my curiosity. That's the nasty thing about reporters. You told him all you've told me?'

'Yes. He didn't know anything about Profiles– Psychological Research Division. He was intrigued. Said he was going to investigate it.' Her lips trembled. 'A couple of weeks later they dragged him off the ice in North Harbour.'

'Sounds as though I was right when Í decided to poke into the activities of INCUBUS – and Hauser . . .'

He stopped talking as he glanced out of the window. Newman put a finger to his lips to warn her not to speak. Standing up, he walked behind the couch into the bay. The Volkswagen van was back. Parked in the same place as before. The cunning sods had pretended to drive off – in case they were being observed – and had then reversed the vehicle into its original position. There was one difference in its appearance. A large aerial had appeared, projected from the roof, an aerial similar to those used by Post Office vans detecting people who didn't pay their TV licence.

Newman frowned at Evelyn to make her continue

keeping quiet. He began a swift and expert search of the room. A Swiss he had once known had taught him how to locate bugging mechanisms. He switched on the radio, continued looking. The bug was attached to the back of the TV set. He held it in his hand, put it back, twiddled the radio knob from pop music to atmospherics, turned up the volume.

'They bugged you,' he whispered. 'Now we'll feed them some disinformation. Be ready to play along with what I say.'

He turned the knob back to pop music, turned the volume down to almost nothing, began talking to Evelyn.

'So you have this aunt in Ambleside you're going to visit?'

'That's right, Bob. I just want to get away from my normal surroundings.'

'Ambleside in the Lake District is a good choice. Of course it's small – everyone knows everyone else and what's going on. But that kind of local gossip will ease the tension out of you. You've decided then to leave today?'

'I just want to leave London as fast as possible,' Evelyn replied, playing along.

'I'll give you a hand with the packing. Then I'll drive you to the station. That way I'll make sure we're not followed. If we are, I'll spot them . . .'

He turned up the volume loud, turned the knob to atmospherics, walked quickly to the window. Within two minutes the automatic aerial was retracted and the Volkswagen drove off.

Newman sat down, deliberately choosing the armchair Grimwood had occupied, leaving Evelyn on the couch.

'What was all that about?' she asked, the anxiety clear in her voice.

'They bugged you, as I said.' He opened his hand. 'They're making them smaller and smaller. It's called progress – the advance of science.'

40

'When could they have done that? I opened the door to them. I was with them all the time . . .'

'Not when you answered the door to me,' he pointed out. 'I am sure one of them attached this little blighter to your TV set in the short time you were showing me in. They're a crafty couple. Professionals. When they reached their van they drove off a short distance in case I was observing them. Then they backed the vehicle, elevated the aerial, listened in and tape-recorded our conversation; that would be my guess. We have to recall what we said, what they now know.'

'And Ambleside?'

'To protect you. They'll be convinced you're off to the Lake District today. That bit I put in about knowing if we were being followed when I drove you to the station will stop them trying to do just that, will keep them away from here. And I handed it to them on a plate. Ambleside. A small place. Everyone knows everyone else. They'll think you'll be easy to find there. They'll scoot off to the Lake District and search round for days.'

'It might work.' She brightened up. 'It *will* work.'

'And they'll be slowed down because they'll have to be discreet. I kept Steve's Walther – I might report that to the police. My guess is a quite different couple will be sent to track you down.'

'They found me here quickly enough,' she reminded him. 'I was back here and less than half an hour afterwards they were on my doorstep.'

'Let's think how they worked that one.' He frowned. 'It suggests some high-powered organization. First, you made the mistake of phoning INCUBUS before you caught your flight from Helsinki . . .'

'I'm sorry . . .'

He dismissed her apology with a curt wave of his hand. 'Let me go on. How they recognized you is what puzzles me. At Heathrow, I mean. I think they followed you here

41

from when you left the airport. What sort of records do they keep at their headquarters for this country in Norwich?'

'You mean about employees? Very detailed. Including photocopies of birth certificates, mortgages – even when they're your own, like mine. And photographs . . .'

'That's it. Those two had a photo to watch for you coming off the plane – which means you must have been followed to Helsinki Airport. Nice people.'

'You said we must think about what they know from bugging us while we were talking after they'd gone.'

'That's important. They know you have talked to me about your secret work. They know I'm investigating the octopus called INCUBUS. That will make my future investigations a little more difficult, but I can handle that. Now I know that they know.'

She stood up, carried a hardback chair close to Newman, sat down, placed a hand on his knee. 'Now. How did Sandy die? I need to know.'

'She was hung up with a rope round her neck. Suspended from a beam in an old bell tower in Suffolk where we'd planned to meet early in the morning . . .'

'Oh, dear God! Sandy . . .'

Newman went on talking fast. 'I was the one who found her. And that makes me number one suspect for her murder . . .'

As if he had triggered off a signal the doorbell rang. They looked at each other. Newman moved her hand, stood up and pressed his own hand on her shoulder to keep her seated. He went to answer the door himself, his right hand gripping the Walther automatic. He had paused in the hall to double-check the magazine was loaded.

Beyond the stained glass window he could make out two male silhouettes. Both tall. At least Grimwood & Co. hadn't returned. He opened the door.

Chief Inspector Roy Buchanan, with Sergeant Warden beside him, stood gazing at him. Buchanan raised an eyebrow before he spoke.

'Well, well. Mr Robert Newman again. We musn't keep meeting like this. People will talk.'

4

Adam Carver had spent longer than he'd expected with *Uno*. The computer was located inside a vault at Level Five – well away from the windowless conference room. Due to an appointment with a major client, he had returned late in the afternoon. Earlier, using the password, he had flashed on the screen all the data on Evelyn Lennox. What had startled him was that she had a sister, Sandra Riverton, who had worked for INCUBUS in Suffolk.

Uno. The nickname had been coined by Hauser himself and Carver found it childish. The President of INCUBUS, shrewd and ruthless, had a naïve streak. Carver had tapped keys and up came the data on the Lennox girl. He stared at it,

Age: Twenty-eight. Nationality: Brit. Description . . .
Occupation: Trained psychologist. Employed Finland.
Division: P–PRD. Rating: A1. Track record: Ultra.
Defects: Related to Sandra Riverton (Sister), employed
INCUBUS, Suffolk, Brit. Zone.

There was a a lot of other stuff he skip-read. It was the final word which caught his attention. *Cancelled*. Followed by a date three weeks earlier. Carver pressed more keys and signed off. The screen went blank, unlike his mind. He sat quite still for ten minutes, thinking.

His mind was in a whirl and he was worried. He then lifted the phone to call Peggy Vanderheld, Hauser's statuesque and hard-bitten personal assistant. When giving interviews to the press Hauser liked to paint a picture of himself as the company's father figure.

'Just because I happen to be President of this company I don't play the Great White Chief,' he was fond of saying. 'My door is always open to any employee who has a problem. Night and day I'm available to the folks who work for us.'

It was a load of crap – like his speech that morning to the executives. His only concern was their future, to help them higher up the ladder? Bullshit. Carver was the Senior Vice President, Banking Loans. A qualified accountant, his official job was to raise funds, find more money. And there were twelve more Senior Vice Presidents across the far-flung empire of INCUBUS. Some were more senior than others.

'Peggy? Adam here. Level Five. I need to see Franklin D. When can he fit me in?'

'That could be difficult. He has a tight schedule . . .'

Damn! Adam had a date with a promising Finnish brunette for that evening. He was confident he'd brought her to the stage where he could lay her. Strike while the iron is hot.

'He asked me to check data on a recent employee. I've checked. He wants me to take action. There are queries before I can do that.'

'Which employee?' Peggy's American voice was a whiplash.

'Evelyn Lennox. Just mention that name to him. Plus I have questions to ask.'

'Hold it . . .'

Adam swore again while he waited. He'd booked a

good table at The Palace. His date had a Finnish boy friend but he knew he was prising her loose. With women you had to keep persisting before they sank into your arms.

'Carver!' Peggy was back on the line. 'Can you come now? Good. Move the butt.'

The connection was broken. Arrogant bitch. They said she carried inside her pretty head more secrets than *Uno*. That she was the only woman Hauser trusted. Had he something on her, Adam wondered as he closed the vault and headed down the corridor walled with stainless steel for the elevator.

Hauser was sitting in his de luxe, specially designed, black leather swivel chair behind a huge mahogany desk in his private office. The walls were panelled in mahogany except for the fourth wall behind him. This was solid glass with a panoramic view over a forest-fringed lake, which was really an arm of the sea.

He took the cigarette holder out of his wide mouth and beamed at his visitor, his Roosevelt smile, warm and toothy. Carver knew for a fact that Hauser had a collection of Roosevelt film clips, that he studied them to perfect the famous American president's mannerisms.

'Your timing is perfect,' Hauser announced. 'Frank has just arrived. Straight from the airport. He's on his way up now. Isn't that nice. A while since you two got together.'

He's playing with me again, Carver thought. Frank Galvone was also a senior vice president. Information and Planning was his division, whatever that might mean. And he was the last person Carver needed just now. The door opened. No respectful knock. Frank Galvone walked in, clad in a snow-covered sheepskin which trailed his ankles, the fur thick with snow. Beyond the window Carver could see a blizzard creaming down, blotting out the sea.

'Hi!' Galvone shook snow from the sheepskin, took it

off, dumped it in a chair. 'Almost as bad as New York here,' he remarked in his low husky voice.

'Frank, you've messed up my beautiful carpet,' Hauser told him mildly and smiled.

Galvone glanced down at the wall-to-wall shag carpet, shrugged. He pressed a button next to the door.

'We have peasants to vacuum the place. Make them work – if you don't want them to spend the day, and your money, sitting with their feet up.'

Peggy Vanderheld, clad in a navy blue form-fitting suit, came into the room. Galvone gestured at the carpet. 'Clean up this mess – and fast. We have a meeting under way.'

She glared at him venomously but went out, came back with the machine, sucked up the snow, left without a word. Carver spoke quickly, nodding towards Galvone's back as the American stared at the blizzard. He said this was something private.

'If it's the Evelyn Lennox problem, go ahead, Adam,' Hauser encouraged him. 'After all, we have no secrets from Frank. By the by, he called in at London on his way from New York.'

'Just a brief stopover,' Galvone said, turning round.

Carver nodded. Why had Frank found it necessary to provide that bit of information?

Galvone was a first generation American with his roots in Italy. Shorter than Carver – five foot seven – he was heavily built with wide shoulders and stocky legs. Clean shaven, his hair was black, as were his thick brows. His face was very bony, cadaverous. His cheekbones were prominent, his nose was long, his chin was aggressive, skeletal. Carver had never seen him smile. His brown eyes were blank.

'Now,' Hauser said genially, 'I have my two top men with me. I always feel comfortable in your presence.'

Carver said nothing: Hauser was up to his usual tactics

– playing off one man against the other. He frequently referred to Carver as 'my potential successor. In a few years he'll have developed a big enough ass to occupy my chair.'

But then Carver had heard that on other occasions he used the same language about Galvone. And he suspected Galvone took the rivalry very seriously indeed.

'OK.' Hauser settled himself more comfortably in his chair. 'Adam, tell us about Evelyn Lennox.' He looked at Galvone. 'He's going to check her out in London. Left the company at a moment's notice, flew back there. We just want to be sure everything is hunky-dory.'

'Why shouldn't it be?' Frank asked.

'Adam will tell us.'

Frank remained standing as Carver was ushered with a wave of the hand to sit down. 'Evelyn Lennox had a sister, a Sandra Riverton, who also worked for us,' he began slowly, staring at the floor. 'Is there a connection between these two?'

'Leave it there,' Hauser said amiably. 'You have to concentrate on the financial side. All you need to do is to make sure she's happy with her pension. Get her general reaction to life. What she's going to do next. You know the sort of thing.'

'I'm not sure I do.'

'You're The Charmer,' Frank interjected with a sneer. 'We all know you have the ladies in the palm of your smooth hand. Wouldn't do to send me.' He made a sound like a sly chuckle. 'I might end up knocking her teeth out.'

'I wouldn't put it past you,' Carver snapped.

'Now that's not a nice thing to say to a fellow vice president. Lost your sense of humour, Adam? It was a joke. J-O-K-E – you do know what a joke is?'

Hauser settled himself even more comfortably. There was nothing he enjoyed more than seeing a couple of his

47

subordinates at each other's throats. Better than a bull fight.

Carver looked at him, caught his fleeting expression, made a great effort to cool it. He nodded to Frank.

'OK. It was a joke. Fair enough.' He turned to Hauser. 'While I was checking the computer I came across a reference to the P–PRD. That's a division I'd never even heard of before. What the blazes does it stand for? What sort of work was Evelyn Lennox engaged on? And why is it coded with initials? All the other divisions have their functions spelt out. Like Frank's. Information and Planning.'

'What the hell has that got to do with you?' demanded Frank.

Carver turned to look at him, showing no particular reaction. Inwardly he was surprised by the vehemence in Frank's voice. Vehemence? Almost vicious fury.

'If I'm to talk to Evelyn Lennox,' he said calmly, 'I need to brief myself in advance with anything she might throw at me.'

'You've got no goddamned right to go poking around in that computer,' Frank snarled.

'Now, boys,' Hauser intervened, 'a bit of push and shove is OK, but you're shoving too hard, Frank. If you can't control your temper you'd better go down to the canteen and help yourself to a drink. Of mineral water.'

There was a snap in his tone and Carver watched as Frank struggled to compose his features. His opponent made a throwaway gesture with his hands, gave a sheepish grin which was more a grimace.

'Sorry, Chief. Those long flights can get to you. Jet lag can creep up on you. Think I'll sit down, rest the body and just listen while Adam tells the tale.'

Jet lag? From a three-hour flight, at the outside, when he'd only flown from London to Helsinki on the last lap? Carver was careful not to comment on the thought. He

48

looked back at Hauser who started talking rapidly.

'I take your point, Adam. Why Sandra Riverton resigned from the company I've no idea. That kind of detail just doesn't reach me. I can't afford to get bogged down in the weeds. But at least you know she did leave. Maybe a coincidence, maybe the two girls talked on the phone, decided they'd both had enough. As to Ed Riverton, all we know is what the police told us. And you have the advantage, Adam, that you talked with this Mauno Sarin. Now, you're briefed, as you put it.'

'Not quite. What sort of work were these girls doing for us?'

'Women are a damned nuisance and I could do without hiring a single female. Their job is at home, in bed and then doing the cooking. But sometimes because they are female they're more suitable for interviewing men susceptible to so-called feminine charm.'

'You mean they were call girls?' Adam enquired.

'Hell, no!' Hauser pounded his huge fist on the desk and glared. 'They were secretarial types – like Peggy. Adam, you've got what you need. Catch the earliest flight down to London, check up on the Lennox twist. OK?'

Hauser waited until he was alone with Galvone, stubbed out a cigarette savagely, lit a fresh one. He took several puffs and Galvone was careful to keep quiet. It was unusual for Hauser to blow his top. When he spoke he seemed calmer and under control.

'You have a job, Frank.'

'Which is?'

'Board the same flight Carver takes to London. Go Economy and make sure he doesn't see you. Follow him, observe him, report back to me personally. Travel Section will tell you the flight he's on.'

'May be difficult to make sure he doesn't spot me.'

'Difficult? Disguise yourself. Fresh clothes. A ski outfit. Goggle glasses. Anything!' He stared at Galvone.

49

'Hell, you've had experience very recently of handling some tricky situations, taking instant decisions, and they came out just the way we wanted them. That's it. Tail Carver.'

5

Inside the living room at 495 Greenway Gardens Buchanan sat in the armchair Grimwood had occupied, legs stretched out, crossed at the ankles. He faced Newman and Evelyn on the couch in the bay. Sergeant Warden sat in the hard-backed chair, notebook at the ready. The conversation continued.

'Would you mind telling me how you heard your sister, Sandra Riverton, had been murdered?' Buchanan asked Evelyn, his grey eyes watching hers.

'I phoned her from London,' Newman said quickly. 'Which is why she flew back immediately from Helsinki.'

'I was asking Miss Lennox.' There was an edge to Buchanan's tone. 'Perhaps you would be good enough to let her answer for herself.'

'You do realize she's not obliged to put up with an interrogation?' Newman rapped back. 'We could show both of you the door. Unless you're charging her with something. That, as I understand it, is the law.'

'I do know my law,' the Chief Inspector replied equably. He rattled some change in his pocket. 'Do you wish to show me the door, Miss Lennox?'

'I am rather upset . . .'

'She's undergone some pretty awful ordeals,' Newman persisted. 'Do you normally question people when they're in no fit state to think clearly? I'm sure it would be best if you both went, deferred this interview until a more suitable occasion.'

'You own this house? Or part-own it?' Buchanan asked in the same mild tone.

'No . . .'

'Then kindly let Miss Lennox take whatever decision she may wish without prompting from you.'

'I really am very upset at the moment,' Evelyn replied, taking her cue from Newman.

Buchanan swung his gaze to Newman. 'A moment ago you referred to *several* ordeals. What did you mean by that?'

'For God's sake! She had just heard in Helsinki her brother-in-law has been hauled out of the frozen harbour. With his throat garrotted, in case you'd forgotten. Then she hears her own sister has been murdered under horrible circumstances. Hence, Chief Inspector, the use of the plural.'

'I have an excellent memory. I had not forgotten about Mr Riverton's death. I hardly would – you told me only a few minutes ago.' Buchanan was speaking in a monotone. 'But you made it sound like more than *two* ordeals.'

He clasped his hands in his lap and waited, studying Newman's reaction.

'I can't help what it sounds like to your tortuous mind. I was referring to both murders. Period.'

'Which is a weird coincidence – since both crimes appear to have been committed within about twenty-four hours of each other.' He look at Evelyn. 'And you said your sister had a similar job to yourself. What was the nature of these jobs?'

'Oh, we were just secretaries. Chief Inspector, I'm flaked out now. Could you leave this for a few days until I'm fresher?'

'Of course.' Buchanan stood up, putting on his coat as

51

Warden stood at the same time. 'I'll try and phone you before we come next time. Please don't bother – we can find our own way out.' At the door he turned and spoke to Newman. 'As for you, I would remind you I am conducting a murder investigation.'

Newman smiled grimly. 'And I'm hardly likely to forget that. Especially after the grilling you gave me at Southwold.'

The hint of a smile appeared at the corners of Buchanan's mouth, a cynical smile. 'And you appear to have calmed down very quickly, Mr Newman.'

On this parting shot he left. Newman followed them as they closed the door. He locked it. 'What did that mean?' Evelyn asked as he came back into the room.

'That he's a very shrewd and dangerous opponent. I'd pretended to lose my temper and he spotted it.'

'Why didn't you tell them about that ghastly couple – Grimwood and Steve? I gathered you weren't going to tell him, so I kept quiet too.'

'Which was smart of you. It would just have confused the issue.' He looked at her. 'That's not quite honest – I want to follow up that investigation myself. I would have told him if I'd thought there was a cat's chance in hell he'd have provided a guard for you – a constable on your doorstep.'

'And he wouldn't have done that?'

'Definitely not, on the evidence of what happened. No one physically attacked you, thank God. These days the Met. are always moaning they're short of staff. Too busy joy-riding in their nice shiny patrol cars to hoof it on the beat.'

'Bob.' She was standing close to him, he caught a whiff of expensive perfume. 'Couldn't you stay with me for a few days in case those men come back.' She paused. 'You could sleep in the spare bedroom.'

And how long would you expect me to stay there?

Newman was thinking. It simply wasn't on. His mind was full of Sandy, of the memory of her hanging like a rag doll. The idea of risking bedding her own sister was repugnant. He shook his head.

'That's not a good idea, Evelyn. I want to devote all my time to finding out who murdered Sandy. The longer I wait, the colder the trail will get. Buchanan could have told you that. Do you know a good locksmith?' She nodded without enthusiasm. 'Then get the locks changed on that front door. Deadlocks. Chubb or Banham. If I call you on the phone I'll ring twice, put down the receiver, do the same thing again. When the phone rings a third time answer it. That guarantees it will be me. Otherwise don't pick it up, no matter how long it rings.'

'Why would they call me?'

'They probably won't. But they just might to make certain you're not here – that you have left for the Lake District.'

'All right, you're going to be busy. So am I. There are the details of Sandy's funeral to be attended to. No, don't offer to help – I can manage on my own. I'm the only family she had left. Will you be attending?'

He refused to be roused by her anger, suspecting she was furious he'd turned down her invitation to stay. As he put on his coat he smiled.

'If there is any way I can help, all you have to do is to call me. And here is my card. Don't forget, Evelyn, I was very fond of Sandy. I was on the verge of asking her to marry me.

'Perhaps in that way she had a lucky escape.'

For the second time he ignored an insult. She was flaked out, as she'd said. Too much horror in too short a space of time.

'Think it over,' he urged her. 'But above all, be careful.'

*　　*　　*

'Now I have another problem,' Tweed announced as he took off his Burberry in his office. 'Since the INCUBUS investigation looks like taking some time to get off the ground I can at least devote my attention to this new one.'

Paula Grey and Monica exchanged glances. It was evening and Tweed seemed excited. He had just returned from a fresh session with the PM at Downing Street. He settled himself behind his desk, wearing his heaviest grey suit. Outside it was a raw bitter February night.

'Why is the INCUBUS problem going to take time to get to grips with?' Paula asked.

'Because it involves a lot of research – maybe months. I have people working on it already but it's a world-wide organization and the structure is complex. Maybe deliberately so, but that's only an educated guess.'

'So what is this new problem?'

'Europe, as you know, is like a boiling cauldron. Frontiers which have held for over forty years are no longer sacred. The Communist apparatus is collapsing everywhere, thanks to Gorbachev. But this leaves some very dangerous and experienced experts without a job. Can you guess?'

'You often say guessing isn't good enough in our work.'

'True.' Tweed smiled at the gentle rebuke, then became grave. 'The experts I'm talking about are the ex-members of various secret services and police forces. Suddenly – overnight – they're not wanted. Worse, from their point of view, some of the top-flight agents *are* wanted – so they can stand trial. Are you with me now?'

'Yes.' Paula looked rueful. 'You're playing a favourite trick . . .'

'Teasing,' Monica interjected. 'Tantalizing us while you lead up to something.'

'A number of the most efficient Communist agents – therefore the most sought after to settle accounts with – have disappeared without trace.'

'Disappeared?' Paula was startled. 'Couldn't they have been secretly shot?'

'No, they've escaped. From several Balkan countries in turmoil. And from what used to be the iron state of East Germany. Western agents – including our own – have verified they have simply vanished. It's worrying the PM and the more reports I study the more my anxiety grows. It has all the hallmarks of a master plan.'

'What on earth could they achieve? They're discredited and have nowhere to go,' Paula protested.

'Can we be sure of that? Supposing they are being formed into a new secret police – with the aim of destroying *glasnost* and *perestroika*? They would be a formidable group – men and women trained in the skills and methods of STASI, the old East German secret police, the Romanian *Securitate*, etc. Europe is in a state of turbulence in the East. Fertile soil for professional activists.'

'Have you any names – specific individuals?' Paula pressed.

'I can give you one which will send shivers up your spine – Ion Manescu. And a Romanian woman in London swears she saw him in the street as he dived into a taxi. A few days ago.'

In Lapland the Lear Executive jet began its radar-guided descent to Rovaniemi airfield in the dark. North of the Arctic Circle, it was always dark in February. Endless night. There were eleven men and one woman inside the cabin. None of the passengers had spoken a word to each other since taking off from Helsinki.

As the jet continued its descent they began to muffle themselves in fur against the subzero temperature on the snow- and ice-covered ground. Fur hats with ear muffs, heavy fur coats, fur-lined boots.

The thin-faced man with a Slavic face in the seat nearest the exit door at the front already wore specially made fur boots of a curious design with pointed toes. He ran a hand over his smooth face beneath his hooked nose.

Ion Manescu felt naked without the curved moustache he had shaved off. He was the first passenger ready to disembark as the jet landed, slowed to a halt. He peered out of the window at the moonlit landscape. Scrubby bushes festooned with ice crystals which gleamed. A barren prospect: more like a moonscape, but the airfield was many kilometres away from the town of Rovaniemi, an airstrip in the wilderness.

The steward opened the exit door when the plane was stationary and dropped the retractable stair ladder. Opposite Manescu a German, Helmut Ziegler, ex-STASI chief in Leipzig, rose to leave the aircraft. Manescu put out a hand to halt him.

'After me, if you please,' he said in German. 'Better that we establish priorities of rank from the start.'

He stood, his bulk barring the progress of the German, who glared. Then, in the light reflected from the snow, he saw Manescu's dark eyes gazing back at him. A veteran of the STASI, he shivered – partly from the icy air flooding inside the machine, but partly from Manescu's expression.

'Please,' Manescu continued and descended the ladder.

The file of other passengers followed him across the iron-hard snow to where a queue of strange vehicles waited for them, engines ticking over. Each vehicle had two enormous thick tyres at the front, two more at the back. In the weird glow of Arctic moonlight they looked like a cross between powerful motor bikes and beach buggies. The maker's name was inscribed along the chassis: Suzuki.

Within two minutes all the passengers were aboard their allotted transport and the cavalcade of machines, engines purring and sputtering sparks, moved off. It headed away from the distant airport building, a single-storey edifice, away from the main road to Rovaniemi, heading east cross-country into the wilderness.

Manescu adjusted his snow goggles as white flakes the size of cats' tails began to drift down. He was satisfied. He had asserted his authority. Always you must begin as you mean to go on.

6

Adam Carver walked out of London Airport and joined the taxi queue. He had travelled Business Class from Helsinki. As he stood in the drizzling rain he welcomed it: the contrast in temperature was huge compared with Helsinki. Here the weather had turned mild. As he waited several women looked at him. One said to her friend in a whisper:

'He's a handsome bastard. I wouldn't mind at all.'

'You're wicked,' her companion responded and giggled, gazing at Carver.

A late arrival came out between the automatic doors, stared at the queue, walked back inside to join the uniformed chauffeur who had been waiting and holding a card. *Mr Shade*. The chauffeur was carrying the passenger's bag but his client had insisted on carrying his executive case himself.

'The car is in the short-term car park. I'll take you to it, sir.'

'Then move. He's in the cab queue. My guess is you've got five minutes,' snapped Frank Galvone.

He had travelled aboard the same flight from Helsinki but in Economy Class, not an experience the Vice President of Information and Planning had enjoyed. He wore a leather beret to conceal his black hair, tinted wraparound glasses and a coat turned up at the collar which masked the lower half of his face.

Information and Planning, he was thinking as he walked up the ramp, shoulders stooped to further alter his appearance. Inside the Dracon think-tank building near Boston off what used to be known as Space Highway, the Division was known to the favoured élite who worked there – academics and strategic researchers – as Information and Action. That was where the master plan was being perfected.

'That guy just getting into a cab,' he said five minutes later as the chauffeur drove out of the car park. 'Follow him, don't lose him. But your first priority is don't get found out.'

Which is one hell of an instruction, Charlie Bone, the chauffeur, thought. Typically American. He was careful not to argue the point as he followed Carver's taxi through the tunnel. Charlie was a cockney by birth but he'd spent time in New York.

And Charlie was probably the most highly paid chauffeur in London. Paid to keep his mouth shut. He had developed a terrible memory for who he drove and where he drove them to. He needed the big money. Charlie had a liking for the girls: high-class Sloane Rangers. And diamonds were a *man's* best friend when it came to making it with the opposite sex.

Behind the closed glass screen of the limousine, separating driver from passenger, Galvone opened his executive case. Disguised as toilet equipment all the apparatus was there – the listening device and several sophisticated miniaturized bugs. Before Carver had left Helsinki Galvone had secreted a tiny bug inside Carver's case.

'495 Greenway Gardens, here we come,' he said to himself.

Evelyn was feeling very lonely when the doorbell rang. She was also wary. She opened the front door on the chain and her eyes widened. Half expecting to see the hideous little creep, Grimwood, with his partner, Steve, the smartly dressed good-looking man standing there was a surprise.

'Yes?' she said.

'My name's Adam Carver. Here's my card.' He passed his embossed visiting card through the gap. 'I remember passing you in the corridor at the INCUBUS building in Helsinki. You were wearing a blue gaberdine suit and a white blouse with a pussy bow at the neck.'

Evelyn rather liked that. She liked his appearance, his manner. And he was a senior vice president. But she was still wary.

'You've come to persuade me to accept the pension, haven't you?'

'No. Look at the card again. I'm on the banking side. I heard you'd left and I had business over here.' He smiled. 'I expect you'll think it was a colossal cheek, but I called the Norwich HQ to get your address.'

'Are you alone?' She peered through the gap.

Carver opened his unbuttoned raincoat and smiled again. It was a pleasant smile. 'Look, no one here but me. No one hidden inside my mac.'

She returned his smile, took off the chain, asked him to come inside. Leading him into the living room, she indicated the armchair for him to sit in. Carver nodded, walked to the window.

'This is a spacious bay,' he said from the far side of the couch. 'Pity it stares out at a row of other houses.'

'That's London.'

Carver stood holding his executive case. He had paid off the taxi, had given the driver a generous extra to drop his suitcase at the Hilton in Park Lane. He frowned as he gazed down the road to where a black limo was parked.

'Could we talk in your kitchen?' he suggested, turning back to her. 'Somewhere we can have running water while we chat?'

Her reaction was as though he'd hit her in the face, then she recovered, left the room and walked into the kitchen at the end of the hall. Turning on a tap, she confronted him.

'Not again, for God's sake.'

He said nothing, perched his executive case on a working surface, opened it, searched it swiftly. He found the bug behind the rear lining, held it up, placed it in the sink, reduced the water pressure to a steady flow and eased the bug underneath it.

'There's a limousine parked down the road,' he told her. 'I think there's a certain individual inside with listening apparatus. If it's who I think it is I'd like to go out there and knock his teeth down his throat. That thing under the tap is a bug . . .'

'I know. I've used them myself . . .'

She stopped speaking and cursed her impetuosity. Carver lifted an eyebrow, said, 'I see. I wondered how you caught on so quickly to the trick of running water which will blot out all our conversation. And that bug must have been inserted in my case before I left Helsinki – without my knowledge.'

'Would you like some coffee and then we could talk?'

That was her desperate need: to have someone she could talk to. Carver said he'd love a cup and carefully chose a stool to perch on well away from the chairs round the table. In that way he wouldn't be too close to her.

He was experiencing a mixture of emotions. Fury at the trick played on him. But above all ironic amusement at how things had worked out. Because he'd found – and shown her – the bug, he'd gained Evelyn's confidence in nothing flat.

In the rear seat of the limousine Galvone was fiddling with his listening apparatus. All he could get was atmospherics, a gushing sound like running water.

He swore foully to himself, then wondered. Was it possible? The Charmer had a great reputation with women, something he secretly envied. But he'd only been inside the place a few minutes. Was it possible Carver was already screwing Evelyn in the bathroom? Maybe later he'd get the information he was after during pillow talk. It was the way Galvone's mind worked.

'. . . so,' Evelyn continued, 'while these two creeps, Grimwood and his pal Steve were here, Bob Newman, the foreign correspondent, arrived. To cut a long story short, he threw them out of the house. Then they came back later in their Volkswagen – which is when Bob found the bug they'd attached to the back of the TV set.'

'And you say this Steve character had a gun?' Carver asked.

He was still perched on the stool while Evelyn sat on the far side of the kitchen table. Don't crowd her, he reminded himself.

'Yes, a Walther something or other. Bob took it away from him and kept it. Later Bob left.' She drank more coffee, put her cup down on the table, looked Carver in the eye. 'I took his advice,' she lied. 'As soon as he'd gone that was when I called the police. They have someone watching this house. Will you excuse me a moment?'

She went back down the hall into the living room, walked into the bay, pulled back one of the net curtains.

To her right, four houses down the street, a black limousine was parked. She dropped the curtain, returned to the kitchen and sat in her chair.

'I have to signal the police at regular intervals that I'm OK,' she continued lying.

Evelyn liked Carver, but he was INCUBUS. After her recent experience she was taking no chances. His next question made her glad she had bluffed him.

'What about that pension document? Did you sign it? Did you agree to accept their terms?'

'Not bloody likely. You think I should accept?' she asked, gazing at him innocently.

'I can't advise you on a thing like that. You must make up your own mind. It's your life.'

She drank more coffee to conceal her expression. Had that been another threat. Subtly phrased, but still a threat? She looked straight at him again.

'Just why have you come to see me, Mr Carver?'

'Adam. I thought we'd agreed that.' He put down his own cup, stood up. 'I came because I liked what I saw when you passed me in the corridor back in Helsinki. Would you have dinner with me? Maybe tonight?'

'Not tonight, Adam. Let me think about it.'

'I'll have to be going. I'm staying at the Hilton. Maybe I'll call you from there.' He took out a notebook, wrote something on it, tore off the top sheet, put it on the table. 'That's the hotel number. Just in case for some reason you want to call me . . .'

She phoned for a taxi which arrived in a few minutes. At the door he saw out of the corner of his eye the black limousine was still there.

Once the cab had left Wandsworth behind it ran into heavy traffic. Carver, his executive case on his knees, the bug inside it, thought over what he'd learned from Evelyn Lennox.

The gun bothered him. Since joining INCUBUS it was the first time he'd come across men who carried guns – outside the States. And he still didn't know any details of Evelyn's job with INCUBUS. She had evaded every probing question on that subject.

As the traffic ground to a halt he glanced round and then behind him. Two vehicles back the black limo was in sight. Impossible to see who the passenger in the rear seat was. Eventually the traffic moved on, crossing the Thames bridge.

When Carver alighted outside the Hilton in Park Lane the limo drove past at speed. Again he found it impossible to identify the passenger.

7

In Lapland the cavalcade of snow buggies bumped and rocked their way through the night over rough terrain. In the moonlight Ion Manescu, sitting in the lead vehicle, peered through his snow goggles at the rolling wilderness. The ground they travelled over was studded with boulders buried in snow-covered moss. In places vehicles which had preceded them along the track had exposed the sterile moss.

Moving in a north-easterly direction towards the Soviet border, they were approaching the shore of an ice-bound lake. Manescu checked his watch. 1 a.m. He glanced at the bearded driver of his vehicle.

'How much further?' he asked in English.

'We are there.'

The bleak landscape would have depressed most

people, but Manescu was used to the winters in Romania. As the driver spoke they crested a low ridge. Below Manescu saw a complex of concrete buildings and a circular tower block surrounded by a high wire fence.

Double gates opened automatically and the cavalcade moved inside the perimeter. Driving slowly, Manescu's vehicle entered a huge cavernous opening where a steel door had risen, again automatically. Inside the cavern fluorescent lights threw a weird glow as the vehicle descended a ramp deep into the earth.

The underground complex had been built in summer, the construction teams working in three shifts round the clock. Manescu had noticed a network of aerials, wires and dishes mounted on the roof. They reminded him of a Distant Early Warning System.

'What is this place officially?' he asked as the buggy turned a corner into a vast garage. Manescu estimated they must by now be three levels below the surface of the earth.

'The most advanced Meteorological Institute in the world. And an Observatory. Here they study climatic changes – and the heavens.'

'And that is its only purpose?' Manescu was puzzled.

'What other purpose could it have?'

The snow buggy pulled up alongside a closed elevator door. The driver switched off his engine as another buggy entered the garage.

'This is where you get off,' the driver continued. 'Don't forget your bag. Go to the elevator and press the button marked minus two. I don't know which section is housed at that level . . .'

Manescu was met by a uniformed guard when the doors opened. The guard, who bore no insignia identifying the Institute, escorted Manescu to a large cell-like room with no window. The moment the elevator doors had opened at garage level a wave of welcome warmth had met the Romanian. His room was equally well heated.

Fifteen minutes later he was escorted by the same guard to a huge theatre-like room on the same floor. Rows of hard-backed tip-up seats occupied the room which sloped towards a high platform. To one side was a large white screen, to the other a wall of milky glass.

'You sit in the front row,' the guard informed Manescu as other members who had travelled in the cavalcade began to filter into the large room. No one was offered a seat in the front row except Manescu.

The room was dimly lit by indirect illumination. The guards distributed glasses of mineral water to the occupants of the seats and withdrew. A minute later a picture was flashed on the screen. Manescu stared. It showed Eastern Europe like a smashed jigsaw, all frontiers zigzagged. Then a distorted voice began speaking, his silhouette vaguely seen behind the milky glass. Something wrong with the glass – like a mirror in an amusement hall which contorted the viewer – made it impossible to guess his real appearance.

'All of you seated here tonight are engaged in a great crusade,' the voice began. Manescu thought he detected the twang of an American accent. Which told him nothing. Half of the people in Europe spoke English with that accent. The voice continued.

'A crusade to bring back order, stability and discipline to the world. Eastern Europe – the Balkan states, Czechoslovakia, Hungary, Poland, Bulgaria and Romania – is in a state of chaos and turmoil and turbulence. That political amateur, Gorbachev, talks of a European homeland from the Atlantic to the Urals. Our vision is much greater. The chance is there to create a Western homeland from the Pacific coast of the United States to the Urals. But that homeland must be controlled and organized from New York . . .'

The hypnotic voice paused. Behind the opaque glass screen Franklin D. Hauser mopped his sweating forehead. The heating was turned up high to dull his audience's senses, to make them more receptive to what he was saying.

'Every individual here tonight has a key part to play in this great plan. You have special skills and experience which will help us to achieve our objective. Others will follow you to this training ground, but you will form the leadership. We are creating the most effective secret police the world has ever seen. You will be allocated certain countries to operate inside. And you will be paid huge sums to complete this work. Those of you who wish will one day be provided with new identities and luxurious homes to live in. Inside the United States . . .'

The voice paused again. Manescu leaned forward, tried to get some impression of the shape behind the glass. Impossible. He was impressed by what he'd heard so far, but how was all this going to come about? As though there had been thought transference, the voice continued.

'How is all this to be achieved? By money. Billions of dollars are at our disposal. The broken states I have named are in a condition of near ruin. Secretly we shall buy controlling interests in their strategic industries. This means we must control the governments of these states. By bribery – all men are corruptible – and by removing permanently any so-called idealists who stand in our way. You have had experience in that form of action. Now I come to the main task of all.'

The voice vibrated with power and confidence. The unknown man was a first-rate orator – Manescu recognized that. He sensed a wave of excitement among the people behind him as the audience kept silent, hanging on every word.

'The major task is to take over Russia,' the voice

thundered. 'A difficult task, you think? No! Gorbachev has no idea of what he is doing, of the forces he has unleashed – forces we will harness and control. He has announced that private enterprise will be allowed to flourish. *We* will provide that enterprise. The American way. Corruption has been the way of life for years with certain powerful people. If necessary, to win our campaign we will rekindle that familiar flame. We already have agents inside the Soviet Union reporting back to us. That empire is crumbling. We must create a fresh one to take its place, as a counter to one billion Chinese, and we shall control the new Russian state. We may well create an independent Ukraine – the movement exists, the UTS, based in Munich, Germany. With the huge funds we shall place at its disposal the next problem Gorbachev will face is the collapse of his empire – and we will pick up the pieces . . .'

A fresh pause. Manescu had the impression the apparition behind the opaque glass wall was drinking from an absurdly shaped vessel. And behind him he had heard gasps as the voice outlined the plan for Russia.

'But,' the eerie voice continued, 'to ensure the success of this plan I must be sure all of you are fit to carry it out. Which is why you are here. Buried beneath the Arctic snows, you will be subjected to a series of ordeals, tests. This will show whether you have the stamina and brains to perform your tasks. Do not expect a comfortable time. But remember . . .' The voice dropped. 'Moscow is the ultimate objective, and the rewards of those who lead this gigantic campaign will be enormous. Good-night . . .'

Someone started clapping. Manescu wondered whether it was one of the guards, but if so it wasn't necessary. Behind him there was a crescendo of applause, and before it could stop the guards were ushering the members of that sinister audience to their rooms.

Escorted to his own room, Manescu looked at the

guard and pointed to the changes which had taken place in his absence. Two litre bottles of mineral water had been placed on a small wooden table with a hard-backed chair. Also on the table was a large notebook and several biro pens.

'What are those for?'

'From now on,' the guard informed him, 'you will be confined to this room and no one will enter it for forty-eight hours. You have toilet facilities, a bed to sleep on. The light will be left on for the whole time. The notepad is for you to write down any ideas which might aid the crusade the Conductor outlined.'

'The Conductor?'

'The man who delivered the speech.' The guard paused by the door. 'This will be kept locked. No food will be provided. And please give me your wristwatch.'

'Why?' asked Manescu, guessing the answer as he unfastened the watch and handed it over.

'So you will have no way of knowing how much time has passed, whether it is night or day, even which day it is. The other visitors are living under the same conditions.'

Without another word the guard closed the steel door with a clang and Manescu heard the key turn in the lock. The ex-Director of the Romanian *Securitate* smiled to himself as he recalled a passage from the speech. *This will show whether you have the stamina and the brains . . .*

In another cell-like room further along the corridor Irina Serov, once the only woman colonel in the Soviet KGB, now jobless since being thrown out in a Gorbachev purge, slid a comb tucked inside her tights into her hand and worked on her hair.

The guard allocated to her had removed all her make-up kit from her handbag, a subtle attempt at demoralization. She stood five feet six tall in her high-heeled shoes, her long hair was dark, and she was the kind of thirty-five-year-old woman men turned to look at when she passed them in the street. She had long shapely legs and had been known in Moscow by her nickname, 'The Smooch'. During her tour of duty in England she had killed two men without any risk of being apprehended.

She wrenched the cap off one of the two mineral bottles, took a brief sip. The water must be made to last. She could go two days without sleep and was amused by the test she was undergoing.

She sat at the table, picked up one of the pens, and began work. At the top of the first sheet she wrote the subject of her first notes. *Intimidation.*

Muffled in furs, Franklin D. Hauser left the complex in a snow buggy which drove him to a helipad a kilometre away. He had no desire to linger any longer in this white Arctic hell.

A construction company controlled by Hauser had built the Institute complex. The finance had been provided by one of his banks in co-operation with French and German organizations to give the place an international reputation. But neither of his partners had the remotest idea of the existence of Levels Two and Three.

With a sense of relief he climbed aboard the waiting Sikorsky, equipped with skis, which would fly him back to Helsinki. He peered out of the window as the machine rose into the now-moonless night.

'Well,' he said to himself, 'I've started the action. Now I must keep the momentum of the operation going.'

8

Newman timed it so he would arrive back at Greenway Gardens after dark. It was eight in the evening when Evelyn opened the door on the chain, then let him inside. He carried a small bag and she misunderstood the purpose of his visit as they sat in the curtained living room.

'You've decided to stay with me?'

'No. I've decided to get you out of here. I thought about what you told me – your job with the Profiles Division, and what happened later to those two Finn manufacturers. On top of that, the couple of thugs who came here to force you to sign the insurance document, which I've read end to end . . .'

'And there's been another visitor since you left.'

He listened carefully while she recalled the arrival of Adam Carver and her conversation with him. She showed Newman the visiting card she'd kept. He glanced at it, looked at her.

'That does it. The final straw. Why should they send a senior vice president to check out what must be, if you'll pardon the description, a minor cog in such a huge enterprise? The hard men came first, then the softly spoken and sympathetic type. Oldest ploy in the world. And you told him you hadn't signed the agreement.'

'Was that a mistake?' she asked anxiously. 'I'm beginning to feel under siege.'

'Doesn't make any difference. The first two knew that. I think this Adam Carver will try to charm you into signing. If you refuse again, what next? There have already been two murders.'

70

'Now you're frightening me.'

Which was Newman's deliberate intent. Instead he pressed harder while she was in a fraught mood. 'Since I left you I managed to trace another ex-employee of INCUBUS. Don't ask me how. Lives in another part of London. I visited him and he closed up like a clam. Wouldn't even give me a hint about what his job had been. He was edgy. Wanted to get rid of me fast.'

'Why do you think he was like that?'

'He'd obviously signed the document, agreed to receive a big fat pension – and keep his mouth shut. He was frightened when I mentioned Fraternity & Equality Insurance, showed me the door. Something pretty devilish is going on. Which is why you're packing a bag, leaving here tonight.'

'Where for?'

'Didn't you say Sandy had a place at Southwold in Suffolk? I never actually visited her there. We used to meet a lot here in town, go out for a meal.'

'The cottage isn't in Southwold,' she said slowly. Newman could tell she was thinking over his suggestion. 'Sandy always said Southwold,' she continued. 'More people know where that is. But the cottage is at a place called Walberswick. She had a Southwold phone number. Who's ever heard of Walberswick?'

'I have. It has a main stem simply called The Street. And nice houses, if I remember rightly. Plus two or three hotels. Very near the coast. You drive to the end of The Street, bear left and drive to the car park. Over to the right is rough dune land, a big area before you top a ridge of shingle. And Bingo! The sea.'

Evelyn smiled, something she rarely did in Newman's experience of her, brief though it might be.

'I can see you know Walberswick . . .'

'It's well off the beaten track,' he continued. 'I'll drive you up there tonight. You have a key to her cottage?'

71

'Yes. You think I'll be safer there?'

'Sure of it. Get packing . . .'

At ten o'clock at night The Street was a deserted tree-lined tunnel illuminated by the headlights of Newman's Mercedes 280E. There were lights in some of the beautiful houses on either side but all of them were upstairs. People went to bed early in Walberswick.

'Slow down,' said Evelyn, seated beside him. 'We're close to the cottage.'

'We'll come back to it. I want to call in at one of those hotels to check something. Here's a nice looking place. Leave the heaters on. Back in a minute . . .'

Before she could reply he had jumped out of the car to walk up the drive to the hotel. The wind hit him the moment he left the vehicle, a ferocious gust off the nearby sea which nearly lifted him off his feet. A storm was brewing up.

'Can you give me a double room for a couple of nights?' he asked the ancient receptionist. 'I'm on my own but I like space. My case is at a friend's house down The Street. I will pay you in advance,' he ended, hauling out his wallet.

He signed the register with a false name and address. *P. Ashbourne, 17 Lever Road, Bournemouth.* The precaution probably wasn't necessary, but on the off-chance that more thugs from INCUBUS came sniffing round, they wouldn't know he was in the area. They had shown very thorough organization so far.

'What was all that about?' Evelyn asked as he got behind the wheel.

'Had a private phone call to make,' he lied. 'Back to the cottage.'

'It's called Rose Bower. Drive slowly. You can park in the drive, or even go on round the back.'

The cottage was an attractive picture postcard by the

light of the moon shining between scudding clouds. Thatched roof, two storeys, the second had more mullion windows hunched inside the thatch. He drove round the back, switched off the engine, reached for the key she was holding.

'I'll go in first,' he said casually. On his way up the paved path between walls of rose bushes he picked up a piece of old iron pipe with his gloved hand. There was always a weapon available if you used your eyes. He unlocked the old heavily studded front door, pushed it open. Evelyn reached over his shoulder, switched on a light, and gasped.

'Wait here,' Newman ordered.

Beyond the doorway you walked straight into the main sitting room. It was a scene of havoc. Drawers had been pulled out of military chests, left on the floor. Chintz-covered cushions had been ripped open, left lying on the floor, stuffing scattered. A chintz-covered settee had been upended, the lining torn open.

'Oh, my God!' Evelyn whispered. 'They've been here, too.'

'Stay just inside the door while I explore . . .'

He went swiftly through the house, still holding the piece of piping. The break-in had not surprised him too much. Beyond the sitting room, a large area with an old brick fireplace set back in a spacious alcove, piles of cut logs flanking it, a narrow passage led to the kitchen and a small study.

Both rooms had received the same brutal searching treatment. He returned to the passage, ran lightly up the narrow twisting staircase, checked three bedrooms, the bathroom and the toilet. Nothing had been overlooked. He ran downstairs and Evelyn had collapsed into an armchair.

'The bastards!' she said between her teeth. 'Wrecking Sandy's old home.' She looked up. 'You didn't find anyone?'

'Lord, no. They're long gone. Must have happened some time after Buchanan and his sidekick came here.

They found the key in her handbag in the Jag.'

'But there's no sign of forced entry. Or is the back door . . .?'

'Firmly closed and locked. These jokers will be experts with skeleton keys. You wait here. I'm just taking my case to that hotel. I booked a room while I was there.'

'But you could stay here . . .'

'I could,' he agreed. 'But this is Sandy's house. She once lived here. I'd sooner not, if you don't mind. Back in a minute. I'm helping you to clear up. Don't argue. Bolt the front door after me till I get back . . .'

As he dumped his case in the pleasant bedroom, lifted the lid and left it at that, he reflected. He hadn't strictly told Evelyn the truth. He had seen the outside of Rose Bower. Sandy had been redecorating the place, had forbidden him to enter. 'Until it's all finished and ready for you,' she had said with her glowing smile. The moment he'd entered Rose Bower the smell of fresh paint had assailed his nostrils. He had almost broken down. No, he could never spend a night in that cottage. Quite apart from the problem that Evelyn seemed to like him.

When he returned she had cleared a space in the kitchen, had coffee ready. They drank it amid the ruins, not saying anything. Newman put down his large mug.

'It's freezing in here. First thing, I'll get that fire going in the sitting room. I'd sleep there tonight, if I were you.'

He insisted on staying until the cottage was as ship-shape as could be managed. At least there was little evidence remaining of the break-in. He said good-night to Evelyn quickly and that he'd be back after breakfast in the morning.

'We could go and explore Minsmere,' she suggested. 'That's a Royal Society for the Protection of Birds Nature Reserve. The migrant widgeons should still be there. I doubt if they've flown north yet in this weather.'

'Good idea. And again, good-night . . .'

74

'Before you go, Bob.' She ran to the door. 'What do you think they could have been looking for – the people who ransacked her cottage?'

'No idea,' he lied.

The receptionist at the hotel had given him a key to the front door and his mind was a chaotic mixture of emotions and thoughts as he walked past it towards the shore. He was well wrapped up against the weather. Clad in a heavy military-style trench coat, turned up at the collar, he had a waterproof hat rammed down over his forehead. The storm was increasing in fury as he turned left towards the car park, beyond any houses, then made his way to the east on to the scrubby dunes. He had walked along this track with Sandy, arm in arm, and as the wind beat in his face he recalled the weather had been similar.

A five minute rough walk in the moonlight took him to the top of the shingle ridge. As he crested it he flinched. Surf from giant waves crashing a few feet away splashed his face. Braced against the storm as it howled, he promised himself something.

'I'll burn the bastards who did that to Sandy.'

Newman had very little sleep that night. He had lied to Evelyn when he'd denied any idea of what the ransackers were looking for. He was convinced he was holding what they sought in his hand.

A red clothbound diary written in her handwriting. He had known where to look for it when he'd left the bell tower after finding her corpse. Going over to her parked Jaguar, he had opened the driver's door, bent down and felt under the seat. The diary was attached to the underside with sellotape. He'd torn it free, pocketed it, had not mentioned its existence to Buchanan. Suppressing evidence in a murder investigation, they called it.

To hell with them. He was conducting his own

75

investigation. And, as Tweed had predicted to Paula in a similar context, he expected it would take him months to unravel the affairs of the world-wide octopus, INCUBUS.

He read again some of her notes. *January 12. Bennington, Swindon. Machine tools. James Archer, Managing Director, sole owner of company. Profile completed, submitted to Division, January 31. Takeover bid, February 20. Note: Archer has daughter, Julia. April 5. Manningham Electronics, Thames Valley. Miniaturized microchips. Chairman: Gavin Manningham. Profile completed, submitted May 2. Takeover bid, May 28. Note: Manningham has a mistress* . . .

There were similar entries for six other companies, all in strategic industries, including two small private banks. Newman yawned. God, he was flaked out. He checked the time – 3 a.m. Undressing quickly, he cleaned his teeth and flopped into bed. The last thing he did before he fell fast asleep was to slip Sandy's diary inside his pillow.

Another day, another storm. Tweed stood behind the heavy net curtains masking the windows of his Park Crescent office, watching the trees in distant Regent's Park shuffle and shudder under the wind's onslaught.

'I've collated quite a lot of information from the researchers,' Paula commented sitting at her desk.

'I'm getting there, too,' Monica said, arranging a series of coded fax messages from Europe.

'So what does it amount to?' Tweed asked, returning to his swivel chair behind his own desk.

'You were right,' Paula continued. 'It does look as though some top Communist agents in the security services in various East European countries have vanished into thin air. We can't be sure, of course. It's pure chaos out there, but one man has, I'm sure, got away.'

'Which one?'

'Ion Manescu, evil genius behind the *Securitate*.'

'I'd already decided we have to check on him closely. On the spot. Subject to your report, which you've just given. Guy Dalby is due here any moment. Flying in from Vienna. By now he knows his sector.'

Despite the arrival of *glasnost*, Tweed had kept in place his extensive network across Western Europe. The situation was too fluid, the future too uncertain for any relaxation yet.

After the tragic murder of Harry Masterson in *The Greek Key* crisis, Tweed had shuffled some of his four sector chiefs. Erich Lindemann, German, was still controlling the Scandinavian sector with a forward penetration zone – Northern Russia. Harvey Wilson, promoted swiftly from field agent, had replaced Paula's deceased husband as controller for Germany, Holland and Belgium. Penetration zone: Poland and Czechoslovakia. Reg Finch, another swift promotion, forty years old and very decisive, had taken over Dalby's old sector in the Mediterranean covering France, Spain, Italy, Turkey and Switzerland. Penetration zone: Libya and the Middle East.

There was a knock on the door, Tweed called out come in, and Guy Dalby entered. Based in Vienna, he was controller of the ultrasensitive Balkan sector – covering Austria, Yugoslavia and Greece. He also had the most tricky penetration zone: Hungary, Romania, Bulgaria and the Ukraine.

'Spot of bother?' he enquired jauntily as Tweed indicated he should sit in the chair beside his desk. 'Message had a mildly urgent ring.'

Dalby, dressed in a conventional grey suit, whipped a cow-lick of dark hair over his forehead. Of medium height and build, he had an air of self-confidence which irked Paula, although she recognized his first-rate brain.

'Ion Manescu,' said Tweed, coming straight to the point. 'You'll have heard of him?'

77

'Heard of him?' Dalby laughed, a hollow laugh. 'He was one of the top men we tried to keep a close eye on – when we could. He's a past master at keeping his whereabouts secret, laying false trails. A dangerous, ruthless and cruel character. Personification of evil. He was close to Ceausescu – and at the same time kept Moscow informed. Ceausescu didn't know that, but we did. If he'd been born an American he'd have been high up in the CIA – and still informing Moscow . . .'

'You mean he's pro-Russian?' Tweed interjected.

'Lordy, no!' Dalby was amused again. 'Manescu's only allegiance is to himself. He kept in with the Soviets in case Moscow ever prevailed in Bucharest – plus the extra money he undoubtedly obtained.'

'Where is he now?' Tweed asked quietly.

'He's performed another of his well-known vanishing tricks.' Dalby made a conjuror's gesture. 'Now you see him, now you don't. Rumour hath it he escaped the country when the revolution revolved. Or he may secretly be under guard in Dracula's castle. Perfect place for him.'

Tweed had taken to doodling. On his pad he drew a fearsome vampire face with fangs, then looked up.

'I need to know for certain whether the Romanians do have him. Alternatively, has he escaped; and if so, his destination.'

'You don't want much, do you? I send in a couple of men?'

'I want you to go yourself. I've arranged with a friend who owes me a favour that I'll supply the supervisor for medical equipment being flown to Bucharest. You'll be that supervisor.' He handed Dalby a slip of folded paper. 'Name and phone number. The consignment leaves tonight from Stansted.'

'Who does he think I am?'

'I was just going to tell you. Usual cover. Special

Branch. Checking a new drugs route – in connection with an IRA group. Just hint at it.'

'Don't think I'd say it outright, do you? I'd better move. Report back to you when I get back to Vienna. If I do.' He stood up, waved at Monica, winked at Paula and was gone.

'That man is too clever by half,' Paula commented. 'I don't think he knows he's not my favourite person.'

'He knows,' Tweed told her, 'which is why he winked. To wind you up.'

'Isn't it taking a big chance, sending a man like Dalby inside Romania? With all the information locked inside his head?'

'It would have been unthinkable not so long ago,' Tweed agreed. 'But they'll welcome him with open arms, bringing them medical aid. He'll make sure they do. And on top of everything else he's a brilliant linguist. Now, all we can do is wait for his report and get on with more work.'

'If you say so,' Paula said dubiously.

The trouble was, Tweed was thinking, Paula had a blind spot where Dalby was concerned. Under that flippant attitude he liked to show at Park Crescent was a mind like quicksilver. Also, among other languages, he spoke Romanian – although Tweed doubted he'd let anyone in Bucharest know that.

'The one advantage of that appalling business of the cottage being broken into,' Newman told Evelyn as they drove away from Minsmere Nature Reserve, 'is they're unlikely even to think of looking for you there.'

'Are you sure?' she asked nervously.

'I can't be absolutely sure,' he admitted. 'But look at it from their point of view. Rose Bower belonged to Sandy – with their obsession for recording details about employees they would know that. They've been there to search for something – whatever – they thought she had. Either they found it or they didn't. But they'll have crossed that place off their list.'

'I have enjoyed today,' she said wistfully.

They had spent the time wandering round the Reserve, watching the widgeon ducks and other wildfowl paddling in the lagoon close to the sea. The sky had been an azure dome, the air fresh and unpolluted. They had eaten a packed lunch prepared by Evelyn. Newman had kept the conversation general, fending Evelyn off when she tried to bring it on a more personal basis. He had decided to drive back to London to check the companies register in the City.

'Do you have to go so soon?' Evelyn pleaded as the car rocked over a series of ramps.

'You'll be safe as long as you stay in the Walberswick area. If you want a change, there's a nice pub at Dunwich. You turn right when we hit the road at the end of this track to Minsmere – instead of left, as we shall, to get you back to Walberswick. But don't go near Southwold,' he warned.

Some bizarre quirk led Newman to take a route back to London past the bell tower where Sandy had died. The Coroner's inquest had been held in Southwold the previous day and he had attended with Evelyn.

Chief Inspector Buchanan had given evidence tersely, in a dry tone. Investigations were continuing. He had no lead as yet. The outcome was as expected. 'Murder by person or persons unknown . . .' As he said the words the Coroner stared at Newman, who stared back. As soon as it was over Newman had driven Evelyn away immediately.

It was night when he turned down the A1120, drove

through Yoxford and continued along the winding country road. There was no other traffic and he kept his headlights undimmed. Sweeping over the ploughed fields the beams showed a blanket of frost forming. The night was cold, the air bitter. It suited his mood.

He was approaching the track leading to the bell tower, a dark grim silhouette in the moonlight, when he saw a great glow of light to his right in the distance. Livingstone Manor, the English country residence of Franklin D. Hauser. As he came closer he saw the old Georgian mansion was illuminated with lights in all the windows. Downstairs the windows were masked by curtains but upstairs the curtains were drawn back. He slowed down.

His eyes narrowed as he saw the outline of a helicopter by the side of the mansion. Newman had spent three days at the hotel in Walberswick – mainly to attend the inquest but also to soothe Evelyn as far as he could. On the day of the discovery of Sandy's body he remembered Buchanan had called at Livingstone Manor, had been told Hauser was in Finland. He also recalled there was a heliport near Beccles to the north.

Was Hauser now in residence? He could have flown by private jet to an East Anglian airfield, been driven from there to the heliport, boarded the chopper and flown to the manor. It was just a chance.

He pulled up in front of the high iron grille gates barring the entrance to a drive, saw in his headlights a speakphone set into one of the brick pillars.

'Robert Newman here,' he announced after pressing the button. 'To see Mr Hauser, but only if he's free . . .'

9

Franklin D. Hauser sat in a large Regency chair, wearing evening dress, in the large living room at the front of the house. The windows overlooked the long drive to distant entrance gates. The parkland was laid out with a smooth lawn. Bordering the lawn was a wall of trees with a huge oak at one corner.

'So, tell me,' he said, addressing Adam Carver, 'how did you get on with the Evelyn Lennox twist?'

'I lost her,' Carver told him bluntly, standing by a spacious fireplace with a drink in his hand. Half a tree trunk surrounded with logs crackled and flamed, warming his backside as he stood with one hand lifting the flap of his jacket.

'My, my, that was careless of you. Losing the girl you'd been sent to interview,' sneered Frank Galvone, standing closer to Hauser.

'Now, Frank,' Hauser admonished him amiably. 'Let Adam finish his story. I'm sure he has more to tell than that.'

'I talked to her at her place in Greenway Gardens,' Carver continued, ignoring Frank. 'In a few words, she did not agree to sign the insurance document. And she told me some character called Steve produced a gun when Newman, the foreign correspondent, interrupted their tête-à-tête. I didn't know this company hired men with guns.'

'You're Banking,' Frank said quickly. 'Stick with that.'

'Does that mean we employ men with Walthers?' Carver asked, staring at Hauser.

'Of course not.' Hauser was amused at the suggestion. 'I

should add that Frank was talking about America. Security guards at certain plants may well be armed. That's common practice in the States . . .'

He stopped speaking as someone knocked at the door. Galvone called out, 'Come on in,' and the butler appeared with a folded sheet of paper on a silver salver. He held out the salver to Galvone who took the sheet, unfolded it, read the few words on the paper and handed it to Hauser. He dismissed the butler with a jerk of his head.

'Talk of the devil,' he said. 'Newman is outside the gate, asking to see you. I'll tell him to move his ass.'

'Wait a minute.' Hauser's tone was abrupt. He opened a blue folder resting in his lap, glanced through the typed sheets. 'Grimwood reports Newman did arrive and spoilt their act just as they'd got Lennox to agree to sign. And Adam has just confirmed his statement. Always meet the opposition and hear what it has to say. Forewarned is forearmed, as the Brits say. Adam, would you be so kind as to tell Winterton to admit Mr Newman? Thank you.'

Galvone waited until Carver had left the room. 'I think you're making a mistake. You rarely agree to see a newspaper man.'

'Frank, you're an impetuous man. You'll never occupy this chair until you learn to control that impetuosity. You really must study my methods more closely.'

'I know I get it wrong sometimes.' It cost Galvone a lot to say that but he knew he'd blundered. 'But I do get it right most of the time. I think I'll freshen up my drink.'

He poured himself a double Scotch from the antique drinks cabinet. Hauser leaned over, opened a drawer in a desk and slid the Grimwood folder inside. Then, settling himself back in his chair, he lit a cigarette. Galvone hurried to place a crystal ash tray on a small table beside him.

Newman walked into the room followed by Carver. He carried his trench coat over his arm. He'd declined the butler's offer to take his coat: he might want to leave in a hurry. He smiled as he advanced across the room.

'Very good of you to see me, Mr Hauser. Normally I ask for an appointment, but I happened to be passing and saw the lights – and the chopper. I guessed you might just be back from Finland.'

He saw a flicker in the ice-blue eyes behind the pince-nez. Glancing at Galvone he saw something different. The dark eyes were glowing with hostility and the man's whole body had tensed. Hit them the moment you arrive was a favourite tactic of Newman's. Hauser recovered first.

'And very pleasant to meet at last the famous foreign correspondent. I read your international bestseller, *Kruger: The Computer That Failed*. Must have made you a fortune.'

'It did,' Newman agreed. 'Gave me financial independence. But I do a piece now and again. When the subject interests me.'

'I'm forgetting my manners . . .' Hauser introduced Carver and Galvone. 'Both senior vice presidents.' He smiled. 'One day one of them will take over from me. The question is, which one?'

'Well, I think that's your decision.'

'Frank, get Mr Newman a drink. What's your poison? Then you can tell me what you want.'

Newman thanked him, shook his head, sat in the chair Hauser ushered him to with a wave of his large hand. 'I am hoping you'll agree to an interview for *Der Spiegel*. At your convenience,' he added blandly.

'I can afford to give you fifteen minutes now. Then I have guests arriving for dinner. Shoot.'

Newman took out his notebook, glanced at Galvone and Carver. 'I always interview a subject on his – or her – own. It's the only way it works.'

Hauser beamed. 'Adam, Frank, maybe you could find something to occupy your time elsewhere. Preferably something profitable for the company.'

84

Galvone stepped forward, laid a hand on Newman's shoulder. He was surprised at the hard muscle he felt under his strong grip. 'Before we go I'd better check this guy for a piece – or a tape recorder.'

'The uniformed guard in the hall did just that.' Newman looked up at Galvone. 'Frank, kindly remove your hand or I may remove it myself. Painfully.'

'Try it, smart ass . . .'

'Your impetuosity is showing again,' Hauser remarked. 'Do I have to remind you Mr Newman is a guest? An honoured guest?'

As he spoke he pressed a concealed button in the arm of his chair. The door at the end of the room opened swiftly and the butler appeared. Hauser called out as though asking for the tea to be served.

'Winterton, could you confirm the guard gave Mr Newman the normal check before he came in here?'

'Oh, yes. He did, sir.'

'Thank you, Winterton. That will be all.' Hauser looked at Newman. 'My apologies. But success in this world seems to breed envy which, in its turn, can breed hostility. A sad state of affairs, but it is so. Security has to be total or useless.'

Galvone had removed his hand and stepped away several paces. He glared at Newman and then left the room with Carver. Newman stiffened his back against the chair and smiled. 'About your security. The guard on the gate at the entrance to the drive should really have checked me. If an intruder eliminated him with a weapon and managed to get inside this place you'd be in trouble.'

'Thank you. What do you wish to ask me?'

'Why are you extending your activities to Europe and what are your plans?'

'Very modest. Mr Newman. A small investment – for INCUBUS – in certain companies to give us a toehold inside the Common Market. A sideline, you might say.'

'Really? Bennington Machine Tools in Swindon. A key firm in a key industry. Manningham Electronics in the Thames valley. A company with the most advanced products in western Europe.'

'Really, Mr Newman,' Hauser waved his cigarette, but again Newman had detected that brief flicker behind the pince-nez. 'I'm Chief Executive and President of a large international organization. I never get buried in the weeds. I concern myself with general policy. You expect me to know all the details of what is happening in a legion of divisions?'

'You have a reputation for being a master of detail. The companies I mentioned are important acquisitions.'

'The names mean nothing to me. You'd haved to consult Adam Carver – or Frank Galvone.'

'One of whom may – or may not – succeed you some day?'

Hauser threw back his large head and chuckled. 'You are so observant. You noticed my little ploy. Keeps them on their toes.'

'You said your investment in Europe is modest. What about Timo Metsola's electronics outfit in Finland – where you've just flown back from? It seems to me you're spreading your net very wide.'

'Again the name means nothing to me.' Hauser's mood had changed. He stubbed out his half-smoked cigarette savagely in the ash tray. 'You'll have to be careful with this article, Mr Newman. Careful you get all your facts right. I operate in the American way. I'd sue you, strip you bare without a second thought.'

'What is your general strategy in the new fluid situation in Europe?' Newman pressed on.

'To provide more employment where I can. I regard INCUBUS as a brotherhood of man. My only role in life is to help my fellow men and women, regardless of race or creed. You may quote me.'

'And regardless of the business methods you use?'

Hauser pressed the button in his chair. 'This interview is becoming tedious, is terminated. I had expected better of you.' His manner was aggressive, his tone hasrsh. 'Have a care in future. Better perhaps that you retire, enjoy the fortune you made from your book.' He stared across the room as Winterton entered. 'Please show Mr Newman out – he is leaving immediately.'

'And thank you for the interview.'

Newman smiled as he stood up, pocketing his notebook and pen. He walked rapidly across the gleaming parquet floor, slipping on his trench coat as he left.

In response to the two presses of the chair button Galvone hurried in to the living room. He knew from the expression on Hauser's face something was wrong. And tobacco ash was spilt down the front of his evening shirt. Galvone pulled out the display handkerchief from his top pocket.

'Excuse me, Chief,' he fawned and used the handkerchief to flick away the ash. 'Something wrong?'

'Robert Newman has just left. He'll be walking down the drive now. He's investigating us, Frank. And he's getting close. I don't like that. I don't like that at all.'

'So I'd better deal with the problem immediately?'

'That's up to you, Frank.' He turned a steely gaze on his subordinate. 'I don't wish to get meshed in the weeds – use your discretion.'

'He's driving a Merc. 280E. The guard biked down the drive and checked it out . . .'

Galvone was half-running from the room as he threw the words over his shoulder, closed the door, ran down the hall and into the night.

*   *   *

Just outside the grille gates – which had opened automatically at his approach and then closed behind him – Newman was lying on his back under his car. He aimed his pencil flash, checking the underneath of the chassis. It seemed unlikely they would have placed a bomb so close to Livingstone Manor, but it was better to be sure than dead. He hauled himself over the gravel clear of the chassis, stood up, opened the front passenger door, pulled the lever which unlocked the hood.

With the hood open he made a swift examination of the engine. Nothing there either. He took off his trench coat, shivered in the cold, shook the dirt off the coat, put it on again and slipped behind the wheel. Despite the bitter night he lowered his window before starting the motor.

He was driving away from the grounds of Hauser's estate when he heard a different engine sound. The sound of the helicopter's rotors starting up. He pressed his foot down, sped along the country road which was free of other traffic. He drove with his headlights undipped to see the endless curves in good time. Bare hedges like barbed wire showed in the beams.

The chug-chug of the chopper was growing louder, coming up fast behind him. A minute later he saw it flying past well over to his right at a height of about two hundred feet. It flew on, red and green lights flashing, then it descended, disappeared.

Newman frowned as he recalled a snatch of conversation with Buchanan during a break in his interrogation at Southwold on the day Sandy's body was discovered. Hauser's name had cropped up and Buchanan had shrugged as he put down his mug of foul-tasting coffee.

'I sometimes think these super-rich men like to show they have made it. Hauser not only has a twenty-acre estate at Livingstone Manor. A constable in Yoxford told me he also owns two hundred acres of farmland to the west of his country retreat . . .'

And now, Newman thought, I'm driving west of that estate. So maybe it was somewhere on that land the chopper has put down. He had been driving at high speed when the helicopter flew past him. And they probably know I'm travelling in this car. He reduced speed considerably, dipped his headlights, began to crawl round the bends, his right foot poised over the accelerator.

He travelled like this for some distance, meeting no other traffic. The moonlight shone off the frost settling on the fields and a wave of mist like sea surf was beginning to rise on either side of the road. He turned yet another corner and saw in the distance a rare copse of evergreen trees close to the road. He stopped, switched off the engine and listened.

Had he imagined it? He could have sworn he'd caught the sound of another engine, a weird noise – a clanking, groaning ratchety sound. The silence of a cold windless night was all he heard now. He switched on the engine and drove on.

He had increased his speed to between forty and fifty miles an hour. Suddenly he wanted to get well clear of the area. He was approaching the copse of trees, a dark island by the side of the road. Because of the chopper's flight he was watching closely and he blinked as his eyes located movement. Something huge emerging from behind the copse, heading for the road. And, much louder, a blasting roar, the sinister clanking sound repeated.

He was ten yards from the copse when the origin of the roar appeared. An enormous tractor with giant wheels was driving across his path. He had a split second to decide. He rammed his foot down, the Merc. responded, shot forward like a torpedo. The yellow monster was almost on top of him, two great lights like enormous eyes now switched on. Newman kept his foot down. To his right the tractor loomed over him, the agent of destruction. Newman's Mercedes skimmed past the revolving wheels with inches to spare. In his rear view mirror he saw the solid yellow wall blocking the whole road. He sped on . . .

· Behind the wheel of the tractor Frank Galvone swore foully. He had misjudged the speed of his target by no more than a fraction. Cursing again, he began reversing the machine back up the farm track towards the hollow where the helicopter and its pilot waited.

Newman, with the murder of Sandy foremost in his mind, having passed the fatal bell tower within the past two hours, was shaken by the encounter. His normal reaction would have been to swing the car in a U-turn to return and tackle the driver of the tractor. But he had no idea how strong his back-up might be. And he was no longer armed – he had hurled the Walther taken from Steve into the sea at Walberswick, followed by the magazine he'd first extracted.

Five minutes later he saw the lights of a village pub. The Nag's Head. He parked his car among a dozen others, out of sight of the road, and walked inside.

An old pub with beamed ceilings, smoke-blackened, and a log fire crackling and spitting inside a deep alcove. The place was crowded. Mostly locals. Agricultural workers, their trousers fastened to their ankles with bits of string or bicycle clips. He leaned on the stained wooden bar. The landlord was a short round-headed red-faced man.

'Good evening, sir. What can I serve you?'

'A Scotch. And some water, please.'

The landlord placed the glass in front of Newman, pushed a jug of water along the bar, studying him.

'Stranger to these parts?'

'Yes.' Newman paid for the drink. 'I've just inter-viewed a man called Franklin D. Hauser.' He diluted the

Scotch, sipped at his glass. 'I hear he's not too popular round here.'

He was aware of sudden hush among the men on either side of him. A heavily built man in a corduroy jacket edged closer to him on his left. His elbow nudged against Newman's side.

'You just finishin' that drink and then pushin' off, Mister?'

'What's that 'e said?' Another voice, this time on his right. A six foot two giant with black hair and eyebrows joined over the bridge of his large nose. 'You tellin' Jed you don't like Mr 'Auser?'

'I may have another drink, I may not,' Newman replied, looking at Corduroy Jacket.

'Best make it one and then shove it as Dan said.'

The giant, Dan, lifted Newman's glass and held it close to his mouth. He grinned, showing bad teeth. 'Drink up now, there's a good boy.'

'Put that glass down carefully,' Newman said quietly. 'And I should warn you I'm ex-SAS. If I have to defend myself I'll try very hard not to kill you – but with my training. And I didn't say I disliked Hauser. I said I heard he wasn't popular. That was in Yoxford. I wondered why.'

'Yoxford!' Corduroy Jacket laughed sarcastically. 'What do them yokels know.' He spoke across Newman to the giant. 'I'd put that glass down very carefully if I were you. We mistook the gentleman's attitude.'

The glass was placed gently back on the counter in front of Newman. He drank a little more and then asked his question.

'I gather Hauser is well-liked around here. I'm not surprised,' he lied, 'but will someone tell me why he's liked so much?'

'Generous with his money.' The landlord intervened, relieved there wasn't going to be any trouble. 'Give you an example. We had trees down in a storm. Cottages damaged. No insurance. Who comes along and says he'll pay for everything to be put to rights? Mr Franklin D. Hauser.'

'Very generous, as you say.'

'That's not all,' broke in Corduroy Jacket. 'Anyone who gets behind payments with the mortgage round 'ere, all 'e 'as to do is tell the Manor. Mr 'Auser helps out. You travel round these parts, you'll find folk 'ave nothing but good to say about Mr 'Auser.' He leaned closer and Newman detected evidence of many pints of beer on his breath. 'And they'd go a long way to 'elp 'im if ever 'e 'ad a problem.'

'Well I'm glad you told me.' Newman swallowed the rest of his drink. 'Obviously I was badly misinformed in Yoxford. I must be off now.'

As he drove through the night, heading back to London, Newman was anxious to get clear of Hauser's 'province'. The American was clever, he'd give him that.

Posing as a philanthropist, he had distributed largess on a big scale to the locals. This provided him with an army of allies – and potential spies – surrounding a wide area of the Livingstone Manor estate. Newman wondered whether he employed the same method in other parts of the world.

It also occurred to him that this precaution eliminated the likelihood of ever finding a witness who had seen Sandy arriving in her Jaguar at the bell tower close to dawn. The word had probably been passed around already: see no evil, hear no evil. Which led to a fresh thought.

Assuming Sandy had been murdered because of her connection until recently with INCUBUS, the murderer could be one of Hauser's close associates. Hauser had struck him as a man who moved with great caution. No hired killers for a one-time job. Too risky.

My God! he thought. I could have been in the same room with the murderer back at Livingstone Manor. Newman had noticed Adam Carver seemed the athletic type, very fit and strong. On the other hand there was Mr Frank Galvone. His first impression of Galvone had been of a mobster, but Newman had met other reasonably honest Americans holding high positions who had made the same initial impression. The fact that both men had been at Livingstone Manor intrigued him. What was it they said about a murderer returning to the scene of his crime?

All these disconnected thoughts were roaming through his mind as he drove through the middle of the night close to his flat in South Ken. Hardly any other traffic about at 1 a.m.

He was so close to his flat in Beresforde Road that he had reduced his speed to a crawl, searching for a parking place. The huge articulated truck with a separate cab for the driver appeared out of nowhere, moving at high speed, lights undimmed and aiming straight for him. He attempted evading action but it was too late. The monster slammed into the rear of his car. Despite the fact he was wearing his seat belt he was hurled forward. His skull cracked down on the steering wheel.

Forcing his head up he found everything was blurred. He had braked automatically, which was probably a mistake. Through the shimmer he saw the huge octopus eyes of the juggernaut grow dimmer. The vehicle was backing away. It turned a corner and vanished. Then he blacked out.

10

81°F. 27°C.

The heatwave which had started in May was continuing to roast London in June. Tweed was clad in shirt sleeves and a pair of lightweight slacks as he stared out of his office window. It was mid-morning and tourists were trudging under the blazing sun towards Regent's Park.

Monica was sweltering despite the fan revolving on her desk. All it seemed to do was circulate the warm turgid air. Tweed turned quickly as the door opened and Paula arrived. He sensed she was excited.

'Bob's jogging in Hyde Park. Isn't it wonderful? He discharged himself from the hospital. When he's had a bath at his flat he's coming here.'

'A drink to celebrate,' Tweed said. 'Champagne.'

'Not until he's arrived,' Paula replied. She sank into the chair behind her own desk. 'Three ribs broken and concussion. Now he's as strong as an ox. He's been through a lot.'

'It wasn't the ribs that worried me,' Tweed replied, sitting in his swivel chair. 'He was fit, I was sure he would mend. But the concussion was a dicey business.'

'That's what the doctor kept telling us,' Paula recalled. 'And he was very insistent Bob had to stay under his care until the headaches went away. They were murder for him, I could tell.'

'It was that truck driver who was intent on murder,' Monica interjected grimly. 'And, of course, what do the police do? They find the truck abandoned a mile away, that it had been stolen. No sign of the driver.'

The phone rang and Paula grabbed hers first. She spoke briefly, put it down and grinned. 'Bob is here. On his way up.'

Newman came in with a faraway look. Paula was immediately concerned. She jumped up and ran forward, guided him to the armchair.

'The headache's come back?' she said.

'Nope.' He grinned at her. 'Sorry if I was in a brown study. I feel fine. I was remembering some of the facts I built up from the data you brought me. I used the phone a lot while I was in that private room. In Sandy's notebook – the one I'd found in her Jaguar that morning at the bell tower – there was a reference to Dracon. I know what it is now. INCUBUS has a think-tank called Dracon based outside Boston. All the ideas come from there. And Ed Riverton was the vice president running it. He gave me a hint when I interviewed him in Helsinki not long before he also was murdered.'

'So why do you believe he was killed in that fashion?' Tweed enquired.

'Because he got worried about what they were planning – all those cranky academics Hauser employs. The trouble is I've no idea of what they were planning.'

'Doesn't get us much further then,' Tweed observed. 'We do have a lot of data on that banking colossus. Collected while you were on holiday . . .'

'Some holiday, thank you very much . . .'

'Did you know it's the biggest bank in the United States?' Tweed persisted. 'Bigger even than the Bank of America. It has enormous resources, and controlling interests in key outfits all over the Western world.'

'Power.' Newman paused to drink from the mug of coffee Paula had made. Champagne could come later. 'Power,' he repeated. 'That's the driving force behind Hauser. The acquisition of more power than anyone else in the world. I've been contacting some reporter pals.

Building up a jigsaw. Oh, by the way, Chief Inspector Buchanan is on his way here. Hope you don't mind?'

'Why should I mind? But I'd have thought you might,' Tweed commented. 'He's been here twice since you were carted off to hospital. You still seem to be his prime suspect.'

'So, when you're in a corner, take the bull by the horns – in this case the bull being Roy Buchanan. Questions I want to ask him. With your assistance – and Mauno Sarin's. He's still chief of Protection Police in Helsinki, I hope?'

'He is, but I don't see . . .'

'You will.'

The phone rang, was answered this time by Monica. Paula was watching Newman: he looked remarkably fit. And he exuded an aura of physical energy and driving power. All the old bounce was back. Monica cupped her hand over the phone.

'You've got your chance now. Buchanan is downstairs.' She looked at Tweed. 'All right to let him come up?'

'Wheel him in . . .'

Chief Inspector Buchanan walked in wearing the same grey suit followed by the wooden-faced Sergeant Warden. He glanced at the assembled company as though surprised to see so many people. Tweed ushered his guests to chairs, then sat back, leaving the field clear for Newman.

'Chief Inspector, have you got any further with your investigation of the murder of Sandy Riverton?'

'I usually ask the questions.' Buchanan sounded amused. 'As you've raised the point, no. In one way I wouldn't expect to find any witnesses – since what happened took place close to dawn. In another, I would. It's a farming community – agricultural workers rise early.'

'But you tried?' Newman persisted.

'Yes, and met a wall of silence.'

'Which doesn't surprise me . . .' Newman recalled briefly his experience at The Nag's Head a few hours before he ended up in hospital.

'Interesting.' Buchanan paused. 'But that doesn't give me any direct link with Hauser, who probably has nothing to do with the crime.' Another pause. 'Except for the murder of Edward Riverton, her husband – which Tweed has informed me about while you were in hospital.'

Of all those seated in the office only Buchanan seemed impervious to the heat. He crossed his long legs, the picture of relaxation as he studied Newman, his grey eyes half closed. Warden was enjoying himself in the background: it was a new experience to see someone else tackling Buchanan rather than the other way round.

'That took place in Helsinki,' Newman pointed out. 'A long way from Suffolk.'

'True. But when you've handled a number of homicide cases you learn to recognize a pattern. There are similarities between the two murders which, incidentally, I gather took place twenty-four hours apart.'

'What similarities?'

Buchanan settled himself more comfortably. 'Sandra Riverton was killed at a remote place at a remote hour. Mr Tweed knows Finland and tells me Edward Riverton's body was dumped into the icebound harbour in the dark. At a time when no one would be venturing out. The methods also suggest a similar technique, although I may be stretching a point.'

'Stretch it for me,' Newman urged.

'Sandra Riverton was killed by a rope round her *neck*. Edward Riverton was killed by garrotting his *neck*. A vulnerable part of the human anatomy. And a certain way of murdering someone.'

'I still don't see where you're going.'

'I think you do.' A grim smile. 'I said earlier the crimes were committed twenty-four hours apart. That time element intrigues me. Time for the same man to complete his work in Finland, then catch a plane to London and hire a car to take him to Suffolk. Also, I have found Mr Hauser has a Lear jet which flies him across the world plus a Sikorsky helicopter which I saw taking off from the grounds of Livingstone Manor. And there is a heliport south-east of Beccles, just north of the area.'

You have been a busy bee, Newman was thinking. But why are you telling me all this? The answer to his unspoken question came as Buchanan continued.

'Mr Newman, were you thinking of flying to Finland during the near future by any chance?'

'No, I wasn't. Why do you ask?'

'Just letting my mind wander.' He glanced at Tweed who was saying to himself, That's a laugh. You never let your mind wander in your life. 'Just a thought,' Buchanan added.

'But there was something behind the thought,' Newman insisted.

'Well, it might be interesting if someone like you were to nose around INCUBUS headquarters in Helsinki, ask some questions. Of course, you'd have to track down the right person.'

'Ask what questions?'

'Again, I think you know. Was a member of their staff in Helsinki during the night of Edward Riverton's murder? And was that same person *absent* the following day? That is, the same day Riverton was dragged out of the harbour. Someone who flew to Britain, so they were over here at the time of the Sandra Riverton crime.'

'You don't want much, do you?'

'Just a suggestion. Now, if that's all I'd better leave. At the moment I'm up to my neck in the Camden Town murder.' He stood up, refusing Tweed's offer of coffee. At the door he looked back at Newman. 'If you found someone such as I have just described it would let you off the hook.'

'So I'm still your number one suspect?'

'Let's just say, Mr Newman, that in so many murder enquiries the culprit turns out to be the person who discovered the body. Goodbye, Mr Tweed . . .'

On that note he left the room, descended the staircase, handed the identification form to the guard, went outside with Warden to his unmarked parked car. Warden asked the question as he settled himself behind the wheel.

'So you still think it could be Newman?'

'I have an open mind until further evidence comes to light. I certainly left Newman with that impression.'

'What was all that Finland business about, Chief?'

Buchanan smiled drily. 'If Newman is innocent he'll want to clear himself. I asked the Assistant Commissioner to let me go to Helsinki and he refused. Said I must concentrate on the Camden Town case. So maybe Newman can go in my place, do the job for me.'

'You think he can cope?'

'He's ideal for the role. A very experienced foreign correspondent, he'll be highly skilled in interrogating people. It was his profession for so many years – not unlike my own.'

You sly bugger, Warden thought. He was careful not to voice the thought aloud.

'Back to the Yard,' ordered Buchanan.

'So where does dragging Buchanan here leave you?' Tweed asked.

'It tells me I'm still his chief suspect. That was what I was really after. But he gave me more than I'd expected.'

'Which particular aspect?'

'The Finland business,' Paula interjected. 'Bob is going to fly to Finland. I can tell from his expression. And,' she continued firmly, 'I'd like to go with him. Women sometimes see things men miss. Don't forget I've done the bulk of the research on INCUBUS.'

'I'll think about it,' Tweed told her. 'It could be dangerous.'

'We've had this conversation before,' she flared up.

'And it was dangerous when we were in Germany. And on a previous operation it was damned dangerous in Rotterdam. So I'm not to be coddled like a twelve-year-old, thank you very much. 'Or,' she played her trump card, 'have you become old-fashioned? Women can't do a man's job?'

'I said I'll think about it,' Tweed responded, refusing to rise to the bait. 'And we don't know whether Bob is going to Finland yet.'

'I think it's my next port of call,' Newman replied. 'But first I'd like all the dope Paula has dug up on INCUBUS . . .'

He stopped as the phone rang again, Monica answered it, and again cupped her hand over the phone.

'It's an American. A Mr Ward Dexter. He says you're expecting him, that you were informed he would be coming a few months ago. He's waiting for you at Brown's Hotel.'

'Tell him I'll be there within an hour.'

Tweed paced the room, wiping moisture off his forehead as Monica relayed the message. The heat was becoming torrid and under his armpits his shirt was pasted to his body.

He was also recalling that Guy Dalby, sector chief for the Balkans, had earlier reported from Vienna. In Bucharest Dalby had been told by a totally reliable source that Ion Manescu, brutal *Securitate* chief, was alive. 'He escaped to God knows where,' Dalby had stressed. 'But he was very much alive when he vanished . . .'

'Mr Dexter will be waiting for you,' Monica said.

'The tempo is beginning to accelerate,' Tweed commented as he slipped on his linen jacket. 'That sounds like the secret aide sent personally by the US President. Now I'll find out what is really worrying Washington. A separate problem from yours,' he said to Newman.

11

Tweed caught a cab, told the driver to drop him at the Piccadilly entrance to the Burlington Arcade. He strolled up the long arcade, pausing frequently to peer in shop windows at the expensive goodies. He also glanced back the way he had come.

Emerging from the top of the arcade, he turned left and slipped inside Brown's Hotel in Albemarle Street. He walked swiftly to the reception counter midway down a long hall leading to Dover Street. A good hotel to stay at: apart from the excellence of its discreet service it had two exits. Mr Ward Dexter was in Room 144.

Tweed took the elevator the receptionist guided him to, stepped out, walked along the deserted corridor. He rapped three times on the door of Room 144, it was opened a few inches. A man with dark hair and thick eyebrows opened it a few inches.

'Mr Dex—'

Tweed stared as the man opened the door wide. He would be in his early fifties, was tall and well built with a craggy face. Beneath the strong nose was a dark moustache, thin and slicked down, which gave him a Latin look. It was the ice-blue eyes which told Tweed he was right.

'Come in,' the man said impatiently.

The door closed behind Tweed as he scanned the luxuriously furnished double room which overlooked Albemarle Street. He walked to the window and gazed down through the net curtains. Of all the people he had expected from Washington 'Dexter' was the last person.

He turned round to gaze at Cord Dillon, Deputy Director of the CIA.

'A rough diamond,' Paula called him. 'The manners of a bull elephant,' was Monica's elegant description.

'You've grown a moustache, I see,' Tweed remarked. 'And what have you done with your hair, for Pete's sake.'

'You recognized me quickly?' Dillon asked aggressively.

'No, I didn't. What have you done to yourself?'

'Grown myself a moustache, used hair colourant on it – as I did on my hair. If you didn't check me out who else will?'

Tweed sat down. The Cord Dillon he had known had a shock of thick brown hair and was clean shaven. The sunken cheeks which emphasized his cheekbones, the thin tight-lipped mouth were the same but they merged with the Latin appearance – further highlighted by the cut of his lightweight suit.

'What are you wearing?' Tweed asked as Dillon poured glasses of Perrier water. 'Thanks, it's a thirsty day.'

'The suit came from Italy. Let's cut the cackle. I'm on my own. When I say that I mean I'm operating without back-up. Even the Director has no idea I'm here.'

'Who does know then?'

'The President.' Dillon padded heavily across the room to sink into a chair next to Tweed. Even his walk was changed: normally he'd moved like a man with springs in his feet.

'Who else?' Tweed asked.

'No one. Just the President. I'm not joking.'

'Why this incredible degree of secrecy?'

'I want to stay alive . . .'

Tweed was stunned. He was talking to one of the toughest, cleverest Americans he had ever encountered. He had never expected to hear Cord Dillon make such a statement. Dillon gave no sign of being frightened, but Tweed sensed he was like a coiled spring.

'Could you elaborate on that a little?' he suggested.

'Sure. But first – so you know I'm *bona fide*, as the Uzbeks say – read this document.'

Tweed was relieved the American had not lost his rare sense of humour. He took out of a thick envelope a sheet of thick paper. The top of the sheet was embossed with the great seal of The President. The authorization was brief and addressed to Tweed. He ran his eyes down the typed message. A passage attracted his attention.

Cord Dillon is travelling as my personal representative with instructions to report back to me about this subject directly and without reference to any intermediaries however highly placed.

Below was the signature of The President. Tweed refolded the sheet, slipped it back inside the envelope and handed it to Dillon.

'Why did you say "I want to say alive"?'

'Because INCUBUS has penetrated the US government at all levels. It has infiltrated the CIA and the FBI. Hauser is a billionaire several times over. We've only rumours to go on but the sums he's paid out are astronomical.'

'Bribes?'

'Yes. He's established a power structure inside the Washington power structure. The President feels himself in a state of siege. We can no longer trust anyone. They might belong to INCUBUS.'

'So why have you come here?' Tweed demanded.

'Because it's in Europe we think we can bring him down with all his works. Franklin D. Hauser. We suspect he's operating illegally. We need absolute proof of that. Rumours say he's co-operating with some strange bedfellows. But who they are we don't know. Goddamnit, Tweed, we don't know a bloody thing!'

'Then we'd better start to find out exactly what he is up to. Especially in Finland.'

'Why would he choose Finland?'

'The perfect neutral base, would be my educated guess. It's a long way north – apparently out of the mainstream of the chaos which is afflicting Eastern Europe. We need a plan of action – to find out what Hauser is doing. He's built a big HQ in Helsinki, has another building in Turku, the second city. And he spends a lot of time in Finland.'

'So we go there, start something, blow his operation wide open.'

Typical of Dillon's tendency to use bull-at-a-gate methods. Not always. Dillon was clever, experienced. But he was under stress – because he was working on his own. Normally he directed a large team. Maybe it also highlighted the difference between the British and the American temperament, Tweed reflected.

'I'd go easy, Cord,' he warned. 'Keep under cover. I can't come yet – but Bob Newman is possibly making the trip there. If he agrees, the two of you could travel in harness.'

'The foreign correspondent? We don't get on. And he's a lone wolf character.'

'What cover are you travelling under?'

Dillon grinned, drank more water. He was calming down under the influence of Tweed's self-controlled personality, his off-hand way of talking.

'Officially I'm attached to the *Washington Post*. As a roving foreign correspondent . . .'

'And if someone checks back?' Tweed asked quickly. 'You've said only the President knows . . .'

'The paper's editor will back me up. He thinks I'm investigating the world drug trade. Which covers my ass.'

'Then it would be ideal for you to travel with Newman. He certainly doesn't dislike you,' Tweed continued, shading the truth. 'But only if he agrees. Wait here a few days, then Newman will contact you, again providing he agrees. If not, I'll contact you myself.'

'I can't sit on my rear for long, hanging round this ancient hotel. It's quite a place, I'll give it that. Service is very good. Must have been built in Georgian times.'

'Not quite.' Tweed suppressed a smile. 'But Agatha Christie used to stay here.'

'You're not going to tell Newman what I've told you?' Dillon demanded.

'I'll have to. Look, Bob Newman has worked with me as you well know. He's fully vetted.'

'OK.' Dillon sounded dubious. 'Don't forget I'm staying here as Ward Dexter. And you won't be saying anything to that ponce of a boss you've got, Howard?'

'Howard isn't included in the magic circle on this one. Sit tight . . .'

Otmoor, north of Oxford, is a bleak lonely wasteland of sour fields with few trees. Newman drove along the narrow road he'd turned on to off the B4027 at no more than thirty miles an hour. Beside him sat Paula, checking her map and acting as navigator. In the rear sat a restless Cord Dillon.

'We're crawling on our bellies,' the American complained. 'You do know where this Archer guy lives now?'

'Yes, we have a general idea, Mr Dillon,' Paula replied tartly. 'Keep a lookout for Begonia Cottage.'

'Begonia! Sounds like a spaghetti joint,' Dillon growled. 'You really think this trip is worth it?'

'If I didn't we wouldn't be here,' Newman told him. 'And it gets you out of London . . .'

'But we were tagged. That silver Chevrolet was following us. Make no mistake about that, brother.'

'And I spotted it the moment we drove off from my flat,' Newman rapped back. 'I told you about my holiday in hospital. That episode shows the opposition knows where I live. I spotted it and lost it at that last roundabout. Whoever was tailing us will never find their way inside Otmoor. And if they do we'll see them coming miles away.'

Which was true, Dillon admitted to himself as he glanced out of the rear window once more. The road – little more than a track with deep ditches on either side – was elevated above the surrounding countryside. No other vehicle was in sight as far as the eye could see.

'Newman,' he persisted, 'you're sure you've got this right – about Bennington Machine Tools being taken over against this Archer's wish by INCUBUS?'

'I'm sure.'

Newman left it at that. He hadn't thought it necessary to recall for Dillon's benefit the tragic death of Sandy, the notebook he'd found secreted under the seat of her Jaguar parked close to the bell tower. The notebook which recorded her interviews with Archer of Bennington, Swindon, and Manningham Electronics in the Thames valley.

Newman slowed down, stopped outside a cottage set well back from the road so Paula could read the name. He had his window down. The heat was overpowering, the sun glared out of a clear blue sky, the inside of the car was like an oven. He wiped his forehead, his hands.

'Holly Place,' Paula said, reading the name board. 'The wrong place.'

'Let's get a hustle on, I'm baking,' snapped Dillon.

'We all are, Mr Dillon,' Paula said amiably as Newman drove on.

In the distance was a large L-shaped residence, also well back off the road. It had a newly thatched roof and was enclosed inside a privet hedge. Newman slowed again and saw the name himself. Begonia Cottage. All the research he had done, using the phone while in hospital, had paid off. Providing the owner was at home. Then he saw the mullion windows were open.

* * *

James Archer was a tall man in his sixties, white-haired and clean shaven. He wore horn-rim glasses and had an air of authority. He had reluctantly agreed to let Newman and Paula into his home after some persuasion.

They sat in armchairs in a low-beamed room at the front while Archer perched in a rocking chair. Paula glanced up and saw cobwebs in the corners, a whole network. If there was a woman in the house she was sloppy, and that didn't seem to go with Archer.

'So, you're the foreign correspondent, Mr Newman. What can I do for you?' Archer enquired, rocking gently.

'Over two years ago you sold your company, Bennington Machine Tools, to Columbia High Multi-Machines Inc. – a subsidiary of INCUBUS Inc.'

'I see you've done your homework,' Archer replied after a slight pause.

'May I ask why you sold out?'

'I decided to retire, enjoy life a little more. Columbia offered me the market price.'

'And yet, when I got in touch with some of your business friends in Swindon they all expressed great surprise. They said you'd told them you'd never sell, no matter how much was offered.'

'You *have* done your homework.' The rocking stopped, the chair was suddenly still, as motionless as the man who sat inside it.

'How is your daughter, Julia, these days?'

Archer froze. A shot in the dark but it had struck a target. He stood up slowly, asked if they would like coffee, made his way out of the room when they accepted the offer. Paula stood up, whispered to Newman that she would be back and followed Archer. Newman stood up, stared out of the window. He could just see his Mercedes with Dillon seated in the back. It had been decided three people might overwhelm the man they were calling on.

Paula found Archer in a small kitchen at the rear of the

cottage. He stood with his back to her, watching a percolator. She was wearing a brightly flowered summer dress, high necked and with short sleeves. She leaned on the working surface and peered at him. There were tears in his eyes.

'Mr Newman hasn't come here to upset you,' she said gently.

'What has he come here for then?'

'He's investigating INCUBUS. He thinks there's something very wrong with that mammoth organization, with the methods it uses. He wants to expose it before the whole world, but he needs your help.'

She left it at that, opened a cupboard, found coffee cups, a jug, milk and sugar, and laid a tray. He dabbed at his eyes, blew his nose, then emptied the percolator's contents into the jug.

'No, I'll carry the tray,' Paula insisted.

'It's your dress,' he said. 'My wife had a dress very like it. She'd have been wearing it on a day like this.'

'And now your wife . . .' Paula began as they entered the living room and she placed the tray on the table, then began to fill the cups.

'She's dead.' Archer sat in a hard-backed chair, very erect. 'The stress of the enforced take-over was responsible. I'm certain of that.'

'Enforced?' Newman enquired as he picked up a cup.

'You were very direct. You seem honest. I've nothing more to be frightened of losing. My wife, as I told you, is no longer with us. And my daughter, Julia, is thousands of miles away, in another country which I won't name. She's married someone in that country so her surname is changed. She's safe.'

'What happened about that takeover?' Newman asked quietly. 'And I saw you glance at my car. That man sitting inside is from the *Washington Post*. He also is investigating INCUBUS, as I am.'

'I'll tell you the whole horror story. You were right – I had no intention of selling. I told that to the American who came to my office and made the offer. A small brute with dark hair and a face like a gangster. A Mr Moroti. An hour later – after I'd rejected the offer – I get a phone call . . .'

He lifted his cup and swallowed more coffee. Paula refilled the cup as he continued, his voice stronger.

'I get a phone call,' he repeated, 'from someone else. An Englishman with a smooth voice. He says they met Julia when she left her secretarial college in Swindon. That she is in good health at the moment, but health is a precarious commodity . . .'

Archer's expression was grim, his mouth closed tight briefly as it came flooding back to him.

'I can remember his exact words. He went on to say all that was necessary to solve the small domestic problem was to be sensible. Just to accept the business deal.'

'You could have contacted the police,' Newman suggested.

'I was warned against that. The Englishman said all my telephones were tapped with a sophisticated device, that I was being watched. They gave me two days to decide – two days of hell.'

'So no one knows about this until now?'

'No.' Archer snapped his fingers. 'I forgot something very important. A week before Moroti called a girl arrived at my office after making an appointment. She said she was from the American magazine, *Leaders of Mankind*. Wanted to do an article on how I'd built the company from nothing. I know it must sound like an ego trip, but I thought the publicity might help the company with more export orders . . .'

'Could you describe this girl?' Newman asked.

'Yes. Very attractive. In her mid-twenties, I'd guess. She was small, no more than five foot five tall, I'd guess.

She had the most beautiful blonde hair. It draped over her back.'

Newman felt sick. He had just described Sandy.

'Go on, please,' he said.

'She asked me a lot of personal questions as well as about my business. My family. I mentioned I had a daughter, Julia. It was only later I suspected this was how they'd obtained their detailed information about me. My routine, where I lived, the fact that Julia was taking this secretarial course.'

'So you never went to the police. You discussed the situation with your wife?'

'We stayed up all night. It was a diabolical dilemma. Should we risk the police? Amelia – my wife – was against it. The point was what they offered valued the company at its market worth. The bastards had done their research.'

'So you sold out to them – and kept quiet.'

'Yes, wouldn't you?'

'Probably. Julia was unharmed when she was returned?'

'Yes. But very frightened. And they'd told her that if she ever talked about her experience I was liable to have a very nasty accident, probably fatal.'

'I see.' Newman looked at Paula. 'I think we ought to leave Mr Archer in peace. Unless you have something to ask.' He looked at Archer. 'I don't intend to mention your name – at least not until we've destroyed INCUBUS.'

Archer jumped up. 'Destroy the bloody bastards root and branch!' He looked at Paula. 'I apologize for my language.'

'I'd have used something stronger,' Paula told him.

12

Peggy Vanderheld stood quivering with fury, silhouetted against the picture window in Hauser's Helsinki office. Behind her the sea glittered as the sun reflected off the waves.

'I'm sure you take my point,' Hauser continued from behind his desk. 'Trust is the first quality I require in those who work close to me.'

'How was I to know the goddamn file was that confidential?' she raged. 'You told me to take the Riverton file down to the vault. I noticed the serial number wasn't right. So,' she drew herself up to her full height, her tight black dress clasping her full figure as though the material was pasted to her, 'so,' she repeated, 'I opened it to check the photograph and saw it *was* Ed Riverton's. That was when you walked in.'

'And what else did you check?' he enquired, his voice soft. 'The biography, maybe?'

'I never saw the goddamn biography. I only saw the first page which, in case you've forgotten the system, shows the subject's photograph, age, length of time spent in the employ of the company, when he – or she – joined us, when he – or she – left us. Unless, of course, they're still with us.'

He ignored the sarcasm, rolled his shirt sleeves higher up his strong, thick arms. Christ, it was hot. He was studying her as he performed this action. He was inclined to believe her: her anger was a natural reaction to his accusation that she had been prying into data which was not her concern.

'It's the heat,' he said eventually and gave her his big smile. 'You know I never could stand humid heat. Who

111

would imagine we'd get this kinda heatwave this far north?'

'You can ask someone else to take the file to the vault.'

'I'm asking you to take it for me – because you always have my full confidence as my personal assistant. And I think the time has come to consider extra reward financially for your loyalty. Thank you, Peggy.'

He watched her leave the room. She would be in a glow of appreciation. Hauser prided himself on his ability to manipulate human beings. He sat thinking about her. Maybe she *had* held her position for long enough. It was his policy never to keep staff below executive level too long – it eliminated the danger of their learning too much. I'll put the skids under her, he decided. Soon . . .

In the elevator Peggy Vanderheld was steaming, and not only with the heat. She knew the signs. He's getting ready to fire me, she thought. So how can I kick the bastard in the balls first?

'Frank, our plans for penetrating Europe and Russia are well under way. I think it's time we increased surveillance on all arrivals into Finland.'

Galvone nodded to Hauser and walked across to the picture window. Heat shimmered in a boiling haze over the sea. He wore a short-sleeved shirt and pale cinnamon slacks. His large feet were shod in trainers. Hauser noticed again that Frank was very physical, could hardly keep still for more than a few minutes.

'We already keep watch on all the air and sea ports,' he reminded his boss. 'And I study the lists of known visitors.'

'That's the point, Frank. We need to be on the look-out for unknown visitors. Use our travel company's film unit. We have reached a sensitive stage in the operation. So get pictures taken of everyone coming in. Then study the films they take.'

'Consider it done.' Galvone sat in a chair, wriggled his feet. 'How are things going in the Soviet Union? A hard nut to crack. They're suspicious of foreigners.'

'It's already cracked.' Hauser was in an expansive mood. 'We have Angel in place, so we don't have to use foreigners, as you called them.'

'Angel? Sounds like a woman. You don't trust women.'

Hauser smiled, waved his cigarette holder. 'Angel is a man, a member of the Politburo in Moscow.'

Frank whistled. 'That must have taken some delicate handling, to get a man at the very top in that secret society.'

'More open now, Frank. This is the era of *glasnost*. And some men at the top in little old Moscow are not sure how it is going to work out in the end. So dollars, especially in a bank account outside Russia, is mighty appealing. Gives a kinda insurance policy for the future.'

'Can I ask who this Angel is?'

'You just did.' Hauser puffed at his cigarette. 'And that was a mistake, Frank. Not like you to poke your big nose into areas that don't concern you. Your area of operation is Europe. I'm dealing personally with Russia. My, my, I am surprised.'

'Sorry, Chief,' Galvone said hastily. 'It just slipped out. I was so stunned you'd managed to pull off such a coup – but I shouldn't have been surprised, remembering how you built up the company from nothing.'

'Which I did . . .'

A dreamy look came over Hauser's large face. He was going back to La Jolla, the small town in California about ten miles north of San Diego on the Pacific coast. The place where he was born. The place where he had founded a small bank. And slowly he had extended his grip. The huge leap forward had taken place in the eighties when he had used junk bonds to enlarge his empire at a fantastic pace – until suddenly it was realized in the States that Hauser controlled the largest private financial institution in the republic.

Hauser, who worked by instinct, unloaded his mountain of junk bonds in the late eighties – and converted it into a mountain of money. He bought politicians at the lowest level – and the highest. Several state governors were tucked away safely in his pocket.

In the corridors of Congress the name 'Hauser' was whispered behind closed doors. What would be his next move, they all wondered. And everyone tried to climb on the bandwagon. INCUBUS was the next decade. INCUBUS was power. But power presided over by a benevolent father figure whose only motive was to do his best for humanity. He had said so. Himself . . .

'Ion Manescu has perfected the new East Expansion Division,' Galvone reported. 'He has sent representatives to Budapest, Bucharest, Prague, Warsaw, Sofia and Berlin. They're already establishing commercial cells in those areas.'

'Reprentatives, commercial cells.' Hauser chuckled. 'I like the terminology – considering their real purpose.'

You would, Galvone thought. You invented the terms yourself. Hauser had a passion for intrigue, for disguising sinister moves by using commercial jargon.

'They all passed the special training course at Kemijärvi,' Galvone continued. 'With special emphasis on tough strong-arm methods.'

'The American way,' Hauser commented approvingly. 'If you're going to compete you remember the game is winners and losers. We're winners. What can stop us – stop us establishing control from the Pacific coast to the Urals – especially with the help of Angel?'

'What can stop us?' Galvone repeated. 'I'll set up the film units on all access points to Finland.'

* * *

On Otmoor Archer followed his guests down the garden path to the front gate. Newman sensed he had something he wanted to say and wasn't sure how to put it as he opened the gate for Paula.

Over Otmoor a dirty mist like marsh gas was rising above the depressing fields. The sun was squeezing the last moisture out of the deserted landscape. A heavy silence filled the air and Newman suddenly realized he had heard no birds sing since they entered the area.

'My daughter, Julia,' Archer began, his hand on the gate.

'What about her?' Paula encouraged him with a smile.

'I don't communicate with her. Not by letter or over the phone.'

'I'm sorry to hear that. Don't you get on?'

'Oh, yes, the relationship is very good. She's bright – she was at Bristol University before she went to the secretarial college. She's a graduate.'

'So what's the problem?'

'Fear. As long as they don't know where she is they can't touch me. They wanted me to stand by as a consultant. I refused. That was after I'd sold out and sent Julia to . . . overseas. You won't try and find her, will you, Mr Newman?'

'You have my word. Under no circumstances. And your own name, your company, will also not be mentioned until I've stopped Hauser in his tracks, destroyed him.'

'You really think you can do that?'

'I'm going to have a damned good try.'

It was Paula who had helped Newman with his research during his stay in hospital, who had traced Gavin Manningham, ex-owner of Manningham Electronics in the Thames valley area.

She had travelled to Maidenhead to his old address and the new occupants of his small mansion had no idea where he had gone. Paula had persisted with the wife and had obtained the address of the housekeeper who had looked after Manningham's home. She had invited the housekeeper, a Mrs Parsons, to have dinner at a nearby de luxe hotel. She had soon realized Mrs Parsons had a liking for gin and tonics. After six drinks the housekeeper confided in Paula, gave her the new address.

'Sacked me without even a bonus,' she complained. 'And that after six years' faithful service. I saw his fancy woman by chance one day. Crossing the bridge on to Riverboat Island, she was. Wearing a very expensive new outfit. Not short of a pound when it came to putting clothes on *her* back, I can tell you . . .'

Newman had left Otmoor and was now driving back towards London, guided by Paula to Riverboat Island in the Thames. A weird island, they found as they walked the last half mile – after leaving the Mercedes in a car park with Dillon seated in the rear.

'I don't know why I came,' he snapped just before they left. 'Why can't I come and see this guy for myself?'

'Because I spoke to him on the phone and he sounds a tough customer. Not the type to talk if too many of us arrive like a delegation. He may not talk at all . . .'

In this assumption Newman was wrong. They crossed a wide roadbridge over a backwater of the Thames, the only way of reaching the place. Boats were moored to the main bank, mostly small powerboats with a few dinghies. The Lodge, as Manningham's new home was called, was a large bungalow which had obviously been built within the past couple of years. Manningham, a burly fifty-year-old with an aggressive manner and a paunch, met them as they descended the far side of the bridge. He was carrying an iron bar and his welcome was far from warm.

116

'You're Newman. I recognize you. What the hell is all this about?'

Newman decided the gentle handling of James Archer wouldn't work with this type. The direct approach was called for.

'It's about INCUBUS, the way they grabbed your firm. I am researching a series of articles for *Der Spiegel*. That's the leading German news magazine . . .'

'I know. What's the angle?'

'I'm building up an *exposé* on the methods they use, how they victimize people all over the world. How did they pull it off with you?'

'Come in and I'll show you.' He had been studying Paula's figure. 'Who is your friend?'

'My assistant, Paula.'

'That's a new name for the relationship. Follow me. Don't touch the wire fence – it's electrified.'

'Is that legal?'

'I didn't bother to ask. There are warning notices as you can see . . .'

The interior of The Lodge was like a show house, flashily furnished, expense no object. The living room overlooked a landing stage with a small power cruiser moored. The room had black leather armchairs and couches scattered on a wall-to-wall pink carpet. Silver cups – golfing trophies – crammed the mantelpiece over a huge arched brick fireplace. Framed photographs of Manningham swinging a club decorated the lime green walls. Their host saw Paula gazing at the carpet.

'Phoebe chose that. Great isn't it? Anyone want a drink?'

They both refused and Manningham poured himself a large Scotch as Paula sank carefully into a vast armchair which enclosed her. Manningham perched on a black leather stool by a well-stocked bar with a large mirror behind it. He opened the conversation with a clenched fist gesture.

117

'They're gangsters. Damn Yankee gangsters. Phoebe is up in town, buying more clothes, spending my money, so this is a good time to tell you . . .'

It was the same story as Archer had told but the sinister technique had varied. A Mr Vicenzo, an American, had met Manningham at his office. The description again matched that of Frank Galvone. Vicenzo had offered the market price for Manningham Electronics. Manningham had said he wasn't for sale, but he might consider double the figure offered.

'Who was he representing?'

Newman interjected the question quickly. Manningham was in full flood, downing his drink and pouring himself a fresh one. The answer was Columbia High Multi-Machines Inc. It was the same outfit Archer had told Newman that made the bid for Bennington. Newman's detailed researches in hospital had come up with the fact that this company was a subsidiary of INCUBUS.

Vicenzo had gone away. A few days later an Englishman had spoken to him on the phone, saying an envelope of pictures Manningham might find interesting were on the way by express registered post. That it would make life a lot happier for Manningham if he closed the deal at the price offered.

'I kept some of the photos that came in that envelope. They wanted them all back when I agreed to sell – at their price – but I said I'd spilt coffee on some of them and thrown them away. You have to understand I'm getting a divorce from my wife. We were separated at the time – the woman in the photographs is Phoebe. Two taken outside a flat I'd rented for her.'

Newman examined the five prints, handed them to Paula and lit a cigarette when Manningham told him to go ahead. The prints showed the same woman. Leaving a shop, outside a block of flats. One close-up taken with a

118

zoom lens. The ugly factor about each print was someone had fashioned a rubber stamp showing the crosshairs of a sniperscope rifle. In each case the rubber stamp had been positioned on the prints so it was aimed at Phoebe's back, the centre of her chest. On the close-up the crosshairs stamped her blonde-framed face.

A high-class tart, Paula thought. A brazen expression. She must have spent half an hour making herself up. Paula spent two minutes putting on her face first thing. But clearly Manningham was in love with the girl. She handed him the pictures.

'They scared me. I admit it,' Manningham told them. 'I was frantic that they'd found out about the flat, where she lived. And then those hideous photographs.' He finished his drink.

'Before this Vicenzo came to see you did, by chance, you have any unusual interviews with an American flavour?'

Manningham stared. 'My God! That girl . . .'

Again it was a repeat performance. The girl who had interviewed him for *Leaders of Mankind*. And the description he gave of the girl was a perfect portrait of Sandy. The same formula all over.

They left Riverboat Island a few minutes later, walked over the wide bridge in silence. Paula was the first to speak.

'It's hideous,' she said. 'The technique they use. And Manningham dare not call the police because they convinced him his every move was being monitored. Which makes it even more diabolical because he's a tough nut.'

'Oh, it's diabolical,' Newman agreed grimly. 'But first we must dig deeper, get much closer to INCUBUS. And the answer probably lies in Finland.'

'Helsinki next stop?'

'I think so. But I've decided to press Tweed to let you come with me. You handled Archer well – and two men

119

and a woman travelling together attract less attention.'

'We're going to let Cord Dillon come with us then?'

'Yes. We may need back-up – Dillon isn't a man I like but in a tight corner he's formidable.'

'So we all fly direct to Helsinki?'

'Not direct,' Newman said as they approached the car park. 'We go in by a roundabout route. Via Sweden. Someone may just be waiting for us to arrive.'

The following day Tweed announced his decision to Monica as they sat alone in his office. He was feeling the heat and kept mopping his forehead and hands.

'I'm going to send Marler to Finland to nose around and see if he can find out where the missing men have vanished to. Men like Ziegler of the STASI and Manescu of the *Securitate*.'

'Why Finland?'

'Because I'm getting reports from Europe that a new underground route has been established. It runs from the Balkans and Central Europe to Travemünde, the German port on the Baltic.'

'Where would they go from there?' Monica asked and looked at the wall map of the continent.

'They could catch the ferry to Helsinki. That way they would disappear without trace. In the present state of chaos no one is checking the passengers on that ferry crossing.'

'Shouldn't Newman know about this?'

'Definitely not. We are running two separate investigations. One into INCUBUS and all its activities. That problem is being tackled by Newman, Paula and Dillon. Marler will be searching for these vanishing men ...' There was a knock on the door. 'Come in.'

Marler was in his early thirties, slim in build, wore an expensively cut sports jacket. Fair-haired, he was clean shaven and had a strong face. Only five feet seven tall, he spoke in a high pitched drawl, a public school accent he often emphasized abroad. Foreigners viewed him as the typical Englishman, a bit of a dandy. It put them off their guard. They would have felt more cautious if they'd known one of his qualifications was that he was the most deadly marksman in Western Europe with a rifle.

'Mornin' to you.' He perched his backside on the edge of Paula's desk, swung his legs. 'I was up till three ack emma memorizing those files you gave me. I've returned all of them to Central Registry. I concentrated on Ziegler and Ion Manescu. He was a big wheel in Bucharest *Securitate*, Mr Manescu. And I got the Engine Room boys in the basement to give me three photocopies of our Romanian friend.'

'Why three?' asked Tweed. 'You'll have to be careful who you mention his name to. He's dangerous.'

'Don't I know it? His track record is a shade beastly — but effective.' He took an envelope from his breast pocket, extracted three photos, laid them on the desk. 'One is the only original picture ever taken of him, the second shows him with a beard as well as his moustache, the third clean shaven. Archie downstairs is quite an artist.'

Monica and Tweed studied the three prints. Monica let out a cat-like hiss.

'It's incredible. He's unrecognizable in the treated pics.'

'Bound to have changed his appearance, would be my guess,' Marler commented and lit a king-size cigarette. 'When I do see him I'll know him — but he won't know me.'

'You should be armed,' Tweed decided. 'Manescu is a killer. The file records he's strangled people with his bare hands in the old days in Bucharest. With the security at airports that creates a problem. Doubtless you'll solve it.'

121

'Consider it solved.' Marler waved an airy hand. 'Is your contact who reported seeing Manescu board the Travemünde ferry for Helsinki reliable?

'Very.'

'You told me about Newman and the tragic death of his girl friend. When was Manescu spotted by that Romanian woman in London?'

'Two days before Sandy Riverton was murdered in Suffolk.'

'Interesting. The file said Manescu spent a year at the Romanian Embassy in London once, that he speaks excellent English. Probably just a coincidence – Manescu's presence in London at that time.'

'The same thought had occurred to me.' Tweed hesitated. 'I haven't told Bob Newman that. He's working on something else. I don't want his mind distracted. He took the death of Sandy very hard.'

'We don't always see eye to eye,' Marler reflected, blowing smoke circles, 'Newman and I. But he's had a tough time, I'll give him that.'

'When can you leave for Helsinki?'

'I've stacked up with Finmarks. I have an open ticket for where I'm flying to first.'

'Where's that?' Monica asked.

'Hamburg in north Germany.'

'That's a funny way to reach Finland.'

'I have my reasons, my dear . . .'

13

The Sikorsky which had flown Hauser from Helsinki to the isolated rendezvous in the Finnish woods stood inside the clearing, its rotors motionless. Hauser walked with Galvone towards the man who stood quite still in the shade of a stand of dense fir trees.

Hauser wore dark glasses, a wide-brimmed straw hat pulled well down over his face. He was carefully not displaying his cigarette holder and wore a floppy khaki drill jacket and baggy trousers of the same material. He was not easy to recognize as Franklin D. Hauser.

'This is Ion Manescu,' Galvone introduced.

'What are my instructions?' Manescu demanded, studying the large man in dark glasses.

'It has been decided to increase the area of surveillance, to widen the ring of protection and observation. We want you to send people to Sweden, to Stockholm. Watch for any arrivals boarding the large ferry ships for Finland.'

'That can be organized within two days,' Manescu replied briskly. 'And I have just the person with me who will be invaluable. Irina Serov.'

'With him?' whispered Hauser. 'He was supposed to meet us by himself. Ask him where this Irina is now.'

Galvone put the question in English. Manescu waved a long slim-fingered hand behind him.

'She is waiting out of sight in the woods. We flew together from Kemijärvi. And we now have fifty agents of different nationalities, all highly trained in the skills taught at the special place.'

'And,' Galvone continued, 'are those agents allocated to treat liberal elements holding positions of influence yet on their way?'

'They are in place already,' Manescu replied, choosing his words carefully.

His lean bony sun-tanned face was relaxed, concealing his high degree of alertness. Instinct told him he was passing some kind of test. He had been careful to answer questions tersely, adding no extra information. But had mention of Kemijärvi been a mistake?

'Ask him when the agents in place will start the anti-liberal operation?' Hauser whispered again.

Galvone put the question to Manescu who stood confidently, hands on his hips, staring at Galvone, never giving a glance in Hauser's direction. He wore a blue check T-shirt, light-coloured slacks. He looked for all the world like a Finn on holiday, which was his intention.

'Today,' Manescu responded, and closed his lips in a tight line which was little more than a gash in the brown hawk-like face.

Hauser turned away, walked slowly back to the waiting Sikorsky. Instead of proceeding at his normal brisk trot, he lumbered up the step-ladder and heaved himself ponderously inside the machine's cabin. There had been too many films taken, shown on TV, of Franklin D. Hauser departing by Lear jet in the States for yet another destination.

At all costs Hauser wished to distance himself from the coming Manescu operation in various ex-Communist European states. When Galvone leapt aboard and seated himself beside his chief Hauser made his unsettling comment before they started up the rotors.

'I'm impressed, Frank. Very impressed with Manescu. He did make one slip, of course – referring to Kemijärvi. But any man is permitted one slip. You think he was telling the truth when the said the anti-liberal operation starts today?'

'It's a sure thing.'

Being an American, Hauser referred to all Socialists as liberals. And they wanted to preserve the nationalized industries. You couldn't do business with – take over – an organization unless it was private enterprise. Hauser took off his glasses, substituted the pince-nez.

'So, when the bombs start to go off the Western press will put it down to hard-liner elements still yearning for the days before Gorbachev arrived. And I really was impressed with Manescu, Frank. Maybe one day we'll be able to bring him out of the closet, give him a new identity, promote him to a senior vice president.'

'Why not?' said Frank without enthusiasm, and gave the pilot the order to take off.

'Any idea who the man in the straw hat was?' Manescu asked Irina Serov as he met her as she dropped to the ground from the branch of a tall fir.

'Franklin D. Hauser,' she answered promptly and flourished the monocular glass she had used to study the man in the hat close up. 'I saw him once when I was with the Washington Embassy.'

'You're certain?'

Manescu grasped her firmly by the arm as he asked his question. Her other hand whipped up like a snake, grasped Manescu by the throat. 'You're hurting me. I don't like that.'

Manescu released her and rubbed his throat. She had a grip like an iron clamp. Irina Serov was an ex-colonel in the KGB – the only woman ever to reach that exalted rank. She had fallen foul of the Gorbachev reforms when a new KGB chief was appointed to clean up their act.

One night she had boarded a small fishing vessel moored at a small port near Yalta. With her pistol at his head, the skipper had sailed across the Black Sea to the Turkish coast. As ordered, he had anchored at night off the port of

Sinop. Irina had promptly shot him, weighted his body, dumped it overboard.

From Sinop she had made her way to Bucharest via Istanbul when Ceausescu was still in power. Here she had first met Ion Manescu who had taken her under his wing – she was an invaluable conduit as to what was going on in Moscow and sympathetic to the Romanian régime.

When Manescu fled Romania after the collapse of Ceausescu and his evil system he had taken Irina with him. Now he stood facing her inside a remote Finnish forest while she gazed back with eyes like the Arctic ice.

Thirty-five years old, she stood only five feet five and had let her dark hair grow long to change her appearance. She had a natural Slavic beauty, a good figure outlined by her tight high-necked dark green blouse – to merge with the forest – and more than one man had fallen prey to her and regretted it, if he had lived to do so. Her eyes had a greenish tinge and her full mouth was compressed with fury.

'We have to go to Sweden,' he said quietly. 'To check on any strangers coming here by that route. Especially we watch for strangers who are hostile – or might be.'

'Then it's a good job I spent time with the Soviet Embassy in Stockholm before they sent me to Washington. When do we leave?'

He was relieved by her reply. He might have been rather less relieved if he could have read her mind. Irina Serov was disillusioned: she cared no longer for Communism, for Capitalism, for any bloody 'ism'. She had one goal in life: to accumulate a huge fortune in dollars, to leave Europe forever and to spend the rest of her life in luxury in America. The realization that she was working for Hauser was opening new horizons for her, but she'd not had time to work out how she could exploit the knowledge.

'For Stockholm?' Manescu replied. 'Tomorrow.'

* * *

In Prague Ladislav Sacher, Minister for Trade and Industry, left Hradcany Castle and walked to his Skoda car parked by the kerb. In his sixties, he had a mane of white hair and a kindly expression. His face was lined after years of 'attention' from the STB, the Czech secret police which had now, thank God, been disbanded.

Sacher was a dedicated socialist who was devoting his considerable influence to blocking the attempts of private firms from the West to establish a dominating position. Especially he was against the Americans with what he called in speeches, 'their Mafia-style methods in business . . .'

Having spent years in prison under the old régime, years that had taken their toll and made him look well over seventy, he got up every morning now, threw open the windows of his apartment, and breathed in 'the good clean air of freedom'.

He carried a stick to aid his ailing right leg which had been broken deliberately by the STB while he was in prison. These days he felt happier than he had at any time in his life. A new era had dawned. A woman walking along the pavement smiled.

'Good morning, Father.'

'Thank you. It really is a wonderful day.'

They all called him 'Father' and he drank in the glowing warmth of the heatwave which comforted his tortured bones. The sun shone out of a clear azure sky. It was good to be alive.

He unlocked his car door, opened it, slid with difficulty behind the wheel, closed the door. A dozen yards away a burly young man, wearing a pale blue shirt, denim trousers and with his goggles adjusted, perched on his moped leant against the kerb. A canvas satchel looped round his neck sagged against his chest.

Sacher turned the ignition key, began to drive slowly away. The man on the moped threw back the flap of his satchel, glanced round, fingered the radio transmitter which would send the signal. He pressed the switch.

The bomb attached beneath the chassis of the Skoda detonated as the signal triggered it off. Sacher's car was lifted into the air by the violence of the explosion, its sides were torn off. Its occupant, the man they called 'Father', was blown into a messy pulp, the corpse unrecognizable, the flesh embedded with pieces of metal.

The man on the moped was already speeding away in the opposite direction. He had no idea that the bomb – with its sophisticated detonating system and the compact radio transmitter – had been smuggled to him by a devious route, via Finland and Germany. Nor that the brain behind the outrage was Ion Manescu. All he was concerned with was the generous fee in Czech crowns now buried under the floorboards of his tiny cottage in the High Tatra mountains.

In Bucharest the sun was not shining. A heavy overcast like a poison gas cloud was stationary over the battered city. The heat was there but in the evening it was humid and sweaty.

Stefan Campeanu, forty years old and a leader of the Peasants' Party, made his way home on foot to his apartment by his usual route, at his normal time. A man of routine, Campeanu had not realized this could be a dangerous habit. It made it easy for an enemy to monitor his movements.

Campeanu was opposed to the National Salvation Front government. Desperate to cling to power, it had agreed to accept help from the US. Campeanu was outspoken in his criticism of the idea that dollars channelled through private corporations should be accepted.

'There are Stalinists at the top of the Front,' he had openly accused. 'We must take no outside help. We must rebuild our shattered homeland ourselves. No to the dollar . . .'

There were still old parts of Bucharest surviving despite the bulldozers of Ceausescu which had torn down the old to build huge concrete cubes. Campeanu walked with his head down, deep in thought as he plunged into a dark narrow back street which was little more than an alley. His feet followed his well-trodden path home.

Half-way along the twisting alley he had to squeeze past a primitive scaffolding – constructed with wooden posts and three storeys high and heavy beams for planks. The structure was held together with ropes binding the beams to the vertical posts. Darkness was falling rapidly as Campeanu eased his way past the narrow gap.

He heard the first ominous creak, looked up. The clumsy structure – the ropes deliberately loosened – was toppling. Campeanu, an athletic man, began to hurry. Then he heard a shout. Ahead of him a shadowy figure stood a dozen yards away, both arms raised, the hands holding what looked like a gun.

Campeanu stopped hurrying, a fatal pause. The scaffolding tumbled down, burying him under a grotesque criss-cross of beams and posts. Silence descended on the alley. When the press photographers took pictures the following morning their pictures of chaos were somehow symbolic of the chaos which was growing worse in Romania.

Two days later Tweed read the *Daily Mail* spread out across his desk. The pictures told the stories. One showed the small boat capsized in the Danube in Hungary outside Budapest. Two leading liberals had drowned. There were rumours the small boat had been hit by a much larger vessel.

The second picture showed what remained of the wrecked car in Prague, the car which had belonged to Ladislav

Sacher. The headline screamed: 'STB ATROCITY!'

The third picture, the last in the double spread, showed the weird spiked mess of scaffolding in the Bucharest alley. It looked like a modern sculpture. The headline was equally sensational. 'LEADING BUCHAREST LIBERAL DIES IN ACCIDENT?'

'It's started,' he said to Monica who had read the paper earlier.

'The strange thing is all four men were killed within hours of each other,' she commented.

'That is the point. One accident. Two could be coincidence. But three – and the Czech liberal was killed by a bomb – is too much. It's part of a plan.'

'You mean terrorists?'

'No. Who ever heard of any fanatical terrorist outfit being able to organize three assassinations in three different countries within the same twenty-four hours?'

'Then . . .'

'It's not terrorists in the normally accepted sense of the breed,' Tweed said grimly. 'This is terror used as a weapon, an instrument of policy.'

'Can you explain that a bit more?'

'It is terror used *pour encourager les autres*, as the French say. To encourage the others – the other liberal and democratic elements in Eastern Europe to keep their heads down. It's cold-blooded murder carefully orchestrated.'

'But who is behind it?'

'I've no idea. Yet. No proof, anyway. We have to start moving faster. And it suggests the driving force – or someone working for him – has a good knowledge of Central and Eastern Europe.'

'Can you back that up – except as a theory?'

Tweed stood up, began pacing round his office, staring at the wall map of Europe.

'Take the Bucharest tragedy. The man who planned all

these assassinations knows the right people inside Romania to do his murderous bidding. A scaffolding collapses on this important politician, Campeanu. You'd need someone with a good deal of local knowledge to pull that off.'

'And the killing of Ladislav Sacher in Prague?'

'Again, someone has to know who to hire to do the job – and probably how to smuggle the bomb into the country. The same applies to the so-called accident to two Hungarians who were drowned in the Danube. Both were vocal in their belief that Hungary must pull itself up by its own bootstraps. And to stage that collision someone had contact with the skipper of a larger vessel plying the river.'

'You're reaching,' Monica commented.

'Three in three countries is too much,' he repeated. 'But I haven't worked out yet the full implications of the conspiracy. I also think that we may have to send Harry Butler and Pete Nield as back-up for Newman and Paula later.'

'When are they leaving for Finland?'

'Very soon. But first Bob wants to talk to Evelyn Lennox before they go. He has some obsession she hasn't told him the whole truth.'

'And Marler?'

'Already on his way to Hamburg.'

Hauser also was reading the reports but his newspaper was the *Herald Tribune*. Galvone stood beside him as his chief pushed the newspaper aside.

'Well, they haven't linked up the three incidents. Just a wringing of the hands over the ferment which is developing in Europe.' He lit a cigarette, clenched the holder and sat back with an expression of great satisfaction. 'I didn't think anyone in the West would catch on to our ball game.'

131

'To scare the shit out of the creeps opposing our offers to modernize their industries.'

'More than that, Frank. Something far more subtle. This campaign Manescu is managing so well has another important purpose – to make the Brits, the Frogs, etc., nervous about investing in those countries. That way we kill off the competition while we scoop the pool ourselves. Then it will be too late. And talking about timing, we have to create a situation so I can fire Peggy Vanderheld.'

'I reckon, Chief, that intimidation of the competition is a brilliant strategy.' Galvone let the fulsome admiration show in his tone. 'You really have worked this one out and we will scoop the pool.'

Hauser patted him on the arm. 'Nothing to it, Frank. It's just the American way.'

14

'Walberswick is a beautiful village,' Paula said as Newman drove slowly down The Street under the arched trees. 'More like a hamlet, actually – but with some wonderful houses and all different and old. I assume Evelyn knows that we are coming?'

It was late evening, close to twilight, but the heat of the day made the atmosphere baking, the air very still. Newman nodded as they passed one dwelling.

'That's Rose Bower. And Evelyn knows *I* am coming but I forgot to mention you'd be with me.'

'Oh, yes?' She eyed him with a roguish smile. 'Do I gather from that that my presence may not be entirely welcome?'

'All I want you to do is to give me your impression of her later. Now I'm letting you have a look at the sea before we call on her. We're a few minutes early . . .'

He turned left when they had passed the hotels, parked the car in the space reserved for vehicles and they climbed out, stretched, stood looking at the view. The wide belt of dune-land with its hummocks and scrubby grass growing out of the sand was deserted at that hour.

A weird isolated structure like a huge cabin reared up close to the harbour entrance. Two storeys high, the walls made of wood, it had a tiled roof and one half had been refurbished. A gull screeched in the distance, dived over the lake-calm deep purple of the North Sea stretching away to a hard straight line, the horizon. In the distance to the north the cluster of toy-like buildings which was Southwold stood a mile away beyond the harbour.

'Evelyn told me she often comes for a walk among the dunes,' Newman remarked. 'When she wants a change she drives south to Minsmere Nature Reserve, a very lonely spot at night.' He checked his watch. 'Time to call on her. While we are there could you excuse yourself, leave me alone with her for a short while. I want to ask her an embarrassing question.'

Paula looked at him wickedly as she settled herself in the front passenger seat. She smoothed her raven black hair with a slim hand.

'I think I can guess what that question might be. And I'm sure she's attractive.'

'You're an imp,' he told her as he turned the ignition key. 'And yes, she is attractive. To some men I'd imagine . . .'

His friendship with Paula had grown steadily. A friendship without complications. As he drove back up The Street he frowned. A man on a motor cycle, a big Honda, had turned round at their approach, parked by the roadside close to Evelyn's cottage. Newman only caught a glimpse of the man in a dark leather jacket but he looked remarkably like Steve, the thug who had accompanied Papa Grimwood on their visit to Greenway Gardens, Wandsworth.

There was a *vr-o-o-m* of engine sound which murdered the silence. The motor cyclist sped off away from Walberswick, was soon a speck which vanished round a bend.

Evelyn, wearing a flowered summer dress belted at her slim waist and clinging tightly to her good figure, led the way into the low-beamed sitting room. It was neat as a new pin and showed no signs of the going-over it had suffered when Newman was last there.

Tugging at her mane of red-gold hair she turned on her heel and looked Paula up and down. Her quick scan took in the pale blue T-shirt, short sleeved, the short pleated skirt, the long shapely legs.

'So you're Bob's . . . *assistant*?' she said with too much inflection.

'His research assistant,' Paula replied with a warm smile, a shade too warm.

Evelyn came close to Newman, dipped her head sideways. He felt compelled to bend forwards and kiss her on the proffered cheek. Which was, of course, for Paula's benefit.

'Lovely to see you, Bob,' Evelyn said again. 'Drinks for anyone?'

They both refused and sat down as Evelyn became the welcoming host. Newman was careful to avoid the couch, to sit in an armchair. Evelyn sat in a Regency chair, carefully crossed her legs, displaying briefly a glimpse of thigh clad in black tights decorated with butterflies.

'Has anything happened to alarm you?' Newman enquired. 'Any strangers in the village? Any motor cyclists visiting the place regularly?'

'No to the first question. No to the second. No to the last one. The bike gangs never come here. Only one very quiet pub and no shop windows to smash in after they've got drunk. Southwold is different. But there was a motor bike went by a few minutes ago. I didn't see the rider.'

'So you feel safe here? No contact with Helsinki since you arrived?'

'Yes, I feel safe.' A brief hesitation. 'And no contact with Helsinki. Not that I'd expect it.'

'Has anyone been fired recently from INCUBUS Oy.? Someone who might harbour a grudge against the company?'

'Not while I was there,' she said, answering now at her normal pace.

'Who employed there would know most about Hauser's day-to-day work, the orders he gives?'

'Well, there's Adam Carver, a VP in charge of banking. Then Frank Galvone often turns up, another VP. Information and Planning is his division, whatever that might be. But if you're thinking of someone who would talk to you, forget both men. Hauser must pay them big money.'

'Anyone else?'

'Not really.' She puckered her shaped eyebrows. 'There is Peggy Vanderheld. A typical New York career woman. But she's about forty and has been with the company ages.'

'What position does she hold?'

'Hauser's PA. He trusts her. That is, as far as he trusts any woman. His wife left him – and I don't blame her – but apparently since then he's gone off women.'

Paula stood up. 'Miss Lennox, do you mind if I pop out and have a look at your front garden before it's too dark? I love wild roses and your path is clustered with them.'

'Take as long as you like. Leave the door with the lock on the latch so you can get back again . . .'

Newman waited until they were alone. Evelyn pulled

her chair closer to him. Her wide mouth, emphasized with her scarlet lipstick, parted in a glowing smile. She reached out, took his right hand.

'I feel even safer now you're here.'

He hit her with his direct question. 'Evelyn, were you Ed Riverton's mistress?'

She snatched her hand away. 'What makes you say a bloody awful thing like that?'

He counted on his fingers. 'One, when I was having dinner with you and Ed in Helsinki at his apartment I sensed a certain intimacy between the two of you. Two, when I called Ed's Helsinki apartment to tell him about Sandy *you* took the call, you were there again – in his apartment. Three, you went all out to persuade me to call Sandy to break the news about Ed's murder. More naturally one sister would have gritted her teeth and done the job herself. You do have grit. But if you'd been playing about with your sister's husband you might feel inhibited. Enough?'

'You expect me to admit it?'

'You just did. I don't care about your private life. But I'm trying to track down the man who brutally murdered Sandy, your sister. Did Ed Riverton ever tell you anything confidential about INCUBUS? About his job? What was his job, for God's sake?'

'He was very close-mouthed . . .'

'Come off it, Evelyn. Pillow talk. That's when men let their back hair down. And when I interviewed Ed he was on edge, very nervy. He'd need someone as a safety valve – you fit the bill.'

She played with her lace handkerchief, just as she had done at Greenway Gardens. Newman lit a cigarette, blew smoke rings, watched them float up, collapse against a heavy wooden beam. He kept silent.

'He was in charge of Dracon,' she began. 'That's the think-tank for INCUBUS, based outside Boston. He told me he used to catch the train from Penn Station, New York, get off it at a station called Back Bay where a car would be waiting for him. He'd be driven to Dracon which is a complex of well-guarded buildings off what they used to call Space Highway . . .'

'Yes, I've heard of it. What went on at Dracon?'

'Ed said they were a lot of kooks. Academics from the Ivy League universities, planners who were ex-generals lured from the Pentagon for huge salaries, economists. I remember a name. A Professor Hiram Goldstein. He'd written a book.'

Now we're getting somewhere, Newman thought. 'I read the book,' he said. 'The one by Goldstein. *No More Space.* But what did these freaks *do*?'

'They were producing plans for expansion, Ed said. He didn't like the plan Hauser chose. He didn't say why, didn't give me any idea of the plan. But Goldstein had a lot to do with it. Ed told me he'd had a lot of bitter arguments about this plan with Hauser.'

'When did he tell you this? About the arguments?'

'A week before they . . .' She choked. 'Before they dragged him out of the harbour. Not a human being any more. Just a mulch of flesh frozen solid as a rock.'

'That doesn't sound like your phraseology. Who used those very graphic words?'

'A Finn called Mauno Sarin. Some kind of detective. He called on me at the apartment a few hours before I left for the airport. I told him nothing. There was nothing I had to tell him. But I was frightened. It was one reason why I caught the first flight home. I never want to have anything more to do with INCUBUS. There's something sinister going on up there in Finland.'

It was very dark as Newman drove along the road away from Walberswick on their way back to London. Paula sat

137

by his side, checking the map spread on her lap with a pencil flash.

'What did you think of Evelyn?' he asked.

'Do you want me to be nice or honest?'

'Honest.'

'You'll think me catty, but you asked for it. She's a man-hunter. It's second nature to her to check that she's still attractive to men with every one of them she meets. And she wants you. Maybe permanently. Or hadn't you realized it?'

'She wants a protector. And yes, I think she's decided I fit the role. But after seeing that motor cyclist, she may need a protector. So if you spot a public phone box tell me. Anything else about the seductive Evelyn?'

'She's a liar. Does that sound catty, too?'

'Just tell me why you said that.'

'When you asked her whether anyone from Helsinki had got in touch with her, that's when she lied. I was watching her. She hesitated before she answered that one. Perhaps only another woman would have noticed.'

'I noticed. The problem is if we can ever trap Hauser in a situation that's illegal we'll need every witness we can get. Evelyn could be one of those witnesses.'

'Well,' Paula teased him, 'you could always keep in touch – she's quite a flirt.'

Adam Carver returned on foot to Rose Bower for the second time that evening. On his first excursion he'd seen a Mercedes parked outside so he'd turned back, returned to his hotel room further down The Street.

Evelyn peered through the newly installed spyhole after turning on the porch light, unfastened the two fresh locks and gave her visitor a radiant smile. She invited him in, pulled at her hair, relocked the door and followed him into the living room.

'I've had a visitor since you were here this afternoon,' she informed him. 'The handsome and beguiling Bob Newman. Care for another drink?'

'A double Scotch would go down nicely – providing you'll join me.' Carver gazed with open admiration at her figure. 'And I see you've dressed yourself up for me. You look – terrific. Sexy.'

'Really?'

She was pleased as she poured the drinks. Carver was a good-looking bastard, had nice manners, and she liked his warm smile, his smooth ways. Deliberately she'd omitted the fact that Paula had accompanied Newman. He asked the question as she handed him his drink.

'Newman, the foreign correspondent? I see. And what did he want coming to this back of beyond?'

'I got the impression he came to see me.' They clinked their glasses. 'We're just good friends, Adam.'

How unsubtle can you get, he thought, but he grinned, drank half the Scotch, placed his glass on the paper mat Evelyn had provided. They were sitting close together on the couch. He put an arm round her waist, pulled her close, kissed her full on the mouth. She went limp, kept her eyes closed, her hand round his neck. He wiped lipstick off his mouth with a handkerchief, reminded himself to lose it. Evelyn had an expression like that cat which has swallowed the cream.

'How did you find me out here in this back of beyond?' she asked.

'When you didn't call me back from your place in Wandsworth I checked with headquarters in Norwich – to find out where your sister had lived,' he said casually. 'I thought it was worth a try, so I drove up here, booked myself in at a hotel down the road. Hey presto! I'm on your doorstep this afternoon.'

'You don't give up easily, do you?'

'Not where a girl like you is concerned.' Can't lay it on

139

too thick, flattery with a trowel, he thought. 'Did Newman ask questions about your sister?'

'No!' She was annoyed. 'I told you, he came to see me.'

'Understandable. Exactly what I've done myself. Is it just as nice upstairs?'

She gave him a sideways look. 'You can come and see, if you like.'

Paula spotted a phone box near a crossroads. Newman called Tweed, explained the position quickly and Tweed agreed to send Harry Butler to Walberswick within the hour. Newman gave Tweed the name of the hotel he'd stayed at during his earlier visit, said yes, he was phoning from a call box when Tweed posed the question.

'Should he be armed?' Tweed asked quickly.

'Yes,' Newman advised. He'd remembered the Walther Steve had brandished in Evelyn's Wandsworth house.

Driving on, he told Paula that Harry Butler was on the way, that he'd given a brief description of Evelyn so Butler would recognize her, plus her address. They travelled the rest of the way into London in silence. Newman dropped off Paula at her flat in Putney, then drove back to his own place. As he entered Beresforde Road at three in the morning his eyes were everywhere, remembering the juggernaut which had put him in hospital. Which is why he spotted the stationary police car.

It was parked beyond his flat on the opposite side of the road. Two men in the front in uniform and their radio aerial extended. He went inside the building and was not too surprised when the bell rang as he was making coffee. He went into his narrow lobby, picked up the phone, pressed the button which operated the visual screen. Chief Inspector Buchanan was standing outside the closed front door.

'Newman here. I've just got back. It's after three in the morning. What do you want?'

'A brief word with you. Possibly you'll find it helpful.'

'Leave Warden outside, please. I could do without the double act just for once . . .'

He pressed the button which released the lock on the hall door, opened his flat door and said nothing as Buchanan strolled inside. Newman led the way into the large sitting room at the front, gestured towards a couch.

'I'm just making coffee,' he said reluctantly.

'Thank you, but I'm not thirsty.' Buchanan gazed round the room, taking in everything, then spoke again as Newman stepped down out of the galley kitchen with his mug of coffee. 'I'm sorry to disturb you at this hour . . .'

'But your watchers parked in that patrol car radioed in that I'd arrived back. Can we cut this short? I'd like a spot of sleep before dawn breaks.'

'You've not yet left for Helsinki but I have a feeling that you will go there.'

He paused, but Newman was accustomed now to this tactic and said nothing. Carrying his mug of coffee, he sat down on a hard-backed chair by the dining table. He drank some of the hot liquid and felt less weary.

'Just assuming that Hauser is involved in the murder of Sandra Riverton,' Buchanan continued, 'and I emphasize it can only be a vague assumption, there's no hard evidence —'

'Have you even any soft evidence?' Newman snapped.

'Circumstantial, you mean? Well, I've kept coming back to the fact that both murders have certain similarities – as I mentioned to you before. Also they took place within the short time span of twenty-four hours, approximately. Also both victims worked for the same organization.'

'Can we get to the point, please?'

'The point is that if my assumption is right then

141

whoever committed those murders may well be someone close to Hauser.'

'What exactly does that mean?'

'It means that from the little I've been able to learn about Hauser he runs a tight ship. He only allows top people to handle major policy decisions. In short, the murderer would be one of his close associates. So, who is close to Hauser?' Buchanan stood up. 'I thought you might like to bear that in mind. When you visit Finland.'

'Thank you.'

'If you locate the murderer you'll then be in the clear, which you aren't yet.'

'Thank you.'

'Good-night. I can find my own way out.'

'I'd hope so. You are a detective.'

Evelyn was up late the following morning. She looked at the rumpled bed and decided it would have to wait. She felt in a restless mood and after drinking a cup of strong coffee she went for a walk towards the sea.

She wore a white high-necked blouse in preference to one of her low-cut jobs. No point in provoking the locals into talking about her. But her pale blue skirt was short, displaying her elegant legs. She saw the well-built man, in his thirties she judged, for the first time as she strolled across the grassy dunes towards the shingle bank which reared up like a dyke with the beach and the sea beyond.

He wore a shabby blue check shirt, open at the neck, a windcheater, grey slacks and trainer shoes. Round his neck was slung a loop supporting a pair of binoculars. Evelyn veered towards him: she needed the company of a man.

Adam had left her cottage early in the morning. He had said he had to fly back to Helsinki. 'Business, darling. I have to earn my living like the next man, get back to my base . . .'

Evelyn thought his departure was a great bore. And in no way was he like the next man. Not after their night together. Had it been a one-night stand? She had no idea. He'd promised to keep in touch, but didn't they always do that?

'Good morning,' she greeted the well-built man. 'Isn't it a fantastic day? Yet another one. The heatwave goes on.'

'Good morning to you.' Harry Butler raised his deer-stalker hat, revealing his thick brown hair. 'Yes, Miss, it's just great.'

'Mind if I walk a little way with you? My sister died just recently and I'm feeling lonely. What are the binoculars for?'

'Watching birds. A hobby of mine.'

'You've come to the right place . . .'

She said nothing more for a while, waiting for him to talk about himself. Butler, clean shaven and with a poker-faced expression, kept silent. Before leaving London he had been briefed by Tweed, who had supplied data on the area obtained from Newman. When the Minsmere Nature Reserve was mentioned Butler immediately decided on his role.

'Bird watcher,' he had told Tweed. 'Perfect cover. A bird watcher can go almost anywhere in the country without arousing any comment . . .'

As they walked up to the shingle bank Butler was thinking Evelyn would be stunned if she knew he had seen Adam Carver leaving Rose Bower just after dawn, that he'd taken several pictures of Carver with his camera equipped with a telescopic lens. What could be more natural than a bird watcher prowling round close to dawn with a camera?

She would have been equally surprised had she known Butler had already explored all round the outside of Rose Bower. Sleeping in his car parked at an isolated spot,

Butler had arrived at the hotel Newman had recommended and claimed the room he had reserved the night before by phone.

As they scrambled up the shingle bank he zipped his front half-way up to make sure the hip holster carrying his .38 Special Smith & Wesson revolver was concealed. Standing on the crest of the bank Evelyn appeared to slip, caught hold of Butler's arm, then slipped her arm through his.

Butler was thinking getting to know Evelyn had proved a lot easier than he'd anticipated. Which would help him in his protection role. He'd planned to ask her the way to Minsmere but she'd done the job for him. On the other hand as a man he was wary: he liked to make the first move towards a woman himself. Evelyn showed a shade too much initiative for his liking.

'Isn't the view just too wonderful?' she glowed.

'Great.'

He was eyeing the wooden piles which lined the harbour entrance between which a powerful tide was surging in. His experienced eye had found an ideal way for an intruder to get to Evelyn. They came in by boat after dark, moored to one of the piles, did the job, and were away before anyone even knew they had arrived. Walberswick was by no means the out of the way safe refuge it had seemed.

15

All roads led to Finland.

Tweed received the mysterious call on his scrambler line at ten in the morning. The man at the other end spoke good

English, spoke rapidly. He gave the correct passw(
which the PM had told Tweed during his interview wi..
her months earlier. *Endgame*.

'Could you please fly to Helsinki, Mr Tweed? A room
is reserved in your name at the Hotel Hesperia, which we
believe you know. Tomorrow please wait at the end of
North Harbour near the cathedral at eleven o'clock at
night. Alone. We will make contact with you there.'

'And who is this speaking?'

'Lev Frolov . . .' The voice spelt it out. 'You will meet
us, Mr Tweed, at the appointed rendezvous? It is very
urgent.'

'I'll be there, yes. What is urgent? We're on
scrambler . . .'

The line had gone dead. Tweed replaced the receiver
slowly and gazed at Monica. He looked thoughtful.

'At long last the Russians have got in touch. Book me
on a flight to Helsinki today. Yes, in my own name.'

He repeated the gist of the conversation. Monica
listened, looked worried.

'Do you know this Lev Frolov?'

'I've never heard of him. It could be an assumed name.
I thought I recognized the voice, but probably I was
wrong. It has to be someone very high up because it's the
personal representative of the Soviet president – just as
Cord Dillon is of the American president. I've never
known such tight security.'

'You do realize that this rendezvous could be very
dangerous,' she persisted. 'North Harbour is the place
where they found the frozen body of Ed Riverton on the
ice back in February. Shouldn't you take someone with
you?'

'No. The arrangement is I meet my opposite number,
whoever he may be, alone.'

'Eleven o'clock at night. Will it still be light in Helsinki
then?'

'No. At this time of year they have two hours of darkness – between eleven and one in the morning.'

'I don't like the sound of this at all.'

'I'll be careful. Nice of them to fix me up with a room at the Hesperia,' Tweed commented.

'You sound ironic.'

'Well, it's obvious, isn't it? My hosts, if you can call them that, will have the place under surveillance. And after all this time it suddenly becomes urgent. I wonder why?'

'I still don't like it,' Monica repeated. 'The situation inside Russia is so unstable.'

'Just book my air ticket, there's a good girl. And it isn't as though I'm going to Russia . . .'

Newman, Paula and Cord Dillon caught Flight SK526, departing London Airport at 1100 hours, arriving Stockholm, Arlanda airport, at 1425 hours, local time.

Newman had driven them to Heathrow, leaving his Mercedes in the long-term car park. On their way there Cord Dillon was in an explosive mood. He sat alone in the back as he barked out his questions.

'Can you tell me why the hell we're flying to Stockholm – which is in Sweden if my geography's any good.'

'Your geography is OK,' Newman assured him breezily. 'I decided we'd move in on Scandinavia by a devious route for two reasons. First in case there's surveillance on everyone arriving in Finland. INCUBUS is a huge organization, and from what Evelyn told me it's run like a military outfit – with some high-pressure security systems.'

Paula giggled. 'Which explains the fancy dress you have decked yourself up in?'

'He looks OK,' Dillon growled.

Newman wore a baseball cap. He was clad in a jacket

146

made of a loud check material. His trousers, also a loud check, were tucked inside leather boots, knee length. He was sporting a pair of large dark glasses.

'And the second reason?' Dillon demanded.

'You'll find that out after we arrive. And the heatwave is hitting Scandinavia like it is here. You'll find the drive in from Arlanda gives you time to adjust – it takes three quarters of an hour to get into the city . . .'

Aboard the flight after take-off Paula, sitting in the window seat alongside Newman, glanced back. The two seats behind them were empty and they were at the front of Business Class. As arranged, Cord Dillon was three rows back, apparently travelling on his own.

'That book you had almost finished when I called at your flat last night. What was it? You seemed absorbed.'

'Evelyn put me on to it – something Ed Riverton once told her. About the Dracon think-tank which dreams up ideas for Hauser. They have a Professor Hiram Goldstein on the staff. It was his book I was reading. *No More Space.*'

'What is it about then? Come on. Give.'

'Goldstein has obviously been influenced by a man called Haushofer. He was an expert on so-called geopolitics – global strategies. Hitler approved of Haus-hofer. Goldstein argues that the United States is hemmed in from any further expansion to the west – because Japan controls the Pacific Basin. He's worked out that the only direction America can expand in is to the east – Europe and Russia. Hence the title – *No More Space.* To the west. Only to the east.'

'Does that tell us anything?'

'It might.'

'Then tell me what. You've obviously been impressed by that book.' She punched him on the arm. 'I like to know what's going on.'

'Then read the book.'

'I will. But tell me what so struck you.'

'Goldstein refers to *Lebensraum*, living space. Hitler, the history books tell us, made a big song and dance about just that. *Lebensraum*. But Hitler meant living space for people. Just an excuse to conquer all and sundry. Goldstein uses it in a different sense. He means space to expand American business. The new objectives – Europe and Russia.'

'Isn't INCUBUS big enough already?'

'Too damned big. But these billionaires can never stop – get enough. They have to look for new worlds to conquer. I need a nap. I'll skip lunch. Watch the view . . .'

There was no cloud bank to obscure the view and some time later Paula stared down on Sweden from thirty-five thousand feet. A patchwork quilt of brown and green fields. Here and there a large dark island which was a forest of evergreens. Then a series of lakes, the water very still and blue under the glare of the sun: like lakes of ice. She checked her watch. Soon they would be approaching Arlanda.

Ion Manescu and Irina Serov travelled to Stockholm overnight aboard one of the large Viking Line ships which ply between Helsinki and the Swedish capital. They disembarked in the early morning at the quay close to the city centre.

The ancient stately buildings of the city of bridges and waterways gleamed in the sunlight, each building a differently muted colour of stone. The twenty-man team which formed the film unit came ashore separately with its equipment and travelled immediately by hired cars to the locations Manescu had specified.

'Well, we've arrived,' Irina commented as they waited for a taxi. 'Do you think we've covered all major entry points?'

'*I* have,' Manescu informed her, stressing who was in charge of the operation. 'One unit goes to Gothenburg Airport on the west coast. Another to the sea crossings from Copenhagen. Another to Bromma Airport just outside Stockholm – a small airfield but someone may try and get clever. And the main unit will be at Arlanda within the hour.'

'That should do the job for us,' Irina replied.

'Just so long as no one from the Soviet Embassy recognizes you. At one time you did work there,' Manescu warned.

Irina stroked her long dark hair brushed to frame her oval face. She wore tight denims which emphasized her long legs, high-heeled shoes which increased her height, a form-fitting windcheater. Yes, Manescu was thinking, you think you look pretty good, and you do. He wouldn't have minded laying her himself, but he never mixed business with pleasure.

'When I was at the Embassy,' Irina told him in her slow deliberate way, 'my hair was cut short, I wore dowdy clothes as ordered by the military attaché. You really think they would recognize me? Because I don't. And you imagine anyone at the Embassy in those days is still there? You have to be joking.'

'You have the instrument on you? Just in case,' Manescu snapped to reassert his authority.

'Concealed in a special pocket inside my windcheater. I do know my job.'

'The instrument' was a specially designed hypodermic perfected in the laboratories of INCUBUS's Pharmaceutical Division. A very slim needle of hardened glass with a pin-point tip, it contained air and was carried in a protective leather sheath. Irina had only to insert the tip into the target's veins, press the plunger, and death would follow in minutes. With no trace of how the victim had died.

149

Manescu watched as the last team came down the gangway and climbed inside a waiting van with their equipment. Along the side of the van were inscribed the words *Commercial Film & Publicity Unit* in Swedish.

'Here's our taxi,' Irina said. 'It's not far to the Hotel Diplomat.'

'Wait a minute.'

Manescu watched the team stowing the film cameras inside at the rear of the vehicle. He stood there until the last man had climbed aboard and the van doors were closed. It was driven off, crossed the bridge on to Gamla Stan, the island crammed with medieval buildings, and headed north.

'Now we know we have Arlanda, the gateway to Stockholm, covered,' he said and stepped into the taxi.

Marler had flown to Hamburg First Class aboard a Lufthansa plane. He preferred Lufthansa or Swissair for European flights: they were the only airlines which provided first-class accommodation. It was not only more comfortable – first class carried far fewer passengers and made it easy for him to study his fellow passengers.

Disembarking at Hamburg Airport, he was certain he had not been followed. The heat hit him as he left the aircraft but Marler was immune to extremes of climate.

Dressed very much as an Englishman of means in his expensive sports jacket, his silk shirt, regimental tie and well-pressed slacks, he collected his single case from the carousel. In his other hand he carried a long hold-all with the handle of a tennis racquet protruding.

A cab took him to the luxurious Four Seasons Hotel and, as requested by phone, his room overlooked the Binnen Alster, the smaller of two lakes in the centre of the great port. After lunch in the dining room he made a phone call, told the man at the other end he had arrived, and slept until late in the evening. So far he had behaved as the impeccable Englishman abroad.

Just after dark he took a taxi to a restaurant in an old converted warehouse on the waterfront overlooking the river Elbe. The restaurant was a de luxe establishment but the district wasn't. It had begun to drizzle heavily as he got out of the cab and paid it off.

A long line of heavy trucks was parked in the middle of the deserted street lined with more warehouses. In the distance girls tried to shelter under the lee of the warehouses. One of them called out but Marler ignored her as he dashed inside.

Hugo Hildebrandt was waiting for him at a table perched on an upper level looking down on the main restaurant. Beyond the lower level Marler could see a tugboat slugging upstream through the misty drizzle.

Hildebrandt, an arms dealer, was dressed like a prosperous businessman. He greeted Marler amiably, said he was paying, handed him the menu. Hildebrandt was slim and tall with a high forehead. In his forties, he stooped as tall men are apt to. They ordered their meal before Hildebrandt – H.H. as he was known in international circles from Hamburg to Iran – raised the subject of business.

'The merchandise you require is available. At a price, of course,' he said in German.

'Of course,' Marler replied in the same language. 'So, how much?'

'It is not damaged goods, it is new . . .'

'Skip the sales talk. How much?'

'Ten thousand deutschmarks . . .'

'You must be joking.'

'I never joke where business is concerned,' Hildebrandt replied calmly, gazing down into the lower restaurant. 'There is Lisa Krenz, the well-known actress.'

'Three thousand,' Marler snapped.

151

'Now that is what I call a joke.' Hildebrandt started eating. 'The bread is very good here,' he remarked. 'When the bread is good the rest of the meal should be edible.'

'Five thousand deutschmarks. That is my final offer.'

Marler crushed his napkin. Pushing back his chair he stood up prior to leaving. Hildebrandt gestured for him to stay.

'Very well. Five thousand. That is under cost, but for you I make the exception. A small loss . . .'

Marler carefully concealed his surprise as he sat down again. He had expected to go up to six thousand. Hildebrandt was obviously short of cash. An hour later the German led the way out of the restaurant. Marler pulled up the collar of his raincoat as they plunged into heavy drizzle and made for the waterfront.

A small sailing vessel with a wheelhouse aft was moored to the quay. Marler saw the skipper inside the wheelhouse and a burly seaman preparing to cast off. He stayed on the quay as Hildebrandt jumped aboard.

'He,' Marler pointed at the seaman, 'does not travel with us. No more bloody argument.'

He only went aboard as the German shrugged, told the seaman he would see him later, and the vessel chugged through the heavy mist-drizzle into midstream. Marler placed his hold-all behind the wheelhouse as Hildebrandt hauled out from under a pile of ropes a package wrapped in polythene. From it he extracted a dismantled Armalite rifle and a sniperscope.

Marler examined the weapon with the aid of a pencil flash. Not renovated, brand new – so no track record. Swiftly he assembled the rifle, attached the telescopic sight, asked for ammo, loaded the weapon. They were passing a distant lighted buoy, the light blurred in the haze, the buoy bobbing up and down. He aimed, squinted through the sight, pulled the trigger. The light went out.

'They said you were pretty good,' Hildebrandt commented, 'but I've never seen shooting like that. Just so long as I'm never the target . . .'

'Cut the flannel. Now, the handgun.'

Hildebrandt burrowed inside the polythene, produced a 9mm. Walther P38 automatic. He inserted a magazine, handed it to Marler. The Englishman glanced up and down the river: no other vessels were in sight on the murky surface. He checked the weapon, raised it, gripping the butt with both hands, fired at a small piece of driftwood floating down the Elbe, then nodded.

'The five thousand deutschmarks,' Hildebrandt reminded him, his right hand inside his trench coat pocket.

'We do it my way,' Marler said brusquely.

Dismantling the Armalite, he tucked the weapon inside his large hold-all underneath the tennis racquet. The Walther was inserted under the rifle and both were covered with a small travelling rug. He handed the hold-all to Hildebrandt.

'Tell the skipper to pull in at the quay we're approaching by the cab rank. I go ashore, you hand me the hold-all as I give you the envelope. And I want ammo for both weapons. Ten mags. for the Walther. And a hip holster.'

'That will be extra . . .'

'It will not.'

Hildebrandt shrugged again, extracted ammo for both weapons from the polythene roll, handed it over and called out to the skipper to put ashore. Opening his trench coat, he unfastened a hip holster, gave it to Marler. Which meant the weapon it had sheathed was in the arms dealer's right-hand pocket. Marler grinned as he slipped his hand inside the hold-all, came out with the Walther.

'Just a precaution, H. H.'

The exchange took place at the quayside, Marler said

good-night, walked to a cab which was dropping a fare, a heavily made up woman who eyed him hopefully. 'Not tonight, Josephine,' Marler told her and climbed inside the taxi, telling the driver to get moving. Only when he was clear of the quay did he give his destination, the Four Seasons Hotel.

The precaution was useless. Lighting a king-size cigarette, Marler glanced through the rear window, saw the motor cyclist who had been parked near the quay following him. Typical of Hildebrandt: how simple for the motor bike rider to pick them up as they left the restaurant, then cruise along the road parallel to the waterfront, keeping the fishing vessel in sight. It didn't spoil his night's sleep.

The following morning Marler took a cab back to the airport. Carrying his case and hold-all, he avoided the check-in counter, walked inside a washroom. Fortunately it was empty.

He began washing his hands in a basin. The door opened and a burly man wearing denims, a grubby shirt and a black stubble on his heavy jaw came in. Marler recognized him as the seaman he'd turfed off the fishing vessel. Hildebrandt was becoming a bore: he wanted to sell the same weapons again.

'Do anything stupid and I'll slit your gizzard from ear to ear. I'll take that hold-all . . .'

There was a click and the seaman was holding a wide-bladed flick knife. Marler took his hands out of the basin, held up his left hand. With his right he aimed the hair spray canister he'd been holding, pressed the plunger. A jet of hair spray splashed over the seaman's face, into his eyes.

He gurgled, raised his free hand to his eyes, gave a groan of agony. Marler's stiffened right hand chopped down on the wrist, the knife clattered on the floor. Marler dropped the spray, grasped the German by the shoulders, shoved him with great force into an empty cubicle, kept up the momentum. The seaman's skull cracked against the tiled wall at the rear and he sagged at the knees. Marler pressed him down on the seat of the toilet. The seaman crumpled, his head slumping forward into his lap.

Closing the door, Marler picked up his spray, the knife, retracted the blade, slipped both into his pocket. Carrying his case and hold-all, he walked out, dropped the knife into a nearby litter bin, went outside.

He got into the first cab, told the driver to take him to the Hauptbahnhof. At the main station he bought a ticket to Lübeck, was just in time to catch the Copenhagen Express a minute before it moved off. He read Somerset Maugham's *The Painted Veil* as the train sped across the flat fields of north Germany.

Leaving the train at Lübeck, the ancient Hanseatic port on the Baltic, he caught another cab to Travemünde Häfen, terminal for the car ferry to Helsinki. He remembered to make sure the tennis racquet handle was protruding from the hold-all.

At Travemünde he bought a return ticket for the ferry to Helsinki. The heat was ferocious as he boarded the enormous ship. Inside his stateroom cabin he took off his tie, loosened his collar, sat down on the bunk, picked up his book.

No one had even glanced at his luggage. His last thought as he settled into his bunk when the ship was moving was that Hugo Hildebrandt must be very short of cash. Poor chap.

16

Howard, Director of the SIS, arrived back from holiday at his villa in the south of France at just the wrong moment. Tall, plump-faced, his complexion pink, he strode into Park Crescent and met Monica with the Finnair tickets in her hand on her way to Tweed's office. He stopped her on the staircase.

'Someone else off on his hols?' he enquired in his plummy voice. 'Who is desertin' the ship in our hour of need?'

Oh, hell, thought Monica, he's in one of his so-called jokey moods. She paused on the stairs and looked back at her boss. As usual, Howard was faultlessly attired in a new pale grey Chester Barrie suit from Harrods. His shirt was white, starched like armour plating. The scarlet display handkerchief peering out of his breast pocket exactly matched the colour of his tie.

'I've got to deliver these in a rush,' she replied, glancing down at George, the guard, seated at his desk by the closed front door. 'You'll excuse me.'

'What's the great state secret I've stumbled on?' he asked jovially, following her upstairs and into Tweed's office.

'Here are your tickets,' she said, placing them in front of Tweed, frowning over her shoulder.

'Got back a couple of days early,' Howard announced breezily, closing the door behind him. 'The heat in Provence was like the local baker's oven. Off somewhere, are we?'

He sat in the armchair, perched one long leg over the arm and admired his gleaming black shoe. Tweed put the tickets in his pocket, leant back in his chair.

'Something urgent. I have to leave here in five minutes.'

'Good. So we have five whole minutes for you to tell me all about it. Where are you drifting off to?'

'Helsinki.' Tweed stood up, checked his watch, picked up his case.

'Wait.' Howard stood up and Monica frowned. He was going to cause trouble. '*Why* are you going on this trip?'

'A special directive from the PM. I'm sorry, but the lid on this business is screwed down tight. Tighter than I've ever known.'

'I see.' Howard took it with surprising calm. 'I bumped into Pete Nield as I came into the building. He knows Scandinavia. Take him with you. That's an order. It's not safe to have you floating round without back-up.'

'The turbulence is further south.'

'Is it? While I was in France I talked to Pierre Loriot on my way back through Paris. He says some very dangerous characters have gone underground from the Balkans. Professionals. He's heard a tip from a reliable source that they're heading for – Scandinavia.'

'I'm just about to catch a plane . . .'

'I'll not sleep if you don't take Pete Nield. He can travel separately from you on the same plane. I'm not asking about the PM's directive, but I am running this outfit. You know Pete always has a case packed for instant departure and money in God knows how many currencies.'

'He may not be able to get a seat on my flight . . .'

Howard swung on his heels. 'Monica, phone London Airport and book another seat on the same flight. That also is an order.'

Tweed nodded, Monica picked up the phone. Tweed was taken aback by Howard's forceful concern for his safety. He couldn't think of an argument to counter what his chief had said. And he could always lose Nield after they'd arrived. Monica made three calls in rapid succession, then replaced the receiver.

'Pete has a seat on the same flight, ticket waiting for him at the airport. He has a room in the same hotel where you're staying. A separate cab will be here in three minutes to get him to the airport on time.'

'Then I'll be off,' Tweed said and looked at Howard. 'Thank you for your support. I'm not sure how long I'll be away.'

'Well,' Howard told him jovially, repeating a remark Tweed had made earlier to Monica, 'it's not as though you're going to Russia . . .'

Tweed peered down through the window of the Finnair machine as it flew over the Baltic in a clear blue sky. They were passing over the incredible Finnish archipelago, the second largest in the world. Twenty-five thousand feet below, a vast labyrinth of islands spread out on the dazzling blue sea, countless islands of various shapes and sizes stretching out from Turku, Finland's second city. Here and there on the open sea he saw a tiny white streak, the wake of some large ship.

He glanced back down the cabin. Two rows behind him Pete Nield was reading a newspaper. Nield was in his early thirties, a slim, neatly dressed man with dark hair and a small trim moustache. He had boarded the aircraft without even a glance in Tweed's direction.

As the plane began its long descent towards Helsinki airport Tweed counted off mentally the strategy he had set in motion. Newman, Cord Dillon and Paula were also heading for Scandinavia to investigate INCUBUS. He'd no doubt Newman would pursue his search with ferocious energy: the murder of Sandra Riverton had filled him with cold rage.

And my own mission is similar – but different – he reminded himself. I also am investigating INCUBUS, but collaborating with an unknown Russian. It's like penetrating a spider's web, he thought.

Then Marler was also on his way, tracking down the dangerous men who had gone missing from the ex-Communist states. And he had a lead: Ion Manescu had been spotted boarding the ferry at Travemünde which sailed regularly – for Helsinki.

Marler, very popular with the girls because of his distant cynical manner, was ingenious and experienced in locating people no one else could find.

It was a double-pronged strategy for two different problems. Penetrating INCUBUS to find out how that colossus operated. And tracing the vanishing ex-secret police criminals. The comparison between INCUBUS and a spider's web came back into Tweed's mind as the plane began to descend more steeply. Who was the spider at the centre of the web? Was it really Hauser?

'It's a problem we must solve. By any method which works.'

Three men sat in Franklin D. Hauser's spacious office at the top of the glass tower outside Helsinki. Hauser stared out of the window at the shimmering heat haze over the sea. Behind him Adam Carver sat in an executive chair while Galvone prowled across the shag carpet.

'What's the present position in Frankfurt?' Carver asked.

'Egon Schmidt owns this private German bank. He won't sell under any circumstances.' Hauser consulted a red file he held in his hand. 'Evelyn Lennox produced the Profile on Egon. He has a son, Dieter. She had dinner with Dieter at the Frankfurter Hof. Dieter is a playboy, has no interest in the bank, would sell tomorrow. Relationships are bad between father and son. But because Egon has no other living relative the bank would pass into Dieter's hands.' He looked up at the two men. 'If anything happened to Egon.'

'Then the solution is obvious,' Galvone said in his hoarse voice.

'What solution is that?' Carver asked quietly.

'We can discuss that later,' Hauser interjected. 'But we need that bank to get a foothold in Germany. So many key companies in Germany are controlled by the banks.' He put the file on a table, changed the subject. 'Tell us, Adam, how did you make out with the Evelyn Lennox girl?'

'She's still nervous, won't accept the insurance money.'

'That means the twist could start shooting off her big mouth,' Galvone warned.

'I think she regards me as a friend,' the Englishman remarked. 'So I could always go back to her, try a little more persuasion.'

'And you could always set fire to where she lives.'

'That would be drastic and possibly counter-productive. And there is a complication.'

'That we could do without, that we don't need,' rasped Hauser.

'What complication?' Galvone demanded.

'While I was in London I checked with Steve Abbott, the not very subtle assistant to Papa Grimwood. Steve reckoned he saw Robert Newman, the foreign correspondent, with Evelyn in Walberswick.'

'What the hell is that?' Hauser asked, lighting up a cigarette. 'Gentlemen, you may smoke.'

Carver took a cigar from his case, lit it, puffed at it and watched Galvone through the smoke. 'Walberswick is a small village on the Suffolk coast. Where Sandra Riverton used to live. Now her sister, Evelyn, stays there.'

'We shouldn't leave that dame hanging around,' Galvone protested.

'Now, Frank,' Hauser chided, 'you are always so

impulsive. I'm sure Adam has the situation well in hand, will bring it to a successful conclusion.'

'Don't bet on it,' Galvone sneered.

'I never bet on anything – or anyone.' There was a hard edge to Hauser's tone. 'What worries me more than a little is Adam's reference to that nosy foreign correspondent. Newman. I'd like to know where he is now. Check on it, Frank. You stay, Adam. There's something we have to settle without wasting time.'

The machine continued its descent. Flight SK526 was due to arrive on time at Arlanda at 1425 hours. Paula stared out of the window as the arid landscape came up to meet her, a landscape of earth baked bone dry, islands of dense green firs and rocks scattered about, embedded in the earth.

Hardly any sign of human habitation except for the sprawl of airport buildings. Arlanda was growing much larger with each year. Newman opened his eyes, yawned, glanced back at Cord Dillon who already was stirring restlessly.

'He's going to be a problem,' he said to Paula. 'He's action man. Mind you, he's an asset in a tight corner.'

'Why should there be any tight corners? No one can possibly know we're heading for Finland via Sweden.'

'Famous last words. We're landing . . .'

Passport Control and Customs took no notice of them. They walked down steps from a high landing into the main concourse. Dillon, wearing a rumpled grey suit, followed several passengers behind them.

'Must be someone important aboard,' Paula commented as they reached the spacious concourse. 'A film star?'

She waved a hand towards a film unit, four men and a girl with cameras aimed at the incoming crowd, filming

161

the new arrivals. Newman, still wearing his dark glasses, touched the peak of his baseball cap with a mock salute aimed at the unit.

'It certainly can't be us they're interested in,' Paula joked.

The remark startled Newman. As they carried their bags to find the hire car he'd ordered he glanced back. The cameras were still filming the crocodile of passengers trudging down into the concourse. As they emerged into the sunshine the heat hit them like a hammer. Paula slipped on a pair of tinted glasses. The glare was so strong it hurt her eyes. Newman hurried towards a Volvo estate car where a uniformed girl stood holding the keys.

The paperwork took no time at all: the girl seemed anxious to retreat back inside the concourse. Just before they left the kerb Dillon slipped into the rear and Newman drove off, heading along the main highway towards distant Stockholm.

'What caught your eye back there?' Paula asked. 'Just as we walked out of the concourse.'

'That film unit. Why should they be recording everyone who came off the plane?'

'No idea.' Paula fanned herself with a brochure brought off the plane. 'Lord, it's like an oven.'

'You've got the window open.'

'Which is just letting in more boiling air. Anyway, it will be cooler in Finland.'

'And how the devil do we get there?' demanded Dillon. 'Some round the houses route you're taking us on.'

'By ferry tomorrow night. You'll find it a comfortable crossing from Stockholm to Helsinki. Huge car ferries sail the Baltic.'

'I'm a bad sailor,' Dillon complained.

'It will be like gliding over a mirror.'

'You could be wrong about that film unit,' Paula suggested. 'There could be a reason for what they were doing.'

'Well, after we get to the Grand Hotel and settle in there's one way to find out. You can come with me if you want to. Unless you're off to that department store, NK.'

'And how are you going to find out?' Paula enquired.

'To hell with that,' Dillon burst out. 'Why are we going to Finland by that route?'

'We need to be armed, that's why. Now leave it alone.'

'You didn't tell me how you're going to find out about that film unit,' Paula reminded Newman.

'You'll find out this afternoon.'

Paula swore inwardly and gazed out of the window. Already her dress was beginning to cling to her and she couldn't wait to have a bath at the Grand Hotel. The broad highway was bordered at intervals with limestone gulches and beyond them she looked out across fields stretching away, vaguely seen through the heat haze. And she couldn't imagine what Newman had in mind for the afternoon.

Marler walked down the gangway after the ferry berthed in North Harbour, Helsinki. He immediately saw the men with cine cameras aimed at the passengers. He hurried, merged with a crowd, avoided the queue of waiting taxis and walked round the harbour front to the Palace Hotel.

'You have a reservation for me,' he told the girl behind the counter, gave her his name, let the porter take his case but said he'd carry his hold-all himself.

His room overlooked the harbour and he glanced out at the blazing sunshine. He was dressed for the heat: a jacket of a linen suit and slacks, an open-necked shirt. He placed the hold-all in a prominent position on a chair, the handle of the tennis racquet protruding. Pulling a hair from his head he inserted it under the zip which was open a few inches.

He left his case locked where the porter had put it on a rack. If anyone searched the room they'd be interested in the locked case. The hold-all was too openly displayed to attract attention. Then he left his room, walked along the Esplanade and turned south into the old city. In his breast pocket he carried a copy of the photograph of Ion Manescu.

Tweed looked out of the window in his room at the Hotel Hesperia. It was supposed to have a 'sea view' but he had stayed at this hotel before, a modern curved concrete block. He looked down on a tall metal mobile sculpture which revolved in a wind. The air was still and so was the mobile. Beyond the Mannerheimintie, the highway which led into the city a short distance to the east, he could observe the 'sea'. It looked like a small lake and was an inland arm of the invisible Baltic.

A neat orange and cream tram trundled past on its way into town. Which reminded him he wanted to check out the rendezvous point at North Harbour in daylight. He took the elevator down to the lobby, wondering whether he would encounter Pete Nield who was booked in at the Hesperia. There was no sign of him as Tweed crossed the spacious lobby and glanced up at the digital meter above the door which registered the temperature.

82°F. 28°C. He shrugged, thankful that he was wearing a tropical drill suit, walked into the inferno, felt the sun burning the back of his neck. The tram shelter was only a short distance closer in to the city and a No. 4 tram pulled in as soon as he arrived. He boarded it, paid the driver with a Finnish coin, was given a ticket and remembered to punch it with the time and date in another machine behind the driver.

Helsinki was Granite City. Coming in from the airport his cab had passed enormous outcrops of the stone and the buildings were constructed of the same material. The tram cruised past a museum with a sloping lawn. An immense granite boulder protruded from the trim grass. Granite everywhere. The Finns had to be tough to have created such a capital.

Ten minutes later he was strolling along the tree-lined Esplanade leading to North Harbour. Men and women walked slowly in the heat, wearing the minimum of clothing. Tweed reached the tip of North Harbour as a car passed him. He stood on the edge of the quay. Behind him market stalls were doing good business and the waterfront was alive with activity. It would be very different at eleven at night during the two brief hours of darkness Helsinki experienced at this time of year.

Why here? Why at that late hour? There had been no message from Lev Frolov, whoever he might be, waiting for him at the Hesperia. And Howard would have a fit if he knew of the arrangement he had agreed to. It was at that moment that he noticed the car which had passed him was parked close by.

A slim man agile man wearing a scuba diver's outfit was running down the nearby steps. His face mask was in place but something about his movements seemed familiar as he plunged into the harbour, floated and then vanished under the surface of the lake-calm sea. Tweed then realized who the man was.

Pete Nield was an expert scuba diver. He had followed the tram Tweed had travelled in, doubtless driving a hired car. Tweed turned away, began to walk back to the tram stop. Nield was taking his instruction to protect Tweed very seriously indeed. And now he would know the rendezvous.

It was mid-afternoon in Stockholm. The air was like turgid hot gas. The sun was roasting the Swedish capital

165

as Newman drove at speed in the hired Volvo with Paula beside him. He was moving along a two-lane highway with water to the left and apartment blocks to the right perched up behind green lawn slopes. Dillon had stayed behind at the Grand Hotel, was taking a siesta.

'How far is it to this Bromma airport?' Paula asked. 'And why are we going there?'

'No more than fifteen minutes from the hotel. You'll see why when we arrive.'

The road was traffic-free, the lights green all the way. Later they were driving on to a single-lane road past old wooden houses painted bright green or yellow. The houses were one or two storeys high and fronted with small well-kept gardens.

'What is Bromma?' Paula pressed. 'Why do they need it when they've got Arlanda?'

'Arlanda replaced it years ago. Now Bromma is used for internal flights and by some private planes. It's a convenient place for people who want to slip quietly into Sweden. And here we are . . .'

The sign read BROMMA AIRPORT. The reception building was tiny compared with Arlanda. Only two people were in sight and when Newman parked a short distance away and switched off his engine a foetid silence descended. Paula had the feeling they were way out in the countryside.

'I was right,' Newman said grimly. 'I want you to do something for me. Get out of the car, wander inside, wait for a few minutes and then come out again.'

'That man leaning against the van is holding a cine camera.'

'And the name on the van is the same as on a van parked outside Arlanda. Do your thing.'

Newman, who had thrown his baseball cap into the river outside the Grand, lit a cigarette. Paula stepped out of the car, strolled towards the building. She wore shorts

166

which exposed her long shapely legs and a loose blouse. As she passed the van the man stared at her legs, the girl with him dug her companion savagely in the ribs.

Inside Paula found the reception hall was fairly spacious but there was no one about, no staff at the counter, no sign of another human being. She walked over to a window, stared out at the small airfield fringed with fir forest. There was a single runway with an approach runway leading off it. A Swedair plane was parked at the edge. Nearer to the main runway stood a Lear jet. Inscribed along its fuselage was the name INCUBUS.

17

'We're in trouble, Hauser has forestalled me. I've badly underestimated him. From now on it could be dangerous – very dangerous.'

Newman was grim as he spoke to Paula in the luxurious bar of the Grand Hotel. He sat in a comfortable armchair with Paula in a similar chair drawn close to him. Dillon had said he was hungry when he met them on their return, that he was going to get a meal in the restaurant overlooking the waterfront where the boats brought back tourists from the archipelago.

'You didn't say a word all the way back in the car,' Paula reminded him. 'Explain. I told you what I saw. And that couple with the cine camera took no notice of me, never took any film of me.'

'That was because you hadn't just flown in from somewhere. That's what they were waiting for – anyone

coming into Sweden, just as they were at Arlanda, and
they took plenty of film there.'

'What do you think was the significance of that
INCUBUS Lear jet? It looked to be waiting for
someone . . .'

'Or something. Tomorrow I'm going to purchase
weapons. And that's another reason I came this route.
You can't obtain weapons in Finland.'

'But you can here? Is that what you're saying?'

'Yes. Tomorrow I'm going to the Sergels Torg. That's
in the centre of Stockholm, a square where the boys
gather, the boys who can sell you almost any kind of
automatic weapon or handgun.'

'I'd like a Browning,' she said promptly. 'But how can
we smuggle it into Finland?'

'That's the easy part. We're travelling to Helsinki on
the night car ferry. There's no real supervision or
examination of baggage. And it's easier to slip ashore at
the other end unseen from a ship rather than from a plane
at the airport. Again, remember Arlanda.'

'Can I come with you to Sergels Torg tomorrow, Bob?'

'I'll think about it. Also we may stay here an extra day.
I just hope I'm wrong about all this.'

'You're worried because you brought me,' she accused.

'I never said anything of the sort,' he lied. 'Let's go and
get some dinner. Tomorrow is going to be a very busy
day.'

The films taken at Gothenburg Airport in western
Sweden, the films taken at Malmö, the hydrofoil crossing
from Denmark, the films taken at Arlanda – they were all
flown to Bromma by helicopter.

At Bromma the same evening they were carried aboard
the Lear jet waiting at Bromma. The jet took off at nine
in the evening and the machine landed at Helsinki well

before the two hours of darkness descended. They were rushed from the airport to the headquarters of INCUBUS Oy. By 10.30 p.m. they were inside the glass tower.

'Nothing like a good film to watch in the evening,' Hauser remarked.

He was settled in a seat in the cinema at Level Two and to his left sat Frank Galvone. To his right Adam Carver sat upright and alert as the next film began running, the one taken at Arlanda.

'Watch this carefully,' Hauser advised. 'See if there's anyone either of you recognize. If so, give a shout, the projectionist will stop the film, and we'll freeze it at that point.'

Galvone was bored, leant back with his elbows on the rear of his seat. He watched as another flight from London disembarked, trailing down into the concourse. The bright light of the day had given exceptional clarity to the picture.

'See anyone yet?' Hauser enquired, waving his cigarette holder.

'Nope,' said Galvone.

'Freeze!' Carver called out. 'Go back a way, run it slowly, wait for me to call you again,' he ordered the projectionist, 'then freeze it instantly when I call out again.'

'Didn't see anything, Adam,' Hauser commented.

Carver said nothing, leaning forward to concentrate as the film was run in slow motion. A girl with raven black hair came down the steps, walked across the concourse. Behind her a man wearing a loud check jacket and a baseball cap followed. He touched the peak of his cap towards the camera in a typical American gesture . . .

'Freeze!' Carver shouted. The film stopped. 'That man in the check jacket. It's Newman, Robert Newman the foreign correspondent.'

Hauser frowned, clenched his teeth on the cigarette holder. 'What makes you think that? Looks like a tourist from back home.'

'His movements.' Carver sat back. 'You know I study body language. Remember when Newman came to see you at Livingstone Manor that evening in Suffolk? I had a good opportunity to observe him.'

'What do you think, Frank?' Hauser asked.

'Run the film again from where he comes down those steps,' Carver ordered the projectionist. 'Now, both of you, think back to Livingstone Manor. And watch carefully the way he moves.'

There was tension inside the large cinema occupied by only three men. They were leaning forward, staring with great concentration. Carver had no doubt.

'What do you think, Frank?' Hauser asked again.

'I guess that is Newman,' Galvone said reluctantly.

'No guess about it. Adam has a sharp eye. His movements, his gestures identify him positively for me. The cunning bastard, arriving like an American.'

'So what action do we take?' Galvone enquired.

'Oh, the answer to that is obvious. Newman is becoming a dangerous nuisance. First, he visits Evelyn Lennox just as Papa Grimwood is on the verge of concluding the insurance deal. He balls us up on that. Second, he was tracked to the vicinity of where that ex-owner of Bennington Machine Tools lives, whatever his name was. Wherever it was.'

'James Archer. Otmoor,' said Carver.

'Whatever. Earlier, he calls on me at Livingstone Manor. Then he visits that tavern afterwards and asks about me. A good job we have friendly folk in Suffolk. Third, he's turned up now in Stockholm, an hour's flight from here. Frank, send a coded fax to the Swedish office for Manescu. Tell him the situation. The instruction is simple. Find Newman, stop him travelling around.'

'And how do we propose to do that?' Carver asked.

'Leave that problem to Frank. He knows how many beans make five. Get on it, Frank . . .'

Marler had been asked to come back at nine that evening when Mauno Sarin would be available to see him. He had used all his powers of persuasion with Karma, Sarin's deputy, to get an appointment. What had turned the trick was when he revealed he was carrying a letter of introduction 'from a highly regarded friend of Sarin's based in London'.

Karma, a short, stocky dark-haired Finn, looked at Marler across the desk in the office he had taken him to. His English was good and he was obviously the guardian of his chief's valuable time.

'If I could show Mr Sarin this letter . . .'

'Out of the question. The letter is very personal. I must hand it to Sarin myself. But you can show him my card.'

Marler gave Karma the visiting card which carried his name and the firm which was a cover for SIS at Park Crescent, General & Cumbria Assurance. Karma, whose clean-shaven face gave nothing away of what he was thinking, turned over the card.

'There's nothing on the back,' Marler said jauntily. 'It's a visiting card, you know . . .'

Karma had left him alone, returned five minutes later with the news that Mr Sarin could see his visitor at nine that evening. Marler had said thank you for saving his own valuable time and left.

At precisely nine o'clock, still in broad daylight, he had walked back to the headquarters of the Protection Police, a title which concealed their real function: counter-espionage. The headquarters was located in the old city which reminded Marler of Leningrad. The address, Rat-akatu 12, was a grimy four-storey stone block on the

171

corner of Ratakatu and Fredrikinkatu. The windows on the ground floor were made of opaque glass and on the upper floors grubby net curtains masked the windows. It was always very quiet in Ratakatu with very few people about.

The heat was overpowering as Marler approached the entrance. Across Fredrikinkatu was a small open space with half a dozen trees, their leaves drooping. Two seagulls perched on a seat, motionless, their wings flopped. Two stone steps led up to the heavy wooden door with a long metal bar attached at a diagonal angle. Marler peeled the front of his shirt off his chest, carried his linen jacket over his arm as he went inside. Karma was waiting for him and escorted Marler to an office on the third floor. Mauno Sarin, seated behind a desk, rose reluctantly to greet his visitor.

'You can leave us, Karma. Now, Mr Marler, what can I do for you? As you'll see, I'm rather busy,' he continued in English and indicated his desk which was piled high with files and documents. 'Please sit down. I understand you have a letter of introduction?'

Without a word Marler handed over the envelope. He waited while Sarin relaxed a little as he sat down again and scanned the letter. The chief of the Protection Police was over six feet tall. In his forties, he had a balding head, a dark fringe beard, was slim and athletic-looking. His personality radiated an air of restless energy and impatience. His shirt sleeves were rolled up above the elbows.

'I thought it might be Tweed,' Sarin commented, handing back the letter. 'What is the problem?'

Marler produced the Manescu photograph, leaned forward and handed it to the Finn over the carnage of paperwork. 'Would you recognize that man?'

'No,' Sarin said promptly. 'Should I?'

'I'd be surprised if you did. Ion Manescu, ex-member of the Romanian *Securitate*.'

'So, he's in prison in Bucharest, along with the rest of his tribe.'

'No. A totally reliable witness saw him boarding the ferry at Travemünde earlier in the year. The ferry which docks here in Helsinki. He escaped from Bucharest. Just as some others have escaped. Including Ziegler, ex-chief of the Leipzig STASI.'

'I see.' Sarin swivelled his chair and stared through the net curtains at the wall of buildings opposite. Then he turned back to face Marler. 'Why are you here?'

'To track down Manescu, find out what he's up to. Tweed is worried. Too many of the villains from security services in ex-Communist states have disappeared. Maybe up here. You think that's impossible?'

'Unlikely.'

'And yet that terrorist attack on the Lockerbie aircraft had origins in – warnings came from – Finland.'

Sarin gazed at Marler, but his brown eyes seemed focused on some distant thought. Marler waited. He could almost hear the wheels whirring inside the Finn's head. He was deciding whether to reveal certain information.

'It's difficult for us,' Sarin eventually began. 'Geographically we are one of the largest countries in Western Europe – with immensely long borders, to say nothing of the Baltic coast. But our population is little more than five million. And we have a tradition of neutrality.'

'I understand all this,' Marler encouraged him quietly. 'I also realize it must be impossible to watch all potential exit – and entry – points.'

'Exactly.' Sarin began playing with a ruler, twisting it in his hands. 'We have had reports of some highly undesirable people slipping into our country over many months. Always by unauthorized routes. A fisherman in the archipelago off Turku saw a motorboat landing two men at night. It's not possible to seal off routes like that. Have you heard of a company called INCUBUS?'

'The biggest bank in the States. Bigger than the Bank of America.'

'Yes, but they control many other companies outside banking, presumably through their bank. They have a big headquarters to the west of the city, a huge glass tower. They also have established other companies here, providing much-needed employment.' Sarin grinned without humour. 'You could say Mr Franklin D. Hauser is a benefactor.'

'You wouldn't by chance have a list of those companies?'

For Marler it was a shot in the dark. He was intrigued by Sarin introducing the name of the mammoth organization into their conversation.

'I just might have . . .'

Sarin burrowed among the mounds of papers. He extracted a sheet, handed it to Marler.

'There is the list. You can keep it, if you like. It is a photocopy of the original.'

Marler glanced down the list, startled by the number of companies, all with Finnish names. Except for one. He looked up at Sarin, who was again gazing into space.

'This Institute for Meteorological and Astronomical Studies at Kemijärvi. Why would a bank be interested in that?'

'A question I often ask myself. Its construction is a weird story. It was financed partly by two other companies, but the major funding was supplied by INCUBUS Oy . . .'

'Which gave them control?'

'Exactly. A number of construction firms were invited to bid for the job, but the lowest tender came from a construction company controlled by INCUBUS. And the curious thing is they imported Sicilian workers to build the complex. As soon as the project was complete they were all sent back to Sicily in specially chartered aircraft.'

'And Sicilians would hardly speak Finnish,' Marler commented.

'They didn't even speak English. The project was very hush-hush, as you say.'

'And this complex is at Kemijärvi, north of the Arctic Circle?'

'No. That is the nearest large town but the Institute is in a remote spot in the wilderness of Lapland.'

'A funny place to build anything.'

'*They* say it is ideal – for studying weather conditions.'

'Why would a huge banking outfit get involved in such a project?'

'Mr Hauser is a philanthropist.' Again Sartin smiled without humour. 'So our government feels rather obliged to treat him as an honoured guest. He also supports the theatre opposite the Marski Hotel. A man of culture, our Mr Hauser.'

'And a man of money. A shipload of it.'

'That also. A billionaire, I gather. The second richest man in the United States. He spends a lot of time here. I often wonder why, especially in winter.' Sarin looked quizzical. 'Perhaps he likes our climate.'

'You've visited this Institute near Kemijärvi?'

Sarin's expression changed, his tone of voice became harsh for the first time. He burst out, as though impulsively. 'I would like to obtain a search warrant to examine it from top to bottom. But it is more than my job is worth to even make such a request. Certainly it would never be granted.'

'What made you mention INCUBUS when actually we were talking about Manescu?'

Another dreamy look. Sarin couched his reply carefully. 'I suppose it was pure coincidence. Not linked at all. But *if*, and this is pure assumption, if ex-members of the *Securitate*, the STASI, the Czechoslovak STB, etc., *were* finding refuge here – and not a single one has been caught – then surely it suggests a large, well-organized and powerful apparatus with plenty of money must be behind the conspiracy. That, I must stress, is only a theory.'

You artful devil, Marler was thinking: the subtle way you're suggesting avenues of investigation to me. He checked his watch, stood up.

'Thank you for giving me so much time – remembering how very busy you said you are.'

'I am always ready to help my good friend, Tweed.'

Sarin stood up and shook hands. He had a grip like an alligator. Marler turned at the door. Sarin had switched on the overhead fluorescent strip. It was still daylight outside but little of it penetrated inside the room. Sarin was gazing hard at his guest.

'You say you couldn't possibly go anywhere near this Institute in Lapland. I suppose the easiest way to get there is to fly via Finnair first to Rovaniemi north of the Arctic Circle,' Marler suggested.

'Yes, that would be the thing to do. You'd have to fix up transport to get you to Kemijärvi from Rovaniemi airport. And, after all, Mr Marler, *you* are a free agent. My regards to Mr Tweed. I wonder where he is now?'

PART TWO

Angel of Moscow

18

It was dark in Helsinki. It was 11.05 p.m. It was two hours before the sun would rise again. It was deserted on the North Harbour waterfront except for one man.

Tweed stood well back from the edge of the silent quay. The only sound was the quiet lapping of water against the harbour wall, a gentle swishing sound. Behind him the market stalls had disappeared, the bustle of daily activity was no more. He stood listening, his hearing acute. In his right hand he held a canister of hair spray, a weapon Marler had once recommended.

He had not heard a word from Lev Frolov, the man who had phoned him when he was in London, the mysterious man who had set up this rendezvous. Out on the black surface of the harbour a large fishing boat was chugging home, its nets hung out to dry. His night vision was keen enough to make out the nets . . .

'Don't move, Mr Tweed, this is a gun. Drop what you are holding in your hand. Now you can move. Walk towards that flight of steps leading down to the landing stage.'

Tweed began walking slowly; the canister hit the cobble stones with a soft thud. It felt very much like the barrel of a gun pressed against his spine. The voice which spoke good English in a clear whisper, began to talk again.

'I am the emissary from Lev Frolov. Now please walk slowly down the steps.'

'Supposing I don't? Supposing I just stand here?'

'I must remind you, this is a gun. The gun is loaded. We

179

are quite alone and no one will miss you. Not in time. Please be sensible.'

The fishing vessel was very close, its navigation lamps turned on, but somewhere there was another sound, almost muffled by the vessel's engine. A peculiar swishing he could not identify. He walked slowly down the flight of steps, waited at the bottom, watching the incoming fishing vessel which was manoeuvring to berth. A seaman jumped ashore with a rope, looped it round a bollard. Tweed was reassured by the reference to Lev Frolov. That had come through on the scrambler from Moscow. He was not reassured by the gun still pressed against his spine.

The hull of the vessel bumped against the lowest step. So far as Tweed could see there were only two men aboard – the skipper in the aft wheelhouse and a shadowy figure standing at the stern. He was again aware of the silence. The only sounds the water lapping, the vessel creaking.

'Step on board,' the man behind him ordered. 'Please, no tricks.'

Tweed climbed over the gunwale, his captor jumped after him, the vessel's engine increased in power as the seaman ashore unlooped the rope, flung it aboard and walked off up the steps. The fishing vessel moved out into the harbour, headed down the channel for the open Baltic.

The shadowy figure came forward. He wore a smart business suit, was slim in build, tall, clean shaven and had trim black hair. Tweed stared now he could see him better.

'Welcome, Mr Tweed,' the man said, holding out his hand.

'Captain Valentin Rebet,' Tweed responded, shaking hands. 'Several years since we met.'

'I used the name Lev Frolov. It was necessary in the interests of security. And from what you have just said your intelligence sources inside Moscow could be better. I am now General Rebet . . .' He made the statement modestly. 'I have enjoyed rapid promotion under the new régime. Also, I have been transferred from the GRU to the KGB,' he went on in English.

Tweed nodded. He was well aware of all this, but pretended ignorance so Rebet would not know how good his sources were. The Russian was in his late thirties and, as in the old days, had a pleasant smile.

It was at this moment something dramatic occurred – the skipper had his back to them, concentrating on threading his course between the lighted buoys. The man with the gun was also standing with his back to the stern, both hands out of his coat pockets, staring ahead. There was a slithering noise at the stern. Tweed swung round in time to see a man in a wetsuit jump aboard, throw his face mask back and aim his harpoon gun at Rebet.

'No one moves or this man is speared. Throw up your hands, you bastards . . .'

Rebet froze, raised his hands above his head. The man with the gun spun round, saw the harpoon aimed point blank at Rebet, raised his own hands. Tweed spoke quickly.

'It's all right, Nield. For God's sake don't shoot. The natives are friendly.'

'How friendly?' Nield demanded, dripping water and keeping his weapon aimed.

'This is the man I came to meet, Pete.'

'You were supposed to be alone,' Rebet accused with an edge to his voice. 'Who is this?'

'My guardian angel. As you see, he looks after me quite effectively. And you never warned me on the phone that I'd be hijacked. I don't appreciate a gun in my back.'

'It was not loaded.' Rebet spoke to his subordinate in Russian, which Tweed, who spoke the language fluently, understood. 'Take out your gun carefully with two fingers, hand it to Mr Tweed, Andrei.'

Tweed warned Nield not to worry. Andrei inserted a couple of fingers, extracted the gun, holding it by the butt, handed it to Tweed. He examined the Makarov. No magazine. He smiled at Nield.

'He's right. The damned thing wasn't loaded.' He looked at Rebet. 'What happened to my old adversary, General Lysenko?' Again he knew the answer.

'Our president has no time for old Bolsheviks,' Rebet replied. 'He was retired on his pension and spends his days chopping wood outside his tiny house near Odessa. Now can your protector kindly lower his weapon? My arms are aching.'

'When you tell me where we are going.'

Tweed glanced to the west. They had already sailed past the tip of the peninsula which was the end of Helsinki. Soon they'd be heading for the open Baltic and, a bad sailor, he thanked God the sea was so calm.

'I am the contact from Moscow you came to meet,' Rebet said, lowering his voice. 'The president's special emissary. We are very worried about the way the situation is developing. I am taking you to meet someone.'

'Rebet, I asked you where we are going. Tell me or turn this old tub round and take me back to North Harbour.'

'A Soviet corvette is waiting for us outside the limits of Finnish coastal waters. You will be comfortable aboard that ship for our short voyage.'

'To where?'

'Leningrad. Now, may we lower our arms? And your assistant needs dry clothes we can provide at once.'

'It's all right, Pete,' Tweed called out to Nield. 'No need to keep them covered anymore. We're going on a trip to Leningrad.'

The Diplomat Hotel in Stockholm overlooks a stretch of water, as does the Grand. This is yet another arm of the Mälaren, the main waterway which stretches many miles

182

into the interior beyond Stockholm. Irina Serov had a bedroom with a view of the creek which looked like a river. She was sitting in front of the dressing table, brushing her long hair in front of the mirror when she heard the special knock on the door.

'Where the hell have you been, Manescu?' she demanded as the Romanian entered, closed the door, locked it, tossed a travel folder on her bed. 'It's evening,' she raged. 'I've been waiting for hours. What do we do next?'

'You'll have enough to keep you occupied with your special talents from now on,' he told her with a sneer.

He disliked Russians. What Romanian didn't? And especially he disliked Russian women. Above all, he disliked Soviet women who were ex-colonels in the KGB and threw their weight about.

'Well get on with it,' she snapped. 'Why have you taken all this time?'

'I will tell you.' He adopted a lecturing tone. 'First, I visited the INCUBUS headquarters on Sveavägen . . .'

'I was stationed in Stockholm,' she reminded him.

'As I was explaining, I visited headquarters. There was an urgent fax from Helsinki, orders from the top. The target is Robert Newman, the foreign correspondent . . .'

'I heard about him during my London posting.'

'Please keep quiet. Just listen for once. *Newman is here in Stockholm*. He was filmed leaving Arlanda. Following the fax instructions I drove to Bromma Airport. I arrived just as the Lear jet which took our films to Helsinki returned. It brought us – me – photographs of this Newman. We have been ordered at all costs to prevent him reaching Finland.'

'And we know where he is? What route he will take?'

'For God's sake – and mine – stop interrupting. I have already arranged for a team – with one of the photographs – to wait at Arlanda. They have tickets for every flight.

183

But I have been warned he is devious. I doubt if he will use Arlanda. I think he will use the night ferry.'

'To Helsinki?'

'Possibly. So more men, also with a copy of his photograph, will be waiting at the terminal where the boat leaves for Helsinki. We will be elsewhere.'

'May I possibly ask for the location of elsewhere?'

'We shall be waiting at the Vartan terminal where the car ferry leaves for Turku. I have reserved two staterooms in case we see Newman going aboard. Here is his picture.'

'He's good looking.' Irina preened herself in the mirror. 'I might be able to get next to him with my little hypodermic needle.' She frowned. 'Why Turku and not Helsinki?'

'Because as I told you, this Newman is devious. Helsinki is convinced he's on his way there. But does he fly there direct? No! He flies first to Stockholm. You think he will fly direct – or take the ship direct – to Helsinki? I do not think so. The other exits are covered, but we will watch the night ferry for Turku. Tomorrow also if we must.'

It was dusk as Newman drove alone to Sergels Torg. Very little traffic about. He had refused to allow Paula to join him on his weapons expedition. On the seat beside him rested a small suitcase. It contained two crumpled shirts and nothing else.

His shopping list included a .32 Browning automatic for Paula, a .38 Smith & Wesson Special for himself. Dillon favoured a 9 mm Luger. It was a tall order but Newman knew you could buy a wide range of guns at the infamous Sergels Torg.

Sergels Torg was a spacious square open to the sky but about fifteen feet below the level of the surrounding streets. Newman drove slowly down the wide ramp which led into the square and continued straight across it to the maze-like underground shopping complex. He stopped, leant his elbow on the lowered window, switched off his engine and waited. Within two minutes a man wandered towards him. As he came closer Newman saw he was no more than twenty, brown hair cropped close to his head, dressed in clean denims and a clean shirt.

'You wanted something, Mister?' the youth enquired in English.

'Depends what you're selling. No drugs. Maybe you know a guy who sells guns. Handguns.'

'You'll have to come and see my friend. He's inside the subway. Leave your car here.'

'Anything you say, Tosh.'

Newman closed the window, picked up his case, got out of the Volvo, locked it carefully, followed the youth inside the shopping complex. Here and there youths gathered in twos and threes, smoking, apparently just passing the time. Newman knew better.

His own youth took him along an arcade to where a beggar was slouched on the ground, a cap for krone coins lying in front of him. To one side of the man was a shabby duffel bag which presumably contained most of his worldly possessions, to the other an open suitcase of book matches.

'Tell him what you want,' the youth said.

Newman crouched on his haunches and saw the man was much younger than had appeared at first sight. In his twenties, he had a stubble of beard and alert eyes which watched Newman. In a low voice the Englishman itemized his wants. The beggar nodded, looked carefully round, fumbled inside the duffel bag, brought out a Browning. Newman checked the state of the weapon under cover of the flap of his jacket. The Smith & Wesson appeared next, followed by a Luger. The duffel bag was a secret armoury.

185

There was a brief haggle over the price and ammo for each weapon was extra. Newman extracted a roll of Swedish banknotes from his trouser pocket, counted out the amount. In his other pocket was a second roll of money but he didn't need to reveal that. He quickly slipped the weapons and ammo between his soiled shirts, closed the lid, stood up, dropped a coin into the cap and walked away. The youth stayed, obviously to extract his commission for the sale.

Newman thought it had seemed too easy as he dumped the case on the front passenger seat, climbed inside, closed the door. In his rear view mirror he saw a white car with twin blue lights on the roof and the word POLIS along its side. It turned down the ramp, came straight towards him, flashing its lights on and off. He was going to be checked.

The main exit from the square, the ramp down which he had driven, was blocked by the approaching police car. Thank God I know this area well, Newman thought. I'll just have to risk it. Five years in a Swedish prison didn't appeal to him.

He drove forward into the shopping complex, headlights full on. As the police car came closer, siren blaring now, he drove in and out among a series of rounded pillars, skimming them by centimetres. The police car followed. Newman drove along a right-hand arm of the complex, praying there wouldn't be pedestrians. The arcade was deserted. A ramp came into view with an overhead sign. GALLERIAN. He was going the right way. The banshee howl of the siren was magnified by the enclosed space. Newman pressed his foot down, roared up the ramp, emerged into the open, turned the wheel. A few moments later he sped past the building which had been the headquarters of Ivar Kruger, the match king in the 1930s. The police car came close again. He swung the wheel, began driving more slowly down a wide cobbled

186

sloping short cut which descended at a steep angle, not meant for vehicles. His wheels bumped over the cobbles. In his rear view mirror he saw the police car turn, speeding down the cobbles.

Inside the car the driver, Bertil, a short plump officer with a flowing moustache, sat beside his sergeant, Otto. The sergeant urged him to move faster. Bertil obliged, hanging on tight to the wheel. The car suddenly slewed sideways, smashed into a wall, wrecked one wheel as the transmission gave way. The car stopped, the engine gave up.

'Did you get the registration number?' Otto demanded.

'No! Did you?'

'You should have got the number. And you're one lousy driver.'

'OK. You take over the wheel . . .'

Out of sight Newman turned on to the Vestra Tradgardsgatan. Three minutes later, all lights in his favour, he parked at the back of the Grand Hotel, took a deep breath.

Newman, carrying his case, knocked on the door of Paula's room overlooking the Strommen. As she let him inside he heard through the open window the siren of a ship returning from the archipelago, the screech of gulls through the open window. The room was still like a furnace.

Paula wore a T-shirt and a white skirt. At a table near the window Cord Dillon sat holding a handful of cards with an unhappy expression. Newman saw a pile of banknotes on Paula's side of the table near her cards, splayed face down. Dillon glared at Newman.

'You might have warned me. I suggested a game of poker and she said she hadn't played for ages. She's already got two hundred dollars of my money over there.'

187

'You can't win them all. I could do with a drink, Paula.'

He sagged into a chair and while she fixed his large Scotch he recalled for them his experience at Sergels Torg and the later chase.

'After this drink I'm returning the Volvo immediately to car hire,' he went on. 'Those cops may think of checking up on every car hire outfit. If they didn't get the number, and I doubt they did, they know the make. Lucky that car hire stays open late at this time of the year.'

'What about the equipment?' Dillon asked, indifferent to Newman's near escape.

'In this case. Hide it while I'm out.' He drank half his Scotch. 'Thanks, Paula. You've got your Browning.' He felt in his pocket, brought out several heavy polythene packets. 'Ammo for your Luger, Cord. And here are spare mags for the Browning . . .'

'When do we leave and by what route?' Paula enquired, after asking him if he was all right.

'Tomorrow night. I managed to reserve three staterooms earlier today. Aboard the car ferry for Turku. Leaves from the Vartan terminal at nine in the evening.'

EGON SCHMIDT, BANKING CHIEF, KILLED IN FRANKFURT
BOMB BLAST. FRESH RED ARMY FACTION OUTRAGE?

Franklin D. Hauser read the headlines in the *Herald Tribune* with interest. The story which followed told how the banker had climbed into his Mercedes parked outside the bank on the highway to the airport. The theory was that when he turned on the ignition the car was blown to pieces.

Hauser laid the paper on his desk with a sense of satisfaction. Now he could instruct Adam Carver to open negotiations with the playboy son, Dieter. Undoubtedly he'd sell out, so INCUBUS now had a foothold in Germany.

He was at his most affable when Peggy Vanderheld, summoned to his office, walked in. With a wave of his cigarette he ushered her to a chair.

'Yes, Mr Hauser.'

She sat with her legs crossed, her notepad on her lap. She was tense. There had been bad signals recently. And she knew from long experience Hauser was at his most deadly when he displayed such amiability.

'How long have you been with us, Peggy?' Hauser began.

'Five years.' As well you know, she thought.

'And how old are you?'

'Thirty-eight.'

She was sitting up very straight now, her dark eyes staring straight at the billionaire. She knew where this was leading, the bastard.

'So with all that experience, with such a prestigious company, it shouldn't be in the least difficult for you to find another very well paid position?'

'Can we cut the preliminaries?' she asked between her teeth.

'If you prefer so. You know it is my policy to inject fresh blood into the organization at regular intervals? I feel now the time has come for you to look elsewhere for more suitable employment. I can well understand that after ten years you must be bored with the job.'

She said nothing. She was studying the newspaper Hauser had been looking at. Peggy had always concealed the fact that she was an expert at reading newspapers and documents upside down.

'So,' Hauser continued when he realized she was not going to react, 'in your own best interests would it not be better if you gave me your resignation? We will, of course, provide an excellent reference, to say nothing of the generous pension rights with Fraternal & Equality.'

'The bottom line is I'm fired,' she threw at him.

'I don't like to put it that way, my dear . . .'

'Then how the bloody hell do you like to put it, for Christ's sake?'

'No need to get emotional about something that happens every day.' Hauser's manner and tone had changed, had become ugly. 'You have three hours to clear your desk and leave.'

'It may take me longer.' She stood up, threw notepad and pencil on his desk. 'But I'll be out of this octopus of a company by the day's end. And it hasn't been nice knowing you.'

She walked out, closed the door quietly behind her. In the elevator she took a deep breath. One thought was running through her head. How can I get back at the smug bastard?

In his office Hauser took several puffs of his cigarette, then lifted one of his three phones, pressed a button.

'Hauser here,' he said when the voice answered. 'I think we may have a problem with Vanderheld. Get up here fast so we can decide how to handle it.'

19

It was going to be another scorching day at ten in the morning. Marler sat in the hired Saab concealed in a copse of firs on the outskirts of Helsinki way beyond the Mannerheimintie. Below him rose the glass tower which was the headquarters of INCUBUS Oy.

He was high enough to see over the wire fence surrounding the huge building. The camera he held at eye level had a zoom lens and he snapped three pictures of a man with dark hair and thick eyebrows wearing an American T-shirt, pale slacks and trainers. The close-up revealed the man's grim expression, his prominent cheekbones. His expression would always be grim, Marler guessed. And he looked like a gangster, but so many Americans did.

The man walked to a red Cadillac, climbed inside, slammed the door so hard Marler heard the *clunk!* a hundred yards away. The uniformed guard operated the automatic gate in the wire, it swung open, closed as the Cadillac vanished in a cloud of dust.

To be driving a Cadillac he had to be a top executive, Marler reasoned. Now he was on record. Earlier he had seen the largest stretched black limousine he'd ever observed turn into the compound and glide smoothly to the entrance. It had tinted glass windows which made it impossible to see who was inside.

The uniformed chauffeur had leapt out, opened the rear door. The unmistakable grandiose figure of Franklin D. Hauser had emerged, spoken briefly to the chauffeur and disappeared inside the glass tower.

Marler had little hope that sooner or later his camera would snap Ion Manescu entering or leaving. But lying in bed the previous night at The Palace, unable to sleep because of the heat, he had recalled his visit to the Protection Police.

He had been particularly intrigued by the way Mauno Sarin had offhandedly pointed a finger at INCUBUS. He had decided it was worth spending a day checking out the HQ of the banking colossus, recording who came, who went.

Half an hour later Hauser reappeared accompanied by a tall slim man carrying two cases. They disappeared inside the rear of the limo and the chauffeur closed the door, ran to his own seat. Inside a minute the immense vehicle was on the move, disappearing in the direction of Helsinki. Mr Hauser was on the move. To foreign parts?

Marler took another small drink of mineral water from the plastic bottle he'd bought. No point in getting dehydrated. Tomorrow, or at the latest the day after, he would fly to Rovaniemi, north of the Arctic Circle. Objective: the mysterious Institute somewhere out in the wilds.

Aboard the Soviet corvette, *Kalinin*, Tweed had travelled up the Baltic to Leningrad with General Rebet and Pete Nield. Again the sea was as calm as a millpond.

For some reason – Rebet said 'engine trouble', which Tweed did not believe – the vessel made slow progress. Consequently they reached the great city and port during the few hours of darkness. Tweed couldn't be sure whether this timing was to ensure he couldn't spy on certain defences on the banks of the River Neva. After all, Rebet had been an officer of the GRU, the military espionage arm of the Red Army, before being transferred to the KGB. Or was it possible his visit was being kept so secret it had seemed wise to land him in the night?

At the dockside a Volga car waited for them. Rebet was apologetic.

'With my present rank it should be a Zil limousine for a guest of your eminence. But a Volga is far less conspicuous . . .'

Which rather confirmed Tweed's second theory. Heavy net curtains were drawn over the windows as he sat in the back with Rebet. Peering out as the car moved fast he could make out very little. The occasional monument rearing in the darkness like a menacing sentinel. Then they arrived at the Hotel Moskwa at the end of the Alexander Nevski Prospekt.

Tweed and Nield were hustled inside the hotel by Rebet and soon they were shown into a spacious two room suite with windows overlooking the Neva. The furnishings were heavy, old fashioned and almost Victorian. Tweed opened a vast wardrobe and found it full of clothes.

'We, of course, have taken your measurements,' Rebet explained, 'so please make use of anything which takes your fancy while we have the pleasure of your company.

'Why evening dress?' Tweed enquired, fingering the suit.

'There is a reception here,' he checked his watch: one in the morning. 'A reception here tonight,' he concluded. 'That will be an important occasion. You will want to keep your eyes open.'

'Open for what?' Tweed demanded and faced Rebet. 'I have been very patient . . .'

'Please give me a few more minutes of that incredible patience.' He turned to the guard who had accompanied them in the Volga. 'Yuri, please show Mr Nield his suite –which is next door to yours,' he added to Tweed.

For the next ten minutes Tweed watched with a sense of foreboding as Rebet examined the suite with a small instrument like a squat torch. He was 'flashing' the accommodation to check for bugs. Here I am, thought Tweed, inside Russia and no one knows I am here. Now even Rebet seems nervous. It was not encouraging.

Tweed perched his backside on a cushion he'd placed on the wide window ledge. As Rebet continued his meticulous search, paying great attention to the chandeliers, he looked out of the window and watched a bridge lift to permit the passage of vessels downriver. Several freighters, a sturdy stubby-nosed tug hauling a barge train.

Nield returned, wearing a navy blue suit instead of the fisherman's clothes he'd been given aboard the fishing vessel which had transferred them to the *Kalinin*.

'They're well organized,' he whispered to Tweed. 'Rebet must have radioed ahead that I was with you. My wardrobe has a selection of clothes in various sizes. This one fitted me best.' He looked at Rebet who was climbing down from a chair under a chandelier at the far end of the huge living room. 'What's up with him? Checking for listening devices? I thought he was a KGB general.'

'Not reassuring, is it.'

Rebet completed his task in the adjoining bedroom and bathroom and returned. He waved both hands in an apologetic gesture.

'I am sorry for the precaution, but we still have hardliners who try to spy on what we are doing. Nowhere is safe. No one can be fully trusted. Which is why you are here.'

'Why is that?' Tweed demanded with an edge in his tone.

'I am forgetting my duties as host. You would like something to drink? Then, rather than talk now, perhaps you would like some sleep?'

'A vodka for me,' Nield said quickly.

'Yuri . . .' Rebet gave the order in Russian.

'We talk now,' Tweed said. 'I slept on the corvette. I wish to know what this is all about.'

'Treachery.' Rebet perched himself on the arm of a chair, looked at Nield, then at Tweed. 'You know whom I personally represent. You said your companion could be trusted? Can I speak frankly.'

'It would make a nice change,' Tweed said drily.

'I am the personal representative of the President of All the Russias. I report direct to him alone. There are conspirators everywhere. Under the old régime, which I am so glad has gone, we at least had stability. Now we have the most terrible chaos. We have treachery at the very top.'

'What is the very top?' Tweed asked calmly.

'The Politburo.'

Howard walked into Tweed's Regent's Park office and Monica looked up warily. Her loyalty was to Tweed and she regarded Howard, the director, as a man to avoid as far as possible. She waited for him to flop into the armchair, perch one leg over the arm, his normal posture.

'Good morning, Monica,' Howard said quietly. 'Seems quiet with Tweed away. And I'm a very worried man.'

Monica blinked. This was a side to Howard she rarely saw, the sympathetic and – in an emergency – decisive chief. She closed her file.

'Why are you worried, sir?'

'Because we have had no word from Tweed, we have no idea where he is and I'm deeply concerned for his safety. Last night I phoned Mauno Sarin . . .'

Oh, my God! she thought. That's torn it. You've botched up the whole operation. His next words were equally surprising.

'I was very careful what I said to Sarin. I remarked it was a long time since we'd been in touch with him, that it was a long time since he'd seen Tweed.'

'And what did he say?'

'He immediately agreed, asked after Tweed's health, gave me the definite impression he had no idea Tweed was in Helsinki. I find that very worrying. You know who Tweed went to meet? I assumed it was Sarin. It wasn't. Tweed may be in great danger.'

'I'm sure he knows what he's doing.'

As she said the words Monica felt equally perplexed. Sarin was the obvious contact for Tweed to make, even if only as a courtesy gesture. The more she thought about it the more worried she became. Howard was pacing round the office, his brow furrowed. Even though the heat was building up he wore his complete suit. It occurred to Monica she had never seen Howard in shirt sleeves, and then he spoke.

'Whereabouts is Paula at this moment?'

'I'm not sure . . .'

'But you do have a general idea. Of that I'm sure. Tell me.'

Monica hesitated. Normally she would have denied all knowledge of Paula's destination, but her anxiety made her change her mind.

'She's somewhere in Scandinavia. I honestly don't know in which country.

'I checked the visitors' book downstairs. Not so long ago Bob Newman was here. Is Paula with Tweed or with Newman?'

'With Newman. He's making some personal investigation – in connection with the death of his girl friend, Sandy.'

'The murder of Sandra Riverton? So, whatever is going on it's happening in Scandinavia. Tweed needs back-up in addition to Pete Nield. Where is Harry Butler?'

'Protecting Sandra's sister, Evelyn, in Walberswick.'

'This Evelyn – she's been threatened? Attacked?'

'Not so far . . .'

'Then that's it.' Howard was decisive. 'This is an order. Harry Butler must leave for Helsinki at once. No argument. He's worked a lot as a team with Nield. His task is to locate Tweed.'

'A bit of a tall order,' Monica ventured.

'If necessary Harry Butler will visit every hotel in Finland. He's like a bloodhound. Never gives up.' Howard turned at the door before he left. 'And, Monica, if I'm not available and an emergency arises, take a decision yourself. Without referring it to me. I sense the action is in Scandinavia. In my absence, you're in charge . . .'

After he'd gone Monica was stunned for a few minutes.

She had never known Howard hand her such power. Then she sat up straighter, smoothed down her bun of grey hair, stood up to haul Tweed's camp bed out of the cupboard. From now on she would stay in the office twenty-four hours a day. She was no longer nervous – even though she had the strong foreboding that there would be an emergency soon.

It was eight o'clock at night at the Grand Hotel in Stockholm when Newman rapped on Paula's door. She opened it and outside stood Newman and Dillon, holding their bags.

'Are you packed?' Newman asked quickly. 'We're ready to leave for the Vartan ferry terminal to catch the ship for Turku.'

'Of course I'm ready,' she replied as they came into her room and shut the door. 'I've been ready for half an hour. So you've decided definitely we go first to Turku, Finland's second city? Not direct by the ferry to Helsinki?'

'Yes. It's less likely they'll be watching that route. I have your Browning in my bag. They rarely search any luggage but I won't risk you getting caught with a weapon.'

'If you say so. Then what are we waiting for?'

The cab drive to the terminal was uncomfortable. Still daylight, the air was heavy, foetid. Although she had just had a shower, Paula, sitting next to Newman, kept plucking her T-shirt away from her body. The heatwave was getting worse and Stockholm had just endured one of the hottest days of the year.

'If it's a car ferry,' she whispered to Newman, 'why didn't you hire a fresh car?'

Dillon, who sat on her right, heard what she had said and replied, keeping his voice low to avoid the driver overhearing.

'Because Bob is smart. The opposition might think of checking all the car hire outfits. They pass a little money, get the make of car, its registration number. Bob phoned ahead to Turku, made arrangements for a car to be waiting for us there. That's why.'

Paula nodded, glanced at the craggy-faced man who seemed unaffected by the torrid atmosphere. 'Bob.' He had used the name twice, had praised his tactics. Coming from Dillon that was praise indeed. She realized with surprise that the two men were drawing closer together.

The terminal came into sight, still well inside Stockholm. She saw for a few seconds the ship waiting for them. The ferry was huge, a great big five-decker. She'd had no idea such massive vessels plied the Baltic. Then she saw the film unit.

Manescu, dressed in a T-shirt and denims, wearing wraparound tinted glasses with curved lenses, stood a short distance from his camera team. Wandering slowly up and down behind him the dark haired Irina Serov was also casually dressed and her hair was tied in a pony tail. She also sported wrap-around tinted glasses, the standard equipment for directors of a film unit. Her denims were tight, looking as though they were pasted on her long slim legs.

'That man approaching the gangplank is Robert Newman,' she warned Manescu as she passed behind him.

'You're sure.'

'I don't make mistakes.'

She had paused to light a cigarette so she could talk behind her cupped hand. She watched the Englishman moving slowly up the steep entrance.

'Appears to be on his own,' Manescu commented. 'Follow him. You know my cabin number. I've got time to phone Helsinki, get final instructions . . .'

* * *

Cord Dillon had boarded the ferry earlier. Paula climbed the gangplank on her own. When Newman went aboard, holding his ticket, he was met by an attractive hostess who escorted him to his stateroom at the bow of the ship on the top deck. It was a comfortable room and there were bottles of mineral water and orange juice on the table.

He uncapped a bottle of mineral water, poured a glassful and swallowed the lot. The air inside the cabin was like an oven. He heard a gentle tapping on the door, put on his jacket, slipped his hand inside to withdraw the .38 Smith & Wesson, unlocked the door. As he'd thought, it was Paula.

'You saw the discothèque as you came on board,' she teased him. 'And you must have heard the music. All those beautiful lint-haired Finnish girls. Just your scene.'

'I might have a look at it later.'

'Where's my Browning? I feel naked without it.'

'You don't look naked. Unfortunately.'

'Are you making a pass at me, Bob?'

'Bet your sweet life I am.' He grinned drolly. 'And here's your Browning, plus some mags.'

She was examining the weapon, checking that it was unloaded, experimenting with the action. She slid it inside her shoulder bag with the mags., one inserted in the butt. Newman's manner changed.

'You saw the film unit on the dock. We've been tagged. At least I have.'

'And you thought we'd elude them by sailing for Turku.'

'Actually, I doubted it. But it makes it more nerve-wracking for Hauser. I'm stalking him, getting closer lap by lap. A little exercise in psychological pressure. He might just panic, make the wrong move. We've no evidence at all yet linking him with Sandy's murder.'

'But you'll get it. I know you when you're in this mood.'

Newman grasped her arm to emphasize what he was saying. 'One thing I must warn you about. We could be in great danger – now, aboard this ship which takes all night to reach Turku. Another reason why I didn't bring a car.'

'I'm not with you.'

'Think about it. We drive aboard, we're spotted by that film unit, they get the make and registration of the car. And all night it's sitting there deep in the bowels of the ship. How easy it would be for someone to monkey with it, mess up the braking system. Even attach a bomb. You've seen the paper – that report about Egon Schmidt, the well-known German banker, being blown up.'

'Yes, you passed it to me. I don't get the connection.'

'It's a *bank*. A very important private German bank. INCUBUS is basically a bank. Earlier I read a gossip item that Egon wasn't in the market for selling, but his son, Dieter, would be only too happy to sell out. I'm getting to know these people, how they operate. If anything stands in Hauser's way he removes it.'

'So he may try to remove you?'

'Exactly. That's why you mustn't be seen with me. And the same applies to Dillon, which is why he's staying in his stateroom.' He grinned. 'So if you do decide to have a look at the discothèque you can dance with me once. But only once.'

'Unless I find someone more attractive,' she said impishly. 'I can't see we're in any danger at a discothèque – in full view of a whole mob of rave-up teenagers.'

Manescu had sent off the film unit to Bromma to fly the new film to Helsinki. He had phoned Helsinki, had been told by Galvone that Hauser was travelling, so he made his report on Newman to Galvone.

'I'll take the responsibility for this one myself,' Galvone had decided. 'That reporter is becoming a nuisance. And

200

the best way of dealing with nuisances is to eliminate them. I rely on you to see the nuisance doesn't leave that ship . . .'

Manescu hurried aboard just before they removed the gangplank. He tapped in a special way on the door of Irina's cabin, slid swiftly inside to talk to her. The Russian girl sat in front of a mirror, brushing her cascade of glossy hair.

Manescu explained the situation quickly. Irina nodded, slipped a well-shaped hand down inside her jeans, felt the sheathed hypodermic needle. She began to apply lipstick.

'Maybe I can get him to go to bed with me. Men on the loose, a long way from home, are susceptible.'

'I don't care how, but do it.'

The great ferry had long ago left the terminal, had sailed down the approaches to Stockholm, had entered the open sea and was gliding over its smooth surface. Newman, shirt hanging out over his denims, walked into the disco and stood on the edge of the gyrating crowd, lighting a cigarette.

The amplifiers were bellowing out Sinead O'Connor, a blast of deafening rhythm. The strobe lights flashed on and off, a blinding glare converting dancers' complexions rapidly from red to blue, to yellow, to green and back again. It was a bedlam of sound, lights and the thump-thump of the dancers' feet. And to hell with inhibitions.

Paula, her hair tied in a pony tail, her legs encased in soft-soled knee-length boots, appeared behind Newman. Immediately a tall Finn with his shirt open down the front beckoned her on to the floor. She began gyrating grace-fully, keeping a foot between them. As she danced her eyes were everywhere. She frequently swung round to scan the floor, to watch Newman.

201

A trim small Finnish girl with lint hair tapped Newman on the arm. He nodded, said, 'OK,' stubbed out his cigarette in an ashtray, joined her on the floor. He realized at once that she was very good and her green eyes were inviting. She came close, spoke very clearly in English above the bombardment on the eardrums.

'Like to take me out to dinner tomorrow night in Turku?' She smiled. 'It's almost tomorrow now. You're English, aren't you?'

'Go to the top of the class, kiss the teacher, I'm the teacher.'

She obliged, eyes glowing, staying close to him. He spread his hands in a regretful gesture.

'I'd love to, but I'm here on business. Tomorrow night I'll be in Tampere . . .'

The music stopped. Couples paused. Some left the floor. A new fast number Newman didn't recognize started playing. The Finnish girl started to come back but was too late. A small slim girl with long black hair and scarlet lipstick had taken her place. Newman studied the Slavic cheekbones as they moved close together. The girl moved her hands a lot, well-shaped hands. Paula, dancing with a short stocky Swede, had moved closer, kept spinning round, her left hand held by the Swede who was a good dancer. Newman's partner placed both hands on her hips, moved her body slowly, a half-smile on her face. Paula was still spinning and the floor was more crowded as new couples took up more space. The girl with long dark hair pushed her right hand deeper inside her denims, her eyes holding Newman's. Her hand emerged in the crush, she reached out to grasp his wrist. Paula suddenly seemed to become a little drunk. Her body hammered against Newman's partner with force. The other girl lost her balance, began to slip. Paula hammered against her harder. The girl fell over. Couples reached out to break her fall as she slid to the floor. Newman saw the small hypodermic drop from her hand, saw Paula's right boot lift, smash down on the hypodermic, crushing it. Then she vanished in the crowd as the dark-haired girl climbed to her feet. Newman jerked her upright, pushed her into the eager arms of a tall Swede, slipped away out of the milling crowd.

'I'll recognize the little bitch again,' Paula said as she slumped on Newman's bed in his stateroom. 'You did say we could be in danger,' she reminded him as she took the glass of water he offered.

'Saved my life, you did,' Newman commented, sagging into a chair. 'What put you on to her? I need my head examining.'

'She kept glancing up at the flashing lights. I realized she was timing the change to a fresh glare, that brief second when you can't see what's going on. That's when she lunged at you with the hypodermic. I wonder what was in it?'

'Nothing for my health, that's for sure. And she's clever. Had I collapsed on the floor everyone would have assumed I was drunk, or was on drugs. She'd have been long gone. We have to be more careful.' He grinned ruefully. '*I* have to be more careful. And they'll be waiting for us when the ship docks at Turku. I suggest a late breakfast and we'll be last off the ferry. It will be daylight, of course.'

'I think I need some sleep now,' Paula decided, sat up, swung her legs over the edge of the bed, stood up, stretched herself. 'I'd better get back to my stateroom, otherwise I'm going to lose my reputation.'

'Would you mind?' he asked, still sitting down.

'What about Dillon?' she asked.

'I arranged we'd meet in the canteen. He'll wait there until we appear. The ferry docks at seven. So, if you insist on going, I'll see you six-thirty in the canteen.'

'I have to think of Tweed.' She looked at him. 'Sometimes a woman takes a lot of time to make up her mind – especially when she knows two very different men.'

'I'll see you safely back to your stateroom. You're right – we need the sleep. God knows what is waiting for us when we set foot in Finland.'

20

Most people who knew Marler would have said he was impatient, wanted quick results. But Marler, when it was necessary, had the patience of Job. Concealed in his car inside the copse of trees above the INCUBUS HQ outside Helsinki, he had spent two days in the broiling heat, taking pictures at long intervals as people entered or left the building.

Back at The Palace Hotel overlooking North Harbour, he sat in front of the phone in his shirt sleeves, his collar open at the neck. He had delivered several films to a twenty-four-hour development shop. He was confident he now had pictures of all the top executives: he had identified them by the expensive cars they drove.

He picked up the phone and dialled Park Crescent. Monica answered his call.

'General and Cumbria Assurance . . .'

'It's Marler, Monica. Anyone I can talk to – and I'm calling from a hotel in Helsinki,' he warned.

'Understood. As to who you can talk to, only me. Believe it or not, our plummy-voiced upper-crust chief has left me in charge.'

Which meant Howard. Marler was surprised. Monica was good, very good, but Howard usually thought there were only two uses for women, one being to stay at home.

'Monica, I need info. Who is where. That sort of thing.'

At the other end of the line Monica hesitated for only a second. She was there to make her own decisions.

'Marler, our immediate sales director is in your area. But we haven't had any contact from him for days – and I'm worried stiff.'

That had to be Tweed. Marler lit a king-size cigarette, gave himself a brief pause to think. 'I'll do some checking,' he told her. 'Any more of the team floating round?'

'Yes, Paula and Bob are travelling together. They're heading your way. No idea by which route.'

Newman's a lone wolf, Marler thought. Although he doesn't sound too lonely this time. Maybe it was the murder of his girl friend which had made him long for company. No, that wasn't right. Paula could only be with Newman with Tweed's sanction. Which meant they were after someone.

'Anyone else?' he enquired.

'Yes. Harry Butler is flying out as an extra representative. He'll be calling me sooner or later.'

'Tell him I'm at The Palace Hotel, to come and see me. And don't worry. Our sales director knows what he's doing.'

Which was the understatement of the year as far as Tweed was concerned. Monica was speaking again.

'He took Pete Nield with him.'

'There you are. Not a thing to get hot and bothered about. Cancel the first part of that remark, Monica. It's bloody hot here. May call you again . . .'

Monica is clever, he thought as he put down the phone. Anyone listening in to that conversation would assume we were a commercial organization after business. So, the clans were gathering. He opened his door, hung the *Do*

205

Not Disturb notice on the handle, closed and locked the door.

Rummaging in his hold-all he brought out the Armalite rifle, began cleaning the weapon. It helped him to concentrate. And the hair he had laid over the zip had not been moved – no one had searched his room in his absence. The problem was which route would Newman come in by?

The airport? Marler didn't think so. Too obvious. And Newman was a devious bastard. By ferry from Travemünde – the route he'd used? He didn't think so. By car ferry from Sweden? That was the most likely, so he'd meet the ship arriving tomorrow. And Harry Butler? Marler out-ranked Butler but secretly called him The Beaver: Butler was a man who had immense stamina, who kept on working away at his appointed task until he'd done the job. A definite asset.

Marler decided he'd delay his flight to Rovaniemi, to explore this strange Meteorological Institute Sarin had pointed him to. Developments could be about to take place in Helsinki. The one thing which puzzled him was Tweed's whereabouts.

It was early evening in the Hotel Moskwa in Leningrad when Tweed, irked at the passing of time, forced the issue with General Rebet. They were sitting round a large table piled high with food and drink in Tweed's suite. Near a wall sat Pete Nield, keeping a wary eye on the slim Rebet who talked a lot with hand gestures.

'You spoke of treachery in the Politburo,' Tweed began, 'and then you veered off on a different subject. Rebet, I want to know why you brought me here, I want to know now, or I want to be flown back to Helsinki within the next hour.'

'Surely our hospitality has been . . .'

'It has been overwhelming.' Tweed, who had refused any sort of alcoholic drink, sipped his Russian tea. 'But I didn't come here for a holiday. Answer my question.'

'We are holding a large reception in this hotel to which you are invited.' Rebet checked his watch. 'I will escort you to it within the next thirty minutes.'

'Answer my question.'

'I have just done so. That is why you are here – to attend this reception *incognito* . . .'

'*Why?*' Tweed had raised his voice. 'I know that Russians take hours, weeks, even months to get to the point. I am the wrong man to treat in that way. Make arrangements now for me to fly back to Helsinki where you hijacked me. That I will not forget.'

'We know there is a high-level go-between – traitor, if you like – in the Politburo who is secretly co-operating with the military-industrial complex in America to help them dominate the Soviet Union. They see this as a unique opportunity to infiltrate my country, to reduce it to a commercial satellite of the United States. Because chaos has broken loose here. You understand me so far?'

'Yes, but I find the idea fanciful. Continue. Where does the traitor in the Politburo come in?'

'We cannot trace his identity. What I am going to tell you now is top secret. We infiltrated an agent inside Dracon, the huge think-tank located outside Boston. He reported an agent at the highest level was co-operating with the conspiracy. That he went by the code name Angel. We have narrowed down the suspects to three members of the Politburo. Marshal Dimitri Zaikov, Minister of Defence. Anatoli Dikoyan, an Armenian and Minister for Foreign Trade. Viktor Kazbek, a Georgian, Minister of Communications. One of these three men is collaborating with the Americans.'

'I fail to see how he could do that,' Tweed snapped.

'We know that Angel has close links with the Mafia . . .'

207

'The American Mafia? Come off it, Rebet.'

'No, my apologies, I referred to the Soviet Mafia. The underground movement which is so well organized, I fear. The men who are black marketeers, officials who have been bribed with large sums, even members of my own KGB. Angel has woven a web throughout the Soviet Union and these are the people the Americans are using.'

'Surely you can penetrate this movement?'

'We have tried to do so, of course. Agents have been infiltrated into this highly secret organization – and have been found dead. Murdered in a back alley in Moscow, here in Leningrad, in Kiev and so on. We have no inkling who Angel is – but he will be at the reception. All three men I have named will be at this reception. Maybe if you mingle with them you will see something with your fresh eye we have missed.'

'I think it highly unlikely.'

'Our President himself has asked you to try. We are running out of time.'

'I'll do what I can, but I promise nothing.' Tweed looked at Rebet. 'You must be desperate to call on me,' he said with a dry smile.

'We are desperate . . .'

Rebet continued talking as they descended a large staircase of stone. Below, guests in evening dress mingled, many of the women bare shouldered. Tweed could hear the clink of glasses, a babble of voices as Rebet instructed him while Nield followed behind them.

'You can spend most of your time observing. I will be by your side. If I introduce you it will be as Mr Gubenko, our commercial attaché at the London Embassy. You speak Russian well but that role will explain any trace of English accent that is detected.'

'I don't feel like Gubenko.'

'You look like him!'

It was the first joke Rebet had cracked since they arrived. As they edged their way into the vast hall Tweed looked up at the great chandeliers glittering high above his head. It was still daylight outside. To one side of the hall there was a buffet almost sagging under the mountains of food, the immense array of bottles. No sign of a food shortage here.

'That distinguished man with greying hair and pink cheeks is the British Ambassador,' Rebet whispered.

'Keep me well away from him, for God's sake . . .'

Then for a split second Tweed froze. In the centre of the hall a large party was gathered round a tall well-built man who wore pince-nez and flourished a cigarette holder. Franklin D. Hauser.

Tweed had a glazed look, seemed half asleep as Rebet escorted him slowly round the crowded room. But the apparently sleepy eyes never left Hauser or his companion. Marshal Zaikov was a short burly man who frequently made some humorous remark and Hauser would throw his head back and roar with laughter. In full dress uniform, Zaikov was clean shaven with a bull-like jaw and never stopped waving a clenched fist. Drawing closer, Tweed was surprised to hear Hauser speaking fluent Russian. The intensive research had not revealed this ability.

As the evening progressed Hauser began to circulate. Tweed sipped at his vodka as a great bear-like man with a black beard and a mane of black hair approached Hauser. They moved into a corner to avoid the crush. The bear-like man hugged Hauser, kissed him on both cheeks, then began to gesticulate. The man was a dynamo of energy, even more so than the American.

'The Georgian?' Tweed whispered.

'Yes, that is Viktor Kazbek, Minister of Communications. A man who likes women, plenty of women.' Rebet shrugged. 'But then he is a Georgian. They have great appetites for food, drink, all the good things in life.'

Tweed nodded, refused a waiter's attempt to freshen up his glass. Hew watched as the Georgian constantly touched Hauser to emphasize a point. Very little sign of inhibition there. Tweed stood quite still for a quarter of an hour while the two men conversed non-stop. Hauser certainly had a way of getting on with other nationalities.

'You would like to talk to someone? Maybe a beautiful woman?' Rebet suggested.

Tweed shook his head, raised his glass to his lips, held it there without even sipping. The Georgian had made way for a very different type of personality. A small slim man, faultlessly dressed, his dark hair brushed carefully back from his high forehead, sporting a trim moustache, was shaking hands with Hauser who had moved away from the corner.

'The Armenian?' whispered Tweed.

'Yes. Right again. Anatoli Dikoyan, Minister for Foreign Trade. He travels a lot in the West, trying to fix up barter deals. We are in a bad way here.'

'His background?' Tweed asked abruptly.

As Rebet gave him a pen portrait Tweed watched the Armenian, who, because of his small stature, had to look up at Hauser as he spoke non-stop to the American. His slim hands gestured frequently to emphasize a point. A clever man, Tweed decided, as Rebet spoke.

'Dikoyan is a brilliant politician. He has adapted himself to every change of régime. He was one of the first to admire the extraordinary man who would ultimately become our new President. He is fluent in four languages, one of them English. He has a genius for always staying in the background so no one can ever point the finger and say he was one of the Old Guard . . .'

210

The crush of people was beginning to move towards double doors which had been opened into the next salon. Rebet nodded towards the shifting mass.

'There will now be a banquet. You are invited. I hope you'll agree to attend?'

'Of course. I want to watch all three men. Do you know when Hauser leaves Russia?'

'After the banquet he flies straight back to Helsinki. He is not a man who stays here long.'

'And I have already seen him talking to the man you call Angel,' Tweed whispered.

'You mean you have identified him?'

Rebet could not conceal his astonishment. Tweed smiled, shook his head.

'After the banquet I may know. Especially as Hauser is leaving immediately it ends.'

'You are being very mysterious, my friend. One other problem is troubling us. A number of the key figures in the old security apparatus in various countries have disappeared. Including some of our own. This is highly confidential, Comrade.' Rebet had lowered his voice so Tweed only just caught what he said. 'A woman from my new organization, a colonel, too, Irina Serov, has vanished. We think she crossed the border into Finland – but that is a guess.'

'And the other key figures?'

They talked as they drifted towards the banqueting salon in the wake of the excited alcoholic crowd.

'One name we have heard several times is Ion Manescu, a tartar in the Romanian *Securitate*. There are names from the German STASI, which has been dissolved. My agents can find no trace of where these people are vanishing to.'

'But any strong evidence that they are going anywhere?'

'The numbers.' Rebet chuckled without humour. 'One

might have fallen down a hole in the ground. Also two. But it would need a very big hole to swallow up those who have performed this disappearing act. With all the troubles we have with so many of our republics it is worrying. Now, I must keep quiet . . .'

As in the old days the banquet went on for hours. Tweed was careful to sip at the variety of drinks put before him, asking frequently for more mineral water. And all the time he sat next to Rebet and ate small portions, his eyes kept glancing towards Hauser who had the place of honour to the right of the head of the table. Their official host was Marshal Dimitri Zaikov who occupied the end seat, ate huge quantities, drank litres of alcohol and told jokes.

Half-way down the opposite side of the table and close to Tweed sat the huge jovial figure of Viktor Kazbek. Constantly proposing toasts, he drank a great deal less than he appeared to. His dark eyes swept the guests, caught Tweed's, paused. Then Kazbek raised his glass and Tweed followed suit, nodding to the dynamic Georgian, sipping, looking away.

The diminutive figure of Dikoyan was paying great attention to an attractive woman who sat facing him. Tweed watched while the Armenian entertained his friend. As the banquet ended guests stood up, began chatting in groups. Hauser, Tweed noted, hurried from the salon escorted by guards, presumably on his way to the airport. Rebet, who had stood up with Tweed, seemed to read his mind.

'The motorcade is waiting for Hauser. He never hangs around for longer than he need. He'll be in the air within an hour.'

Dikoyan appeared at Tweed's side, was introduced by Rebet, and smiled cordially.

'I know London well,' he began in his quick way of speaking in English. 'I remember well catching the train from Charing Cross for a weekend in Bournemouth, Britain's Yalta nestling by the sea. A beautiful place.'

'Except that you must have travelled from Waterloo.'

'Of course!' Dikoyan threw up his hands in apology. 'So many stations in London . . .'

After a few minutes' lively conversation he disappeared in the crowd. Tweed glanced at Rebet.

'I thought he was devious. That reference to Charing Cross was a trap – to see if I really had been attached to the Soviet Embassy there . . .'

He broke off as the huge bulk of Viktor Kazbek loomed over him. Again Rebet made the same introduction in Russian. Kazbek stared at Tweed, asked Rebet to repeat the name.

'Igor Gubenko, commercial attaché to London,' Rebet replied.

'I am so pleased to meet you at our little party. Mr . . . Gubenko? Have I got the name right now?'

'Yes, you have.' Tweed stared straight back up at the glowing dark eyes of the bearded Georgian. 'You enjoy being Minister of Communications?' he enquired.

Kazbek threw back his maned head and roared with laughter. 'I enjoy it? Who on God's earth enjoys being a Politburo member these days, except the boss, maybe.' He tapped the side of his hooked nose with a large forefinger. 'Now I am being wicked. You quote me, Mr . . . Gubenko, and I get the sack. Now I am in your power!'

Another roar of laughter, his thick mane shook, he slapped Tweed on the back, grinned, exposing gold teeth and turned to kiss the hand of a fat woman.

Rebet drifted towards the exit and Tweed followed slowly, turning his head to survey the room. Nearby stood Marshal Zaikov, a motionless stocky figure with a face like Siberia. He was watching them and for a moment

213

Tweed felt sure he was going to come over to talk to them. Then the soldier seemed to change his mind. His eyes caught Tweed's for a fleeting moment and he moved in the opposite direction.

Rebet waited until he had escorted Tweed and Nield, who had sat a few places away, to their rooms before he asked Tweed the question.

'That's it. Hauser has gone. I believe you wish to return in the morning. You will be flown to Helsinki.' He paused. 'Have you any inkling as to which of the three men is Angel?'

Tweed said good-night to Nield, opened his door, turned and gazed at Rebet. The Russian had asked the question casually but Tweed sensed his anxiety. He shook his head.

'I am sorry but I really have no idea,' he lied. 'But thank you for the hospitality. It was worth a try.'

Had he told the truth, had Rebet asked him the reason for his identification, he would have replied, 'It was the absence of something I observed . . .'

21

Newman, Paula and Dillon were the last three passengers to disembark from the Silja Line ferry at Turku. After a late breakfast aboard they had assembled in Newman's stateroom and the argument had broken out.

'We're going ashore together,' Newman announced. 'With no attempt at concealment.'

'That's crazy,' Dillon had growled. 'After all the trouble we've taken to slip into Finland unseen.'

'I'm inclined to agree with Cord,' Paula had commented.

Newman had been firm, even aggressive. 'Listen, we tried and what happened? My invisible man act was a flop. They have the whole area cordoned, all entry points watched. You think it will be different here at Turku? Well, it won't be. So I'm changing the strategy. Let them see us – and we'll see them. I'm not picking up the hired BMW until early in the evening. Then we drive like hell along Highway E3 from here to Helsinki.'

'I still don't get it,' Dillon rasped. 'I don't agree with it . . .'

'Either come with us or make your own way there,' Newman told him brutally. 'Your choice. But remember, we now have guns. We can protect ourselves. And three is a formidable group if we come under attack during the drive.'

'And what, may I ask,' Dillon persisted, 'do we do during the day while we wait for evening? Give them a good chance to spot us, lay plans for an ambush? Stroll round Turku openly? Maybe have lunch at a hotel? More public exposure?'

'Exactly that,' Newman told him. 'Now it's time we went ashore. I know Turku. We'll dump our bags at the station, then take a look at old Turku. That's a collection of old wooden houses showing Finland as it was a hundred years ago. Relax, always in the open. That's what we're going to do. On second thoughts I'll hire a second car – which we won't use. It's psychological warfare – to throw them off balance.'

'What the hell does that mean?'

'That the one tactic which confuses the opposition is the unexpected.'

Irina Serov, wearing white shorts, a white blouse, a pair of tinted glasses, a wide-brimmed straw hat which concealed her hair, bare legged and shod in trainers, watched

215

as Newman walked out of the car hire firm. She slipped inside quickly as the girl behind the counter was completing a form, read it upside down.

'Can I help you?' the receptionist asked, looking up.

'I'd like a brochure showing the cars available and prices, please . . .'

Once she was outside in the steaming heat she looked round for a convenient doorway. Further along the street Manescu, also clad in casual clothes and wearing a straw hat, followed Newman as he joined Paula and Dillon.

Irina slipped inside the doorway alcove, felt inside her capacious shoulder bag, brought out a miniature walkie-talkie. Extending the aerial, she contacted INCUBUS Oy. in Turku.

'Joanna Star speaking. The subject has hired another white Volvo station wagon. Registration number . . . He has not driven the car away, so presumably he is still attending the convention. Over and out . . .'

Paula spoke casually as Newman joined them. 'You do realize you were being watched?'

'Girl in a straw hat and tinted glasses. Could be the one who tried to kill me last night at the disco – except that she's taller.'

'She's wearing trainers with specially elevated heels,' Paula informed him. 'And the little darling moves in the same way. She followed you into the car hire place.'

'Great. She'll have checked and report we're travelling in the wrong kind of car.' He looked at Dillon. 'Don't look back – we're now being followed by a man slouching along in a straw hat.'

They were strolling along together in the middle of Turku. The buildings were a mix of new and old, mostly three or four storeys high, so they were not shielded from the sun. The traffic in Turku was quieter than in Stockholm: they could even cross the street almost whenever they wanted. Newman nodded, glanced back and led the way to a bar on the far side.

'Time for a drink. Whatever else you have, order some mineral water and drink the lot. We must guard against dehydration. And it will be fun to see what Straw Hat does.'

'I don't like this cat-and-mouse game,' Dillon said as they sat at a window table. He waited until the waitress had taken their order. 'I'd like to shove Straw Hat into one of those alleyways, squeeze his throat until he talks, then make him unconscious.'

'And give away the fact that we know what's going on?' Newman grinned, shook his head. 'We're playing innocents. We think we've shaken them off. That way they'll make a mistake.'

'I don't think INCUBUS makes many mistakes,' Paula observed when the waitress had delivered their order. She sipped her orange juice through a straw. 'Do you think it was such a good idea leaving our weapons in the cases we deposited in the station lockers?'

'Oh, definitely.' Newman was in a good humour. 'That way we can't get caught by the police. Whoever is running the surveillance operation on us might just get the idea of giving the police an anonymous tip. They catch the three of us with guns and that's it. The Finns don't like strange people in town tooled up with guns.'

Dillon grunted. 'And I've got sand in my shoes – or whatever that stuff was we walked through prowling round those old cabins.'

Newman stiffened, then relaxed. He gazed out of the window across the street at the men's outfitters shop where Straw Hat was taking his time examining the merchandise. But his expression had frozen and only Paula realized what had happened. Dillon's reference to sand. It had shot back into Newman's mind his girl friend, Sandy, and he was reliving the nightmare dawn in Suffolk

217

when he'd discovered her hanging by her neck in the bell tower.

Earlier his mind had been concentrated on outwitting their pursuers, which had driven the horror into the background. Now he sat with his jaw muscles clenched tight and a blank look in his eyes. Paula knew that look, had seen it only once or twice before. Newman was feeling like murder.

Franklin D. Hauser's Lear executive jet had flown him back from Leningrad and landed him at Helsinki airport. The waiting bullet-proof limo drove him straight to INCUBUS Oy. HQ. He hurried out of the car into the building, in a rush as always.

Concealed inside his car in the copse overlooking the HQ Marler snapped off three shots with his camera, recorded in his notebook the time. Early that morning he had met the Silja Line car ferry from Stockholm, had checked each passenger off the ship. No sign of Newman: he had guessed wrong. Was the reporter coming at all? he asked himself.

On the top floor Galvone was waiting for his chief. Seeing his expression, he began talking at once as Hauser settled himself behind his desk. No small talk: get to it.

'Newman has arrived in Finland.'

Hauser's expression froze. He reminded Galvone of one of the great faces of four American Presidents carved out of the stone cliff at the summit of the Black Hills in South Dakota.

'Here in Helsinki?' he demanded, his voice harsh.

'Not that bad . . .'

'How bad? Get to it.'

'Newman is in Turku. Arrived on the ferry from Stockholm this morning. Manescu and Serov have the situation in hand. Newman has hired a Volvo, is expected to drive

218

here soon. He has people with him. A man. A girl.'

'Why didn't they do the job on the ferry?'

'Serov tried. She just got unlucky.'

The door to Hauser's penthouse office opened and Adam Carver strolled in. It was early evening but the Englishman looked fresh as paint, ready to start a new day.

'We're in conference,' Hauser snapped.

'I just got in from Germany. Egon Schmidt's bank is ours. I persuaded the surviving son, Dieter, to sign a preliminary agreement. There'll be more paperwork but the bank is yours. You have your foot in the German door.'

'Good.' Hauser was pleased but impatient. 'You'll be tired. Go and freshen up. Then stay in your office. I want to see you later.'

He waited until he was alone with Galvone. Leaning back in his chair he stared at his subordinate.

'Frank, this is an order. Finish him off. No way must he reach Helsinki . . .'

Inside a café opposite the car hire firm Irina, the last customer, sat making her second cup of coffee last out. A waitress came to her table, said they'd soon be closing. Irina told her she was waiting for a friend she expected any minute. She passed the waitress a banknote, a generous tip.

Five minutes later she saw a BMW drive out with Newman at the wheel, the girl beside him, the second man in the back. She extracted her pocket walkie-talkie from her shoulder bag, extended the aerial after checking the waitress had disappeared. 'Joanna Star here. The subject is driving out of town. Not the Volvo I reported earlier. He's changed cars. Now in a cream BMW. Registration . . . Over and out.'

Manescu walked into the café as she finished her coffee and prepared to leave. She told him what she had reported to INCUBUS Oy. HQ in Turku.

'It's all arranged,' Manescu assured her as they walked into the street. 'Orders from the very top. They'll die on Route E3.'

'You've been this way before,' Paula said as they left behind the outskirts of Turku. 'How far to Helsinki?'

'Exactly a hundred and fifty-eight kilometres. Take us about a couple of hours.'

'Where are we staying in Helsinki?' Dillon demanded from the rear.

'Decide when we get there,' Newman said tersely. 'Not the Hesperia if we can avoid it. I've stayed there before. Just leave it to me, there's a good chap, Cord.'

Paula glanced at Newman. Ever since Dillon had made the remark which had reminded the Englishman of Sandy, Newman's manner had been polite, his mood grim. They were speeding along Route E3, a two-lane highway each way. Very little traffic as behind them the sun sank into lower orbit. Paula checked the dashboard.

'What are the speed limits in Finland?'

'Sometimes 80 kph, sometimes 100. Further along there's a special stretch called The Highway. There you can ram your foot down a bit. 120 kph.'

Again he was terse. Hands on the wheel relaxed, Paula noted. Newman was a superb driver but she sensed the tension inside him. Was it because they were approaching their objective – Helsinki? That Newman couldn't wait until he confronted Hauser? Newman's thoughts were really miles away. He was recalling what Chief Inspector Roy Buchanan had said. The points he had made.

Try and discover which top executive was in Helsinki when Ed Riverton had been garrotted, his body dragged off the ice in North Harbour. Try and pinpoint an executive who had been *absent* from Finland when Sandy was murdered at the belltower in Suffolk. Hope that the same man fitted both situations.

Paula looked out of the window as they drove through countryside. Stands of great firs, the sky luminous with that pearl-like and crystal-clear light you only saw in Finland. The firs reared up like silhouettes, their edges sharp-cut against the sky. Dream-like land . . .

'We're moving on to The Highway,' Newman commented.

Paula was aware they were racing much faster, again checked the dashboard. 120kph. 75mph. The BMW glided along, adding to the dream-like atmosphere. This is pure heaven, Paula thought.

'There's a huge truck coming up behind us,' Dillon warned. 'I saw a name splashed along the side as it came round a curve. INCUBUS Oy.'

'A juggernaut,' Newman replied calmly. 'And I have seen it. Moving up on us like an express train . . .'

Paula twisted in her seat, strained against her belt to see the vehicle. It was enormous. It had a separate cab for the driver attached to the mammoth load behind it. They were now separated from all traffic coming in the opposite direction by a high shrub-covered bank. She looked at Newman, saw his lips were pressed tightly together.

'Trouble?' she asked quietly and reached inside her shoulder bag, her right hand gripping the butt of her Browning.

'Could be.'

Newman's tone had become laconic. He glanced in his rear-view mirror, then grinned at Paula. The juggernaut was bearing down on them like a battleship, far exceeding the speed limit even for The Highway. Behind the driver's cab the immense load swayed ominously and slowly from side to side. Then with a burst of speed the juggernaut overtook them on the left, was driving alongside them, looming over Newman like a mountain. He dipped his head briefly, caught a glimpse of the driver on the far side. A stocky man hunched over his wheel, wearing a peaked cap, dark glasses. The vehicle began to move closer, the driver turning his wheel inches at a time.

Paula hauled out her Browning, leaned forward. Newman had his window lowered all the way to counter the hot foetid air of evening. Paula dipped her own head, raised the gun barrel.

'Put that thing away! Newman snapped. 'You want us arrested for murder?'

'So,' Dillon called out from his seat, 'we're going to be the meat in the sandwich . . .'

'Thanks for the vote of confidence,' Newman rapped back.

There was still about one foot between the two speeding vehicles. The gap was closing second by second. To their right, on Paula's side, ran an endless steel barrier, closing off the inner lane from a slope descending to a wall of firs. She saw it all in a blur – the canvas covering of the juggernaut moving towards them, the highway ahead with not a vehicle in sight. She had obeyed Newman, thrusting the Browning back inside her shoulder bag, her right hand moist and slippery on the butt. Every muscle in her body seemed to scream with tension, the tension of waiting for the impact as the juggernaut smashed into them, hurled them against the steel barrier, the sparks flying as metal collided with metal, the awful moment when she felt the barrier give way, the BMW begin to turn turtle . . .

Newman again dipped his head briefly, saw the driver inside the cab change his grip on the wheel prior to swinging it in a large arc to his right. Nineteen drivers out of twenty would have tried to race ahead, ramming their foot down, but Newman was the twentieth man. He had heard the deep-throated boom-boom of the juggernaut's souped up engine. No chance of out-racing it. He did the dangerous unexpected thing. He reduced speed as rapidly as he dared, waited for the skid – and there was no skid. The driver in the cab had swung his wheel, was cutting across Newman's bow to crush him against the steel barrier. Newman took his second lethal risk. He rammed on the brake. The BMW came to a shuddering halt. Paula glanced back at Dillon. The American had braced himself with his left hand against the back of her seat. His right hand held his Luger, muzzle pointed towards the left. The driver of the juggernaut had turned his massive load inwards, knowing the collision with the BMW would cushion him. But the BMW had vanished. He saw the steel barrier fly towards him, felt the vehicle crash against the barrier, heard a wrenching sound as the barrier gave way, tried desperately to turn his wheel. Too late.

Newman, rubbing his aching right arm inside the stationary BMW, watched as the juggernaut destroyed the barrier, began to topple sideways, turn over as it rolled down the slope. It hit the wall of firs like a cannon firing, three firs tilted sideways, there was a brief moment of silence when the only sound was the ticking over of the BMW's engine, then the motionless juggernaut burst into flames, cremating the driver as the flames soared up in a gigantic torch consuming the tilted firs.

Newman glanced in his rear-view mirror. No traffic coming up. He drove on, pressing his foot down until the speedometer reached 120 kph. With one hand he lit a cigarette: the only sign of any reaction to what had occurred. Paula knew he normally never smoked when driving. She relaxed her grip on the Browning, took a deep breath, wiped her hands on a handkerchief, looked back at Dillon.

The American's craggy face showed no indication of what they had just experienced. He winked at Paula.

'I'll be ready for a drink, I guess, when we reach

Helsinki,' he remarked. 'I wonder what happens when we get there.'

'We need a lucky break,' was Newman's only reply.

22

Peggy Vanderheld had cleared her desk, had left INCU-BUS Oy.'s HQ forever. She had taken a taxi to her apartment overlooking the sea, which she still thought looked more like a lake.

She sat by the window, drinking a dry martini, still seething over the way Hauser had treated her. Her apartment was in a block near the end of tram stop No. 4 coming out from the city. It was located only a short walk from the Hotel Kalastajatorppa up the hill, a weird complex of buildings which some Finnish architect had designed so it looked as though it grew out of the granite it stood on. Maybe she would go there for dinner.

No, she decided, I have a ticket to the theatre opposite the Marski in town. I want to be among a lot of people. She sat gazing down at the scrubbing platform, a wooden structure projecting into the sea at two levels. Wooden rails surrounded it.

Peggy had often watched Finnish women working on that platform in the morning, dipping their carpets in the sea water, then scrubbing them clean on wooden tables. It was incredibly hard work and yet many of the women who used it were middle class. The thought had just passed through her mind when the bell rang.

'Hell! Who's come to bother me when I want to do a Garbo?'

She operated the speakphone, asked who it was.

'Peggy, it's Adam Carver. I'd really appreciate it if I could have a word with you. I know you must be raging at what they did.'

'OK. Come up. If you must . . .'

She pressed the button which released the lock on the door to the main lobby. Checking her appearance in a wall mirror, she had the door open when Carver, looking very smart in a cream silk suit, entered.

'You'd better sit down, I suppose.'

She was damned if she was going to offer him a drink. But she recognized she had mixed feelings towards Carver. Certainly he was a handsome brute, but she mistrusted his British charm. He gave her what she supposed was his winning smile and sat in an armchair. She chose a hard-backed chair and crossed her shapely legs.

'Well, what is it?' she demanded.

'Don't be like that. I thought we got on pretty well when you were with the company.'

'Everyone has their illusions.'

'I don't necessarily agree with everything Hauser does, you know.' He gazed at her. 'You really have the most superb figure, if I may say so.'

'You just did. Who am I to argue with a vice president?'

'This is getting us nowhere . . .' He smiled again.

'So goddamnit, let's get somewhere. Let's get to the point of why you came here.'

'INCUBUS is willing to offer you a very generous pension.'

'Which I'll take because it's owing to me. Nice to be referred to like an old horse put out to grass.'

'Peggy! Please! I didn't imply anything like that. You're still a young woman. With your track record you could get any job you want. And I didn't get the chance to explain – INCUBUS is offering you double the pension you're expecting.'

Her eyes narrowed. She stroked her dark hair. 'And what is the catch, Buster?'

'A good question. Nothing more than your signing the usual agreement which forbids revealing any information picked up while you were in the company's employ. No talking about it. No newspaper interviews. No writing your memoirs for a big fat advance from New York.'

She stood up. 'You know something. You just gave me a great idea. Glad you called, Adam. And now, if you'll excuse me, I have a ticket for the theatre and I have to change.'

He stood up slowly. 'But what about what I just said? I'd like a reaction before I go.'

'Just like that? You have to be joking.' She opened the door. 'I'll give it some thought. May take some time. Nice knowing you . . .'

Carver left the apartment block and walked slowly up the street to where he'd parked his car. He rubbed his freshly shaven chin. Was he losing his touch? He'd felt sure he could twist her round his little finger.

He climbed behind the wheel, sat staring at the deserted street. A No. 4 tram appeared in the distance, trundled to its terminus a hundred yards away. Carver picked up his mobile phone, dialled Hauser's private number.

'Adam here, sir. The problem is unresolved. Difficult to foretell how the subject will react . . .'

'You're saying negative?' Hauser rasped.

'Up to a point. At the moment . . .'

'You're saying negative,' Hauser repeated. 'Get back here fast. I want a full report.'

Newman had decided against the Kalastajatorppa. Too many painful memories. He had stayed there years before when his wife had been murdered in Estonia. He could do without that on top of Sandy's death. Not the Hesperia: he had stayed there before. Which left three hotels – the Marski, the Intercontinental and The Palace. He chose the latter.

Waiting in the lobby for Paula and Dillon – Newman was an expert at swift unpacking – he found arriving back in Helsinki he was reliving earlier experiences. He needed a drink. Wandering into the bar the first person he saw sitting by himself at a corner table was Marler.

'Large Scotch, please,' Newman ordered at the bar.

He carried his glass as he strolled round as though unsure where to settle. As he reached Marler's table he appeared to stumble, spilling some of his drink on the table top. He took out a handkerchief, talking as he mopped up the liquid.

'Sorry to mess up your table. Not like me to be clumsy, but I'm bushed. Just got in after long drive.'

Marler waved a hand. 'Be my guest. Take the weight off your feet . . .'

To an onlooker it appeared to be a chance meeting between two strangers, Englishmen who were glad to encounter a fellow-countryman. Newman sat down, blew out his cheeks in a gesture of relief.

'Thanks.' He lifted his glass. 'Cheers!' He lowered his voice as he placed the glass on the table. 'The INCUBUS octopus lot have just tried to kill me twice.'

Marler grinned. 'They must be amateurs. If I'd been hired by them you wouldn't be there drinking Scotch.'

'I love egomaniacs,' Newman responded. 'And don't be surprised when Paula and Cord Dillon walk in. We're travelling together.'

'Dillon? The deputy director of the CIA. Care to enlighten me.'

'Can't. Not about Dillon. Tweed's orders. Sorry. But I can tell you why I'm here . . .'

He gave Marler a concise account of his investigation of

INCUBUS, including his interviews with the two Englishmen who had been forced into selling out to the corporation against their will. Briefly, he described the two attempts on his life, told Marler how he had obtained weapons. Marler stroked his fair hair, said nothing while Newman explained, then extracted from his jacket pocket an envelope.

'Care to see my holiday snaps, chum? Taken in secrecy from a point overlooking INCUBUS's HQ west of the city. No idea who is who, but I didn't see the man I was looking for.'

Newman looked at the glossy prints, identified certain people as he handed each print back.

'That's Adam Carver. English. Met him when I called on Hauser at his Suffolk home, Livingstone Manor. Not a mile from where I found Sandy hanging by her neck. He's a vice president. And this one is Hauser, which you probably know from seeing his picture in the papers. This thug is Frank Galvone, another vice president. These two I don't know. Now, this handsome-looking brunette . . .'

He stopped speaking as Paula entered the bar with Dillon.

'Don't stare, Cord,' Paula warned, 'Newman's in the far corner. And somehow he's met up with Marler of all people. I think we had better stay away.'

'Suits me, honey. Don't too much like either of them. Even if they are two tough pros. Let's have a drink together, get our nerves back into shape.'

It was the first hint Paula had that Dillon, always outwardly calm and unruffled, had been affected by the terror on The Highway. She accepted his offer gratefully and they took their drinks to a table well away from where the two Englishmen sat.

Newman nodded to Marler. 'Paula is smart. They're

228

pretending they don't know us. Which probably suits you. Now, you were about to say something.'

'I've identified that handsome-looking brunette. She's American, was Hauser's highly confidential personal assistant, until he gave the lady her marching orders, which she doesn't like one little bit. Peggy Vanderheld. I even know where she lives in Helsinki.'

'How the devil did you work that one?'

'Charm, old boy. I followed one of the Finnish secretaries home in my car one evening. I thought she might just be my type. She stopped at the Marski bar for a drink. I went in after her. We got on fine over a few drinks. She thinks I'll soon bed her. I'm not sure I need go that far. Want the details?'

'Of course I do. Stop being tantalizing. Give me the lot.'

'The Finn girl told me Peggy Vanderheld knows more about INCUBUS operations than any other employee below the rank of vice president. She also told me Vanderheld is blazing with hatred about the way Hauser kicked her out. She's still in Helsinki. I even managed to wheedle Vanderheld's address out of my girl friend.' Marler took out a small pad, scribbled on it. 'Here it is, if you think it'll be of any use. You know Helsinki pretty well, don't you?'

'Yes.'

'Then the easiest way to reach her apartment block is to catch a No. 4 tram. Go to the end of the line, get off, walk down towards the sea and it's the last block on the right. I got that out of the girl friend, too.'

'Thanks, Marler. This could be the break I've been hoping for. I suppose you'd laugh in my face if I asked you what brings you out here?'

'No. I'm tracking some dangerous ex-secret police types – thrown out of a job when Communism collapsed in the Balkans and East Germany. One is Ion Manescu . . .'

'The Romanian. I've heard of that bastard. Expert in a

nice line of torture among other talents. Why look here?'

Marler told him about the sighting of Manescu boarding the Travemünde ferry reported to Tweed, the ferry sailing for Helsinki. About his interview with Mauno Sarin, Chief of the Protection Police, who had deviously pointed him towards INCUBUS.

'So that's why you were watching their HQ?' Newman remarked.

'It was a long shot and it didn't come off. Here is the only picture ever taken of Manescu.'

Newman studied the photograph, frowned, gazed round the bar to where Paula and Dillon were engaged in deep conversation. Then he studied the print again and finally looked up at Marler.

'I can't be sure. I'm probably wrong . . .' He hesitated.

'Go on,' pressed Marler.

'While we were hanging around in Turku waiting for evening before I drove here we were followed. I was sitting inside a café with Paula. This character I called Straw Hat was pretending to examine the clothes in a men's outfitters on the other side of the street. It was very hot and for a few seconds he took off his hat to mop his forehead. It was bloody hot, as it is here. I caught a glimpse of his face and it looked damned like this photo. But without a moustache.'

'He could have shaved that off,' Marler said quickly. 'How can you be sure he was working for INCUBUS?'

'Because, as I told you, it was an INCUBUS juggernaut which tried to turn us into mashed potato on Route E3. That links Straw Hat direct to INCUBUS.'

'Of course.' Marler went to the bar, ordered fresh drinks, came back and sat down again. 'It's strange,' he continued, 'but before I saw Sarin I'd have said we were working on two separate operations. Now I wonder. Where do you think Ion Manescu will turn up next?'

'If it was him, here in Helsinki.' Newman stood up,

folded the sheet of paper with the address on it, put it in his wallet. 'This information about Manescu should go to Tweed.'

'He's disappeared,' Marler said quietly. 'I called Monica and she said he'd come here. I checked every hotel two days ago. No trace.'

'Check them over again,' Newman advised.

'Where are you going? I'm staying at this hotel, incidentally.'

'I was about to ask you that. Where am I going? To talk to Peggy Vanderheld.'

The theatre opposite the Marski was a modern circular edifice, its walls covered with creeper. Peggy Vanderheld, wearing a chestnut-coloured suit, left the theatre and walked to the No. 4 tram stop. A large brown Buick moved from the kerb, crawled slowly after her.

She boarded the tram and looked out of the window as it moved out of town. She was on the right-hand side and watched people strolling in the green park, the huge granite boulders rearing up out of the earth. Behind the tram the brown Buick drifted in its wake.

She couldn't make up her mind what to do about Hauser. While watching the performance her mind had been free of problems. Now they all kept flooding back. A double pension? That was a load of money for life – if she kept her mouth shut. Screw that, she thought, I want to kick Hauser in the balls. That mistaken remark Carver had made about not writing her memoirs for a big fat advance from New York had opened up new horizons.

The tram left the city behind, entered a wooded suburban area. She was the only passenger to leave the tram at the end of the line. With her mind in a whirl she didn't notice the Buick which had parked a dozen yards

231

up the road. Nor did she see the cream BMW parked beyond the stationary tram near the sea.

Inside it Newman sat behind the wheel, all the windows open in an attempt to counter the torrid heat of late evening. He recognized Vanderheld at once from the photo Marler had shown him. Earlier he had pressed the button for her apartment outside the locked front door. No answer.

He sat quite still as she entered the block. He had noticed the brown Buick, a big job, which had followed the tram and then parked. No one alighted from the vehicle. Beyond the amber-tinted windscreen he saw the silhouette of a chauffeur wearing a peaked cap and dark glasses.

He waited a few minutes, closed the windows, got out, locked the car and walked up the steps to the entrance. Once again he pressed the bell on the speakphone alongside the card with *Vanderheld* inscribed in neat script.

'Who the hell is it now?' a feminine voice with an American accent demanded.

'Robert Newman, foreign correspondent. I'd much appreciate ten minutes of your time. It concerns an investigation I'm making.'

A pause. Newman carefully said nothing more.

'An investigation into what?' Vanderheld demanded.

'Something too serious for me to discuss standing in the open.'

'Ten minutes. Not a second more.'

A buzzer sounded. Newman pushed the door open into the lobby, heard it close automatically behind him as he ran up the staircase. She was standing in the doorway of her apartment, ready to slam the door in his face. Instead she stood aside and he walked in to a modern apartment, comfortably furnished without clutter. A place for everything and everything in its place. The home of a professional businesswoman. He perched on the arm of the chair she ushered him to.

About five feet nine, Newman estimated, a slim figure clad in a lightweight brown suit. Sheer black tights, high-heeled shoes and a mass of coiffured black hair. Good bone structure, a full mouth, bright red lipstick. Early forties and a handsome woman. She stripped off her jacket, exposing well-formed breasts, placed it carefully over the back of a chair.

'I recognize you from pictures I've seen in the papers a few years back. You've worn well.'

'Thank you . . .'

'An investigation into what?'

She stood gazing down at him from a distance of six feet, her hands on her hips. There was a challenging note in her tone. She lit a cigarette, remained standing, one arm beneath her breasts, the other holding the cigarette.

'An investigation into INCUBUS.' He took a quick decision, began telling her about the murder of Sandy, the proximity of Livingstone Manor, the murder of Ed Riverton, his interviews with the two English businessmen forced to sell out.

'Why come to me?' she asked. 'What is there in it for me?'

'Your chance to get back at Hauser. I blast his operation wide open in *Der Spiegel*. But I need information. Hard facts.'

'I'll think about it. Where can I reach you?'

'I'm staying at The Palace.'

'And why, may I ask, Mr Newman, are you doing all this? I recall you wrote that huge international bestseller, *Kruger: The Computer That Failed*. That must have made you financially independent for life.'

'It did.'

'So why? You don't need to work as a foreign correspondent any more. *Why?*'

'I told you,' he reminded her. 'Because of Sandy. I think Hauser is linked to her murder. If he is, I'm going to bring him down.'

'I see.' She stubbed out her cigarette while Newman watched her. He rather liked Peggy Vanderheld. She was attractive, had brains and guts. 'Come back and meet me here tomorrow night at the same time,' she decided. 'I'm going out to the theatre again. I want to sleep on all this.'

He stood up. 'Sleep well . . .'

Newman settled himself behind the wheel of the BMW. The brown Buick was still parked further up the street. As he cruised past it slowly he glanced at the driver. The chauffeur was slumped in front of the wheel, peaked cap dipped over his head. He appeared to be asleep.

Newman had a good look at the vehicle. It was a very large American job: a LeSabre estate wagon. A four-door car, it had brown wood bodywork below the tinted windows, sleeping space in the rear and a chrome rack on the roof.

As Newman drove on through the late evening, still in daylight, the main stem of Mannerheimintie traffic-free, the air crystal clear, into the city and past the Marski Hotel, the heat so intense his shirt was pasted to his back, he wondered about Tweed. Where could he be at this moment?

23

Tweed sat with Nield in the basement restaurant beyond the bar area in the Marski. They had flown in from Leningrad and Tweed had chosen the Marski because he'd never stayed there before.

'Nice to get back to familiar food, Pete,' he remarked as he tucked in to fried chicken and saffron rice. 'Finnish cooking is marvellous.'

'And that salad we started with was quite something. It fascinated me watching the girl mix it so skilfully . . .'

They occupied a curtained banquette at the far end of the restaurant so they were able to talk openly. Nield was relieved to be back in Finland but Tweed seemed more interested in his meal. Occasionally he would stop to look at three postcards – on the back of each he had written a name. Kazbek. Zaikov. Dikoyan. It helped him to sift his thoughts by having the names in front of him.

'Which one?' asked Nield.

'Difficult to be sure . . .'

Tweed looked up as a well-built, clean-shaven man in his thirties, wearing an open-necked white shirt and grey slacks stopped at their table and looked back at Tweed. Harry Butler. Nield goggled at the appearance of his old partner. Tweed shifted his plate and glass further along the banquette and merely invited his subordinate to join them.

'What brings you up here, Harry?' he enquired.

'Howard was worried about you – really worried. He ordered me off the job of protecting Evelyn Lennox in Walberswick and sent me here in case you needed reinforcements. And Monica is out of her mind with anxiety about what's happening to you.'

'Not any more. I made a brief call to her as soon as we got back to Helsinki. We've been abroad.'

'You're abroad now,' Butler pointed out in his impassive way.

'There's abroad and abroad.' Tweed smiled. 'Pete would agree with me, but don't ask him questions. How did you find me?'

'By checking every hotel in Helsinki daily since I arrived. I said you were a business associate and I wasn't sure of the date of your arrival.'

'Very diplomatic. And I'm glad you're here – although I'm not happy about Evelyn being left unguarded. But your presence is welcome. I have a feeling that when the crisis breaks it will explode here. We may need every man we can get.'

'Then you'll be glad to hear Marler is based at The Palace. Monica called me at the Hesperia and told me where to contact him.'

'That's a big plus,' Tweed commented as though the information that Marler was in Finland was news to him.

'And that's not all,' Butler continued in his placid manner. 'Marler told me Bob Newman and Paula came in recently. They're also staying at The Palace. What they are here for I don't know.'

Tweed nodded. He realized Butler had been careful not to ask why. Butler was reliable: he knew that at times Tweed operated several groups independently on a cell system similar to that used by the Russians. One cell might have a different task from another. Only Tweed decided the moment when battle had to be joined, when his forces must be merged into one big spearhead group to attack the target.

'No coffee for me tonight,' he decided. 'I need the sleep. Harry, stay at the Hesperia so I can call you the moment an emergency arises.'

'You're expecting one soon?' Nield asked.

'Once Hauser discovers the opposition is on his doorstep – that's when the balloon goes up.'

The following day Peggy Vanderheld phoned Newman at The Palace. She had slept badly the previous night, her mind churning over her problems. She was still unsure whether to blow the whistle on Hauser to Newman.

'I'd like you to delay calling on me at where we met yesterday,' she said crisply. 'I find my theatre ticket is for tomorrow night,' she lied. 'So I'm going out of town to see a friend. Maybe I'll see you tomorrow night. Don't do anything until I call you.'

'Anything the lady wants . . .'

Newman put down the phone in his room and frowned. No point in pushing a woman – you had to let her take her time, make up her mind one way or the other. And he and Paula had an appointment to see Tweed at the Marski late in the afternoon. The sooner Tweed knew about the two murderous attempts on his life the better. And what could go wrong during a twenty-four-hour delay?

The weather changed in late afternoon. The azure dome of sky vanished. The sun no longer shone. A heavy overcast hung over Helsinki and the murky sky looked like grey smoke. The atmosphere became horribly humid, pressing down on the city like an iron lid.

Peggy Vanderheld had heard the weather forecast and when she left the theatre again in late evening she was prepared for the heavy drizzle which had begun to fall. Over her brown suit she wore a cream raincoat bought at Stockmann's, the leading Helsinki department store. Wrapped round her dark hair she was protected with a highly coloured scarf she had also purchased at Stockmann's.

She was walking towards the tram stop when she noticed several yards ahead another woman of similar build who also wore a raincoat exactly like hers. Well, Stockmann's must sell a lot of them. What surprised her was the woman also had exactly the same scarf wrapped over her head. Peggy *had* thought the scarf was exclusive when she chose it. At the time it had been the only one on the counter. Presumably all the others had already been grabbed earlier. I suppose she's also wearing the brown suit I got from Stockmann's, she thought ruefully.

The woman in front of her was boarding a No. 4 tram. Peggy ran to catch it: they came only infrequently. Out of breath, she jumped aboard, purchased a ticket from the driver, slid it inside the slot machine which stamped the time and sat down.

The woman dressed so like her was sitting five seats in front of her. Peggy was so absorbed in thinking about Newman she never noticed the brown Buick which had been cruising behind the tram. As it approached the last stop but one she never saw the Buick suddenly speed up, overtake the tram, driving on to a point near the last tram stop.

Peggy glanced out, realized it had stopped raining, decided she needed a little exercise. Unusually, she left the tram at the last but one stop. Vaguely she was aware that the other woman dressed so like herself was still aboard.

Her long legs carried her swiftly along the tree-lined sidewalk. The air was fresher now, the goddamned humidity had evaporated. Earlier it had been like moving through treacle. As she turned into her apartment block entrance she was vaguely conscious her 'twin' was walking down to the shore near the scrubbing station. No one else about.

She took a quick shower, smoked one last cigarette, fell into bed and seconds after her head hit the pillow she was asleep. The sound of police cars woke her at seven the following morning.

Curious, she pulled back the curtains of the window overlooking the sea. She stared at another glorious sunny day in amazement. Clustered round the scrubbing board platform area was a cordon of police cars. A crowd of early risers, some men carrying briefcases stood close to the cars. Dressing quickly, she went downstairs and walked to see what all the fuss was about.

More police cars were arriving, uniformed men jumping out, trying to form a barrier to hold back the crowd. Peggy walked slowly forward. A lint-haired girl clad in denims and a windcheater open at the front was scribbling in a notebook. Peggy stood beside her.

'What is going on? Why are you making notes?'

'You live in that apartment block?' the girl asked, pushing her glasses further up her nose. 'I thought I saw you come out of it.'

'Yes, I'm a resident. I have an apartment . . .'

'Did you hear anything unusual in the night? Or maybe in the evening late on?'

'Why? Who are you?'

'I'm a reporter on the newspaper *Iltalehti*. A woman has been murdered on the scrubbing platform. She was garrotted.' The girl drew a finger swiftly across her throat. 'Then, from what I can gather, the back of her skull was bashed in.' She looked round. 'Oh, God, here comes the TV crew.'

Peggy glanced over her shoulder. A white van had pulled up a few yards up the hill, well clear of the police cordon. The rear doors opened, men carried out a wooden platform with two steps leading up to its top. A man with a mobile TV camera jumped up the steps, aimed the camera over the heads of the crowd, took pictures, jumped down as a man in a linen suit and a hard-faced woman began talking to him.

Peggy strolled over to the van, climbed up the steps and had a perfect view of the scrubbing platform. Police photographers were taking pictures. On the lower level of the scrubbing platform sprawled the lifeless body of a woman, face down. Peggy gazed at the horror, hypnotized. She was looking at *herself*.

It was the woman in the cream raincoat like her own. Round her head was the highly coloured scarf, again like her own. But the garish colours seemed stronger in the brilliant sunlight. The scarf was soaked in blood. As if in a nightmare Peggy recalled how the woman had got off at the last tram stop, the one she always got off at. Except that last evening she had left the tram one stop earlier. She saw the woman walking down the street towards the sea . . .

She felt faint, almost toppled off the perch. Before anyone saw her she forced her stiff legs to go down the steps. She walked slowly up the hill, went through the entrance to her apartment block in a daze.

She sat inside her living room for half an hour, smoking cigarettes. Then she picked up the phone after consulting the directory.

'Palace Hotel,' a man's voice said.

'I want to speak to Mr Robert Newman who is staying with you . . .'

'Newman here. Who is this?'

'Peggy Vanderheld. Newman, could you come and see me at my apartment tomorrow evening? Same time as you called before.'

'I'll be there.'

24

'So you bungled the job,' Hauser shouted at Galvone. 'You let Newman reach Helsinki alive despite my specific order. Frank, it's not good enough. I'm beginning to worry about you.'

The two men sat inside Hauser's office. Beyond the picture window the sea was dark and hostile, large waves rolling in to the shore. Galvone sat opposite his chief with the desk between them. Hauser tilted his jaw, clenched his teeth on his cigarette holder.

'We don't know Newman has come to Helsinki,' Galvone ventured. 'OK. He was on Route E3 driving in this direction from Turku . . .'

'So where the hell else would he go? And Manescu isn't the hot shot he was bummed up to be.'

'You could talk with him. He's in the building . . .'

Hauser erupted. 'Here! Are you mad? There must never be any direct link someone could trace between people like Manescu and INCUBUS . . .'

'I had to take a quick decision,' Galvone said defensively. 'Manescu was worried about the truck fiasco when it tried to run down Newman . . .'

'Well at least the schmuck of a driver is dead,' Hauser said savagely.

'True. No danger of him talking. As I was trying to explain, Manescu drove here to report to me because he was worried. It was a complete surprise to me when he turned up here. No need to worry, I've put him in a locked room at Level Five . . .'

'Then get him out of it. Now! Drive him to the airport. Get the chopper to airlift him back into the jungle where I met him. You've bought a summer house in the woods and he can simmer there until we need him again. Ziegler is out there too?'

'Yes. I bought three summer homes in the same area. Very remote. The others are there – including the two Czechs, who were STB men, three more *Securitate* and Irina Serov.'

'Serov was with Manescu. How come she went into the woods while Manescu blunders in here!'

'Well . . .' Galvone had hoped this question wouldn't be asked. 'Irina has a mind of her own. She *was* a colonel in the KGB. She decided she should vanish . . .'

'So!' Hauser exploded. 'She has more savvy than Manescu – more than you. It looks to me as though maybe we ought to put Irina in charge of the whole operation. Yes, I like the idea.'

'Manescu won't like it,' Galvone warned.

Hauser, shirt sleeves rolled up above the elbows, exposing his powerful arms, leaned forward. He spoke with the cigarette in his mouth, a sure sign of his wrath.

'Frank, who cares a shit what Manescu likes? What he likes is the big money I'm paying him. For that he takes orders and likes *them*.'

'He did organize those bombings in Prague, Bucharest and . . .'

'Frank! We don't talk about things like that. Now go down to Level Five and get Manescu to hell out of my HQ. You can manage that?'

'I'm going now . . .'

Alone in his office, Hauser took out of a drawer a copy of the Finnish newspaper, *Iltalehti*. Splashed over the front page was a huge photograph of the woman lying on the scrubbing platform. Hauser had had the text translated and the typed English version was inside the newspaper.

242

He read the first few words of the article again, his face grim.

Anna Jarva, secretary who worked with a well-known Finnish firm of timber merchants, was found murdered . . .

Anna Jarva! The wrong woman had been killed. So his own ex-personal assistant, Peggy Vanderheld, was still walking around alive. And with all those company secrets locked up inside her clever skull. What made it worse was that Carver had reported she didn't seem interested in the double pension he had offered her. That was what had triggered off Hauser's decision that something should be done about Vanderheld. Something permanent.

Galvone unlocked the door at Level Five and walked into a luxuriously furnished room with a bathroom leading off. Manescu was sprawled on a couch, reading an American comic paper. The bony-faced Romanian looked up at his visitor and went on reading the comic.

Galvone padded over to him slowly, reached down, took away the comic. Manescu, his face tanned from the sun, wore a check shirt, slacks and special shoes with concealed metal tips in the toes. Strapped under his left trouser leg was a sheath with a knife: he was right-handed and the sheath was attached to the inner side of his leg.

'Time to return to the backwoods,' Galvone told him.

'What about Newman?'

'We can work something else out later. At the moment you must leave this building unseen. Collect your satchel and follow me . . .'

At the exit to the building Galvone ordered Manescu to stay inside. He strolled out and the glare of the sun blinded him. He shielded his eyes, looked carefully round. No one in sight. The car park was almost empty. His red Cadillac was parked next to Hauser's stretched black limo and there were a couple of other cars. He ran back into the vast entrance hall.

'Come out now. Follow me to the Cadillac, get in the front passenger seat as soon as I unlock. Make with the feet.'

Inside the Saab parked in the copse of firs above INCU-BUS's HQ, Marler was drinking out of his plastic bottle of mineral water when he saw below the man emerge. It was the last day Marler was going to keep up his surveillance. The interior of the Saab was like a furnace but Marler was tireless. He reached for the camera with the zoom lens, aimed it, lowered it.

'I already have you in my photo album, Mr Frank Galvone,' he said to himself.

He was relaxing when he suddenly sat up straight. Something odd about the way Galvone was staring round. Marler reached for his camera again. Galvone disappeared inside, came out again almost at once as Marler aimed his camera. But his time he was not alone.

'My God!' Marler said to himself. 'At the last moment, on stage Mr Ion Manescu . . .'

Manescu was also blinded by the sun's glare. He stopped to haul dark glasses out of his pocket, perch them on his nose. During the time it took him to do this Marler snapped off six shots. And there behind Manescu's head was the company sign, INCUBUS Oy.

Galvone walked back, grabbed Manescu by the arm, hurried him to the Cadillac. There was a brief pause while he unlocked the car, then Manescu disappeared inside the front and Galvone ran round, jumped in behind the wheel, slammed the door and fired the engine.

Seconds later he was driving at speed past the gate the guard had opened, skidding round on to the road and roaring off out of sight in the direction of the city.

'Terrible driving,' Marler commented to himself. 'And

about time I left. That camera shop will have to work fast producing these new prints.'

Hauser was in a mood of cold fury when Galvone returned from seeing Manescu aboard the helicopter. Outside it was still daylight. Galvone had prior warning of Hauser's state of mind when he saw the number of cigarette butts crushed out in the crystal ash tray.

'Manescu is a world away from Helsinki,' he reported.

'Goddamnit! That was a real balls-up on Route E3, Frank. You even used an INCUBUS juggernaut – which Newman must have seen. That ties us in to the attempt on his life.'

'Manescu organized that. But you can't blame him either. Had he hired a truck he'd have had to show identification and you wouldn't have wanted that. Even if he'd used one of the Turku staff to do the hiring they'd have had to provide identification. That would have been dangerous.'

Hauser lit a fresh cigarette, regarded Galvone through the smoke. It had always been the same right back from the early days when he'd sweated to accumulate the money to bid for a tiny bank in La Jolla in California. If you wanted a job done properly, you had to do it yourself.

Now his organization was so vast he had to rely on executives to carry out his instructions. And even though he handed out the biggest pay cheques of any company in the world they were still second rate. He sat back, forced himself to relax. He'd faced plenty of crises before and come through triumphantly. This one would be no different. Now he was thinking calmly and fast.

'The first thing to do is to locate Newman. Put as many men on the job as necessary. Check every hotel. And I do mean *every* hotel. We have his photo. Run off a whole load of copies. He may be staying under another name. Use money to get receptionists to talk, show them his picture. I

245

want Helsinki turned over. Don't you interrupt me, Frank. Manescu gave you descriptions of the girl and the man who came off the Turku ferry with him? Good. Tell the bastards who go out to use their eyes for once. I wish to God I could do the job myself. Frank, why are you still sitting there? Get on it. Now!'

The phone rang as Galvone left the office. Hauser picked it up, asked his operator who the devil it was now at this hour? 'A Mr Robert Newman, sir . . .'

At The Palace Hotel Newman was perched on the edge of his bed. In shirt sleeves, the windows wide open, he mopped his forehead with one hand while gripping the phone with the other. His tone was harsh.

'That you, Hauser?'

'Franklin D. Hauser speaking.'

'Let's cut out the bullshit, shall we? I'm at The Palace. I think it's time we met again, talked. Tomorrow suit you?'

'Certainly, Mr Newman. What time would you suggest? At your convenience, of course.'

'Noon. At your headquarters. Is that OK?'

'I shall look forward to renewing our acquaintance. Could you give me some hint as to what we'll be discussing?'

'Information I've dug up about your operations. Noon tomorrow. Good-night, Hauser.'

In his office Hauser put down the phone, then called his operator and told her to intercept Galvone before he could leave the building. A few minutes later his vice president hurried into his office, then stopped. Hauser was gazing out of the window. It was the first time Galvone had ever seen his chief look stunned.

In his room at the Marski, Tweed listened while Newman gave him a terse account of his experiences since leaving

London. On a nearby couch sat Paula, chin cupped in her hand, listening. Cord Dillon occupied a chair against the wall where he could watch his three companions.

Newman checked his watch as he concluded his account. 'I'll have to leave in a minute. An appointment with Vanderheld.' He grinned. 'Oh, by the way, I borrowed Harry Butler. He's parked outside Peggy Vanderheld's apartment block. I don't want her doing a disappearing act.'

'I think this meeting with Hauser is impetuous, too early in the game,' Tweed informed him.

'Don't agree.' Newman's expression changed, became stubborn. 'His minions tried to kill me twice, as I've told you. And,' he looked at the couch, 'the second time Paula and Cord would have died. So Hauser is a billionaire. So what? I think I threw him off balance. He's had the initiative so far – tracking me across Europe. Time I confronted him.'

'You have absolutely no evidence to link him with any misdemeanour, let alone assassination attempts,' Tweed persisted. 'What we need is hard evidence. You're going in with not one damn thing to hit him with.'

'I've made the appointment.' Newman stood up. 'And it was an INCUBUS juggernaut which tried to mow us down.'

'Which they will already have reported as stolen. If I could I'd take you off this operation, Bob. You're too personally involved – with the appalling murder of Sandy driving you on.'

'You can't take me off anything,' Newman snapped. 'I don't belong to you – or your organization.'

'Cool it, Bob,' Paula said quietly. 'Tweed is only thinking of your safety.'

'Safety first?' Newman rapped back.

'From where I sit Tweed is right,' Dillon interjected with unexpected support. 'You have to time these operations. You're charging about like a mad bull.'

'OK. So that's what I'm doing.' As he turned to leave Newman spoke to Paula.

'Sorry I snapped at you. I realize you're concerned.'

'And next time,' Tweed told him, leaning forward, 'kindly ask my permission before you hijack Butler.' He paused. 'Even so, I think you got that right. Vanderheld may just prove to be the weak link in Hauser's chain.'

'Newman is in town,' Hauser told Adam Carver as they sat next to each other on a couch in the penthouse office. 'I was just about to have every hotel checked to see if he was here when what the hell do you think happens?'

'No idea.'

Adam Carver was wary. He sensed Hauser was in a rage and he'd always trodden carefully on these rare occasions. You never could be sure which way the American would jump in a crisis situation.

'The bastard actually phones me here, suggests he comes to see me tomorrow. He even tells me he's staying at The Palace.'

'No reason why he shouldn't,' Carver responded smoothly. 'He'd guess you'd check his whereabouts so he tells you . . .'

'He's got a lot of gall.' Hauser quietened down. 'You're a Brit. What's your impression of Newman? You had a chance to assess him that night he dropped in on us at Livingstone Manor.'

Carver lit a cigarette with his strong, well-shaped hands. He gave his answer a bit of thought.

'Very experienced in grilling people. A lone wolf. Used to operating on his own – his days as a foreign correspondent, a top one, would teach him that. He knows his way around. A determined and resourceful opponent.'

'Sound as though you admire the crud,' Hauser grumbled.

'I'm simply saying he's a man it would be a great mistake

to underestimate.' Carver was cool as ice while Hauser stood up and prowled restlessly round the huge room. 'Another point,' he continued, 'it would also be a great mistake to alienate him. He carries a lot of clout with the media.'

'Maybe.'

Carver kept quiet. He had answered the question without frills. He was wearing a pale grey silk suit and he uncrossed his legs and adjusted the crease. He had half a dozen silk suits. The trouble was they creased easily and cost him a fortune at the cleaners. But they impressed women and Adam Carver was a great ladies' man. He had mistresses in London, Brussels and Frankfurt.

'Time to go over on to the offensive,' Hauser decided. 'Pussy-footing isn't my style. So this is what we do next . . .'

25

It was late evening, the light that glorious clarity you only found in Finland glowing over the fir-fringed sea, as Newman got off Tram No. 4 at the last stop. Parked on the far side of the road was the hired BMW, opposite the apartment block where Vanderheld lived.

Butler sat behind the wheel with the window down. His hand was tapping a tattoo on the window ledge. For a brief moment as Newman glanced across the road he gave the thumbs up sign. Peggy Vanderheld was safe.

She answered the speakphone immediately, released the front door, and again was waiting for him in the doorway to her apartment. He smiled, walked inside and she closed and locked the door. She was wearing a

form-fitting black dress which outlined her figure provocatively. The garment was strapless and her beautifully
shaped shoulders were bare, the colour of ivory. Newman
was never sure what kept the damned things up. Watch it,
he warned himself. This time his reception was quite
different.

'Do sit down, Mr Newman. What would you like to
drink? Tea, coffee, or something stronger – maybe that
would be a nice idea?'

She waved an arm towards a large cocktail cabinet
which was now open, exposing a huge array of drinks,
including just about every known liqueur as far as Newman could see.

'A strong Scotch wouldn't go amiss. I've had a some-
what trying day.'

'I think I'll join you. Straight up? Fine . . .'

As she poured the drinks he glanced round the room.
On the occasional table close to the couch she had
ushered him to lay a copy of *Iltalehti*. The newspaper was
spread out exposing the front page with the huge photograph of Anna Jarva sprawled on the scrubbing platform.
Peggy followed his eyes as she sat beside him, handed him
his glass.

'That should have been me,' she said and clinked his
glass.

Newman had noticed that when she was pouring the
drinks her hand had trembled, tinkling the bottle against
a glass. He studied her as he sipped his drink. She looked
good, make-up skilfully applied, but he thought he detected dark circles under her eyes.

'What did you mean when you said that?' he enquired.

'That murdered woman is wearing clothes just like I
wore on my way back from the theatre . . .'

Speaking rapidly, her voice slightly high-pitched, she
described in detail her journey from the moment she left
the theatre, ending with the moment when she had

250

stumbled down the steps from the TV platform after seeing the body. Newman listened in silence, his eyes holding hers, registering every minute of her macabre journey.

'I see,' he said eventually. 'And you're convinced . . .'

'For Christ's sake!' she blazed. 'Isn't it obvious? Hauser sent a hired assassin to kill me. Because I know too much about his crooked operation.'

'Crooked? Now do you really mean that?'

He let the scepticism show in his voice deliberately and the ploy worked. She swung round on the couch until she was almost touching him, her dark eyes glaring.

'I worked for INCUBUS for ten years, five as Hauser's personal assistant. I ought to know how they run that outfit. Hauser divides the world into winners and losers. OK. A lot of people do that but it depends on the methods you use. He'll use any method on God's earth to get something he's after – and a few maybe God never heard of. I could see he was going to kick me out weeks before it happened. He was too nice to me. So I gradually built up a dossier of items of his more shady operations. I took photocopies of documents – so after I'd gone he wouldn't realize I had those records. Including a highly secret file on some creep called Popescu . . .'

'Who did you say?'

'Popescu. Damned stupid name. Comes from some-where in the Balkans. Is it important?'

'Might be. Anything might be.' Newman kept his tone casual. 'Popescu. Sounds Romanian.'

'It is. He came from Bucharest.'

'I'm surprised that Hauser, a man I've heard plays his moves close to his chest, let you in on so many sensitive topics.'

'He didn't. I overheard things. And he's normally careful but he has an advanced electronic intercom he

251

sometimes forgets to switch off. I made tapes of some of his confidential conversations.'

'Where is –' He nearly said Manescu. 'Popescu now?'

'No bloody idea. I do know he travelled some route planned by one of his executives . . .'

'Which one?'

'That I don't know. As I was saying, Popescu came in aboard a ferry from Germany direct to Finland. And he wasn't the only one who used that route.'

'Where are those tapes you mentioned, that dossier? Here in your apartment?'

'God no! INCUBUS have turned over more people's apartments to search for something than I've had hot breakfasts. I've stored them in a deposit vault in a Helsinki bank. Not the bank I normally use. I could take you there, hand them to you. The material will sink Hauser. What do I get for it? I could make a lot of money writing a book and selling it in New York.'

'Except you'd never live to complete the book. The vital thing now for you to do is to vanish. I'll think of somewhere if you'll trust me.'

'I have an option?'

Newman indicated the newspaper picture. 'What do you think?'

'I suppose you're right. You propose I go into hiding?'

'Yes. With protection.'

She stood up, went over to the window, looked out, came back and sat close to Newman. He lit a fresh cigarette for her and saw her hand tremble. She took a deep drag.

'I have news for you. I'm being watched at this moment. A guy in a white BMW on the other side of the street.'

'That's my protection for you. The chap's a pro. His name is Harry Butler, in case for some reason he calls on you.'

'My!' She leaned closer to him and he caught a faint whiff of perfume. 'You do look after a woman. I'd like to show my appreciation for that . . .'

'Then perhaps you can answer a tricky question.' Newman had recalled what Chief Inspector Buchanan had said to him back in England. 'I don't suppose you brought any appointments diaries with you and put them in that safety deposit.'

Peggy studied the end of her cigarette. 'As a matter of fact I did. Not that it was really necessary. I'm blessed with an encyclopaedic memory for dates. I can reel them off for months back.'

'Let me test you. I'm trying to identify an executive at the INCUBUS HQ here who was absent on two dates. On *both* dates, I stress. Although you probably don't know about the movements of Popescu . . .'

'I do. I read his file before I photocopied it. Shoot.'

'One date is the day an executive was here in Helsinki – I put it badly a moment ago – I stress was *here* on the night when Ed Riverton was murdered . . .'

'That I recall. And the other one?'

'It was a date close to that one . . .' He gave her the date when Sandy was murdered in the Suffolk bell tower, trying to keep his tone offhand. Then he waited while Peggy stared into the distance. He could almost hear the wheels revolving inside her mind.

'Let me get this straight,' she said after awhile. 'You want someone who, as far as I know, was present the night Ed Riverton was garrotted and thrown into North Harbour. You also want the same person who was *absent* from Helsinki, maybe abroad, on the date you specified?'

'That's exactly what I'm after.'

'Tell you later. After I'm sure of the protection.'

*   *   *

Newman was late up the following morning, was finishing his breakfast in The Palace dining room at 9.30a.m. when Marler joined him.

'Losing your grip, old boy?' Marler greeted him. 'I had my breakfast at seven and I've done a day's work already.'

'Bully for you,' Newman responded without enthusiasm.

'I've got some additions to my photo album in my room. Care to see them? When you've eventually finished, of course.'

'Of course.'

Reluctantly, Newman admitted to himself that Marler looked very chipper. He wore a well-cut tropical drill suit, an open-necked shirt, a pale red silk cravat. His complexion was tanned. He vibrated energy as he lit a cigarette.

'You were damned late in last night, Newman,' he commented. 'I checked in at midnight and your key was still with the concierge. Still no excuse for spending half your life in bed. Oh,' he continued breezily, 'Tweed phoned me. He's nearly going spare – couldn't contact Harry Butler.'

'I know where he is. I'll call in at the Marski and give him the good news.' He finished his coffee. 'Let's look at your new pics. Probably all out of focus, as usual. You're a lousy photographer.'

Which wasn't true: Marler was as expert with a camera as he was with a sniperscope rifle. But the two men had never really liked each other and frequently exchanged insults – just to show nothing had changed.

In Marler's room Newman waited while Marler lifted up the false bottom of his suitcase, revealing a secret compartment. He took out an envelope, produced the three photos of Manescu which had been treated in the Engine Room in the basement of Park Crescent.

'I've seen these before,' Newman complained. 'Mane-scu as he was in Bucharest with a moustache, then minus the 'tache and finally with a beard. What's the point?'

'I took these late yesterday evening looking down on INCUBUS's headquarters.'

He produced six more prints and watched Newman's reaction. Newman stared at them, noted the INCUBUS Oy. sign behind the head of the man Marler had snapped. He looked up.

'This links Ion Manescu directly with Hauser's mob.'

'And Mauno Sarin did point me in the right direction when I visited the Protection Police at Ratakatu. Frankly, I didn't think he was right – and those pics were taken just before I gave up.'

'You didn't by any chance photograph any of their cars?'

'As a matter of fact, chum, I did just that. Mainly to fill in time. Got a shade boring sitting in my Saab hour after hour.'

Marler dived into his envelope again, produced more prints. Newman examined each colour shot. He came to the last one and whistled softly, then held up the print.

'This one of a big brown Buick. That was in the car park?'

'On only one occasion while I was spying on them. A chap in a chauffeur's uniform drove it away. Didn't bother to snap a minion. Seemed pointless.'

'Pity. But you've done marvels.' He looked at Marler. 'I have to visit Tweed at the Marski now. Can I borrow these pics of Manescu – the lot? Plus the one of the brown Buick?'

'Be my guest. Just let me have them back, there's a good chap. My regards to Tweed. Thank the Lord he's surfaced – I somehow found the time to check a few hotels trying to locate him. I'll drop round to see him later. Gentlemen first.'

*   *   *

Tweed stood staring out of the window of his room at the traffic while Newman brought him up to date on recent developments, concentrating on his interview with Peggy Vanderheld and the arrangements he'd made for her safety. Paula sat perched on the edge of the bed, taking it all in.

'Now don't blow your top,' Newman continued. 'I decided we had to move quickly to protect Vanderheld. Butler has taken her aboard a flight to Stockholm. From Arlanda he'll drive her in a hired car to a cottage on the island of Örno in the Swedish archipelago. From what she told me, as you'll have gathered, she's in great danger, and she's a key witness. Harry flies back to Helsinki this evening, so he'll be here if you need him. No time to contact you.'

Tweed swung round. 'You did the right thing. But how did you obtain use of this cottage on Örno?'

'I know the people who own it, a Swedish couple. They have a luxury apartment in the centre of Stockholm. I phoned them and they said I could use the place as long as I liked. Butler will call on them for the key, then drive Peggy via the ferry to the island.'

Cord Dillon had been sitting on a hard-backed chair tilted against a corner of the wall. He made his first comment.

'I guess Newman has done very well. He's secured a potential witness. And he moved fast – hiding Vanderheld away after one attempt on her life was smart.'

'A *potential* witness,' Tweed repeated with a hint of scepticism. 'What about the dossier she spoke of, the diaries, the tapes? Where are they now?'

'Still in the safety deposit in some bank here in Helsinki.'

'Which one?'

'No idea. She wouldn't tell me. But this arrived for me at The Palace this morning by special courier.' Newman produced a key. 'The trouble is I have no idea which bank she used – and, as you know, safety deposit keys are anonymous. Peggy said that was her insurance policy – that we'd continue to guard her while we didn't know where the evidence was.'

Dillon sighed. 'That's one smart cookie.'

'Have you by any chance a copy of her signature?' Tweed enquired.

Newman shook his head. 'No, I thought of that. After she'd told me just before Butler flew her to Sweden. She had told me this key would be delivered today. I asked her to sign a statement that she was travelling with Butler of her own free will. She refused.'

'As I told you,' Dillon repeated, 'one smart cookie. The fun will come when we transport her to the States. Hauser has things pretty well tied up there. We don't know who we can trust. She'll have to be guarded every moment before she testifies in court against Hauser.'

'If she ever does,' Tweed warned him. 'We've got to move in another direction. We need more.'

'Isn't it lucky we have more?' Newman replied. He took out Marler's photographs. 'Manescu has surfaced . . .'

Again Tweed listened in silence as Newman explained how Marler had obtained the pictures. Tweed polished his glasses on a corner of his handkerchief, standing quite still, then walked over and examined the prints with Dillon at his side.

'My congratulations to Marler,' he said eventually. 'These tell *us* that Manescu – and probably Ziegler and the rest of the ex-secret police thugs from various countries – has been recruited by Hauser. So, it's a step forward in our information. But I doubt that these photographs would stand up in court. In Britain.'

'Or in the States,' Dillon said. 'A good attorney could argue they were fakes. And what do they prove? That one

257

man wanted in Romania made a brief appearance at INCUBUS headquarters. Hauser could say that the man gave another name, that he applied for a job with their security apparatus and was turned down. I could kill the case myself.'

Newman stood up. 'Marler is coming over to see you,' he told Tweed. 'Meantime, I have an appointment to keep – with Mr Franklin D. Hauser.'

Paula jumped up. 'I'm coming with you, Bob. I may notice something you'd miss.' She gave him a big smile. 'The well-known feminine instinct. And my powers of observation aren't bad either. Give me five minutes to change and I'll be with you.'

'I don't like the idea,' Tweed said quickly but she had unlocked the door and left the room.

'She may be right,' Newman argued. 'And nothing deadly will happen to us at INCUBUS's headquarters. I'll drop a remark that the police know where we've gone.'

'Still don't like it,' growled Tweed.

He stood gazing out of the window, hands clasped behind his back until Paula returned in less than five minutes. She wore a form-fitting, knee-length printed linen dress with a floral design. Sleeveless, it exposed her shapely arms and round her waist was a leather belt. The ensemble was completed with flesh-coloured tights and gold high-heeled shoes.

'Lady, you look pretty damn sexy,' Dillon commented.

'Thank you, sir.' She curtsyed.

'Both of you, have a care,' Tweed warned.

When they had left he paced backwards and forwards. Dillon sat down in the hard-backed chair in the corner, tilted it.

'You know,' he remarked, 'that bluff Newman is pulling about the police knowing they're there may not work. Hauser does have all his marbles.'

'I agree. I've been thinking about just that.' Tweed went to the phone. 'Which is why I'm calling Mauno Sarin. He's rather fond of Paula.'

26

A high-speed elevator shot Newman and Paula up to the penthouse floor. When the doors opened a woman remarkably like Peggy Vanderheld in poise and manner waited for them in a business suit. Crisp, competent, controlled, the main difference was her blonde hair.

'Mr Hauser is ready to see you now, Mr Newman.' She looked at Paula. 'We were expecting you to come alone.'

'Paula Grey, my assistant. She travels with me most places.'

'I see.'

The woman eyed Paula up and down briefly and her look conveyed a world of understanding. She led them into a vast office with a huge picture window overlooking the sea. The glass doors were open and beyond was a large balcony. Hauser was sitting behind his desk, dressed in a pale blue suit. Adam Carver stood close to the balcony and his eyes lit up as he saw Paula.

'Welcome to INCUBUS, Mr Newman.' Hauser stood up, walked swiftly round his desk, held out his hand. In his left hand he held his cigarette holder; his trademark, Newman thought. 'This is the second time we have had the pleasure of meeting. I trust life has treated you well since last we met?'

'This is my assistant, Paula Grey.'

'And from my point of view it was worth Mr Newman

sparing his valuable time to come and see me so I could meet you, my dear. Come and sit with me on the couch. What would you like to drink?'

'Mineral water, please,' said Paula.

She was aware that the other man by the balcony was studying her with frank interest and pleasure. She disliked his method of scrutiny intensely, felt almost naked under his gaze.

'A double Scotch for me,' said Newman, choosing a high-backed chair facing the couch.

'I'm forgetting my manners,' Hauser went on in the same affable tone. 'This is Adam Carver, one of your countrymen – and Vice President of Banking Operations.'

'Hello,' said Paula and left it at that.

Carver held on to her hand a little too warmly for her liking but she smiled as though enjoying herself. Carver then fetched the drinks as Hauser adjusted his pince-nez higher up the bridge of his strong nose. Since they had entered he had been the soul of amiability, as though meeting Newman again was one of the most pleasurable moments of his life. He stretched an arm along the top of the couch behind Paula who sat between the two men when Carver joined them on the couch.

'To answer your question,' Newman said, holding his glass, 'it has been hazardous in the extreme.'

'What has?' The beaming smile slipped for a fraction of a second.

'You asked if life had treated me well since last we met.'

'Oh, that.' Hauser sipped his martini. 'Hazardous? I'm sorry to hear that. The life of a foreign correspondent, I suppose?'

'A little more than usual. Including surveillance of our movements non-stop. Plus an attempt to kill me aboard the ferry to Turku. To say nothing of nearly being crushed to death by a juggernaut on Route E3. Little things like that.'

'My, my. This sounds dreadful.' Hauser assumed his statesman's expression. 'It does sound as though you've provoked a determined enemy, Mr Newman.'

Adam Carver leaned forward, after watching Paula's crossed legs. 'Maybe you should seek some kind of protection, Mr Newman. Yours sounds a dangerous occupation.'

'Oh, I can look after myself.' Newman stared at Hauser. 'To give you one example, I told the police I was visiting your headquarters. They like to know where I am after what happened.'

'Really? You surprise me. I'd have said this was one place where you could feel perfectly safe.' He beamed at Paula. 'You feel quite safe, I hope, my dear?'

'Depends what you mean by safe,' she responded, gazing sideways at Carver.

Adam Carver took her by the arm. 'I think maybe Mr Newman has business to talk over with Mr Hauser. Come and look at the view from the balcony. It's especially spectacular on a day like this . . .'

She allowed herself to be guided on to the balcony which was wide and stretched beyond the window opening. Carver led her to a swing seat at the far end, still holding her arm with one hand while he grasped his drink with the other. Paula glanced over the rail before she sat down. The sheer drop was like a precipice, brought on a feeling of vertigo.

'Sit down, please. A lot of people find this height a trifle awesome.'

'Or awful?' she suggested sweetly as he sat beside her.

'You have a way with words. I like your dress. Perfect for a day like this.' He took hold of her left hand. 'Really you're dream-like.

She withdrew her hand, smiled. 'That belongs to me.'

261

'Very good.' He grinned. 'I know this may sound a bit fast. But would you like to have dinner with me tonight? I admit I'm overstepping the mark but I'm appalled that this may be my only chance.'

'I'll think about it.' She sipped her drink. 'I've thought about it. Collect me from the lobby of the Hesperia. Seven o'clock. Tonight.'

'Great . . .'

Inside the office Newman had refused Hauser's offer to join him on the couch, staying in the high-backed chair. He was inwardly experiencing a sensation of cold fury. Meeting Hauser again brought back to him their last interview way back at Livingstone Manor, the image of Sandy in the bell tower hanging from her extended neck, her eyes and tongue protruding.

'You might like to know I've talked to the ex-owners of Bennington Machine Tools and Manningham Electronics – both of them forced by illegal methods to sell out to your organization,' he said brutally.

There was a brief flicker in the cold blue eyes. Hauser then raised a hand to his forehead as though trying to recall something. He smiled broadly, waved his hand in a dismissive gesture.

'Neither name means anything to me.' He leaned forward and smiled again. 'You must realize that with a company as large as mine I delegate many small deals to my executives . . .'

'I didn't say they were small companies. Why did you make that assumption?' he demanded aggressively.

'Can't say I too much like your tone, your attitude. And I think you ought to be careful of throwing around that word "illegal". I have an army of attorneys. They could ruin you tomorrow.'

'They could try. But the publicity could be damaging to your whited sepulchre reputation.' Newman sipped a little of his drink. 'It might even ruin you tomorrow. I don't think you yet control the world's media.'

'Mind if I take off my jacket?' Hauser beamed again. 'It really is a very hot day. Ah, that's better. Now let's get down to the bottom line. Let me give you a few words of advice, Mr Newman. I get the impression you're thinking of going up against what is a global organization, an international world-wide power structure . . .'

'*Power*. That's the key word, isn't it? Money no longer means much to you – you're so loaded you think you've got the Midas touch. What you get your kicks out of now is the acquisition of more and more power. At anybody's expense. No holds barred . . .'

'Business is a jungle,' Hauser interjected, his facial muscles tensed.

'Oh, I know that. The whole of life is. But in moderate degree. You're bringing the jungle into the whole of Europe. At least I'm damned sure that's your plan. You're Public Enemy Number One, Hauser. Men and women are just counters to be moved on your huge chessboard, to be thrown away when they're no longer any use.'

'Women?' Hauser's tone was contemptuous. 'Marriage is a trap women lay for men. OK. So one time a hundred years back they were subservient to men – for centuries they were. So to protect themselves they developed all kinds of devious techniques to influence and control men. Understandable – that way they survived. What's the situation now? We have Women's Lib triumphant. Equality and all that crap. But still they use their devious techniques, exploit their feminine charms.' He folded his arms covered with light-coloured hair. 'But not with me they don't. No, sir.'

Newman half closed his eyes. He had hit a nerve. Maybe it was the billionaire's experience with his ex-wife? But he also spotted Hauser was guiding him away from the main point at issue.

'Not only power,' Newman continued in full flood. He was facing the man he was convinced was responsible for Sandy's brutal murder. 'Money, too, is your god. You can't get enough of it. Now you've taken over Egon Schmidt's private bank in Frankfurt. The *late* Egon Schmidt . . .'

Again he saw the hostile flicker as Hauser gazed straight back at him. The temperature in the room was rising rapidly, and it wasn't only the sun's heat.

'I'm beginning to think you could become a minor nuisance,' Hauser commented, stubbing out a cigarette, inserting a fresh one in his holder, lighting it. 'You're naïve, Newman. No idea what you're up against. I could squash you like a fly.'

'You could try,' Newman agreed. 'Seems to be a sensitive subject – the Schmidt bank. The first step in moving on to take over Germany?'

Hauser flushed with fury. He leaned back against the couch, tilted his jaw, making a supreme effort to regain self-control. He smiled, made a gesture towards the balcony with his left hand.

'I trust you have Paula Grey's best interests at heart? I have noticed it's a long way down off that balcony.'

Newman froze for a couple of seconds. Hauser was attempting to provoke him, but the implied threat infuriated Newman. He stood up, walked out on to the balcony. Paula was perched on the swing seat while Carver leaned towards her.

'Paula,' Newman called out, 'I think we've exhausted our welcome.'

She jumped up and Carver followed her. They hadn't reached the entrance when the door to Hauser's office burst open. Mauno Sarin, tall, athletic in his stride, walked in while behind him on his heels came Karma, his assistant, his right hand in his pocket. Newman felt sure he was gripping a handgun.

'What the hell is the meaning of this? Who are you?' Hauser demanded. 'You can't storm into my office like this . . .'

'I just did. Protection Police.' Sarin flipped open a folder. 'I have a warrant for the arrest of Robert Newman.'

Sarin said nothing until he was driving his Saab back into the city. Beside him sat Newman while Paula occupied one of the rear seats. Sarin drove fast, just inside the speed limit. He frequently glanced in his rear-view mirror.

'Well, no one is following us.' He glanced at Newman. 'I must say you have a habit of walking into the lion's den.'

'What about the warrant for my arrest? On what charge. And how come you turned up when you did?'

'No warrant. No charge. Just an excuse to get you out of that place. Tweed called me, said he was worried, could I help out?'

'You arrived very quickly,' Paula said to the small stocky Karma who sat beside her.

'Mauno was driving,' Karma replied with the ghost of a smile.

'What the devil did you hope to accomplish? Taking such a risk?' Sarin demanded.

'Exactly what I did accomplish. I rattled Hauser's cage – he was fit to explode when you arrived. If I'd had a few minutes more he was so worked up by what I said he might have let something slip.'

'Gratitude!' Sarin drove with one hand, fingered his fringe beard with the other. 'I tell the most blatant lies and I get a kick in the rear.' His tone was mocking.

'I'm grateful,' Newman told him. 'Frankly, it was getting a little ugly. The swine had just threatened Paula.'

'Then maybe we could swear out a complaint against Hauser which would give me the chance to question him about some of his operations.'

'I'm afraid not. He's clever. He phrased the threat by implication. He has an iron nerve even in a rage. He was trying to provoke me. I hit him pretty hard verbally – it may cause him to make a blunder. Object of the exercise. I was pretty convincing for a certain reason . . .'

Briefly, he told Sarin about the February dawn in Suffolk when he had discovered Sandy hanging in the bell tower. Sarin listened as they started down the Mannerheimintie, his expression blank.

'So,' Newman concluded, 'history can repeat itself in the most macabre way. The last time I was here I was hunting down the killer of my wife Alexis – and you'll well recall our trip across the Baltic to Estonia. Now I'm determined to identify the murderer of Sandy and I find myself in the same part of the world. Finland.'

'Very curious, and nothing personal, but we could do without your presence. It always brings trouble.' Sarin's voice changed. 'I'm very sorry to hear about your girl friend's death. I gather that's what is driving the motor on this visit. Do you mind if we call in at the Marski? I said I would let Tweed know when you and Paula were safe.'

He swung across the road suddenly in front of an advancing tram and Paula closed her eyes in horror. When he parked outside the Marski Newman let out his breath. Now they *were* safe. From Mauno's driving.

'Thank you for looking after Paula and Bob,' Tweed said to Sarin after the Finn had told his story.

Earlier they had heard from Newman an account of his meeting with Hauser. Sarin had listened with great attention and Paula noticed he was staring into space as though taking a decision. Dillon sat in his usual place on a chair in the corner. He had been introduced to Sarin as Ward Dexter, a commercial attaché on his way to join the American Embassy in Helsinki. He disguised his position cleverly, remarking to Sarin:

'London told me to contact Mr Tweed so I could get the lowdown on the situation here. Of course our interests do not always coincide. INCUBUS is a major force in the US and I have to adopt a neutral stance in these matters. A question of diplomacy, Mr Sarin.'

'I understand,' Sarin looked at Tweed. 'My own position is very similar to Mr Dexter's. A neutral stance. May I suggest that if you have the spare time you may find a visit to the remarkable Meteorological Institute complex near Kemijärvi interesting? I must go now.'

Karma opened the door for him. Sarin paused and turned, before leaving, to make one more remark.

'I would appreciate it, Tweed, if you would keep me informed of any further developments in case I can assist you.'

Tweed showed his anger as soon as the two Finns had left the room and Pete Nield, who had remained silent, had locked the door. He glared at Newman.

'That was a very dangerous and foolish tactic – to stir up Hauser in the way you did. God knows what might have happened if Sarin hadn't arrived.'

'What might have happened is Hauser would have blown his cool and told me something,' he snapped back. 'Give me a little credit for not mentioning Ion Manescu, the fact that we have photographic evidence that Romanian *Securitate* was inside the INCUBUS building. And God knows why you didn't show those pictures to Sarin. He's trying to get something on Hauser, something his government simply can't ignore.' Furious, he wiped sweat off his forehead before going on. 'And I gave no hint that we're holding Vanderheld, that she has information which could rock INCUBUS to its evil foundations.'

'That is what she says,' retorted Tweed. 'Has it occurred to you she could be bluffing? To get the protection you've provided her with? She thinks one attempt was made on her life . . .'

'No *thinks* about it,' Newman retorted. 'Her story links up with the picture in the paper. She actually showed me the outfit she was wearing. It fits the description given in that news report.'

Tweed was still glaring. 'She could have gone to Stockmann's and bought that outfit ready to show you. She had time to do just that . . .'

'Another thing you're forgetting,' Newman threw at him, 'is the brown Buick I saw parked outside her apartment – which links up with the picture Marler took. Same registration number as the car I saw parked outside her place. What more do you want? Hauser's head on a platter? And another item you missed. You should have shown Sarin the picture of that car and I'd have made a statement to what I saw.'

'What more do I want? Tweed repeated quietly. 'Some hard evidence.'

'Cool it, Newman,' Dillon advised. 'Tweed is right. Showing those pictures to Sarin would have bought us nothing. It's not Sarin's fault – he is in hock to his government – this country has to tread carefully. Russia is in turmoil. They can do without a breach with Washington.'

'The trouble, Bob,' Tweed explained in the same controlled tone, 'is that your motive is revenge. Naturally your only thought is to track down the man who murdered Sandy. That is blinding you to the bigger issue. Investigating INCUBUS. That has top priority.'

'Not with me any more!'

Newman stood up, wrenched on his jacket, ready to walk out. He caught Paula's eye.

'Bob,' she said, 'can I come over and see you and Marler at The Palace. I have something to tell you, something you'd like to know.'

'OK. Be my guest.' He paused before Nield unlocked the door for him. 'Paula, you're welcome. Even for a drink . . .'

There was silence as Newman left, a silence which continued for several minutes. Paula stood up and stared out of the window, her arms crossed. She was appalled. She had never witnessed such a blazing row between Tweed and Newman. She glanced over her shoulder. Tweed was cleaning his glasses, watching her with a quizzical expression.

'Thought I got it all wrong, didn't you?'

She walked slowly towards him, her eyes half closed. 'What are you up to? I know that expression. You're up to something. My Lord! You were putting on an act. You weren't losing your temper at all. Give. Now, please.'

Tweed glanced round the room at Dillon and Nield. He put on his glasses, settled back in his chair. He's giving himself time to decide something, Paula thought, still standing as she gazed down at him.

'You wound him up,' she accused.

'Yes, I did,' Tweed admitted. 'Let's face it. Newman is already wound up like a coiled spring, bent on revenge. Nothing is going to change that, stop him. To bring down Hauser is not going to be easy.'

'So why do we want to bring him down?' Paula prodded.

'Because *we* know he's using the ex-secret police who have been vanishing off the face of the earth. Marler's pictures of Manescu prove that to me. And it won't be only the *Securitate*. It will be the STASI, the STB from Czechoslovakia and God knows who else. If he's using them in Finland it's only a matter of time before he infiltrates them into Britain. So we have to stop him.

Because INCUBUS doesn't stop at murder – the horrible death of Ed Riverton shows that. He knew about Dracon, the think-tank outside Boston. He probably knew all about the plan – Hauser's plan to control a lot of the world. And one of the murders took place in Britain – Sandra Riverton. No one, nothing is safe while Hauser is operating.'

'But why use Bob Newman?'

'I'm not using him. He undertook the job himself. And don't forget he – together with yourself – have dug up more information than I have so far. It was Newman who visited the old owners of Bennington Machine Tools and Manningham Electronics in Britain – and got them to talk. It was Newman who deliberately provoked the attempts on his life – to smoke out the opposition. The three of you – Newman, yourself and Marler have provided me with pointers as to what Hauser is up to. And this,' Tweed said grimly, 'is now a duel between myself and Franklin D. Hauser.'

'With Bob in the front line?'

'Yes. I've launched him as a missile – a torpedo, if you like – against INCUBUS. Because he's getting results – and can look after himself. Are you satisfied?'

'You're wily, you're devious,' she said, crossing her ankles, her arms, staring at him.

'You know any other way of fighting a man like Hauser? And something interesting has happened. I started out with two quite separate investigations, as I thought. One, Newman and Cord here investigating INCUBUS's activities. Two, Marler on the trail of the vanishing secret police. Now both investigations have merged.'

He stopped speaking as someone tapped in a certain way on the door. Tweed nodded to Nield who unlocked the door. Marler walked in.

'On the dot, as always,' he said jauntily, 'for our meeting.'

'We need more data on INCUBUS,' Tweed said immediately. 'So how do we go about getting it?'

'I do a recce,' Marler said, perching on the arm of a chair Paula was sitting in. 'I fly to Rovaniemi north of the Arctic Circle, spy out the ground a bit. If that Meteorological Institute looks as peculiar as Sarin suspects, then maybe we organize a strike force to go up there, turn the place over.'

'The problem,' Tweed pointed out, 'is to work out how a group of people can move around in the wilderness without arousing suspicion.'

'Haven't worked that one out yet.' Marler stood up. 'First thing is the recce. I'm good at playing the Invisible Man.'

'Nothing like knowing you can pull off anything,' growled Dillon. 'You could end up in a box the way these people operate. I was inside that car when the juggernaut came at us.'

'Have faith, dear boy,' Marler assured him. He turned to Tweed. 'I'll fly up there in a jiffy, if that's OK.'

'Best to fly up in a plane,' Paula teased him.

'I agree,' Tweed decided. 'But be cautious . . .'

'I'd like to go with him,' Paula chimed in. 'No argument, if you please. That is, if Marler is happy.'

'Welcome aboard,' said Marler.

The phone rang as Tweed was about to protest. He picked it up. The voice at the other end did not identify itself but Tweed recognized the distinctive tone of General Valentin Rebet.

'I need to see you urgently. There has been a development you should know about. I can meet you at a rendezvous in the Finnish archipelago . . .'

'No!' Tweed's tone was abrupt. 'In Helsinki or not at all.'

'Would you consider Turku? Please. I do not wish to be seen.'

'Yes.'

'There is a colony of old wooden houses, a creation of Turku a hundred years ago . . .'

'I know it.'

'By the entrance to the colony at, say, twelve midday tomorrow?'

'First I must know something of what this is about,' Tweed demanded.

'Take my word for it. You will want to hear my news.'

'I agree to the meeting.'

'Thank you so much. It is a crisis situation.'

Tweed put down the phone. Paula was watching him closely. 'I asked you if I could go with Marler. That phone call. Was it trouble?'

'No. And you can go.' He looked at Dillon. 'Cord, you wanted to contact your embassy. Now might be a good time. Paula, why don't you go to lunch with Marler, plan your trip?'

Tweed waited until he was alone, locked the door and noticed Newman had left his pack of cigarettes. He took one, lit it, one of his rare cigarettes. He had felt the need to be alone, to sort out his thoughts.

Everything was happening at once. Nield sat silent by the wall sensing his chief's mood. Yes, everything was moving faster. Manescu had been located, was employed by INCUBUS. Had he any connection with the newspaper reports of bombs going off in various countries? All the victims were key liberal statesmen who might have stood in Hauser's way.

On top of that Newman had spirited away a vital witness to a safe refuge. Peggy Vanderheld. Butler was due back any time now. Newman was on the rampage, must have rattled Hauser's cage. That would, Tweed had no doubt, trigger off a violent reaction.

Then there was this mysterious Institute located in the Arctic Circle. How the devil could they transport a strike force up there if it came to that? Tweed stubbed out his half-smoked cigarette. Of course! Newman had by chance given him the solution. He picked up the phone to contact Monica. They would need certain equipment.

But, as he dialled, Tweed couldn't get out of his mind what Rebet had said. Am I right about the identity of Angel, he asked himself once more. And Rebet's last words were unsettling.

'It is a crisis situation.'

27

'Frank, I want you to fly to the Meteorological Institute and double up the security.'

Hauser was restless, exuding an aura of impatient energy as he prowled in his shirt sleeves round his office. His subordinate, sprawled in a chair, legs stretched out, ran a hand through his thick black unruly hair.

'Security is very tight now,' he ventured. 'What's on your mind?'

'What ought to be on yours. Goddamnit, you know what happened. Do I have to work out everything myself? Yes, I do. Always have had to. Get your bloody legs out of my way. I'll spell it out like I would for a child of ten,' he raged.

'I'm listening . . .'

'Then keep your trap shut and do just that, you crud. Listen! OK?'

Galvone stiffened. Crud? Did he really have to take all these insults his chief hurled at him? Then he remembered the money he was being paid. Yes, he did. He listened, his dark eyes narrowed as he responded tersely.

'OK.'

'I'd just asked you to launch a big tracking operation for Newman. Next development? Newman has the gall to arrive here, to tell me he's digging up dirt I thought was buried. He's very active, that nosy Brit. His next objective may well be a visit to the Institute. If he gets into the wrong area we're in trouble, big trouble. So, to hell with the security you've installed. You get up there fast in the jet. You do what I tell you. You double the security.'

'I'm on my way . . .'

'Keep your butt in that seat until I say you can go. I've just had an idea. Something's been bothering me, my instinct has never been wrong before. We're missing something. Newman has all his marbles, but he's a newspaperman. I think behind him there's another brain directing this operation against me. Before you fly north organize a dragnet – check all the hotels in this little town. The men you instruct are looking for new arrivals during the past week. Brits or Americans.'

'I'll get it moving. Anything else?'

'Yes. The campaign to take over Europe to the Urals. We're mounting a vast bombing operation to create more chaos – then we move in on certain areas we haven't touched yet. I want Irina Serov, Manescu and Ziegler flown out of the forest to Turku. They stay in hotels. You provide their papers. I want them there tomorrow. So any opposition has to be neutralized. Meantime I'll walk down another avenue.'

'Which one is that, if I may ask?'

Galvone stood up. Hauser, despite the heat – there were damp patches under his armpits – was in full flood, at his most dynamic. Lusting for action.

'You just did ask.' Hauser was still prowling like a panther. 'Adam Carver has fixed dinner tonight with that twist who came with Newman. Paula Grey. So Adam can

274

get her drunk, bed her, pump her. Maybe that way we'll hit on the mastermind behind this investigation into the corporation. Make with the feet, Frank. I think I'm homing in on the real enemy.'

Tweed lunched with Paula and Dillon at the Marski restaurant in the basement. They occupied a banquette at the end of the restaurant and Tweed, who ate quickly, had finished his plate of fried chicken coated with sesame seeds and saffron rice. Harry Butler, who had just returned from Sweden, sat in an outer seat facing Tweed.

'Peggy Vanderheld is holed up in that cottage on the island of Örno in the Swedish archipelago,' he reported. 'We may see her back here. She's restless, an energetic lady and didn't like being left on her own.' Butler's normally poker-faced expression showed a hint of embarrassment. 'She seems to have taken a fancy to me. I don't believe that,' he went on hastily. 'I think she just wants male protection next to her.'

'It would be very dangerous if she did come back,' Tweed mused.

'I did my best to get the idea out of her head,' Butler told him. 'But I thought we needed an insurance policy, so I let her know she could find me at the Hesperia. If she flies back I'm sure she'll come straight to me.'

'Did the best you could,' Tweed assured him. He looked at the others. 'I've been trying to put myself in Hauser's place after that confrontation he had with Newman. I think we've got to keep on the move, leave the Marski today.'

'And go where?' asked Dillon, pausing between mouthfuls.

'To the Hesperia, where Butler's staying. But we register under false names. All three of us.' He opened the briefcase he'd brought with him, slipped an envelope

275

across the table to the American. 'There's your new passport, not that they check much here. You're now British.'

Dillon took out the passport below the level of the table, flipped it open to the page with his name and a photograph opposite. He grunted.

'Lawrence Dawlish. Sounds like a faggot. And I know I've an ugly mug, but this is ridiculous.'

'It's the kind of picture which could fit almost any clean-shaven man. And they never look at it, as I said. Here is yours, Paula. Your real photo. As you know, we have a selection at Park Crescent. I brought several in case of need. I've another for myself. I'm Martin Baker. We move after lunch. Just a precaution . . . It could save our lives.'

Tweed caught a train to Turku the following morning for his meeting with General Rebet. Pete Nield came with him after an argument which Nield won. Tweed used the railway because it was easier to slip unobserved out of Helsinki as opposed to using the airport.

The main station was close to the centre of Helsinki. Its façade had a weird 1930s look and Tweed assumed it must have escaped the destruction of World War II. He timed it so they arrived at the colony of old houses in Turku a few minutes before the noon rendezvous with the Russian.

To kill time he wandered among the old wooden houses with Nield, trudging up the sloping cobbled streets between the wooden cabins. No traffic was permitted inside and it was oddly quiet and deserted. The weather had changed again and dark storm clouds like an invading army were rolling in over Finland's second city. Inside the colony Tweed had the sensation of being miles away from the twentieth century.

At noon they had wandered back to the entrance and a taxi, the word spelt *taxsi*, pulled up. General Rebet stepped out by himself, wearing a dark overcoat and a

276

peaked cap. As he paid off the driver, Tweed thought he looked more like a Finn. What the devil had he flown here from Leningrad for?

Newman was concealed inside the same copse overlooking INCUBUS Oy. HQ which Marler had used. He had asked Marler to draw him a map of the layout of the area and Marler, without asking what Newman was up to, had obliged. Arriving at 8 a.m., it was an hour before Newman saw what he had been hoping for.

A large stretched black Mercedes limo was driven close to the entrance to the building. A uniformed chauffeur jumped out of the vehicle, opened the rear door and immediately Hauser emerged with another figure. Through the lenses of the binoculars he had borrowed from Marler, Newman focused and identified Hauser positively. He had recognized the American from his walk but his garb puzzled Newman. Normally dressed in an expensive business suit, Hauser was clad in a rumpled windcheater, baggy denim trousers and a peaked cap pulled down over a pair of dark glasses. No pince-nez? He looked like a seaman.

'What's going down?' Dillon asked, seated in the rear of the BMW.

'Hauser going places . . .'

'And the guy with him?'

'Adam Carver. Hardly the fashion plate this morning. He's wearing denims, a scruffy windcheater like his boss. There they go . . .'

The automatic gate in the wire fence was opening, the limo was driving through the exit, turning towards the city. Cord Dillon grunted. From the Hesperia he had called Newman at The Palace when Tweed said he'd be absent, maybe for the day.

'What are you doing today?' Dillon had asked. 'I'm redundant. Can I help?'

Newman had decided that maybe some back-up wouldn't do any harm. And Dillon was as involved in breaking INCUBUS as he was. He'd told the American to be with him in fifteen minutes or he'd be gone.

Now as the limo disappeared from view Newman started up the BMW, let it glide down the spiral road which emerged on to the highway nearer the city and beyond INCUBUS. Within two minutes he had picked up the limo which was moving just inside the speed limit.

Dillon felt under his armpit where his Luger rested inside the shoulder holster. It was safer carrying the weapon on his person rather than leaving it in his room back at the Hesperia. He was glad he'd taken the precaution when Newman strapped on his own holster containing his Smith & Wesson just before they'd left The Palace.

'Expecting trouble?' he asked as Newman drove on.

'Aren't you? After what happened on The Highway?'

'So what's your plan of operation?' Dillon demanded.

'Stick to Hauser like glue. I stirred him up yesterday. I think sooner or later he'll react. That's how he got where he has. On top of the world.'

'Owns half the States, the bastard,' Dillon growled. 'That we don't like. They say he has a third of the Senate in his pocketbook. What's the problem?'

Newman had sworn half under his breath as he swung the car off the highway into Helsinki and followed the limo away from the centre of the city. They were driving with parkland on either side: wooded ground with grassy hills over which pathways wound out of sight. Newman nodded to his right.

'In a moment you'll see a really crazy old house with turrets. Like something out of Disneyland and very old. One of the houses which Russian Tsarist generals used as summer residences a hundred years ago when Finland was a principality of Russia.'

Dillon stared out of the window. Beyond some trees a weird house painted white was perched up on a knoll, four storeys high with elaborate balconies and circular turret towers at the corners.

'And that,' Newman told him, 'is Hauser's town house. How he managed to buy a national monument is probably quite a story.'

'Passed money to the right bureaucrats?'

'That wouldn't work in Finland. My guess is he's built so many plants here, provided so much employment, the government are naturally sympathetic to him. Same technique as I found he employed in Suffolk back in England for miles round his home there, Livingstone Manor. Play the philanthropist, recruit an army of spies and allies. Yes, I think there is a problem coming up within the next half hour.'

'Which is?'

They were well clear of the city, were driving along a highway which passed between gulches of granite outcrops. It almost reminded Dillon of the Wild West. Here and there an isolated house, a small lake in front of a cliff wall. Granite again, of course. Granite City. In the distance the black limo was moving round a long curve.

'The problem,' Newman informed Dillon, 'is that we're on the way to the airport. The locals call it Seusta. Looks as though Hauser is flying off somewhere. This car can't take to the air.'

'We board his flight.'

'I don't think so. My bet is he'll use the Lear jet. And it looks like some secret meeting. Hence the mess of clothes Hauser and Carver are wearing. To avoid recognition . . .'

'Checkmate. You were right,' Dillon commented as Newman parked the BMW.

They had arrived at the airport, the black limo had

dropped Hauser and Carver who hurried inside the building. Newman jumped out with Dillon, slid a press card from his wallet, tucked it under the windscreen wiper. It might work.

Inside the small airport building – small by comparison with Heathrow or Frankfurt – he walked rapidly after Hauser and Carver who ignored the normal departure route. From a window he watched the two men hustling over towards a Lear jet which was being refuelled.

'Checkmate,' Dillon repeated. 'Shit.'

'There may be a way . . .'

Newman walked back to a door marked *Security* in Finnish and Swedish. The latter language he could understand. Knocking on the door, he opened it, walked inside, closed it, leaving Dillon outside. He flashed his press card.

'Liaison with Protection Police,' he said to the uniformed officer who looked up from behind a counter. 'I need the flight plan for that Lear jet out there. Call Mauno Sarin at Ratakatu if you want to. We need to follow that jet.'

'Then we'd better not waste time making phone calls. The flight plan is for Turku. A scheduled flight takes off for the same place in fifteen minutes. You'd better hurry.'

'Thanks a lot. Sarin will be grateful . . .'

They bought tickets, caught the scheduled flight with minutes to spare. Newman thanked God there was no known terrorist problem in Finland – so no security apparatus to detect the guns they were carrying. The door was closed as they sat down, the motors hummed into high pitch and they were off, moving down the runway.

'And when we get to Turku?' Dillon whispered as the machine lifted into the dazzling clear blue sky.

'We just hope this beats the jet. If it does we can pick up where Hauser is going, track him to his destination.'

*   *   *

'Adam, this goddamn outfit I'm wearing reminds me of those days when I worked as a longshoreman on the San Francisco waterfront,' Hauser remarked as the jet left the ground.

'You've come a long way since then.'

'Yes, it's been one helluva journey and it's not over yet. Want a drink?'

'Just mineral water,' Carver replied. He liked to keep his mind clear. 'What is this meeting we're attending? And I should be back in Helsinki this evening. I have a date with Paula Grey. Of course,' he added quickly, 'if necessary I can stand her up. She'll be that much more eager when I make a new date.'

'Don't do that, boy. You could extract valuable data from that dame. You'll be back in Helsinki late this afternoon.'

Hauser sipped at his bourbon. The interior of the jet was luxurious. They sat side by side in leather armchairs. In front of Hauser by the bulkhead was a fully stocked cocktail cabinet with a door which opened and closed at the press of a button. In front of Carver was a telephone linked to a sophisticated communications system using a satellite. With this phone Hauser could call any of his companies spread out across the world and the conversation would be scrambled and automatically decoded at the other end. The jet was a flying HQ of INCUBUS.

'This meeting,' Hauser began, 'is top secret.' He paused, sipped more bourbon. 'I brought you along in case we have to discuss prices, even negotiate a final deal. I do doubt the latter, the people we're dealing with think time is a weapon to wear down the impatient. So I'm offering them a deal they can't refuse.'

'Do I sit in on it with you?'

'I think not. These are very security-minded people. So security minded even the people back home where they've come from don't know they're in Turku.'

281

'So nothing recorded, I assume?'

'You assume right, boy.'

'How do we organize liaison with each other, if necessary?'

'I'll leave them in one room, come through to check with you in another.'

'Can you be a little more specific?' Carver pressed. 'It helps if I know in advance what's going on. I'll be quicker with answers for you.'

Hauser paused again. 'You might as well know. It's a Soviet trade delegation – interested in my forming private companies inside Russia. We hold fifty-one per cent of the equity – which gives us control, as usual. It's all new to them so I have to lead them by the hand.'

'You must have worked to pull off a deal like that,' Carver remarked, encouraging more revelations.

'It's a long upward haul. Those peasants are living in the last century. I once had dinner with a top bureaucrat. He'd lived in the West, was decently dressed. When the soup came he scooped it up, shovelled it in his mouth.' Hauser demonstrated, dipping his head, working his elbow. 'Peasants,' he repeated. 'And the three men I'm flying to meet are top people. Time we civilized them.'

'Where in Turku is this meeting taking place then?'

'The last place you'd expect to find three top Russians. In the two cabins we bought in that colony of old houses . . .'

After buying a ticket, General Rebet entered the compound of old houses, shook hands with Tweed, with Nield.

'I suggest we stroll round this strange place,' he said after checking his watch.

Nield dropped back behind the two men. His right hand rested inside his jacket close to the Browning automatic tucked inside his belt. He had borrowed the weapon from Paula.

'Crisis was the word you used,' Tweed said, coming straight to the point. 'What's happening? Why are we here?'

'To witness a meeting between Franklin D. Hauser and three members of the Politburo. Kazbek, Marshal Zaikov and Dikoyan. And I still don't know which one is Angel, the traitor.'

'But you hope to find out this time?'

Rebet shrugged as they walked up a cobbled ramp-like street with cabins on either side. 'My informants – who are risking their lives – found out the meeting would take place here, who was coming.'

'How are these three men travelling? Presumably they don't want the Finns to know. Certainly Marshal Zaikov's presence would cause a furore with the Finnish government.'

'That's the intriguing part. Their mode of travel. Two of them – and I don't know which two – are flying in by Aeroflot to Turku airport. Their cover is the trade exhibition opening in Turku today. They're travelling in a separate compartment aboard the aircraft. Also aboard is a low-level trade delegation visiting the fair. The two Politburo men will go straight to a car which will drive them here.'

'And the third man?'

'Whose identity I also don't know. He's flown to Tallinn in Estonia across the Gulf of Finland. From there he's travelling by fast power cruiser to one of the islands in the archipelago. There he transfers to a fishing vessel for the short voyage to Turku.'

'A complex route. Sounds like Angel.'

'I agree. The problem will be to identify which of the three arrives here on his own.'

Tweed stopped alongside Rebet. They had almost reached the summit of their climb. A rope, waist high, barred their way. A man dressed in working clothes held up his hand. He spoke in English.

'Work proceeding repairing the street. You can't come any further this route today.'

A dozen paces behind the two men Nield took a firm grip on the Browning. He had noticed the bulge under the shoulder of the workman's clothes. Did Finnish workers normally carry handguns?

Tweed nodded, gazed beyond the rope. Two large wooden cabins stood close together with only a tiny alley separating them. Behind heavy net curtains all the main curtains were closed. And despite the storm clouds gathering it was broad daylight. The two men turned back.

'We've found the meeting place,' Rebet whispered.

'I think so. But when?'

Rebet checked his watch. 'They are due here in fifteen minutes from now.'

The Finnair machine made a smooth landing on the Turku runway. A mobile staircase was brought out. As Newman descended with Dillon following he glanced up at the sky. A Lear jet was coming in to land. They had beaten Hauser to it by minutes.

'I'm staying here,' Newman said as they entered the reception hall. 'You go outside and grab a cab. Give the driver a large tip. Tell him you're waiting for another passenger . . .'

Newman walked back to a window overlooking the airfield. As the jet landed, slowed to a halt, a black limo drove out to meet it. Hauser seemed to favour black cars. He used his binoculars, focused them on the rear of the Mercedes, memorized the registration number, walked quickly outside to where Dillon stood by a cab.

'They're leaving any moment, Cord. Get in.'

Inside the cab Newman gave precise instructions to the cab driver, including the registration number. Casually he mentioned they were reporters, that they were interested in the two passengers in the limo, that they were checking out a story.

'I understand,' the driver replied and drove off, then stopped.

As the limo passed them he followed without making it obvious, keeping a reasonable distance behind the vehicle. After they had travelled a short distance the driver spoke over his shoulder.

'They look like they are heading for the settlement of old houses. Maybe you have heard about them?'

'We have heard about them,' Newman said as the cab slowed.

Tweed and Rebet had positioned themselves inside one of the cabins open to the public close to a window. It was dark inside the room, the furniture was heavy and ancient in keeping with the turn of the century. The guardian of the cabin, deciding they were harmless, had left them alone.

'Here, I think, comes Hauser,' Newman said.

Carver jumped out of the vehicle the moment it stopped, bought two tickets and walked into the colony with Hauser. The two men walked straight to the cobbled avenue leading up to where repair work was supposed to be taking place. Rebet checked his watch again.

'This operation is being carried out with great precision. My three are due any moment now.'

Pete Nield, who stood behind Tweed, stared out of the window as a taxi pulled up. He stiffened as the door opened and gently nudged Tweed in the back without letting Rebet see his signal. Tweed kept his expression blank as he watched Newman and Dillon pay off their driver, buy tickets and enter the compound.

Inwardly he was fuming. What on earth did Newman think he was doing? How could he have turned up here at this sensitive moment? Swearing to himself, he preserved his blank look as the two men walked swiftly to the cabin facing the building Tweed watched from. They both kept out of sight and Newman peered round the corner. Tweed guessed he was observing the progress of Hauser and Carver up the hill towards the meeting point.

'Those two visitors seem to be taking a great interest in Hauser,' Rebet remarked.

'Probably INCUBUS guards,' Tweed suggested. 'Hauser doesn't travel many places without protection.'

'I suppose you're right,' Rebet responded dubiously. 'And now we have another taxi coming . . .'

Newman had heard it too. He grabbed Dillon by the arm and they slipped inside the open door of the cabin before the cab reached the entrance. They're doing what we are, Tweed said to himself: observing from under cover.

The cab stopped and three men stepped out, one of them paying the driver. Dressed in lightweight raincoats, they all wore caps. Tweed stared as they entered the colony. *Three* men. Marshal Zaikov, Viktor Kazbek,

Anatoli Dikoyan, still managing to look neat and trim in a shabby raincoat and a cap.

'Damn!'

Rebet slammed one clenched fist into the palm of his other hand. 'All three turned up together. Now I have no idea which is our target.'

'Someone played it clever,' Tweed suggested. 'Came ashore from that fishing vessel very early, then waited in a taxi at a prearranged rendezvous until the other two arrived and then joined them to come here. The only thing wrong with that theory is how would he explain his devious route to the other two?'

'I can tell you that at least. There's unrest in Estonia, as you know. One Politburo member was going there to check out the situation secretly. That reason would satisfy the other two, neither of whom are Angel. The trouble is, I don't know which one went to Tallinn.'

Nield had tactfully moved to another window to give Tweed and Rebet privacy. Now he called out softly.

'Two more taxis arriving.'

The three Soviet Politburo men had disappeared up the same avenue which Hauser and Carver had walked up. Marshal Zaikov had marched straight up on his own, followed by Dikoyan and Kazbek who walked side by side, Tweed noted.

Seven men piled out of the two taxis. Several had bottles protruding from their pockets and a couple did a little dance on the pavement while the drivers were being paid off. Rebet leaned closer to the window, his mouth tight.

'My God! Those are Soviet KGB guards disguised as seamen. I recognize some of them. They're protecting those three men – I thought it was odd the way they turned up alone. They'll all be armed.'

Tweed was disturbed. Newman and Dillon were still hidden in the cabin opposite. And he had earlier seen Newman pull down his jacket. Tweed knew that gesture: it was to ensure the gun he was carrying was concealed. This was an explosive situation.

'They're being clever,' Rebet commented bitterly as the seven men bought tickets and rollicked into the compound. They were giving a perfect imitation of a group of seamen who were not drunk but were enjoying a brief period of leave ashore. Several put their arms round each other as they plodded up the avenue which the three Politburo men had walked up.

'That really checkmates us,' Rebet said.

'Not necessarily,' replied Tweed. 'Do you know whether Angel will return by the same route he came in by?'

'Piecing together the bits of data from my informants, yes. He has to. Officially he flew to Tallinn. So he must fly back to Moscow from Tallinn.'

'Using exactly the same route?' Tweed persisted. 'First the fishing vessel, then transferring to the power cruiser to reach Tallinn?'

'The same. In reverse.'

'Then let me have a word with my associate.'

Tweed walked across to the window where Nield stood watching the outside world. He lowered his voice as he gave the instruction.

'Pete, you saw those three arrive shortly after Newman and Dillon? Good. Now this will be difficult, but it's also vital if you can work it. I want you to leave here, look for some transport to follow the taxi which takes those three men away from here. One of them will somehow detach himself inconspicuously from the others who will go to the airport. I want you to stick to that third man like a leech. He will leave Turku aboard a fishing vessel to rendezvous with a big power cruiser somewhere in the archipelago. Understood so far?'

'Quite clear.'

'If you can, I want you to follow him out to sea as long

as possible. As well as transport, buy a camera. I need you to bring back photos of that third man.'

'Got it.' The formidable mission was taken in his stride by Nield. 'Only one objection – I'm here to protect you. I can't be in two places at once.'

'Newman and Dillon are in that cabin over there. They can take your place.'

'Then I'm on my way . . .'

'You have enough money?'

'Plenty. For what I need.'

Tweed watched the slim agile figure of Nield walking swiftly towards the entrance. It was obvious he had already worked out how he was going to handle the difficult and dangerous job Tweed had given him.

Tweed strolled by himself across to the cabin opposite. Out of the corner of his eye he saw the distant summit of the avenue he'd climbed with Rebet. Three of the so-called seamen were leaning up against the walls of cabins just below the roped-off area. That left four: they would be guarding the other sides of the two cabins. He would have given a lot to know what was going on inside. The door of the cabin opposite was opened, Newman beckoned him inside, closed the door. Dillon was standing by a window, the Luger held by his side.

'May I enquire what the devil you are doing here?' Tweed enquired.

Newman, making no apologies, told him how they had followed Hauser from his HQ in Helsinki. Tweed listened, sat down and nodded.

'I suppose I can't blame you . . .'

'I should hope not,' Newman rapped back. 'Our job is to detect what Hauser is planning. Who were those peculiar characters who arrived recently?'

'Emissaries,' Tweed replied enigmatically.

'Your friend across the way is in trouble, maybe big trouble,' Dillon called out. 'He peered out when you left the cabin, must have been seen. A couple of those thugs have just gone inside . . .'

'He must be protected. At all costs,' Tweed ordered.

Newman and Dillon ran past him, opened the door, walked slowly across. Newman glanced up the avenue, saw the other men in the distance were talking, their backs to him. He pushed open the cabin door slowly, his .38 Smith & Wesson in his hand. Dillon followed, the Luger still by his side.

The atmosphere inside the cabin was heavy with the humidity which had descended on Turku. Rebet stood against a wall, facing the two men, his hands raised as Newman and Dillon entered silently. Both men facing Rebet held Makarov pistols aimed at Rebet. His voice was firm as he spoke.

'Starkov, I'm ordering you and your companion to put away those guns . . .'

He had spoken in English, seeing Newman and Dillon entering the cabin. In response both men took firmer grips on their pistols, aimed them point blank at Rebet.

'I wouldn't if I were you . . .' Newman began.

The first man spun round, his Makarov aiming at Newman. A shot rang out. The Russian was falling when his companion, who had turned round when Newman spoke, waved his pistol towards Dillon. A second shot rang out and he sagged to the plank floor beside his colleague.

Rebet ran forward, bent down, checked the neck pulses of both men. He shook his head as he straightened up.

'They are both dead,' he told Newman. 'I have to thank both of you for saving my life. But we must leave here quickly.'

Newman picked up one of the Makarovs, shoved the muzzle into a leather cushion on a couch, pulled the trigger. He did the same with the second Makarov, turned over the cushion to hide the bullet holes, pressed a pistol into the right hand of each Russian, took a bottle from the pocket of one man, spilt vodka over the mouths of the corpses, left the bottle on a table. Had the other guards heard the shots? A plane had flown overhead at that moment. Rebet stood still, watching Newman with interest.

'Now let's be careful getting back to the other cabin,' Newman warned the two men.

He opened the door, peered up the avenue. Some kind of argument seemed to be going on at the far end of the avenue, men gesticulating, their backs turned. He beckoned to his companions, ran over to the other cabin. Tweed opened the door, let the three men inside, closed the door quietly.

'What happened? Where are the two guards?'

'Dead . . .'

Newman explained tersely what had taken place. Rebet made his comment when Newman had finished.

'He saved my life – both of them did. And it was a brilliant trick to make it look as though they'd shot each other. It might work when they're found.'

'Which could be any time now. We have to get away from here,' Tweed said decisively. 'If we can unseen. Immediately . . .'

'What's happened to Pete Nield?' Dillon asked.

'He can look after himself. I said we must get well clear. Now!'

Newman led the way. He checked to make sure the guards were still absorbed and saw two of them strolling slowly down the avenue towards him. They must be wondering where their comrades were. He waved towards Tweed who was watching from the doorway which faced the exit. The four men hurried out of the colony and Tweed ran towards a taxi parked further up the street. The four men jumped inside, Tweed told the cab driver to take them to the Akateeminen Bookshop, the first place which came into his head in the centre of Turku. As the cab moved off he glanced through the rear window. No sign of any guards as the taxi turned a corner.

'We're safe,' he whispered to Rebet. 'As Wellington said at Waterloo, it was a damned near run thing.'

'But we are still no closer to identifying Angel,' Rebet whispered back.

'We may be soon.'

As he said the words Tweed was worried about Pete Nield and the task he had given him. It could be a great deal more dangerous than he had anticipated.

29

Pete Nield returned to the colony of cabins fully equipped. He was riding a powerful Honda motorcycle he had bought second hand. His suit jacket was neatly folded away in the rear carrier and he wore a leather jacket, a Martian-like helmet with outsize goggles. Pulling up at the kerb a short distance from the compound entrance, he lit a cigarette.

He had spent a lot of money but fortunately Tweed insisted his agents carried a generous supply of the local currency when abroad and Nield had been loaded with *markkaa*. After purchasing the Honda he had sped to the port area. The skipper of a small fast fishing vessel had taken little persuading to make his craft ready for immediate departure when he saw the size of the fee Nield was offering.

'Half now, half when we've completed the job,' Nield had insisted.

Paula's Browning automatic was shoved down his belt

inside his jacket. It was a damned hot day for a leather jacket, he thought as he smoked his cigarette, but he had to look the part of a courier. He had also purchased a Japanese camera with a zoom lens, now tucked away in the front carrier.

All I can do is sweat and wait, he thought as he wiped moisture from his forehead.

The humidity was building up. Black clouds sealed off the sky but heat still radiated up from the street. Nield was accustomed to waiting: it occupied half his time on a job. He had just stubbed out the cigarette when he saw three men hurry inside a taxi they must have phoned for.

A great bear of a man with a mane of black hair and a beard of the same colour. A much smaller slimmer man who moved quickly and gracefully. A stocky heavily built man who marched with a military tread. The cab drove off. Nield pressed the starter button, followed.

Had he been there to witness it, Tweed would have admired the military precision of the departure. Shortly after Nield had left two more cabs arrived. Seven men occupied the vehicles. Four men entered the first cab, two carrying one of their number who sagged and appeared drunk. Three more occupied the second cab and again one man, also smelling of vodka, was carried inside. The two cabs then took off along the same route as the first cab.

Several minutes later a black limo driven by a chauffeur pulled in at the kerb. Hauser appeared at the foot of the avenue with Carver. Hauser had heard of the discovery of the two corpses and looked warily around before diving into the rear of the limo, followed by Carver. As the taxi left the kerbside Hauser gave an instruction to the driver and turned to Carver.

'Adam. I'm dropping you at the railroad depot. Take a

train back to Helsinki for your dinner with the Grey woman. I have work to do at headquarters here. I'll fly back by the jet later . . .'

Pete Nield stared through his goggles as the cab ahead slid to a halt in a quiet part of town on the outskirts of Turku. He slowed, moved into the kerb, fiddled in his satchel hung across his chest as though checking a delivery.

In front of the cab he'd followed another cab was parked. He watched as the door of the cab with the three men inside was opened. A van masked his view for vital seconds and then he saw a blurred figure disappearing inside the cab parked in front.

He whistled under his breath. A switch. Which one to track now? The humidity was fogging his brain. Of course! Tweed had said follow the third man, the one who detaches himself from the other two. How the hell had Tweed foreseen this manoeuvre?

He started away from the kerb as the first taxi drove off. He checked again in his wing mirror. The same two cabs he had observed behind him earlier were still following. It was a great relief when he checked a minute later and the two cabs were no longer there. They had to be something to do with the cab he'd left behind.

Several minutes later he smelt salt in the air and a waterfront came into sight. The cab in front moved slowly along a quay. Everywhere loomed a forest of masts, swaying slowly. A strong breeze was blowing. Nield eased his machine down the quay, saw the cab stop alongside a large fishing vessel, cruised to a stop beside his own smaller craft. The wheelhouse was aft and the tough, wizen-faced skipper inside waved to Nield.

The Englishman nodded in response, swung his leg off the saddle, took hold of the Honda and heaved it aboard the vessel. Jumping after it, he hauled a sheet of canvas to

294

conceal the machine. Taking off his helmet, he tucked that underneath the canvas. Next he stripped off the leather jacket, shoved that out of sight. Burrowing under the canvas he opened the rear carrier, extracted his folded jacket, slipped that on. It was surprisingly chilly on the waterfront. Then he hauled out his camera from the front carrier and placed it carefully under the canvas for easy access. Nield was noted for his meticulous attention to detail.

He jumped back off the heaving vessel on to the quayside and fingered his trim moustache as he watched the silhouette of the passenger from the cab disappear aboard the fishing vessel. The skipper of his own craft, who spoke English and had told Nield his name was Savola, had already started up his engine, which chug-chugged gently.

A few minutes later Nield thanked his lucky stars he had taken precautions, had completely changed his appearance – two more cabs appeared after the first one had driven past him back to the city. They cruised past him and stopped by the vessel where the third man had gone aboard. They looked like the same two cabs he had seen in his wing mirror to Nield.

Lighting a cigarette, his back to the wind, he watched as seven men emerged and went aboard. Two appeared to be blind drunk. They were carried aboard. Nield pursed his lips. The third man must be important to be escorted by so many guards. He frowned as two guards reappeared on the quayside to stretch their legs. They had lost their loping seamen's walk, were moving up and down, erect and brisk. His skipper, Savola, joined him on the quay.

'That big fishing job further up this quay is the one I want you to follow,' Nield told him.

Savola, a short heavy-set individual with broad shoulders and a wide mouth under an aggressive nose, reminded Nield of old films he'd seen on TV of Edward

G. Robinson. He smoked a curved pipe which was hardly ever alight. He grunted, looked up the quay, took out some matches and lit one, passing it over the pipe bowl.

'That's the *Alskär*. We're a community, we all know each other. Skipper of the *Alskär* told me he was hired by the Soviets – some oceanographic team carrying out research. So they say. Spying more likely.'

'Does he know about me?' Nield asked, deliberately phrasing the question positively.

'How could he? I didn't know that was the ship I had to follow until now. And the fee you paid gives you complete secrecy. What you asked for you get.'

'You can keep up with the *Alskär*?'

Nield looked at Savola's much smaller vessel, the *Skäret*. It was a midget compared with the Russians' ship.

Savola puffed at his pipe. 'I can race him to the Kattegat if I have to. That engine you can hear is powerful. And my *Skäret* had a complete overhaul two months ago. Skipper of the *Alskär* is mean about maintenance.' He knocked out the dottle from his pipe, crushed it under his huge boot. 'And maybe we'd better get aboard. *Alskär*'s engine has just started up.' He unlooped the ropes from the bollards.

Nield followed the skipper into the cramped wheelhouse. It gave him a better view of the target vessel. I hope they don't mind their pictures being taken, he thought as the *Skäret* nosed its way away from the quay, heading out for the archipelago and the open sea.

It was the twenty-first century. After dropping off Carver at Turku railway station Hauser was driven to INCUBUS's HQ in Turku. Another cylindrical building, the walls constructed of opaque blue glass, it towered twenty storeys high. The largest building in Turku.

Hauser sat in the weird interrogation room on the top

296

floor. Seated at a table which supported a console, he faced a one-way window. He could see into each of the three rooms behind the long sheet of glass. The occupant of each soundproofed room could not see him.

By operating switches on the console he could communicate with each person sitting in the three separate rooms, one at a time. Hauser had a microphone suspended at mouth level, as had the three people he could see so clearly.

In the right-hand room sat Helmut Ziegler, ex-STASI chief in what had been East Germany. In the centre room, erect in her chair, was seated Irina Serov. Ion Manescu sat inside the third room. Hauser was addressing Irina Serov.

'My name is Morrow. I am your boss. Would you be prepared to go back underground inside the Soviet Union, Irina?'

'Such a trip would have to be most carefully planned.'

'It would be. You haven't answered my question.'

'First, tell me what my task would be. Then I will answer you.'

Gutsy bitch, Hauser thought. He pushed the pince-nez further up his nose. Yes, he had been right to choose her as chief of the subversive operations.

'Explosives have been smuggled inside the Soviet Union. I want these used to disrupt Russian rail traffic. To bring more chaos so they need help and technical advice desperately. On my terms. You would choose the strategic points to place the explosives. You would choose the people to plant them. Your answer, please.'

'I think it would be possible. There is growing unrest in almost every republic. The chaos would provide perfect opportunities to use the explosives, to create more chaos. I suggest we concentrate on the Trans-Siberian Railway and all rail routes out of Moscow, which is the hub of the system. One question, Mr Morrow. Through which zone do we smuggle the explosives into Russia?'

Hauser hesitated. Irina had impressed him. She sat so confidently, clad in a tight-fitting blouse and a short skirt revealing her excellent figure. She's every man's woman, he was thinking.

'The explosives dump is already established,' he told her. 'Here in Finland. We moved it from Lapland in the north across the Soviet border.'

'A perfect choice.'

'But before you take charge of that operation there is something else I want you to do here in Finland. A seduction job. I'll come back to you in a minute.'

Hauser switched off the communication with her room, switched on the right-hand room. Ziegler was short in stature, heavy in build. In his forties, clean shaven, his fair hair was trimmed *en brosse*. He had thick eyebrows which almost met in a bar above a pug nose, a tight mean mouth and an aggressive brutal jaw. He stirred restlessly in his chair until Hauser gave him his instructions.

The organization of unrest, mob demonstrations, bomb attacks, all inside Germany. The trouble had to be laid at the door of a revived terrorist group, the Red Army Faction. More than that, Ziegler had to contact the UTS, the Free Ukraine movement based in Munich. If it appeared the Ukraine, the second most important republic in the Soviet Union, might break loose the Soviet president would have his hands full, would not notice Hauser's penetration of his country.

Hauser switched to the bony-faced Ion Manescu. His orders were brief.

'You have to keep the Balkans cauldron bubbling. Targets – Budapest, Sofia and Bucharest. Set those places on fire . . .'

His instructions to Manescu completed, he turned again to Irina who still sat erect, staring at the mirror facing her as though she could see the man who was talking, the man who called himself Morrow, the man whom she was convinced – despite the distortion of his voice – was Franklin D. Hauser.

'Irina,' Hauser began, 'we shall shortly identify the mastermind behind the opposition to us operating in Finland. When we do I want you to meet him as a woman who escaped from Moldavia, the area Stalin grabbed off Romania at the end of the Second World War. I'm sure you have the personality, the equipment physically, to get him to talk . . .'

She's as sexy as the devil, he thought when he'd finished. He blanked out the console. The job was done. All hell was about to erupt across Europe and Russia.

It was fortunate Pete Nield was a good sailor. The *Skäret* had travelled far from the mainland, was threading its way through the archipelago in heavy seas. The fishing vessel pitched and tossed as large waves swept towards it, climbing a surf-topped crest, plunging down into the next trough.

Holding on to a rail alongside Savola who gripped his wheel, Nield was fascinated by the archipelago. A labyrinth of channels, they weaved a course between countless islands of varying sizes. Some were large with a few wooden one-storey houses, their walls painted bright red. What must it be like living in such solitude, Nield wondered. Others were mere giant brown boulders, whale-backed with waves crashing over them. They rounded the point of one large island and the *Alskär* again came into sight.

Savola was showing great skill in navigation, sailing up a channel which took him out of view of the Soviet-hired vessel, emerging later to bring the target into view once more. As the *Skäret* swayed Nield steadied himself against the rear of the wheelhouse, the binoculars he had bought in Turku pressed to his eyes. Guards jumped close in his lenses. In his mind's eye Nield had a clear recollection of the three men who had arrived by themselves at the Turku colony. Not one of them had appeared so far. And how the hell am I going to take pictures with this tub bobbing like a cork, he wondered. Assuming the third man ever did show.

'Could we get a little closer?' he asked.

'Yes,' Savola replied. 'But if we do they may know we are following them. So far we are just a fishing vessel heading for the best hunting grounds. You have seen other ships so why should they think about us? But if we get closer . . .'

'Will the skipper of the *Alskär* betray us to the Russians?'

'No.' Savola spoke with his teeth clenched on his curved pipe. 'He is paid to transport the so-called oceanographic team. He has no interest in making trouble for me. We all have to live together, to fish another day.'

'Then get closer . . .'

They were leaving the archipelago behind, were approaching the open sea of the Baltic. Islands were becoming fewer and fewer, and none were inhabited. In the far distance the horizon was a hard line as black as ink where a solid mass of clouds assembled overhead. Green rollers continued to surge towards the *Skäret*, sunlight had broken through. But leaving behind the archipelago, Nield realized, meant a greater chance of exposure to the Russians. No other vessels were now in view except the *Alskär*. And they were closing fast on their quarry.

Oddly enough, as they sailed into open sea its surface became calmer. Nield took hold of his camera. He slid back the door of the wheelhouse. Savola glanced at him.

'Be careful. They are Russkies.'

'I'll be all right . . .'

The wind had dropped as Nield leaned against the side

300

of the wheelhouse, aimed his camera. A guard's head jumped into the viewer. The guard had binoculars trained on the *Skäret*. He lowered them and there was a sudden flurry of activity aboard the larger vessel. More guards appeared. Nield held his ground.

'Watch out!' shouted Savola, who had slid open the door.

His keen eyes had seen one of the guards holding a rifle, the muzzle aimed at the *Skäret*. Nield had also spotted the weapon. He remained where he was, peering through the camera. The *Alskär* was sailing now with very little motion, which would help the marksman. Savola swung his wheel over, altering course abruptly. Above the sound of the engine there was the sound of a clatter, like pebbles hitting the gunwale. Bullets. The sudden change of course had saved Nield.

Through the viewer, Nield saw a different figure appear on the desk of the *Alskär*. The third man, his features clear and sharp. Nield continued taking shots as Savola weaved from side to side, as the rifleman continued firing. More clatter, again like pebbles hitting the hull.

'Bastards!' shouted Savola.

Nield bent down, picked up something from the deck, hauled the door open, rushed inside the wheelhouse, slammed the door shut, gripping his camera.

'Job done!' he called out to Savola. 'We can go back . . .'

'If we survive.'

Another rifleman had appeared. The third man was pointing at the *Skäret*. Nield grinned. 'Got you, you thug.' The *Skäret* was swinging through a hundred and eighty degrees fast. As it headed back towards the archipelago Nield was staring through the rear window. The riflemen were still firing, Savola was weaving again. Nield saw the calm water near their wake disturbed by projectiles hitting the sea. He opened his left hand, showed what he had picked up from the deck.

'Rubber bullets. Of course if one had hit me in the eye or the throat that would have been it.'

'We go home?' Savola suggested.

'We go home,' Nield agreed.

30

'Don't punish yourself, Bob,' said Paula. 'Poring over that diary of Sandy's you found in her Jag in Suffolk isn't going to tell you anything more. You must know it off by heart now.'

Newman was sitting in a chair in his room at The Palace while Paula curled up like a cat on his bed. It was hot and humid, felt like a storm was coming. 28°C. the forecast had predicted. That was 82°F. Newman, clad in an open-necked shirt and slacks, looked at his hands. They were covered in moisture. He wiped them on the back of his slacks, went on checking through the diary. He came to two pages stuck together. He'd missed them before.

Using his fingernails, he prised the pages apart, stared at the entry.

Porvoo. That's how he said it was spelt when I told him I'd overheard a reference to the word. He said it was some place in Sweden. I don't believe him. He tells lies . . .

'God! And I missed it,' he said aloud.

'Missed what?' enquired Paula, jerking upright.

'This entry. The two pages were gummed together – like they sometimes are in a diary. I suppose I was still so stunned at the time I didn't spot two pages were missing.'

'Give!' commanded Paula. 'And explain.'

He handed her the diary open at the pages, stood up and drank some more mineral water. He paced round the room and it was like walking through treacle.

'The handwriting is Sandy's,' he went on. 'I wonder who the *he* was she refers to. And whoever it was she was too right. He is a liar.'

'Sorry. Am I being thick?'

'It's not a big place so, like most people, you've probably never heard of it. But Porvoo is *not* in Sweden – so why did someone think it necessary to lie about where it is?'

'And where is it? Stop being tantalizing.'

'It's an ancient port no more than forty to fifty miles from here. East of Helsinki along the continuation of Highway E3. I think I'm going to look at that place. I'll see if Marler is in.'

'Can I come too?' she asked as he picked up the phone.

Marler tapped on the door a few minutes later. Newman felt rumpled and creased with the heat: as usual, Marler looked fresh as paint in his tropical drill suit.

'I was having a siesta,' he announced. 'Bored with having to wait for Tweed to get back from wherever he's pushed off to. Said would I wait till we had more data before I flew to Rovaniemi. I didn't agree – the way to collect data is to move around, but Tweed is Tweed. How's the most beautiful girl in the world?' he asked Paula.

'Not in a mood for phoney flattery. Too hot . . .'

'Marler,' Newman interjected impatiently, 'when you visited Mauno Sarin he showed you a list of Hauser's companies in Finland. Was one of them in Porvoo?'

'No,' said Marler promptly. 'Why?'

Newman explained about the diary. He handed it to Marler who glanced at the entry, raised his eyebrows, gave back the diary.

303

'Not much to go on,' he commented.

'I'm going to check it out,' Newman said stubbornly, slipping into his shoes.

Opening a drawer, he carefully removed neatly folded shirts, took out the shoulder holster, strapped it on, sheathed the Smith & Wesson, put on his jacket, checked his appearance in the mirror. Marler raised his eyebrows at Paula. She was standing up, hands on her hips.

'I said can I come too, Bob?'

'I suppose so. Marler, you're invited. You helped me locate that copse above INCUBUS's HQ.'

'I can't imagine why. I must have been bowled over with an excess of generosity. Where is Tweed, by the by? Anyone know?'

Newman kept his expression blank. After the confrontation with the two Soviet guards earlier in the day he had flown back from Turku. Partly because he was worried about Paula. Tweed had stayed on in Turku. Anxious about Nield, he had taken a cab to the waterfront. Dillon had insisted on staying with him.

'You need protection,' he said. 'I have a gun, and now Nield is away somewhere you'd be on your own . . .'

'As far as I know he's safe. Outside Helsinki for the moment,' Newman replied. 'Are you or are you not coming with me to Porvoo?' He had collected the BMW which was still parked at the airport on his return.

'Might as well.' Marler sounded dubious. 'Can't really see the point – all on the basis of a note in a diary. And INCUBUS, as I told you, doesn't have a company there. Still, you need someone to look after you.'

'You can get me back here by seven?' Paula queried. 'I've my date with Adam Carver. Of course you can,' she went on, determined not to be left behind. 'And probably nothing will happen at all while we're there . . .'

* * *

With Paula beside him and Marler in the back, Newman drove across the bridge over the river into Porvoo. Glancing downriver towards the sea he saw a collection of single-storey wooden cabins perched at the edge of the water. Each cabin had a wooden landing platform projecting over the river, several with old boats moored to them. The whole atmosphere of Porvoo was so different from Turku's colony of old wooden houses which had an artificial air.

'I like this place,' said Paula. 'It's really old and small. It reeks of what Finland must have been like one hundred years ago.'

Newman parked the BMW, locked it up as Paula and Marler stood looking round. The sun was glaring out of an azure sky in the late afternoon. On the north side of the town old cobbled streets climbed steeply between more wooden houses, many with walls painted rust red and dark roofs. Crocodiles of tourists were trudging wearily up towards the top.

'Where do we start?' Paula asked briskly.

'The waterfront,' Newman replied.

'Why, old boy?' asked Marler.

'I'm not sure why. Instinct. And not so much of the "old boy". Now, let's get moving.'

He led the way across the main road and they walked down a cobbled road behind rows of cabin-like houses which he'd seen crossing the bridge. Narrow cobbled streets, little more than alleys, led down between the houses to where the river flowed. Newman walked purposefully on. Paula had to hurry to catch up with him while Marler trailed behind, smoking one of his king-size.

Paula glanced at Newman as she trotted alongside him. He looked grim. She looped an arm through his.

'Slow down. You look like murder. It's rereading that diary, isn't it?'

'I feel like murder.'

305

'Do you really think there's any point in poking around here? Nothing I can see will help us.'

'So we ask questions. That used to be my job. I'm still good at it. Let's start now. Here.'

A grizzle-faced fisherman was sitting on a wooden stool, tending his nets. He looked up as Newman stopped in front of him, holding several banknotes between his fingers.

'You speak English?'

'Some.'

'I have been asked by INCUBUS to write a history of their activities. You know what they do in Porvoo?'

The fisherman's hands stopped working his nets briefly, then he resumed work after glancing at the banknotes. He took a little while before replying.

'I have never heard of this company. I don't know anything.'

Newman walked on closer to the waterfront. Paula waited until they were out of earshot of the fisherman before she asked her question.

'You think we're getting anywhere?'

'Yes. He was lying. Didn't you notice? He referred to "this company". I never told him INCUBUS was a company. So why should he lie? I think we've stumbled on something. Let's try this chap.'

He stopped by the side of a fisherman caulking his rowing boat. The same question. The same quick glance at the money, at Newman. The same expression of ignorance. Newman walked on, Paula by his side, Marler still trailing the rear.

They walked quite a distance, parallel to the river, and the landscape became wilder, less inhabited. Still some way from the sea, Newman had questioned three other fishermen. Always the same negative result, always the sensation something was being concealed. Where had he experienced this before? God! Suffolk. In the area round

Livingstone Manor. Newman felt the long hand of Franklin D. Hauser reaching out to Porvoo.

It was then that Paula's sharp ears caught the sound of an engine approaching slowly behind them. Then another sound. Someone whistling, a steady persistent whistle. Marler. She glanced over her shoulder. Behind Marler a motor cyclist was cruising slowly, bumping over the rough ground, the rider dressed like a fisherman. Marler cupped his hand in front of his stomach, beckoned for her to join him, a gesture invisible to the motor cyclist. She told Newman she'd join him in a minute, that she ought to have a word with Marler.

'What is it?' she asked, strolling beside Marler.

'Chap on the motor cycle behind us. He's been shadowing us for the past ten minutes, watching the two of you.'

'You don't think he could be an INCUBUS thug?' she asked, alarmed.

'No idea. Let's see how things develop. No other fishermen in sight.'

As he spoke the motor cyclist rode slowly past them. When he reached Newman he stopped the machine, jumped off and began to push it alongside Newman. He would be in his thirties, Newman estimated. A fresh-faced man with thick dark hair and a five o'clock shadow round his firm chin.

'You've been asking questions, I understand,' he said.

'Have I? So what?'

'You've been asking the wrong people.'

'So I gather.'

Newman was careful not to show any eagerness. He continued walking, the motor cyclist continued pushing the motor bike beside him. There was silence for a couple of minutes.

'Ask me the questions,' the fisherman suggested.

Newman repeated the question he'd put to the other

fishermen. His companion remained silent. Newman produced the banknotes and held them in view. The reaction was unexpected.

'I don't want your money. How do I know who you are? You could be an agent of Hauser's.'

'True. Sensible of you to be so careful.' Newman produced his press card, handed it to the man. The fisherman stopped, screwed up his alert eyes. Newman realized he had never seen the form of identification before. He took a chance.

'I'm Robert Newman, a foreign correspondent. I'm investigating INCUBUS Oy. I think there's something wrong with that corporation.'

'There is.' The fisherman handed back the card. 'I fished for INCUBUS until a few months ago. Here you fish for INCUBUS or have a bad time. They threatened me, told me not to fish for them anymore.'

'Go on. I'm interested.'

'Out there,' he waved a hand towards the sea, 'they have a huge factory ship for processing frozen fish. The *New York*. It is the most advanced factory ship in the world. We supply the fish, take them well out to sea to the factory ship. It cleans, guts, freezes and packs them. They even have the refrigerator trucks on board . The *New York* is like a giant car ferry. They have constructed a large ramp on the coast by a road. Every now and again the *New York* comes inshore – the water is very deep where the ramp is – and trucks drive ashore and on to their destinations for delivery.'

'Sounds like a legitimate operation. Legal,' said Newman.

'Something funny is going on. The *New York* always lands its trucks after dark. No one is permitted near that ramp when the *New York* is unloading. That is one reason I was told I had lost my job. I watched the unloading and the guards caught me.'

'Guards?'

'Men with rifles. And no one is allowed near the factory ship after they have delivered the fish. I was curious and sailed close after I'd unloaded my catch. Aboard they have more guards with rifles. I was seen. They opened fire but I got away. The trouble is someone must have had binoculars. They identified my vessel. That factory ship is used for something more than freezing fish.'

'Information should be rewarded,' Newman said producing the banknotes again.

'I said I didn't want your money,' the fisherman said vehemently. 'I want to hit back at Hauser. And there is something else which puzzles me. I have a cousin in Kemijärvi. That is north of the Arctic Circle, on the way to the Meteorological Institute and the Soviet border.'

'What else is there then?' Newman prodded as the man hesitated.

'I was staying with my cousin and saw an INCUBUS refrigerated truck passing through east on Route 82. Who out there would want all that frozen fish?'

'I have no idea. It does sound strange.'

'You might be able to check one of their trucks if you go back quickly to Porvoo. An INCUBUS truck broke down. It was repaired but when I came through Porvoo an hour or so ago I saw the driver in a café having lunch. You might catch up that truck in your BMW.'

'Any idea which route it follows?' Newman produced a map and the fisherman traced a route. 'Through Lahti and then north along E4?' Newman remarked. 'How do you know that?'

'Because one night I followed a truck on my motor cycle. You will have to move fast before he leaves Porvoo. If he has gone – the truck was parked just round the corner where you left your BMW – you might catch up with him.'

'Thanks. Thanks very much.' Newman turned to join

Paula and Marler who had stayed behind as Paula pretended to examine some wild flowers. 'And take care of
yourself – these are tough people.'

With Newman at the wheel they were driving through
wild forested country and Paula gazed, fascinated, at the
lonely wilderness of dense fir trees going on forever as
Newman sped along a superbly surfaced road. Through a
gap in the trees she caught a glimpse of an idyllic lake, a
sheet of pure blue water with not a sign of human habitation. Finland just went on and on, a haven of peace and
beauty with pollution unknown.

They had rushed back to Porvoo, found the truck had
gone, had jumped inside the BMW and now they were
following the route the fisherman had described. Paula sat
with the map on her lap and was acting as navigator next
to Newman. Marler sat in the back, making discouraging
remarks.

'You know,' he began again, 'I can't see we're going to
find anything – just supposin' we ever find the truck. I
think this trip is a bit loony.'

'Thanks for the vote of confidence,' snapped Newman.

'Any time, old chap. Any time.'

Paula glanced at Newman. His expression was still grim
and he stared ahead as they rounded a long curve hemmed in by the walls of forest. No other traffic in either
direction. Pure bliss, Paula was thinking. Where else in
the world could you find such dream-like country to drive
through all by yourself . . .

Her musings were interrupted without warning. The
curve had ended and a straight stretch of highway sprawled into the distance. A half-mile ahead was a large truck.
As the gap closed she saw it was a large refrigerated
truck. Across the rear of the vehicle was the logo.
INCUBUS.

310

'Well, I'll be damned.' Marler leaned forward. 'Take back all I said. Never thought we'd catch the blighter.'

'The next decision is how do we handle it,' Newman commented.

'Pull in by the side of the road, if you please,' Marler requested.

Newman, wondering what he had in mind, pulled up, switched off the engine. Paula, her window down, was stunned by the silence of the forest which she could *hear*. This was paradise.

'Now, listen to me,' Marler went on. 'I'll tackle the driver . No argument. The INCUBUS lot have photographs of you both. God knows how many with those film units you told us about at Arlanda and the Stockholm ferry terminal. They have no pics of me at all. So we change places. I drive and you two occupy the back. When we get close both of you go into a clinch. They'll have circulated the photographs they took of you. And those trucks have large wing mirrors. OK?'

They were outside the car, changing position, when Paula looked at Marler. His expression was businesslike.

'You don't have a weapon to defend yourself,' she pointed out.

'But you're wrong there, my dear.'

Marler hoisted up his left trouser leg. A leather sheath was strapped to the inner side of his slim leg. He hauled out a large knife with a vicious-looking blade, then shoved it back into the sheath.

'Finnish hunting knife,' he told her. 'Available at all good hardware stores in Helsinki. You must have noticed.' He looked into the far distance along the ruler-straight road. 'Nothing coming. Let's get cracking . . .'

Glancing in his rear-view mirror, he saw the road was deserted behind them and drove off. As he got closer to the truck he realized it was trundling along at a steady but unexciting pace. He stared through the windscreen.

'They have a load of aerials above the cab. Perhaps they are in touch with Mars.'

In the rear Newman had gone into a clinch with Paula. He whispered, 'Might as well make this convincing,' and pressed his mouth to hers. In his mirror Marler observed their faces were hidden. He accelerated, pulled alongside the large truck, saw to this surprise there was only the driver. No guard beside him. Perhaps it was a clever display of innocence? But what were they guilty of?

Marler began tooting his horn. On. Off. On ... The driver, short and stocky, stared at him. Marler grinned, gestured over his shoulder, then waved to the side of the road, continuing his nerve-wracking barrage of horn tooting. The driver shrugged, slowed, pulled in to the side, stopped.

Marler stopped just short of the cab, nipped out of the car. He was standing by the cab, looking up as the driver opened the door. He grinned again.

'I say, do you speak English? Jolly good. Thought I ought to warn you. Your bally registration plate is hanging off the rear. End up in the road any second. A patrol car might get excited. You know what they're like. Anything to fill up their little notebooks ...'

As he was speaking the driver lowered himself on to the footplate, down on to the road. Marler hauled out his hair spray canister with his left hand, pressed the button and spray squirted into the driver's eyes. He yelped, lifted both hands to his eyes.

'Jesus Chr —'

He never completed the expletive because Marler's clenched right fist rammed up into his jaw. The impact knocked him backwards and Marler grabbed him under the armpits as he sagged unconscious. Newman and Paula had dived out of the BMW and ran up to him.

'He's got a whole load of communications gimmicks inside,' Marler warned as he heaved the man back inside the cab. 'Including a microphone and some gimmicks I haven't seen. Stay there a sec.'

Climbing into the cab he searched the pockets of the inert body. He found the bunch of keys in a jacket pocket, held them up.

'Bingo! Now let's see which one unlocks the doors at the back . . .'

He had to try four keys before the lock turned. Reaching up to the handle, he swung the right-hand door open and hauled himself inside. The door had the appearance of a safe vault and icy air met him as Newman followed. Paula stayed outside to warn them if other traffic appeared.

Marler swung up the steel catch on what appeared to be a large consignment of frozen fish, stared down inside with the aid of a pencil flash. He let out his breath between his teeth. He scooped up a handful of grey plastic dough and moulded it, his teeth chattering with the intense cold. Paula opened the second door from the outside. She peered inside.

'You'll freeze to death in there,' she warned. 'The air flowing out feels like the Arctic.'

'It's better with that other door open,' Newman called out. 'And we can see what we're doing.'

He had opened another metal container and stared at the contents. He looked up as Marler brushed past him, jumped out of the truck, ran to the BMW, came back with a cleaning cloth. Newman bent lower over the open container and froze.

'Marler, come here.'

'What is it?'

Marler had been wrapping his cravat round a large ball of the grey dough. He came to Newman and gazed down inside the container. Newman straightened up.

'Unless I'm very much mistaken those are sticks of gelignite. And they're sweating. You took a course of

313

explosives at the training house Amersham in the Chilterns.'

'That's jelly,' Marler said tersely. 'Let's get clear of this truck. It's a ticking time bomb . . .'

'Maybe we should check a few more cases?'

'And maybe we should not. My guess is they all contain explosive. Let's hoof it.'

'What have you got there?' Newman asked.

Marler was stuffing his cravat inside his jacket pocket and jumped into the road. He gestured for Newman to get a move on.

'Semtex, the plastic explosive, is my guess. Luckily it is harmless without a detonator and all the gadgets.'

Marler fetched more cleaning cloths from the BMW, twisted them into skeins as he stood by the cab. 'Give me a bit of help,' he said to Newman. 'We have to immobilize the driver in case he regains consciousness while we're gone.' Climbing inside the cab he checked the pulse of the slumped figure. 'Good pulse rate. He's just out cold for a little longer.'

Newman turned the driver over, held his hands behind his back while Marler tied his wrists together with the makeshift ropes. They then tied together his ankles. Newman looked at the dashboard which was more like a console. He picked up the microphone, smashed it against the floor and they both jumped to the ground, closing the cab door.

Paula appeared from the rear of the truck. She ran to them and spoke quickly.

'I've closed the doors at the back. I heard what you said.'

'Better lock them,' said Marler.

He ran to the rear of the vehicle. Paula took her map out of the BMW and marked it with a cross.

'Mauno Sarin,' Newman said as Marler returned, holding aloft the bunch of keys. 'We have to contact him fast.'

'There was a phone box about ten miles back the way we came,' said Paula.

'Don't get into the car,' Marler warned. 'I want both of you to run a hundred yards up the highway, get as far away as you can before I start up the car. It's just possible the engine vibrations might send this lot sky high. No, don't argue, Newman. Get Paula out of the way. *Now* for God's sake . . .'

Gasping for breath – running in the heat was strenuous – Newman and Paula stopped further up the highway and waited. As the sun beat down on them the tension built up. Newman wished he'd insisted on taking over the wheel. Marler sat behind the wheel alongside the front of the truck. Paula clenched her hands into fists as they waited for the sound of the engine starting up.

What the hell was Marler waiting for? Newman wondered. He reached for Paula's right hand. She unclenched her fist, entwined her fingers with Newman's, gripping him tight. The silence which had seemed so wonderful now pressed down on her like a menace. She prayed it would be all right, prayed with all her might.

Behind the wheel Marler had a fresh unlit cigarette between his lips. He glanced up at the truck. Within the next few seconds he would either be alive or a mess of debris scattered over the countryside. No point in hanging about. Newman was right: they had to contact Sarin.

Paula and Newman stood close together like statues. She was trembling. The silence was broken with the sound of Marler turning on the ignition. It sounded like a thunderclap to Paula. God! The truck was exploding . . .

The BMW slid smoothly away from the truck, drove slowly towards them. Marler executed a U-turn and pulled up alongside them. They jumped into the car, Paula grabbing the front passenger seat, picking up her map. With the unlit cigarette still in his mouth Marler drove slowly back, glided past the stationary truck, continued slowly for a couple of hundred yards and then rammed his foot down.

31

Newman and Marler called on Mauno Sarin at Ratakatu at nine the same evening, as previously arranged when Newman had phoned him from the isolated box on the highway. Sarin was standing behind his desk, nodded to Marler, came round his desk to shake hands with Newman.

'I hope your visit this time is different from a few years ago when we travelled to Estonia together.'

'As I told you earlier, there àre grim similarities,' Newman replied and left it at that. 'What's the news about that INCUBUS refrigerated truck?' he asked as he sat in the chair Sarin had ushered him to.

'You would like coffee?'

Sarin looked at Newman, at Marler, who was also seated in a hard-backed chair. There were no frills, little comfort, in the austere Mauno Sarin's office. Both men shook their heads. Sarin settled himself behind his desk, began twiddling a pencil between his fingers.

'I responded to your call immediately,' Sarin began. 'I despatched six patrol cars, each with two armed men. When you handed the phone to Paula Grey she described the location perfectly. The patrol cars arrived,' he glanced at a typed sheet on his desk, 'thirty-five minutes after I received your call. They found an INCUBUS truck. The driver was asleep in his cab, said the extreme heat had affected him.'

Newman frowned, leaned forward. 'Yes. What about the explosives? Go on.'

Sarin waved the pencil like a schoolmaster. 'The patrol car men checked every container in the truck. Frozen fish in every one. No sign of explosives . . .'

'I don't believe it,' Marler interjected.

'You have to believe it. So there is no hard evidence to back up your story.'

'Oh, yes, there is,' Marler snapped. He took out the folded cravat, exposed the ball of dough-like substance, handed it to the Finn. 'I took that myself out of one of the containers. Newman was there, can vouch for what I say. Semtex.'

Sarin stared at the grey ball, pursed his lips. He pressed a button under his desk. A short dark-haired Finn appeared after knocking on the door.

'Karma, take this material downstairs to our explosives expert. Ask him if he can identify it. At once, please.'

Newman waited until they were alone before he asked his question.

'Did the patrol car people describe the driver?'

Again Sarin glanced at the typed sheet. 'Yes, they did. A tall lean-faced man with a moustache. In his fifties.'

'They switched drivers,' Marler protested. 'Ours was short, stocky, in his early thirties.'

'They switched trucks too,' Newman intervened. 'How the devil did they do it so fast? How did they know?' He recalled the interior of the truck's cab. 'I should have thought of it. The dashboard has a complex console system. I smashed the microphone, as I told you. But with a consignment of high explosives they'd have a sophisticated system of keeping an eye on the truck without being obvious, without having a car with guards behind it. What do you think, Marler?'

'Only explanation for their vanishing trick. Quite possibly they had OK signals sent at five-minutes intervals by

317

the driver. There was a load of communication equipment on top of the cab. They're clever. When they suspected something was wrong they sent out another truck, probably with two drivers and several guards. One of the fresh drivers then drove off the explosives truck while the other one parked where we'd left the first one. He pretended to be asleep when the patrol cars arrived. Do you believe us?' he asked Sarin.

'Just a minute,' Newman broke in. 'We left the keys to unlock the rear doors inside that phone box, as we said we would when we phoned you. Did anyone pick them up?'

'Yes. A patrol car picked them up.' Sarin opened a drawer, showed them a bunch of keys. 'Every key was used to try and open the rear doors. None of them fitted.'

'Of course they didn't,' Marler told him.

'And,' Sarin went on, 'there are no markings on these keys to link them with INCUBUS.'

'I'd noticed that,' Marler responded. 'Mind if I light a cigarette?'

'If you must.'

'Do you believe us?'

'What is there to believe?'

There was a knock on the door. Karma entered with his normal lack of any expression. He waited.

'Well?' demanded Sarin testily. 'Any news?'

'Yes. It is Semtex. No doubt about it.'

'Thank you, Karma. That will be all.'

Newman seized his opportunity. 'Also a reliable source told me he'd seen an INCUBUS truck driving through Kemijärvi in the Arctic Circle. It drove on east towards the Meteorological Institute you told Marler about. How much frozen fish do they consume there? And can't your Coastguard people go aboard that factory ship I mentioned on the phone?'

'No. It operates well outside Finnish coastal waters.'

'Then we won't take up any more of your valuable time.'

'And can I take that?' Marler asked, also standing up, reaching out a hand towards the Semtex Karma had left on the desk.

'No, you cannot.'

They left behind a very worried and frustrated Mauno Sarin.

'Why did you try and get hold of that Semtex?' Newman asked as he drove the BMW away from Ratakatu.

'Oh, you never know when it might come in useful. And I do know how to construct a detonator and a timer. Any hardware shop in Helsinki has the equipment – household – I can convert.'

'Except you haven't any Semtex.'

'Shame on you. You weren't very observant when we were out on that highway examining the truck.'

Marler opened the glove compartment. Inside was a cleaning cloth wrapped round what looked like a brick. He peeled away a portion of the cloth, showed Newman its contents. A brick-shaped quantity of grey dough-like material.

'Semtex. Enough to cause quite a devastating blow-up. And I wonder how the fair Paula is enjoying her dinner date?'

Paula wore an exuberant orange print dress decorated with white sunflowers. She had carefully chosen a long-sleeved dress with a high necked collar so that no part of her anatomy was bare for Carver's roving hand to touch.

'I know a marvellously romantic place out of town,' he had said when he met her in the lobby of the Hesperia.

319

'I've brought my Cadillac so we can get there in no time. You'll love the restaurant, the view over the sea.'

'Thank you.' She had given him her best smile. 'But I've already booked a table in your name at my favourite restaurant. The Palace. And that overlooks the harbour.'

'I see.' For a few seconds he couldn't conceal his annoyance, then he rallied. 'Sounds great. The Palace it is. Let's move. Have a drink in the bar first to warm us up. Although, looking at you, I'm warmed up already . . .'

Carver was wearing an off-white silk suit and a white tie. She thought he looked like a paint salesman but carefully refrained from saying so. Over the dinner table he openly admired her with his eyes but she pretended not to notice his close attention. She waited until they were eating the main course before she broached the subject.

'We have a mutual friend. Evelyn Lennox. I understand you went to see her at her cottage in Walberswick.'

He paused briefly before replying. 'I did know her but only briefly.'

'Really?' She sipped her Chablis. 'She told me you also visited her at her place in Wandsworth. That's in London.'

'I know it is.' He had snapped out the words. 'I mean I did see her there as well. It was a business relationship.'

'I didn't gather that from her. You chased after her up to Suffolk when she didn't visit you in London. Those are her words, not mine.'

She smiled again. Sipping her wine she thought his dark eyes grew even darker, more penetrating. He thinks he can hypnotize a woman, she thought, enjoying herself.

'I think maybe she embroidered things a bit,' he suggested.

'Maybe.' She didn't sound convinced. 'Of course she had a lot to upset her. First the murder of her brother-in-law, Ed Riverton.' She gazed out of the window. 'Weird to think they dragged his body out of that harbour last February.'

'The conversation seems to have taken a macabre turn. I took you out to enjoy yourself.'

'Oh, don't worry. I'm having the time of my life. Then almost at the same time her sister, Sandra Riverton, was found murdered as well. Which way round was it? Did Ed die first or was it Sandra?'

'I'm sure I have no idea. Has anyone? But you're right. Evelyn was, naturally, rather thrown by those grisly incidents. I tried to comfort her.'

'Really? Good for you. But I thought you said it was a business relationship.'

'Well, it was. But she was in a bit of a state. Had to confide in someone, I suppose.'

She hit him again. 'That surprises me. Evelyn isn't the confiding sort of girl. And I wouldn't have thought you were her type. I could be wrong, of course.'

The smooth man of the world was floundering under Paula's onslaught. He wiped his mouth with a napkin, eyed her warily, took a large drink of wine, refilled her glass, then his own.

'Maybe after dinner we could go for a drive outside Helsinki,' he suggested. He glanced at her. Had she had enough to drink yet to mellow? Some of the girls these days had heads like rocks. 'The scenery is superb and it would give us a breath of fresh air.'

'Except the air outside is like the inside of a hot oven.'

She withdrew her hand from the table as he reached out to take hold of it, picked up her fork and smiled.

'This is an excellent dinner. Do you often take girls out? Probably not. Your job must take up most of your time. So I don't imagine you're used to feminine company.'

He didn't like that either, she could see. The image of an experienced Casanova was slipping fast. He started

321

eating quickly, furious, and made no reply as she chattered on, breaking off briefly to drink half her refilled glass of the Chablis.

'Adam, what do you actually do at INCUBUS? Buried in paper work most of the time? Is it boring?'

'No, it isn't.' He put down his knife and fork, wishing he hadn't replied with such vehemence. She was dangling him on a string, damn her. 'I'm Vice President of Banking Ops. I handle very large sums of money, sums you've probably never even dreamt of.'

'So you were involved in the takeover of Egon Schmidt's bank in Frankfurt. I read about it in the paper.'

'That was a straightforward business deal.'

'Was it?' She twirled her glass, watching him over the rim. 'The father, Egon, was determined not to sell out. Then he goes and gets killed when his car blows up. Which leaves the way open for you to make a deal with son Dieter, who was always willing to sell. That bomb must have smoothed the way for you, Adam.'

'The Red Army Faction terrorists killed him. One of those coincidences which happens in business.'

'But the Red Army Faction lot denied they'd had anything to do with it.'

'They would, wouldn't they?'

He refilled her glass, ordered a fresh bottle. How the hell had the conversation taken this twist? Setting out to seduce Paula, he had been coaxed into talking too much about INCUBUS. As she drank more, he waited and then threw at her the vital question.

'We've been talking too much about me. It's you I'm interested in. Who do you work for? Who is your boss? Difficult to work for, is he?'

'I work for an insurance company.' She looked straight at Carver. 'Ed Riverton had a life policy with us. I'm here to find out what happened to him. The policy could be null and void under certain conditions.'

'And you're the boss of the outfit?'

'Heavens no. Martin Sheffield is,' she said, making up the first name which came into her head. 'And he's a peach to work for.'

'He's with you now? Here in Helsinki?'

'Half the time I never know where he is. He's a regular will-o'-the-wisp. No, I don't think I'll have a dessert or coffee. I think I'd like to go back to my hotel.'

'The Hesperia? I'll drive you there.' He called for the bill, produced a credit card, dealt with the paperwork. She waited until he had finished.

'Thank you for the offer, Adam. Sorry to break up a lovely evening. I've enjoyed every minute of it. But I'm tired. And I've got a headache coming on. Must be the heat. And I'll go back in a taxi. Don't push me.'

No way was she going to climb back inside his bloody Cadillac. As they stood outside waiting for a taxi in the humid air of late evening Carver struggled to control his frustration.

'At least I can see you again,' he began confidently. 'I'll give you a buzz at the Hesperia. Next time we can go anywhere you choose.'

'Maybe. Thank you again for a superb meal.'

She dived inside the taxi before he could kiss her on the cheek. She didn't wave to him as the cab moved off. Settling herself, she smiled. Newman wasn't the only one who could stir up the pot.

Sitting behind the wheel of his parked Cadillac Carver hammered his fist against the dashboard. The bitch! But with a bit of luck he could get back at her, teach her a lesson she'd never forget.

32

Hauser had flown back from Turku in the evening, had climbed into the waiting limo at Helsinki Airport. The chauffeur drove the bullet-proof Mercedes to Hauser's town house, the weird turreted edifice Newman had pointed out to Cord Dillon when they had followed Hauser to the airport.

Inside the house, after a shower and a change of clothes, Hauser had climbed to the turret room he had converted into a combined office and living room. He poured himself a slug of bourbon, was sipping it when the phone rang. Adam Carver had arrived, wanted to see him.

'Then tell him to drag his ass up here . . .'

The room was eight-sided and Hauser stood looking out of a window at the deserted park while Carver reported on his dinner with Paula Grey. He would like to have edited the version of their conversation over dinner but he knew that Hauser had an uncanny knack of sensing when a man was leaving something out.

He was also annoyed that as he began talking Frank Galvone came into the tower. Hauser told him to sit, to listen, to help himself to a drink if that would help him keep his trap shut. Hauser was not in the best of moods.

Irina Serov had flown back with Hauser but, for security reasons, she had waited half an hour after Hauser left the Lear jet. She had then taken a taxi to a company apartment near where Peggy Vanderheld had lived.

Hauser had ordered Manescu and Ziegler to travel to Helsinki by train. Each had been given a different address in apartments at Setula near the airport. Hauser was assembling his forces.

Carver continued his report while Galvone poured himself a drink, then leaned against a wall, holding the glass in fingers covered with black hair. He watched Carver with a cynical expression.

'Sounds like you boobed it,' he commented when Carver had finished speaking.

Hauser rounded on him viciously. 'Frank, I thought I asked you to keep the trap shut. How are things up at the Institute? You're just back from the Arctic Circle?'

'Flew in an hour ago, Chief.' He smiled with satisfaction. 'Security has been doubled. Really tightened up. I had to kick a few people in the crotch to waken them up. They're awake now. Anyone who tries to snoop around will end up as duck soup.'

'Take that grin off your ugly mug. No security is one hundred per cent. How many times have I to repeat it? Listen. Both of you. We have another problem. Locating the opposition. And there is one – look at how we saved that truck out of Porvoo. I told you about that, Frank, when you called me from the airport. Adam, I'll explain that incident later. Due entirely to my persistence we may have identified the opposition. Including the top man.'

Hauser walked across to a Turkish table inlaid with marble chips of various colours. It was eight-sided, to match the design of the turret. Hauser had an obsessively precise mind. He picked up a sheaf of typed sheets.

'I have here a list of Brits and Americans who arrived at hotels in Helsinki during the past week.'

'How on earth did you get hold of their names?' Carver asked in a tone of admiration.

'Adam, why do you always want to know how we operate even when it's something outside your sphere?

325

Hell, it was easy. I sent a team round the hotels with plenty of money. We've been careful to see we have friends planted in the major and medium establishments. I checked through this list while I was changing. Something came out of your abortive conversation with Paula Grey. She said her boss was Martin Sheffield. OK?'

'OK.'

'But it's not OK. No one of that name is registered at the Hesperia.' He looked at Galvone. 'Now Adam said when he asked Grey the name of her boss she said Martin Sheffield. She's staying at the Hesperia – but she's just moved there from the Marski. And at the same time a Martin *Baker* moved in at the Hesperia. A Brit. You know, Adam, when you spring a question like you did, the person who wants to disguise a name often uses the same Christian name and alters the surname. Now Adam,' he said sarcastically, 'you've just had an exhausting evening so push off to bed.'

He waited until he was alone with Galvone. Inserting a cigarette into his holder he lit it.

'Frank, that Grey woman knows too much. Some of the things she asked Adam about were too sensitive for my liking – the Schmidt bank takeover, for example. We have to find out more of what she knows.'

'Sure. How do we go about it?'

'We kidnap her, using Adam as bait, you schmuck.'

'You didn't mention the idea in front of Carver.'

'No, I didn't, did I? Think my memory is going? He won't even know the part he's playing. I sensed he's taken a fancy to Paula Grey. Now push off yourself . . .'

Hauser smiled to himself as the door closed. He was skilled at the game: never let the right hand know what the left hand is doing. And vice versa.

He took out a small box from a drawer, extracted a circular filter instrument, screwed it on to his phone. Manufactured in one of his laboratories outside Boston, it distorted the voice. He dialled the number of the apartment where Irina Serov was staying. When she answered he used her code name.

'Sonia, this is Morrow speaking. Name of the subject you contact is Martin Baker. Got it? Staying at the Hesperia. Get next to him tomorrow. He could be the top man causing me a little trouble., Do your stuff. All the way if necessary . . .'

Tweed arrived back from Turku late with Nield and Dillon. It was ten o'clock when he arrived at the Hesperia. He'd had nothing to eat for hours but he was tireless. Before ordering from room service he made a number of calls.

Two were to rooms in the hotel – to Paula and Harry Butler. Then two more, this time outside calls to The Palace to Newman and Marler asking them to come and see him at once. He looked at Dillon as the American came out of his bathroom, drying his face with a towel.

'Nield will be here in a minute. The others are coming in from The Palace. Time we had a full-scale conference.'

'I'd like something to eat. You seem to exist on mineral water. I'm going to my room for a fresh shirt. Be back soon. Don't forget the food.'

Tweed paced round the room when he was alone, hands clasped behind his back. Nield was the first to arrive.

'Couldn't talk to you on the train. Wasn't sure Dillon was in on the third man business.'

'Tell me . . .'

Tweed continued pacing as Nield talked about his experience aboard the *Skäret*. When he said he could describe the third man Tweed made a dismissive gesture.

'You say you can get the photos developed at a shop which prints and develops in a few hours in the morning. Wait until you show me the pictures . . .'

He broke off as Paula came in. 'That was quite an

327

evening I had with that Carver. He's too clever by half . . .'

Again Tweed listened while she relayed to him the conversation in detail. He frowned when she had finished.

'You took a chance, raising some of those issues.'

'Oh, I lied like a trooper. Especially about Evelyn Lennox being a friend of mine. As you've probably guessed, I recalled what Bob had told me about Wandsworth and his trip to Walberswick. As to taking a chance, I thought the plan was to stir up INCUBUS, unsettle Hauser.'

'You did a good job,' Tweed decided.

He broke off as Harry Butler arrived. He glanced at his old sparring partner, Nield. 'On your hols? Lazing in the sun while I do some real work?'

'You wouldn't have enjoyed being with me this afternoon,' Nield retorted.

Butler sat down, looked at Tweed. 'Since I was left behind like a spare wheel I decided to poke around. I hired a Saab, drove out to the airport. Turned out to be a hub of action. Spent the whole day there, a very long day.'

'Do you think you were seen?' Tweed enquired. 'I was counting on there being four people INCUBUS doesn't know exist. You, Nield, Marler, myself.'

'Shortly after I arrived,' Butler reported in his matter-of-fact way, 'I saw an airport official in a pale blue uniform throw his cap into the back of his car, then go back inside for something. I was wearing a blue jacket, the nearest I had to their uniform. I pinched the cap, walked inside the concourse. The owner came out, never noticed his cap was gone, drove off. All day long people thought I was an airport official. Merging into the background you call it.'

'Clever,' Tweed commented. 'What did you see?'

'Hauser and Carver arriving in a whacking great limo. Recognized them from Marler's photos. Then Newman and Dillon arrive. Hauser and Carver board a Lear jet,

328

take off. Newman and Dillon catch the flight to Turku . . .'

'I never saw you,' interjected Newman who had arrived with Marler.

'You weren't supposed to. Can I get on? Then that brown Buick LeSabre, turns up. Six tough-looking thugs jump out, board two Sikorsky choppers, take off, head north.'

'Reinforcements for the Meteorological Institute,' Tweed suggested.

'No idea. But we know now they have two helicopters on the payroll. I then hang around for hours, moving about so I'm not conspicuous. This evening the Lear jet arrives back. The black limo is waiting for Hauser when he walks rapidly from the jet. For a big man he can move. I notice the retractable staircase you leave the jet by is still in place. I decide to follow Hauser. The limo drives him to a house out of Disneyland. I can locate it for you on a map . . .'

'We know where it is,' Newman told him. 'But now we know where Hauser is. Sorry.'

Butler had a large audience as he made his terse report. Paula, perched on the end of the bed, listened attentively. Newman sat astride a chair, watching him. Marler was leaning against a wall, twiddling a cigarette between his fingers. Nield stood with his arms folded. Tweed also was standing, his eyes fixed on Butler, registering every detail.

'Because of that staircase still left in place, I drive back to the airport. I'm lucky. I arrive just in time to see a woman leaving the jet. The brown Buick is back. She gets into it and I follow it into Helsinki, then – sorry about this – I lose her.'

'Description, please,' requested Tweed.

'Difficult. She's wearing those big tinted goggle glasses, a scarf wrapped round her head. She's slim, medium height. I wondered about that last bit – she walks as though she's wearing elevated heels.'

'So she could be small?' suggested Tweed.

'Could be. By then I reckon I've seen all I'm going to at the airport. So I drive to the railway station.'

My God, Paula thought, he never stops. No wonder they nickname him The Beaver.

'I've left my cap on a counter at the airport,' Butler explained. 'I take off my jacket and hang around that station. I see you, Tweed, get off a train with Dillon. Then I see someone else I recognize from the photograph get off the same train after you two have gone. Mănescu. And with him is a tough-looking thickset character with a brutal jaw. Looks Teutonic. Then, Bingo! The brown Buick turns up and they jump inside it. I follow the Buick to a place called Setula near the airport, fairly near anyway. Mănescu slips away into an apartment block. The Buick drives off with our Teutonic friend and I've lost him.' He drank mineral water from a glass Paula had put by his side. 'That's it.'

'That is indeed a lot.' Marler whistled with admiration.

'The brown Buick,' Tweed said. 'Who was driving it?'

'Uniformed chauffeur each time. He gets around.'

Tweed sighed audibly. Paula looked at him and saw he was still fresh and alert.

'Why the sigh?'

'The precision of it all,' Tweed commented. 'Hauser is a top-flight organizer. I suppose that's how he got to the top of the world.' He looked at Butler. 'Those six men you saw board the two helicopters. Any idea of nationality?'

'Mittel-European. Slav types. Could be Czechs, Romanians, Bulgars. Who can tell the difference?'

'The vanishing men,' Tweed said half to himself.

'Isn't it about time we planned what we're all going to

330

do next?' drawled Marler. 'We have to stop waiting sometime.'

'We move when the moment is right,' Tweed told him. 'And I said we needed more data. Today we have accumulated more than I ever dreamed was possible. Newman and Marler with Paula discovered Hauser is transporting huge amounts of high explosives north. Maybe to somewhere near the Institute.'

'Maybe to the Institute itself,' Newman suggested. 'It was Hauser's construction outfit which built the place.'

'Butler,' Tweed continued, 'has provided data about where a number of key people are, that they've come in to Helsinki. Harry, are you sure you saw Manescu get off that train? Was it a positive identification?'

'Positive. He wore a beret and a scarf wrapped round the lower part of his face. In this heat! The scarf slipped for a moment and I saw him full face. I've studied the only photo of Manescu taken you showed me. That is until Marler snapped him leaving INCUBUS's HQ. I studied that pic of him without his moustache. Manescu got off that train, is now at Setula. A half-hour's drive from where I'm sitting.'

'Not good news,' Tweed commented. 'Hauser is assembling his forces.'

'Let's not forget,' Newman intervened, 'one of the main objectives. At least as far as I'm concerned. Who murdered Sandy back in Suffolk? Find the killer, make him talk and we have Hauser over a barrel.'

'I agree. Everything is linked together now. The murder of Sandy, the murder last February of Ed Riverton, and the botched attempt to kill Peggy Vanderheld. On top of the murders we have the explosives. On top of that we've the newspaper reports of three assassinations in Prague, Budapest and Bucharest. And Manescu's presence merges the two original investigations – one into INCUBUS, the other into tracing the whereabouts of the

331

professional villains who escaped from the *Securitate*, etc. INCUBUS almost certainly has been recruiting them.'

'So,' Marler said impatiently, 'it's time I made my recce of that mysterious Institute. And I've found out how I can do just that?'

'How?' demanded Tweed.

'This morning I was up early, went to the Akateeminen Bookshop to buy some maps of Lapland. I overheard a couple of women talking about a tourist excursion tomorrow to the Institute. They leave by coach from the Intercontinental next door. Mostly English, I gathered. They're a few places short. I propose to join that tour. Coach takes the party to the airport mid-morning. Perfect cover.'

'I'll think about it. Let you know in the morning.'

'I'd like to have a positive answer now.'

'In the morning.'

Tweed answered automatically. Watching him, Paula realized his mind was far away. He was on the verge of taking a major decision. Tweed straightened up.

'Everyone had better get some sleep. Tomorrow I may move all of us into the same hotel. I think the time has come to mass our forces. I feel Hauser breathing down my neck. So off you go.'

'What do you mean?' asked Dillon, who had been quiet up to now. 'Breathing down your neck?'

'This sudden influx of some dangerous characters into Helsinki. I think Newman achieved his purpose when he went to see Hauser at his HQ. He disturbed him. Now Paula has rattled Carver, who will undoubtedly report back to his boss. Hauser is preparing something nasty for us. Off to bed . . .'

Paula stayed perched on the bed until she was alone with him. He looked at her, wondering what she had on her mind.

'If Marler goes to the Institute with that tourist party

332

I'd like to go with him. Don't argue again. A couple, a man and a woman are less noticeable.'

'I'll let you know in the morning. Now, I want to think.'

Left to himself, Tweed paced slowly round his room. It had been a long active day but he still felt fresh. He was sorting out the data, the fresh pieces of the jigsaw which he had found out during the day. Newman was right: a lot hinged on identifying the murderer of Sandy and Ed Riverton. The same man, Tweed was sure.

When he eventually went to bed his thoughts still wouldn't leave him alone. He had a strong instinct he'd taken the decision to marshal his forces too late. Hauser was going to strike savagely.

33

The next morning Irina Serov arrived very early at the Hesperia. She had bleached her hair blonde, wore four-inch high-heeled shoes, had piled her hair up, applied mascara to make her eyes look larger and had light green-tinted glasses perched on the bridge of her Roman nose.

She waited until a male receptionist was free, approached the counter with her prepared story. The receptionist gazed at her with interest. She wore a tight-fitting sleeveless blouse which hugged her figure and a pleated mini-skirt. He had seen her legs as she entered.

'I wondered if you could help me?' In her slim hand she held two banknotes. 'I'm trying to get a job with a Martin Baker who is staying here. But I don't know what he looks like.'

'I do,' the receptionist said quickly. 'He's probably

having breakfast on the first floor. I called his room a few minutes ago and there was no reply.'

'I haven't had breakfast,' she said in a husky voice, staring at him. 'If you could possibly see your way to pointing him out to me . . .'

The receptionist accompanied her up to the first floor. In the elevator she hugged her shoulder bag closer, checked to see the flap was unbuttoned. The receptionist pointed out the guest to her, refused the tip.

'Maybe we could have a drink together?' he suggested. 'I go off duty at six.'

'So I'll be here at six. Thank you so much . . .'

The dining room had long tables which could seat eight of the guests. People sat where there was a place. The dining room was fairly full but the seat next to Martin Baker was vacant. She collected bread and jam from the buffet, stood behind the empty chair.

'Do you mind if I sit here? There aren't many free places.'

Tweed looked up, pulled out the chair for her, she sat down.

As he piled butter and jam on a piece of roll Tweed's mind was elsewhere. He was thinking of General Valentin Rebet who had parted from him in Turku. He suspected the Russian was still in Finland: Rebet had made a point of asking Tweed if he was staying on in Helsinki.

'I'm Sonia Drayton. I arrived last night from Turku.'

Tweed noticed her superb legs. Because she was sitting the skirt had slid further up. With mock modesty she pulled at the hem. She had seen his glance.

'Martin Baker,' he replied. 'What were you doing in Turku?' It was something to say. His mind was still miles away.

'I worked for a corporation called INCUBUS. I left them. They are losing staff. A Peggy Vanderheld left

334

their Helsinki office at about the same time.'

'What kind of a corporation is that? I've heard of them somewhere.'

Tweed drank coffee, had shown no reaction except mild interest. Inwardly he had woken up, focused on where he was, on his attractive breakfast companion. She spoke in a soft appealing voice with a trace of accent.

She seemed to read his mind. 'You may have noticed I have a faint accent. It's Austrian. My father was English, my mother came from Vienna.'

'What made you leave this corporation? INCUBUS, did you say?'

'Yes. It is the world's largest bank. American. Bigger than anything in Japan, which gives some idea of its size. Actually I was sacked. So was Peggy Vanderheld. Now they want me to sign a pensions agreement. A generous one. I can't make up my mind whether to do that.'

'Why not?'

'You look like a businessman. I need someone neutral I can talk it over with. Is there somewhere quiet we could talk after breakfast?'

Marler had risen early at The Palace, had eaten breakfast, returned to his room. Now, while Paula watched, he held his Finnish hunting knife by the tip of the blade. On the far side of the room he'd placed a block of wood on the carpet. He had picked up the block from the grass verge the previous day when Newman was using the isolated phone box to call Mauno Sarin. He threw the knife from shoulder height. The tip hammered into a small circle he had drawn with a pen on the block.

'Bull's-eye!' called out Paula. 'Where did you learn to throw a knife?'

'In Arizona. A member of an Indian tribe taught me. They use knives to carve wooden sculptures for tourists.'

He retrieved the knife as Paula unlocked the door in response to a rapping tattoo. Newman walked in. He wore a peaked check cap and tinted glasses. Paula relocked the door as Marler retrieved the knife, slid it inside the sheath strapped to his leg, hid the block of wood inside a wardrobe.

'When do we leave to join the party at the Intercontinental?' he asked.

Earlier Paula had arrived with a message Tweed had preferred not to pass over the phone. He had agreed they should explore the Institute. His condition was that Paula could only go if Newman as well as Marler travelled with her.

'We take a cab to the Intercontinental now,' Marler said. 'Are you carrying that Smith & Wesson?'

'Nice to know it doesn't show.'

'And I got my Browning back from Nield,' said Paula. 'I have it in my shoulder bag. You're expecting fireworks?'

'With INCUBUS you never know. And they'll have trouble recognizing you.'

Paula had taken a leaf out of Irina Serov's book after listening to Butler's description of her. She wore a scarf round her head concealing her raven black hair and a pair of tinted glasses. Everyone was wearing them to shield their eyes against the glare of the sun. Marler had insisted they both disguise themselves, pointing out that he was the only one present INCUBUS had no idea existed. He checked his watch.

'Let's get moving . . .'

With the other tourists, mostly middle-aged English with a few young Finns, an hour and a half later they were airborne aboard scheduled Finnair Flight AY 424 which took off at 12.05 p.m. Newman and Paula sat alongside each other while Marler sat behind them in the window seat.

It was a smooth flight over a vast flat landscape with fir forests and ice-blue lakes scattered about like some crazy jigsaw puzzle. They had one stopover at Oulu near the coast of the Gulf of Bothnia then flew on to Rovaniemi.

Landing at the small airfield amid a wilderness of scrub and rocks they appeared to be miles from the town. It was at this remote airfield after a fifty-minute flight that the tourist party was transferred to a Fokker Friendship aircraft, a smaller machine powered by props.

After the aircraft had taken off, heading east, the courier, a lint-haired Finnish girl dressed in a smart grey suit, took over. 'Call me Irene,' she said in English as she walked down the central aisle. 'We are now flying towards the Soviet border over Lapland . . .'

Paula peered down out of the window, checked her map. They were flying over Route 80 which led to Kemijärvi, the town where the Porvoo fisherman had seen an INCUBUS refrigerated truck driving on east towards the border. She glanced behind and Marler appeared to be asleep. His half-closed eyes missed nothing below as he tilted his head sideways.

Paula looked down a little later, saw a large lake with wispy forest clinging to its granite sides plunging into the still water. The courier was talking.

'We are now passing Kemijärvi to the north. As you will realize the plane is descending. An airstrip has been constructed by INCUBUS Inc., the large philanthropic corporation which was largely instrumental in creating the Institute you are visiting . . .'

Marler glanced round. All the passengers looked pukka. He slipped a small Voigtlander camera out of his pocket as the plane glided down. A complex of modern buildings built of concrete spread out below. In the centre was a tall circular building which reminded him of the INCUBUS HQ in Helsinki. He took several shots

337

while the courier's back was turned. She swung round, came up to him.

'Excuse me, sir. Are you taking pictures? That is forbidden by INCUBUS. It is only by courtesy of the corporation that we are permitted to use the airstrip.'

Marler grinned. 'No pics. I've forgotten to insert the film.' He slipped the camera into his pocket.

'That's all right then, sir. It is the regulation . . .'

The machine dipped as a concrete runway came up to meet it. Newman glanced at Paula. He had an awful premonition he should not have allowed her to come.

Irina had been invited up to his room at the Hesperia by Tweed. He had checked the lobby, found it was crowded with a party of French tourists. As they stepped out of the elevator he clapped a hand to his forehead.

'Miss Drayton . . .'

'Sonia, please.'

'Sonia, do you mind sitting on that couch for a moment? They said there was a message for me at reception before I went to breakfast. I'll be back in a minute . . .'

Irina sat on the couch in the large corridor, relieved to be on her own for a short time. She had received a body-blow shock. While serving with the Soviet Embassy in London six years before, General Lysenko of the GRU had come briefly on a secret visit. From a window in a safe house near Regent's Park he had suddenly called out to her to join him. He had pointed down into the street. 'That man running to that waiting taxi. You see him clearly? Good. Remember that face. He is Tweed, Deputy Director of the SIS . . .'

That had been in the last days of the Cold War – when Lysenko was Tweed's chief adversary. And Irina had just been promoted to the rank of colonel in the KGB. Now, only half an hour ago she had sat down next to Martin Baker, and only when he turned to face her had she recognized him as Tweed.

Irina was thinking fast. She had discovered the identity of the top man behind the opposition to INCUBUS. A much more dangerous man than she – or Hauser – had ever anticipated. Extreme measures were called for.

The elevator doors opened and Tweed emerged, smiling. He led the way to his large room, unlocked the door, ushered her inside and to a chair facing the window. He sat in a separate chair, his back to the strong light.

'Now, what did you want to talk to me about? I can give you half an hour. I have an important business appointment then, I'm afraid,' he said affably.

'The document I have to sign to obtain this generous pension contains certain conditions. For life. If I break the conditions clauses I forfeit the pension.'

'What are these conditions?'

'That I never tell anyone about my work – or anything I learned while in INCUBUS's employ.'

'Could be a precaution against industrial espionage,' he suggested, gazing at the wall.

'But some of the things I had to do were awful.' She hesitated. 'I had to seduce certain businessmen INCUBUS wished to influence. It was blackmail. That is a crime.'

'It most certainly is,' Tweed agreed.

'And yet the pension is very generous. And I can take any other job I wish to without forfeiting the rights.'

'Why did you come to Helsinki from Turku?' he asked suddenly, watching her.

'To be interviewed for a job with an entirely different type of firm. I go to see them later today.'

'Have you evidence of these criminal activities?'

She hesitated again. 'Yes. Photocopies of certain letters which incriminate INCUBUS. I left them where I'm staying. I could bring them to you tonight at six o'clock. If that would be convenient.' She smiled and looked innocent and pathetic. 'I'm sorry to bother you, but you seem so kind.'

'Then I'd better see these photocopies before I can advise you what to do.'

'Thank you. I wonder if I could use your bathroom?'

'Of course. Through that door . . .'

As he walked to the window he heard her lock the door. Inside she looked swiftly round. A full bottle of indigestion mixture unopened on the glass shelf above the basin. Next to it a glass contained a tube of toothpaste tilted at an angle. The toothbrush was in another glass.

Tweed had struck her as a man meticulous about personal hygiene. So far he had not cleaned his teeth after his breakfast. Opening her capacious shoulder bag, she took out a small oxygen mask with a five-minute duration. She placed it over her face, slipped the strap over the back of her head to hold it.

Next she took out from a special pocket a small cylinder with a screw top. Inside was a hypodermic containing potassium cyanide in solution. INCUBUS seemed to be able to supply anything; she had no idea the device had been produced in a laboratory outside Boston.

Through the goggles she saw her sinister image in the mirror over the basin. She studied the angle of the tube of toothpaste tilted in the glass, lifted it out, unscrewed the top, placed it on the edge of the basin. Unscrewing the top of the cyanide container, she extracted the hypodermic, inserted the slim needle inside the toothpaste tube, pressed the plunger. Withdrawing the needle, she quickly screwed on the cap of the toothpaste tube tight and placed it back inside the glass at the same angle.

Carefully she slid the hypodermic back inside its protective tube, screwed the top on, slipped it back inside her shoulder bag. She went quickly to the window, opened it silently and wide, still wearing the mask. Despite handling the cyanide so carefully she had been warned of fumes being released.

She left the window open while she flushed the lavatory. Turning on the cold tap, she washed her hands, leaving the tap running while she dried her hands. She removed the mask standing near the open window, tucked it away inside the shoulder bag, closed and buttoned up the flap. Only then did she close the window quietly, turn off the tap, unlock the door and walk out.

'See you tonight then at six,' Tweed said, standing by the window. 'Good luck with your job interview. What firm is it?'

'Akateeminen Bookstore,' she said swiftly.

'On the selling side?' he asked, walking forward to open the door.

'No. Admin. For one of the directors. Thank you so much for your time . . .'

Tweed closed the door, stood for a moment. He could taste the remnants of his breakfast. He hadn't cleaned his teeth. He walked into the bathroom.

He stood quite still, looking round, his eyes slowly checking everything. Nothing seemed to have been moved, tampered with. He frowned, puzzled. He made a quick search to see if anything had been left behind. Nothing. He turned on the cold tap, picked up the tube of toothpaste to unscrew the cap.

Harry Butler sat at the wheel of the BMW Newman had driven to the Hesperia while Marler and Paula had taken a taxi to the Intercontinental Hotel next door. Tweed's instructions given on the phone to his room during the few minutes he had absented himself from Sonia Drayton had been explicit.

'A woman in her thirties will leave the hotel in half an

hour or so. Bleached blonde hair, shoulder length, wearing a tight-fitting pale green sleeveless blouse, a cream pleated mini-skirt. Good figure. Oh, her hair is piled on top of her head at the moment. She might drop it before she leaves. She may or may not wear green-tinted glasses. Clear, Harry?'

'There can only be one like that. Height? Weight?'

'Medium height at first glance, but she has four-inch heels. Slim build. Follow her. Don't lose her. Need to know where she goes. Leave it to you . . .'

Butler removed his jacket. It was early yet but the heat was building up. It was going to be another hot day. He watched gaggles of tourists crawling out of the hotel exit. Some stopped to talk, appeared to argue. Shall we go on that long trip in heat like this?

His target walked out ten minutes after Tweed had called him from the phone in the lobby. She walked with a confident strut which just stopped short of a call girl's posture. She's pleased with herself about something, Butler said to himself.

She climbed into the next taxi to disgorge more guests with luggage. Butler switched on his engine, watched the cab head along the Mannerheimintie away from the city. As he drove Butler tried to put his finger on what it was about the girl he found familiar. No good. Forget it – and it would come back to him.

Two things gave him her identity. The apartment block near the end of tramline No. 4 where she was dropped at. And the strut had gone. Nothing marks a person more than their movements. This was the girl who'd left the jet the previous day, Hauser's jet.

Tweed turned the screw cap on his toothpaste tube. The first turn. He paused, frowned. He recalled that when Sonia Drayton had used his bathroom he had heard the

342

tap running until a moment before she emerged. And yet she had dry hands. More sinister, Tweed never screwed the cap of his toothpaste tube tight. It had a tendency to stick so he always left it a trifle loose. Now the cap had been screwed down tight. And the glass holding the tube was slightly moved, exposing the circular mark it had imprinted on the shelf.

He screwed the cap on tight, placed the tube carefully back inside the glass. He looked at the full bottle of indigestion mixture. It did not appeared to have been tampered with. He left the bathroom.

Picking up the phone he dialled Mauno Sarin's private number. The Finn answered immediately.

'You'll recognize my voice, I expect,' Tweed began.

'Yes? A problem.'

'Could your forensic people check certain items from my bathroom? I suspect either poison or explosive – I suggest the items are handled with care.'

'Karma, since you know him, will be on his way over as soon as this call is completed.'

'Tell him to ask for Martin Baker. I'll wait in until he arrives . . .'

34

The Meteorological Institute complex loomed over the airstrip. The tourists disembarked via a mobile staircase. Paula, Newman and Marler lingered behind the crocodile and formed its tail. Irene, the courier, explained in a lecturer's tone as they filed past her towards the entrance:

'I'll have to describe what is going on in most of the

different departments. Nearly all the staff are on holiday.'

'But not all of them,' whispered to Newman. 'Look up at the roof.'

'I saw. I saw him.'

A man standing on the flat roof of the five-storey building was peering over a wall, examining the tourists with a pair of binoculars. As they entered the building each tourist was handed a pass with a clip to attach it to themselves by a sour-faced male receptionist.

'We are going to see the Planetarium first,' Irene called out. 'Not a correct name really. It shows various satellites orbiting above the Arctic Circle. . . .'

They walked into a vast chamber which was almost dark and had a huge domed roof. The courier switched on the tape recorder which began to identify the satellites in English, German and French. The tourists stood huddled together, staring up as their eyes became accustomed to the gloom.

'Satellite Astra is now appearing,' intoned the echoing voice.

An object like a spiked football appeared, was tracked by a spotlight as it moved slowly in an arc just above the rim of the dome. Marler left the group, began wandering round the chamber, looking up frequently as though seeking a better view. He came to a heavy steel door with a handle inset into the circular wall. He tested the handle. It refused to budge.

As the voice droned on he was joined by Newman and Paula as they strolled round the perimeter of the chamber. It was surprisingly cool and Paula guessed it was air conditioned. Hauser had spent a fortune on this showbiz monstrosity. Standing with his back to the wall, Marler tried the handle of a second door. Locked tight. He strolled further round the chamber. Everyone else, including the courier, was staring upwards as the constellations began to twinkle in the roof of the dome. Followed by Paula and Newman, Marler strolled a few yards further. Again he stopped, his back to an inset plate of metal, wide, stretching above head height with a razor-thin split in the centre. No handle. Only a slot waist high. For a computer card. He slipped his credit card from his wallet, inserted it inside the slot, began to fiddle it at various angles. Sometimes it worked.

Paula checked the group of tourists. All heads craned upwards as another satellite came into view. The recorded voice droned on. The tourists were becoming hypnotized by the unending spectacle way above their heads. There were forty of them. With a bit of luck no one would miss three people if they could find some way to explore other parts of the complex. She heard a faint whirring noise, the movement of well-oiled machinery.

'You've opened it,' whispered Newman. 'Let's risk it. Quick.' He turned to Paula. 'You wait here . . .'

Marler stepped inside the large cage-like elevator which had appeared behind the open doors. Newman slipped inside, Paula followed. Marler's eyes whipped down the control panel. Level Four was at the bottom. He pressed the button. The doors slid closed. The elevator began to descend.

Marler looked up, checked the ceiling, the walls of the elevator for spy cameras. Nothing. The elevator continued its descent. Paula slipped her hand inside her shoulder bag, gripped her Browning automatic. Newman withdrew his Smith & Wesson from its holster, held the gun by his side. The elevator stopped, the doors opened.

Marler peered out. He was gazing along a curving corridor, the walls of grey metal, the floor coated with ribbed rubber, which would muffle their footfalls. Which way? To the left or right?

To his left he saw the corridor appeared to end with a windowless door. In the other direction it disappeared round a curve. To the right, he decided. He motioned his companions to stay inside the elevator a moment longer. Stepping into the corridor he saw there was a control panel in the corridor's wall. He beckoned for them to come out. When they all stood in the corridor he pressed the button for Level One. The doors closed and the elevator began its return journey to the so-called Planetarium.

'Then if someone comes along they won't wonder why the elevator is down here,' he whispered to Newman.

'Agreed. Don't let's hang about.'

Marler began walking down the wide corridor slowly, looking everywhere. He looked up, stopped, moved close to the wall and gestured to Newman and Paula to do the same. He pressed himself against the wall, waited for them to reach him. He pointed upwards further down the corridor.

'Surveillance camera. The lens hasn't a wide enough angle to take in the whole width of the corridor.'

Newman knew Marler was an expert on surveillance equipment. They moved forward. Paula slithered forward along the surface of the wall, couldn't take her eyes off the lens which looked like a gun. When she had passed it she glanced at the wall. Dust free. The eerie nerve-wracking silence was broken only by a faint humming sound. Air was being extracted from the corridor; fresh air was being fed in. A noise which reminded her of a visit to Sizewell nuclear power station in Suffolk, south of Walberswick. Which in return reminded her of Newman's description of the horrific murder of Sandy. Could there be any connection between that atrocity and this weird complex in Finland?

Marler stopped again and his companions froze. He was staring at the wall a few feet ahead of where he stood. Newman moved close to him. Marler turned round, gesturing as he whispered.

346

'Electronic beam across the corridor. Waist high. Break that and a flaming alarm system is activated. We have to crawl under it.'

Dropping to his knees, he edged his way forward, keeping his back low. Newman followed, standing up again beside Marler. Paula took a deep breath, shortened the strap of her shoulder bag, slung it against her chest. Crawling forward she watched the innocuous-looking glass button embedded in the wall. It reminded her of an evil eye. She forced her body lower, reached the two men, stood up, gasping with tension.

'We'll have to watch our step for those things from now on,' Marler warned.

The corridor continued its endless curve. Marler guessed they were moving round the perimeter of the tall circular building he had seen from the air as the Fokker came in to land. At widely spaced intervals there were closed doors in the opposite wall, windowless doors. He hoped to God no one would walk out from one of them.

Bringing up the rear, Paula was beginning to suffer from claustrophobia. Level Four. They were buried deep inside the Arctic earth. Entombed. She had a sudden overwhelming urge to scream. She put a hand over her mouth, swallowed rapidly several times. Marler stopped again, held up his hand. What the hell was it now? she wondered.

'Devilish clever security system,' Marler whispered calmly. 'Another electronic beam – at ankle height.'

He pointed downwards. He glanced over his shoulder, grinned at Paula when he saw her face. Gave her a mock salute.

'Watch me,' he warned.

He walked forward, then raised one leg high, like a soldier goose-stepping. He moved his other leg in the same way, stood looking back. Newman imitated his movements. Paula looked down, saw another of those evil glass eyes inches above floor level. Her legs aching with tension, she lifted them over, one by one. Marler clapped a hand on her arm, gripped it.

'Good girl. Keep it up. Not much longer now.'

He walked forward again, sliding along the wall as he spotted another surveillance camera positioned above the centre of the corridor. Paula slithered along the wall with her arms. Her hands were moist. Frequently she glanced back. She had lengthened the strap of her shoulder bag. Wiping her right hand on her backside, she slipped it inside the bag, gripped the Browning. Newman paused, looked back at her.

'I presume you're keeping a sharp lookout behind you?'

'For Christ's sake!' she blazed in a low hiss. 'I've been checking every ten seconds.'

'OK.'

Paula was surprised. Normally she would have expected it would be Newman who realized she was petrified. But it had been Marler who had understood. Then she remembered Sandy. Newman's mind had become one-track. Could she blame him for that?

For Paula their journey round the corridor was becoming a nightmare. She had a vision of their walking round it forever. With no way out. Then she grasped what was disorientating her. The continuous movement in a vast circle, the horrific thought that they would find themselves arriving some day at the elevator which had brought them down into this hell.

She frowned. The flat surface of the corridor was no longer moving on the level, it was climbing, climbing like one of those inclined walks at London's Heathrow Airport on the way to the final departure lounge. The incline increased. They negotiated yet another waist-high beam by crawling under it. The upward slant of the corridor continued.

Marler paused, again held up his hand. Another beam? No. Now he was pointing ahead. The corridor ended. Two doors, closed and with safety bars, masked what lay beyond. Marler bent down, dropped to his knees. Paula was puzzled. He was staring at something on the rubberized floor under one of the overhead fluorescent lights embedded in the curved ceiling. And that's another thing that's driving me crazy, Paula thought. Everything curved. No straight surfaces.

Marler reached out a tentative hand, scraped his fingers over a darkish patch, sniffed at it. He stood up, walked back to Newman who stood back to the wall, revolver by his side. Marler showed Newman the fingers of his right hand.

'Wheel marks. A large vehicle. A smell of petrol. They bring trucks into this corridor. A wide gauge tyre.' He looked up. 'A very large truck could pass under the roof, could edge its way down the corridor – it's wide enough. I kept wondering why they needed all this space.'

'Then let's see what's beyond those doors.'

'If we can open them . . .'

Oh, God, no! Paula thought and clenched her teeth.

Newman gripped the Smith & Wesson in both hands as Marler gently eased up the safety bar of the right-hand door. He pushed at the heavy weight slowly. The gap widened. Newman, with Paula peering over his shoulder, gazed through the gap.

'It's the biggest garage in the world,' Newman commented, keeping his voice low.

They were looking into an immense underground garage with squat support pillars running away into the distance, row upon row. Parked on the concrete was a huge assembly of INCUBUS trucks, like an endless series of convoys preparing for an invasion. The INCUBUS Oy.

349

logo stood out clear under the powerful overhead fluorescents. A large number of trucks in two separate rows had strange lettering on their sides.

'What's written on those trucks?' Paula hissed.

'It's Cyrillic,' said Marler. 'Russian.' He understood the language. 'The words say State Transport.'

'What's going on here?' Newman wondered.

Marler had his head poked through the gap, his head tilted to one side. He listened for several minutes, put a finger to his lips so no one would talk.

'I don't think there's anyone about,' he said eventually. 'Let's explore, see what they're up to . . .'

For Paula it was an enormous relief to emerge from the confines of that horror movie corridor into the spacious cavern. No windows to the outside world: they were still below ground. A long way below. Maybe still at Level Four.

She followed Newman and Marler, holding on to her Browning. The two men kept to the left-hand wall of the garage, walking down a passage between the garage wall and a long line of trucks. There was a smell now of oil mixed with petrol. The lack of anyone else about was uncanny, but still Paula welcomed the space.

Half-way down the garage Marler paused. He pointed to the huge grille doors of a giant elevator large enough to take one of the trucks. All of the vehicles were refrigerated, Paula observed.

Newman tapped Marler on the shoulder, then moved sideways between two trucks across to the first row with the trucks carrying Russian lettering on their sides. He had spotted one truck with the rear doors open. Marler shrugged, moved off further down the garage past one of the squat pillars. Paula followed Newman.

He approached the truck cautiously, peered into the back. Empty of any guards. He crept along its side to look inside the cab. Empty. He walked back to Paula who had stayed at the rear.

'Let's take a look inside,' he said. 'See what merchandise we have this time.'

Paula jumped aboard and Newman followed. Both rear doors were wide open and there was plenty of light. She lifted the hasp of a long metal container, raised the lid, gazed inside. Taking a spare scarf from her shoulder bag, she emulated Marler's earlier treatment of the same grey and dough-like substance. Scooping up large handfuls of the material which reminded her of plasticine, she wrapped a considerable quantity inside her scarf, put the scarf back inside her bag.

'What are you up to?' Newman asked.

He had moved over to look inside the container after opening a larger box. He almost laughed when he saw what she had discovered, although there was nothing amusing about the substance.

'More Semtex,' he commented. 'God! They must have obtained it by the ton.'

'Evidence,' Paula said, taking out a large handkerchief.

She scooped up a much smaller amount and wrapped it inside her handkerchief. Then she stuffed this into the shoulder bag. She straightened up, caught his wry smile.

'What's so funny?'

'Come and look – and remember that truck north of Porvoo. You've taken Marler's place. A repeat performance for me.'

She stared down into the large box he had opened. Now she could recognize some of the deadly toys so-called civilized man produced. The sticks were neatly stacked in rows.

'Gelignite,' said Newman. 'Let's get out of here . . .'

The guard appeared from nowhere as they jumped from the truck. A lean bony faced man with high cheekbones who might have been Manescu. Except he wasn't. Another of the Romanian *Securitate* who had disappeared from Bucharest, Newman thought grimly. His Smith &

Wesson was inside the shoulder holster. The guard held a Colt .445, gripped in both hands, aimed point blank at them. The end of the muzzle looked like the mouth of a cannon. Newman knew that with one bullet the weapon could carve a great hole out of its target, hurl the victim back like a hammerblow. The Romanian spoke in broken English.

'Raise hands high. Sit on truck. Drop to ground.'

Paula and Newman did exactly what they had been told. The guard was standing about twelve feet away from them, too far away for Newman to risk a grab for the weapon. Paula cursed inwardly that the Browning was nestling inside her shoulder bag. They straightened up, raised their hands again. It was horribly silent in the huge cavern.

'Now you walk slowly to wall,' the gun muzzle waved towards the inner wall of the garage, 'and you face the wall.'

Paula walked slowly close to Newman. His proximity was a source of comfort to her. They were going to die – she had no doubt of that. The guard spoke again as they stood facing the rough concrete.

'The man faces me . . . slowly. The girl faces wall.'

Newman turned slowly through a hundred and eighty degrees. The guard braced himself, feet wider apart, took a firmer grip on the Colt with both hands. He squinted along the sight, the muzzle aimed at the centre of Newman's chest. He grinned, showing bad teeth.

'After shooting you I make love to the girl before I shoot her. Do not move!'

Newman had stiffened at the hideous threat. Something shiny, catching the overhead lights, flashing through the air, plunged into the guard's back. Marler had appeared from behind a pillar. The guard grunted, had a look of sheer disbelief. He dropped the Colt and half-turned round, staggering. Newman saw the knife protruding from his back, inches of the blade penetrating the target. The guard's hand flopped by his side. He swayed for a moment, then toppled backwards, hit the concrete floor with a heavy thud, driving the knife deep into his body. He lay still as Marler ran forward lightly on his feet.

Paula, sweat streaming down her back, turned round. Marler was bending over the guard. He checked the neck pulse, glanced up, his tone offhand.

'Dead as doornail. Newman, get me one of those cloths out of the truck. Thanks. Paula, you'd better not watch this.'

She was wiping her moist hands, mainly to conceal the fact that they were trembling. She gripped them tightly together. She forced herself to watch: if she couldn't stand this she wasn't up to her job.

Marler stood up, crouched down again, wrapped the cloth round the section of the blade still exposed. He took a deep breath, heaved with all his strength at the handle. It was hard work: withdrawing a knife from a body. The blade emerged slowly, Covered with blood, then jerked free. Standing up. Marler used the cloth to clean the blade, walked to the truck, shoved the soiled cloth beneath other cloths, pulled up his trouser leg, slipped the knife back inside the sheath. He brushed concrete dust off his trouser leg where it had brushed against the pillar he had concealed himself behind. His manner suggested it was all in a day's work.

'Let's get out of this place,' he said briskly. 'That truck elevator is our best bet. Must lead to the outside world.' He looked at Newman. 'First give me a hand with this scum.'

Between them they half dragged, half lifted the guard. Carrying him to the truck Newman and Paula had explored, they shoved the corpse well under the chassis. Marler brushed off his hands, straightened his jacket, then stood quite still. The huge elevator was moving up, out of sight.

'Someone coming down,' Marler commented. 'We'd better get ready to prepare a reception committee . . .'

Paula, standing in front of the elevator shaft, about six feet back, had insisted on acting as bait. Vehemently she had pointed out that whoever was coming down would be thrown off balance to see a woman waiting. Reluctantly, Newman agreed.

The tension again rose as there was a loaded pause. The elevator was stationary at some upper level. For Paula it seemed hours before anything happened. She stood with her hand holding the Browning inside her shoulder bag.

The whirring noise began again. It seemed an age as it slowly descended. Paula guessed it had climbed to the top level. The outside world, she hoped. Expecting to see a large truck she was startled when the elevator appeared, came to rest. Beyond the grille gates stood a short thin-faced man wearing denims and a jacket. He reacted swiftly. A gun seemed to jump into his hand. A Mauser aimed at her stomach. He used his free left hand to open the gates, stepped out, rapping out the command in English.

'Take your hand from that bag slowly. If it is not empty you lose your belly.'

She carefully withdrew her hand, releasing her grip on the Browning. His face had the same racial appearance as the guard Marler had eliminated. High and prominent cheekbones. He took another step closer to her.

The muzzle of Newman's Smith & Wesson hammered down with great force on the side of his head, with such force the barrel bounced off the split skull. He sagged forward and Paula jumped sideways as he sprawled on the concrete. Newman checked his pulse, shook his head at Marler.

They dragged the body under another nearby truck after Marler had extracted spare magazines for the weapon from the guard's jacket pocket. He then picked up the Mauser, checked the gun, shoved it inside his belt behind his jacket.

'Now for the nasty part,' Newman remarked. 'Going up in that elevator and seeing what's waiting for us at the top.'

Paula glanced at him with curiosity. At one time he would have been upset by the grim episodes they had just experienced. They had all noticed a change in his character since his traumatic secret journey into East Germany in the days of the Cold War. His reaction had become *Now for the nasty part.*

Inside the elevator Marler briefly studied the control panel. From the top downwards there were three buttons and then a key at the bottom.

'Intriguing,' he said. 'Buttons for Levels One, Two, Three. A key to operate the elevator down to Level Four. I think I'll take that when we reach the top. No point in leaving behind evidence that someone went down to the garage – and it might come in useful later.'

He pressed the button for Level One. As the elevator began its ponderous climb Paula experienced tension again. What new danger might be waiting for them at Level One? She forced herself to ask the question which had puzzled her.

'How on earth do those monster trucks reach Level Four?'

'Found the exit,' Marler replied, staring at the grille gate. 'I reached the end of the garage. There's a huge tunnel curving out of sight. The floor climbed steeply. Solid doors at these levels.'

Beyond the grille they could see, as they passed each level, solid steel doors. The place was like a fortress. The elevator slowed even more, stopped at Level One. An agonizing pause for Paula. Then the doors slid back with the grille. Marler's right hand was inside his jacket, gripping the Mauser. Newman had slipped the Smith & Wesson out of its holster, thrusting the gun inside his belt under his jacket. Paula blinked as the harsh glare of Arctic sunlight hit her. They had arrived at ground level.

Beyond the elevator was a concrete-floored compound with a massive building on the other side. No windows. Like a vast blockhouse. Marler peered out, looking both ways. He beckoned them to follow after pocketing the key for Level Four. Marler had lost all sense of direction: they could go either way. He pointed to a cavernous opening in the blockhouse.

'See that opening? That's where the trucks drive out and in to reach Level Four.'

'I thought they couldn't just use the elevator,' Paula said. 'It would take forever to send down the number of vehicles down there. So why do they need the elevator when they have the tunnel?'

'My guess,' suggested Newman, 'would be an emergency exit and entrance in case a truck with explosive blows up in the tunnel and blocks it. Mr Hauser is nothing if not efficient. And we move to the right. This curved wall is the outside of the same building where we walked forever along that corridor. With luck we may arrive back at the airstrip one day.'

'Good thinking,' commented Marler.

At his urging they kept close to the wall: Marler had remembered the guards on the roof they had seen disembarking from the aircraft. At intervals there were porthole windows at shoulder height. Marler ducked to creep beneath them and his two companions followed his example. Compared with the cool interior it was like an inferno in the open air. The sun beat down on them mercilessly. They passed a long narrow alleyway carved out of the building: inside were huge metal waste bins.

They had moved a few yards further on when Marler held up his arm.

'Someone's coming. A lot of people. Back to that alley. Fast!'

Paula ran back with Newman at her heels, dived inside the alley. She ran deep inside the narrow space, hid herself behind one of the bins. Newman and Marler concealed themselves behind bins closer to the entrance. Marler watched the end of the alley from behind his bin.

A team of guards appeared – all of these in uniform – strolled past the end of the alley. Not one glanced into the alley. Bloody woodentops, thought Marler, and thank God for that. When the last man had passed he crept to the exit, followed them part way round the wall. He returned quickly to the alley.

'All clear. There were twenty of them. Heavy security on this complex. They all had holstered handguns. Curious for a so-called Meteorological Institute. They went into the vehicle elevator. Chap in front was holding a key.'

'They were heading down for Level Four then,' said Newman. 'We were lucky. They must all go to lunch together, leaving behind just a couple of men.'

'And they'll wonder where they are. They'll look for the two missing men,' Paula interjected. 'Do you think we'll get out of this place alive?'

'Let's keep moving,' Newman told her.

They were following the curving wall when they started to pass the first door they had come to. It opened suddenly. Marler reached for the Mauser. A large woman wearing a wide-brimmed straw hat and a wild orange dress which enveloped her like a tent walked out. Of uncertain age, she beamed at Marler, who recognized her as one of the tourists.

'I'm Mrs Fairweather,' she gushed. 'An appropriate name for this climate, don't you think? You've got fed up

357

with the endless walking too, I expect. And those awful tape-recorded voices blaring at you non-stop. It's all simply too much. I told Irene I must get some fresh air. She tried to make me stay but I insisted. George, my husband, says that when I insist the world had better take notice.'

'I'm sure he's right, dear lady,' Marler agreed, smiling.

'I expect you know we continue following this wall to the right. Irene told me three times as though I was some kind of village idiot. *To the right!* Like someone blaring at you through a megaphone. You're sure you want to leave now, she kept asking. She showed me the passage leading to that door. Once you're outside you can't get back, she went on at me. The door automatically locks so you can't change your mind . . .'

They followed the wall as Mrs Fairweather gushed on and Marler smiled agreeably. He had shoved the Mauser back out of sight just in time. Behind them Newman and Paula kept silent. Mrs Fairweather talked enough for four people.

'Of course,' she gushed on, 'the Planetarium was interesting. I expect you were as surprised as I was when Mr Talking Machine revealed the satellites were weather satellites near the end. We'd all thought they were Soviet spies in orbit. The others are getting fed up and want to come back. We spent too long in the Geological Research Department. That was when it got boring. A crashing bore. And no refreshment. Irene said there would be refreshments on the flight back to Rovaniemi. Oh, look, there is our plane . . .'

The airstrip had appeared. The mobile staircase was still in place. Marler followed Mrs Fairweather up the steps, sat down beside her. He could think of no more excellent cover.

Paula checked her watch as she settled in a window seat with Newman two rows behind Marler. She checked her watch again. Newman knew what she was worrying about. Sooner or later the twenty-man strong team of guards would find their dead comrades. That was when the plane would be stopped from taking off.

Five minutes later the crocodile of tourists appeared, marching determinedly to the plane, hurrying aboard to take their seats. Irene looked depressed. Mrs Fairweather whispered in a voice which half the aircraft could hear.

'You see! I started the revolt. I knew they were all as fed up as I was.'

'You're a tonic,' Marler lied cheerfully.

Paula stared out of the window at the entrance to the complex. She felt certain guards would appear at the last moment. The mobile staircase was moved away, the pilot started his engines, the props began spinning. Paula was still watching the entrance. She stiffened. Three uniformed figures were running towards the plane, windmilling their arms, mouths open as though shouting some orders.

'Whatever they want it is too late. We are *leaving*!' Irene shouted.

Paula heard the slam of the passenger door. The Fokker moved forward, gathered speed down the runway, took off into a cloudless sky. Within thirty seconds the Institute was a toy complex far below as the machine headed back for Rovaniemi.

'You know, Mrs Fairweather,' drawled Marler, 'I'm most grateful you cut short the tour. It was boring. It was *dead* boring.'

35

'You are saying there has been an intrusion at the Institute, Frank?'

Hauser's voice was dangerously calm. He sat behind his desk in the turret tower of his strange home which he used when he was working out his next strategic manoeuvre. Beyond the French windows perched a balcony with an elaborately decorated grille railing. Galvone was striding backwards and forwards nervously, hands in his trouser pockets.

'News just came through over the phone,' he reported. 'Two guards were killed in the garage at Level Four . . .'

'Go on,' Hauser said in an ominous tone. 'Don't feed me it piece by piece.'

'A quantity of Semtex has disappeared from one container aboard a truck. They think the intruders joined a tourist party visiting the Institute.'

'And you had just been up there to double the security. Or so you told me. What went wrong? Do I have to lean on you?'

'Listen, Chief.' Galvone spread his hands in a pleading gesture. 'I left orders all guard teams were to take meals in shifts, to leave half a team on duty. The garage team had lunch together, presumably so they could talk to each other, play cards. They left only the two men behind – the men who were killed. Strictly against my instructions.'

'If you say so, Frank. Stop walking about. Park the butt, for Chrissakes, while I think.'

Hauser lit a cigarette. He was seated in his shirt sleeves:

360

at six in the evening the heat was ferocious but Hauser had
learned to live with extremes of climate. He was thinking
about Irina Serov. She had shaken him in the morning
when she'd told him that a man called Tweed, Deputy
Director of the Brits' Secret Service, was staying at the
Hesperia. He had located the mastermind – who by now
should be dead. Hauser wasn't sure Irina had done the
right thing. How would the British Prime Minister react to
the news?

He had another anxiety. Including the raid on the truck
north of Porvoo, two lots of explosive had disappeared.
Hauser had no doubt now it was the same opposition
who'd grabbed more explosives from the Institute. Evidence – which maybe they'd show to the Finnish Government. Most men faced with the situation would retreat.
That wasn't Hauser's way. Under pressure you attacked.

'Frank, we're in a crisis situation. Operation Urals has
already started. Look . . .'

He pushed a copy of the *Herald Tribune* across the desk
and waited while Galvone read it. It was a major headline.

TRANS-SIBERIAN RAILWAY SABOTAGED.
EXPLOSION BLOWS TRAIN.

Galvone read the text. Over a hundred people were feared
dead. 'Extremists and Terrorists' were blamed by the
Soviet authorities. As Galvone read on Hauser stared out
of the window. Irina Serov would never make such a
mistake. She'd have arranged detonation after the train
had passed. The sooner he sent her back inside Russia to
take charge the better. The first consignment of explosives
had been smuggled over the border too early.

'What do we do now?' Galvone asked.

'We go ahead with Operation Urals. This time under the
guidance of someone who knows what they're doing. What
happened at the Institute today means we must transport
all the explosives across the frontier into Russia fast.

361

You're in charge. And you're going to be busy, Frank.'

'That's OK, Chief. What else?'

Galvone was relieved Hauser had switched away from the fiasco at the Institute, didn't want him to return to the subject.

'A contingency plan to move our centre of operations out of Helsinki to the HQ in Stockholm. At twelve hours' notice. All the secret files, the key staff. I'm trying to calm down the Finnish government by offering them three million dollars to build a super icebreaker. But they're so goddamn sensitive about their neutrality they may not play along. The main thrust now is to get Operation Urals moving. A woman will be in charge of the team, a Sonia Drayton. Now, why's your backside still in that chair? And send Adam Carver up pronto . . .'

Alone, Hauser checked over in his mind the different elements of the jigsaw he was juggling. The late Mr Tweed obviously had a team with him in Helsinki, the team which had caused trouble at Porvoo, now up in the Arctic Circle. He needed an execution team. He'd hold back Irina Serov to control the team. It would comprise Manescu and Ziegler, men who wouldn't hesitate to organize permanent accidents for the opposition. In a tight corner, *accelerate*.

Tweed had had a busy day. Monica had phoned from London giving him details of the flight bringing in the equipment he had requested. Butler had driven Tweed and Nield in the BMW to the airport.

Tweed had escorted the equipment through Customs, signing the release as Martin Baker. The boxes had been loaded inside the BMW. They had then driven to a warehouse behind North Harbour Tweed had rented. He helped them to carry the boxes inside.

'Should I ask what this stuff is?' Nield had queried.

'It's equipment for a film unit. Newman gave me the idea

when he described how they had been tracked and recorded at Arlanda and the ferry terminal from Stockholm to Turku. By film units.'

'I still don't see,' Nield persisted.

'I couldn't see how we could explore that Meteorological Institute in the Arctic Circle. When I heard from Newman that fisherman at Porvoo had seen a truck pass through Kemijärvi heading east towards the Institute I felt sure it was the base for some operation. Everything depends on what Newman, Marler and Paula tell us when they arrive back.'

'If they arrive back,' Butler said grimly. 'We aren't playing with pussycats.'

'They'll survive. Harry, did you hire that van? Are the posters and pass cards being printed?'

'They are. And the van is at the back of this warehouse. You can't see it because I covered it with a sheet of canvas.'

'Mind if you tell me what you're doing?' asked Nield.

'Butler is getting streamers printed with National Film Unit printed on them in Finnish and Swedish. Two will be attached to the van. While at the airport I arranged to charter a plane if necessary. The passes are for fake identification.'

Butler closed the warehouse doors, attached two padlocks and they climbed back inside the BMW. As they drove away Nield, anxious for action, put his question.

'What next?'

'I'm waiting for Monica to call me. She's researching INCUBUS non-stop through every available source and contact. She might just come up with key data . . .'

At five o'clock during a torrid afternoon Tweed took a call from Mauno Sarin. The Protection Police sounded very serious.

'Could you drop in at Ratakatu at say 6.30 this evening?

Forensic have come up with results I would rather not relay over the phone.'

'I'll be there.'

Five minutes later the phone rang again. It was Newman, calling from Helsinki Airport. He sounded tired, tense.

'Just to let you know we're back. We have information. Top priority. We could be with you in thirty minutes.'

'See that you are. Not only the heat is building up. I have to leave here at six . . .'

He turned to look at Butler and Nield who were were seated in chairs. Nield, always casual, was sprawled, legs stretched out in front of him. Butler sat upright, alert.

'There could be a blonde woman calling here about six – you followed her back to that apartment, Butler. I'm not sure she will appear, but if she does she'll ask for me at reception. Then she'll try and leave. I wanted her grabbed outside and kept on ice. Where, is for you to decide.'

'I'll recognize her,' Butler said. 'I'll describe her to Pete so we both know what she looks like. Maybe we should go down into the lobby now in case she turns up early.'

'Good point,' agreed Tweed. 'She might do just that . . .'

With minutes of their leaving he took another phone call. This time it was a long one from Monica, reporting the results of her research so far. Tweed made a lot of notes. At one stage she repeated what she had just said.

'That house and the power cruiser belonging to Hauser are in the Swedish *western* archipelago. Not the one off Stockholm. It runs off the coast north of Gothenburg nearly up to Norway.'

'I've got it. And the name of the anchorage. Go on . . .'

He had just finished the call, put away his notebook, when Newman and Marler arrived. He checked his watch. Newman said Paula had rushed to her room to have a bath, began his report of their journey to the Arctic. To begin with Tweed sat listening but as the story progressed he stood up, pacing slowly round the room, taking in every word, his expression grave. Marler produced Paula's handkerchief enclosing the substance she had scooped out of the container, but he did not mentioned the scarf containing a much larger quantity. He had deposited that inside the wardrobe in his room before he joined Tweed.

'I'd better take that with me to my appointment,' Tweed said and stuffed the handkerchief with its contents inside his jacket pocket.

He waited as Newman unlocked the door in response to a gentle tapping. Paula walked in, her step brisk, the hint of a smile on her face.

'Guess what? I've got another date with Adam Carver. He said he'd been calling me all day. He's coming over for a drink. I'm to meet him outside the Intercontinental at six this evening.'

'Is that a good idea?' queried Tweed.

She punched him playfully on the arm. 'I haven't fallen for that cardboard matinée idol, if that's what you were thinking. If anything, it appears to be the other way round.'

'Why go?' Tweed persisted.

'All part of your campaign to throw INCUBUS off balance. And I might coax him into letting something slip.'

'Just be careful.'

Tweed checked his watch again. 'I congratulate all three of you on your Arctic Circle trip. You may have brought back just what is needed to stir the Finnish Government into taking action against Hauser. But everyone must be careful. I'm beginning to get inside Hauser's head – his reaction to the events at the Institute may be violent.'

* * *

Tweed sat silent as he faced Mauno Sarin across his desk at Ratakatu. The Finn reminded him of a studious tonsured monk with his balding head, his fringe beard. Sarin was in a serious mood.

'It is fortunate you didn't clean your teeth early this morning. Forensic have reported your tube of toothpaste is laced with a lethal quantity of potassium cyanide.' He smiled with humour. 'Their precise way of expressing themselves. Cyanide is lethal. The indigestion mixture is harmless.' He perched his elbows on the desk, clasped his strong hands together. 'Now who could have tampered with that tube?'

'A Sonia Drayton,' Tweed said promptly. 'I can give you her address.'

He explained tersely his encounter at the breakfast table with the bleached blonde, told Sarin that she had alleged she was an ex-employee of INCUBUS. He omitted that she had also said she would return to the Hesperia at six.

'INCUBUS again,' commented Sarin.

'You will repeat that remark after I tell you about the visit Marler and Newman made to the Meteorological Institute today . . .'

Tweed omitted any reference to Paula – who was on his conscience because of her journey into mortal danger. Sarin listened, his brown eyes fixed on Tweed. At the end of his report Tweed produced the handkerchief containing the substance Paula had collected. Sarin pressed a button, Karma appeared.

'Have that checked immediately. I suspect our explosives expert will be familiar with it by now. An answer quickly, please . . .'

Karma was back in less than five minutes. He laid the handkerchief with its contents on Sarin's desk.

'Semtex. A positive analysis. You don't need me for the moment? Thank you.'

Sarin poked at the dough-like substance with a long finger. 'As you predicted. INCUBUS again.'

'Surely it's time you went after Hauser,' Tweed demanded acidly. 'How much more evidence do you need?'

'There is a problem. Hauser this afternoon offered the government three million dollars to build a giant ice-breaker. They are considering the offer. Please!' He held up a hand as Tweed began to protest. 'The trouble is an individual can choose his neighbours, a country can't. I would like, myself, to deport Mr Hauser . . .'

'How much more evidence do you need?'

'Let me finish. It is a strange coincidence that Hauser has made this offer so soon after your associates discover explosives in two different areas directly connected with INCUBUS. I think he is a good poker player.'

'Explain that.'

'My government is indebted to Hauser for the employment he has supplied us with. We can't simply throw back his offer in his face. But we have a highly unstable Soviet Union on our doorstep. They might not like our accepting such a massive sum outright from Washington. So it is stalemate for the moment.'

'I said how much more evidence do you need?'

'I personally am extremely worried about your discovery of this Semtex. Not once, but twice. But are you prepared to put Mr Marler in open court, stating his profession, to tell his story? Bearing in mind who you are, and that Marler is a member of your Service?'

'No, of course not. But . . .'

'Then we have no evidence yet we can use. Newman alone is not enough. We need *two* witnesses, one to confirm the other's story.'

'Then we'd all better go home.'

'Were there any casualties during this secret examination of the Institute complex?'

'No,' lied Tweed promptly.

'I would be glad if you would continue your enquiries but if necessary I will deny ever saying that.'

'Thank you for all your support,' Tweed said savagely as he stood up to leave.

The streets were quiet as he walked back between the old granite office blocks. After his interview with Sarin at least they knew where they were. On their own.

The news that hit him when he returned to the Hesperia made him realize how much on their own they were.

36

Paula found Adam Carver waiting for her in a deserted area near the rear of the International. Newman had tried to accompany her, but she had refused. She was far more likely to extract information from Carver on her own.

'You're looking terrific,' Carver greeted her. 'And I was worrying you wouldn't turn up. Let's make this an evening to remember. Have dinner after a drink.'

'We'll see. After a drink . . .'

She had just replied with the traditional feminine wait and see tactic when she heard a car, burning rubber, coming up behind her. She swung round. A brown Buick jerked to a halt. The doors flew open. Three men wearing stocking masks, holding handguns, jumped out. One man ran to Carver, who looked astounded, told him to face the blank wall, rammed the gun into his back.

At the same time two other men rushed to Paula. One placed the muzzle of his gun against her skull, the second grabbed her arms, forced them behind her back. She felt the steel of handcuffs round her wrists, heard the click of locking.

She looked quickly at Carver. He was staring over his shoulder, the astonishment now replaced by rage. She was hustled into the rear of the large car. Doors slammed. The gunman holding Carver kicked his legs from under him, he sprawled on the concrete as the gunman leapt into the car. The Buick backed, turned, drove out past the Hesperia on to the Mannerheimintie.

The sheer audacity of the attack had taken Paula's breath away. The two men in the back were half-sitting on her, one holding a large hand over her mouth. She stared up at the sinister figure with the stocking mask as the Buick roared off away from the city.

Tweed was hot, sticky, frustrated as he paid off the cab and entered the Hesperia. Newman and Marler were sitting in the lobby. They jumped up as he came in and he wondered why they were waiting for him.

'Something's happened,' Newman said crisply. 'Better we tell you up in your room . . . '

'Well, what is it?' Tweed asked as he locked the door of his bedroom on the inside.

He peeled off his jacket, slung it over the back of a chair, which was uncharacteristic of him. His shirt was pasted to his back. He jerked it out and let it hang outside his trousers. Again uncharacteristic. He flopped in a chair.

'Get on with it. Incidentally we get no help from Mauno Sarin.'

'We've managed quite nicely on our own,' Marler observed.

'Butler phoned,' reported Newman. 'He and Nield grabbed Sonia Drayton. She came in at a quarter to six, headed for reception . . .'

'To check up I was dead.'

Tersely, Tweed told them of the findings of Forensic at Ratakatu. Marler whistled softly when he told them about the potassium cyanide.

'So it's a good job we've got her,' Newman continued, as he sat facing Tweed. 'Butler wrapped it up on the phone but this is it. He put his arm round her and rammed the end of his pipe into her back, told her it was a gun. They took her away in the BMW.'

'Where to?'

'The warehouse where you stored the film equipment down by the waterfront. That's a clever idea – using a film unit to—'

'Never mind about that,' Tweed snapped. 'Was it clever to let her know the location?'

'She doesn't know where she is, what route they took. I gather Nield blindfolded her as soon as they were driving off in the car. They're trying to get her to talk – with a tape recorder at the ready. No rough stuff, of course. But no food. Just mineral water. So far nothing. She's told them nothing.'

'I wonder whether we ought to hand her over to Sarin for attempted murder – of me,' Tweed mused. His mind was flitting about. 'Where is Paula?'

'Getting Adam Carver drunk with her wiles,' Marler said.

'Damn it!' Tweed punched one clenched hand into the palm of the other. 'We need more data. Something to convince Sarin he has to move.'

He's in a rare irritable mood, Newman thought. The phone rang and he picked it up. Tweed reached out for the extension phone by the bedside, lifted the receiver at the same moment. Maybe Sarin had changed his mind. He stiffened as the distorted voice at the other end began speaking.

'I wish to speak to Mr Martin Baker.'

'Not available,' snapped Newman. 'I'm his assistant.'

'You are a member of his organization?' queried the bland voice.

Newman scribbled a note on a pad, handed it to Tweed. In spite of the distortion he thought he recognized Hauser from the way he pronounced certain words. He'd had two conversations with the INCUBUS president. Tweed read the note, *Hauser*.

'I told you I am his assistant, his chief deputy,' Newman said into the receiver. 'What is this all about? Who is speaking? I don't take anonymous calls.'

'You will take this one. Your chief's girl is with us. I'll describe how she is dressed . . .' An accurate picture of what Paula had worn followed. Newman nodded to Tweed, confirming the description was accurate as the voice went on. 'I will be holding the girl as a hostage. If there is any further interference in our industrial operations you will, as a first present, receive through the post her right hand. Do you understand?'

Tweed held up a hand to stop Newman replying. He was in a state of greater fury than either Marler or Newman had ever witnessed. He fought for a moment for iron self-control. When he spoke his voice was implacable, the grimness apparent in the way he spoke slowly, with great determination.

'Hauser, this is Martin Baker speaking.'

He paused to let that sink in. There was a long pause at the other end of the line. His statement had thrown the voice off balance. He continued.

'You are quite right. We do have an organization. You have already experienced its power. With the explosives truck north of Porvoo. With the penetration of the so-called Meteorological Institute. I warn you now, Hauser, if the girl is harmed in any way I will hunt you down if I have to follow you across the face of the earth. You will not sleep. You will look over your shoulder

371

everywhere. There will be no place you can hide.'

'Hauser?' The voice sounded as though it was trying to be mocking. 'I have never heard of the name . . .'

'Release the girl immediately. Unharmed,' Tweed ordered. 'You will be hounded out of Finland. I promise you. Our resources are unlimited. We are ruthless professionals.'

'This conversation ceases now. I will give you an hour to think it over. I will then call you again. Just hope the hostage will not be tortured in the meantime . . .'

The line went dead. Tweed replaced the phone with great care. Neither Marler nor Newman had ever seen such an expression on his face. He looked like a hanging judge, staring into the distance, hands clasped lightly together.

'You didn't play our strongest card,' Newman told him. 'We have Sonia Drayton. She attempted to murder you. She'll have information on INCUBUS which Hauser won't want revealed.'

'I'm aware of that.' Tweed's tone was ice cold. 'I am going to hit him with that when he calls back. At the moment he's in a state of shock – because I'm still living. It's strange – I can think like Hauser, subconsciously foresee his next move. And I believe the reverse is also true. We think of kidnapping the Drayton woman – he thinks of kidnapping Paula.'

He was still staring into space when Marler spoke.

'You know when you arrived back we were waiting for you in the lobby. I thought I saw Adam Carver outside. Someone who was the spitting image of the photographs I took of him leaving the INCUBUS HQ. He looked in a bad way, went off towards the Intercontinental. Think I'll go and look for him. He was the man Paula went to meet . . .'

'No! I'll go,' snapped Newman.

He was out of the room before anyone could react.

Like Tweed, it was a dreadful blow to him that Paula, of all people, should be in the hands of thugs who didn't hesitate to kill.

Stepping out of the elevator, he moved swiftly outside, crossed the path leading to the International, walked into the hotel and instinctively headed for the bar.

'Martin Baker – Tweed – is still alive,' Hauser told Galvone. 'That I didn't expect. And bloody aggressive too. You're sure the hostage girl is secured?'

He was pacing round the turret tower, beefy arms folded across his chest. Galcone knew he was disturbed: it was not working out as planned. Yet.

'She's secure,' he assured his chief. 'Locked away in an apartment out at Setula near the airport. Three tough guards with her. Orders not to touch her. Yet. What I can't figure out is why you didn't let Adam Carver know he was bait. He may not be pleased when he gets back. I don't care a cuss,' he added, 'but he's a key executive.'

'I didn't let him know because I think he's sweet on the girl,' Hauser lied. 'And not knowing meant he'd act the part better. That guy Baker, Tweed or whatever his goddamned name might be, is a tough bastard.'

'He'll crack. They all do under pressure.'

'You're right, Frank. Next time I call I'll turn the screw a little tighter, make the bastard crawl. We do this the American way.'

Inside the waterfront warehouse Butler put down the phone. Marler had just called, had asked questions, had told him by implication about Paula. Butler was fond of Paula.

Sonia Drayton was tied to a heavy chair they had found with other old furniture stacked at the rear of the building. She was tied at the ankles, one leg to each front leg of the chair. Her arms were bound behind her back, roped to the chair. She wore a blindfold.

Nield had parked the BMW in a corner of the warehouse, was keeping watch through a window smeared with muck and dust. He turned as he heard noises. Butler was removing the gag, holding a cardboard carton of mineral water to her lips. Important she didn't get dehydrated. The interior of the warehouse was like a furnace.

'If I had some food,' Drayton said, 'I might tell you a few things which would interest you.'

'You'll talk, anyway,' growled Butler. 'When your stomach is screaming for food.'

'What's happened? You sound tougher, less human.'

'I feel tougher, less human.'

Butler applied the gag again, tying it a little tighter this time. It was the first occasion for a long time when Irina Serov had felt frightened. When they questioned her earlier she had refused to tell them anything. She had expected them to slap her around, but they had not laid a hand on her. Now she was worried: her captor's manner had changed, he had sounded ugly. Was it retaliation for the death of Tweed? But how could they have identified her?

Butler wandered over to join Nield, peered out of the window. He wished to God he was out there, searching for Paula.

Imprisoned in a strait-jacket, Paula was streaming with sweat. Thrown on to what felt like a couch, her eyes were covered with a coloured handkerchief. She had counted three men; only two had spoken to her, in English, but with a Mittel-European accent. More *Securitate*? Not a reassuring thought. But she had made herself relax – straining against the jacket used up valuable energy.

374

She was surprised she didn't feel in a state of terror. But she was confident Tweed would find a way of rescuing her. One thing puzzled her: that look of total surprise, then fury, on Adam Carver's face. If he had lured her into the ambush his reaction when it took place was odd, very odd.

What the hell is going on? she wondered. Time seemed to have stood still. Not knowing what the time was bothered her more than anything else. She had only asked them the time once.

'Maybe time to die soon, lady,' had been the reply.

Newman found Adam Carver sitting by himself in a corner of the International bar. It was quiet at that hour and Carver was out of sight of the barman. Newman bought himself a glass of champagne, sat down on the banquette next to Carver who was nursing his chin with his right hand.

'Evening, Carver. Have a tiff with Paula?'

'Good God! It's you, Newman. How the devil did you know I was here?'

'Easy. You had a date with her to meet outside. Where is she?'

'She . . . er . . . stood me up.'

'A handsome chap like you?' Newman sipped at his champagne, put the glass down. 'I can't believe it.' His voice hardened. 'I don't believe it.'

'You can get stuff—'

'You can talk,' Newman's right hand grasped Carver's short collar below the throat, twisted it, banging his head back against the wall, 'or I'll throttle you. Talk! Now!'

'Let go . . . can't breathe . . .' The grip relaxed a little. 'She was hijacked . . . Three men in stocking masks. One held a gun on me. Smashed my chin against the concrete wall. Look at my bloody jaw. I'm still dizzy – or you

375

wouldn't find it so easy to push me around.'

Newman looked at Carver's chin. There was a nasty graze along the side of his jaw. He clenched his fist as though about to punch Carver through the wall, then opened his hand, shrugged.

'All right. Talk. How did they take her away? And I like quick answers.'

'In a brown Buick. I didn't know that was going to happen. For your information it was a bloody great shock.'

'So naturally you informed the police? Gave them your description of the Buick? Sounded the alarm?'

'I'm still in a state of shock.' Carver drank more Scotch. 'It all happened so quickly. And I thought it might be dangerous to inform the police . . .'

'Why?'

'They may ask for a ransom. Don't kidnappers make it a condition the police aren't informed? I could have been putting her life at risk. For Christ's sake, Newman, I'm as worried as you are.'

'Believe that, believe the moon is blue.'

Oddly enough Newman found himself reluctantly believing that Carver *was* telling the truth. But at the same time he couldn't rid his mind of a feeling of dislike, distrust, of Carver. He finished his champagne, stood up, left with a blast.

'Well, I can tell you one thing. I'm going to do something drastic. Very drastic.'

Cord Dillon, who had taken a shower, was sitting with Tweed when Newman arrived back. His craggy face was as grim as Tweed's. He had just listened to the latest developments. The American liked Paula and secretly he was pessimistic about her chances.

'I propose we form a strike force,' Newman began.

'Nield can look after the Drayton bitch. Butler can come back to join Dillon and myself.'

'A strike force?' queried Dillon. 'Against who, what and where?'

'Hauser's crazy house. We take out Hauser himself. Give me half an hour alone with him and he'll talk. Boy, will he talk.'

'Don't like the idea,' Dillon objected before Tweed could react. 'Hauser will be heavily guarded. Too few of us to launch an assault. It could end in the death of Paula.'

'I agree with Cord,' Tweed said quickly. 'Cool down, Bob. Storming Hauser's citadel is no way to handle this.'

'Then what the hell is the way?'

'Leave it to me. That's an order.' Tweed's manner was cold. 'And you stay here until the phone call from Hauser comes through. I think I can do a deal with him.'

It was strange, Tweed thought as they waited. This was his first confrontation with the enemy. He had no intention of underestimating his opponent, but he had steeled himself to stay calm.

'I don't see how you're going to persuade him to let her go,' Newman snapped. 'And I did find Adam Carver sitting in the bar next door. I twisted his arm verbally. Said he was there when the kidnap took place, that he was rammed up against a wall by a gunman wearing a stocking mask. He does have a badly grazed jaw. The whole episode seemed to come as a great shock to him. You'll think I've lost my marbles but I believed him.'

'Why?' rapped out Dillon.

'Mainly because of where I found him. In a bar close to where they snatched Paula, drinking, in a state of shock. Had he been involved, known what was going to happen, he'd have disappeared long before this.'

'Makes sense,' Dillon agreed reluctantly. 'The guy who organized it could be Frank Galvone. A near-gangster

Hauser recruited from Chicago.' He saw Tweed raise his eyebrows. 'I did do my homework before I crossed the Atlantic . . .'

He stopped speaking as the phone began ringing. Tweed checked his watch. Half an hour after the previous call. Not an hour as Hauser had said. More psychological warfare. He deliberately let the phone ring a number of times before he picked it up.

'Martin Baker speaking.'

'Do you agree to my conditions?' the distorted voice asked. 'Or do you want her right hand delivered by special messenger? She is right-handed. The conditions are you cease all activities against us, withdraw your soldiers back to Britain. OK?'

'No, I don't agree to any of it. And don't interrupt me, Hauser, I have news for you. We are holding Sonia Drayton in a safe place.'

A pause at the other end. 'Who is this Sonia Drayton?'

'You know perfectly well who she is. She tried to murder me. Cyanide. We have the evidence. You'll do exactly as I tell you or Drayton is handed over to the Protection Police. She has already provided damaging information about your organization, information which was tape recorded. I will immediately give her to the police. With the tape. The Finnish government doesn't like people who compromise its neutrality. People who smuggle explosives into their country. People who employ murderesses. It's all on the tape.'

Another longer pause. Tweed guessed Hauser was using another line to call Drayton's apartment.

'I doubt if I'll agree,' the voice resumed. 'What do you propose?'

'Oh, you'll agree. Or face the Finnish government throwing you out of Finland lock, stock and barrel. There is going to be an exchange. Your hostage for mine. Plus the tape.'

'We might consider that arrangement. In a week's time . . .'

'Nothing doing. The exchange takes place before midnight this evening. Or Drayton and the tape go to the police. I'm not negotiating any more. Make up your mind. Now!'

A further pause. 'It will be difficult to bring in our package tonight . . .'

'No, it won't. You're holding her within half an hour's drive of this hotel.' Tweed was gambling on the data Butler had provided when he had followed Manescu and Ziegler from the railway station to Setula, to an apartment block not so far from the airport.

A brief pause this time. Hauser was absorbing the shock of realizing how much information his opponent had.

'After dark then,' he decided. 'Between midnight and two tomorrow morning . . .'

'Absolutely not. It will be dark during those two hours. That is why I said before midnight. My patience is wearing thin.'

'Then we have to agree the location. In the forest outside Helsinki. I'll give you directions . . .'

'Absolutely not.' Tweed's tone was firm, detached. 'The location for the exchange will be the scrubbing board platform at the end of tram stop No. 4. Where you murdered the wrong woman – Anna Jarva instead of Peggy Vanderheld.'

'Don't know what the hell you're talking about. The names mean nothing to me. The location is agreed. There had better not be any police there or your girl . . .'

'No police. Time for the exchange ten o'clock. 2200 hours. And the hostage had better be in perfect shape. I will have a doctor to examine her before the exchange is completed. You can take the same precaution. Now I want to get some dinner. Have you got the arrangement quite clear?'

'I agree the exchange, the details. Go f— yourself.'

The line went dead. Tweed replaced the phone. Marler, who had sat in a corner all this time, motionless as a part of the furniture, spoke.

'How the devil did you get him to agree? And to the location I suggested?'

'Because I realized he's in the middle of launching some major operation. Those explosives you discovered at the Institute. So close to the Soviet border. And this news in the *Herald Tribune*.' He passed the newspaper to Marler. The headline glared at him.

TRANS-SIBERIAN RAILROAD SABOTAGED.
EXPLOSION BLOWS TRAIN.

'That,' Tweed went on, 'links up with the murders of leading moderate statesmen in Prague, Budapest and Bucharest. Now Hauser is starting to destabilize Russia. I have a contact who confirms my view, a contact from inside the USSR. With the Soviet President distracted by more problems the way is clear for Hauser to infiltrate Russia, to gain a commercial stranglehold on their economy.'

'Then you gambled on Hauser being so concerned with this campaign he couldn't afford to risk being thrown out of Finland?' Marler suggested.

'Exactly,' said Tweed.

'Then let's hope to God the exchange is successful,' Newman commented.

'And that reminds me.' Marler jumped up. 'Gentlemen, I have to leave you. I have to make certain preparations which Tweed has agreed. Precautions to protect the exchange.'

At 9.45 p.m. a No. 4 tram stopped at the end of the line outside the city. The last two passengers alighted, Butler very close to Sonia Drayton, keeping pace with his prisoner as they walked down the pavement towards the sea and the scrubbing board platform.

'One wrong move,' Butler warned in a harsh voice, 'and it will give me great pleasure to blow a hole right through your middle.'

They walked slowly, like lovers. Butler had his left arm clasped round her waist. His right hand beneath his jacket held the Luger borrowed from Dillon, the muzzle pressed against her side. She had a long silk scarf they had discovered in Paula's room. It was draped over her shoulders, tied at the ends below her thighs. It concealed the fact that her wrists were now bound with cloth in front of her.

Irina was surprised by the viciousness in Butler's voice. He could not forget that this woman had tried to murder Tweed. They were arriving early deliberately – in case INCUBUS men were concealed in Peggy Vanderheld's apartment which overlooked the scrubbing board. It was only one reason why Tweed, after discussion with Marler, had chosen this rendezvous before taking the second call from Hauser. It seemed likely the INCUBUS group would have a key to the Vanderheld apartment – and watching from it they would see there were no police.

'Then you won't get Baker's girl friend back and he'll be lonely in bed at night,' she rapped back lewdly.

'Clean out your filthy mouth.'

Butler rammed the muzzle into her and she grunted with pain, kept silent. Thank God for a clear sky, Butler thought: dusk, let alone night, would not ruin visibility. Marler had said that was important. They walked across the deserted road, stepped on to the wooden planks of the platform, down on to the lower level projecting over the sea.

It was still very hot. Butler could feel the dampness of Drayton's T-shirt. They stood looking out to sea. The only sound was the lapping of the water against the piles supporting the platform. There were still the relics of a red stain on the planks. The blood of Anna Jarva who had died instead of Peggy Vanderheld. Murder had been committed where they stood.

More like a large lake than a sea, the distant shores were fringed with a wall of dark firs. There was an atmosphere of peace only to be found in Finland. No boats on a surface reflecting sunlight like mercury. The only entrance to this huge lagoon-like stretch of water was a channel from the Gulf of Finland which couldn't be seen to the south.

'What do you do if they don't bring her?' asked Irina.

'Hand you to the police. Charge, attempted murder . . .'

Butler was suspicious she was diverting his attention. He tightened his grip on her waist, turned to face the shore, swinging her round with him. The No. 4 tram was a small oblong, its rear growing smaller as it headed back to Helsinki. Maybe they were waiting for that to go away.

'We'll move around a bit,' he said.

He could see no sign of life in the apartment block on the second floor where Vanderheld had lived. To their right a bank of tall reeds rose out of the water, quite still. There was not a breath of moving air. Inland from the reeds was a dense tangle of undergrowth. Butler took her over close to it, glanced inside the tangle, walked her back to the platform. Somewhere a machine was approaching.

Standing on the lower level he watched the helicopter coming into view from the south, coming closer. A

Sikorsky. He had seen Sikorskys at the airport. On the side of the fuselage he saw the INCUBUS logo.

'They could be bringing her in aboard that chopper,' he commented.

'How the hell would I know. It's your party, Buster.'

'Where did you pick up that awful Americanism from?'

'From—' She clamped her mouth shut.

She had been going to say *from Hauser*, Butler thought as he watched the Sikorsky descending, over-flying them, then cruising at low level over the surrounding land area. He grinned without mirth.

'Just checking, your friends.'

'I don't know what you're talking about.'

The chopper had vanished, its engine sound fading in the distance. Butler checked his watch. Two minutes to ten. They were cutting it fine. Then he heard another faint engine sound behind him. He swung her around again, stared out to sea. A large cabin cruiser was crossing the water at high speed, trailing a white wake. Butler looked over his shoulder, stared up the tramline road to where a side road branched off to the right up a hill leading direct to the Hotel Kalastajatorppa. That road was important.

Another No. 4 tram had trundled to the terminal. A single passenger alighted, walked towards the platform. A lean man wearing a cream linen suit, a straw hat and carrying a brown bag. Walking as though he had small stones inside his shoes, he stepped on the platform. A middle-aged man with horn-rim glasses and a reedy voice.

'Are you Mr Butler?'

'Yes.'

'I am Dr Winter. Mr Baker is most persuasive ...' Butler felt Drayton stiffen. It was the first news she had had that Tweed was definitely alive. 'This is most

383

irregular,' Winter continued. 'I am supposed to examine a hostage, a woman. It is almost unbelievable. A hostage – in Finland.'

'It is,' Butler agreed, 'but it has happened. Put the bag on the platform. You may make the hostage takers nervous. And they may be arriving now with your patient.'

He turned round and the two-deck cabin cruiser was moving more slowly, almost drifting inshore. Near the prow of the vessel stood a girl with raven black hair, very erect, a blindfold across her eyes, her hands behind her back.

'There's Baker's precious tart,' sneered Irina. 'Now . . .'

She broke off, winced, stifled a groan of pain. Butler had again rammed the muzzle into her side. He had felt like pulling the trigger. There were four men on the foredeck, all with scarves pulled up over the lower part of their faces. One stood beside Paula, gripping her right arm, the other three had one hand behind their backs.

The engine of the cruiser was ticking over, the bow no more than fifty yards from the platform. Another man appeared on the upper deck, a loud-hailer held close to his mouth.

'Set Sonia Drayton free. We want to see her wave her hands about. Then she walks to the edge of the platform. When she is there we bring our boat to the platform. We let our prisoner free. She steps ashore as Sonia steps aboard . . .'

'Get stuffed!' Butler shouted back. 'You think I'm falling for that one?'

He had an uneasy feeling the man with the loud-hailer was talking too much, that it was a cover for some premeditated action. He remained where he was, his arm firmly round Drayton's waist.

'I said release her,' Loud-Hailer repeated. 'We are not staying here all evening. This is your last chance to obtain her freedom. Take your arm off her. Are her hands free? Wave to us, Sonia, if you can.'

'Don't move one inch,' Butler whispered.

'You have to do something, Buster,' Irina mocked him.

There was a sudden burst of another engine. Hidden in the reeds aboard a power boat, Marler peered at the cabin cruiser as Newman jumped ashore, Smith & Wesson in his hand. He moved through the dense clumps of undergrowth, crouched low, found what he was searching for, settled on his haunches to wait.

From his vantage point Marler could see the three men with one hand behind their backs were concealing guns. Earlier he had collected the power boat he had hired from a firm at North Harbour. He had also bought from them a chart. Moving at speed, he had left North Harbour, swung round the tip of the peninsula on which Brown Park stood, had steered the boat inside the channel into the arm of the sea overlooked by the Kalastajatorppa, had headed for the scrubbing board and hidden the boat inside the reeds an hour before rendezvous time.

He perched the barrel of the Armalite rifle on top of the perspex screen of the open wheelhouse. The boat he had hired was equipped exactly as he had specified. A microphone was close to his mouth. A small megaphone was mounted for'ard. The cabin cruiser's engine had been cut out. For a moment it was very silent, then his voice boomed out over the gentle purr of his own engine.

'The three guards standing on deck will keep quite still. They will drop the guns they are concealing at once. 'Or,' his voice increased in power, 'I'll blow you into the water.' He fired two shots. One bullet, carefully aimed, shattered the wheelhouse window, missing the helmsman. The second bullet thudded into the deck.

385

'Drop the bloody guns!' Marler yelled.

The three men froze, uncertain how to react. Then one man dropped his weapon. A moment later the other two followed his example.

'Free the hostage's hands!' Marler thundered.

A third bullet hit the deck close to one of the guard's feet. Merged behind the reeds, Marler was that most unnerving of terrors, an invisible target. The guard alongside Paula took out a key, unlocked the handcuffs. Paula stretched her aching arms, waved both hands aloft.

On the platform Butler shoved his Luger inside his belt, produced a penknife, reached under the scarf, slit the cloth binding Drayton's wrists. Seconds later the gun was again pressed against her side as she waved her free hands.

'Bring the cruiser slowly up to the platform,' Marler commanded. 'Try and run for it and you're dead . . .'

Another bullet through what remained of the glass backed up the threat. The cabin cruiser's engine started up, the vessel moved slowly forward, its hull bumped the edge of the platform, the engine was cut.

'The exchange takes place now,' Marler called out in a confident tone. 'You may all live to see another sunrise if you don't play tricks . . .'

A further bullet thudded into the deck. Marler reloaded the weapon, peered through the 'scope. Paula stepped on to the platform, passing Drayton who stepped aboard. Neither woman gave the other as much as a glance.

Sonia Drayton was hurried below decks as the engine was started up. Grabbing Paula by the arm, Butler hurried her off the platform towards the tangle of undergrowth. She took long strides, easing movement back into her legs.

'Can you ride a bicycle?' Butler asked.

'To get away from that lot I'd ride a penny-farthing.'

A lot happened so fast it was a blur of movement. Newman was dragging the three bicycles Marler had hidden in the undergrowth into view. The cabin cruiser was speeding out across the sea. A motor cycle appeared, a Honda ridden by Pete Nield, a long chain with heavy iron links looped over his handlebars. He had hired it earlier in the evening on Tweed's orders.

Marler watched as they cycled off up the road, Newman in the lead, Paula behind him, Butler bringing up the rear. Paula was pedalling furiously, ramming down her aching legs. She cycled in London frequently from her apartment to Park Crescent: it was quicker than using a car and sitting in a traffic jam.

A brown Buick raced into view down the road from the north. Full of men, it turned to pursue the cyclists, to run them down. Nield rode his Honda alongside the car, threw the chain just ahead of a front wheel. The chain coiled round the wheel, the Buick swung round in a crazy circle, stopped, as Nield followed the cyclists. Marler aimed his Armalite, found he couldn't target the man getting out of the Buick: the tangle of undergrowth masked his view.

The man outside the car swore foully as he fought to free the chain too quickly, then took more care, pulling the chain loose, hurling it towards the scrubbing board. The cyclists had disappeared, turning right up the hilly road past several foreign embassies. As she pedalled after Newman Paula sensed there was a new emergency: she had heard the car's tyres screech as it revolved in a circle.

'Keep moving!' Newman shouted over his shoulder. 'We haven't much time left.'

She didn't answer, saving her breath for her exertions. Newman reached the top of the hill, saw the BMW parked off the road, heard the Buick coming up behind them. He leapt off his bike, let the machine topple, grasped Paula's arm as she left her own machine, half dragging her into the section of the weird Kalastajatorppa complex on the side of the road nearest the sea. On the opposite side of the road where the BMW was parked was the other section of the hotel. The Kalastajatorppa was an architect's fantasy, a series of stone block-houses which seemed to grow out of the granite it was built on.

Newman and Paula, followed by Butler, were disappearing inside the hotel when the brown Buick topped the hill summit and screeched to a halt. Slumped behind the wheel of the BMW, a cap pulled down over his head, Tweed sat quite still as he watched four men pile out of the Buick, run inside the hotel. He switched on the engine, sat up straighter, gripped the wheel, waited.

Inside the hotel Newman led Paula to a flight of steps leading underground. At the bottom a nightmare tunnel stretched into the distance. Its walls were covered with white polystyrene, carved into shapes like ice. Paula recalled the claustrophobic atmosphere when she had explored the underworld beneath the Rhône glacier in Switzerland. The tunnel ahead was deserted, the atmosphere horrific.

'What the hell is this?' she gasped as she ran alongside Newman.

'Tunnel for guests linking both complexes. Goes under the road, emerges inside the other section of the hotel. Keep moving . . .'

They were three quarters of the way along the tunnel, Butler at their heels, when they heard the urgent clatter of feet running down the steps leading to the tunnel behind them. Newman ran faster, forced Paula to keep up with him, still grasping her arm. She was almost out of breath when they reached the second flight of steps. She glanced back, saw men coming down the tunnel.

They rushed up into the large reception hall, ran across it out into the open. Newman guided her to the BMW, threw open the back door. She stumbled, trying to get

388

inside too quickly. In his wing mirror Tweed saw the four men emerge, run to the Buick. He was worried. He had hoped they wouldn't have to use the second contingency plan he had worked out with Marler and Newman, who knew the layout of the hotel – that they could have jumped inside the BMW as soon as they reached the top of the hill. The arrival of the Buick had forced Newman to use the diversion. As Paula managed to climb into the rear, followed by Newman, Butler dived into the front passenger seat. Tweed saw the Buick was already moving towards them to block their escape.

'We'll never get away,' said Paula, looking through the rear window.

The Buick had been driven forward at speed, was now turning through ninety degrees to ram the side of the BMW. Tweed watched it, his foot on the brake. The Buick rushed towards them, Paula braced herself for the moment when it would slam into the side of their car. Tweed glanced to his left at the massive granite boulder he was parked alongside, timed it carefully. Foot off the brake – thank God the BMW was automatic – foot hard down on the accelerator, gear in reverse. Paula watched in horror as the huge brown projectile hurtled towards them. Tweed backed swiftly. The timing was in fractions of a second. The BMW cleared the boulder. The Buick's driver saw what lay ahead too late. Almost scraping Tweed's front bumper, the Buick roared at top speed, slammed with great force into the granite. The impact was so great the vehicle shuddered.

Tweed turned the wheel, drove on to the road, down the hill towards Helsinki. Behind him Nield skidded to a halt in front of the crumpled Buick, held the Browning, borrowed from Paula's room, by the barrel in his left hand. He smashed the butt against the windscreen. The shatter-proof glass crazed, making the world in front of the driver opaque. Nield raced off at speed, huddled low in his saddle.

38

In his bedroom at the Hesperia Tweed told Dillon what
had happened. The American had earlier become aggressive
in his attempt to join them. Tweed had been firm, brusque.

'The Deputy Director of the CIA risking exposure? If it
all goes wrong, exposure of your presence in Finland to
Mauno Sarin? The answer is no!'

'But it's all right for you to go? Deputy Director of the
SIS?'

'It's my girl they've got . . .'

Now Paula was relaxing from her ordeal in a bath while
Newman, at her request, sat in her bedroom. She had felt
the need for company, for someone to talk to beyond the
half-open door.

'It's been one hell of a day for you,' Newman commented.
'First the flight to the Institute, the scene in the Level Four
garage. You must be just about at the end of your tether.
And then the grim experience of being kidnapped.'

'The bath is helping. I appreciated the way you let me
watch while Marler retrieved his knife from that guard. I
know he told me not to look, but he didn't expect me to
take any notice of him. I appreciate the way you both treat
me as a member of the team.'

'You are a member. Fully paid up.'

'And you left that bit out when you told Tweed.'

'Deliberately. Marler and I decided that beforehand –
we both felt Tweed would have disapproved. And Tweed has
amazing reflexes. The way he timed backing out of the way
of that Buick. And cool as a cucumber on the way back here.'

'Talking about the kidnapping . . . No, Bob, it will help me to get the experience out of my system, the trauma. Looking back on it, I don't believe Adam Carver had a clue about what was going to happen. I think they used him.'

'I rather agree with you. I found him in a bar after we knew they'd grabbed you. At the Intercontinental of all places. I half-throttled him to screw information out of our smooth-talking vice president. I'd say he's pretty strong but he didn't resist. Seemed in a genuine state of shock.'

'What do you make of him?'

'I'm not sure, but he doesn't seem to fit in to that outfit as a banking chief. He's a bit of a mystery to me, something there I can't put my finger on.'

Midnight. An hour later, it was dark; the brief two-hour night Helsinki experiences in July had begun. Everyone was assembled in Tweed's room. Dillon, Paula, Newman, Butler and Marler, who had taken the power boat back to its mooring in North Harbour.

No one felt like going to bed, keyed up by the events of the day. Tweed had ordered ham sandwiches, mineral water and champagne from room service. Paula was keeping going on sheer nervous energy. Tweed swallowed the last of a sandwich and spoke.

'That kidnapping – and the swift way Hauser decided to release her – may be a significant turning point.' He looked at Paula. 'I'm appalled you had to go through that experience but, if it's any consolation, it tells us something we might not otherwise have realized.'

'And what is that?' Paula asked.

'Hauser is on the eve of launching some major operation he couldn't afford to have interfered with. Sonia Drayton may know something vital to his plans.'

'So the usual waiting period while you accumulate data is over?' she suggested hopefully.

'I think it is. Time we organized our bogus film unit and paid a visit to that so-called Meteorological Institute. And this time you stay home, Paula.'

She was about to protest when the phone rang. Everyone stiffened, looked at each other. Who could be calling at this hour? Tweed picked up the phone, the operator said she had a Mr Smith on the line for Mr Baker.

'Put him on.'

'I think you'll recognize who this is speaking,' a familiar voice said. Rebet. 'I hope I haven't woken you up but it's an emergency. We need to meet. Urgently.'

'When?' Tweed asked.

'Tonight. Or rather, this morning. Within the hour. I will be waiting in a black Saab at the top end of North Harbour.'

'At what time?'

'Are you dressed?'

'Yes.'

'Can you make it by one o'clock?'

'Yes.' It sounded like General Rebet but Tweed was in a cautious mood. 'Mind telling me the name of the hotel I stayed at when later there was a reception, followed by a banquet?'

'The Moskwa,' the voice answered immediately.

'See you at one o'clock.'

Tweed put the phone down. The others watched him curiously. The conversation had been so monosyllabic. Paula assumed it must be one of his secret informants, identity known only to Tweed. Newman reared up violently as soon as Tweed announced what he was going to do.

'I have to leave you. Please stay here, finish your meal, finish off the drink. God knows you've earned it. I'm driving myself to an appointment – just made on the phone as you heard.'

'What appointment? Where?' demanded Newman, standing up.

'As it happens,' Tweed told him reluctantly, 'at the top of North Harbour where they hold that market in daytime.'

'Great!' Newman put his glass on a table. 'Same place as where Ed Riverton was murdered, garrotted, also in the middle of the night.'

'My contact is trustworthy,' Tweed replied stiffly.

'Well, you're not going alone.'

'I think my contact would expect me to be alone . . .'

'Doubtless he would.' Newman was strapping on his shoulder holster, checking his gun. 'We've run enough risks in the past twelve hours or so. So have you. You're supposed to arrive alone. Fine. You drive, I'll hide in the back of the BMW.'

'It's parked at the rear of the Intercontinental,' Nield informed them. 'I moved it there. No point in advertising our presence.'

'Got the car keys, Pete?' Paula enquired, standing up. 'Good. Toss them to me.'

She caught them in mid-air. Staring at Tweed, she handed them to Newman. She brushed her hands together, as though to say: that's that.

'I've been through enough myself today,' she snapped at Tweed. 'Now you'll do as you're told. Bob goes with you in the back.'

'I used to think I was the boss,' Tweed lamented in a mock timid tone. 'I appear to be out-voted.'

'You goddamn well are,' Dillon told him gruffly. 'Night assignations are always dangerous.'

At 12.30 a.m. the streets of Helsinki were traffic-free except for a solitary cream BMW, occupied apparently only by the driver, who turned into the tree-lined

Esplanade. The street lamps cast a weird glow, creating large areas of shadow where anything might lurk. The driver's window was open, as were the rear windows on both sides. Newman wanted to hear, to see, to be able to shoot, if necessary. Tweed cruised slowly along the deserted street. Not the sign of a living soul anywhere.

He was almost thirty minutes early for his meeting but Newman had insisted they arrived in the vicinity well before time.

'If anyone is waiting to surprise us we'll surprise them,' he had ordered.

Tweed crept the car away from the Esplande and along the waterfront. At Newman's whispered command he stopped, left his engine running. Moored round the waterfront were many vessels, lights at their mastheads swaying gently. There was always a wind at North Harbour. Sometimes a raging gale, sometimes a gentle breeze as there was tonight. Newman told him to turn off the engine, listened.

He heard the sea lapping against the quayside, a creaking from several wooden boats. Quiet sounds in the otherwise sinister silence. Tweed glanced round like a man out for a breath of fresh air. He couldn't see any out of the way movement.

'Start the engine,' Newman whispered. 'Drive around the side streets up towards the cathedral. If you see anything, warn me. We have time to check out the whole area.'

Tweed turned left up a one-way street, continuing to cruise. He bumped over a tram line. The side streets were darker, shrouded in the deepest shadows beyond the pools of light cast by street lamps. For Tweed this was a novel experience – the dark. Ever since arriving in Finland he had gone to bed by daylight, woken up to it.

He completed a slow circuit of the old buildings, drove back on to the waterfront, checked the time by the dashboard clock. 1 a.m. A black Saab was parked by the quay, its engine turned off. Without turning his head – hardly moving his lips – he reported to Newman.

'My contact has arrived.'

'Is he alone?'

'Appears to be. I think he'll keep his word.'

What bothered Tweed was the Saab was parked by the quayside steps leading down to the landing stage where he had been hijacked by Rebet before being taken to Leningrad. He pulled up alongside the Saab, a few feet away so the driver couldn't see inside the rear of the BMW. He was careful not to use a name as he called out to General Rebet.

'Move your car away from the quayside. Park it on the far side of the market area. Then we can talk.'

Tweed had surveyed the harbour and could see no moving vessel but was taking no chances. He drove on slowly, watched Rebet in his rear-view mirror as the Russian moved the Saab across the wide concourse, parked it in the shadows of a building. Tweed performed a U-turn, drove towards the Saab, stopped close to the wall of the building.

'Leave the engine running,' Newman whispered.

'No. He has to trust me.'

Rebet was walking towards him, wearing a sports jacket and slacks. Tweed left the car quickly to meet him, to keep him away from the BMW. In his pocket he carried the photographs Nield had taken of the third man aboard the *Alskär* during the chase through the Turku archipelago into the open sea. When Nield had brought the developed and printed pictures to Tweed he had grinned, holding them behind his back.

'Write down on a bit of paper who you think the third man is.'

Tweed had obliged, Nield had handed the pictures to him. As Tweed looked at the prints Nield had chuckled.

'You guessed right . . .'

Tweed did not shake hands with the Russian and they began to stroll up and down the cobbled open space. Tweed took the initiative.

'What is this emergency? And where have you been hiding yourself?'

'In a safe place here in Finland.'

Which meant the heavily guarded Soviet two-hundred-man Embassy on the way to Brown Park, Tweed thought. The Russian, taller than Tweed, looked very slim in his well-cut outfit, younger in his roll-top sweater.

'The emergency,' Tweed prodded.

'You heard about the explosion on the Trans-Siberian Railway? We haven't caught those responsible but we know the saboteurs were infiltrated across the northern border.'

'Northern?'

'The Finnish frontier. A thousand miles or so long. Finland has a small population, a vast land area. And the explosives came in the same route the saboteurs used – via Lapland. We think we know where. We hear a huge consignment of more explosives is due to cross the border tomorrow. That is, today. It's after midnight.'

'How on earth does someone smuggle in explosives in large quantities, into Finland?' asked Tweed.

He knew very well. Newman had discovered the route when he visited Porvoo with Paula and Marler, when he heard about INCUBUS's factory ship operating outside the coastal waters. He was testing the Russian's knowledge.

'Probably through the archipelago,' Rebet replied. 'It wouldn't be too difficult – it's an incredible labyrinth of islands. The Finnish authorities could never guard the whole area. That we understand.'

'How can you be sure about this explosives consignment? About the precise timing – tonight?'

'I'm not identifying him but we have an agent inside the so-called Meteorological Institute east of Kemijärvi. He reports a great convoy of trucks with guards – who are undoubtedly also saboteurs – will slip across the border tonight. And this links with another movement. One of the three Angel suspects is touring the northern frontier on his way to Murmansk.'

'This man?' Tweed asked quietly, producing the photos.

Rebet examined them under a street lamp. He looked at Tweed in surprise.

'You know? We can't be sure. His presence could be a coincidence.'

'No coincidence,' Tweed said briskly.

Without naming Nield, he told Rebet how a member of his team had tracked the third man through the Turku archipelago, aboard a fishing vessel obviously heading out to transfer their secret passenger to a Soviet ship bound for Tallinn.

'And you guessed who Angel was in Leningrad when you watched Dikoyan, Kazbek and Marshal Zaikov talking separately to Hauser?'

'Yes. Some day I may tell you why.'

'We thought the Red Army was restless about *perestroika* and *glasnost*.'

'We may be able to give you some help with the operation from the Finnish side . . .'

Tweed explained in detail the plans of the fake film unit which would be travelling to Lapland later that same day. Rebet listened as Tweed told him a few members of his team would be armed.

'We are leaving the Soviet border open to let the convoy through,' he warned. 'Your team should all wear white coats. I now reveal a top secret since you have co-operated so fully with me. You will be careful who knows this?' Rebet stressed.

'Of course.'

'Soviet paras will be waiting for that convoy. Your team could cross into Russia without realizing it. I am catching the first Aeroflot flight from Helsinki to Leningrad this morning. I shall then fly on to the north opposite Lapland. I will warn our troops to watch out for men in white coats, that they are friends.'

'Who knows? We may help to drive them into your arms.'

'That is what I am hoping.' Rebet stopped walking, turned to Tweed, held out his hand. 'Do not forget, Soviet paratroopers, an élite force. It could be very dangerous.'

'I think we've coped with our ration of danger so far.'

39

Dawn spread its eerie light over Helsinki shortly after 2 a.m. Tweed, leaving Newman to park the BMW, returned to his room to find everyone waiting for him. Paula, keeping herself awake by sheer will power, stifled a yawn. Tweed appeared still fresh.

'Who doesn't need sleep?' he asked cheerfully, glancing round. 'There's a job to be done. Keep you up until the morning.'

'It is morning,' Paula commented.

'I meant until eight or nine ack emma.'

'What's the job?' asked Marler. 'I can get by without sleep for two days.'

'And you'd be ideal for the job.' Tweed was moving about, full of bounce now action was imminent. 'I want

398

someone to watch INCUBUS Oy's HQ. There could be activity. You know where to watch the place from.'

'I'll do it . . .'

'Draw me a plan,' Dillon interrupted, 'and I'll keep an eye on them. I've been out of things all day.'

'Not you, Cord,' Tweed said. 'Not for this surveillance job. You could do it. Don't doubt it for a moment, but for a while longer you have to stay under cover. Remember your instructions.'

'Keys, Newman,' Marler said, holding out his hand as the reporter arrived back. 'You parked the BMW out back?' He looked at Tweed. 'I'm on my way. Report back about ten?'

'Not a moment later. We're leaving aboard the chartered plane for the Arctic Circle.' He continued giving orders as Marler left. 'Butler, Nield – I want you up at six. Come to my room. We have to drive in your hired Saab to the warehouse to collect the equipment for the film unit. As soon as Stockmann's is open one of you buys seven white coats. Better get some shut eye, all of you. You may soon feel a bit tired after yesterday.'

'A bit?' Paula remarked, standing up. 'You must be joking.'

'Sorry. I wasn't including you. You've had the toughest day any one of us has gone through for a long time. Get off to bed. Sleep well.'

Newman waited until they had all gone. He had the stamina of an ox, still didn't feel like sleep. He poured some mineral water for Tweed out of a bottle which had rested in the ice bucket alongside the champagne bottles.

'We were lucky during the hostage exchange,' he observed as Tweed drank. 'At that hour there were no guests from that hotel with the unpronounceable name floating around down by the scrubbing board. And none in reception when we rushed through it to reach you – even the receptionist was absent.'

399

'Lucky,' Tweed agreed. 'Paula seems OK. At nine this morning I have to soothe Dr Winter who came to check Paula. Says he never got near her.'

'No time,' recalled Newman. 'We were too busy escaping. And Paula looks pretty good.'

'I'll keep Winter quiet with a large fee,' Tweed decided. 'He's one of the few English doctors in Helsinki. I'll tell him it was an operation the police want kept quiet. Which is why nothing will appear in the press.'

'I think sending Marler out to INCUBUS at this hour is a waste of time. The place will be shut up. What's the idea?'

'First, Hauser moves about a lot, jets all over the world. He's spent far longer in one place – Helsinki – than he normally does. I got this from the data Monica fed to me. He could be moving on. Second, he's near the end of a risky and sensitive operation in Finland. I'd expect him to clear out in case it blows up in his face. Literally.'

Without revealing Rebet's identity, he told Newman what the Russian had explained to him. What they might face if they were close to the border, the precautions he was taking. The only factor he omitted to mention was the existence of Angel.

'Today,' Tweed ended, rubbing his hands together, 'will be one of frenetic activity.'

'That's nice. Yesterday you'd call a rest day?'

Inside his penthouse office at INCUBUS's HQ Hauser was supervising the removal of all key files locked away in steel cabinets. Each was labelled with a coded designation of its contents. Male staff were heaving cabinets out of his office towards the elevator.

It was 2.10 a.m. For a moment Hauser glanced at Carver and Galvone, then looked out of the picture window. The rising sun was casting a pearl-grey light on the smooth sea which made it look like a leaden lake.

'I'll miss this view,' he said nostalgically.

'I suppose someone will let me in on the secret of where we're going to when they feel like it,' Carver commented ironically.

Hauser closed the door behind the last workman who had temporarily left the office. He poured a large glass of mineral water, drained it.

'OK, boy,' he said to Carver, 'time to let you in on the secret. We're moving our centre of operations to the HQ in Stockholm.'

'Nothing is labelled with its destination,' Carver pointed out.

'For security reasons. Addressed labels are prepared, will be attached while the trucks are en route to the airport. Attached only by trusted staff. You know how I operate. I turn up where I'm least expected.' He swivelled his gaze. 'Frank, hadn't you better be leaving to take charge of Operation Urals?'

Hauser waited until he was alone with Carver. The president of INCUBUS had his shirt sleeves rolled up above his elbows. He was personally supervising the movement of top secret filing cabinets. If you wanted a job done properly you had to do the goddamn thing yourself.

'Adam, you fly today to Stockholm aboard the Lear jet. It will be carrying the key filing cabinets. I'm making you personally responsible for supervising the unloading and transport of them to the vault at our Stockholm HQ. The Lear lands at Bromma Airport – away from prying eyes.'

'We'll need a vehicle to carry them from Bromma . . .'

'All arranged. A truck will be waiting. You take them to our HQ in one of those high-rise office blocks on Sveavägen – high-rise for Stockholm.'

'I didn't see any identification to separate the key cabinets from the others.'

Hauser clapped a hand on his shoulder. 'All taken care of. Green labels will be attached aboard the truck for the jet downstairs. The rest of the stuff travels air cargo by scheduled flight.'

'When are you coming? You are travelling to Stockholm?'

'I travel incognito under a different name aboard another scheduled flight later. I have to be out of Helsinki by midday.'

'What is this Operation Urals?'

'Questions! Questions! Haven't I told you before you ask too many? Get down to the garage area and make sure those jerks attach a green label to every cabinet. On your way.'

Hauser inserted a cigarette into his holder as Carver left the room. Hauser radiated confidence but he was a worried man. The plan to rescue Irina Serov, to hold on to their own hostage, had gone badly wrong. Tweed had foreseen his strategy, had out-manoeuvred him with superior strategy. Hauser shrugged his massive shoulders. So Tweed had scored a brownie point.

He smiled as he thought of his opponent's chagrin when he eventually discovered the entire INCUBUS apparatus in Finland had disappeared. Oh yes, he could out-smart Tweed.

Sitting inside the car perched in the trees above INCU-BUS's HQ, Marler watched through the viewer of his camera. At three in the early morning, now broad daylight, he studied the intense activity.

Men in overalls carried filing cabinets to one of the waiting trucks parked in the compound outside the garage area. There seemed to be some division of labour. Adam Carver was standing by one truck as cabinets were heaved inside.

Other men were lugging cabinets to two other trucks and Carver appeared to have no interest in these vehicles. Marler twiddled an unlit king-size between his lips and waited.

Occasionally he sipped water from a plastic bottle. He could do without food but already it was very warm: had it ever cooled down? Marler settled in for a long wait. He had infinite patience, had learned to develop that virtue as a marksman waiting for his target to show.

Nearly two hours later, at 5 a.m., Carver climbed into the cab beside the driver. The vehicle drove forward, the automatic gates in the wire fence opened, the truck came out, turned in the direction of Helsinki.

'You're for me, Laddie,' Marler said to himself.

He started the engine, drove down the road out of sight of the HQ, joined the main road. Keeping well back – there was no traffic to speak of at that hour – he kept the truck in sight. Soon he realized it was heading for the airport as the truck barrelled along the highway between the granite outcrops.

Marler was driving the hired Saab. The opposition would be familiar by now with the cream BMW. He arrived at the airport as unloading was beginning. Driving past, he pulled in at the kerb, locked the car, strolled inside the concourse.

Even at that hour there were a number of tourists waiting for flights. Mostly young back-packers, sprawled in seats, fast asleep, a growth of stubble on the men's chins, the girls in crumpled denims and creased blouses.

Marler picked up a brochure from a pile on the counter, pretended to be studying it. A wheeled trolley laden with filing cabinets marked with green labels was pushed past him. The presence of Carver outside did not bother him: so far Carver had never seen Marler.

Through a window he watched the trolley being propelled out to the waiting Lear jet. The men in overalls had a

403

hard job manoeuvring a cabinet up the retractable steps inside the jet. Marler decided it would be too risky enquiring where the jet was bound for. He heard another truck arriving.

Half an hour later the cabinets aboard the second truck were being handed over to Cargo for transport aboard a scheduled flight. Marler waited until the team went back for another load, approached the cargo supervisor.

'I have a consignment arriving a bit later for you. I hope it arrives in time. Can I check departure time of that plane you're loading?'

'For Arlanda, Stockholm? Departs 7.30 a.m. Will be on time.'

'Thank you,' said Marler.

He walked outside and a third INCUBUS truck was drawing up at the kerb. He paused to light a cigarette. Two men jumped out of the cab, ran to the rear, unlocked the doors. A team inside began unloading at once. Conducted with military precision, Marler thought as he climbed behind the wheel of the Saab and drove away.

Tweed was freshly shaven, fully dressed, when he opened his bedroom door to Marler. In a chair sat Paula, also dressed for the day. Marler swallowed a yawn.

'You people don't get much sleep, do you?'

'Too excited,' Paula told him.

'I have to leave for the warehouse with Butler and Nield,' Tweed said briskly. 'What have you found out – if anything?'

'Hauser is evacuating the Helsinki HQ . . .'

He described what he had seen, kept it short, to the point. Tweed was drinking mineral water as he finished.

He put down the glass, walked to the window. It was going to be another glorious day. The metal mobile sculpture was motionless. Not a breath of wind. It was going to be bloody hot.

'Stockholm,' he said after a moment. 'I thought he might be running for it, dissociating himself from Finland considering what will soon be happening in the Arctic Circle.'

'I am coming with you all,' Paula said firmly.

'No, you're not,' Tweed informed her. 'Change of plan – because of Marler's news . . .'

'Because you think this expedition is too dangerous for a woman,' Paula blazed.

'Because,' Tweed countered calmly, 'I now have a job for you which could be even more dangerous. Because you know the area. Because I know you would never let me down.'

'What job?'

'I want to be sure you can disguise yourself. You may be travelling with members of the opposition who know you – who have pictures of you. In short, I want you to fly to Stockholm, preferably aboard the 7.30 a.m. flight, providing you can get a seat. If you do board that flight, wait at Arlanda, wait when you arrive. Before you leave Helsinki phone one of the twenty-four-hours-a-day hire firms, arrange for a car to be waiting for you at Arlanda. After they've unloaded the cabinets Marler has told us about, follow them to their destination.'

'I'd better get moving . . .'

'Wait. First, go to your room, disguise yourself. Come back and let me see how you look . . .'

Within minutes she had returned. Tweed and Marler stared at her. Paula had tucked most of her hair under a tight-fitting straw hat, had changed into a grey skirt and a long-sleeved cream blouse. But the greatest transformation was the pale shade of face powder she had applied, the large pair of horn-rim spectacles she was wearing. And no lipstick.

Marler chuckled. 'God! You look like a schoolteacher.'

'That's the general idea,' Paula snapped.

'I congratulate you,' said Tweed. 'When you arrive in Stockholm book rooms for all of us at The Grand Hotel, if they have the space. If you have to fix us up elsewhere, leave a message in a sealed envelope for me.'

'The Grand?' Paula objected. 'Bob and Cord Dillon stayed there with me when we were on our way here.'

'No matter. If Hauser checks, finds we have arrived on his heels, so much the better. Pressure, that's what I'm putting on him from now on. Pressure and more pressure. Better get moving.'

Marler waited until she had rushed off. 'It is a dangerous assignment you've given her. Is that wise when she's recovering from her kidnap ordeal?'

'One reason why I asked her – apart from the fact that I do need her to do the job. She'll be working on her own – which she's very good at. That alone will help the ordeal to fade.'

'And now we're heading for the Arctic Circle. It could be quite a battle.'

'A ferocious battle.'

40

The heatwave was scorching London. At Park Crescent Monica had all the windows open. It made no difference: the air was still, not the ghost of a breeze came inside. She was sitting with Howard, explaining her extensive research on INCUBUS and Franklin D. Hauser.

'I had trouble locating this house he has in Sweden close to Norway in the western archipelago – that's north of Gothenburg. Most people outside Scandinavia think there is only one, the archipelago outside Stockholm.'

'I do know some geography,' Howard bridled.

'Good for you.'

Howard smiled. With so many of his key staff away the barriers between himself and Monica were coming down. As a major concession to the heat Howard sat in shirt sleeves, an informal state of dress Monica had never known before. She ran a hand over her bun of grey hair and continued.

'It is a large house, very remote as far as I can see. I had to get this chart from a contact at Lloyd's to locate Skalhamn.'

'What's that?'

'The tiny cove below where the house stands.' She pointed to the chart. 'There it is. Well out of the way. My contact at Lloyd's phoned a friend in Sweden. Apparently the house looks like a major communications centre. A tangle of weird aerials on the roof, plus a satellite dish.'

'Where does that get us?'

'If you'll wait till I've finished. Hauser also has based there a large yacht – the kind of boat Onassis used to live on. The *Washington IV*. When he's not jetting across the world Hauser travels around a lot in that vessel. And it is equipped like a floating communications platform.'

'Hauser is in Helsinki so far as we know,' Howard objected.

'But I've checked his movements in recent years as far as I can. He jumps all over the globe like a grasshopper – so he may leave Helsinki. Tweed will want to know about his haunts.'

'And that's it?'

'Heavens, no! The best is yet to come. He has offices in

Oslo, Stockholm, Copenhagen, Amsterdam, Brussels, Frankfurt, Paris, Geneva, Vienna, Madrid, Lisbon, Milan, Athens. Also in Singapore, Auckland, Sydney, Montreal. And in South America and Japan. Do you want me to go on?'

'That is the best?'

'No, I've been saving the gem for last. Livingstone Manor in Suffolk. Apart from Boston, New York, and a host of other cities in the States. Livingstone Manor *is* the gem,' she repeated.

'What about the place?'

'It appears to be the real HQ from where he controls and directs his world-wide empire . . .'

'Sounds most unlikely.'

'That's the clever part. It's supposed to be his country home in Britain. Who would suspect it was the centre of the INCUBUS spider's web?'

'I wouldn't, for one. What is all this?'

'Livingstone Manor is very large, has extensive grounds. Underneath the ground floor is a labyrinth of converted cellars. They're like catacombs. The whole area was reconstructed, the security is tight. He has installed the latest sophisticated cipher and coding machines. A very advanced telephone scrambler system has been secreted in one huge room. More sophisticated than the hot line between Downing Street and the Kremlin.'

'How on earth do you know all this?' Howard asked in an incredulous tone.

'I have a friend in an insurance company who covers the equipment. He only gave me the tiniest hint but I followed it up.'

'And how did you do that?'

'I obtained from the same friend the name of the electric company who had installed it.'

'Don't tell me he spilt all these beans to you.'

'No. I didn't even try that route. Instead I phoned one of Tweed's close friends in Special Branch. He owes Tweed. It's all the old boys' network. You use it yourself at that club of yours.'

'Never mind about that. Go on.'

'I gave the Special Branch man the name of the electrical firm and he went to see the managing director. I gather he had to twist his arm, but I didn't want to know about that. Guess what?'

'I'm not partial to guessing games,' Howard retorted, for a brief moment his old stiff self.

'The Special Branch man obtained from this managing director a complete specification of what they had installed at Livingstone Manor. He, the managing director that is, became worried he had broken some regulations. He came up with the information I've supplied.'

'And they installed the cipher machines?'

'No. They must have been made inside INCUBUS' laboratories in Boston on what used to be Space Highway. But one of the top electrical supervisors wandered round this underground labyrinth beneath Livingstone Manor. He was at Bletchley during the war – working on the ENIGMA cipher machine the Nazis were using. He found a steel door open and looked inside. No one was about. He saw the cipher machines, reported what he'd seen to his managing director.'

'I see.'

Howard was impressed, almost appalled. Bloody nerve. In the middle of the English countryside. And in Suffolk – where he had his own country retreat on the rare occasions when he paid his obligatory visit to his wife, Cynthia.

'Nothing illegal about it, I suppose. Unfortunately.'

'No,' Monica agreed. 'But highly significant. As I said earlier, I'm convinced Hauser has moved his operational centre from America to Livingstone Manor . . .'

She broke off as the phone rang. She listened for a short time, put a hand over the instrument.

'We have two unwelcome visitors. Chief Inspector Buchanan and Sergeant Warden. They're waiting downstairs and have asked to see Tweed.'

'Tell them to go away, that he's not here.'

'Not wise,' Monica said firmly. 'We ought to find out what they want. Forewarned is forearmed.'

'Oh, all right, if you say so . . .'

Howard himself was surprised at the transformation in the relationship between himself and Monica. He had always before regarded her as the ageless woman who looked after the files. Now he was treating her as an equal.

Buchanan was at his most official when he entered, Sergeant Warden was his normal poker-faced self. Howard did not stand up. Dismissively, he waved them to sit down.

'I'm Howard, Tweed's superior. Tweed is away. If you can make it brief I would appreciate it. We are rather busy.'

'Aren't we all?' Buchanan, appearing not to notice Howard's lack of welcome, and relaxed, crossing his long legs. Warden took out his notebook, rested it on his lap.

'Anything said at this interview is off the record,' Howard snapped. 'Kindly remember where you are.'

'Oh, we're very conscious where we are,' Buchanan told him amiably. 'But I would remind you, Mr Howard, since I am confident you must have heard, that I am investigating a particularly brutal murder. Namely that of Sandra Riverton in Suffolk.'

'And I read in the paper,' Monica chimed in, 'that you've caught the Camden Town murderer.'

'Quite correct.' Buchanan politely swivelled in his chair to address her. 'So all our energies are now released to continue the investigation into the Sandra Riverton case.

Not that we ever ceased our interest.' He paused. 'Did you know that Evelyn Lennox, Sandra's sister, has been attacked in her cottage at Walberswick?'

'What on earth has all this to do with us?' Howard demanded.

'I'll explain,' Buchanan continued patiently. 'The person who discovered Sandra's body hanging from a bell tower was Robert Newman. You know where he is at this moment?' he asked suddenly.

'No idea,' Howard snapped. 'No contact for some time.'

'The point is,' Buchanan went on relentlessly, 'within twenty-four hours Ed Riverton, Sandra's brother-in-law, an American, was also brutally murdered in Helsinki. And I detect a similarity in both MOs. Murder by garrotting the neck, murder by hanging from the neck.'

'Fail to see the connection.'

'I'm coming to that. Sandra Riverton had worked for INCUBUS, who have an office in Norwich. She had resigned two weeks before she died. Ed Riverton was a top executive with INCUBUS. Evelyn Lennox also worked for INCUBUS.'

'How is she?' Monica asked. 'Is she seriously hurt?'

She felt illogically conscience-stricken. At Tweed's request she had withdrawn Harry Butler from Walberswick and his job had been to protect her.

'She was lucky.' Buchanan changed his phraseology. 'She was resourceful, plucky. It was evening. A masked intruder appeared in her hall. He must have picked the lock to get into the place. They grappled in the hall, Miss Lennox was bruised but broke free. She fled into the kitchen where she had some water boiling in a pan. She threw it at her attacker, at his masked face. He screamed, ran for it. Lennox thought from his build he might be a man called Steve who visited her some time ago at her Wandsworth home.'

411

'He works with a man called Papa Grimwood,' Monica told him.

'And how do you know that, if I may ask?'

'Bob Newman told me . . .'

'Lennox gave us a good description of her attacker's build,' Buchanan added. 'It also pretty well fits Newman's.'

'That's ridiculous,' Monica burst out.

'It would be,' Buchanan agreed, stretching out his legs, 'if I knew Newman was a long way from the scene of the attack at the time.'

So that's what you've been building up to, Howard thought. He waved a hand.

'So far as we know Mr Newman is out of the country.'

'So far as you know? That's not good enough.'

'It will have to do for now.'

'Chief Inspector,' Monica broke in to divert him to another subject, 'is Evelyn Lennox under police protection? Whoever did this awful thing might come back.'

'Yes, he might. The local police have agreed to your suggestion. The trouble is all they can spare is a PC who visits Walberswick on his bicycle, that he will call in at Rose Bower to make sure Lennox is all right. I'm afraid it's rather a flimsy form of protection.'

'Then find Papa Grimwood and this man, Steve,' Monica said.

'We're looking. So far no trace of them.' He handed Howard a card. 'When Newman gets back from wherever he is I'd appreciate it if you'd give me a call.'

'Why can't he give you a call himself?' Howard suggested in a bleak tone.

'Better still.' Buchanan stood up, Warden followed his chief's example. 'Thank you for your co-operation, sir. Perhaps now you can see the connection?'

'Not entirely,' Howard responded. 'Thank you for calling.'

'That's all right. And we can find our own way out . . .'

'Don't forget to hand in your passes. Or otherwise even you won't get past the guard,' was Howard's parting shot.

Monica could hardly contain herself until they were alone.

'You see! I was right about Livingstone Manor. It's in the same area as Walberswick where that girl was attacked. Sooner or later the action is going to move back to Livingstone Manor.'

'I do wish Tweed would get in touch,' Howard said irritably. 'I wonder what he's up to now?'

41

'He's an expert executioner,' Hauser said.

In the turret room at his house overlooking the park he was taking files from a wall safe, stuffing them inside a briefcase. The files were records of various key industrialists who owned companies he was determined to buy up in Britain and Europe. The files had been compiled by Sandra Riverton and Evelyn Lennox pretending to compile profiles for the American magazine *Leaders of Mankind*.

His reply had been in answer to a question posed by Iris Reynolds, the girl sitting on the edge of a couch while she watched him.

'Why have you decided to fly Ion Manescu to Stockholm?' she had asked him. 'I thought he was going with Galvone and Ziegler to see the explosives convoy safely across the Soviet border.'

Iris Reynolds was the new identity given to Irina Serov

by Hauser. She had arranged her bleached blonde hair so it framed her face. Combed down over her forehead, it changed her appearance from the woman who had visited Tweed at the Hesperia. She wore a flowered print dress, a wide-brimmed straw hat, flat-heeled shoes – reducing her earlier heights by inches. She looked very English and carried a doctored British passport.

'Manescu,' Hauser went on as he slid more files into the case, 'is travelling by scheduled flight to Arlanda. I'd like those photographs now.' He put them inside a cardboard backed envelope, inserted the envelope in the case.

'The only member of the opposition we haven't pictures of now is the man on the motor cycle who helped to foil our trap at the scrubbing board. You'll travel aboard the Lear jet with me. When we reach our destination you can help produce an Identikit of Tweed. As you saw, we have photos of the man who guarded you standing on the platform. The schmuck was filmed from the cabin cruiser with a telescopic lens. There may be others but they'll be back here, trying to locate us.'

Irina marvelled at the American's energy. He now had shown full confidence in her after the long apprenticeship: it was the first time he had let her know his identity.

'One thing I don't understand,' she said carefully, 'is why I'm not yet being sent into Russia to run Operation Urals.'

'You've phoned your agents in München, the Free Ukraine movement. Your agents are placed in Poland and Czechoslovakia. They'll all be crossing the border into Russia, they know where to pick up the explosives, the targets.' He paused briefly, stared hard at her with his icecold eyes. 'That is a fact, I hope.'

'I have done all that,' she assured him.

'Then maybe later we'll fly you to Istanbul so you can slip across the Turkish border to keep them active.'

'One more point,' she ventured. 'That attractive girl you exchanged me for. You think she'll stay here?'

He grinned cynically. 'Could you imagine Tweed having the audacity to send her after me? Bearing in mind how many pictures we have of *her*?'

Waiting aboard the Lear jet at Helsinki Airport, Adam Carver checked his watch again. When was the damned thing going to take off? They were hours behind schedule. He swallowed some more mineral water. The jet was air-conditioned but the heat seemed to penetrate inside the aircraft.

A small canvas-covered truck drove towards the jet. Carver frowned. All the cabinets had been put aboard ages ago. What could be coming out to the jet now? The truck arrived, turned a half-circle, backed to the foot of the steps. Carver stared in disbelief. The canvas flap had been lifted from the rear, two people appeared, boarded.

Hauser wore a peaked cap of the type once favoured by German students, a British sports jacket with a small check design, a pair of well-creased grey slacks, dark glasses. He parked the unknown girl with him in a seat at the front of the jet, walked back to settle in an armchair next to Carver.

The step ladder had been retracted, the door closed; the jet engines were growling, building up power. Hauser clutched the bulging briefcase in his lap. It contained enough information to blackmail over thirty industrialists and copies of the earlier reports by Sandra Riverton and Evelyn Lennox. The profiles on firms already swallowed up, details of the techniques used. A briefcase of dynamite.

'It's mid-afternoon,' Carver protested. 'And I'd no idea you'd be travelling with me.'

'Now you know.'

Hauser grinned to himself. Keep them all off balance – and it was good security not to let even his closest associates know what was happening next.

'I suppose we are going to Bromma?' Carver asked as the jet moved down the runway.

'Bromma is our next destination,' Hauser agreed.

He turned away to conceal his wolfish smile. Well, they were at least putting down at Bromma for a few minutes. And he had fooled that bastard Tweed.

'At last we have some questions we can put to Hauser. To grill him,' Mauno Sarin said with satisfaction to Karma.

It was the news from the Finnish traffic police about the brown Buick wrecked at the Kalastajatorppa which had given the Finn the lever he had been looking for. Sarin had told them to leave it where it was, had driven at speed with Karma to the scene of the 'accident'.

'Surely someone must have witnessed this,' he said when they stood looking at the vehicle, its bonnet telescoped against the granite boulder.

'I haven't found anyone,' reported Karma who had arrived earlier. 'The guests were enjoying themselves at a dinner dance in the main restaurant across the road. But I found this taped to the underside of the front passenger seat.'

A Luger. Fully loaded. In Finland you don't travel with handguns. Karma had used the hotel phone to check the registration number on the intact rear plate. The Buick was registered to INCUBUS. Sarin wasted no time.

'Drive me to their headquarters. Fast . . .'

Arriving at the tall circular building they were surprised to find the automatic gate open and no sign of a guard. No sign of any staff. The switchboard was unmanned.

Sarin had pressed the elevator button for the penthouse floor. As they stepped out he was struck by the silence.

His long legs took him swiftly to Hauser's office. Opening the door he walked inside, stared.

The furniture was still in place. What attracted Sarin's attention were rectangles of dust-free marble on the floor against the walls. Spaces where filing cabinets had stood. He opened several drawers in the outsize desk. Empty. He looked at Karma.

'If that phone is working call the airport. Hauser has a Lear jet.'

Karma found Hauser's personal phone was still connected with the outside world. Probably a private line which bypassed the switchboard. Sarin walked rapidly through the other offices, returned as Karma put down the phone.

'The place has been evacuated,' Sarin commented.

'And the Lear jet took off mid-afternoon after being in a holding area all night and since early morning.'

'Destination?'

'The flight plan was for Bromma Airport, Stockholm.'

'So he's run for it. I wonder why? You may as well know I told the Minister about the Semtex Marler says he took from an INCUBUS truck north of Porvoo, and the second lot from a truck in an alleged hidden garage at the Institute.'

'How did he react?' Karma enquired.

'At first he said he'd take it under consideration. In other words, do nothing. Or so I thought. Yesterday I heard the government had turned down Hauser's offer of the three million dollars for a new icebreaker. That was signalling to Hauser he'd better be more careful.'

'Could be the reason he's left Finland.'

'Unless there's a more sinister reason. Assemble a team of men to fly to the Arctic Circle. I'm going to take a look at that Institute for myself.'

'Half our people are on holiday – it is July,' Karma warned. 'It will take time.'

'So have the team ready for tonight.'

*   *   *

Newman was disturbed to discover the plane Tweed had chartered was a Fokker, a machine powered by propellers. He sat alongside Tweed as it took off from Helsinki Airport in late afternoon.

'Sounds like a bloody sewing machine,' he commented.

'It was the only machine I could get,' Tweed responded. 'And it's large enough to take all of us in comfort – plus the equipment.'

Marler sat opposite, staring out of the window. His Armalite was easily concealed among the fake film unit's load of cameras, lights and canisters of film. Butler and Nield sat beside each other near the front of the aircraft. Cord Dillon sat alone, his craggy face grim as the machine soared into the sky, heading north.

There had been an animated argument between Tweed and the American alone in Tweed's room at the Hesperia prior to departure for the airport. Tweed had marshalled all his reasons why Dillon should not go.

'You're the US President's personal representative . . .'

'And he sent me to Europe to get enough evidence to destroy Hauser in the courts back home. What could be more damning than proof he's transporting explosives into the Soviet Union? Goddamnit, hear me out! I'm coming with you if I have to shove this Luger in your back . . .'

Eventually Tweed had given in. Dillon's case for joining them was overwhelming. Reluctantly, he had agreed.

One thing which worried Tweed as the Fokker continued to climb, leaving Helsinki far behind, was the few weapons they carried. Dillon had his Luger; Marler his Armalite; Newman his Smith & Wesson. That was it. No, there was another weapon: Marler had given Butler the Mauser and the spare mags taken from the second guard at the Institute. One rifle, three handguns. A meagre strike force.

Before leaving for Stockholm Paula had offered her

Browning. Tweed had insisted she kept the weapon. It was bad enough sending her off on her own on a dangerous mission. At least she should be armed.

On two empty seats at the rear of the machine were six white coats purchased from Stockmann's. And those, Tweed reminded himself, were vital life savers to identify the fake film unit. His mouth tightened at the prospect before them on the Finnish border. Operating just over that frontier: Soviet paras.

Due to the regulations the Fokker had to land at Oulu on the coast of the Gulf of Bothnia. Tweed peered out of the port window. A small airfield. No sign of the town. Just one tiny airport building designated *Oulu* over the entrance. No other aircraft. Butler returned from the pilot's cabin with the bad news.

'The pilot says we have to wait here. Weather conditions. A storm is coming in fast. It may be for a while.'

'How long is a while?' Tweed demanded.

'No idea. Oh, he also had a met. report from Rovaniemi. Temperature 33°C. That's 91°F.'

'But that's hotter than Helsinki,' Tweed protested to Newman. 'Rovaniemi is north of the Arctic Circle.'

'Didn't anyone tell you?' Newman replied with a droll smile. 'It often is hotter in the Arctic Circle.'

'Charming. Meanwhile we're stuck here. Might as well eat while we're stationary . . .'

He had hardly finished the sentence when the storm broke. Beyond his window forked lightning flashed non-stop. The spectacle was punctuated by tremendous thunderclaps which seemed to shudder the aircraft. Sheets of tropical-like rain hammered the tarmac, bouncing off its surface, flooding the area. Rain lashed the windows like a flail of whips.

'Just what we needed.' Tweed sighed.

Butler and Nield acted as stewards, serving ham sandwiches from coolbags. Tweed was ravenous. With his sandwiches he drank mineral water. Dillon, holding a paper plate piled with sandwiches, left his seat, walked up to where Tweed sat.

'This delay going to screw up our schedule?'

'The beach buggies waiting for us at Rovaniemi airport will just have to move faster,' Tweed told him.

'Ever tried to drive one of those things? Tried to make them move faster?'

On this optimistic note he returned to his seat. There was no point in continuing the conversation – thunder crashed like a continuous banging of giant cymbals, rain was still streaming down in sheets, more like a cascade from a deep waterfall. Lightning flashes flared as Tweed finished his meal, checked his watch.

'Has to stop sometime, I suppose,' Newman remarked.

Tweed grunted, closed his eyes for a nap and fell fast asleep. He was woken by the starting up of the motors. He looked out of the window and it was a bright summer's day. The Fokker moved forward, gathered speed, took off and turned in a circle. Through the window Tweed saw a vast distance – out across the sea to the west was the coast of distant Sweden. The plane continued climbing, heading away from the sea north-east for Rovaniemi.

'Are you satisfied with the arrangements?' Newman asked. 'This is going to be a tricky operation.'

'The Admin. Officer at the Institute is a Mr Palonen. Paula had a long talk with him on the phone yesterday. Gave him the impression we are filming for a TV documentary. They always fall for TV. Palonen said the Institute had just been closed for redecoration . . .'

'That would be Hauser. Trying to keep people away from the place while the convoy of explosives is moved.'

'Exactly. Paula went on talking, said would it be OK if we took pictures of the outside and the surrounding countryside. Palonen agreed to that. So he is expecting us.'

'And supposing we need to make a quick getaway? Hardly a situation for beach buggies.'

'Which is why when I chartered this machine I also fixed up for the hire of a Sikorsky and a pilot. An S61. Takes eighteen passengers.'

'So why didn't we travel in that?'

'Because it wasn't available until this evening. I also obtained from them a Verey pistol with orange flares. Marler has it. If we're out in the wilderness – which I suspect we shall be – we can signal to the S61 where to land to take us off.'

'You seem to have thought of everything,' Newman commented as Tweed peered out of the window at a blue rope which was a river winding its way across the flat sun-bleached plain far below.

'Except for the unexpected. Thank God Paula isn't with us.'

Hours earlier Paula sat in her hired Volvo outside Arlanda airport. Knowing it would take time to unload cargo from the aircraft which had flown her from Helsinki, she had not hurried with the courier who handed over the car to her.

Now she sat peering from under the brim of her straw hat at the waiting INCUBUS AB truck. The heatwave was burning Sweden and she had all the windows open. An hour later she saw trolleys stacked with filing cabinets being trundled towards the truck where the automatic rear platform had been lowered to street level.

Half an hour later the truck was belting down the highway through open country towards Stockholm. Paula was careful to keep some distance back: it was a good three-quarters of an hour's drive from Arlanda into the city centre.

The highway reminded her of the drive into Helsinki from the Finnish airport. It stretched into the distance between limestone outcrops until she reached the outskirts of the Swedish capital. She closed the gap.

Sveavägen. Near the end of the wide street was Sergels Torg. A few hundred yards before reaching that notorious square where on their outward journey Newman had purchased weapons, Little Manhattan sheered up to her right just beyond where she was parked. Five nineteen-storey slabs of white stone; the tallest office blocks in Stockholm.

Paula watched as the filing cabinets were moved inside one of the towers. Over the entrance was the logo INCUBUS AB. She sat behind the wheel as though waiting for her boy friend. The charade was not difficult to keep up as several Swedish youths approached one by one and chatted her up.

Paula began to worry as the elevated platform was raised, the truck drove away. Delivery completed. If those cabinets were so important why weren't they accompanied by a top executive?

I'm missing something, she kept thinking. What is it?

Then she remembered Bromma, the small airport the other side of the city Newman had driven her to when they were in Stockholm on their way to Finland. Paula had a flair for recalling routes. She drove through the city, headed along the highway to Bromma.

The airport seemed as quiet and lifeless as it had when she had last explored it. Parking the Volvo, she walked inside, across the deserted concourse to the window she knew overlooked the airfield. She stood stock still for a moment, hardly able to believe her luck.

'Bull's-eye!' she said to herself.

Extracting the small pair of binoculars she always

422

carried in her shoulder bag, she focused them. The Lear jet stood in almost the same place it had been parked before. And along the fuselage stood out the logo. INCUBUS.

She moved to one side of the window, raised her glasses, waited. The door was open, the retractable staircase was leading to the ground. Five minutes later she saw a man appear, walk stiffly down the steps. A large man, he wore a peaked cap, a British-type sports jacket, grey slacks and dark glasses. It took Paula a moment to recognize him. More something about his movements than his mode of dress.

'Good God! Hauser!' she said under her breath.

Hauser was stretching his arms, walking up and down, when a second man appeared. Slimmer, he ran down the steps, paced slowly up and down alongside Hauser. Paula had no trouble recognizing him. She pursed her lips.

'Mr Casanova himself. Adam Carver.'

She lowered the glasses, slipped them back inside her bag, waited. It was obvious they were not waiting for a car to take them into Stockholm. Marler had told her enough about Hauser's meticulous organization and timing for her to realize a limo would have been waiting *before* the jet landed. Mopping her forehead with a handkerchief, she prepared to wait some more.

'I thought when you said we were flying to Bromma we'd be occupying the Stockholm HQ,' Carver said as he strolled alongside his chief. 'What's next on the menu?'

'The cargo of filing cabinets which travelled by scheduled flight to here are routine. Tweed seems good at gathering information. His job, I guess. So we let Mr Tweed think we have flown to Stockholm when he wakes up to the fact we're no longer in Finland. Let him waste his time, not mine.'

423

'Well, if it's not a state secret, what is next on the menu? Where are we going?'

'To somewhere, boy, Tweed knows nothing about. Time we got aboard. The pilot should have checked that flashing light by now.'

He hauled his bulk back up the steps, walked inside the cabin, sagged into his arm chair. Jesus Christ! It was bloody hot.

'So make it a mystery tour,' Carver said irritably as he sat beside him.

'Gothenburg, boy. That's where we're going to. Gothenburg on the west coast of Sweden.' He lifted a hand as the pilot appeared at the exit to the control cabin, waved it forward.

'Get this hunk of scrap metal off the ground,' he growled.

Inside the airport building Paula watched as the jet became airborne. She waited until she saw the direction it was taking. West.

She was walking out of the entrance when she heard a shutter being pushed up. Swinging round, she saw the reception counter had just opened. A fair-haired and good-looking man in his thirties was arranging some papers. She rushed across the concourse as though she had just arrived.

'Is Mr Hauser's jet still on the ground? The INCUBUS Lear jet.'

'Just took off. You missed him by minutes.'

'Oh, Lord! I have a vital file he thinks he has with him outside in my car. I'm Peggy Vanderheld, his PA. I'll have to fly after him. He'll go crazy when he discovers he hasn't got it. And the hell of it is I got to the office late on Sveavägen so I don't know where he's off to now.'

'I shouldn't disclose flight plans, lady.' He was examining her with more than a little interest. 'Will you be coming back to Stockholm? Maybe we could have a drink together one night?'

'Well . . .' She gave him a winning smile. 'I'm just arrived from England. I don't have many friends. So maybe yes. But first I have to catch up with Hauser.'

'I never said anything to you.' He leaned over the counter, his face close to hers. 'Gothenburg.'

42

It was midnight north of the Arctic Circle in Lapland and broad daylight. The sun would remain above the horizon for twenty-four hours a day between June 16 and July 18. Tweed found the incredibly clear and ghost-like illumination weird.

The three beach buggies with their huge tyres were moving at speed through the wilderness. The manager of the firm Tweed had phoned in Rovaniemi had said he might be able to supply machines with souped-up engines. He had succeeded: the three cumbersome-looking buggies rocked from side to side as they plunged down an arid slope.

Newman and Marler were in the first machine with Newman behind the wheel, driving full out. In the second buggy, following him, Tweed sat beside Butler who was driving at the same teeth-shattering speeed. Behind them followed Nield, driving with Dillon seated alongside.

'This is like Macbeth's blasted heath,' Tweed shouted to make himself heard above the roar of the engine.

'It is blasted rough country,' Butler retorted. 'I hope Newman is heading in the right direction.'

'The man who hired out these things supplied a compass as I requested. Marler has a map.'

'I wonder if he can read a map?' Butler queried sarcastically.

Butler didn't too much like Marler. Tweed stared round as the file of machines raced on, holding on tight. The light was like high-powered moonlight and the country like a moonscape. The ground was covered with rocks protruding from its surface, rocks coated with lichens. A few stubby trees were little more than undergrowth growing in small miserable clumps. A wilderness. No landmarks. Low bare hills rose ahead.

'Why didn't we use the Fokker to fly us to the airfield at the Institute?' Butler called out. 'We'd have made much better time.'

'Because I couldn't persuade the pilot to fly on without referring back to Helsinki air control. That might have been dangerous. And in any case he had total interference with atmospherics on his radio.'

He stopped talking as the buggy began to climb the slope of one of the low hills. More rocks. More stunted trees. The ground covered with shrivelled moss. Tweed thought the world might look something like this after an atomic blast. Ahead of them Newman had stopped just below the summit, was standing up to peer over the top. Butler drew up alongside him, followed by Nield's buggy. Tweed stepped down on to spongy ground thankfully as the engines were switched off. He stretched his cramped legs, his aching arms, mopped his sweating forehead.

'And to think, we're only four hundred kilometres south of the Arctic Ocean.'

'I haven't done too badly,' Newman commented, binoculars pressed to his eyes.

'Let me have a shufti,' said Marler and took over the binoculars.

'What can you see?' Tweed asked as Dillon stood beside him.

'The Institute – a long way behind us. I bypassed it deliberately. We were way behind schedule. Take a look yourself when Marler has torn himself away from my binoculars. And the target is in sight . . .'

Tweed ignored the offer of binoculars. He had exceptional eyesight. With Dillon, Butler and Nield he walked the few paces to the summit, looked down over a vast landscape. The white buildings of the Institute complex were standing at a far lower level to the west, reminding him of their toy-like aspect Newman had described returning from his earlier visit.

What excited him was the convoy of ten trucks wending its way along a track to the east. He took the binoculars Marler handed him, stared through the lenses. Inscribed in Cyrillic along the sides of each truck were the words *State Transport*. They had located the INCUBUS convoy on its way to the Soviet Union. Tweed was appalled as he considered the amount of explosives, the havoc it could cause. Hauser was planning on creating a state of total turmoil and destruction so later he could walk in as a saviour. On his own terms.

'See that prominent hill,' Marler said, checking his map. 'It is 656 metres high – and inside Russia.'

'We are so close?'

Tweed was startled. He could see no sign of fortifications, no indication of where the frontier ran. Except for that prominent hill. Gazing at the luminous light he knew he shouldn't be here, so near to the border. And neither should Dillon. Howard would have a fit if he had known. But Tweed was enjoying the experience. Back in the field after many years. It took him back to the old days when he was a field agent. Then he frowned. The convoy had halted. Why? Had something disturbed them?

He swept the general area of the border again. Nothing

427

which betrayed the presence somewhere of Soviet paras from even this height. His binoculars picked out an unmanned watchtower. He could see inside the cabin perched at the top of the stilt-like support legs. Empty.

'Something is going wrong,' Newman said grimly. 'That convoy is still on Finnish soil, looks as though it may not be going any further.'

'Maybe we ought to encourage it,' Dillon suggested, producing his Luger. 'To keep moving.'

'So long as someone is waiting for it,' Tweed replied.

Troubled, he wondered if Angel had succeeded in his task. Maybe the frontier *was* wide open for the trucks to move into Russia and disappear to their various destinations. Marler had no such doubts.

'Time we got after that convoy, prodded it into moving. A few bullets flying round their cabs should encourage the drivers no end. Tweed, may I suggest you drive your buggy? Butler has the Mauser. Nield can stay behind his wheel – Dillon has his Luger.'

'And what about us?' Newman snapped. 'I have a Smith & Wesson. In case you've forgotten.'

'Never forget anything, chum,' Marler replied. 'But I have the Armalite. You stay with the wheel.'

'Let's get moving,' Tweed ordered. 'The first two buggies drive along the right side of the convoy when we catch it up. Nield drives along the left side – trap them in a crossfire, make them panic . . .'

Tweed settled himself behind the wheel as Butler jumped into the passenger seat. Newman was already rocking and slithering down the steep eastern slope at speed as Tweed started his engine, followed. It was the worst ground they had crossed. The slope was littered with boulders. Tweed avoided many of them, weaving in and out, but there were some he couldn't avoid. Only the enormous tyres of the buggies could have negotiated such territory. Frequently he had to wipe a damp hand on his white coat. His body was streaming with moisture – the effort of driving the buggy, the Arctic heat, above all the fact that the white coats were of the type worn by house surgeons. Too heavy.

The convoy was still stationary. They were approaching it from the rear as they reached the lower part of the back-breaking slope. With luck, Tweed thought, they won't see us until we're on top of them. The element of surprise was even more likely to cause panic.

'Aim to miss, for God's sake,' Tweed warned. 'We want the drivers alive to get those vehicles moving east.'

Butler had hauled out his Mauser, holding it in one hand to check it while he used the other hand to grip a bar. There was every chance that otherwise he would have been hurtled from the buggy which was swaying and bucking like a ship in a storm.

'Got the message,' Butler shouted back.

Newman's buggy was slowing down. Tweed realized he was doing this to mute the roar of his engine as they came closer to the tail of the convoy. Tweed reduced speed.

Still perched above the vast spread of landscape although now much lower on the long slope, Tweed was surprised at how close they had come to the prominent 656 m high hill. Inside Russia. He realized the lead vehicle in the convoy had stopped just short of the frontier.

He also had a good view of the track which continued on over the border with no apparent barrier, an equally good view of the terrain inside Russia. Very small scrub covered hills, deep rocky gulches and narrow crevasses just beyond either side of the track. Still not a sign of any human being, of Rebet's paras. Again he wondered had Angel tricked his own people, even tricked Rebet?

'I'm going to let rip in a minute,' Butler said.

'Not until we're alongside the lead vehicle. And miss the petrol tank, we want the trucks kept moving,' Tweed warned.

'I do know my job,' Butler protested mildly. 'That is exactly what I planned to do.'

In the third buggy Dillon, like Tweed, was frightened and exhilarated at the prospect of some active service once more. Better than sitting behind a desk in Langley, Virginia, sending out one poor schmuck after another into the firing line.

In his wing mirror Tweed saw Nield peeling off over to the left to take the convoy from the far side. Tweed checked his watch. He was thinking of the Sikorsky he had arranged to fly into the area to take them out. It was going to be a damn' near-run thing. Marler could be up to his neck in action when he should be signalling the pilot with his Verey pistol.

Newman opened up his engine, raced forward at all-out speed, racing past the first nine trucks of the convoy. Tweed saw Marler, holding the Armalite, bracing himself for his first shot. He raced his own buggy forward as Butler held on to the bar with one hand, rested the arm holding the Mauser across the bar, the muzzle jumping up and down. How the hell could he hope to aim a shot in the correct direction?

Newman rammed on his brake as he drew alongside the cab of the first vehicle, turned the wheel. The buggy skidded in a half circle, stopped. Marler was now facing the two men inside the driver's cab. He aimed his rifle, the two men ducked, he fired, high and at an angle. The windscreen shattered, spilt glass over the bonnet. Newman drove slowly back along the convoy, swerved to avoid Tweed's buggy while Marler continued firing the Armalite over the roofs of the trucks.

Nield arrived on the far side of the lead vehicle as the driver started his engine. Dillon loosed off one shot from his Luger, aiming above the two men's heads through the cab which had both side windows down to counter the heat. Nield drove on, turned on to the track to spin round. His engine stalled. The lead truck picked up speed, rumbled towards Nield to slam into the buggy. Nield tried twice to start the engine, got it going at his third try, drove off the track seconds before the truck crushed him. Dillon loosed off another shot.

From Tweed's buggy Butler was firing his Mauser as the other truck engines started up, aiming across the bonnets as the whole convoy began lumbering forward. Tweed suddenly observed Newman's buggy driving straight for the frontier, the foot of the 656 m high hill.

'What the devil is the crazy fool doing?' he burst out.

'Someone on that hill,' Butler said laconically. 'And no one is shooting back at us from the convoy. Didn't expect that . . .'

'None of those men aboard the trucks will have arms – they're probably dissident ex-KGB men who slipped out of Russia soon after the new president took over. Now they're going back as trained saboteurs. So no arms – in case they're stopped later and searched. What man on the hill?'

'Pull even further away from the convoy and you'll see him. A little way up, standing in front of a huge rock and waving a white flag. I saw him for a few seconds when you were turning . . .'

Tweed drove the buggy away from the track. Stopping it, leaving the engine running, he stood up to get a clear view. The last truck of the convoy was crossing into Russia. A hundred feet or so up the side of the hill stood a man waving a white flag. He lowered the flag and at last Tweed understood why the convoy had waited.

It had been waiting for the all clear signal, the waving of the flag. Marler was running forward to the base of the hill, reached it, began climbing, carrying his Armalite in his left hand. Butler saw Tweed lean forward, stare fixedly.

'Oh, my God!'

'What is it?' Butler asked.

Out of one of the rocky gulches close to the last truck a group of men were springing to life. Men in army camouflage. The Soviet paras. The large man on the hill stooped, straightened swiftly, holding a machine pistol. He aimed it at the paras directly below him. It would be a massacre.

The man was large, looked huge even at a distance, a man with a mane of thick black hair, a black beard. Viktor Kazbek, the Georgian, the Minister of Communications. He raised the barrel of the machine pistol, hugged the stock into his massive shoulder.

A single shot rang out, echoing in the sudden silence of Lapland as the engines of the trucks died. The engines of the beach buggies had been turned off. Kazbek swayed, a second before he could press the trigger, sending a lethal fusillade down on the unsuspecting paras below. Kazbek stiffened, seemed about to step back from the edge, then his huge flamboyant figure toppled, fell down the sheer face of the hill, crumpled over a jagged rock on the ground. Marler removed the Armalite from his shoulder, scrambled back down the hill, walked with a jaunty step back to the beach buggy where Newman waited.

Butler looked behind the buggy into Finland. He stared for a moment, gripped Tweed by the arm. Tweed looked in the same direction. In the distance a vehicle very like a Land Rover was stationary on the track. Two men. One standing up, holding something to his eyes. The strange light flashed off something. Binoculars.

As he watched, Newman drove his buggy back with Marler by his side, stopped next to Tweed's machine. He pointed to the Land-Rover. Tweed nodded, seemed indifferent.

432

'They could be some of Hauser's men, watching how the operation went,' Newman asserted.

'They undoubtedly are.'

As he spoke the standing man sat down. The vehicle performed a U-turn, built up speed, racing back westward towards the Institute. A dust cloud floated up from the sun-scorched track, hiding the Land-Rover.

'Shouldn't we get after that?' Newman pressed.

'No.'

'But they will report to Hauser the operation had failed.'

'Which is exactly what I was planning on,' Tweed replied enigmatically. He turned to face east. 'I think I see a familiar figure. All of you wait here.' He looked at Marler. 'I congratulate you on your marksmanship. You brought down your target just in time.' He jumped out of the buggy.

'I'd better come with you,' said Newman.

'No, this is a rendezvous I must keep alone . . .'

General Valentin Rebet was wearing full military uniform as he beckoned Tweed forward, staying on his own side of the border. He must be sweating like a bull, thought Tweed. Rebet held out a hand.

'So it was Kazbek. How did you know in Leningrad?'

'Quite simple. So obvious you missed it. Hauser talked at the reception before the banquet with Dikoyan, with Marshal Zaikov, with Kazbek. But when he was with the first two he was in a middle of the room, surrounded with people. For his chat with Kazbek they moved into a corner. That huge Georgian hugged him. Undoubtedly Hauser slipped something to his Angel. Money? Details of the operation inside Russia? We'll probably never know. I thought it significant Kazbek was Minister of Communications.'

'Why, if I may ask?'

'You may. The most effective way of throwing the

433

Soviet Union into chaos is to disrupt communications. The telephone system. Radio stations. Above all, the railways which are so important to you. Hence the first explosion on the Trans-Siberian Railway.'

'I am grateful to you, Tweed. We are checking the trucks. So far every container opened has been full of explosives. That convoy must hold enough to blow up half Russia.'

'And don't forget, some must already have been smuggled in. You will have trouble for a while. Has Hauser concluded any trade deals with Moscow?'

'Yes. At the conference held secretly in Turku. He is opening banks, supermarket chains.'

'Close them down. Have nothing to do with him. I must go now.'

Tweed had heard the chug-chug of an approaching chopper. Over his shoulder he saw Marler firing his Verey pistol, saw the orange flare explode. The S61 was descending rapidly, close to where the beach buggies were formed up in a laager formation.

'Please give my warmest thanks to your marksman,' Rebet said quickly. 'He saved a whole unit of paras. Kazbek would have massacred them. Of course, we had back-up units further behind the frontier. And welcome to the Soviet Union. You have one foot on our territory!'

Tweed withdrew his right foot, shook hands, ran back to where the Sikorsky had landed, its rotors slowing, then stopped. Tweed noticed there were two pilots for the large machine. Marler came forward.

'You might like to know I trained my binoculars on that Land-Rover. The man standing up was Frank Galvone.'

'Who probably directed the whole operation. Who will report back to Hauser it was a fiasco. Everything now is working out as I hoped.'

'What does that mean?' Newman demanded.

'The kidnapping was significant. To be precise the easy

way they released Paula. That told me something big was afoot. My strategy has been to drive Hauser out of Finland. No more questions. Board the machine . . .'

The spacious cabin which could take eighteen passengers gave them plenty of room. Marler sat next to Tweed who was gazing out of the window as the Sikorsky lifted off, turned away from the border. He borrowed the binoculars from Marler. It was a relief to be aboard the chopper, away from the drumming beat, the vibrations of the beach buggy.

'What are you looking at?' Marler asked.

'We left just in time. Several beach buggies full of men are approaching those we left behind. I can see Mauno Sarin in the lead vehicle. I have saved him a great deal of trouble.'

'How do you mean?'

'Finland naturally treasures its neutrality. If a huge quantity of explosives – so easily smuggled in ashore from Finland's long coast – had been discovered, it would have compromised their relations with Russia. And there is enough turmoil across the Baltic without Finland being dragged into the inferno.'

'What next? Newman is sitting all by himself. Why?'

'He's thinking about who murdered Sandy. I'm thinking about destroying Hauser. Maybe the two objectives are linked.'

PART THREE

Whirlpool of Terror

'I've just heard, Adam, that cretin Steve did a screw-up with Evelyn Lennox.' Hauser clenched a beefy fist, punched the air in the huge living room as though felling Steve. 'The Norwich HQ tells me he attacked her in her cottage at Walberswick, bruised her, and she got the better of him. Now he's had to go under cover – the police are after him.'

'Unfortunate,' Carver commented.

They were sitting in the L-shaped living room of Hauser's house perched on a small clifftop at Skalhamn - Shell Bay – in the western archipelago of Sweden. Landing in the Lear jet at Gothenburg, the waiting limo had taken them north, followed by a truck transporting the secret filing cabinets.

The weather had changed drastically. The big picture window at the end of the room looked out over the Skagerrak and the North Sea beyond. A storm was raging. An army of thirty-foot waves was rolling in, crashing against the rocks below the house, splashing the picture window with brown spume.

'Dramatic, isn't it, Adam?'

Hauser walked over, glass of bourbon in his hand, to get a closer look at the turbulent sea. Offshore, the anchored *Washington IV*, an enormous white cabin cruiser, pitched and tossed as the giant waves swept under it. The window was also L-shaped, continued along the southern wall. Hauser looked down but the projecting clifftop masked his view of tiny Skalhamn where a powerboat was moored safe from the storm.

'Evelyn Lennox,' Hauser continued. 'I think you ought to go see her again, persuade her to sign the pension agreement, solve the problem. She's a hole in our defences.'

'I thought we were sailing to Harwich. We won't make it until the storm abates. You want me to fly over from Gothenburg?'

'The met. forecast says the storm may move on. We'll wait it out a day or two . . . Who the hell can that be on the phone?'

Hauser stood to take the call. Adam straightened out a crease in his trousers, shot his cuffs to display the gold cuff-links, then watched the American. Hauser's eyes behind the pince-nez were bleak, his mouth a tight line. His reactions were monosyllabic.

'Yes, Frank . . .'

'No . . .'

'No . . .'

'OK,' he concluded. 'Get your ass over here to Skalhamn. For Chrissakes, it's my house north of Gothenburg. Catch the first flight. Bed down at an airport if you have to. Get over here yesterday . . .'

He slammed down the phone, drank more bourbon, refilled his glass. Carver kept quiet as his chief paced up and down the long living room, expression grim, big feet hammering into the pile carpet. He sank into a chair.

'Operation Urals is a bust.'

'What operation is that?'

'None of your goddamn business. Frank says Tweed is responsible. How the hell he got into the act I'll never know. But I do know we're going to have to do something to discourage that guy.'

'And how do we go about that?'

'*We* don't get involved. That's Frank's territory. We'll sail for Harwich soon as Frank gets his carcass into this house.'

'The storm may still be raging. Look out of the window.'

'I've looked. The storm will have stopped by then.'

Hauser spoke as though he could command the waves. He tilted his jaw, his mind racing. He'd decided by the time he'd put down his glass.

'We'll definitely sail for Harwich. Then to Livingstone Manor by car. That old English country house is my most modern and advanced communications centre in the world. Tweed will never guess I've moved back on to his own doorstep.' He waved his cigarette holder. 'Equally important, all communications can be sent via the cipher machines. There isn't a code-breaker on the planet who can penetrate the system.'

'You seem to have Tweed on the brain,' Carver ventured.

'Hell, no! Tweed is just one more opponent to be outwitted, outmanoeuvred.'

Hauser perched his large buttocks on the arm of a chair and smiled. It was an effort. Carver had hit a sensitive nerve. Hauser was undergoing an experience he had never known before. Tweed was becoming an obsession with him. Only to himself would he admit it was Tweed who had driven him out of Finland, had made him flee like a fugitive to the west. Well, Livingstone Manor was one place Tweed would never dream of locating him. Come to that, the bastard would never find Skalhamn.

'They won't be moving any more of those filing cabinets out to the *Washington IV*,' Paula said to Linda. 'Not while this weather keeps up . . .'

The two girls were crouched together in the cleft of a rock above Shell Bay. Both wore yellow oilskins with hoods pulled well down over their heads. So far they had served as reasonable protection against the lashing rain. The rock face, looking inland, afforded further shelter against the fury of the storm.

Paula had travelled a long way and fast since seeing the

441

Lear jet take off from Bromma. Driving back to Arlanda, she had handed in the Volvo, bought a ticket to Gothenburg, caught a flight to Sweden's second city and west coast port. She could hardly believe her luck when as the SAS plane came in to land she saw the Lear jet parked at the fringe of the airport.

Arriving in Gothenburg, she had booked a room at the Sheraton, a very modern hotel with a vast interior and rooms on several floors looking down on the restaurant at ground level. She had been lucky again when she phoned one of Tweed's network of informants and researchers spread over Europe.

Linda Sandberg had left her apartment nearby and reached the hotel as Paula finished unpacking. Paula had taken to Linda, a tall slim girl in her late twenties with a waterfall of golden hair framing her excellent bone structure. They had talked for half an hour.

'. . . so I do know about this Franklin D. Hauser,' Linda had said later. 'Not many people know he has a super house at Skalhamn. That's a tiny place even a lot of Swedes don't know exists, but I drive round the coast of the archipelago when I get time off from my job with the advertising agency. Skalhamn is way up north, well on the way to Norway . . .'

Linda's car had been in a garage awaiting maintenance but she knew a car hire outfit close to the hotel. She had warned Paula a storm was predicted so while Paula hired a red Mercedes Linda had gone to a shop, purchased sweaters and oilskins.

It was early evening when Linda drove along a winding road through wild country where brown stone cliffs rose in the distance with dense black fir forests scattered at frequent intervals. They had turned off at a lonely signpost with the legend *Skalhamn* along a narrow road when Paula saw the INCUBUS AB truck ahead.

'Slow down,' she warned. 'This could be dangerous.

442

Are we far from this Shell Bay?'

'Pretty close,' said Linda as she slowed the car.

'If you can, park the car out of sight when we're within walking distance . . .'

Linda had parked the Merc inside a forest and they had walked the last half mile when the Swedish girl pointed to the upper half of a house showing at the top of a small cliff. As she pointed, a black limousine appeared near the cliff edge, vanished.

'That's Hauser's house,' Linda said. 'And it looks as if he might be inside. I once saw him arrive at Gothenburg airport and a car like that picked him up from his jet. The chauffeur has just moved it into the garage. I think the storm is about to break . . .'

They were walking along a very narrow winding road hemmed in by rocks. Linda grasped Paula's arm, put her other hand to her mouth for silence. They crept forward, peered round a rocky bluff and Paula had her first view of Shell Bay.

The anchorage was tiny, scooped out of the brown rock rising up on both sides. Shaped like a sea shell it had a neck-like entrance, a minute stone jetty with a power boat moored below an iron ladder attached to the jetty wall. The INCUBUS truck had backed close to the ladder and men in overalls were lowering a steel filing cabinet held by ropes into the power boat. Paula thought she saw a green label attached to the cabinet. A second cabinet was lowered and this time Paula was certain it had a green label. Two men shinned down the ladder as the ropes were released. The engine of the power boat purred into action, the craft was steered slowly through the entrance.

Linda pulled at Paula's arm, guided her up a narrow defile out of sight of the anchorage. Suddenly they were looking out at the open sea where a big white cabin cruiser rode at anchor. The power boat picked up speed, left a white wake behind its stern, headed for a platform and staircase slung over the hull of the cruiser. They watched as the cabinets were transferred aboard.

'Time to put on our oilskins,' said Linda. 'I felt spots of rain. It's starting.'

Over the sea the sky was black as ink. The full fury of the storm broke suddenly. Lightning flashed. Thunder pealed like the drums of some celestial orchestra. The clouds opened and Niagara flooded down. The power boat, returning to the anchorage, had trouble manoeuvring back behind the shelter of the jetty. It just made it as the wall-like waves started sweeping in. Paula lowered the binoculars she carried in her shoulder bag, shoved them inside, closed the flap. Through the lenses she had made out the name of the ship. *Washington IV*. That was when she made her remark:

'They won't be moving any more of those filing cabinets out to the *Washington IV* . . .'

'Better get back to the car,' said Linda.

They ran all the way, saved from being drenched to the skin by the oilskins. When they had stripped them off and Linda was settled behind the wheel, she turned on the ignition. Nothing happened. She tried six times to start the car and each time the engine died on her.

'Great. Maybe the engine's overheated. We drove here at quite a lick.'

'I'm sorry,' Paula told her, 'it could be dangerous staying here.'

'You said that before we started out. It's more fun than writing advertising copy. Let's eat those sandwiches you got the hotel to make up. We could be stuck here.'

In the living room Hauser had the radio turned on low, waiting for the next met. forecast. Adam, who insisted on regular meals, hating the American habit of gobbling down fast food snacks, was eating the dinner prepared by the housekeeper. He wondered who the second place was laid for. A slim girl with bleached blonde hair walked into the room and Hauser introduced her as Iris Reynolds. She wore a tight blouse which hugged her figure and a mini-skirt exposing shapely legs. Adam stared at her in open admiration, grinned at her as she pulled back her chair at the table.

'Take that look off your face or I'll kick you in the crotch,' she said pleasantly.

Adam nearly choked on his food. Attractive women didn't talk to him like that. He glared at her across the table and their eyes locked. Iris held his stare, no longer smiling as the housekeeper laid her meal in front of her. Adam was disturbed: the eyes seemed to stare right through him, like a hangman measuring him for the drop.

Hauser was amused. 'Iris is coming with us to our new headquarters.' He looked at the housekeeper. 'Bring me a hamburger wrapped in paper. I'll eat it with my hands. And plenty of fried onions.'

'Who,' asked Adam, to change the subject, to ignore Iris, 'if anyone, will be travelling with Frank? Or maybe I shouldn't ask?'

'Goddamn well shouldn't ask. Told you before – you ask too many questions. I can't figure out why.'

Hauser was continuing his usual tactic of letting executives know only as much as they needed to. Ion Manescu would be flying with Galvone. The two men would then fly on from Sweden to London Airport. Who would dream of looking for an ex-*Securitate* chief – or an ex–STASI leader – inside an old English country house? And Galvone would bring Helmut Ziegler with him.

Adam Carver seemed at once to read his mind. 'If Frank flies here we may be gone when he arrives.'

'We will be. So I leave a note for him with the housekeeper. "Contact Dr Livingstone immediately." That will give him the message.'

'A bit of a long way round for him to get there.'

'So he has some exercise. Do the schmuck some good . . .'

An hour later the storm subsided as suddenly as it had broken. Through the picture window the sight was spectacular. The huge waves became smaller, the late evening sky lightened, the surface of the sea became an oily calm. Hauser ordered the loading operation to be resumed.

'We sail tonight to Harwich, we keep moving . . .'

Inside the Merc, under the cover of the fir forest, Linda lowered a window. The storm had gone away, the air was very cool. Paula found it a strange experience after the heatwave to feel almost cold and shivery. She pulled over her head the sweater Linda had bought.

The silence of the forest was unnerving. The only sound was the steady drip of raindrops from the spreading branches which reminded her of the wings of some huge evil birds. Linda turned the ignition key. The engine burst into life first time.

'I'm going back to take a final look,' Paula said. 'Now, no protests! You stay with the car, keeping the engine ticking over. And one person is far less likely to be seen. I do know the way now . . .'

She walked along the road which was no more than damp: most of the downpour had drained off the cambered surface into the fields on either side. Unencumbered by the oilskin, she climbed agilely up the rock cleft to the point where it overlooked the sea. She whipped out her binoculars.

The power boat was moving out from Shell Bay, heading across calm water which resembled a vast endless lake. Besides the helmsman the craft carried three passengers. She easily recognized in the lenses the bulky figure of Hauser, the far slimmer Adam Carver. The third passenger was a woman. Something about her seemed familiar, then she got it. Her mind flashed back to the horrific episode when she had been exchanged for another hostage on the scrubbing platform. This was the woman she had been exchanged for. As they approached the landing stage slung over the side of the hull she switched her gaze to the ship.

At the masthead on top of the huge control cabin a flag was being lowered, the flag of convenient Panama. As soon as it had been hauled down a fresh flag was hoisted. The Red Ensign. Paula had seen enough.

She scrambled down the rock cleft, ran back along the deserted road to where Linda waited anxiously in the Merc. The Swedish girl waved as Paula approached her, opened the front passenger door.

'God! Am I glad to see you safe and sound.'

'That's nice of you,' Paula jumped into the car. 'I'm OK. Could you drive me straight back to the Sheraton? I have an urgent phone call to make.'

44

Tweed seemed tireless. Even Marler marvelled at his endless stamina as he sat with the others in Tweed's room at the Hesperia. Newman and Butler sagged in armchairs; Cord Dillon was asleep on a couch. Only Pete Nield also looked fresh as he gazed out of the window. In the late evening, tourists in shirt sleeves, the women clad in dresses creased by the heat, trudged wearily along the Mannerheimintie. With the windows open the atmosphere was still torrid. The metal mobile drooped stationary as Tweed listened on the phone, taking notes.

He was talking to Monica who said she had been trying to contact him for hours. He listened without interrupting, occasionally reassuring her.

'Yes, I'm still here. Go on . . .'

Monica was showing great ingenuity in passing information to him, wrapping it up in seemingly innocuous data about insurance. Eventually he thanked her, put down the phone, turned round.

'Bob, Chief Inspector Buchanan is on your tail again. He called on Monica and Howard, wanted to know where you were. Apparently he's cleared up another murder case and is now concentrating on the murder of Sandy.'

'About time he damned well did . . .'

'Wait, there's more. Evelyn Lennox, the girl you interviewed in Wandsworth – and later was being guarded by Butler in Walberswick – has been attacked.'

'And Buchanan suspects me? Why on earth . . .'

'Do wait till I've finished. Lennox was attacked in her cottage by a masked figure but she fought him off. She thinks it was a man called Steve . . .'

'That thug?' Newman made a gesture of disgust. 'Surely the Yard can track him down.'

'He's gone under cover. What we have to do concerns me – and it's a lot. I hope you haven't forgotten Peggy Vanderheld, maybe *the* key witness. Butler, your next job is to fly to Arlanda, hire a car, drive to the island of Örno, pick her up, take her back to Arlanda, fly with her at the earliest to London, take her to Park Crescent, leave her with the guard in the hall, pick up a gun, drive her to Walberswick to Evelyn Lennox's cottage. You know where it is. Guard both women. They may have interesting things to tell each other.'

'I'd better get my ticket for the first flight tomorrow now.'

Butler was on his way out when Tweed stopped him. He included all his team in the next order.

448

'Everyone, including you Butler, has to get rid of all the weapons. Dump them in the harbour, anywhere. But get rid of them.' He nodded to Butler. 'All right, you can go now. And I'll visit Walberswick myself to question Vanderheld. By then she will be thoroughly frightened.'

'Why?'

Butler paused near the door. Tweed's mind was moving like lightning. He had thought of something else.

'Because Evelyn Lennox will have told her of her own experiences with INCUBUS. She'll be more than ready to talk to me.' He looked across at Nield. 'On second thoughts I want you to go with Butler. Lennox and Vanderheld are the only two witnesses who may be able to bring down Hauser.'

'Let's hope Evelyn Lennox is still alive,' Newman said grimly. 'Is she under guard? Surely Buchanan has thought of that.'

'He's done his best. The local bobby on his bike is calling in on her.'

'Heaven help us,' Newman commented. 'We're dealing with pros. Let's hope you get there in time, Harry.'

'You have a point, Bob,' Tweed decided. 'So Butler, you fly to Arlanda, pick up Vanderheld. Nield, change of plan. You fly direct to London, go to see Monica. She will show you the location of Lennox's place in Walberswick, Rose Bower. Then drive straight there. Bob, can you give Pete a brief letter identifying him to Evelyn?'

Dillon sat up. 'I heard what you said about weapons. I'm wondering how to get rid of this Luger when I don't know Helsinki all that well.'

'I was about to suggest something,' Marler intervened. 'It's almost as difficult to get shot of a gun safely as it is of a corpse. If everyone hands me their hardware I can do the job.'

'How?' Tweed demanded.

'I still have hire of that power boat I used when Paula

449

was kidnapped. I'll put them in a hold-all – including my own dismantled Armalite – and weight it with a length of chain or something. I take the power boat well out to sea, drop the hold-all overboard.'

'The best idea,' Tweed agreed. 'Don't forget spare mags.'

Dillon handed over his Luger and ammo; Butler his Mauser; Newman the Smith & Wesson. He held on to it for a moment.

'Tweed, the people we're up against will be crawling with guns. Why leave us naked now?'

'I'll explain that later.'

'As Paula would say, be cryptic.'

Marler put the weapons in an empty drawer, left the room, was back in no time with a leather hold-all. He placed the guns inside, zipped it up, sat down, lit a cigarette.

'What's next on the agenda?'

Butler and Nield had left the room. Tweed checked his watch. It was later in the evening than he'd realized. They had landed at Helsinki Airport on their return from Lapland early that morning, had flopped into bed as soon as they reached the Hesperia and The Palace. They had slept until almost midday: Tweed had told the operator at the Hesperia not to put through any calls before struggling into his pyjamas. An almost unprecedented action.

He had let his team alone during the afternoon, summoning them to his room late in the evening. Now he had been fooled by the fact that it was still daylight. He opened his mouth to reply to Marler and the phone rang. He replied as he reached for it.

'We're flying to Stockholm. That's where you reported those INCUBUS filing cabinets were being flown to . . .'

The caller was Monica. Again he listened for several minutes. This time he took no notes. He thanked her, said he'd call her back, replaced the receiver, looked at his team.

'Fresh change of instruction. Cancel Stockholm. What I thought might happen has – Hauser, Adam Carver and the girl who tried to kill me have sailed from the west coast of Sweden. Undoubtedly heading for England. I'll check in a minute. Paula has done a magnificent job . . . .'

He gave them the gist of Monica's report. Paula had called her from the Sheraton in Gothenburg, had described what she had seen at Sveavägen in Stockholm, her trip to Bromma, and her experiences with Linda Sandberg at Skalhamn.

'. . . so,' Tweed concluded, 'we can now assume my plan worked better than I could ever have hoped.'

'What plan?' Newman demanded. 'Tell us this time, for God's sake.'

'We were always handicapped coming to grips with Hauser in Finland – because of its understandable desire for absolute neutrality. I aimed all along to frustrate any operation he was carrying out – to drive him west. Into Sweden I expected, but the plan worked even better. We have driven him back to England – where he is under British jurisdiction.'

'You wily bastard,' was Dillon's comment.

'But are you sure?' Newman pressed.

'With luck I shall be during the next hour. The Harbour Master at Harwich, a Jonas Heathcoate, is a friend of mine.'

'Where does that get us?' protested Newman.

'Paula has reported seeing Hauser, Adam Carver and a girl I suspect who tried to murder me here boarding Hauser's millionaire's cabin cruiser. I mentioned that before – but not that Paula had seen it with her own eyes. It is a question of geography. The port closest to Livingstone Manor where such a ship – the *Washington IV* – could dock is Harwich.'

'He could have sailed off anywhere,' Newman persisted.

'Except that earlier Monica phoned, told me her researches had revealed Livingstone Manor is equipped with some of the most modern communications equipment in the world. Including cipher machines. Hauser is getting wary – he needs a foolproof method of communication we cannot penetrate.'

'You never told us about this earlier call from Monica.' Newman snapped. 'All this data about Livingstone Manor.'

'I don't believe I did.' Tweed smiled drily. 'But when I first knew all this Hauser was in Finland.'

'So,' repeated Marler, 'what's next on the agenda? As if I didn't know,' he added.

'I'll tell you after I've phoned Jonas Heathcoate. Just contain your impatience.'

He took out a small notebook with an index, turned to the letter 'H', dialled a number, waited. There was an atmosphere of growing tension in the room. Newman as well as Marler had guessed what he was checking. Tweed had to speak to several people before he reached Heathcoate. He identified himself, reminding the Harbour Master of the last time they had met. Newman leaned forward, his hands clasped tightly together. Livingstone Manor . . .

'. . . yes, Jonas, that's the vessel,' Tweed continued. 'The *Washington IV*. A big white cabin cruiser. It belongs to the banker, Franklin D. Hauser. What was that? Could you repeat it? The line isn't good. The *Washington IV* docked at Harwich early this morning? And Hauser was met with a black limousine? That's a dangerous habit of his – he's setting himself up as a target. Bullet proof, you said? It had better be from his point of view. Thanks, Jonas. I owe you one.'

Tweed put down the phone, wiped his clammy hand, looked at the others.

'You heard all that, I imagine? He must have arrived at Livingstone Manor hours ago.'

Marler whistled in admiration. 'How do you do it? You wouldn't have an informant planted inside INCUBUS?'

'I have taken a lot of trouble to think myself into the mind of my opponent. To foresee his every move. I sense he's doing the same thing with me. So why should I need an informant?'

'And next on the agenda?' Marler repeated for the third time.

'Obvious, isn't it? We all fly back to London tomorrow, plan the next stage of our campaign against Hauser. He has walked into my cage.'

The following morning at Livingstone Manor Hauser was leaving the cipher room when he found Adam Carver in the corridor. He pushed his pince-nez further up his strong nose and his mouth was pouched unpleasantly.

'What the hell are you doing poking around down here?'

'I came to find you.' Carver, immaculate in a lightweight pale grey silk suit, was poised and confident. 'I have the balance sheet figures of Egon – or rather, now Dieter – Schmidt's bank we bought in Frankfurt. You said you wanted to see these figures.'

'Later.' Hauser slammed shut the security door leading to the cipher room. 'How did you get down here? There's a security door at the top of the steps. You don't have a key.'

'Someone must have left it open. I'll be ready to show you these figures when you are.'

Hauser waited until Carver had strolled off up the cellar steps out of sight. Dressed in short sleeves and slacks, he took out a bunch of keys, opened the door to the suite next to the cipher room, walked inside, closed the door.

The suite was luxuriously furnished, had a living room, a bedroom, a bathroom. It was also air conditioned. On a couch was sprawled Ion Manescu. It was doubtful whether his old *Securitate* associates in Bucharest would have recognized their ex-chief.

Manescu had had his hair trimmed very short before he had flown from Helsinki with Galvone. He had a pair of large horn-rim glasses perched on his beaky nose which gave him a professorial look. He was smoking a cheroot as he swung his legs to the floor, clasped his strong bony fingers, waited.

'Frank says you left him at London Airport, that you hired a car. You arrived here half a day after Frank. So what the hell did you think you were doing? Where did you go?'

'I drove up into Suffolk, didn't I? Before I came here I cruised, stopped at a few English pubs, listened to the locals, picked up a little more English accent.'

'English pubs where?' demanded Hauser.

'Lavenham, Southwold . . .'

'You went into that area? Are you crazy? I told you to avoid that part of the world. Why did you do it?'

'I've just told you.' Manescu had no intention of being intimidated by the American who stood over him. 'And no one took any notice of me. I can pass. Isn't that what you wanted?'

'You took a helluva a chance going into that area. Don't do it again unless I tell you to.'

His manner changed, became affable. It was these switches in mood the Romanian found it difficult to adapt to. And Hauser had the habit of assuming his genial personality when issuing important – even dangerous – instructions. When he had finished talking Hauser turned to leave the room, spoke once more as he unlocked the door.

'OK what I told you? And don't discuss the problem with Carver or Galvone.'

'OK,' agreed Manescu.

Time to light a fire under Galvone. Hauser locked the door leading to the cellar complex. Clenching his fists, he walked into the big living room with the arched window at the front. Galvone was standing, gazing out of the window. The sun was burning Suffolk as the heatwave went on. The storm at Skalhamn had been a freak, Hauser was thinking. He looked at the glass in Galvone's hands.

'Bit early to start getting smashed. You're going to need a clear mind, for God's sake.'

He had been looking for something to set the tone. Walking to the cocktail cabinet, he poured a large glass of mineral water to ram the point home.

'You screwed up with Manescu at London Airport. Christ, Frank, can't you even escort sensitive material?'

'I was amazed at how different he looked. He was keen to merge into the Brit background. That's what we want, isn't it?'

'I'll tell you what I want, Frank,' Hauser roared. 'I want people who aren't laid back about their jobs. When I give an order, you carry it out. I want men who wake up in the morning ready to bite the ass off a bear. Talking about bears, you really screwed up in Lapland. Did those explosives get through or didn't they?'

Galvone paused, feeling he was walking on a quicksand. He had felt compelled to report to Hauser what he had seen from the Land-Rover. You didn't lie to Hauser – if you wanted to survive. But under pressure you could shade the truth.

'Most of the trucks had crossed the border before I saw signs of the intervention . . .'

'Intervention! Soviet paras you said earlier. Don't play

455

word games with me. They were waiting for that convoy. Who tipped them off? My best bet is that bastard, Tweed. It's lucky we smuggled a big consignment through earlier.'

'You've seen the newspapers?' Galvone asked, hoping to divert his chief. He pointed to the *Daily Mail* on a table with its shrieking headline. 'That really is sensational.'

Hauser nodded. He looked down at the paper, his arms folded across his chest. That did give him some satisfaction.

KGB HQ IN KIEV BLOWN UP. UNREST GROWING.

'What is the plan?' Galvone enquired.

'You've read the story, I guess. The blue and red flags of an independent Ukraine are flying everywhere. No sign of the Soviet flag. The UTS – the Free Ukraine movement based in Munich – is active. What is the master plan, you meant?'

'That's what I meant.'

'I have a vision. One day not long from now, the dollar will be the world currency. The dollar will replace the rouble. Hell, any tourist to Moscow will tell you the locals pester them for dollars. They even have bars in Moscow where some of the ten thousand prostitutes look for customers – providing they can pay in dollars. Prostitution isn't illegal in Russia. It's their largest growth industry. They even have police girls dressed in civilian clothes, often sitting on a stool next to a call girl in these bars in the top hotels.'

'But you said it was legal,' Galvone pointed out.

'Your hearing is improving. The police girls are simply there to make sure there's no trouble for foreign tourists while they take their pick. Dollars, Frank – the key to a home for human beings stretching from the Pacific coast of the States to the Urals.' Hauser puffed at his cigarette, waved the holder, changed the subject in the swift way Galvone found disconcerting.

'Talking of money, has that private bank, Street & Braithwaite, down in Southampton, decided to sell out to us?'

'I called the Norwich HQ. They said Leopold Street said no. Apparently there's an empty shop right next to the bank. Easy to break into.'

'Then maybe Mr Street needs a little encouragement. We have that load of Semtex in the basement here for cases like that.'

Galvone stood up. 'You want me to organize a sweetener for the guy?'

'Why the hell do you think I raised the subject? Wait a minute,' he called out as Galvone strode towards the door. 'Another bone I have to pick with you. How did you get here so quick? I told you to go to the house at Skalhamn.'

'Oh, that.' Galvone made a throwaway gesture with his large hands. 'Knowing how you jet around, change your plans, I called the house from Helsinki Airport. The housekeeper opened the envelope you'd left for me, read out the message. The reference to Dr Livingstone told me you'd moved on here. So we flew direct to London Airport – myself, Manescu and Ziegler. You've hidden Ziegler away somewhere here?'

Hauser flushed with fury. He bit hard on the holder to regain self-control. Seeing his expression, Galvone stood stock still. Hauser strode forward, a thick index finger pointing, jabbing.

'You could be on your way out. The hard way. I've told you before, you obey my orders. Don't start thinking, taking your own decisions. Ed Riverton did that and someone did me a favour. You delivered Ziegler. That's the end of it so far as you're concerned. Adam Carver knows how to do what he's told.'

'Adam knows his job,' Galvone agreed in a conciliatory tone.

'And Adam is doing a job at this moment.' Hauser smiled. 'But sometimes I wonder about Adam. Better collect that Semtex, drive down to Southampton.'

'I suppose it's OK to use a bomb? We are in Britain.'

'Jesus!' Hauser clapped a hand to his forehead. 'Do I have to do everything myself? Call in at London Airport on the way. Wait for an Irish to check in at the Aer Lingus counter, pinch his passport. You started out in Chicago as an expert pickpocket. Leave the passport in the shop. The Brits will think it's the IRA.'

Alone in the living room, Hauser smiled with satisfaction. The Evelyn Lennox problem would be solved soon now.

45

Panic!

Evelyn Lennox stared out of the mullioned window in the living room at Rose Bower. She could hardly believe her eyes. A red Jaguar had pulled up by the front entrance at the end of the garden.

'It's Adam Carver! You said he was in Finland . . .'

'He was,' Butler replied tersely. He looked at Pete Nield. 'Hustle Peggy upstairs. Stay with her in her bedroom . . .'

Nield was moving, taking Vanderheld by the arm, hurrying her into the hall, up the narrow staircase. Butler moved away from the window, walked quickly to an open door. He turned before he went into the next room.

'I'll leave the door open a crack. I'll be able to hear all that's going on. Don't let him know we're here – and not a word about Vanderheld. You've no idea where she is. Can you handle it?'

Evelyn nodded. 'Yes, I can . . .'

'Of course you can. Let him talk. If you're alarmed, say something about Southwold. I'll be in here in a flash . . .'

Evelyn took a deep breath. The door bell was ringing. She smoothed down her mini-skirt, glanced at herself in a wall mirror, fiddled with her hair, went to the door, opened it.

'Surprise!' Carver grinned. 'Hope it's not the wrong moment to call. I tried to phone but you're not in the book.'

'Ex-directory.'

Evelyn swallowed. She thought Adam had never looked more handsome. His face and hands were tanned brown. He wore a smart beige silk suit, a blue striped shirt, plain blue tie, matching display handkerchief, hand made brogues. The tan emphasized the perfect bone structure of his face. He held a small posy of flowers.

'These are for you. Although I expect you've more than enough flowers.' He glanced back at the hedges of wild roses bordering the path. 'I just wanted to bring you a little something.'

'They're lovely. Thank you so much. Come into the living room. That chair is comfortable.'

She carefully didn't look at the door leading to the small study cum library where Butler was hiding. She knew he was armed with a Smith & Wesson. He had showed her the weapon to reassure her when he arrived. And upstairs Nield was carrying a Browning .32. The weapon he favoured most, like Paula.

The posy was a problem. Normally she would have taken it into the kitchen, filled a vase with fresh water, but she dare not leave Adam alone in the living room with

Butler so close. Picking up a vase off the table, she took out the flowers it held, dumped them on the hearth, arranged the posy in the same vase.

'I'll put fresh water in later. What would you like to drink?' she hurried on. 'Orange, lemon, lime juice? Or something stronger?'

'Lime juice will do very nicely. I've got a thirst like the Sahara. Are you all on your own here?'

'Yes, but I enjoy the peace and quiet. There was one rather nerve-wracking incident . . .'

She handed him his drink, sat down, crossed her legs and told him about the masked attacker without mentioning the resemblance to Steve. He had trouble tearing his eyes away from her legs and then listened with a grave expression, holding her eyes with his own.

'That's quite dreadful,' he said when she had finished. 'Surely you reported it to the police, asked them for some protection?'

'Yes, I did. But all they could spare was the local bobby who cycles here occasionally and calls in to see I'm all right. I probably disturbed a burglar and he lost his head. Not to worry.' She smiled. 'Ancient history. How is the banking business?'

'Oh, we're still taking over everyone in sight – that is, everyone who wants to meet our price. It's becoming a mania with Hauser. Buy, buy, buy.'

'You don't like the Americans?' she asked quietly.

He hesitated. 'Well I do find them rather brash. They seem to think they do everything better than anyone else can. Which isn't the case.'

'If you don't like them, why do you go on working for them?'

He gave her the disarming smile which always made her feel weak and yielding. 'Frankly, for the money.' He moved his fingers as though counting banknotes. 'Where else am I going to get a job which pays that sort of money?'

'Money isn't everything.'

'Wasn't it Rockefeller who said that?' He smiled again. 'Look, I really came here to ask you out to dinner one night. Maybe at The Swan over at Lavenham. It's not so far – that Jag eats up the miles. I'd drive you home afterwards, of course. I'm trying to persuade you.'

'I know you are. When?'

'That's great. What about sometime next week? Thursday any good?'

'It might be. All right, I'll say yes. On one condition.'

'Name it.'

'If something crops up I may have to delay it. So I need some way of getting in touch with you. A number I can call. Where are you based now?'

He hesitated again, briefly, took a card from his wallet. Scribbling a number on the back he handed it to her.

'There was one other thing before I go. The Pension Fund. I've been asked by Equality and Fraternity whether you'd now sign the agreement . . .'

'Hence the briefcase.' Evelyn indicated the case he had perched against the side of his armchair. 'So now we come to the real reason for your visit.'

'No!' Adam was vehement. 'I was coming to see you for my own personal reasons, to ask you out to dinner. I had to tell Hauser where I was going – he keeps us all on a tight leash. He shoved the papers at me, told me to ask you while I was here. I don't give a tuppenny damn myself. Incidentally they've upped the amount payable each month.' He wiped his moist forehead. 'Wish I'd never brought the subject up now. And I don't like that insurance outfit any more.'

'Why?'

He leaned forward. 'Because I was always told it was an independent company. Recently I discovered by accident it's a subsidiary of INCUBUS. More of Hauser's business trickery.'

461

'You can leave the agreement with me. I'll have to consult my accountant.'

'That I can't do.' His tone was apologetic. 'If I don't return with the agreement I'll be scalped. Let's forget the whole idea. Dinner's still on?'

'Unless I call to say I can't make it.' She looked at the calling card for the first time. 'I see you are based at Livingstone Manor now. I thought that was one of Hauser's country homes.'

'He's fitted it out as a business headquarters. I suspect he likes playing the squire of the manor. Which is amusing considering he's a billionaire.' He checked his watch, stood up. 'I think I've taken up enough of your time. Hope to see you Thursday next week. I'll call for your about seven.'

'We'll see.' Evelyn smiled as she escorted him to the front door. 'Your Jag will be pretty hot by now.'

'You're right.' Carver pulled a pair of kid gloves from his pocket, slipped them on. 'The wheel especially will be burning hot for the first few miles. See you . . .'

She waited until the car had disappeared before closing the door. Butler was waiting for her in the living room. She poured him a cooling drink.

'What do you think?' she asked. 'Was the real reason for his visit that beastly pension?'

'Oddly enough, I don't think so. He had some other reason for calling on you.'

'Being as cynical as I can, I agree with you. Strange the way he showed hostility to Hauser – almost as though he was sending me a message.'

'I'm going to call Tweed immediately, report the incident.'

At Park Crescent Tweed took the call from Butler, listened, thanked him for calling, put the receiver down.

His room was so crowded extra chairs had been brought in.

Paula had just finished telling them in detail about her experiences in Sweden. Starting with her arrival at Arlanda, watching the filing cabinets being unloaded at INCUBUS' HQ on Sveavägen in Stockholm, her drive to Bromma, her later arrival with Linda Sandberg at Skalhamn and what she had seen there.

She had an attentive audience. Monica took notes. Newman and Marler sat listening. But the man who sat quite still, his grey eyes never leaving hers, who listened most closely, was Chief Inspector Roy Buchanan. Beside him Sergeant Warden took his own notes. Tweed was the first to speak when she had finished. He told them about Carver's visit.

'... but what was even more interesting was what Butler told me about Nield. Pete travelled up to Walberswick on a motor bike. Yesterday he was driving slowly round the beach area. He's worried someone could come in by sea. On his way back to Rose Bower he saw a Ford Cortina dawdling past the cottage. It then did a U-turn, drove back towards the A 12. Nield followed at a discreet distance on his Honda. Later the Ford was stopped by lights in open country and Nield drew alongside it, got a good look at the driver. He swears it was Ion Manescu.'

'The terrorist you told us about,' Buchanan commented.

'More a saboteur than a terrorist. Like all of us, Nield has studied those pictures Marler took of Manescu leaving INCUBUS in Helsinki. He didn't twig immediately, but the driver glanced at him before driving off and then Nield was sure. Says the Romanian has had his hair cut much shorter, was wearing large horn-rims.'

'Any idea where he drove on to?' Buchanan asked.

'That's interesting too. Nield followed him when the

Ford turned on to the A1120, through Yoxford. Then he turned back, afraid Manescu would spot his tail.'

'If I remember rightly,' Buchanan suggested, 'Livingstone Manor is located further along the A1120.'

'It is,' Tweed agreed. 'Which makes the direction Manescu was driving along it significant.'

'I'd like to get the position quite clear in everyone's mind,' said Buchanan. He stood up, began walking between the chairs, addressing no one in particular, rattling loose change in his pocket. 'At the moment I am investigating three murders, albeit one out of my jurisdiction – in Finland – but I'm convinced the same hand committed all of them.'

'Three?' Tweed queried. 'Which three?'

'First that of Ed Riverton in Helsinki, second that of Sandra Riverton in Suffolk, and third that of the man called Steve who accompanied the man called Papa Grimwood when they visited Evelyn Lennox in Wandsworth.'

'So you found the thug, Steve?' Newman asked.

'Yes, but a very dead Steve, unfortunately. We traced him through underworld informants to the East End of London. Specifically to an address in the Mile End Road. We were just too late. The body was secreted behind the locked door of a disused cellar.'

'And the link is he was employed by INCUBUS?' suggested Tweed.

'The link,' Buchanan continued as though no one had spoken, 'is the cause of his demise. He had been garrotted.'

He paused. There was dead silence in the turgid atmosphere of the office. Buchanan wore a grey business suit and seemed unaffected by the heat: the temperature had risen into the eighties. Buchanan leaned against a wall, folded his arms, continued.

'Every killer – assassin might be a better word in this case – inadvertently leaves behind his trademark. Here we have a killer who always goes for a particularly vulnerable part of the human body. The neck.'

'I think we get the drift,' Tweed said, anxious about what he might say next.

Buchanan went on remorselessly. 'The American in Helsinki, Ed Riverton, was garrotted.' He stared at Newman. 'Sandra Riverton was hung by her neck until she was dead.' It was a brutal thrust and Newman froze. 'And now we have this Steve, also garrotted. I have little doubt that when we identify the murderer of one of those three victims we shall have found the murderer of all three. That is the present position.'

He sat down, stretched out his legs. As he waited he was watching Tweed.

'I think my next move,' Tweed began, 'is to travel up to Walberswick. I want to have a long talk with Peggy Vanderheld. She will know more about people connected with INCUBUS than anyone we can get at.'

'I would like to be present,' Buchanan said simply.

'If you promise to keep quiet. Not otherwise. And only if Vanderheld agrees to your being present. Since she is an American citizen you have no jurisdiction over her. Come to think of it, neither have I. Certainly we have no evidence she is guilty of any crime. I can only hope to coax her into talking.'

'And you are experienced in interrogation,' Buchanan remarked. 'Not only in your present position. I do know that before you joined this organization you were one of the most successful Yard superintendents with Homicide.'

Tweed smiled wryly. 'That was a little while ago. Are you agreeable to come under the conditions I laid down?'

'Quite agreeable.'

'May I come too?' asked Paula. 'The presence of another woman might help. If she bridles I'll leave you with her immediately.'

'Again, on that condition, yes.' Tweed's manner

relaxed. 'My interview with Vanderheld could be the turning point in what started out as an investigation into INCUBUS, an attempt to trace what had happened to missing members of one-time Communist secret police services like the *Securitate*. Now it is a murder investigation.'

'A triple murder case,' Buchanan emphasized. 'We are hunting a mass murderer.'

Cord Dillon, seated on a chair tilted against the wall in a corner, had remained silent. Introduced to Buchanan as 'Mr Dexter, an official of the State Department', he spoke for the first time.

'And I need evidence to put Mr Franklin D. Hauser out of business.'

'Maybe the solution to Chief Inspector Buchanan's problem will turn out to be exactly what you also need,' Tweed said. 'Any more comments?'

'I rather think it might be an amusing idea if I drove up to Suffolk by myself,' interjected Marler. 'Nothing exciting – just to mooch around Livingstone Manor. After dark, of course.'

'Be very careful,' Tweed warned. 'I have the strongest foreboding Hauser is about to strike back. The trouble is we don't know what he will choose as his target. I think we should now leave for Walberswick.'

46

Hauser crashed his clenched fist on the desk in his large study overlooking the grounds at the back of Livingstone Manor. His eyes glowed with rage and frustration. Facing him, Carver wondered whether this was another exhibition staged by a natural actor.

'Why couldn't you persuade the Lennox bitch to sign the agreement?'

'She said she wanted time to think it over. If I could have left the agreement with her she might have changed her mind.'

'You know we never leave documents like that lying about for prying eyes. God knows who she might have shown it to.'

Carver, seated erect in a hard-backed chair, kept quiet. He didn't think it wise to let Hauser know Evelyn had proposed keeping the agreement to let her accountant examine the papers. Why add fuel to the flames?

'Well, there we are.' Hauser smiled, tilted his jaw.

'Why is Evelyn Lennox so important?' Carver asked.

Was Hauser a schizophrenic? he was wondering. His changes of mood were bewildering. Hauser was beaming now, leaning back in his executive chair as he waved his hand.

'There you go again, boy, asking questions about departments of INCUBUS which don't concern you. Maybe I'll send one of our female staff to have a word with Evelyn. Woman to woman. Might work,' he went on genially. 'Who can tell how women will react? They don't even know themselves. Would you have a map of that area. Adam?'

'Yes, I do.' Carver extracted the map from his breast pocket, handed it to his chief. 'Suffolk is a complex area. It's easy to get lost.'

'No, spread the map out. Mark on it with a cross in pencil where Evelyn Lennox lives. Then the young lady I send can find her way there. That is, if I decide to send anyone. You haven't a pencil? When I was young and starting out in California I always carried a pencil and a rubber. Here you are. You're a well-educated guy. I'll bet you've got three or four gold pens on you but no pencil. Shame on you.'

Carver disliked the patronizing tone Hauser liked to adopt. He bent over the map, marked the location of Rose Bower with a pencil cross. He had no inkling that his chief's banter was to cover up the significance of the pencilled cross. Afterwards it could be rubbed out – a vital piece of evidence destroyed.

'Thank you, Adam.' Hauser folded up the map. 'No sign of anyone else at the cottage while you were making up to Evelyn? No? I just wondered.'

Carver was startled, kept his expression blank. How the devil could Hauser have guessed he had asked Evelyn out to dinner? The man was a mind reader. It was unsettling, worse than when Hauser was in a rage. Hauser came round his desk as Carver stood up, clapped him on the shoulder.

'Later I may have a serious mission for you. You do it right and there's a big bonus coming. Off you go, play with your bat and ball . . .'

Hauser waited until Carver had left and his expression was grim. Taking out a bunch of keys, clutching the folded map, he walked from his study down the long hall, entered the living room, inserted a key into the locked door leading to the cellar complex.

Irina Serov looked up from the English novel she was reading as Hauser entered the suite next to where Manescu was quartered. Elegantly stretched out on a couch, she let Hauser have a good look at her legs before she stood up.

'I have a difficult job for you,' Hauser began, spreading out the map on a table. 'See that pencil cross? Take this rubber with you. When the job is done be sure to erase the cross, throw away the rubber. A girl lives at Rose

468

Bower in a hick place on the coast called Walberswick. The cross shows Rose Bower – crappy name – which is where she lives.' He straightened up, smiled down at her. 'And that is the problem – she's still living . . .'

Irina, driving a hired Ford Escort, turned off the A 12 on to the B 1387 where the signpost carried a single word. *Walberswick*. She was carrying a driving licence in the name of Iris Reynolds, a calling card with the same name and her occupation. *Beautician*.

The card had been printed in one of the rooms in the cellar complex at her suggestion before she left Livingstone Manor. She guessed that a lot of INCUBUS employees were carrying cards with fake names. And in the heat the ink had dried quickly when she had left it face up in the passenger seat.

She also had perched on the same seat an expensive-looking wine-coloured executive case. The necessary ingredient had been supplied from the pharmacy in another cellar room which, like the other rooms, always had the door locked. Which was a good idea, Irina thought as she drove along the deserted country road. They had enough stuff in that so-called pharmacy to poison the whole of Suffolk.

She slowed down as she passed the first house, slowed a little more as she drove out of the sun glare into the shade of a tunnel of trees. She was checking the name of each residence as she crawled through the tunnel. She nearly missed her target because this name was almost covered in creeper. *Rose Bower*.

She continued to crawl as she glanced up the path between hedges of wild roses, checked the windows downstairs and the dormer windows in the thatched roof. No sign of life. Still cautious, she drove on, checking both sides of the road for hidden watchers. Hauser had said the girl lived alone. But Hauser hadn't visited the place and she didn't trust that fashion plate creep, Adam Carver. She had seen him when she had peered from her cabin door aboard the *Washington IV* during the night crossing from Skalhamn to Harwich. Carver had not seen her but as he had walked down the companionway she had heard Hauser call out. 'Adam, I want to talk with you . . .'

She reached a point where a panoramic view of the glittering sea appeared. In the distance a man and a woman stood on a shingle bank, staring out to sea, their backs turned. She swung the wheel, drove back to Rose Bower.

Butler was in the lavatory, coping with a bout of constipation, when Evelyn saw the small slim girl walking up the garden path. She dashed from the living room to the door, peered through the spyhole. She saw an attractive face framed with blonde hair. Before the visitor could ring the bell she opened it on the chain.

'I am so sorry to bother you,' Irina began, 'but I am lost. I must have taken the wrong turning. Have you a map you could show me? This heat is getting me down.'

Evelyn slipped off the chain, invited her inside, took her into the living room. On a sideboard stood a large jug of punch, freshly made. Butler had told her Newman was coming to see her. 'With some friends . . .'

Evelyn had decided she must have some refreshment to offer. After the long drive from London in this heat the visitors would probably appreciate a pick me up. Irina settled back in a chair, her handbag on her lap, the flap undone.

'I've been driving round for hours,' she explained. 'I don't supposed you could let me have a drink of something? I'm almost dehydrated.'

'I've just made some punch. Or you could have a fruit drink. Lime juice . . .'

'A small glass of punch would be wonderful. Providing you're joining me.'

'Well, a small glass for both of us. Where are you trying to get to?' she asked as she poured from the jug, then placed it back inside the ice bucket.

'Southwold. I suppose I'm miles away.'

'No, you're very close. If you drove down to the end of this road to the sea and looked north across the entrance to the harbour you could see it in the distance. But driving there is a bit complicated. Let me show you on the map . . .'

She traced the route for her guest. Irina nodded, smiled.

'That's very clear. Thank you so much . . .'

Settled back in the armchair she stiffened suddenly. Evelyn was still standing as she spoke.

'Oh, Lord! I'm a beautician. Don't think I'm trying to sell you anything,' she added hastily. 'Not after your helpfulness. But I've left my case of samples outside your front door. I put it down by the door to ring the bell . . .'

'I'll get it. I'm sure it will still be there.'

Evelyn left the room. Irina lifted the flap of her hand-bag, took out the white paper packet, emptied the cyanide powder into Evelyn's glass, lifted the spoon Evelyn had left on a plate, quietly stirred the drink. When her hostess returned she was flopped back in her chair.

'Here is your case. It's very smart-looking. You don't want to lose that.'

'How kind of you.' Irina lifted her glass to drink, smiling again. 'Cheers!'

Evelyn reached for her glass of punch, changed her mind, picked up another half-filled glass.

'I'll finish my lime juice, then enjoy myself. I feel like something with a bit of a kick.'

471

Irina drank her own punch, put down the empty glass. She opened her executive case, took out a small box, handed it to Evelyn. Closing the case, she stood up to go.

'That's a little thank you present. I could have been driving round in this heat for hours. I must go now.'

'Chanel No. 5!' Evelyn was looking at the small box. 'This is quite unnecessary . . .'

'Don't you like it?' Irina asked moving towards the door. 'They are free samples for special customers – and I rate you in that category.'

'I still think it's too generous, but thank you – and it is my favourite perfume.'

She opened the door and began walking down the garden path with her departing guest. Suddenly there was an ear-splitting barking of such savagery Irina jumped and looked to her left. At the border of the garden a strong high wire fence divided off the two properties. The barrier continued at right angles halfway down the next front garden, turned again to form a box. Behind the wire crouched a large dog; an Alsatian? The animal, teeth bared, was foaming at the mouth.

'Don't worry,' Evelyn reassured her, 'it's well fenced in. The owners have gone to fetch the vet. He's going to put it down. It's gone mad. Could be the heat . . .'

She stood by the gate as her guest drove off towards the A 12 in her Ford Escort. Evelyn peered over the gate towards the sea. Pete Nield had taken Peggy Vanderheld for a walk along the sand dunes. The American woman seemed restless, had to have regular walks.

Going back inside, Evelyn closed the door, remembered to attach the chain. Even that brief sojourn in the heat of the day had made her thirsty. She went into the living room, picked up her glass of punch. I need a pick me up myself, she thought, as she raised the glass.

*   *   *

Newman was grim faced as he drove his Mercedes 280E along the A1120 heading for Yoxford. Beside him sat Tweed and in the back the only other passenger was Paula. Tweed glanced at Newman, saw his expression, guessed accurately what he was thinking, kept silent.

They were approaching Livingstone Manor's long drive to their left. Already Newman could see the old church perched on the hill with its isolated bell tower, the place where Sandy had died horribly. He reduced speed, began to cruise at thirty miles an hour.

'Coming close to Livingstone Manor, are we?' Tweed asked.

'Yes.'

'If there are guards at the entrance lodge they may spot us.'

'Let them.' Newman's tone was cold, remote. 'Let the bastards know we're coming after them. They've walked into your trap. Let them sweat.'

'Oh I'm sure they're doing that already,' Tweed replied, trying to lighten the atmosphere, 'in this heat sweating has become a way of life.'

'That's not what I meant.'

'We know,' said Paula quietly. 'We do know, Bob.'

A hundred yards behind them, adjusting his speed to Newman's, Chief Inspector Buchanan drove a Volvo station wagon. He liked plenty of room for his long legs. Beside him sat Sergeant Warden in his shirt sleeves. For Warden this was a great concession to the heat.

Newman slowed the Mercedes even more as they began to pass the sprawling estate of Livingstone Manor. At the lodge gate a guard was wiping his wet forehead. The car meant nothing to him. Paula looked to her left and beyond the closed grille gates she saw several vehicles drawn up near the front of the mansion with the central arched window.

'One red Jag,' she said. 'One cream Cadillac. And one

stretched black limo. Mr Franklin D. Hauser must be in residence.'

'Three cars, I know,' said Tweed.

Paula blinked. She had not seen Tweed move his head one inch as he stared ahead along the road. But she had experienced this before. Tweed seemed to be able to see more out of the corner of his eyes than most people observed staring straight at something.

'Pity that mansion is spoilt by the load of communications equipment on the roof,' he remarked. 'Monica was right – or rather, the electrical supervisor grilled by Special Branch was right. That place has as much sophisticated communications junk as we have at Park Crescent. Alarming thought.'

'At least it confirms it is a key headquarters,' Paula remarked.

Tweed checked his watch. 'I just hope nothing has happened to either of our witnesses at Walberswick.'

'How could it?' snapped Newman. 'With Butler and Nield on guard.'

'I'll just be glad when we get there and find they're all right. How much longer before we do get there?'

'Roughly half an hour,' Newman said and lapsed into silence.

Butler hurried into the living room. He had thrown on his jacket to conceal the holstered Smith & Wesson. As he entered Evelyn raised the glass she was about to drink from in a salute.

'I heard voices,' Butler said. 'I got here as soon as I could.' He looked at the empty glass on the table. 'Who came? Where are they now?'

'A girl who had lost her way. A beautician. The heat was getting her down. She left her samples case outside the front door. I fetched it for her. She was genuine. She even gave me this bottle of Chanel No. 5 . . .'

'*Don't drink that!* Now, put the glass down carefully on the table. Tell me exactly what happened . . .'

Butler's normal poker face had a concentrated look as he listened to her account of the visit, his head turned to one side as he visualized everything which had happened.

'. . . so you see, she was quite harmless,' Evelyn concluded. 'And, as you can see, she drank her own punch . . .'

She broke off as the Alsatian next door began snarling, barking its head off. She grimaced at the sound.

'I told you the people next door have gone to fetch the vet to put down that dog. It gets on my nerves.'

'Have you a shallow bowl? The sort of thing a dog could drink out of?'

'Yes. Why? Sorry, you must have a reason. As a matter of fact I kept the one I had for my own dog. It got run over and I couldn't bear to have another one in the house.'

Butler grasped the handle of the coal shovel lying in the hearth. In his other hand he carried her glass of punch and followed her into the kitchen. She was just putting a plain white shallow china bowl on the table. He poured half the contents of the glass into the bowl.

'I'm going out of the back door. Could you go into the front garden and distract that animal, keep it there for a few minutes. For heaven's sake keep well back from it.'

He stepped out of the back door where the high wire fence continued along the border of the garden next door. He walked half-way along the lawn, bent down close to the wire, placing the bowl by his side. The dog was shrieking its head off at the front.

The ground was so hard, so sun baked, it took him several minutes to shovel a shallow hole under the fence – shallow but deep enough to push the bowl through to the other side. Standing up, he rattled the metal shovel along the wire, back and forth. The sound of the dog barking stopped for a few moments, was resumed as Butler continued scraping the wire. He jumped well back from the barrier as the Alsatian appeared.

Evelyn came rushing back through the front doorway, shut the door, fixed the chain, ran along the passage into the kitchen and out through the back doorway. Butler gestured with the shovel.

The Alsatian, dripping foam, glared at him with startling red eyes, bloodshot. Then it saw the bowl. It sniffed at the intruder, stood for a short time staring at the liquid. Then it bent its huge head, began lapping up the contents. Suddenly it jerked its head up, a shudder ran through its body, it opened its jaws, gave one muted howl, stiffened from head to tail, fell over sideways, hitting the ground with a heavy thud. It lay quite still, the sun shining down on it, roasting the corpse.

'Oh, my God!'

Evelyn's right hand flew to her mouth. She stood still for a moment. Butler took her arm, guided her inside the house. She thanked him, walked like a zombie to the living room, collapsed into a chair, staring up at Butler.

'That could have been me.'

'But it wasn't.' He gave one of his rare smiles. 'You and I have to come to an arrangement. You promise never to let anyone into the house yourself – or I'll stop going to the toilet . . .'

She laughed, with only the faintest touch of hysteria, then giggled. Jumping up, she threw her arms round him, hugged him. He gripped her shoulders reassuringly as she released him.

'We have a sample for the Forensic merchants left in the glass. Now I'm going to empty the jug of punch you so carefully prepared down the lavatory.'

'And after all the trouble I took to concoct it.'

That was when Butler knew she wasn't going to slide

into a state of shock. He had emptied the jug, was flushing the toilet, when the door bell rang. Evelyn ran into the lavatory, playfully tugged at his arm.

'Someone at the door. Do your duty, Harry.'

Peering through the spyhole, he saw Nield standing arm in arm with Peggy Vanderheld, looking at the rose hedge while they waited for the door to be opened. Standing in the entrance, Butler stared cynically at their posture.

'Enjoying yourself, Pete?' he enquired.

Even though tanned, Nield flushed. Peggy disengaged her arm and gazed boldly back at Butler. Clad in a form-fitting skirt and a short sleeved blouse she looked sexy and knew it.

'All's well?' Nield asked in an over-hearty tone.

Butler's mind moved like lightning. Tweed was coming to interrogate Vanderheld, should arrive soon. Maybe a jolt would help to loosen the tough American woman's tongue.

'Oh, sure,' he replied. 'Everything's fine. Of course we had a little bit of excitement. A girl called while I was in the loo and tried to poison Evelyn. Go through to the kitchen and take a peek out of the back door – see what happened to that mad dog next door when I fed it the drink meant for Evelyn. It's quite an education . . .'

47

Tweed stepped out of the Mercedes Newman had parked in front of Rose Bower. He scanned the area, his experienced eye judging the security – or lack of security – of the location. Newman locked the car and waited as Tweed walked back to where Buchanan had stopped his Volvo.

'I'm going in now. I'll do my best to persuade her to let you be present but I guarantee nothing. Someone will come shortly to let you know.'

'It's up to you. I'll wait here,' Buchanan replied.

Tweed looked at Warden who was about to get out of the car. He already had his notebook in his hand.

'I don't think your presence will help the interview at all,' he said crisply.

'You mean you want me to stay in the car like a guard dog?'

'If you wish to put it that way, yes.'

As he strode away Tweed was sure Buchanan had suppressed a smile. Butler had emerged from the cottage, was talking to Newman. He listened while Butler told him about the attempt on Evelyn's life. Outwardly he seemed unaffected by the incident.

'Where is Peggy Vanderheld?'

'Nield has her in the guest bedroom at the back upstairs,' Butler told him. 'They are expecting you.'

'Then I'd better get on with it . . .'

The living room door was closed as he entered the cottage, ran up the narrow stairs. Nield met him at the top, pointed to a closed door.

'She's in there. You've heard about the attempt to kill Evelyn Lennox this afternoon? Good. And,' he lowered his voice, 'that Butler told Vanderheld. Thought it might soften her up for you. She's a pretty gutsy lady.'

'You stay on the alert here on this landing but not near this door. I'm expecting another attempt – maybe on the lives of both women, once they know Evelyn is still alive.'

'How can they know that?'

'No idea. But they will . . .'

Tweed knocked on the closed door. A soft American

478

voice called 'Come in', and he entered a small bedroom with an angled and beamed ceiling, closed the door. Whatever he had been expecting it was not this. Peggy Vanderheld was reclining on a double bed, her shapely legs stretched out below her mini-skirt, her breasts tight against a close-fitting white blouse, the first three buttons undone. She appeared to be wearing nothing but her skin under the blouse. Perched up against a pillow, she studied Tweed through half-closed eyes. Her thick, jet black hair was splayed over the pillow. She's trying to sex me up, Tweed decided.

'My name is Tweed, Chief Claims Investigator of General and Cumbria Assurance. I'm probing into the death of Ed Riverton in Helsinki. He carried a very large policy with us. Also into the death of Sandra Riverton, who also carried a policy with us. May I sit down?'

'Perch on the edge of the bed if you like.'

'I think a chair might be more comfortable. Thank you.'

'How do you think I can possibly help?'

'The investigation has widened its scope. To get at the truth we're having to investigate the company you once worked for. INCUBUS. Incidentally, in a car outside is Chief Inspector Buchanan of New Scotland Yard. He is in charge of the Sandra Riverton murder case. I would like him to be present, if you agree.'

'Wheel him in. If I don't like him I'll tell you and he can piss off.'

'He won't ask you any questions.' Tweed opened the door, called out to Nield, went back into the room. Vanderheld had slid off the bed, was standing in front of a wall mirror, brushing her hair. She straightened her slip of a skirt, sat in a chair, crossed her legs as Buchanan strolled in.

'This is Chief Inspector Buchanan,' Tweed introduced. 'He is here strictly as an observer.'

For a moment Buchanan stood still, his grey eyes meeting Vanderheld's, then he walked forward, held out his hand. 'Miss Vanderheld.' Her shapely hand was surprisingly cool, her grip firm.

A formidable woman, Buchanan thought as he chose a chair in a corner, out of her direct line of vision. She had the most compelling dark eyes and when she spoke he found her voice very feminine, enticing. Her unbuttoned blouse emphasized her beautiful neck but Buchanan also noticed the excellent bone structure, the strong chin.

'So you're investigating the whole INCUBUS apparatus,' she began, addressing Tweed. 'In that case I may have interesting facts to tell you. Hauser runs the entire world system. Personally. If that bastard goes, INCUBUS collapses.'

'What about his top executives?' Tweed asked.

'Messenger boys with big titles.' Her full lips curled. 'Take Adam Carver. Vice President of Banking Operations! He can't buy a hot dog stall without Hauser's say-so. He is a front man who smooth-talks through a deal already set up by Hauser. And for that he's paid $300,000 a year. Another thing about Adam – Hauser likes having a well-educated Englishman at his beck and call. Why? Because Hauser came up from nothing in California, had little formal education. Sometimes I wonder how Adam spends his days when he's not seducing some floozie.'

Her tone was vicious. Tweed wondered whether Adam hadn't paid sufficient attention to Vanderheld.

'What about Frank Galvone?' he asked.

'Frank!' Her voice dripped contempt. 'Did you know he was scum on the streets of Chicago when Hauser hired him?'

'Yes. Occupation: professional pickpocket, strong-arm man.'

Vanderheld looked surprised. 'You seem to know a lot. You wouldn't have a man on the inside?'

'Unfortunately, no,' Tweed responded immediately. 'But I've done my homework. Please go on – you were talking about Galvone's background, his work at INCUBUS.'

'Officially he's Vice President of Strategic Planning. The titles change at Hauser's whim. Another $300,000 a year for another messenger boy. He's Hauser's hatchet man, but again he can't take a shower without the nod from Hauser. He flies about the world a lot. Sandra Riverton told me that when he visited the Norwich HQ everyone was shivering in their shoes. He puts on the pressure, keeps the staff working all-out.'

Buchanan leaned forward. 'If I might ask a question?'

Vanderheld looked at him, gave him a slow smile. 'Depends on the question, Buster.'

Tweed heaved an inward sigh of relief. Obviously she approved of the Chief Inspector's polite, quiet manner.

'You mentioned Sandra Riverton just now. Was she visiting Helsinki when you had this conversation with her?'

'No. It was over the phone. She'd had a long session with Frank. She told me she was limp with exhaustion after the experience. In Norwich, that was. He'd fired questions at her non-stop about her job, whatever that was. He stayed several days but I don't think she saw him again.'

'Thank you. I wish everyone I met answered with such precision.'

He settled back in his chair, withdrawing from the discussion. Tweed's technique of interrogation intrigued him: the way he was playing on her fury at being summarily dismissed, a fact he cleverly had not referred to. He relaxed again, listening as Tweed put his next question.

'In Helsinki you mentioned a Mr Popescu to Bob Newman.'

'Nicolae Popescu is a creep. I only saw him once when he had just arrived in Helsinki, months ago. I was coming up to the penthouse floor in the elevator, the doors opened and I saw him. Hauser moved in the way to conceal him and I pressed the "down" button before Hauser saw me. I don't know why, but I felt I wasn't supposed to see him.'

Tweed produced an envelope, extracted a number of photos he had previously shown to Buchanan at Park Crescent. He handed them to Vanderheld and she pulled her chair forward so their knees were almost touching. Buchanan watched the effect of their proximity on Tweed. Not a blink. She looked through them, quickly. All her movements were brisk.

'This one,' she said handing back one print.

'You're sure?'

Tweed held up the photo so Buchanan could see the one she had chosen. The picture of Ion Manescu.

'Positive. I said he was a creep. He was creepy. Not someone I'd like to meet in a dark alley.' She paused. 'Look, when this interview is over does the protection for me continue? Specifically, will Pete Nield stay with me while Hauser remains free?'

'Yes,' Tweed said promptly. 'You have my personal guarantee. What made you ask?'

She reached under the counterpane covering the bed, pulled out a large polythene wallet containing a green file. She handed it to Tweed.

'I took out some insurance when Hauser fired me after all those years. That is a photocopy of the file on Popescu. Ridiculous name, but he's anything but ridiculous. When Hauser gave me the file to put in the vault he said Popescu was Austrian. I ask you! Austrian – it sounds one helluva more like Romanian to me. That file records he speaks good English, that he was an attaché at some embassy in London for a year. Nationality of the embassy is deleted.

You see now why I checked on the protection?'

Tweed smiled, looked at her dark eyes which stared straight back at him. Almost hypnotic.

'You wanted to be sure of me before you gave me the file. Very sensible.' Despite the heat inside the claustro-phobic bedroom, he kept his voice casual. 'Just as a theory, let us suppose Hauser was capable of organizing a murder. Would he hire an outsider, a professional assassin?'

'You think he's done that?'

'At the moment it is a theory.'

She sat back in her chair, kicked off her shoes, grasped both arms of the chair with her hands, crossed her legs and one of her feet brushed Tweed's trousers. He pre-tended not to notice. Her face had become like carved stone.

'I'm not answering any more questions. This is getting me in too deep. I thought that Robert Newman was going to be present. That was the message Pete gave me.'

'What has gone wrong? Tweed asked quietly.

'You have. You're some kind of insurance man – if that's what you really are.' She glanced at Buchanan. 'Sitting over there is a high-ranking detective. Now you're talking murder. If a reporter was present – someone really from the outside world who can't be intimidated – then I might talk. Put up or shut up.'

'Give me a moment,' Tweed said amiably. 'We thought you'd feel overwhelmed with three people.'

He went to the door, opened it. So Vanderheld could hear he called out to Nield to fetch Newman immediately. He waited until Newman, wearing his shirt open necked, his sleeves rolled to the elbows, appeared. He ushered him inside without a word.

'Hello, Peggy,' Newman greeted her with a droll smile. He leaned against a wall, folded his arms, crossed his ankles, the soul of relaxation.

483

'Give me a cigarette, Bob,' Vanderheld said. 'And maybe you'd light it for me.'

Newman obliged, handed her the cigarette. She took a long drag, blew out a smoke ring.

'Now I'm relaxed.' She looked at Tweed. 'You were saying?'

'Assuming Hauser wanted to organize a murder – or a series of murders – would he hire an outsider, a professional assassin?'

'No. Never. He'd keep it in the family – a phrase he often uses referring to INCUBUS. Maybe a top executive, maybe someone professional but on the payroll. That way he keeps complete control – because he's paying them a fortune. Definitely someone on the inside, close to the top.'

'So,' Newman intervened, 'I'll ask you again the question I asked in your apartment in Helsinki before we moved you out to Örno, with a guard, and probably saved your life. Remember Anna Jarva, the poor woman murdered on the scrubbing board, the woman who happened to be dressed just like you, who travelled on the same No. 4 tram.'

'What question?'

All her attention was on Newman now. Her full red lips were slightly parted, showed the tip of her tongue. My God! Buchanan was thinking, you do like to arouse men, to make sure you still have the power to do so.

'Can you check from your records,' Newman asked, 'who was present in Helsinki the night Ed Riverton was murdered. Who – providing it's the same man – was *absent* from Helsinki the following night when Sandra Riverton was murdered in Suffolk. Or are the records, maybe your diary, still locked away in that Helsinki bank you told me about?'

'I don't need written records.' She leant back, arched her chest. 'I have a photographic memory. That was why I lasted with Hauser five years. He couldn't abide a PA who had to look things up in files.'

'I'm still listening,' Newman assured her.

'Adam Carver fits. He was in Helsinki the night Riverton was garrotted. The following day he flew off somewhere. No idea where.'

'Anyone else?' Newman pressed.

'Frank Galvone. I remember when I left the building I saw a light in his office. Said he was working late. The following day he was away for forty-eight hours. He looked bushed when he got back.'

'That's the lot?'

'No, it isn't. Nicolae Popescu was sacked out on a bed at Level Five. His door was open a fraction – it was a cold night, ice cold. The heating in the corridor was going full blast. I caught a glimpse of him as I took some files to the vault.'

'And the following day?' Newman persisted.

'I had to deliver some important papers to catch a flight from Helsinki airport. I saw him queueing up to catch the direct flight to London.'

'Peggy, your memory is quite extraordinary. You are sure of these facts?'

'That's right, Buster. That's what they are. Facts . . .'

'Leaves us just about where we were,' Tweed said as he descended the staircase. 'Three possible suspects.'

'Not quite,' said Newman grimly. 'I can't prove it but I think I've identified the killer.'

'And how have you done that?'

'Since I can't be sure yet I won't say any more. I can be cryptic too, Tweed.'

Paula met them in the hall. During the drive to the cottage Tweed had persuaded her too many people might overawe Vanderheld. Which wasn't his real reason: he

485

had suddenly realized the presence of another attractive woman might make Vanderheld bridle. After his visit to her at the Helsinki apartment Newman had described Vanderheld as 'a powerhouse of sex . . .'

'How did you get on with her?' Paula asked, excited.

'So, so,' Tweed replied. 'I sense you have something else on your mind . . .' He broke off as Butler appeared from the living room.

'Harry, I want you to tell Chief Inspector Buchanan all about what nearly happened to Evelyn. Take him out into the back garden. Then show him the state of that dog – and give him the sample for his Forensic people.'

He nodded to Buchanan who had followed them slowly down the stairs, slotting into his mind the general layout of Rose Bower. As Butler led the way to the kitchen Tweed followed Paula into the living room. Evelyn, who had heard their voices, was filling glasses with lime juice.

'I am bone dry,' Tweed admitted as he sat down. 'Thank you. Are you feeling better after your nerve-wracking experience? My name is Tweed.'

'Much better, Mr Tweed. If you'll excuse me for a moment, I want to fetch some more lime juice. I've been taking glasses out to Sergeant Warden.'

'What is it, Paula?' Tweed asked when they were alone.

'I want you to show her that picture of Irina Serov you wouldn't tell me where you got it from.'

Tweed drank more lime juice, considered her request. He had been given the photo in confidence by General Rebet during his stay at the Hotel Moskwa in Leningrad. Because the dissident had been a colonel in the KGB, Rebet had wanted the defection kept quiet. Very Russian.

'Why to Evelyn?' he asked.

'Because we've been chatting about her ordeal while you were upstairs. Something about the description she gave me of the fake beautician made me think of that photo. She doesn't need to know who it is.'

'I'll think about it. I can't see Hauser risking bringing someone like that into this country. Buchanan mustn't know about that picture. I've been careful that he didn't see it. Lord, I hope you're wrong.' He lowered his voice. 'Vanderheld told us Manescu has visited Britain more than once. A frightening thought.'

He stopped speaking as Evelyn reappeared with a jug of fresh lime juice. He let her refill his glass. Talking a lot was a thirsty business in the late afternoon heat.

'Miss Lennox,' he began, 'I have a photo here I'd like you to look at. You might just have seen this woman in the vicinity of Walberswick at some time.'

Paula stood beside Evelyn as she examined the print. She frowned, puckered up her mouth, held it further away.

'I don't think so,' she said eventually. 'Although there is something familiar.'

'Place the print on that drum table,' Tweed suggested. 'Then use your fingers to cover the dark hair so you can only see the face.'

He drank more lime juice. Even inside the shaded interior the temperature was high. He looked round the comfortable room, furnished with chintz-covered chairs and matching curtains. Normally he disliked the material but it suited the beamed ceiling, the large brick alcove fireplace.

'I'll be damned,' exclaimed Evelyn. 'Now I'm certain it is that awful beautician woman who tried to poison me. It was the bleached blonde hair which fooled me – makes her look quite different. Who is she?'

Tweed was prepared for that question. 'A woman wanted for involvement in insurance swindles. This is the first time she's resorted to attempted murder. You haven't taken out an insurance policy on your life recently, have you?'

487

'No, I haven't. How on earth do you think she came to pick on me?'

'Maybe there was something in what she said. She was lost, came to the wrong address. And I'd appreciate it if you didn't mention this to Peggy Vanderheld. We can't be sure of anything so it's important to keep her nervous – alert. Of course, that fake beautician might have come from INCUBUS's insurance outfit, Fraternity & Equality.'

He wished he'd thought of that explanation earlier. The heat must be fogging my brain, he thought. Buchanan came into the room followed by Newman.

'Don't worry, Miss Lennox,' he assured her, 'I'm not here to ask a lot more questions. Only one.' He produced a large button, showed it to her. 'You worked in Helsinki for quite a time, as I understand it. I sent back Sergeant Warden to search the messy floor of the bell tower where Sandra Riverton was murdered. You can see threads attached to the button. It has the Daks symbol on it. I suspect it was torn from a British warm while Riverton was struggling for her life. Anyone you knew in Helsinki who wore a British warm?'

'Hauser does in winter. He buys a lot of British clothes. And wasn't it bitterly cold here when my sister died?'

'It was,' Newman intervened bleakly. 'Can I look at that button? Thank you.'

'Someone else wore a British warm in Helsinki,' Evelyn recalled. 'Why do I think it was a foreigner?'

'You tell me,' Buchanan suggested.

'No good. It won't come back to me.'

'It is the only solid item of evidence,' Buchanan remarked, taking back the button. 'I didn't ask Vanderheld – she's American and I'm not sure of her. She talked just a little too much. If you do recall the owner of another British warm perhaps you'd call me at this number.'

He gave her a card, walked down the garden path towards his Volvo. Tweed drank some more lime juice, thanked Evelyn, walked out into the heat.

'I'm worried,' he told Newman as they strolled between the hedges. 'Nield reported identifying Manescu in that car he pulled up alongside on his motor cycle. Now Evelyn has positively confirmed the presence of Irina Serov in the area. Hauser is preparing something very nasty indeed.'

He asked Newman the question nagging at him as they drove back to London followed by Buchanan and Warden in the Volvo.

'You said you'd identified the assassin among those three suspects Vanderheld listed. May I ask what gave you the clue – always assuming you're right?'

'Something Buchanan said at Park Crescent before we left for Finland. You pride yourself on your memory, so just play back that conversation in your mind.'

48

IRA BOMB MISSES SOUTHAMPTON TARGET.

Hauser read with satisfaction the headline in the late edition of the *Evening Standard* Galvone had bought during his drive back from the Hampshire city. The story below told how the bomb had been placed in an empty shop next door to the private bank, Street & Braithwaite. The assumption was they had hoped to blast a way inside the bank and make off with a large sum of cash to swell IRA funds. The reporter theorized the bomb had detonated not close enough to the adjoining bank's wall.

489

'You've done good, Frank,' he said, throwing the paper on to his desk in his study at Livingstone Manor.

'Must have scared the shit out of the bank's directors,' Frank agreed smugly.

'You've not finished yet,' Hauser snapped as Galvone started to leave the room. 'But first come down with me to the map room . . .'

Inside the cellar labyrinth he unlocked a door, beckoned Galvone to follow him. The room was empty as he walked over to a huge wall map of Europe and Russia. Red pins were stuck into different cities. Warsaw, Budapest, Sofia, Belgrade and Bucharest . . .

'That shows where the next major explosions will detonate. The outfits I want to take over will be anxious to sell to me before they're blown up. We have to create turmoil before we can establish American control.'

'Why Belgrade?'

'You really must keep in closer touch with the situation, Frank. That is, if you're going to continue to be of any use to me.' He smiled. 'I never have this trouble with Adam. Yugoslavia is falling apart. The province of Slovenia is screaming for independence. Always keep the pot on the boil.'

He spoke as though it was a normal business deal. The fact that the bombs would be timed to explode at lunchtime on weekdays – when maximum casualties would be caused – was for Hauser an obvious ploy to bring about more chaos.

'The other job you have,' he went on, 'is to double check the security here at Livingstone Manor. I've a feeling that Tweed will get to know I'm here. He's dangerous – well, so am I. Move the big feet, Frank.'

It was probably just as well that Marler was immune to the heat. He spent an active day preparing for his exploratory assault on Livingstone Manor.

He planned to penetrate the defences at three in the morning. Morale was always at its lowest ebb, guards on duty would be weary. He spent a long time in the East End of London. At a none too salubrious address off the Old Kent Road he met Alfred Higgins by appointment.

Alf Higgins, as he was known to his mates in the underworld, owned a small watch-maker's establishment. He did just enough legal business to make it impossible for the police to haul him in for questioning. Alf's real skill lay in his up-to-date knowledge of alarm and security systems. He was also an expert locksmith, which was a euphemism for picking locks and opening the doors to houses and safes which were supposed to be impregnable. Marler had used his services on several illegal occasions before and knew he was a slippery customer. He also knew he'd have to listen to the same lecture.

'Sit yourself down in that armchair. Real comfy, Mr 'Enderson,' Alf greeted his client. 'Not your real monicker, 'Enderson, I'll be bound.'

Marler took one look at the decrepit armchair in the dimly illuminated room – dimly because of the grimy windows. He perched himself on a polished wooden stool instead, folded his arms.

'Henderson I said, Henderson it is. Just like last time. I want you to break into a large country mansion which is heavily guarded. By men, by the latest security systems . . .'

'Installed by who?'

'A British firm. They really know their stuff.'

Alf, seated in an ancient rocking chair, scratched his thatch of grey hair. Needed a trim, Marler thought – made him look like a farm labourer. Which was all to the good since they'd be travelling together in Suffolk. He was a small man with skinny arms and legs. His face was like a walnut, wrinkled and brown. Age, impossible to guess – somewhere between forty and sixty. His best feature was his hands with long sensitive fingers. The lecture came.

'You said, "I want you to break in." You know my rules, Mr 'Enderson. I never goes inside. That way I've never gone "inside", if you gets my meanin'. All right?' He chuckled at his little joke. 'I make sure you get into this mansion. I loan you the equipment you'll need to open any lock easy. But I stays in the car while you're breakin' the law. I'm law abidin' and wouldn't dream of bein' found on private property.'

'Understood,' Marler said brusquely. 'What equipment? I emphasize the place will be like a fortress.'

'Costs more, does a fortress. We can talk about the dibs later. Want some beer? Bloody 'ot.'

'No, thank you,' Marler replied, observing the greasy glass Alf was drinking from. 'What equipment?' he repeated.

Perched on the stool rather like a pixie, Marler was wearing an old lightweight navy blue suit. It didn't show the dirt. He glanced round the room full of junk. The room had probably once been a bar. A stained wooden counter ran behind his host, the counter almost covered with old clocks, none of which appeared to be working. More clocks and old watches were piled on the shelves behind the counter. The floor was covered with spare parts, boxes of tools with the lids open. Hardly a square foot of free space. Which would make it almost impossible for the police to search the place. Like sifting through a council rubbish dump.

'There's two kinds of security lock,' Alf said suddenly. 'These security burks think if they make a lock complicated they've kept everyone out. Just the opposite. If they used lots of bolts they might earn their big fat fees. There's the combination lock – what you get when you come across most wall safes. Come to that in a mo' –

let's see what we do with deadlocks first.'

Higgins was wearing a surprisingly clean linen jacket with large pockets. He delved inside the right-hand pocket, brought out three apparently ordinary keys of different sizes. Only the colour was peculiar, had a fluorescent tinge. He nodded towards the door leading direct to the street.

'Take these, open the door. And they ain't the proper keys for that door.'

Marler looked at the heavy wooden door. It had three locks. Higgins believed in his own security. But there were also four large bolts which had been shot closed after Marler had entered the premises. He took the keys, looked at Higgins.

'How then?'

'You're 'oldin' magnetic keys. One of them will slide inside any security lock. Fiddle the key gently, see what 'appens.'

Marler shrugged, dropped off the stool, walked up to the door. First he opened the four bolts. Taking the three keys, he held each one close to the top lock, found one which seemed the right size, inserted it, fiddled it gently as instructed. He heard the lock opening. He chose another key for the second lock, performed the same action, again heard the lock open. The same key worked on the lowest lock. He turned the handle and the heavy slab of wood opened.

'Lordy!' he said under his breath.

'Better lock up,' Higgins said, leaving his rocking chair.

He held a bunch of keys, attended to the locks, shot the bolts back in to the closed position. Moving light-footed in his trainers, he bent down at the far end of the counter, pushed aside a heap of boxes, exposing a large safe.

'Keeps all my money in that, don't I? You can 'ave it if you open it. This might 'elp.'

From his left-hand pocket he produced a small circular

instrument with a thick base. He showed Marler the other end. It was hollow, appeared to be fitted with a series of flanges of diminishing size. Higgins handed it to Marler.

'Try your luck, matey. Insert the hollow end over the combination. Again be gentle when you fits it. When you feel it lock on, press the button in the base and wait. And that safe 'as the latest combination lock. The company what makes it guarantees security. Stupid burks . . .'

Marler crouched down, studied the instrument for a moment, carefully slipped the hollow end over the combination lock, felt a slight pull as it locked on. He pressed the button in the base, clasped his hands, waited crouched on his haunches. He heard faint clicking noises. Very rapid, one after another. Then silence.

'Well, get on with it,' urged Higgins. 'You're where you're not supposed to be. Don't 'ang around.'

Marler turned the safe handle, pulled the door open and stared at the contents. Nothing. It was empty. Higgins bent beside him, closed the safe, twisted the instrument slightly to the right to release it, dropped it in his pocket.

'Those three keys . . .' Marler began.

'Magnetic, like I tell you. Sucks the tines of the lock open. The security lot make their locks of metal, think that makes it safer. Those keys are my own invention. Made them meself in a friend's engineering shop. Sometimes I thinks I ought to patent them.' He chuckled again.

'And the combination thingumajig?'

'Ah, that.' Higgins looked sad, drank more warm beer. 'Like to tell you I made that. Be a lie. Got it off a Yank friend I'd done favours for in Philadelphia. Very expensive to buy, I'd say. If you knew where to buy it from. 'As a tiny built-in computer in that base. It's battery operated. I'll fit a new battery so it's nice and fresh for you. Eight hundred nicker the whole job,' he said quickly.

'Eight hundred pounds! You must be joking.'

'And no rough stuff. You'll 'ave to 'andle any of that.'

'I can. I will. Four hundred pounds. And it's getting damned hot in here, so make up your mind. I could go elsewhere.'

'Don't be barmy. And get keys like I got? And the thingumajig?'

'Five hundred. In cash as last time.'

'Only deal in cash. You knows that. Tax people can read cheques. Can't read cash – not if they can't find it. Six hundred nicker. Final offer. There's the door. I'll even unlock it for you.'

'All right, Scrooge. Six hundred nicker. Oh, there will be alarms. Electronic beams. I'm sure of it.'

'I'll handle them. All included in the six hundred nicker. Only 'cos I like the look of your face. When?'

'Tonight. I'll call for you at 11.30. After dark. In a blue Ford Cortina. Don't keep me waiting. Here's four hundred in fifties on account. And don't forget to bring *all* the equipment. Now unlock that bloody door before I suffocate.'

Marler's brief call at Newman's South Ken flat in Beresforde Road turned out very differently from what he had expected. Newman listened to him, heard about his plan to break in to Livingstone Manor:

'. . . so as you visited Hauser there back in February, I hoped you'd be able to give me some idea of the layout inside. Maybe draw me a plan of the part you saw.'

'Yes, I will do that.' Newman lifted his glass of fruit juice and then grinned. 'On condition you let me come with you and this Alf Higgins.'

'That wasn't on my agenda . . .'

'It is now. If you want that ground plan. And I noticed some of the security system.' Newman's manner changed, his voice became sombre. 'Don't forget my girl friend,

495

Sandy, was killed by one of Hauser's men in an especially horrible way. And I'm convinced now since Tweed told me what Vanderheld said before I sat in on the interview – convinced that Hauser gave the order for Sandy's execution. Because that's what it was.'

'Tweed would say you were too personally involved to get mixed up with me on this trip.'

'I'm personally involved up to the hilt. Take your choice. I can draw that plan, tell you something about the security, maybe save your life. We're not dealing with pussy-cats.'

'I had realized that.'

'So do I draw the plan?'

'Yes, please. And I agree, this may take two of us to do the job. Even then, it will be dangerous.'

Marler wandered to the large bay window at the front of the large Victorian living room. Beyond the net curtains was the church of St Mark's, the trees and the grass in the garden surrounding it. Not a normal London view.

'This is the plan,' Newman said after a few minutes. 'I can only give part of the ground floor. Hauser's study appeared to be at the back – I saw a door open at the end of a long passage. The key is probably the huge living room. When I was talking to Hauser I noticed Galvone leaning against an almost closed door in the inner wall here . . .' He pointed with his pen. 'He quietly closed it. I think that leads down to the cellar complex Monica described to us during the meeting with Tweed this morning.'

'I was going to drive up for a quick recce of Livingstone Manor, but you've been there. They have guard dogs patrolling the grounds?'

'No, I don't think they do. They seem to rely on human guards. The windows are wired up, but I couldn't see any security round the heavy front door. Mind you, it has three locks.'

'Any bolts?'

496

'No, why?'

'Just wondered. This chilled champagne is good. Lanson? Your favourite brand?'

'I find it goes down well. One more serious factor. I'm proposing to go armed.'

'Sensible chap,' Marler drawled. 'So am I. Not the Armalite for this job.' He opened his tropical drill jacket, showed the butt of the .32 Browning nestling in his hip holster. Pulling up his left trouser leg, he exposed the strapped sheath, the handle of a hunting knife protruding. Reaching into a pocket he took something out, slipped it over the fingers of his right hand.

'Knuckle dusters?' Newman queried. 'You're expecting close-quarter combat.'

'If we meet anyone they have to be eliminated quietly.'

He slipped off the knuckle dusters, dropped them in his pocket, raised his glass.

'Here's to success.'

'To survival,' Newman amended. 'And the obtaining of evidence to bring down Franklin D. Hauser.'

As they drank Newman reflected the normal hostility between himself and Marler had vanished. For the moment. Maybe it was the hot weather? The phone rang. Marler picked it up as Newman nodded. It was Tweed.

'Put Newman on, please.'

'And what can I do for you?' Newman asked.

'Whatever you're planning you're on your own. Remember that. And take care. I predict we're approaching the final crisis.'

'Tweed sends his love,' Newman joked as he put down the phone. 'When exactly do we launch this break-in operation?'

'Zero hour 3 a.m. On the dot, if you please . . .'

'What are you up to now?' Paula asked.

She was wearing a pale fawn mini-skirt, pale red tights

497

and a short-sleeved white blouse as she perched on the edge of her desk. The atmosphere inside Tweed's Park Crescent office was torrid. He replaced the receiver.

'Just checking. Marler *is* with Newman at Bob's flat.' He looked at Monica. 'Rather obvious – Newman draws a Smith & Wesson with his certificate of use from the armoury. Marler takes a .32 Browning. And they're together.' He glanced at Cord Dillon perched on a chair in a corner. 'You need evidence, solid evidence, against Hauser.'

'I sure do. Something the Justice Department can nail him with forever. I hope these two ladies realize that officially I don't exist this side of the pond?'

'Both are trustworthy. The question is unnecessary.'

'When did you realize Marler was also up to something?'

'As soon as Monica told me he had been here early this morning. That he had extracted from her all the information she had obtained about the cellar complex at Livingstone Manor.'

'You could have stopped them,' Paula accused.

'They can look after themselves.' Tweed's voice hardened. 'Hauser breaks every rule in the book. Terrorizes companies he wants into selling out. Transports explosives into the Soviet Union. We're not going to outwit a man like that by playing it strictly legal. And he's a world menace.'

'You sound unusually vehement,' Paula commented.

'Look at these newspaper reports, for God's sake.'

He spread out different papers over his desk. He jabbed a finger at the headlines.

BOMBS EXPLODE IN BALKANS.

CAR BOMB KILLS LEADING ROMANIAN LIBERAL.

CHAOS IN BULGARIA.

YUGOSLAVIA BREAKING UP.

BOMB AT KIEV KGB HQ KILLED TWENTY.

'Since the lid was taken off by the Soviet President all stability has gone,' said Tweed. 'Europe has become a whirlpool.'

49

'Evelyn Lennox will be one stiff corpse by now,' Irina reported. 'What is my next assignment?'

'You've seen the newspapers.' Hauser waved a hand towards the papers spread out over the living-room table at Livingstone Manor. 'You're just completed a task which worried me for quite some time. Your next assignment? To stir up the cauldron boiling over in Europe and Russia. Specifically, I'm flying you to Münich in the next few days. From there you control the assault on the Ukraine.'

'And until then?'

'You stay under cover in your suite.'

'Hauser took out his bunch of keys, walked to the door leading to the cellars, unlocked it, led the way down. On his return he pressed a switch on his intercom.

'Frank, get your ass in here. Inside thirty seconds.'

He unfolded the piece of paper Serov had given him. On it was noted the phone number of Evelyn Lennox. Earlier they had found she had an ex-directory number. While in the hall of the cottage Irina had observed the number. Hauser held it out to Galvone as the American, dressed in a T-shirt and slacks, hustled into the room.

'Frank, call this number, ask to speak to Evelyn Lennox. It probably will get you no place. She's dead.'

'Then why am I calling?'

'You really aren't too bright sometimes, Frank. To make sure she is dead.'

'And if she isn't and comes on the line? She'll recognize my voice. She did work at the Helsinki HQ.'

'Frank, amazing as it may seem, I do remember that. If she did come on the line, recognized you, OK. It steps up the pressure. Now, call a dead lady . . .'

Galvone dialled the number. It rang for some time before it was answered.

'Yes, who is this?' a woman's voice enquired.

'I wish to talk with Evelyn Lennox.'

'You're talking to her. Who *is* this?'

'We're not selling anything,' Galvone said quickly. 'We are operating a survey on the Greenhouse menace. You live near the coast. What are your views?'

'I'd first like to know who is calling, please.'

'I can't hear you too well. Atmospherics. It's a very bad line. I'll call you back . . .'

Galvone rammed down the receiver. He looked grimly at his chief. Hauser was not a man who liked bad news.

'That was Evelyn Lennox I just spoke to. I recognized *her* voice. She's about as dead as I am . . .'

'Maybe less so,' Hauser snapped viciously. 'You're quite sure?'

'I told you. I know her voice.'

'Then we'll have to do something very final about her. I want you to organize a squad of four men – no, six men – in two cars to visit Rose Bower in the middle of the night. She may have protection. The squad is to be armed with the weapons the IRA often use. Kalashnikov automatic rifles – and tear gas pistols.' His voice was rasping. 'Assault that goddamn Rose Bower. You don't go. Choose a tough squad leader. When they've done the job set the place on fire. Take gasoline. Rose Bower goes up in flames. Get on it, Frank.'

'Six men away from here will dilute the security – you told me to double it.'

'Do what you're told!' Hauser jabbed a finger at

500

Galvone. 'You think I want an argument from you? I can get that from other cretins.'

'Then can I bring in some dogs to patrol the grounds during the night? I know a guy in Norwich who could supply . . .'

'Frank! I've told you a dozen times before. Use dogs and the guards rely on them. All intruders need are hunks of poisoned meat and all *you've* got are dead dogs. I want human dogs who stay alert and hungry. Why are you still standing there?'

Hauser felt restless when Galvone had gone. He also felt harassed and harried. Why? The Lennox problem would be solved in the night. He was launching the most ambitious campaign of his career, the campaign to control a 'home' from the Pacific to the Urals, a campaign which was well under way. So why?

He inserted a fresh cigarette into the ivory holder, lit it and left the room. He walked down the passage to his study, walked inside. To alleviate the heat of the afternoon the French windows were open to the vast spread of grounds at the back. He walked outside, down the steps from the wide stone terrace on the lawn.

The grounds were surrounded with a wall of fir trees. At the end of the lawn was a circular concrete helipad. A small Sikorsky helicopter stood on the helipad, fully fuelled at all times with a roster of pilots on duty round the clock.

Behind him along each of the perimeter paths armed guards followed the bulky figure at a discreet distance. Hauser reached the Sikorsky, boarded it and the two guards ran to join him. One sat at the front, the second made his way to a seat at the rear. Hauser occupied the single armchair as the pilot appeared for orders.

'Hank,' Hauser instructed, 'fly this thing over a place called Walberswick. A hick village on the coast north of here. Circle over it until I tell you to fly back here.'

501

'Yes, *sir*!'

Hauser had at last put his thick finger on what disturbed him. There had been no reaction anywhere from Tweed. So what was the bastard up to? He was becoming obsessed with his antagonist.

Sergeant Warden dashed into Chief Inspector Buchanan's office at New Scotland Yard. He clutched two documents in his hand and his manner was triumphant.

'It's all right, sir.'

'What is all right? And you shouldn't rush about in this heat.' Buchanan leaned back in his old wooden swivel chair, clasped his hands in his lap and continued in a dry tone. 'Sit down, compose yourself, tell me about it.'

'I've got the two search warrants. One for Adam Carver's flat in Chelsea, the other for Frank Galvone's pad in that de luxe block near Regent's Park. We could go there now.'

'Hardly to both places at once. There is a distance between them.'

Buchanan opened a drawer. He took a plastic bag from it, extracted a large button with the Daks symbol and several strands of black thread entwined inside the metal shank at the back. He held it up to the light.

'Our only clue to the murderer of Sandra Riverton. I wonder.'

'Don't follow you, sir.'

'Sandra Riverton was murdered close to dawn on a bitter February morning. That sort of weather the murderer might well have worn a British warm. But that coat, if it still exists, might well be in Helsinki.'

'Only one way to find out,' Warden said with unusual eagerness.

'Then there is the third suspect Vanderheld mentioned in my presence at Walberswick. Ion Manescu.'

'A Romanian. Surely he'd never possess a British warm, sir.'

Buchanan was amused. 'Because he's a foreigner? Tweed told me Manescu was attached to the Romanian Embassy in London several years ago. What makes a man look more English than wearing a British warm? Only one problem.'

'What's that, sir?'

'I contacted Interpol. They told me Manescu is dead.'

'Bit of a teaser that. Tweed got it wrong then?'

'Possibly. Yet one of his men positively identified Ion Manescu, hair trimmed short, behind the wheel of a car in the vicinity of Livingstone Manor a few days ago. My experience of Tweed is he is usually correct. Time we made the effort. Adam Carver's flat in Chelsea first. And it was Tweed's handmaiden, Monica, who traced both unlisted addresses.'

At Rose Bower Butler made his fifth effort to get through to Tweed on the phone. It was with great relief that he heard Monica's voice, identified himself, heard her say:

'It's Butler. Sounds urgent. He had trouble reaching us . . .'

'Am I glad to hear your voice, Tweed. There's been a couple of important developments. Frank Galvone phoned Evelyn – obviously to make sure she was dead. I let her take the call while I listened on the extension . . .'

Butler relayed the conversation between Galvone and Evelyn word by word from memory. Tweed listened, was not surprised, but kept the reaction to himself. His brain was thinking in top gear, assessing the implications as Butler ended his report.

'Harry, Hauser now knows Evelyn is still alive. Prepare for a much heavier attack on the cottage. I've already arranged with a friend at Special Branch to send a courier by car. He'll be bringing you two machine pistols with plenty of ammo. If you decided to move everyone to a new location, do so. And the courier is also bringing you a mobile telephone – so wherever you decide to go you can contact me.'

'Thanks. That's not all. I told Evelyn to let Vanderheld know about the Galvone phone call. She then told me she had three more files here. One on Adam Carver, one on Galvone and a more detailed one on Manescu. She didn't leave them in a Helsinki bank.'

'Then give the files to the courier. Tell him to drive to Park Crescent immediately on his way back. Will you be leaving Rose Bower?'

'Let me have a quiet word with Pete before I decide.'

'It's your decision. And good luck.'

Paula jumped up from behind her desk. 'I've just remembered something else I saw at Skalhamn. The *Washington IV* had a helipad on the aft deck – and a small Sikorsky parked on it. I don't know whether it's important.'

Tweed reached for his phone, dialled a number. He looked at Paula.

'I'm calling Heathcoate, the Harbour Master at Harwich.' He spoke into the phone, asked for the Harbour Master and again had to wait.

'Heathcoate? Sorry to trouble you again. This is Tweed. That ship the *Washington IV* – has it by any chance a chopper on its aft deck?'

'You do seem well informed. It did have one when it berthed.'

'*Did?* I thought you said a black limousine took Hauser away. Maybe I misunderstood you?'

'You understood me perfectly. I was surprised he hadn't used the Sikorsky. Then later I saw mechanics working on it. Looked as though something was wrong with the engine. It's all right now. Must be. It flew off this morning, hasn't been seen since.'

'Thank you . . .'

'Hold on. Don't suppose you're interested, but I've just been informed the *Washington IV* expects to put to sea tomorrow morning. Supplies are being taken aboard.'

'Thank you again.'

He told Monica and Paula what he had heard. Paula was pouring more tea into his cup. He drank half the contents: his thirst seemed endless.

'Everything seems to be happening at once,' Paula commented. 'The tempo is accelerating all round. Newman and Marler on the move. And I don't like the sound of the situation at Rose Bower.'

'I fear the crisis is very close now,' Tweed said gravely.

50

The Sikorsky flew low over Walberswick, slowly circling the area. Hauser stared down out of the window. Serov had reported she'd killed Lennox. What had gone wrong? What was it about this place?

Impossible to locate the cottage, Rose Bower, from the air. The machine flew over the sand dunes and the beach where tourists gazed up at the chopper. Hauser saw the narrow entrance channel leading to the harbour. Boats were moored a fair way inland: the entrance consisted of wooden piles bordering the narrow neck of the channel. No boats moored there.

He nodded to himself. Once again he had to go and look at the target, to spot the weak point. God knew why neither Carver nor Manescu had reported back the safest way to approach Rose Bower. The sea was calm, small waves lapped at the entrance, rolling into the channel, merging further inland into the smooth surface of unruffled water. He gestured to the for'ard guard.

'Tell the pilot to head back for Livingstone Manor. I would appreciate it if he'd use what passes for his head. Fly direct inland before he alters course, flies south for the helipad. Get to it . . .'

As soon as the machine had landed he jumped out, dipping his head to escape the rotor which was still revolving slowly. He strode back to the study entrance, saw Galvone coming out to meet him.

'Everything is fixed, Chief, for the assault on Rose Bower . . .'

'Come inside. Change of plan. There's only one road in to Walberswick off the main highway.' He sat in his chair, very erect as he stared at Galvone who stood in front of him.

'So, Frank, that means there's only one way out, for Chrissakes. Can't you read a map? The assault squad could be trapped. The obvious approach is from the sea. Cancel the attack overland. Send the squad to Harwich, tell them to board the *Washington IV*. They take the big powerboat – and make sure they have the large rubber dinghy with outboard. They wait till after dark, then move up the coast to Walberswick.'

'Might be difficult to find Walberswick in the night.' Galvone suggested.

'My God! Do I have to draw a blueprint with every tiny detail? The skipper provides them with a chart. With the six-man squad travels one of the seamen who knows the coast. I've cruised along it often enough.'

'They're still waiting to leave.' Galvone checked his watch. 'I'd better send them off by car so they do have plenty of time.'

'By car?' Singular? You're a case for brain surgery. If six men turn up at Harwich together, board the vessel as a team, they may be spotted by the Harbour Master. They are a tough-looking bunch.' He smiled, not pleasantly. 'So Frank, they travel to Harwich at intervals, in three cars, two men to a car. Got it?'

'Sounds sensible.' Galvone, about to leave, hesitated.

'You've something on your mind. Spit it out.'

'All that explosive – the Semtex – we have in the cellar. Shouldn't we shift it away from here?'

'Why? It's the last place anyone would think of looking. And I carry clout here. The factories I've built in depressed areas provided employment. We move it out as it's needed in Europe – stashed in frozen food containers. The Brits are watching for drugs and explosives coming in, not going *out*.'

'It was clever bringing in the stuff gradually from Libya in private luggage from the *Washington IV*.'

Galvone had decided it was time to soothe Hauser. Once again he had miscalculated the psychology of his boss.

'Sure it was clever, Frank. Something you'd never have dreamed up. Which is why I'm a billionaire and you're getting by on $300,000 a year. Now go organize the new plan for that squad. And remember, they're strong-arm men, so not too bright in the head. Spell it out very clearly.'

Alone in his study he strolled restlessly. He had been careful not to let Galvone know the *Washington IV* was due to sail early the following morning. There should have been someone snooping round Livingstone Manor by now, maybe even calling on him. The apparent inactivity of Tweed was getting on his nerves.

Inside Newman's South Ken flat at Beresforde Road Marler sat up on the bed in the small room at the front leading off the living room. He had just woken from taking a catnap. He swung his legs on to the carpet, stood up, tucked his shirt back inside his slacks, went into the living room en route to the bathroom.

Newman was walking round the large room, hands in his trouser pockets. He checked his watch as Marler appeared.

'You should get a bit of kip, chum,' Marler advised.

'Sleeping in the daytime just knocks me out.'

Marler swilled his face with cold water in the bathroom, combed his hair. When he returned to the living room Newman was still pacing. Marler straddled a dining chair, lit a cigarette.

'Your trouble goes back to the days when you were a foreign correspondent,' he observed. 'Always on the move. You're like a caged panther. Relax.'

'Don't feel like it. We'd better have something to eat. There's a hotel nearby where we can get a near edible meal. You wouldn't want to sample my cooking – not that I feel up to boiling an egg in this heat.'

'And since I'm not partial to food poisoning, I agree. We go out.'

Marler was aware of the tension inside the flat as he put on his jacket. Newman was wondering what might be waiting for them at Livingstone Manor.

Chief Inspector Buchanan made a detour before visiting Adam Carver's flat. He was intrigued by the difficulty of tracing Papa Grimwood, the man who had accompanied the dead Steve to the original interview at Evelyn Lennox's flat in Wandsworth.

He parked on a yellow line in the side street off Shaftesbury Avenue in front of the entrance to the only INCUBUS offices in London. Warden made his obervation as Buchanan locked the car.

'We're on a yellow line.'

'I had noticed. Where else do you suggest we park? We're not causing an inconvenience in this quiet street. Let us see whether we can dig up some information here. When you called you said they'd never heard of Fraternal and Equality.'

Buchanan showed his warrant card to the rather dim-looking girl receptionist. He spoke to her as he might to a sixteen-year-old, but politely.

'I want to see the managing director of Fraternal & Equality Insurance. If you've never heard of it I'll see whoever is in charge here.'

'That's Mr Humble. Only appointed a few weeks ago. I'll tell him you're here.'

Buchanan followed her as she knocked on a door with the top half an opaque window of glazed glass. Everything about the place had an old fashioned, run-down atmosphere. A deliberate ploy?

He walked in behind the girl and a middle-aged man wearing gold rimmed glasses glanced up from behind his old wooden desk, frowning at the intrusion.

'It's all right now,' Buchanan told the girl, 'I'll take over from here. If you'd be good enough to close the door and go back to reception.'

'You can't come in here like this.'

Humble was an appropriate name, Buchanan decided as he again showed his warrant card. The managing director had a squeaky voice. Trying to show indignation, he sounded ridiculous. Buchanan hauled forward a rickety chair, sat down cautiously. Warden, notebook in hand, leaned against a wall.

'I don't understand what you could want,' Humble went on. 'We haven't had a break-in or anything like that. Perhaps you have the wrong address?' he added hopefully.

'Company records in the City show this address as the registered office of Fraternal & Equality Insurance. So

509

you must be managing the company,' Buchanan said, framing the statement positively.

'It is a small part of our business, as I understand it. I'm new here . . .'

'Papa Grimwood is one of your chief operatives. He goes round with a man we've identified as Steve Reilly.'

'I've never heard of either of those names.'

'Then you won't mind our looking at your employment records, I'm sure. Of course, you can refuse. But then I would obtain a search warrant – and inform Mr Franklin D. Hauser of my action.'

'I've never seen Mr Hauser. I'd sooner you didn't communicate with him.' Humble was agitated. 'Certainly you can examine the employment records. No search warrant is necessary. I am only too anxious to co-operate with the police. But it could take you some time. There are a lot of ledgers.'

Buchanan glanced at Warden who had just finished scribbling in his notebook. The sergeant nodded, confirming that he had carefully recorded the managing director's statement.

'A lot of ledgers,' Humble repeated. 'The one thing I know about Mr Hauser is he doesn't trust computers. He says they can be "hacked" – I think that's the word. We store them in this back room. Please come with me . . .'

Beyond the doorway Buchanan and Warden stared. The room was lined with wooden shelves. The shelves were jammed with ledgers, wall to wall. Humble excused himself, left them alone. Buchanan stripped off his jacket, placed it over the back of a wooden chair which had seen better days.

'Come on, Warden. We'd better make a start. At least the spines of the ledgers have a description.'

'Funny, sir,' said Warden, following his chief's example, 'I thought INCUBUS was one of the most modern organizations in the world.'

'It is. This is just a front outfit, but from the few spines I've read so far it's Fraternity and Equality . . .'

It took them ages to locate the Executives ledger. Buchanan found Leopold Grimwood. With an address in Pimlico. Warden noted down the details.

'Why is Grimwood so important?' he asked.

'From what we've heard this so-called pension fund is a form of blackmail and extortion. If we can break down Grimwood we may just get the evidence for a case against Hauser. I stress the word "just".'

'Where to now?' Warden asked as Buchanan settled behind the wheel of their car.

'Carver's flat in Chelsea first. Heaven knows when we will reach Galvone's apartment near Regent's Park. And after all that work, radio in Grimwood's address – with a request that a couple of men are sent to bring him in for questioning.'

Warden was reaching for the microphone when the message from Tweed transmitted via the Yard reached Buchanan.

For the fifth time Paula stood up from her desk and gazed out of the window at the night, her arms folded. Tweed looked up from the old file on his desk.

'You're restless.'

'I know.' Paula swung round as Monica watched her. 'I can't keep still. Surely there's something we can do – instead of just sitting around waiting.'

'It's getting to you, isn't it?' Tweed smiled. 'So if it's getting to you what effect do you think it will be having on Hauser? I've been on his tail ever since I arrived in Finland. He'll guess I've tracked him back to England by now. He's smart. So he'll expect me to do something. Instead nothing happens. It's what one of our famous generals once called masterly inactivity.'

'It's driving me up the wall,' Paula snapped.

'So let's hope Hauser is up there with you.'

An hour later the Special Branch courier arrived with the files Peggy Vanderheld had handed over to Butler. He apologized for the long delay. Traffic jams, the traffic solid during the holiday season. Tweed opened one file, his mind elsewhere.

He was worried about Newman and Marler. He took the decision suddenly. Picking up the phone he dialled Buchanan's number at the Yard. A policewoman answered and Tweed thought the voice was familiar.

'Sergeant Murray-Browne speaking. Can I help? Who is calling?'

'My name is Tweed . . .'

'Hello, Mr Tweed. I came with Chief Inspector Buchanan to see you once when Sergeant Warden was off colour. Is there something I can do to help?'

'I need to speak to the Chief Inspector urgently.'

'I'm afraid he's been out on a job for hours. I might be able to contact him. He has a radio in his car.'

'The message is urgent. He knows the Chief Constable of Suffolk. I don't know the new man. Could he contact the Chief Constable, ask him to send as many patrol cars with armed officers as he can muster to the vicinity of Livingstone Manor? No screaming sirens. A silent approached is vital.'

'I'll pass on the message as soon as I can reach him on the radio. Is that all, Mr Tweed?'

'That's all. Emphasize the officers should be armed.'

He turned his attention back to the files. He was skip-reading the last one when Cord Dillon came into the office. Monica asked him if he'd like some coffee and he said he'd be grateful. He sagged into a chair. Tweed handed him the files.

'These came in from Vanderheld. She's been holding out on us. They're fascinating, but I can't see anything

512

which could put Hauser in the dock, here or in America.'

'I can tell you that would be near impossible without reading them – although I'm going to do that. Hauser has so many judges in his pocket I doubt we'd ever get a conviction. But I'll look . . .'

Five minutes later the phone rang. Tweed picked it up, wondering who it could be at that hour. It was Marler.

'I'm calling just before we leave Newman's flat. He's in the loo. Have you got – or do you think you'll ever get – evidence to put Hauser behind bars?'

'Odd you should ask that now. You must be psychic. Is there a reason?'

'I always have a reason for asking a question. Are you going to answer it? And I'm in a hurry.'

'Hold on thirty seconds.' Tweed looked at Dillon. He knew the American had taken a fast-reading course. He was already scanning the remaining pages of the last file. 'Cord, what do you think now you've looked at the files?'

'What I thought before. One or two things stand out – but a smart attorney could rubbish them. And Hauser has the best attorneys in the States on his payroll.'

Tweed took a deep breath, removed his hand from the phone.

'The answer is no.'

'Thank you.'

The connection was broken. Tweed put down the receiver, stood up. He looked at Paula.

'I'm driving out to Suffolk myself now. You can come if you want to. I don't want to get back and find you swinging from the proverbial chandelier.'

'Action at last.'

Paula opened a lower drawer in her desk, took out her bag, slipped her .32 Browning inside with spare mags

513

under cover of the desk. As she stood up she saw Tweed checking his 7.65 mm Walther automatic. She had hardly ever known him to carry a gun. He slipped it inside his jacket pocket as Dillon also stood up.

'And I'm coming with you folks. No argument. Something is breaking. I can smell it.'

'Will we arrive soon after Newman and Marler?' Paula asked.

'Not by a long chalk,' Tweed told her. 'Not the way Newman drives.'

51

At two-thirty in the morning Hauser was working in his study, checking the clauses in the agreement for the sale of the Street & Braithwaite bank in Southampton. He had been careful not to let either Carver or Galvone know that he was sailing aboard the *Washington IV* by 7.30 a.m. Destination: Boston.

He couldn't be sure why his instinct told him it was time to leave Britain. He disliked the decision: his HQ at Livingstone Manor was ideally equipped. But he had survived so far by always obeying his instinct. He pressed the intercom switch.

'Adam, come and see me. My study. Now.'

Another inconvenience was having the French doors shut and locked. It was becoming unbearably foetid inside the room. But with only four guards available he had sensed it would be foolish to leave those doors open.

'What can I do for you, sir?' Adam asked as he stood in front of the desk.

He noticed Hauser was freshly shaven, had changed his clothes. He assumed it was the heat. Hauser pushed the sheaf of papers across the desk.

'Make an appointment to meet with Street today. See him while he's still shocked by that IRA bomb. Don't come back without his signature on the agreement.'

He studied Carver. The Englishman was clad in one of his silk suits, a pale blue check. No wonder he could make it with almost any woman. Well, he was going to have to do without his dinner date with Evelyn Lennox. Unless he wanted to dine with a corpse.

'I'll take this into the living room, master it before I get a few hours' kip.'

'Use the library upstairs. Not the living room. I want to use it myself for a conference. Get moving.'

A conference? At this hour? Carver shrugged to himself as he climbed the wide winding staircase from the hall. The billionaire seemed to live without sleep. The secret of his success, Carver thought as he closed the library door, settled himself in a chair and began studying the agreement.

The phone rang just before Hauser left his study. He let it ring several times. He wasn't expecting a call at this time of night. He picked up the receiver.

'Who is it?'

'Mr Franklin D. Hauser, I believe. This is Robert Newman. Hope I'm not disturbing your beauty sleep – I thought there was something you ought to know.'

'Say your piece, then drop off a cliff.'

'I thought you'd like to know a vital clue has been discovered in the investigation into the cold-blooded murder of Sandra Riverton. A button torn from a Daks overcoat. From what we call a British warm. The button carries the Daks symbol.'

'Are you drunk? What the hell is this?'

'I found the button among the straw at the bottom of

the bell tower where she was murdered. I've left it there. It's evidence for the police to find when daylight comes. Sleep well . . .'

Hauser cursed as the connection was broken. He stood for several mintues thinking, then walked rapidly down the long passage to the hall. Turning into the living room, he unlocked the door, closed it behind him, ran down the steps and along the flagstones of the cellar passage floor. Opening the door to Manescu's suite, he walked inside. The Romanian was again stretched out on the couch, reading a newspaper. As Hauser came in he was loosening his necktie, taking it off to combat the heat. He stood up slowly while Hauser waited: he expected swifter demonstrations of respect from his minions.

'Some problem?' Manescu enquired.

Waiting for an answer, he played with the necktie, twisting the cloth into a rope-like skein. His swarthy chin was disfigured with a dark stubble.

'Get a shave,' Hauser snapped. 'That's your first problem. And I've had a phone call from that crazy reporter, Robert Newman. Says he's found a button torn from what he called a British warm inside the bell-tower. So, when it's daylight, maybe you'd better poke around, see if you can find any button. And then later in the afternoon you're flying to Belgrade. Keep the cauldron on the boil. Your ticket is in the pseudonym you're operating under at the moment.'

He threw down the airline folder on a coffee table. At the door he turned round.

'I'm leaving this unlocked. Don't start prowling inside the house.'

Continuing along the passage, he unlocked the door leading to Irina Serov's suite. She was fully dressed, seated in front of her dressing table mirror. Dropping her lipstick, she jumped up to face the American.

'Change of plan. Like Manescu, you're leaving earlier –

this afternoon. You catch a flight for Munich. Here is your ticket. You know what you have to do. Set the Ukraine ablaze. And this door will stay unlocked. You leave at eleven in the morning.'

'Understood . . .'

She was talking to the air. Hauser had gone. He climbed the steps, closed the door, walked to his desk in the living room, pressed the intercom switch.

'That you, Frank? Get down here. Adam, you heard what I said? Why aren't you here then?'

Hauser was seated behind his desk when the two men entered. He wiped the back of his thick neck with a handkerchief. How did Adam Carver keep so slick-looking in this heat? But it was good to have someone around who kept himself smart. Galvone was freshly shaven, but otherwise he looked a crumpled mess in his soiled shirt and denims.

'I just had a phone call from Newman,' he told them. 'In the middle of the night. He's crazy as a coot – I think he was bluffing too. Said he'd found a button torn from a British warm on the floor of that bell tower. That he'd left it there for the police to find in the morning. A pretty feeble war of nerves. But that tells me Tweed is back. So what the hell is he and his gang of killers doing?'

Adam Carver thought that remark was priceless – coming from Hauser with Galvone standing in the room. Hauser looked at Carver.

'You've got your red Jaguar fuelled up with gasoline for your trip to Southampton in mid-morning?'

'A full tank,' Carver assured him.

'Frank, you're flying back to Helsinki. To open up that HQ again. Tweed will never guess I'd make it operational so soon. There's your ticket. Don't miss the flight. Now, leave me alone, both of you.'

Fetching a jug of ice water from the fridge built in with the cocktail bar, he poured a large glass, drained it. He checked his watch. He'd dealt with everything now. No, there was one more vital detail to check. He walked down the passage into his study, unlocked the French windows, nodded to two guards as he hurried across the lawn to the chopper stationed on the helipad.

'That machine OK?' he shouted up to the pilot.

'Ready and rarin' to go.'

'Show me. Lift off, then land again.'

The rotors spun, the engine throbbed, the chopper elevated, circled over the grounds, made a perfect landing on the helipad. The pilot slid back the window, grinned.

'Satisfied?'

'Take that smirk off your face. Complacency I can do without. You'll be flying me to the *Washington IV*?'

'Sure thing, sir. Just came on duty. Met. reports indicate a smooth flight.'

'It had better be.'

Off the coast of East Anglia the powerboat was stationary. The helmsman waited as six heavily built men put the big dinghy with the outboard over the side, transferred to it weapons with silencers, tear-gas pistols loaded with lethal nerve gas shells, then climbed aboard themselves.

The squad leader carried a map of Walberswick with Rose Bower marked with a pencil cross. They'd moor the dinghy to the harbour entrance, make their way across the sand dunes to The Street, the country road where Rose Bower was located. Do the job, set fire to the place with the cans of gasoline already stashed aboard, head back for the dinghy. He estimated the job would be accomplished in thirty minutes. At the outside.

The man at the stern started up the outboard. He steered the dinghy for the harbour entrance. It was a moonless night. That would just help a little more, the leader of the squad thought, as the dinghy rode the small waves and the wooden piles came closer.

Marler had lied to Tweed when he told him Newman was in the loo. Newman had earlier driven to the Old Kent Road to collect Alf Higgins. As soon as the Mercedes had arrived back Marler, carrying a large canvas satchel with an adjustable strap, had climbed in beside Newman. Higgins, hands clenched tightly, sat silent in the back for most of the journey.

They were driving across Suffolk before Newman asked his question in a whisper. The headlight beams, undimmed, illuminated a traffic-free road lined with hedges. For the last hour they had not seen a single other vehicle.

'What are you carrying in that heavy satchel?' Newman asked.

'A couple of gadgets Alf gave me,' Marler whispered back. 'Plus some toys I brought back from that explosives course I attended at the country house near Amersham.'

'You're expecting to use that stuff?'

'No idea. Until we get there, see what the set-up is. Be prepared is my motto. Didn't know I was once a Boy Scout, did you?'

'A less suitable member I can't imagine . . .'

He slowed down as they came within a mile of Livingstone Manor. The clock on the dashboard registered 2.30 a.m.

'We're nearly there,' he told Marler.

'I know. Didn't I tell you? One evening after we returned from Finland I drove out here alone on a recce. It was after Monica told me about the cipher machines and all that equipment she'd found Hauser had installed.'

'What kind of a recce?' Newman pressed.

'Oh, the normal kind. After dark I penetrated the

grounds, circled Hauser's Georgian mansion. I counted nine guards. We'll have to tread a little carefully. And if we meet one of those guards leave him to me. I called in at a sleazy night club on my way to your flat. The type of place the so-called aristocracy patronizes for their illegal kicks.'

'What the devil are you talking about?'

'With luck you'll never know. We should park the car – turn in to that field behind those trees. We're close. Take a deep breath, Newman, it's starting . . .'

Butler had led Evelyn and Peggy to the bottom of the back garden behind Rose Bower. Now their eyes had become used to the dark they could see where they were placing their feet safely. Each woman wore a high-necked overall supplied by Evelyn. Over their heads they had pulled pale grey waterproof hoods Evelyn used for gardening in damp weather.

'Find some protective clothing if you can,' Butler had asked Evelyn earlier. 'And two pairs of slacks – if you think one of yours would fit Peggy . . .'

Both women now wore slacks under the overalls as Butler held up a hand to halt them. It was the appearance of the helicopter flying low over Walberswick which had warned both Butler and Nield that they might all be in mortal danger before the night was out.

Butler, wearing gardening gloves, carefully parted clumps of brambles at the edge of the garden, held them while the two women passed through. They waited on the verge of a field and Butler showed them their hiding place.

'There's a large ditch almost covered over with grasses. I want you to lie down in it, pull the grasses over yourselves and keep very quiet. Even if you hear men coming don't move a muscle. And you may hear bursts of gunfire.

That will be me shooting at them. Whatever you do, don't get curious, look up to try and see what's happening . . .'

He waited until both women were stretched out inside the wide ditch. Leaning down, he pulled more grasses over them. There had been no rain for weeks so the ditch was bone dry. The only problem was it could be crawling with insects. He hoped the protective clothing would shield them from any creepy-crawlies.

'Where is Nield?' Evelyn whispered.

'He's out front, keeping watch. I'll be nearby. You may be there for quite a time. Try and relax.'

'Maybe you'd like us to go to sleep?' Peggy called out ironically.

'That's right,' Butler told her. 'Have a nice nap.'

He crept back along the side of the garden, stopped at a point half-way to the house. Looping his weapon over his back, he climbed an old oak tree he had discovered earlier. Perching himself in a crook between two thick boughs, he checked his field of fire. From here he was able to cover the entire back garden. Any men exploring the back garden would be point-blank targets for his gun. He settled down to wait.

Marler was also high up a tree he had climbed at a corner of the spacious grounds. Before leaving the Mercedes he had stripped off his jacket and donned a boiler suit of a neutral colour which merged with the foliage. From one of the capacious pockets he had extracted binoculars and he was scanning the grounds close to the mansion.

He had sat on a branch for over half an hour and was puzzled. During the whole of that vigil he had only seen three guards patrolling. They moved round the house separately and so large was the mansion each man reappeared at intervals of ten minutes.

During his previous recce he had counted nine guards. At that time they had patrolled in pairs – two couples moving close to the mansion while the rest prowled across the grounds, frequently walking the perimeter. One man had passed under his tree, but no one ever looked *up*, a phenomenon he had observed in the centre of cities.

Where the devil were the other six guards? Marler doubted that they were all inside. If so many men were available the smart thing was to position the majority outside. *If* they were available.

It was then he noticed the absence of something. There were only three cars parked on the gravel circle by the far corner of the house. A red Jag. A stretched black limo – undoubtedly Hauser's. And a red Cadillac. When he had watched before he had counted nine cars of various makes. Marler's patience was endless: to make sure he waited a little longer.

Inside the Mercedes Newman's patience was anything but endless. He sat with all the windows open, drumming his fingers on the wheel, checking his watch every five minutes. In the back Alf Higgins stirred.

'These jobs take time,' he observed. 'Can't rush 'em. That way you get caught. Mr 'Enderson knows his stuff.'

'Glad to hear it,' Newman said brusquely.

'Knew a chap like you once,' Higgins went on obstinately. 'Was doin' a job in Lunnon. I told 'im 'e was in too much of a bloody 'urry. Case the place proper, I says. Wouldn't listen. Know where 'e is now? Servin' a ten-year stretch in Strangeways.'

'A very comforting thought at this moment.'

'Just tryin' to be 'elpful. Why not get out, walk about a bit? Some people gets stiff, sittin' in a car.'

Newman decided he would take this bit of advice. Opening the door, he stepped out on to the grass. He walked slowly back to the road, listening for any sound of traffic coming. And Marler appeared, having approached without making a sound.

'Time you started working for your living, chum,' he told the irate Newman.

52

Pete Nield stood outside Rose Bower, holding a large briefcase he had borrowed from Evelyn. It was very quiet in The Street, so quiet he could *hear* the heavy silence of an early morning when the air was still turgid with the heat of the previous day.

He looked back at the cottage he was supposed to guard. There were no lights, the front door was locked and bolted. Nield was fighting with his instinct. He had followed it so often before and been proved right.

Taking a firmer grip on the briefcase, he left his post, began walking rapidly towards where the village ended, towards the sea. As he turned on to the track leading to the wilderness of dunes and grasses a hint of a breeze touched his face. He quickened his pace, leaving behind the darkened houses.

He stopped suddenly, undecided. Butler was relying on him to provide back-up. And the two men had been partners in more than one desperate situation. It seemed like an act of desertion. As he stood there, about to turn back, the only sound was the gentle whisper of the grasses, moved by the breeze. The only sound? He waited a moment longer, certain his ears had deceived him.

Then he heard it again. The faint sound of an engine. From the direction of the sea, the enemy. Since his first exploration of Walberswick as a refuge he had always been convinced the sea was the enemy. He moved off the track, plodding as fast as he could across the rough territory of the dunes, the treacherous powdery sand. He climbed one dune to try and get a view over the long barrier of the shingle bank.

He blinked, closed his eyes, opened them again quickly. Above the barrier a belt of calm sea stretched away. He caught the wisp of white as the faint engine sound died. The wake of a powerboat? Or was it all his imagination? He looked back. Butler would be on his own if they came by car, pulled up outside Rose Bower and rushed the cottage.

Much against his will he plodded on over the dunes, the tang of salty air much stronger. Then he was climbing the slippery shingle bank overlooking the beach and the harbour entrance. He stood there, alone in the world of the night and the sea, staring out to catch a glimmer of navigation lights. Nothing. He waited, checked the illuminated dial of his watch. It had taken him ten minutes to reach this spot from the cottage. He would wait three more minutes and then run all the way back, stumbling over the dunes.

He heard the faint burst of the engine starting up – but it had a different sound from the earlier one. He sat on the shingle bank, decided he could still be seen as a silhouette through night glasses, huddled down behind the top of the bank.

A fresh burst of another engine starting up, which promptly died. What the hell was going on? Now he could identify the chug-chug of an outboard motor approaching the harbour. The skipper of the powerboat, the mother ship, had tested his engine, switched it off. But the chug-chug was growing louder.

Now he could see the growing arrow wake of the incoming boat. From his jacket pocket he hauled out the night glasses Tweed always insisted his men carried. Crouched out of sight, he focused them just in front of the wake. God! It was an outsize rubber dinghy. Powered by an outboard. Six men aboard. All wearing what looked like pea jackets, peaked caps. Carrying what looked like automatic rifles.

Nield felt a surge of exhilaration. He had guessed right. The attackers were coming in from the sea – as he had always predicted they would. If they were hostile. Nield was in a dilemma. It was summer. Tourists sometimes liked a novelty. Sailing across a millpond sea in the middle of the night. And he couldn't feel sure they were carrying automatic rifles.

The dinghy loomed larger, seemed to be heading straight for the harbour entrance. Nield gritted his teeth in frustration. How to be sure they were not getting ready to sail down the entrance between the piles, aiming for their berth further inland after an evening cruise up the coast? Then he remembered the powerboat.

He stood up in full view, cupped his hands, bellowed at the top of his voice:

'Cut your engine immediately or I'll blow you out of the water . . .'

He dropped flat behind the bank as he ended his warning. And as he dropped the bullets began to fly from the dinghy, a steady fusillade which was alarmingly accurate. One silenced bullet winged past the right side of his skull as he disappeared below his makeshift parapet. He heard others hammering the shingle in front of him. One pebble whipped into the air, spun down within inches of his left foot.

Nield hauled the Uzi machine-pistol out of the briefcase. The weapon, brought by the Special Branch courier, held a magazine of forty rounds, fired at a rate of six hundred rounds a minute. Nield rested the muzzle on top of the shingle bank, aimed at the lower hull of the rubber dinghy, pressed the trigger. A hail of bullets hammered into the craft, above and below the waterline.

Nield rammed in a fresh mag, saw the dinghy topple to starboard, empty the six men into the sea, capsize, vanishing below the surface. He fired again, aiming above the bobbing heads, some of which were swimming towards the shore. They reversed course, began swimming out to sea, in the hope of reaching the distant powerboat, no more than a speck to Nield's eyes.

He inserted a new mag, opened fire again, aiming always over the bobbing head, the flailing arms. He saw two heads sink without resurfacing. Not from his fire – must be poor swimmers.

He stood up to get a better view. Four heads now, then another one sank into oblivion. Nield shoved the Uzi back inside the briefcase. Time to get away from there quick. He took one last look out to sea. Only two of the bobbing heads remained in view. Nield turned away, shrugged.

'So what?' he said to himself. 'They were all killers, bent on massacre.'

When he entered the back garden of Rose Bower, in search of the two women, Butler jumped down from the oak tree.

'You look tense,' he commented. 'Run into anything?'

53

Marler, Newman and Higgins crept along the front of the mansion close to the wall. They had climbed the same tree, dropped over the wire fence surrounding the estate, approaching Livingstone Manor from the outer perimeter.

Marler had given the go-ahead after seeing a guard disappear round the side of the building. They had ten minutes to get inside before another guard appeared. The windows they were passing faced out from the living room: Newman recalled this fact from his visit in February. He whispered the information to his companions.

'I'll check to see if there's any one in there,' Higgins whispered back.

From his pocket he produced an instrument like a stethoscope, plugged one end against a pane of glass, listened through the earpiece at the other end. Newman checked his watch. They were way behind schedule: Marler had taken so long before returning to the Mercedes. And now Higgins was taking up more time. He pulled gently at the rubber sucker, freed it from the glass.

'No one in that room.'

'How can you be sure?' Newman demanded.

'Very sensitive, this gadget. Can pick up a man turning the pages of a newspaper. Shifting 'is position in an armchair. I guarantees it. No one in there. Now open that front door,' he told Marler. 'Don't 'urry it . . .'

Newman swore inwardly. They'd had an argument earlier before leaving the Merc. Higgins had insisted the front door was the place no one expected a break-in. He examined the solid slab of wood, the edges with the aid of a pencil flash.

'No alarms. Get stuck in.'

Marler confronted the three locks, selected a key for the lowest lock, inserted it slowly, cocked his head to listen. He heard the lock opening. He had the other two locks open faster than he'd expected. Higgins handed a small torch-like instrument to Newman. He whispered the warning.

'That's the little jigger I tells you about in the car.

Detects electronic beams. Switch it on and it kills the beam for thirty seconds – and no alarm goes off.'

'And you're coming in with us . . .' Marler began.

He was too late. Higgins had sprinted past the curtained windows masking the lights behind them, was taking off his jacket as he ran. Presumably to form a cushion when he scaled the wire fence, climbed back into the tree.

'I'll take over,' Newman said. 'I know the layout.'

He held his Smith & Wesson by his side in his right hand and hoped to God he wouldn't have to press the trigger. Its silent use as a blunt instrument was a different matter. He turned the handle slowly, eased the door open. Well oiled, it made no sound. The gap widened and he had a view of the large hall, the deserted staircase curving upwards, the long passage leading to another room at the back. The door to the room was open and there was a light on inside.

He checked his watch. Nine minutes. A guard would come round the front very soon. Jerking his head to Marler, he stepped over the doormat – in case there was a pressure pad underneath. He closed the door very carefully as Marler stood against a wall, his right hand by his side, his left concealing a small canister. Both men were wearing rubber-soled shoes as Newman crossed the hall, peered inside the living room. Higgins had been right: it was empty.

Leaving the door open, he went inside. There were no electronic beams in this room: he had observed that on his previous visit. He gestured towards the door let into the inner wall. Marler studied the lock, tried one key. No result. Selecting another key, he fiddled it, again heard nothing. The third key was too large. Newman reached past him, turned the handle slowly, pushed. The door opened, exposing a flight of stone steps leading down into the cellars.

'Let me do a quick recce,' Marler whispered.

Newman waited in the shadows at the head of the steps as Marler crept down them. The stone-flagged passage was illuminated by overhead fluorescents. Holding the 'torch' in front of him, Marler moved down the long passage, passing several alcoves and side passages in darkness.

The guard walked out of a room ahead of Marler, stood, stared at the intruder as Marler slipped the torch inside a pocket. The man was a giant, well over six feet tall, built like a quarterback. In his early thirties, he had his hair trimmed to a stubble. Ex-Marine, Marler thought.

The guard, wearing a singlet and slacks, grinned as he looked down at the small, compact Marler. Eat you alive, he was thinking. He walked forward, huge fists clenched, a holstered gun on his left hip. He expected Marler to back away. Marler ran forward, his right hand with the knuckle dusters over his fingers slammed up, crashed into the large jaw. The guard staggered, dazed, dropped his head as Marler skipped to one side, brought his stiffened left hand down in a chopping movement against the side of the guard's neck. The guard toppled forward, his jaw smashed into the flagstones. He lay still.

Newman ran forward. Marler was checking the neck pulse. He looked up.

'Dead as a doornail. He hit the floor like the Empire State falling. Help me drag him into a side passage . . .'

They had hidden the guard inside the darkness when Marler reached into his pocket. He brought out a small packet, stuffed it inside the guard's trouser pocket.

'What's that?' Newman asked.

'Crack. I bought several packets of the filthy drug at a night club. If he's found while we're still down here it will be assumed he was on drugs, took an overdose, fell and smashed his jaw on the flagstones.'

'Let's explore,' Newman said.

They were further along the passage when they heard the sound of a door opening behind them. Marler had his satchel close to his back on a shortened strap. He followed Newman into the gloom of a side passage. Voices. Feet walking away slowly. Newman peered out. A girl and a man. Faces turned towards each other as they talked. He had studied their photos. Irina Serov and Ion Manescu.

'How do they keep this place so clean?' Manescu asked.

'Servants from th.. ~tside. Locals. But they're here in the daytime only. Hauser won't let them live in . . .'

They walked up the steps. Sounds of the door opening and closing. Newman realized why the door wasn't locked. For some reason the two terrorists – saboteurs, to use Tweed's description – were free to roam around tonight.

'We'll explore some more,' said Newman.

Half-way down the long passage they detected a beam. A red light flashed on in the top of the torch. Marler switched it on. They walked past electronic eyes embedded into the stone walls at ankle height. Just beyond was a locked door.

Marler only succeeded in opening this lock with the third key. They walked into an arched cellar. Stacked along both walls were familiar boxes stencilled with the words 'Frozen Fish'. Marler opened the lid of one box, stared at the grey dough-like substance. Newman lifted another lid. More of the grey dough.

'Semtex,' said Marler. 'I phoned Tweed before we set out. He told me no one could bring Hauser to justice.' He swung his satchel round to his chest, unfastened the strap, placed the satchel on the floor, opened the flap. 'You go outside, close the door, hide in the passage opposite, watch my back.'

530

'What are you going to do.'

'Move, we're short of time . . .'

Newman went outside, closed the door, slipped inside the dark side passage, waited. He seemed to wait for ever and kept checking the illuminated dial of his watch. He heard Manescu and Serov walking back down the passage. Serov was talking, her voice surprisingly feminine and seductive.

'That walk in the grounds was a relief. Now for sleep. We have flights in the afternoon and I want to arrive in Munich fresh. I'll be radioing instructions from there well into the night . . .'

Newman heard one door close, then another. They had separate rooms. He checked his watch again. What the hell was Marler taking all this time over? Newman was determined to be well away from Livingstone Manor by dawn.

The door opened, Marler paused, satchel slung over his back, waited until Newman emerged and beckoned. Closing the door, Marler used the same key but found he couldn't relock it. Something he had forgotten to check with Alf. He glanced further down the passage.

'That door is open a bit,' he whispered.

'Time we left . . .'

'Only take a moment to have a peek inside.'

Marler pushed the door open wider, saw the room was deserted, walked inside. Newman followed, stared at the huge wall map of Europe and Russia, the red pins stabbed into various famous cities.

'My God!' he explained. 'These are the targets for the bombs going off all over Europe. You read the papers.'

'Sometimes. I see there's a pin for Kiev. KGB headquarters was blown up the other day. At least twenty dead.'

'Hauser is a monster,' Newman commented. 'Nothing stands in the way of his pursuit of power. Destabilize,

531

then move in to rebuild on the ruins – rebuild American-style.' He looked at Marler. 'What's that thing you're holding? Looks like a mobile pocket telephone.'

'Complete with press button numbers. Designed by our boffins in the Engine Room at Park Crescent.' He pulled up an aerial. 'They're clever johnnies. This chap is a radio transmitter to detonate a bomb. And there's rather a lot of explosive, I'd say, in that cellar next door. I press the numbers for the right code – in this case 142 – and the radio signal is transmitted to the bomb.'

'You fixed all that up while you were in the cellar?'

'Not quite. I had a device inside my satchel. Involved a certain amount of advance preparation. You've forgotten the Semtex I pinched from the truck north of Porvoo, then later from the Lapland Institute. Hadn't we better take our leave of this de luxe millionaire's property, as the estate agent chappies say?'

'Immediately. What is that transmitter for?'

'Purely a precaution. In case we meet a little opposition on the way out. When I've explained the position I think they'll be happy to escort us off the premises.'

'Then let's move. Now!'

Tweed drove the new Volvo station wagon Howard had sanctioned at speed along the winding road. Beside him Paula clung to the hand grip as he swerved round a long bend. In the rear seat Cord Dillon sat chewing an unlit cigar.

'I think we're pretty close to Livingstone Manor now,' Paula said. 'I recognized that bend you've just flown this aircraft round.'

'I'm worried,' Tweed snapped, keeping up the same speed. 'We haven't seen any police patrol cars. They should be in position by now.'

'They may be concealed,' she mused. 'Although the

532

way you're driving I'd have expected one to stop you.'

'Lord knows what risks Newman and Marler are taking – and Hauser is totally ruthless. You're right, we're very close. I'll turn into this field, park behind the copse of trees over there.'

Paula sat up straighter. Tweed had parked, switched off the engine.

'Look, there's Bob's Mercedes . . .'

She jumped out, ran to the stationary car. A figure stirred in the back, opened the door, stepped out. He touched his forelock.

'Mornin' to you, ma'am. George Budge at your service,' said Alfred Higgins. 'Just 'aving forty winks. Stupid to drive at night when you're tired. Your feller doesn't 'alf get a move on . . .'

Many miles behind Tweed, Chief Inspector Buchanan was also exceeding the speed limit. It seemed to Warden seated beside him that they were negotiating dangerous bends on two wheels.

'We'll get there eventually, sir,' he ventured.

'*Eventually* may be too late. I took too long persuading Tweed's assistant, Monica, to tell me where she thought Newman had gone. He's a man motivated by revenge for the murder of his girl friend, Sandy. I think he's identified the killer.'

'You can't be sure of that, sir.'

'I'm not sure, I'm certain. So was Monica. It's that damned coat button.'

'Well, you're behind the wheel.'

'Your powers of observation astound me,' Buchanan responded and rammed his foot down further.

54

Marler and Newman had almost got clear of Livingstone Manor when they ran out of luck. Marler had climbed the tree at the corner of the estate, dropped to the ground. Newman was following, climbing the trunk from branch to branch when he heard the sound of automatic rifle fire. He glanced back. One of the guards had appeared, must have seen the movement of the foliage, had perhaps found the front door unlocked.

Bullets spattered the foliage as Newman desperately moved faster. A shower of leaves whisked across his face. That was close. He reached the overhang branch, risked a final look back. A second guard held a rifle to his shoulder. As he dropped the foliage was shattered with a hail of gunfire.

'Across the road,' Marler shouted as Newman dropped beside him. 'The ground rises. There's another tree copse. If we can reach that we can mow them down as they cross open ground . . .'

They ran across the hedge-free road straight into a field of wheat, ran uphill planting their feet flat to avoid turning an ankle. Marler moved like a four-minute miler with Newman close behind, climbing all the time. They dived inside the copse, Marler looked up, chose an exceptionally tall chestnut, began to shin up it with the agility of a monkey, his satchel flapping against his back.

As Newman climbed after him he heard a car start up from the direction of Livingstone Manor. It drove closer, then moved further away for a short distance. Newman heard the engine sound change and not far away it seemed to be driven on a course parallel to the one they had taken running up the hill. He paused, tried to see the car, but the foliage smothered his view. The engine stopped as he followed Marler who was climbing an incredible height.

He found Marler straddled across a branch with an open view clear down the hill, over the grounds and beyond the roof of Livingstone Manor. Marler had binoculars pressed to his eyes. Newman perched on the same thick branch, leant against the trunk of the tree.

'Hauser is running for it,' Marler warned. 'He's got a small chopper, Sikorsky, I think, at the end of the estate. He's boarding the bloody machine.'

'He's going to get away. The top man always escapes,' said Newman.

He leaned forward. Police patrol cars had appeared out of nowhere. One was approaching the open grille gates as a guard ran out. The guard aimed his automatic rifle at the car, shattered the windscreen. The offside door opened, a policeman jumped out, steadied himself behind the boot, fired twice. The guard was thrown back against one of the stone pillars, leaned there for a moment, sagged to the ground. Other policemen were jumping out of cars as another guard appeared, raised his weapon. One shot rang out. The guard dropped his weapon, slumped to the ground.

The firing ceased, was replaced by another sound, the whirring of the chopper's rotors. The machine elevated slowly from the ground, hovered, then turned south towards Harwich. It was then Newman noticed Marler had his radio transmitter in his hand. The helicopter was passing over Livingstone Manor as Marler punched out the numbers. *142*.

Newman had just checked the time. 5 a.m. Dawn would break at any moment. But first a false dawn broke. The

chopper was still flying over Livingstone Manor when the
world erupted. A tremendous BOOM murdered the last
of the night silence, disturbed now only by the steady
chug-chug of the chopper. The mansion came apart, was
hurled upwards in flying chunks of masonry. The
shockwave of the detonation shook the helicopter, which
suddenly seemed to hover. A flaming curtain of red
soared upwards, enveloping the machine. Newman saw it
sink into the shattered relic of the mansion which now had
only two walls standing. He thought he saw Hauser's
chopper hit the ground a second before one of the walls
crumbled inwards, burying it. Then the smoke came,
blotting out the carnage.

'This little jigger has a range of over two miles, I'm
told,' Marler remarked. He looked where the mansion
had once stood.

'In any case, it was second-rate Georgian architecture.'

Newman was clambering down the tree, smashing off
twigs in his rapid progress. Marler stared down, called
out.

'Where are you going?'

'I have an appointment. With a murderer.'

55

It was going to end as it had started. In the same place. At
the bell tower. For several days Newman had thought it
would be like this. What he was not prepared for was how
like February it would be.

Dawn was breaking in the east, bands of deep blue and
gold. Another heatwave day. Toiling up the track he

536

stopped, almost transfixed, disbelieving. Parked near the gaunt bell tower was a red Jaguar. Just as Sandy's red Jaguar had been parked when, buoyantly on a bitter frosty February day, he had strode up this same track to meet her.

He shook himself, like a man emerging from a nightmare. Tired, dirty, clothes torn, hands bleeding from twigs which had grazed his hands, he took a deep breath, strode faster up to the bell tower.

It was the same, but it was different. Before it had been winter, now it was glorious summer, a summer Sandy would have loved. He flexed his aching fingers as he came over the last rise, saw inside the bell tower. Moving on to the grass verge, he advanced silently.

Inside the bell tower a man was on his knees, his back to Newman, scrabbling among the straw, searching for something. Newman was within two yards of the bell tower when the man glanced over his shoulder, jumped to his feet.

'What was that terrible explosion?' asked Adam Carver.

'You've messed up your nice silk suit,' Newman said in a cold voice. 'Would this be what you are looking for?'

He held up the button he had torn from his own British warm, the button carrying the DAKS symbol. Carver waved both hands in a gesture of incomprehension.

'What are you talking about? Why should a button concern me?'

'Because Sandy tore this button from your coat when she struggled for her life before you hung her like a common felon from that beam up there. Up there, Carver. Above your head.'

Instinctively Carver glanced up. Newman moved forward. Carver looked for escape, stared through one of the arched openings, saw the car approaching, bumping up the track. He turned, grasped the sides of the ladder, ran

537

up it. Newman reached for his ankle, missed it, began mounting the shaking ladder himself.

Looking up he saw Carver's foot aimed at his head, ducked just in time. Carver continued his climb, reached the wooden platform close to the hanging beam. He was in such a rush he slipped on the straw scattered across the platform, sprawled full length.

Newman stepped on to the high platform as Carver jumped up, faced him. Newman showed him the button a second time. Both men stood quite still for several seconds.

'You're Hauser's hired assassin,' Newman told him. 'You killed Ed Riverton, garrotted the poor bastard, then threw him into the ice of North Harbour to be crushed by the icebreaker. You're a fast mover, I'll give you that. You next caught a plane to London, drove up here after making an appointment with Sandy for dawn. You want to know how I eventually knew it was you – not Galvone, not Manescu?'

'All right, Brain Box,' Carver sneered. 'How *did* you know it was me?'

'Because,' Newman said, hiding his sadness, 'it had to be someone with an appearance, a personality she would trust. That ruled out Manescu and Galvone. You've a way with women, you louse. Under that nice silk suit you're pure filth.'

'Jealous, are we?'

As he spoke Carver stooped swiftly, scooped up a handful of straw, threw it in Newman's eyes. Newman was blinking when Carver rushed him. Instinctively Newman grabbed Carver round his body with both arms to save himself. Both men were so intent on their struggle they failed to realize the car approaching the bell tower had reached it. Buchanan had grabbed a British warm off the back seat, had run inside the bell tower in time to hear the conversation, Carver's admission. He stared up as

Warden followed him. Cupping one hand, Buchanan called up to Newman.

'We have Carver's coat minus the missing button. Forensic confirmed the button's from his coat. He'll stand trial . . .'

Grim faced, he saw the grapple continue on the rickety platform constructed of single wooden planks without any protective rail. Carver hooked a foot behind Newman's ankle to trip him. Newman hung on, freed his right hand, thrust it under his opponent's jaw. He jerked his hand up savagely. Carver toppled, recovered his balance, not realizing he was at the edge of the platform with an abyss below. Newman kneed him in the groin. Carver grunted with pain, loosened his grip, clenched his right fist to slam it into Newman's throat. His feet slithered over the edge. His right hand grabbed for Newman's throat. He dropped off the platform as Newman countered the grab by grasping his arm.

Carver fell, almost dragged Newman with him. Newman had braced his legs to take the strain, crouched, still grasping Carver by the right arm. Only Carver's body above the shoulders was level with the platform. The greater part of his body hung suspended in space. Newman gazed down into the terrified eyes of the killer.

The silk sleeve began to come apart at the shoulder. Newman continued holding on to the right arm, feeling the material slowly slithering through his grasp. His eyes were cold, almost devoid of expression as he watched the sleeve ripping loose stitch by stitch. There was a long moment when it looked as though Newman might haul the hanging man back on to the platform. Then the sleeve parted company with its owner. Carver let out a high-pitched scream as he plunged down. His body performed a semi-somersault in mid-air, then like a swimmer he dived down head first. Buchanan heard the awful sound of the skullbones smashing against the flagstone floor of the tower. Carver lay sprawled motionless, like a broken rag doll.

Newman stood up slowly, holding the sleeve, walked forward with an effort of will, forced himself to descend the shaking ladder rung by rung. At the bottom he stood quite still, not looking at the corpse. He was gazing at the red Jaguar, the spitting image of Sandy's.'

'I'll drive you back to where Tweed is waiting by your car. Let Tweed drive you back,' Buchanan said.

'I can drive myself . . .'

'But you won't. That's an order. And I'm sure Tweed won't let you. This is Carver's coat. We found it at his Chelsea flat. One button missing. Strange that he never realized how incriminating a missing button could be.'

'Strange,' Newman agreed and let himself be led to Buchanan's car.

His mind was so dazed he had no idea what Buchanan was talking about.

Epilogue

'I've come to say goodbye.'

Cord Dillon held out his hand to Tweed in the Park Crescent office. Tweed paused, shrugged, shook hands without enthusiasm.

'You've guessed it?' Dillon suggested.

'Guessed what?'

'Why we wanted Hauser finished. His whole apparatus wiped out. Which is what will happen now he's gone.'

'Go on.'

'The infrastructure of the Soviet Union is on the verge of collapse. The railways are crumbling for lack of maintenance. The telephone system hardly works – a lot of their equipment was installed before 1918. Try to make a call from Moscow to Leningrad and you'd better allow a day to get through. Then maybe you won't.'

'So?'

'The subway in Moscow, once their pride and joy, is also crumbling. Stand on a station platform and watch water dripping through the cracks in the walls. Do I have to go on?'

'The whole place is collapsing?'

'Exactly. And Hauser – after scaring them to death – was going to rebuild Russia into a new America. You think we want that? After seventy years of Communism? Russia is going off the map. Will become a Third World country.'

'And that suits you?'

'Down to the ground. No more worry as to who takes

over. Makes no difference. Hauser was going to spoil all that. Now we can just sit back and watch it happen. You knew?'

'I guessed. Because all the time you were with me your function was mostly that of observer. You didn't do all that much to help. Isn't it time to catch your flight?'

'Guess so.' Dillon looked across the room. 'Goodbye to you, Paula.'

'Goodbye,' she said.

'Is that a good idea?' she asked when they were alone.

'It wasn't a good idea to let Hauser take over,' Tweed replied.

'I mean to let Russia collapse,' she persisted.

'If it does we'll have an even grimmer situation to cope with.'